DEUS

DEUS

Philip Boast

HEADLINE

First published in 1997
by HEADLINE BOOK PUBLISHING

10 9 8 7 6 5 4 3 2 1

British Library Cataloguing in Publication Data

Boast, Philip, 1952–
    Deus
    1. London (England) Fiction
    2. Historical fiction
    I. Title
    823.9'14 [F]

ISBN 0 7472 1725 4

Typeset by Palimpsest Book Production Limited,
Polmont, Stirlingshire
Printed and bound in Great Britain by
Mackays of Chatham PLC, Chatham, Kent

HEADLINE BOOK PUBLISHING
A division of Hodder Headline PLC
338 Euston Road
London NW1 3BH

For my wife, Ros

Corruptio optima pessima

When the best is corrupted, it becomes the worst

One

The Miller's Daughter's Son

Alice's tale

London Bridge, 2 February 1832

This is my story that I must tell. Listen, listen, you must hear.
Who are you?
Alice, me.
Are you there?
Can you hear me, are you deaf? Can you see me, are you blind?
Where are you?
Born six hundred years ago and more, another place, another time, another world, and fell in love.
Are you dead?
I am Alice, I am alive, I do not die, I love Jack still. I am the sound of breaking seas, I am the wash of the wind in the trees, I love him. I am the rattle of hammers on stone, I am the sigh of footprints in the snow, I love him. I am the woman who weeps, I am the man who wakes. I am the gentle Cathar who prays in a cave. I am the gleam in a bird's eye, I am the mouse that nibbles on cheese. I am the black cat that flees in the night, I am the call of the crow from winter's white rooftop. I am the river's rush, I am the echo in the arches, I am the bridge. I am your nightmare and your dream.
Are you here?
Do you hear me now? Do you see me now? I am everything you touch. I am the water in your mouth, I am the air you breathe. Where am I? I am you.
Who made the world?
The Devil.
Does your story begin with the Devil?
No, but both God and the Devil were there that night, and good and evil, and chance. And the miller's daughter.

Stone Bridge, Abbot's Littlebourne, Kent
Innocents' Night, 28 December 1163

So you see, my story begins with the miller's daughter stealing forward through the last night of her life, in the dark, through the falling snow, towards the bridge. I was not there, being myself a newborn babe, but I can imagine this scene as clearly as seeing it, because later as a girl growing up I knew the village and the bridge (now long gone, shoddy work) better than anyone, except Jack. By our time the low arch at the west end was silted with reeds and bulrushes and known as the Kissing Arch by certain youngsters, and as Kissing Alice by Nick, and there were less lovely names too, but I won't tell you those now.

I'm seeing the falling snow.

Heylewise was her name. Not Héloise, that's French. Her father was Alured, big and friendly and stalwart and Saxon to his proud backbone, although he and his mill and his wife and his children, even Heylewise the apple of his eye, all were the personal property of the Frenchman, the abbot of St Augustine's. Like most of the rest of the village, for that matter. Like me, then. Before I belonged to the Temple.

I can see the snow falling like bitter white feathers out of the dark, draping a white veil over Heylewise's face and her shoulders and over her long black hair like a long white cloak. I never knew her, but I can imagine what she felt as clearly and sharply as though I see her feelings. Fear. Despair. Loss.

Anger.

Her footsteps stole through the snow towards the mason's lodge. Heylewise had not been seen in the village since the summer, they say. Not even her father had seen her. He believed her killed.

What actually happened was worse. She fell in love.

Here she is, slim again, her bare, bruised feet made big and soft by the fallen snow, the veil of it concealing all sign of her presence, staring at the candlelit lodge where Jack's father sits drinking. The lodge is always built as near the centre of the bridge as possible, for everyone knows ghosts cannot cross running water. Often the bones of a child are sealed among the bridge stones for good luck.

She reached out her fingertips to the door, then lowered her hand.

Jack's father wasn't a bad man. Myself, I doubt he originated an evil thought in his life. He was human, that's all.

Everyone remembered – he never touched a drop after that coming Twelfth Night – how in those days Jack's father had what they call a good drinking singing voice. He liked the sound of himself, and doubtless he was singing that Innocents' Night, and I can imagine his lonely voice drifting through the thin walls into the snow.

Perhaps he stopped and heard the silence. Too drunk to hold back, perhaps her name bubbled up from the bottom of his brain.

'Heylewise?'

She turned away from the lodge, stole away in her footprints, and the falling snow covered them, and it was as if she had never been.

It was dawn. The stream wriggled like a black vein between clean white villages and snowy watermills towards the new stone bridge. The basket was swept beneath the foaming arch, almost capsized in the standing waves,

4

turned round three times. A man's hand reached down from the bridge and plucked it up.

Imagine yourself inside the head of Jack's father, the man he was in those days. Look out through his eyes. Think the world of yourself.

He knew at once such pretty work belonged to a girl. He'd keep it and sell it, or pass it on to his wife.

But, he thought, it might belong to someone much more interesting.

He knew all about girls, he had a way with them, and they all trusted him, except his dear wife.

Jack's father, a stonemason with a roving, appreciative eye, looked round for a response equally roving and appreciative for the return of the lost basket, but he saw no one. The only movement was the river and the cows drinking by the old ford. He smiled in case some beautiful young creature watched him from the trees, too shy to come forward, crinkled his eyes attractively. He had a lovely smile, he knew how to melt hearts. He had grown heavy with middle age and his daily gallon of the abbot's ale, but his eyes were still what women noticed, dark blue, with large dark centres. He saw well at night.

'There's three temptations I can't resist,' he called. 'A bargain, an opportunity, and a pretty girl.'

Alfred Mason saw his handsome reflection returning his gaze from the water swirling below the bridge. He crossed himself superstitiously, glimpsing for a moment someone bloated and swaying, a basket clasped to his chest and ale froth clinging to his lips, wearing stone dust like grey mortality in his hair. He looked like an old man, worn out. The parapet was unfinished and his foot slipped over the edge, showering stone dust into the gleaming black water. He sat down with a bump.

He put down the basket beside him, wiped his lips, finished off the dregs of ale and felt better.

Legs dangling, he caressed the stonework tenderly with his rough hands. The bridge he had built over the Little Stour (come spring he would take off the straw protecting last year's work, finish off the parapets and build a shelter for the monk who would collect the toll) crossed the river on three arches irregularly spaced, each of a different size, and the western arch was very low. There was no particular reason for this design, Alfred knew, except that it was God's will. The bridge had wanted to grow this way, the bridge piers had found the patches of hardest ground to support their weight, the central arch had wanted to be wider because that was where the deepest water was found. God the Master Mason, the Grand Geometer who built the world, allowed His work to take on natural shapes. God did not place His hills evenly or smooth their sides, or make His rivers of equal depth and width and length. For a human builder to impose symmetry on God's work was the sin of pride. A mason's work must follow the patterns and rhythms of nature. It was his job to find the shape God had put in the stone.

The basket was empty but for an old lumpy rug, dark red in colour, clumsily folded. He called again, but saw only the bare trees, black river, white snow.

I know what Alfred was thinking, I know what they're like, even the best of them. He was thinking about his sex, dreaming of some willowy vision of a girl beckoning him from the trees, and he goes over and she's all coy but so grateful to him for returning her basket, and he takes her in his arms and we know what happens next.

What actually happened was that Alfred belched, then wiped beer froth from his mouth for the second time. He struggled to his feet, forgot about the basket, left it on the edge. He closed the gate of the mason's lodge, or ark, locked it with an iron key, and walked off the bridge, then remembered the basket and fetched it. Yawning, he trudged home between the white ploughlands and pig woods of

Abbot's Littlebourne, came past the old wooden church to his cottage. He hated days on which it was too cold to work, or he was too drunk. The door stuck, as usual. He pushed with his shoulder, and almost fell down the step inside.

There they are. Jack's mother Cristina stood close to the fire, busy, bare to the waist, suckling Jack at her large milky breast. She was a lovely, difficult woman, I knew her well in her old age, and I can just see her face tightening at the sight of Alfred staggering in the doorway and falling down the step. This was the way things were between them in those times. Then the weary lines would flood over her face. She complained about the cold and he was letting the heat out and when was he going to fix the door and where had he been? 'And who have you been drinking with?' Her eye fixed on the finely-made basket. She demanded, 'What's that? Who's that for? Who gave that to you?'

Alfred realised she might go on like this for hours. He had a stroke of genius. He held out the basket.

'It's for you,' he said. 'It's a gift.'

Cristina's eyes filled. It was as simple as that. She fell silent, and despite her broken teeth and stinking breath, he kissed her. He eyed her exposed breast, her fine dark nipple with one white drip of milk squeezing from the tip. Cristina knew he didn't see anything else, his son, or her, or think of her except for that one thing about her, as though her swollen breast was all she was. 'You only think of one thing,' she said. Like father, like son, *I* say.

The sight and heady feminine smell of his wife made Alfred so hot he forgot the snow clinging to his boots and his breeches, forgot the basket under his arm, and he reached for her with his free hand.

'You can't. It's wrong. It's disgusting,' she sighed. He squeezed her rump, touched her hard nipple with his soft tongue. 'I'm nursing,' she said. 'It's fornication, it's not allowed. You'll have to confess.'

He slid his cold hand between her thighs warm from the fire. 'I'll confess,' he grinned, 'but I'll be in Heaven first.'

He opened his breeches, hoisted her skirt. With the tip of her little finger she disengaged baby Jack from her breast and laid him on the rug in the basket to be safe during her husband's attentions. Close to her eye as she endured the business, the rug twitched.

Then she saw the rug move.

Cristina pulled aside one corner, revealing a tiny pink hand curled into a fist.

She screamed, and the rug kicked beneath Jack as she hauled him off it, then it kicked again so that she almost dropped him. She clung to him and they all stared at the basket. The rug jerked and a pink leg kicked out, then a tiny penis slid into view and then a bellybutton. Finally a pink head gleaming in the firelight, almost bare of hair, was revealed. Then the rug slipped off, and it was as though they had just watched the baby being born.

The baby kicked and cried, eyes and fists squeezed tight shut.

The baby fell silent and still. His eyes opened.

'Holy Mother of God, Alfred,' Cristina said. 'He's got your eyes.'

He did, too. Eyes that would see well in the dark.

They stared at the baby, even Jack with his steady blue gaze, dark-centred, and Cristina looked from one to the other. The two babies looked as close as brothers.

'I swear I didn't know it was in there,' Alfred said.

Cristina reached her hand forward to the baby. Her fingers stretched out as if marvelling at him.

'Don't touch it!' Alfred said, panicking. He tried to cover the baby again with the rug. He wanted rid of it right now. But Cristina held back the rug with her hand.

'He's not newborn,' she murmured. 'The cord has rotted away, so he's more than ten days old. A few weeks perhaps.' She frowned. 'There have been no births in the village. How could some poor girl keep this secret?'

'Someone's playing a trick! I'll take it back.'

But Cristina knelt. 'No one would play a trick on Innocents' Day.' The baby looked at her breast just like her husband had, just like Jack did. It put out its left hand. She hesitated. Suddenly baby Jack twisted against her, suckling, one leg kicking, mouthing her fruitful nipple. He had a scratch on his cheek and she remembered she must cut his fingernails. Cristina groaned with love. She had waited so long for a child that she had grown to accept her husband's infidelities, taking the blame on herself for her barrenness. But since Jack was born, everything had changed.

She told Alfred fiercely, 'Don't lie to me any more.'

He blustered.

She said firmly, 'Who was she?'

'I swear to God I don't know. I never saw . . .'

Cristina put out her finger to the baby, and it curled its tiny fist round her fingertip. Jack's father kept speaking, saying something, some new lie. She interrupted him.

'When you're with them,' she said bitterly, 'do you think of me?'

He laughed. 'With who?'

'With some pretty girl, or somebody's wife.'

He said sincerely, 'There is no one but you, my love.' He crinkled his eyes, then realised with incredulity she did not believe him. 'Yes. It's always you I see.'

'You're such a liar!' she cried. 'It's one of the Woxeston girls, I suppose. The brickmaker's girls, they're no better than sluts. Or Everard Tyler's brood that live by the kiln.'

'Oh, them. No.'

'Was she the miller's daughter, the one at Garwynton Mill?' Cristina nodded, her anger turning to calculation. 'She dropped from sight months ago. You'd like that one, she has a smile. And she has spirit. And now she's stuck you with this for catching her.'

He said earnestly, 'I don't know her. It wasn't her.'

'Someone further afield? Canterbury, perhaps.' Cristina shook her head, weary again. 'It could be anyone. You don't even know, do you? You forgot her as soon as you finished. You'll have to try and find the mother, Alfred. Not for you. For the boy's sake.'

'It's you I love. I told you I don't know who she is. I swear to you I'm innocent.'

'Swear on the bones of the saint in the church.'

He hesitated.

She said sadly, 'Alfred Mason, you look like a good man but you don't care about anyone.'

He said, 'Don't cry.'

But she wasn't crying, he realised. This was more serious than that. She had seen through him and this time she was blaming him for what she saw. She had huge emotions blowing through her, far larger than sexual desire which was love to him. She picked up the new baby and he couldn't stop her. She clasped the babe to her, then knelt defiantly with the two babes suckling her breasts. The babes' faces almost touched. Even their legs kicked in time, and her milk trickled from their mouths as they drank.

'Nicholas,' she said. 'Jack, and Nicholas.'

After Twelfth Night the monk-warden's urchin arrived early, as usual, at the new bridge. The donkey carried the stonemason's weekly allowance of ale in the seven-gallon lidded bucket called an *olla*, but today the urchin ran ahead of the donkey. 'Drowned!' he shouted excitedly to rouse Alfred Mason if he was drunk, not daring to enter the mason's lodge but hoping for a halfpenny or a pot of ale for his news. 'Drowned!' he repeated through the doorway.

Alfred Mason was not drunk. Inside, a pile of shaped stones for the parapet surrounded him. He had finished more in the last week than the previous month. His face was white with stone dust, his lips and eyelids red gashes.

'Drowned? Who's drowned?'

'The miller's girl at Garwynton! Her father found her when he went to clear rubbish from the millwheel. They don't know how long she's been there. Round and round.'

Alfred said, 'Heylewise?' He got to his feet. 'Heylewise?'

The urchin watched him go, then grinned at the ale and helped himself.

Alfred ran along the riverbank. His heart thudded. When he was out of breath he walked, then ran again. The ground became marshy and he ploughed up to his knees in mud and slush. The mill had been built at the pool where the Nailbourne met the Little Stour. Alfred heard the rumbling wheel, the women weeping, he saw the wooden millhouse and waterwheel quivering in their reflections in the millpond as the wheel churned. The sluice gate had jammed open and the miller and his sons beat it with hammers. They kept shoving the women away but the women pushed forward, wailing, trying to help, trying to seize the girl from the wheel, getting in the way. By the look of her she could have been on the wheel since Innocents' Day, a week at least, and everyone knew that her soul would remain locked in her body until she was buried in consecrated ground. The wheel threw up spray from its great weedy slats as it turned, massive, foul, implacable. Alfred came close as if to help, too close, then pressed the back of his hand to his mouth as Heylewise rose out of the water near enough to touch him with her trailing slimy fingers, and she was carried over the top of the wheel, and she was carried down into the water again.

Again she rose up, and Alfred saw she was caught by her long black hair in the slats. She had loved her hair. Her swollen arms and legs waved against the slippery wood as if playing at life. The hammers rattled frantically. Finally the gate slammed down, the roar of water died away to a trickle. The wheel ran on, slowing, and Heylewise rose up for the last time. The wheel stopped. The only sound was the drip of water from the orifices of her body.

The men could not disentangle her. Her mother would not let them cut her hair. They went away for tools to remove the slat.

Alfred stared into her eyes. He was not to blame. He had hardly known her. He could not remember anything about her that made her different, and he had not thought about her when he was not with her. Yet he saw his reflection standing in her eyes, a dark shape with the bright sky behind him, and he felt like a murderer.

Jack and Nicholas, Nicholas and Jack. Years later they even fell in love with the same girl.

You know her, don't you? She's me, Alice.

Alice Lacknail, in those days. Look at me, there in the corner of your eye, the girl in the pauper's smock. Eleven years old, legs and arms skinny as sticks, and a hungry look fixed on my thin dirty face. Can you see me there behind the matted brown curls, the colour of dirt, that cling greasily over my shoulders and arms and my face? Can you see my eyes? The glint of my blue eyes through the filthy curls like a tiny animal trapped in a cave, defiant and ready to fight, but knowing I'll be hurt? That's me. That's all of us, that's our family. We are *nativi*, slaves by birth. We are *neif*, the naive, capable of knowing nothing for ourselves, dumb human animals. Our bodies are not our own any more than the body of a lamb or a calf is its own, we belong to our owner. Us and our work are the property of our lord the abbot. We pay *merchet* for permission to marry, *leyrwite* if we do not marry, *tallage* to live and *heriot* to die, and *toll* to sell any poor thing we possess.

Ma never washed us or cut our hair, nor Mabel, there were more of us than you count on one hand, all girls. Our father was a woodcutter until he lost his thumb to the sheriff. Sometimes we lived in the woods, and sometimes we had a lean-to roof. We hated it under the roof because of the smell of our shit, and our father grunting, or cursing, or crying. He was always hurting but there was nothing wrong with him that anyone could help, except his gone thumb so he could not hold the axe, and that is the sign of a criminal too, so in the village the good folk stoned us because of right and wrong. They called him John Lack-a-Nail, once a criminal always a criminal. In the spring, soon as the dry month came, we girls scattered like a litter of wild mice and slept beneath the trees. The monks owned everything around us, and everything we did and everything we had, when we had anything. When we had nothing we were good-for-nothing, and our abbot granted our service to the Temple lands beyond the Fishpool, thus discharging some small obligation or a debt, perhaps, but doing the Temple no favour, for a one-thumbed man can't cut or plough or hoe, so the abbot had simply discharged useless mouths. He was a cunning man. There were already too many girls in the village for everyone to marry, and we would end up as whores or stealing married men, so the wives stoned us to save their husbands from the temptation of adultery and they were blessed in church for it, and we were outcast though we had done nothing. That was the year Mabel, our eldest, was kicked in the stomach and ailed, and after a little while she died with her baby still inside her. Our sister Mabel was almost as old as our mother, it seemed to us, and when she and her baby slept for ever beneath the leaves, we missed her, though we went and grumbled to her sometimes when we were in trouble. But we were used to looking after ourselves. I think we even liked it that way.

In that same year my youngest sister Noelle was born. Our father had lost only his thumb, remember, not the thing between his legs. That worked fine, in fact Ma said he couldn't stop it. So Noelle joined the rest of us and she didn't die, and next year there would be another, but everyone said Noelle was a bit like me. But she was still only a baby that summer's day, and the stone didn't come whistling over the bushes at Three Oaks From One Root and hit *her* head.

The stone hit me.

My head throbbed, but there was no blood. I sat down with a bump on the path, then realised the danger I was in. When you are lying down or crying, you are helpless. I rolled away, then crawled forward without a sound on my toes and fingers.

Through the bushes I heard a boy's voice whisper, 'You hit her, Jack!'

Another voice replied. The boy called Jack said, 'Of course I hit her.' He sounded offended to be thought capable of missing.

The other boy said excitedly, 'Did you kill her?'

I crept into the mossy V between the two oak trunks on my right, slid over the great root joining the trees, let myself slither quietly down into the bushes. The bushes rustled beyond the third oak. The boys were trying to see me lying on the path, or running away, or hear me crying. Boys like to make girls cry and chase us and frighten us and they sounded disappointed to get no fun.

Jack's voice whispered, 'I can't see her, Nick.'

'Where were you aiming?'

'At her head.'

9

'Where did you hit her?'

'Smack between the eyes! I saw it and I saw her fall over. I knocked her out.'

But they weren't sure. The oak roots stood like great legs and I wound my body between them, crawling forward. The boys were beginning to sound frightened by what Jack had done. They were frightened of girls. They were afraid to look, only peeping in case they saw something awful that would get them beaten, but at the same time they wanted to see the results of their handiwork. The bushes rustled as they moved and I wriggled forward quickly on my elbows. I stopped when the boys' rustling stopped. I could hear them breathing now, and one of them slapped an insect. The boy Jack had called Nick whispered, 'I still can't see her, Jack. Do you think she's dead as a doornail?'

'If she was dead, she'd still be there,' Jack said. A booted foot pushed back against one of the roots, Jack's foot, I saw it move as he spoke. A boy wearing a green leather boot like a man, a proper cobbler's boot, probably old Cobbley's in Lukynden. A boy like that would eat two square meals of meat a day, on proper bread. My head throbbed with pain and hunger. He said to his friend, '*I* threw the stone. *You* go out and look.'

'No, Jack, you!' Nick said. Then he added, 'Suppose she's really dead?'

Jack said firmly, 'She isn't dead. She's a serf. People like her are hard as rocks. They have rocks in their heads. They've been slaves since Roman times, they were enslaved by King Lovernios, it's in their blood, they're born to it. If you knock them down they get up again.'

I wondered who King Lovernios was.

I crept round the side of them, close enough to touch. I saw an elbow, I could have touched my fingertip to the soft green wool. The fat boys – their skin gleamed with the meat fat of good living – were used to living in a house with walls, perhaps even stone walls. They did not think to look or listen to each side, they did not know the forest. But I know the forest. There are truffles in the forest but you do not see them. There are conies in the forest but you do not hear them. I do.

The boys could not see me, could not hear me. I let my face slide against the dirt, wiped clay between my eyes. My hand came away a little bloody. I rubbed the red slipperiness between my fingers. They would pay.

'We'll stand up together,' Jack said. I heard him swallow. He was nervous. 'On three.' I wondered what *three* was. Something you stood on? 'One,' Jack said. 'Two. Three!' The bushes were thrust aside, the boys stood up.

They were no older than I was.

They were brothers, I saw that at once. Jack stared at the empty path. He exclaimed, 'Where's she gone?'

Nick said, 'She's gone.'

Jack was tall for his age, broad-shouldered, with sun-streaked hair. Nick was a little smaller, darker, but the brothers had the same dazzled, deep-centred eyes, and I thought, they see well in the dark. I wondered if the boys might even be twins, their age seemed so close.

Nick looked behind him. He said, 'Jack, I'm scared.'

I rose up in front of them, rose up over the oak root with arms upraised, shrieking, clay-coloured, leaves stuck to my hair. The boys screamed. I saw the pink insides of their mouths and the whites of their eyes and it was all I could do not to burst out laughing. I turned and ran, ran along Swanton Lane with the dust flying from my feet. They chased me, I could hear them. I looked back, laughing. I could run faster than any fat boys and the woods were my home, but Jack and Nick were almost as fast as I was. Their footfalls behind me were gaining, slower but longer than mine, covering the ground faster. I dodged between the tree trunks into the woods, went one way then another, crouched, and I became the trees and the bushes and the fallen leaves. From time to time I heard the brothers searching, then Jack's voice called out in disgust, 'Let her go.'

I grinned, listening to their complaints fading. I was home.

I hated them.

Anyone with eyes can see that Abbot's Littlebourne is not one place but many. The busiest part of the village is the old elm church, its back broken with age and its aspenwood cross split by the sun. The church overlooks Church Meadow, the new bridge and the Little Stour. The monk on the abbot's bridge charges travellers and pilgrims a farthing to cross, Canterbury being only an hour's walk away, and the shrine of St Thomas our martyr is so popular that the bridge has already paid for itself. Most of the Littlebourne hamlets – Garwynton, Lukynden, Ickham and Wickham, Wadysmede and Telebridge the wooden bridge – follow the Little Stour and the Lampen Stream so folk can draw water one side and shit the other. One or two big houses have their own wells and cesspools. Between the two rivers are the scattered brick pits and tile pits and kilns, the sheep pastures and pig woods, pigsties and rick yards, flax plots and beehives, ploughlands that must be ploughed and meadows that must never be ploughed, all laid down in ancient charters going back to the foundation of the abbey in Canterbury in the first days of Christianity. I don't know what we did before Jesus Christ came here.

The centre of the village is Pevynges Wood. A girl who lives here, as I do, knows everything. I am the pauper queen of my world. Fishpool is as convenient to me as Stone Bridge. Temple Moat and the gallows on Stodmarsh Lane, where the spine of a horse thief still hangs from its skull and moans as it swings on windy days, are as familiar to me as the watermills of Garwynton and Ickham. Nobody sees me, or notices me if they do, or cares about me if they do notice me. Nobody misses me, one of a handful of grimy sisters. I am beneath care.

It took no time at all to find the two brothers. My anger drew me to them like a fish to a hook.

They lived in a stone house near the church. I hid behind the barn. Yvon Piggot the pigman's son walked humming along the rutted track behind the back wall, tapping the three black rumps of his father's hogs with a stick. I let him pass, then came up silently behind him. 'Yvon, where are you going?' I said in a low voice.

He turned with an oath, staring clear over my head, then looked down. 'Oh, it's you. I'm going from Ley Wood to Pevynges Wood, me,' he said. He brushed away the flies that always clung to him and smiled down at me, a genial dung-spattered boy who was almost a man, too gentle for his own good. 'Ley Wood costs too much pannage, see.' Pannage was a tax. Yvon knew about complicated things like that but he slept when he should have been guarding the hogs from thieves, as my father knew well to his benefit, but obviously Yvon did not, since he remained friendly. He walked ponderously backwards after his hogs, smiling, blinking at me. People have done this recently. I am more noticed than I was.

I walked with him, jerked my thumb over my shoulder. 'Who lives there?'

He stopped the hogs and they milled around us, snuffled hopefully at our legs, then rooted for straw and stuff in the manure heap. 'The fine stone house? That's the Master Mason's house.' So the boys' father was Alfred Mason, the stonemason. I knew their names, I knew their father, and soon I would know everything about them. 'Free man, him,' Yvon rambled. I listened impatiently. Everyone knew a stonemason was always a free man, one of the few free men in the village. The monks of course were free, though everything

11

they had was supposed to belong to the abbey, but they lived like lords with agreed rights to wine, beer, meat, cheese, robes, shelter, even money, and had endless opportunities for stealing. They were no better than ordinary people, but they stood between us and God, and that made them powerful. The de Cornhills were London merchants, free because they were rich. Alexander the lord of Downham was free because his family held vast properties. All the rest of us were cottagers, or villeins, or the lowest of the low, serfs. I thought, perhaps my poor father's family really are descended from the Roman slaves who worked the brick pits of Tegham and Downham. Little changes here since Jesus Christ walked our land, they say, not even the shape of our clothes.

'A free man has no lord to look after him,' Yvon said slowly. 'I wouldn't want to be free, would you?'

I imagined it.

'I'd give lands to the abbey,' I decided, 'and I'd wear red and green and yellow clothes all at the same time, and I'd eat sugar.' I had seen a sugar cone once.

'No, that's being *rich*,' Yvon scoffed. 'Being free's not like that. A free man lives by earning money. That's all right if he succeeds. But if he don't succeed, he starves.' He copied me, jerked his thumb at the house over and over, as though he'd never seen the gesture before. 'They're all right now the old man's got himself in order. But I know what I know.' He kept jerking his thumb. He wanted me to ask him what he knew.

'Go on, then, what do you know?'

'Used to be quite a lad, Alfred Mason. Drink. Girls.' He leered, stuck his thumb in his mouth. 'You know what. You wouldn't have been safe.'

I was intrigued. 'What, like the animals?'

'That's right,' he said appreciatively. 'Marriage didn't come into it, I can tell you.'

I understood. He was talking about sin. A free man could get what he wanted from any sensible girl who knew what side her bread was buttered, especially if he was handsome. He could spin her any old lie. A cottager sometimes won a poor sort of freedom by his trade as a thatcher or carpenter or smith, but any girl worth her salt knew a mason was always free, the son of a free mason, born to be a mason. A stonemason's hands did the work of God. His hands built churches – most new churches are built of stone, and even some small bridges are. Every stonemason is descended from Hiram, the mason who built King Solomon's Temple in Jerusalem. Churches and bridges and castles are made to stand by strange knowledge, taught to King Hiram and to Solomon by the demon Asmodeus, and the mason father reveals the secrets of his trade only to his mason son, and only inside the Lodge, and he may never speak of them.

The boys came out from the house into the sun. Yvon stared at me but I ignored him. Through the gap in the gate I saw the boys kicking a ball in the yard between the house and the barn. They didn't have a care in the world. The hogs snuffled around my knees, shoved at me hungrily, but all I saw were those two boys. I said, 'They'll have red meat for supper tonight, and beer, and butter, and white bread.'

Yvon pushed me like the big hog that he was but I didn't look away. 'Envy!' he said.

'It's not envy.'

He knew better. 'They don't drink beer,' he said, to get my attention. 'They don't drink beer, their father don't let them. They drink milk.'

'Milk!'

Yvon picked his nose with his little finger, his other fingers were too big. 'Alfred Mason don't touch a drop of beer himself, nor wine, neither will he let his wife, nor his sons. It's milk for them, or water from the well, or go thirsty. Even though he's got work outside the village, he won't take them with him.

Protects them.' I tried to imagine something as far away as *outside the village*. 'He's in Canterbury, repairing the abbey.' Everyone had heard of Canterbury. I had seen the towers of Canterbury from Higham hilltop, and once the sun gleaming on the town walls too. I knew I would never travel so far away in my life.

I murmured, 'What's he protecting them from?'

'I don't know. Who cares?' Yvon slapped at the hogs with his stick, setting them on their way. He walked after them, forgetting me, then turned and jerked his thumb for the last time. 'Look at them larking about!' he snarled. 'Not a care in the world!'

It was true. Not a care in the world. My head ached. I ran back to Three Oaks From One Root and searched in the dust. The stone that had struck me was gone. Night rose from the ground as the sun fell, throwing three shadows from the tree trunks around me as I searched, then the light was gone and everything was shadow. My fingers found the stone by touch, in the darkness, where it had rolled beneath a root. I sat turning it in my hands, listening to the sounds of darkness closing around me, then cradled the stone to my tummy until it was warm. The warmth was comforting. I would make them care.

From behind the barn I watched them, and planned my revenge. Throw stones, would they? I imagined their house burning and them running with their clothes burning, those two cocky boys who thought they could get away with anything.

I'd teach them to . . . to *think*.

I woke, sweating. My tummy had cramped and the stone was hot and slippery with my sweat where I had pushed it against me. I took deep breaths. *One, two, three*. I could now count to three. I kissed the stone, and the cramps eased.

Jack and Nicholas, Nicholas and Jack. The fat boys were easy to hate. They had a mother and a father who loved and protected them. Though their father was away, they never went hungry, and I realised he must love them so much that he sent them money. He cared about his family even while he was not with them. Perhaps he even thought about them while he worked. They lived in the stone house he had built, respectably close to the church, with a red clay roof that was the first I had seen, and windows with translucent white gauze hung across them. Those confused me until at last I understood the thin material would let the light in and keep the wind out. As a traveller, of course, he knew all the latest innovations. Oak shutters were closed over them at night so no one could break inside. I understood *that*. It was a sure sign they had something worth stealing, coins buried beneath the hearth perhaps, a silver platter or two, perhaps a rug and a proper bed.

Used to be quite a lad, Alfred Mason. Drink. Girls.

Their mother doted on her fat boys. When they left for school she spat on her palm and wiped their hair and faces. She was a busy woman but she looked sad to see them go and happy when they returned for their midday meal – three meals a day!—and she had the food ready, no time lost. I stared at the hunks of cheese, onion, bacon, bread, and my belly whined with hunger. Sometimes in the long evenings she simply sat on the step with her sons, her soft white arms thrown round their shoulders, not working, not fighting, not worried, not starving or drunk, not falling into an exhausted sleep like most people. She was simply talking to them. I could not hear what she was saying.

Nick cut his knee and she bound it in new linen. Jack's boot was holed and she bought him another, threw the old one on the house dump though it could have been repaired. From behind the barn I watched their privileged lives. I watched them rain and shine, following the barn's shadow if it was hot, holding stinking rags from the dump to shelter me when it rained. I could not stop thinking about them, they filled my head. My bare feet sank into the mud and I found the single boot that had been thrown away and wore it like a talisman. When it was dark I hobbled forward into the yard and sat, watching, listening. The door of the barn was locked against thieves but a thin child like me could wriggle between the rough wattle walls and the thatch, and drop down inside. In the stalls I found a cow, a donkey and a small dappled pony, and chickens roosting above them on the rafters. The straw-covered floor was dangerous, I might be trodden on by the animals or surprised by humans, accused of theft, and flogged. I perched on a rafter, sucked an egg dry, and slept with the chickens. In the morning I found a place in the roof where, by scratching aside the clay daub with my fingernails, I could look down on the stonemason's house.

I shook their door one night, like a ghost, and heard their frightened shouts immediately. They had no man in the house, but their mother came outside carrying a candle in one hand and a stick in the other. She stared defiantly into the dark, peering from her pitiful flickering circle of light. She never saw me, I was already gone. I wriggled under the thatch into the barn. The chickens knew me by now and did not stir, and the cow chewed peacefully. The boys' mother stood in the yard shouting threats at thieves whose shadows she thought she saw, and she wouldn't let her boys come out of their house. It was all I could do not to laugh aloud. Someone called her name, probably Agnes the old slut, whose task it was to close the shutters, begging her mistress to come back. Mistress Cristina, Mistress Cristina, come back in your house and be safe.

Her name was Cristina. Soon I would know everything about them.

I followed the boys to school across Church Meadow, the spiders' webs shining like spun silver in the sun, then along the bank of the Little Stour to the trees, then through the trees along the sunken path. I didn't get too close. They looked back but I turned aside. I followed them again. The path had been worn down into the clay by time and use and only their heads showed. It was the perfect place for an ambush. Beyond it was the clearing cut in the undergrowth, opening towards the monk's cell between the yew and the lime where Brother Paulus held his lessons. On the other side of the river I saw the big wooden house of the de la Ley family, the wooden palisade round it making a yard where the farm stock was gathered in at night and led out in the morning. Two rough-looking resentful men argued over a boundary in the middle of a field, accusing each other of moving the boundary stone. The Becles family argued with the Nailbournes over anything, they would argue over the weather if they could find nothing better, and their children did too. I saw sweet little John Woolton, horrid Gilbert's younger brother, their father rich from fleecing, come trudging down from the sheep pastures carrying a wax writing tablet under his arm, and Richard de la Ley crossed the bridge. Poor children were fetching water from the river in pieces of skin held at the corners. A few lucky girls wore skirts that touched the ground, and ignored the boys. Some of the boys broke off to kick a football, impressing the girls with their prowess. The girls giggled, and the victor snatched a kiss. The losers – it was every boy for himself – kicked over a pail of water and there was a fight. Ellen Cowherd's mother broke up the warring factions with great slaps of her hands. To my horror Jack and Nick, faces shining, hair slicked, turned back to watch the fight. They came straight towards me on the sunken path while I stood rooted in front of them, nowhere to run. My heart was in my mouth.

But they pushed by, one on each side of me, without even looking at me, Jack first, then Nicholas.

I held the stone warm to my tummy. I almost dropped it as my hands fumbled. The boys walked on, talking between themselves, pushing at each other over some joke. I drew back my arm and threw the stone straight and

14

true. It struck Jack on the side of his head, drawing a line of blood in his hair, his sun-streaked hair.

'Rubbish!' I shouted at them. 'You're both rubbish.'

Jack rubbed his head. He looked at his hand. He looked at me and frowned. 'Who is she?' he said.

Nick ran at me, and I raced away between the trees. He turned back to his brother. My eyes were full of tears. I ran until I got home in the forest and the lean-to with leaves over it. My elder sister Martha called from the tree, 'Don't go in there.' But I ran in and my father was lying on my mother like a filthy dark mound, and I screamed at him, and he rose up and grabbed me and held me down with his left hand and gripped me as I wriggled and screamed, and he beat me with his thumbless right hand. He threw me into the leaves. 'I told you,' Martha said. I went and sat in the forest where Mabel was buried and talked to her.

'I said they were rubbish,' I whispered, 'and rubbish they are.' After a little while Martha came by, looking gentle. 'They didn't even know who I was,' I told her.

'Who?' She stared at me, then she sniffed me. 'Poor Alice,' she murmured, and her eyes widened knowingly. 'You're one of us now.'

'*I'm not one of you!*' I screamed at her, and ran away between the trees. She called after me but I ran until I could not hear her. When night fell I had only one place I wanted to go.

I perched on the rafters among the chickens, my knees to my chin, and watched the stonemason's house. Like any child, I could perch quite naturally like this, or sit cross-legged in an attitude adults found impossible, for hours on end. But now my legs ached, and my tummy ached too.

I remembered what Jack had said. *Who is she?*

He hadn't even remembered me.

The cockerel crowed, the chickens flapped, it must be the dawning of first light. For me it was still night, my eyes would hardly open, stuck closed, sticky with sleep. I stared blearily at the daylight peeping beneath the eaves, rubbed the white mucus away with my fingers, sucked them. My head ached groggily, then I realised my legs felt as though they had fixed solid, bent double on my perch. A beam angled from the rafter up to the roof, and I had fallen asleep resting my arm against the wood, my head on my arm, and now my neck and my whole body felt stiff enough to break if I moved.

I moved, and my heel slid wetly forward, my leg slipped over the edge. I hung on. There was something slimy beneath me on the rafter.

I had wet myself in the night. It was the first time I hadn't held myself since I could remember, and I was ashamed. Then I saw that the rafter was wet with slippery blood, dark with it, and blood trickled down my white skinny leg like a long thin wound drawn by an invisible knife. A slimy thread of blood swung from my heel, growing longer like red spittle hanging down, then it dripped and a moment later I heard the drop go *pat* against the straw.

I pulled up my leg, stood with cracking knees. I clung to the roof beam and felt myself. This had something to do with babies but I had no idea what it meant. Perhaps the Devil had slept with me. The Devil did sleep with women in the village, he had been seen. There was a wooden picture in the church of a woman embracing a smiling man between her parted legs, but the back of the man's head, which she could not see, bore the Devil's hideous grinning face. Had the Devil come sliding over the rafters to take me while I slept? Had I felt his ice-cold touch in the moonlight, in my dreams? Had I held on to his horny head while he thrust into me, split me apart, and left me bleeding as the sign of sin? I had no one to ask and did not dare. I looked round fearfully, afraid of every shadow. But my flesh was not cold like the Evil

15

One's, I was hot. I was soft and sticky with blood, and more slid urgently through my fingers.

I was not ill. This was Eve's sin, I realised, not my own, it was only a warning. I tore my smock and the rotten fabric gave way easily, pieces of carry-marry held together by nettle stalks. I wiped my legs with the rag and wadded it against me, then moved along the rafter feeling slow and clumsy.

The boys would come soon to let the animals out. I was late already. I crawled down and wriggled beneath the eaves, dropped down behind the gate.

The gate was open and Nick was coming through it. He saw me. His eyes opened wide, his mouth opened to shout. 'Jack!' he yelled. He carried a bucket by its rope handle and his fingers opened on the rope, letting go. I knew I must run but I turned too slowly. I heard the bucket clatter, I felt his hands grab my hair. I pulled forward, he pulled back. I put my hands round his hands and we tugged back and forth, me screaming, my feet slipping in the yellow juice seeping from the manure heap. 'Jack, I've caught her!' Nick shouted. I swore at him. I kicked his knees and pulled away, but he twisted my hair and got behind me. 'Got you,' he said. I wept and fell to my knees and he must have thought he had really hurt me.

I snatched a handful of manure and threw it up.

I heard it spatter. Nick said, 'Ugh!' He let go, wiped his hands over his face, spitting. I laughed at him, then backed away because Jack was coming through the gate looking serious. Then he laughed too, seeing his brother's smeared and speckled face. 'She's shitted you, Nick,' he said cheerfully. I watched them, panting. They had it so easy. What happened didn't mean anything to them, it was just fun. I snatched two deep handfuls from the foul-stinking pile, going in almost up to the elbows, green-brown. 'Don't,' Jack said, and I almost didn't. Then I pelted him.

'You're just pieces of shit,' I shouted at him.

'It's the same girl,' Jack said.

I ran, scooped up stones from the path, ran backwards throwing them. '*You're nothing but rubbish, you're nothing but pieces of shit!*'

When I was somewhere out of sight round a corner, I leant back against a tree. I couldn't catch my breath. The brothers weren't following. My belly hurt and my face sweated and I hated them almost as much as I hated myself.

Still no sign of them. Why not?

I stood in the middle of the track, waiting, then turned and walked off.

This was the church way that led down to the river. Travellers, pilgrims and strangers called it the road to Canterbury from the port of Sandwich. I was already away from the cluster of fine houses near the church and the shacks leaning against the churchyard fence. The filthy hovels that almost encircled the ring of fine houses round the church fell behind me. I looked round alertly, wary of pursuit. Because ours was an ancient village founded at the beginning of time, there were no trees in the fields. Each huge field was an orderly patchwork of different colours, peas, barley, beans, following the contours of the ground. Each long, narrow strip was worked by a different peasant. No two strips of yokeland lying together belonged to the same man, so good land and bad was shared equally. The odd-shaped parcels of land near streams or marshes were called gores. The boundaries were marked with small shrines or crosses to St Augustine, the patron saint of our village, and they were much older than the road, so the road twisted and turned between them, no straight more than a few yards long. Near the rookery some peasants had set up brutal-looking scarecrows to guard their strips, woven of sticks and old baskets like men of straw, and even grown-ups feared them as pagan totems and crossed themselves before treading on that land. The child scarecrows rose with the sun, like the birds, and their cries mingled with the early birdsong.

16

Their mothers would arrive later to weed carefully among the ripening crops. As usual Widow Gore let elecampane weed grow in her awkward third of an acre, the yellow flowers sprawling waist-high over her scraggy knee-high barley, infuriating her neighbours whose neat strips were carefully tended, and there were always complaints against her at the manor court.

I stopped, listening, but the track was empty. I wished I could see further back than the last corner, but the level of the road had sunk between the fields. The sun was already hot. I was very thirsty and I imagined the river and the cool water.

In fact the road had not sunk, the fields had risen. The end of each field was called the headland, the heap of raised soil thrown up by ploughing, rising by a finger's width each year. After so many years the headlands were higher than a man, and the lane wound tortuously between steep banks that hid the fields from me now that I was among them.

Voices echoed over the headlands, but I decided it was just the urchin scarecrows calling out. Then their little voices rose in a miniature storm of anger, sounding just like a flock of sparrows. Something had alarmed them. I scrambled up the bank on to a headland and peered through the long grass.

Nick looked up. He had cleaned his face on his sleeve. His sleeve was dirty. 'We'll get you,' he said.

I spat at him.

I dashed along the headland. The brothers raced below me through the crops, trying to cut ahead of me. The urchin scarecrows ran after them, shouting. Spoiling crops was a dreadful crime, last year two knights who held a joust in the rye were fined for it, though no one supposed they would ever pay. The brothers followed the footpaths between the allotments, but leaping against the skyline as I was I could not have been more clearly in view. The headland turned away from them and the road followed. Ahead of me the stone bridge over the river came in sight beyond the green water meadows and church leys dotted with cows.

I shouted an obscenity at the boys and jumped down into the lane.

I landed lightly but the wheel ruts had dried hard as iron with summer, and my foot slipped. I felt a flash of pain as my ankle twisted. I hopped forward, groaning, I knew I had only a few moments out of sight. Which way should I go? Forward, as they expected, or run back? But that meant going back towards their house. Anyway, I realised, the two of them could cover both ways. Cut round on each side of me. That's what I'd do if I was them.

That was what Jack would do.

My ankle felt weak. I knew if I stayed on the lane they'd catch me. One side of the road was the headland, the other was an impenetrable tangle of green, one of the permanent boundaries begun just after the Flood, at the dawn of time, when Noah laid down the pattern of our land. Ham, Shem and Japhet his sons split young saplings near the root with their axes and bent them over, wove them tightly together, and the saplings grew into trees lying along the ground. By now their branches sprouted upwards towards the sun, split and tightly entwined in their turn, and the mass of them rose up like a wall of leaves. It was a living fence.

I jumped at it, clutched my hands and fingers deep into it, and Nick jumped down into the lane behind me. I dragged myself up the fence, leaves and whippy green twigs pressing against my face, and tried to roll over the top. His hand grabbed at my ankle, the one I had hurt. I cursed him and spat and kicked at him with my other foot and felt his fingers slip. I kicked him again and he let go, then jumped up at me, but I rolled over the top of the leaves and branches, and they bent and I fell down the far side.

I landed on my shoulders and hit my face with my knee. For a moment I felt

17

numb, then I sat up, hurting all over. Around me were big tussocks of grass and cow pats beaded with early-morning dew. I was in Church Ley. I could see the line of trees along the river. I knew Nick would jump down on me from the fence. I could hear him trying to barge through, then I heard him trying to climb up. I rubbed my knee and thought, what's the use? I'll let him catch me, he'll only beat me up.

'She's in Church Ley!' Nick shouted.

He can't get through the fence, I realised. I can get away. 'You're a piece of shit, you,' I said.

The fence stopped shaking.

I chanted, 'Nick, your ma still wipes your arse.' I listened. Nick did not reply.

What was Jack doing? If I was him, I'd cut round and find an easier way into the field. I wondered where Nick was, I couldn't hear a sound from him now.

In the distance Jack leapt over the stile into the far end of the field. His green clothes made him difficult to see among the tall green grass, but I recognised the sun in his hair.

Where was Nick?

I ran towards the river, scattering the cows so that they would get in Jack's way, then ran between the trees and bushes bordering the river. In front of me was a temporary fence made of rough wood hacked into lengths and bound together. I hitched up my smock and the wood creaked as I scrambled over it. Now I was running in St Augustine's Ley. A man leading two oxen shouted at me but I did not look at him, our eyes did not meet, probably he would not recognise me. The other side of the river was Ley Park, where some sorts of monks hunted deer, or had their sport with falcons. I heard the shouts and arguing and gossip of the women who gathered water here. They were the lowest sort, the river's flow being muddy and soiled by the cows at the old ford.

I might not make it that far. I walked, then ran again. My ankle hurt a lot and I limped. Francis Oxworth's black and white dog scampered after me, barking.

Behind me Jack jumped the thistles in Church Ley, then he jumped the rickety fence too, but the top rail broke under his foot. Francis Oxworth shouted at him and waved his stick and the black and white dog turned back from me and yapped at Jack's heels. Jack tripped. Francis shouted, 'I know you, Jack Mason!'

I was well ahead now, in sight of the stone bridge. The mortar had crumbled from between the stones, taking with it the lines of red paint that drew attention to the pointwork, so that the bridge looked gappy and weathered, although it was no older than I was.

I wondered, where is Nick?

Once past the bridge I would hide in the undergrowth by the Nailbourne Stream, and the two brothers would never find me.

Nick leapt out of the bushes. He held his arms wide, blocking the path. I stopped, looked back. Jack was still a long yardland away. I looked on the slope leading down to the old ford for stones to throw at Nick, but the mud had been dried hard as brick by the sun. Whichever way I went, Nick would catch me before I reached the bushes.

He dropped his hands to his sides, watching me, then stepped towards me. He knew he'd got me.

I ran down the slope into the water. He gave a shout of surprise, admiration perhaps. I waded out among the ripples over the old ford.

The river was icy, lovely. The heat of the summer sun beat down on my head and shoulders, the dust melted from my legs in the cool water. I thought, he won't follow me out here. I'm not worth getting wet for. And he can swim no more than I, no doubt.

18

Nick grinned. He splashed into the water, pushed forward against the flow.

'Nick, stop,' I said. I laughed to make him stop while I felt with my toes on the riverbed for a pebble to hit him with. 'I give up, Nick.' But the riverbed was soft slime and weeds, nothing hard. I sank in the mud to my ankles and the river rose over my waist. The stones and rubble chucked across the riverbed to make the ford in Noah's day had been allowed to wash away since the bridge was built, and the water was too deep for me.

Nick said, 'How do you know my name?'

'Oh, that's just one of the things I know,' I bragged. I wanted him to think I knew everything.

'You've been spying on us,' Nick accused. 'Who for?' He thought I was a thief, and I remembered all the things worth stealing in the house. I began to realise how stupid I had been. 'Tom Ratface?' he demanded. 'The outlaws at Tegham Pits? What are you planning to steal?'

I stepped backwards into deep water. The river rose around my chest. 'Steal?' I gasped. I shivered. 'I wasn't going to steal anything.'

'Do you expect me to believe you?' He waded into arm's reach. 'Who told you my name?'

I felt backwards with my foot but there was nothing, nothing but water. I would go over my head if I retreated further. It was time to tell the truth.

'Jack,' I said. 'Jack told me your name.'

Jack looked angry

Jack called from the bank, 'I never spoke to her in my life.' His face was flushed from running, not anger. 'Who is she, Nick? I can't even see her for all her hair and dirt.'

'I'll find out.' Nick ducked me. Bubbles rushed past my eyes, then slowed. His hand rubbed my face underwater. I coughed bubbles, I hated being held down. The water crept icily against my skull as it seeped through my hair. I tried to stand up but my feet could not find bottom. I struggled. Suddenly I struggled wildly, terrified. The harder I struggled, the harder Nick held me down. I had no breath. I heard the sound of bubbles breaking from my mouth, and the splash of my feet kicking spray from the surface of the water echoed down to me as a deep, hollow, booming sound. Weed brushed my face like slimy fingers, I was upside down. I was drowning. A voice shouted, 'Let her go! Nick, let her go!'

A hand found my arm, hauled me up. I spluttered a mouthful of water, gasped for breath in the sunlight. The sun had never been so bright or so perfect.

Jack was in the water. He shoved angrily at Nick. 'What got into you, Nick? What's wrong?'

Jack pulled me to the bank. Even in shallow water I could not find my feet. I could not run away. I could not even stand up. He lifted me up in his arms and dropped me on the riverbank. I lay among the grasses and the sun shone through the treetops above us.

Jack's hand wiped the hair and mud and water from my face.

'But you're lovely,' he said.

Boys have no mercy, they are cruel to anything in their power.

But Jack says, 'What got into you, Nick? What's wrong?'

I did not know what to think as I limped away from the two shocked boys. I coughed water. They tried to follow and I threw pebbles behind me, grass, flakes of dry soil, dust, anything I found. The dust and grass floated on the wind. The old monk who took the tolls reproved the boys from his shelter on the bridge, then Francis the ox-master arrived red-faced, complaining. They were in trouble, I saw, and they'd find no friends in the rough older women fetching water. By the time Nick and Jack got free of them to torment me further, no doubt, I would not be there to be found.

Boys do not grow up, they are vicious little children, they show their strength by pulling the wings from butterflies and the petals from flowers.

But Jack's hand wipes the hair and mud and water from my face.

They throw stones at other boys and at girls and pull our hair and make us cry so they can laugh at us. When Gilbert Woolton pushed Margaret de la Ley into a puddle, she cried. Gilbert pushed me, too, but I swore at him and bit him, and then he called me Alice Lack-a-Nail. Maud and Matilda Lukedale ran away when he threw a stone, but I threw a bigger stone at him. It missed, but there was no one to see him lose face, so he left me alone. They are all the same. I belched water.

But Jack says, 'But you're lovely.'

I crept into my hiding place by the Nailbourne for no reason except that I had decided to hide there earlier. I did what I have done all my life. I cannot change myself. I am who I am.

The sun grew hot as it climbed, then cool as rain clouds covered its glare, and the day darkened. I wove ferns over my head against the rain.

Something more than the weather had changed. I had changed. I was mad. I was so hungry I was weak, but instead of catching or cadging or stealing something to eat, all I could think about was their mother Cristina loving them, their father Alfred's fine stone house sheltering them, the plentiful food they ate with knives, and the feather mattresses they slept on. I was as completely outside their life as a mouse peering through a crack in the wall.

And Nick had thought I only wanted to steal from them. I wanted more than that. I wanted to *be* them. I wanted to feel their soft woollen clothes. I imagined wearing a brown wool dress like Cristina's, that almost reached the ground, and I imagined having children like Nicholas and Jack and being their mother. Jack had paler skin and longer hands. Despite his strength, I thought he was the gentler of the two.

I blinked the drops from my eyelashes. Raindrops pittered and pattered through the trees and the fern covering and slid down my cheeks and down my spine. I was wet through and lonely and alone and filled with despair. Martha saying, *Poor Alice, you're one of us now.* I trudged home to Pevynges Wood. It was no drier inside the lean-to than outside, the smoke clung under the clay and twigs and the rain dripped miserably. Elviva's face was dark with smoke and shiny like rubbed wood. Clothes hung on a stick over the fire, not to dry but because the greasy smoke made them waterproof. Elviva sat on a stump coughing, holding the new baby in her lap, and for the first time I noticed what a pretty child Noelle already was, the small black mole on one cheek giving her face a strange attraction. Elviva followed my eyes. 'Do you want to hold her?'

'No, I don't.' I backed away.

'Don't go. Where have you been hiding?' she demanded. I sulked. 'Hiding's the same as stealing, you know,' she chattered. 'You can't work if you're hiding, so it's theft. You're an *ancilla*, a girl slave, and if you aren't good, the Temple will make you an outlaw.' I shivered. The fire gave no heat, nothing but smoke. Elviva relished her next words. 'No one will shelter you, no one will give you bread, you can be raped and no one will lift a finger to help you, and if you're killed, no one will care.'

I tested her. 'You'll care, won't you, Elviva?'

'Not me. You'll be an outlaw. I won't be allowed to talk to you.'

'Our father should have been made an outlaw for what he did to Mabel,' I said. I touched Noelle's cheek with my fingertip. She smiled. I drew back, alarmed, then smiled too.

'She won't bite you,' Elviva said. She lived for the baby.

'Martha said something I don't understand,' I confided. 'Poor Alice, she said, you're one of us now. What did she mean?'

20

'She meant you're dirty.'

I remembered the excited, knowing look in Martha's eye. I wondered if the exact opposite was the truth. 'No, I'm clean,' I said. Elviva spat with an ugly sound, but I remembered the sun, and Jack's hand, and heard his voice saying, 'Look at her. You've cleaned her, Nick. Her hair is chestnut brown. She has blue eyes.' I remembered the exact tone of his voice as though he was even now speaking the words. Sadness, wonder, excitement in his voice. Almost hunger.

'You're dirty because you're growing up.' Elviva held the baby out for me to take, practical and remorseless. 'Come back to us, Alice.'

I listened to the dark drippy woods. Elviva did not see the raindrops, did not hear her lungs creak and cough, she had forgotten her eyes streaming from the smoke. This was her life, it was all she knew. Her acceptance was a kind of happiness. She would never steal away from here and look for the towers of Canterbury from Higham top, she would never wonder, she would never think. In a few years she would never have existed. Elviva, like Mabel, would not live old enough to marry. Elviva had never, as I had, simply walked into the church on the Sabbath and taken her place among the people standing on the floor of beaten earth beside the aisle, or caught at the priest's murmured, unintelligible mysteries of worship in the foreign language, *Dominus, Amen*, through the screen cutting ordinary folk from the privileged ground of the chancel. She had never asked who the statue on the screen was, and been told by old Peter Plowright that it was Our Lord Jesus on the Cross, and His mother Mary beside Him in His suffering, and the Apostle John. In the churchyard, I noticed, most of the wooden crosses marked the graves of children younger than I was, or children buried with their parents. Elviva did not want to know anything.

I sighed and to please her took baby Noelle unwillingly, cuddled her without affection. It hurt so much to love them when they would soon be gone. I softened. She really was the sweetest, prettiest little thing.

'She's just like you,' Elviva said. 'Like you used to be. She has your face.'

'I don't have a mole.'

'Why are you so unhappy?' Elviva said.

I shot back, 'Why aren't you?'

'It's not fair, is it, you coming back to try and make the rest of us feel wretched.' She smiled sentimentally at me holding the baby. I realised with a dreadful feeling that she was seeing my future, and she saw nothing wrong with it. Like the lambs of Temple sheep or the calves of Temple cows, we were the human offspring of Temple property, our father and mother, so we were as much Temple property as the lambs and the calves, and so would our children be. God had commanded us to multiply like the beasts of the field and the birds of the air. This was the pattern of the world made by God, a place for everyone and everyone in their place. I looked round the lean-to and wondered how all of us got inside at night. How did we lie down without suffocating? It would have been easy to build another lean-to, and there were good dry caves in the Tegham quarries where the clay had been dug out. 'Why don't we do something about it?' I said. But I knew we wouldn't.

Elviva looked disappointed. 'Come back, Alice. Give up. We have to make up for the work you're not doing.' I kissed baby Noelle and handed her back.

I stood to go and Elviva said, 'Why do you hate us?'

Look at you, I thought. Do you think I want to be like you? I'd rather live in a cave.

'Life isn't worth living,' I said. 'It's not you I hate. It's life.'

I pushed outside into the forest. I was crying. I had not meant to cry. I hardened my heart, but the tears flowed out of me as though my heart knew more than I did. A fresh wind had risen with the ending of the rain, blowing heavy drops around me from the trees, and instead of clinging greasily to my shoulders, my hair suddenly lifted in the wind like a bird's wing, no longer stiff and thick but flying behind me in the wind. I turned, and my hair flew across my face in fine chestnut ringlets which I pulled from my eyes with my fingertips, laughing.

I crossed the glade behind Three Oaks From One Root. It was wet beneath the dripping trees but the air in the clearing was dry – my hair was already dry. Then something moved and I saw the two brothers sheltering, or so they thought, beneath the oaks, and I knew chance had not brought them here. They were standing as if they could not sit. Drops showered over them from the leaves and they were thoroughly soaked and miserable. They saw me and came stiffly towards me, as though it hurt them to walk.

'We thought you might be here,' Jack said.

I snatched up a stone and backed towards the tangle of roots and the path. I showed my teeth and hissed.

Nick told Jack, 'I told you.'

But Jack held out his hands to me. 'Pax?' he called.

I put my head on one side. Jack expected me to know the word. Perhaps it was one of the mysterious words Father Humphrey muttered in church, like *Amen*. Or perhaps it was a trick to slow me before they attacked. I hesitated, and felt my bare feet tingle. Horsemen were coming.

'Listen,' Nick said. But I hardly heard his voice for the thump of horses' hooves on the path. Shadows flickered between the trees in the low evening sunlight.

'Help!' I shouted. 'Help me!'

'Shut up,' Jack said, alarmed. 'You'll get us into worse trouble.' He knew as soon as he said it he'd said the wrong thing. I wanted to get them into trouble. Our eyes met. 'Don't,' he said.

'Help! I shouted.

'Don't, Alice,' he said earnestly.

He knew my name. Perhaps Francis the ox drover had recognised me after all, but I did not think so.

'We want you to be with us, not against us,' Jack called. 'You can be one of us. You can be a boy.'

But I was already jumping across the roots on to the path. The horsemen rode into view with the sun behind them. The man on the lead stallion, a white warhorse, rode higher than the others, in a massive oak saddle strapped with iron, large enough for two men to ride. I tripped on the root, sprawled across the path. The warhorse did not shy, or slow its steady walk, or turn aside. Nor would it, unless its rider commanded. I scrambled backwards. Each iron horseshoe thumping down was larger than my head. Behind me the brothers stood rooted to the spot, staring up at the knight in awe.

The warhorse chomped foam from the cruel brass bit as it plodded forward. Lather dripped on me from its mottled lips, steam rose from the heavy leather armour and white canvas that clothed its huge bulk. I had never seen a horse so large, but I knew the long white hairs growing down its legs were called feathers, as though such a heavy horse could somehow fly. Everyone knew the horses of the Knights Templar could fly. The thick red reins and girth were bound with wire so they could not be cut in battle, and the knight gripped them with gloves forged of chain-mail links, heavy wet iron that must have been horribly uncomfortable. His whole body was clad in chain from his filthy red-chafed neck to his pointed feet, and a heavy chain overskirt hung to his knees. His rain-soaked white cloak (secured at the neck by the Agnus Dei, the Lamb of God, the only ornament permitted the Templars) was draped from his shoulders over the rump of his horse, so that the cloak also steamed and stank. Down his front he wore a white tabard woven with a single ornament, the shape of the holy Cross in blood-red, its ends splayed out to make the ferocious symbol of the blood and suffering and humility of Our Lord Jesus Christ.

I knew this man. He owned me.

I heard Nick gasp, 'He's a Templar.'

They are men who, like butchers, live by blood. They are God's soldiers.

Jack ran forward. 'Get out of his way, Alice.' The horse thumped forward another stride. But I stared up.

Once before I had seen this man, the knight Geoffrey de Prudome, riding along the Moat Gate path to Temple Moat. The small Templar castle, or preceptory, was almost hidden behind the moat and trees and a cluster of outbuildings, armouries, stores, barns, a small round chapel like a temple. No doubt the wealthy Grand Master never looked down far enough to notice the ants toiling in his fields, but through the enormous holdings and estates of his order in this country I was his property *nativa*, born and bred, my life worth nothing more than a few pence.

The Master glanced down at me indifferently as he rode, weary no doubt after his long journey from London, and doubtless he had passed many like me on the roadside. From his filthy unwashed face his strange dark eyes seemed to look both ways, a monk and yet a warrior.

He looked me. His eyebrows drew together beneath the brim of his iron helmet, his lips moved under his unkempt black moustache, he dragged on the rein. Oily droplets squeezed through his chain-mail gloves from the rain-soaked leather and cotton undergloves beneath, showing his strength. The warhorse halted in mid-stride, then took half a step back.

The men-at-arms following behind, who wore black or brown, reined in their mounts obediently. Household staff and the foot soldiers and bowmen behind them, wearing dark green, turned aside watchfully. The whole jingling column was brought to a halt. The Master's every movement was an unspoken command. A chaplain wearing pale green prayed. A steward bustled forward officiously to knock me aside with his rod.

But the Master stopped him with a look, then, like most nobles, spoke our common English with the strong foreign accent called French.

'Well, child?'

Child, not girl. He ignored the fact that I was a girl though it must have been obvious to him, the wind blowing my hair across my face, my nipples itching from the wet nettle threads of my smock, my knees showing bare where it was torn. But he spared me only brief, disgusted glances. A Knight Templar knows no woman, he lives in chastity like our lord Jesus Christ. His sisters and even his mother are not allowed to approach the Temple in which he lives, just as the Holy Mother did not approach her Son until the hour of His greatest suffering upon the Cross.

Jack said calmly, 'Alice, sister, for pity's sake come home with your brothers.'

The knight spoke sharply. 'You fear your brothers, child? *Oc?* Is this true?'

This would not do. A girl who feared her brothers was a bad child. I had asked a Knight Templar for help in a childish squabble, and in a moment he would see it clearly. He might kill us all. Jack and Nick stared at me with round eyes. A Knight Templar of the Order of the Poor Fellow-Soldiers of Christ and the Temple of Solomon is the priest of knights, answerable only to the Pope. By papal decree he is excused from all authority on earth, and all taxes and tolls; he is on God's business. Kings and cardinals may not command him, only the Pope. He does not obey the fourth Commandment, Thou shalt not kill. A Knight Templar kills for Christ. He worships God. He protects pilgrims. Nothing more, nothing less.

The sword at the Templar's side reached from his chest to his heel.

It came to me in a flash what I must say. I pressed my forehead to his foot. The Master flinched at my touch. 'Sire,' I confessed, 'I am *pauper et peregrina*, a poor pilgrim. These boys and I are travellers together,' I searched desperately for words, 'travellers made brother and sister by pilgrimage.'

The Master reached down, turned my face up. The chain links on his fingers smelt of sweat and cold wet rain. He held my chin between finger and thumb, stared at me close, then closer. Threads of snot and saliva mingled with the beads of rain clinging to his moustache. His beard straggled over the chin-piece of his helmet, each hair longer than my hand.

'You are young to be a pilgrim.' His eyes flicked from my lips to my eyes. He seemed to look into my soul.

I gabbled, 'Sire, I am walking with my father and mother to the shrine of good Saint Thomas at Canterbury! I lost them in the woods and could not find the path again!'

'Lost? Only lost? Yet you shouted for help.' He wiped his thumb over my cheek, thoughtfully, as though the iron felt out the shape of my bones. At any moment he would see through my story. 'And, as you plainly know that I am sworn to the aid and succour of pilgrims, I begin to suspect you . . .'

'Sire, I shouted for help because I was afraid!' He gave me a blank stare. He did not understand fear. I went on quickly, 'The pilgrims split up to search for me among the trees.'

'Then where are they now?'

'I wandered far. So far that at first I did not recognise these boys, my brother pilgrims, in the darkness of the forest, and I was afraid they were outlaws. So I ran from them and shouted for help. But they are good boys and only wanted to show me the way to the road.'

'A misunderstanding, sire,' Jack said. 'We'll guide our sister back to her father. He'll be overjoyed to see her.'

'That is the truth, sire,' I said.

But the Master shook his head slowly. 'Have I not seen you before?' His frown deepened. 'Somewhere . . . not here. Near here. Where do you come from?'

I could think of not one single other place in the world.

'Outside the village,' Jack said, and I realised his mind had gone as empty as my own, and we almost laughed.

'London,' I said. Everyone has heard of London.

The Master nodded, but did not lose interest. '*Oc*. That may be.' *Oc* is their word for yes. A horse whinnied, breaking his concentration on my face. 'Perhaps it was in London, then. Perhaps I shall see you again.' He relinquished my face from his finger and thumb, but he did not take his eyes off me. His gaze rested on me like heat, but I was so relieved to be released from his touch that I almost fell down. His heel spurs were as long as his foot, sharp as knives. Then he nodded again, touched his spurs lightly to the horse's flanks. 'I wish you safe journey, pilgrim.' The warhorse resumed its steady, stately walk, but the Master looked back over his shoulder at me until the corner hid me from his sight.

The three of us stood without moving until the last man plodded round the corner. The path was quiet again. An owl called.

Jack threw his arms round me, danced me about the path, kissed me as though it was Mayday. 'London!' he whooped. 'She *is* one of us. Throws stones like a boy, runs as fast, even thinks as quick. Marched straight up to him!' Jack clasped his hands over his chest, mimicked a girlish voice. 'Oh, I am a poor *pauper et peregrina*!' His voice broke and we both laughed, then I pushed him away.

'I'm not a boy,' I said. Jack farted and I waved my hand in front of my face. 'And I don't want to be, either.' I looked down the path where the men had disappeared, only the churned mud showing where they had been.

Nick watched us seriously. He was the serious one, the thinker. But Jack was the leader.

'Listen,' Nick said in a low voice. 'Did you see the cross he wore on his chest? On his left breast. They say its red colour is the *sang réal*, it is the tincture of a single drop of Christ's blood. Her hair blew across it every time the wind blew.' He reached out to my hair. 'Her hair touched the blood of Christ.'

The boys touched my hair reverently. The curls slipped softly through their fingers, and we were not quite children any more.

I broke the spell. 'All right. I'll be a boy, if you'll be girls.'

The boys looked horrified. They shook their heads as one, suddenly just boys again. I asked, 'What does *pax* mean?'

'Peace.' Jack looked uncomfortable. 'Francis Oxworth caught us by the river. He thrashed us. It didn't hurt!'

'He thrashed you for what you did to me?'

'No, why should he care about you? For us frightening the animals. It took us till afternoon to catch them.' Jack looked meaningfully at Nick. This was something they had decided. 'You tell her.'

Nick said, 'I'm sorry I held you down in the river.'

'You could have killed me.'

'I didn't mean to.'

'Nick isn't sorry,' Jack explained. 'He was afraid.'

Nick said, 'I was not afraid.'

Jack said, 'You were afraid of drowning.' *You.* Jack was on my side against Nick.

I burst out, 'He nearly drowned *me*!'

'That's what happens,' Jack said. 'You were afraid, weren't you, Nick? You couldn't stop thinking about drowning.'

'I wasn't afraid,' Nick said.

Jack gave him a look. 'We agreed.'

'I wasn't afraid.'

'All right.' Jack shrugged. 'Nick wasn't afraid.'

'Yes, I was,' Nick said. 'I was afraid. Do you forgive me, Alice?' He took my hand.

My heart was racing, but I made them wait. 'All right.'

Jack took my other hand. 'Friends?'

I coloured and looked at them with pride, our joined hands, a ring of friends. The brothers gazed at me anxiously. I made them wait longer this time. 'Friends,' I agreed.

Jack looked pleased. He took his hand from mine and the moment broke. 'Go on, show her your arse, Nick.'

'No, I'm not showing her my arse,' Nick said.

Jack dropped his breeches and proudly showed me the stripes and scratches marking his round white backside.

'Did Francis Oxworth do that?' I was impressed. For the first time I realised that boys have round bottoms, whereas ours are pear-shaped. The stripes I could understand, but the scratches confused me.

'He whipped us. Then our mother did.' Cristina. I thought of her brown woollen dress. It must be hard bringing up two sons with their father so often away. 'She thrashed us because Clemencia Woolton had seen what we'd done and told her. Her long scratchy besom, hazel, birch. That hurt even worse.' I thought, I'll wager being told to apologise to me hurt you a good deal more. Obviously Cristina had known who I was, for she had told the boys my name. But *how* had she known, and why did she care?

I had no time to think of that now, because Jack was wiggling his arse. I said solicitously, 'Is it still painful?'

'Yes.'

I kicked him. He laughed. Nick pulled down his breeches. I kicked him too.

'Good,' Jack said. 'I'm glad we told your knight we were brothers and sister. Now let's go and stone Gilbert Woolton.'

I grew up. I learned that everything that is simple for a child is complicated for an adult, and that if I learned to look around me more, the more I saw. The forest is more than trees, and trees are more than wood and bark and leaves. Life grows from poisonous soil and rotting manure, and the world is larger than Abbot's Littlebourne. God and the Devil are real, and the angels of good and evil are constantly at war beneath us in the underpinnings of our world. Dogs do not have souls but women do. The stars and sun and moon are held in God's arms, with Man at the centre of the universe. It would take a man more than seven thousand years, even on a Templar's flying horse, to ride to the nearest star. In his cramped teaching cell Brother Paulus revealed these truths to Nick and Jack, and they told me. Women, the monk confided, are born for the confusion of men. Woman is an insatiable beast, a continuous anxiety, an incessant warfare, a daily ruin, a house of tempest, a hindrance to devotion. 'He means you,' Jack told me.

'He wants you to be monks,' I said.

'I'm no monk,' Jack grinned. 'Nick is. He'd make a good monk.'

Other matters, apparently, are not so certain. Is the baby growing within its mother blessed with a soul at conception, or at birth, or at baptism? Certainly an unbaptised child is cast down to Hell. But does even the baptised soul see the face of God revealed at the moment of the earthly body's death, or must it await the glory of the Beatific Vision until the Day of Judgement? Jack yawned, lay back in the grass, flicked pebbles in Miller's Pool, and we lay half-awake listening to the churning of the millwheel. Water is the entrance to the world of the spirits, which is why bridges are so important to travellers, and fords universally despised. Jack said, 'My father says the soul cannot leave the body until it is buried in consecrated ground.' I yawned because he yawned, Jack's yawns always had that effect on me.

'Everyone knows that,' I said. Everyone in the forest did. I didn't know if Father Humphrey taught it in church. I think he just mumbled Latin from memory, neither reading the words nor understanding their meaning. I didn't dare reveal my suspicion to the boys, they were more accustomed than I to the services and did not question them. I wanted them to think about me, not God. I was thrilled by their company, and lying between Nick and Jack on the grass I knew life was more marvellous than we can imagine, and that marvels are all around us, all the time, everywhere.

But at first, being a child was simple.

Can you see us running? Can you hear our laughing voices? Jack and Nicholas and Alice, Alice and Nicholas and Jack. Brothers and sister. From a life of misery I came to happiness, out of cold loneliness I found warm friendship. Nothing I could ever do would repay the brothers for their gift, their transformation of my life. Everything I remember of my childhood is of them. They had everything, taller than I was because well-fed, and I looked up to them as though they were made of gold.

I taught them everything I knew.

I taught them hunger. The boys had never thought of hunger before, and it amazed them. I was always hungry. I had no one to give *me* a platter of meat and bread or a bowl of milk still bubbling from the house cow. Nick brought me a slice of beef under his jerkin; I ate it still warm from his skin. Jack slipped me a piece of the goat's cheese. I had never eaten cheese before. They watched me eat, then looked at one another.

'More next time,' Jack said.

'Or she'll eat us too,' Nick said.

'Don't get caught.' I wiped breadcrumbs from my mouth with my thumb, belching.

'We never get caught,' Jack said. He added, 'Hardly ever.' He combed the fingers of his right hand through his hair, his habit.

'She can't be this hungry.' Nick watched me pull at the meat.

Jack said in a low, marvelling voice, 'Look at her. We have to feed her.'

'I'll show you how,' I said.

Each brother was as bad as his twin. They fell out of apple trees together, piled sour apples in my smock, we ran together and ate the apples in any of a hundred secret places I knew, and together, full, we groaned with bellyache.

Feeding Alice, they decided, was fun.

I showed them how to move quietly through the forest. I taught them how to be motionless as lifeless twigs. For all their schooling and numbers, they knew almost nothing. I taught them silence, patience, stillness, speed, everything that was second nature to me. A robin redbreast perched on my fingertip, then as I raised my hand it plucked the worm from my lips, pecking as delicately with its sharp tiny beak as a breath of wind. I taught them to make fish lines of woven grass or tall sinewy stalks of nettle, strong and supple, and hooks out of fishbone, and in which pools of the Little Stour the fish lay. 'Fishbone,' Jack said, looking admiringly at the flapping minnow on the hook. 'I call that catching fish with fish.'

Nick laughed, but Jack's wit was sharp enough to cut him, one day. Too often he thought clever words settled matters, and moved on when agreement had not been reached in the hearts of others. Jack thought the world of himself and thought everyone else did too. I turned my back on him and spoke to Nick, who always listened carefully without interrupting, and did not take his eyes from my own. No one knew the boys better than I.

I taught them how to be shadows, how to twitch the fish line temptingly, when to jerk it tight to bed the hook. A few carp always escape from Fishpool during the winter rains, and I showed the brothers how to lie on the planks of the Telebridge, chew a mouthful of bread to paste, then squeeze it in their hands mixed with the juice of a berry. Reaching my hand down into the Lampen Stream, the carp scented the prize in my fist and rose up, mouths gaping, forgetting my other hand sliding under their slimy bellies, and so they died gasping on the grass. I showed the brothers how to slit the fat carp and gut them and spit them and cook them on a fire without flame or smoke to give us away.

'What did we do before Alice?' Jack asked sleepily.

'We didn't do anything,' Nick said. 'We were lost. Our lives weren't worth living.' He squeezed my hand, yawning, but I sat up to the fire. Leaves whirled from above us and the sun was cool. Autumn was here and I was afraid I would not see the brothers so much in cold weather. Once I crouched, alone, among the dry leaves of Pevynges Wood and watched the smoke leak from the lean-to, and listened to Elviva's cough. My mother came outside, broad and beamy, her face burnished by soot, white runnels down her cheeks where her tears had run, and I saw the woman I would become. Noelle toddled beside her clothed in rags, smiling with my face, made strangely enchanting by the black mole. I smiled just to see her, then shrank back between the trees and ran away.

One evening I dared the brothers to come with me to Fishpool. Not much daring was required. Such illicit projects always excited them and kept them close to me. Jack is not the only one clever and cunning; I see it in him because it is expected of a young man, but he cannot see it in me because I am a girl. Boys are easy to use, and my skill was growing. On a grey rainy evening, twilight made early by the rain, we crossed the little bridge near Three Oaks From One Root and crawled through the soaking pasture to Fishpool. The rain hissed lightly on the waters.

'What do you think Mother would think of us if she knew we were here?' Nick whispered.

Fishpool is several pools joined together, fed from Adrian's Spring. Since Adrian was abbot nearly five centuries ago the ponds have been prized by hungry monks who eat fish on meatless days – one pool for trout, another for carp, dace and rochets together in a small pond, and mature roach transferred to the large pool, a pond of stub eels for stewing and another of shaft eels for baking in pastry. All are covered by nets against herons, kingfishers and thieves like us, and supposed to be guarded by one of the monk-warden's urchins. But not on such a night. Jack crawled up the earth bank, steep to prevent eels climbing out and wriggling in shoals across the fields in search of snails. He lifted the net, slipped underneath and quickly hooked three long eels. He held up the bunch admiringly and we heard their tails whipping in the dark. He whispered, 'I call that catching eels with fish.'

No fish clings more tenaciously to life than an eel, and even after we had skinned them and cut them up, the pieces continued to wriggle. Jack boiled them for us in a little pot, chopping dried parsley with his knife. He was very pleased with himself. I was disappointed. The eel dare had been too easy, and now Jack would be cockier than ever. I finished first and licked my fingers.

'You've never tasted pike, have you?' I said.

He chewed. 'Have you?'

'There's no pike at Fishpool,' Nick said. 'Pike's the knight of fish.'

'Exactly,' I said. 'And I know where they are . . .'

I waited at the back of the house. The evening star winked over the last glow of the sun behind the church, it was a freezing clear night. I had not eaten all day, except acorns like a squirrel, the winter is a hard mistress. I heard Agnes the kitchen slut snoring. Then the shutter moved, and the boys slipped out from the window on to the frozen mud. They cursed the cold, then each kissed my cheeks, so that the two kisses came simultaneously to me on each side from the dark. They pressed soft bread and part of a chine of salt pork into my hand. 'Doesn't your mother miss her food?' I hissed as we clambered over the yard wall.

'She believes Agnes steals it,' Jack grinned, 'and says nothing out of mercy. She knows what it is to be hungry, I think.' Remembering her large white arms and broad hips, I doubted Cristina knew any more of hunger than her boys had. I led her sons across the frosty field ditches in the last glim of day, eating my bread from one hand and meat from the other, took the road past Fishpool and arrived by Moat Gate at the perfect time, the interval of total darkness between sunset and moonrise. The brothers stumbled and swore behind me, they suspected where I was leading them but their pride obliged them to follow. I hissed and they found me. I reached up into the dark, lifted myself up and straddled the tall gate, but Nick grabbed my leg.

'Where are we going?'

'The knight of fish,' I reminded him. 'Born and bred and fed for the table of knights.'

'Temple Moat.' I glimpsed the whites of Nick's eyes. The moon was rising behind the Templar castle and would soon illuminate us. 'She's going to get us into trouble,' Nick said. 'If they catch us they'll beat us. I've already been beaten once for you, Alice.'

I taunted them, 'You aren't afraid, are you?'

'I'm not afraid, not I.' Nick swung his leg over the gate and I heard him jump down into the bushes that lined the track. I grinned. Nothing frightened boys, and perhaps even men, more than showing fear to a girl.

'Nor me,' Jack said. He straddled the gate, then I felt his breath on my face. 'Pike are dangerous, Alice. They're noble fish, they fight, and they have fierce teeth. What are you up to?'

'You can show us how to catch them,' I shrugged.

Jack kissed me on the lips. 'I'll show you,' he said.

'Come on, you two,' Nick whispered in the dark. I realised he couldn't see us, and so did Jack. He squeezed my shoulders, his mouth and tongue moved silently against my lips, speaking without words, then a hot feeling rushed through me and I felt exactly what he was saying. I had always wanted to put my hands in his hair. His fingers slipped to my chest, felt something there, and we gasped in each other's mouths. In the palm of his hand my nipple hardened on my breast, which felt full and soft like Mother's. I was ashamed of myself, pulled away, jumped down from the gate. Jack held me, then let me slip between his fingers until he held only my hand. He did not let my hand go. 'Alice?'

'Jack.'

The bushes rustled, Nick returned. 'What's the trouble?' If we didn't hurry the moon would rise over the castle and reveal our movements as bright as day.

'We've got to get in place before the moonlight strikes the moat,' Jack said 'The ground has been cleared and any movement will show.' I looked up at him adoringly and sensed him wink at me. We even thought the same thoughts. I wished I could see all of him.

He swung down, then held my hand as we crept forward towards the moat. The black jumble of buildings and roof lines was meaningless to me. 'Temple Moat is part of the Preceptory of Kent,' Jack whispered as we crawled. 'The commander of each lodge is called a preceptor. The knights are fabulously wealthy, and they keep these commanderies of stored weaponry and armour in every shire ready for the Pope's call.'

I whispered, 'How do you know this?'

He shrugged. 'Templar walls are built of stone, by masons. Masons used to be a fraternity of monks, you know. My father told me.'

'Told you?'

He hesitated. 'I cannot repeat it.'

'You kissed me.'

Jack made his choice. When we are in love everything seems so simple, so easy, so harmless. 'Masons and Templars are always close, Alice. Hiram the Mason was the builder of Solomon's Temple, built in Jerusalem two thousand years ago, in the early days of the world. Now brother masons are raising the new Temple of the Knights Templar in Jerusalem over the ruins. They uncovered the winding staircase going down beneath the ancient foundations.'

I shivered in the frost but his hand holding mine was hot. It never occurred to us that people were tortured and killed for revealing this information, that William the Bachelor, the Grand Templar Master of Ireland, had been bricked up in a wall for his indiscretion, with a hole large enough for water to be passed through but not food, so that he lived for almost twelve weeks in his agony before expiring. Jack tugged me forward through the darkness, then paused watchfully. I felt but could not see the flattened track in the frosty grass left by Nick's knees. He too had paused here, the marks had melted. I sucked the drops from my fingertips, then whispered, 'A winding staircase? Do the Templars know?'

'Yes, of course. There's always a winding staircase. Even in those days the builder was killed when he completed his work and sealed inside its stones, just as in ancient Egypt.'

I imagined the cold stones coming down over me and settling in place for ever. 'How horrible!' I said, enthralled.

Jack shrugged but I could tell how much he wanted to impress me. 'Even today a cathedral architect, a really good one, is often killed when his work is done.'

'Why?'

'So he can't build a better cathedral somewhere else. Castles have a young girl bricked up in the walls so that her spirit will give the fortifications strength.'

'Why a girl?' I murmured.

'Men create life, but it is brought to flower in women. My father has sometimes found their bones when he's been doing repairs.'

I gripped his hand tight as we crawled forward. Moonlight shone on our right, swinging towards us. We moved forward along a shadow that was the shape of the castle. The castle wall rose over us, the moat gleamed suddenly. We were close.

'Jack, do you think bones are sealed in these walls?'

He chuckled. 'Of course.'

I jerked his hand. 'You're playing. It isn't true. Not a word of it.'

He parroted what he must have overheard. 'Solomon's Temple was built on Mount Moriah, one of the ridges of Mount Zion. The winding staircase found by the masons led down to the Sanctum Sanctorum, the Sacred Lodge presided over by King Solomon, the holiest place beneath the Temple. Long ago Hiram the Master Mason was taken down in chains. He was stripped to the waist and there was a secret ceremony playacting his death and rebirth, just like they do today.'

I was disappointed. 'Then it's just a game.'

'Yes, just a game, Alice. Like your little dares.' He added, 'And your game that just happened, on the gate.' He was ashamed of kissing me and was trying to blame me. I knew why. This was Brother Paulus and his sterile envious teaching about women being insatiable beasts and houses of tempest. Jack, in defiance of his nature, believed what he had been taught. But I believed in Jack on the gate.

'How can you believe I'm horrid?' I was crushed and must have sounded it. 'Didn't you mean it to happen?'

'Your mood changes quickly, doesn't it? Come on, Alice. You're blaming me, aren't you? You kissed me—'

'No I didn't! *You* kissed *me*. It isn't a sin, Jack.'

'Yes, it is. You know all about sin, don't you? All you girls do, you're born to like it.'

I looked at him tearfully. We sounded just like grown-ups. I sniffed and wiped my tears but he paid no attention. I pulled my hand out of his hand and crossed my arms and turned my back.

He whispered, 'Hiram suffered his symbolic death and rebirth in the Sacred Lodge. Then he was led down the vaulted crypts deep below, to the one called Bir Arruah, the Well of Souls. There he was ritually killed, for real.'

'For real?'

'Crucified, in the dark. And his bones were sealed in the stones he had built, and he made his entrance through the grave into eternal life.'

'But *why*?'

'Because Hiram had enlisted the help of his half-brother, the demon Asmodeus, to finish the Temple. Knowledge is sin. All knowledge comes from the Devil. Only faith comes from God.' He confessed, 'All I know is, I wanted to kiss you, I *did*, I *do*, and I'm glad I did.' Jack ferreted my hand into his. 'Pax?'

I decided to be difficult. 'You don't really mean it.'

30

'You know I do.'

'Only words.' I strung him out expectantly.

Jack's lips touched mine. Everything was all right between us again. 'Of course I meant you to,' I whispered. I tousled his hair.

'What I've just told you makes us much closer than a kiss, Alice. One day I shall take an oath to tell you nothing.'

'Oh, when you're a mason? Your silly stories and secret ceremonies. You're as bad as Father Humphrey and his Latin no one understands. The games you men play.'

'Brother Paulus is right,' Jack murmured. 'A girl is a hindrance to devotion.'

A slice of the moon appeared beside the castle wall. We would be illuminated any moment. I whispered, 'Believe in me,' and tugged him into the dark.

We crept to the icy edge of the moat and I felt someone move, warm. 'It's me,' Nick said. He moved almost as silently as I did, learning my craft. We kept to the shadow of a tree as the moon swung over us. No one patrolled the battlements. The moat was not black like normal water, but white. 'It's ice,' Nick said. 'So much for fishing. Let's go home.'

'Make a hole in it,' Jack said. Nick and I looked at each other. Jack crawled along the shadow of the tree on to the ice. The ice creaked. He stopped, then lay down, spreading his weight, and slid forward. I saw his eating knife flash as he made a dark hole in the ice, then levered his sigh. He slid carefully back to us on his belly and sat up.

Nick said, 'Who's got the fishing line?'

I made them wait. Jack chuckled, although his hands and bottom must have been almost frozen to the ice. He knew. I pulled a roll of black twine from my pouch. 'Stronger than grass or nettle,' I informed them. 'Horsehair.'

'Whose horse?' Nick said.

'Your donkey's tail.' I unrolled the greasy loops to reveal a precious iron hook.

'Catching a pike with a donkey,' Jack said. He took the line, spreadeagled himself, kicked off from the bank and slid out along the tree's shadow. Nick and I watched him bait the hook with the mouthful of salt pork I had given him. He dropped the hook through the hole and turned his head towards us, made a yawn. We might be here for hours, for nothing.

The line moved almost at once. 'It's nothing,' Jack said, but he twitched the line as I had taught him, then jerked. Up came a slim silvery fish, its ring of teeth looking as fine and sharp as pins. 'The hook's bigger than the fish,' I scoffed.

'That's not even a pickerel,' Nick whispered. 'It's got to be a proper pike, it's got to be bigger than three pounds, hasn't it, Alice?' Nick is always precise.

'All right, all right,' Jack muttered. He disengaged the hook carefully and dropped the fish back in the black water. I noticed one side of the hole showed a white gleam of moonlight.

I looked up at the roofs showing beyond the moat wall. Because of the nearby clay pits the sloped pitches were of tile, not thatch. Nick put his mouth close to my ear. 'Tiles reduce the risk of fire from burning arrows. The wooden end beams are whitened with chalk for the same reason.' But I wondered if the walls were less for resisting siege than simply to ensure privacy. They were not high enough to withstand a serious assault, though the moat was broad except at the gate on our left, where the drawbridge would come down. Nick whispered, 'The Templars call all their properties lodges, whether they are fortified or not.' By the size of the roofs I guessed the tax barns for storing grain were huge – they levied grain taxes but did not pay them. I noticed a roof of a different pitch. 'That's probably the stables,' Nick whispered. 'They have hundreds of horses. A knight dresses only in white, rides only white horses, and only stallions. He is attended by a triune of three sergeants who wear black and are provided with

31

two horses each. Each sergeant is responsible for a triune of three men-at-arms who wear brown.' I loved to hear the boyish enthusiasm in Nick's voice. Once they discover an interest, boys like to think they know everything about it. Jack listened, but his eyes were fixed on me. He saw me looking at him and grinned, returned his attention to the hole. It was half moonlit now. He moved a little, keeping in the shadow of the tree. A horse whinnied beyond the walls. 'That's the stables all right,' Nick said, but I wondered what had disturbed the animal. Animals sense more than we do.

'Chaplains wear pale green,' Nick said. 'Pale green, the colour of death. The Pope has given the Templars special dispensation to dismiss any priest or chaplain who does not please them.' Not even King Henry was so powerful. 'Apart from the knights, who wear the Cross of Christ's Blood on white, the chaplains alone of the Brethren of the Temple are allowed to wear two colours. They put white gloves over their filthy hands before touching the Host during Mass.'

The horses whinnied, at least two this time. I looked round but sensed no change in the air. The moon shone steadily.

I whispered, 'Filthy hands?'

'The Templars never wash or shave. The Rule of St Bernard forbids it. They are forbidden to hunt, except lions. They are not allowed to wear fur, except sheepskin. They are forbidden women.'

'Why?'

Nick parroted Brother Paulus. 'The sin of Eve. Because of women, the ancient demon denied us the right to live in Paradise.'

Jack sat up. He had shifted to keep in the shadow of the tree. The hole in the ice was moonlit now. I saw the curve of the line stiffen gently, begin to slide out between his finger and thumb. Nick was still talking.

I murmured, 'So they can't have children?'

'Of course not. Their only love is pure love, for God. They fight and pray. That's all they do.'

Jack glanced at me. I realised he always turned towards me now, not Nick, when something exciting was happening. This was the first time I had noticed it. Nick fell silent. Perhaps he noticed it too.

Jack twitched the line. The line continued to run out between his forefinger and thumb. He looked down to check how much he had left. He lifted his other hand, letting the line slide over his palm, then gripped hard, jerked the line. He glanced at me, blew on his fingers. Hot.

The horses in the stable neighed and stamped excitedly. The call was returned from behind us, on the road. I heard nothing more until I put my ear to the ground. 'Hoofbeats, more than one,' I whispered. 'Someone's coming. Let the fish go, Jack.'

'It's big.' He tugged, then the line went slack. His arms worked busily, pulling in the wet dripping loops.

'It's gone,' I said.

He hissed, 'It's coming back towards me.'

I heard the iron gate latch clang.

'Let the line go,' I said. 'Let the fish go, Jack!'

'Keep still.' Nick held my elbow, pointed with his head. Men were moving along the battlements. We could hear their voices but not what they were saying. The line snatched taut again in Jack's hands. He sat without moving, then his back stiffened. The muscles stood out in his arms. With two small kicks he knocked grooves to hold his heels in the slippery ice. He skidded slightly, then his heels dug in and took the strain. One of his feet showed in the moonlight but no one looked in our direction for the moment.

Horsemen rode from Moat Gate along the track towards the castle. We glimpsed their shapes flickering between the bare trees then they emerged on to the open ground we had crawled across, riding swiftly but without haste, three Knights Templar with their heavy white robes flapping a little in the chill night air. The warhorses snorted white breath with a chuffing sound like the blacksmith's furnace bellows. Behind the three knights rode nine sergeants dressed in black, only their pale faces visible, and the occasional flash of a sword or armour, or item of harness.

'Jack, leave it,' I said, but Nick stared at them.

He muttered, 'I was right. They ride in threes, and three times threes.' I pulled him down beside me and we lay without moving.

The horsemen were expected. Someone shouted a command in the castle, a mechanism groaned, and part of the wall seemed to detach itself and swing out. They were lowering the drawbridge. The top of the drawbridge gleamed suddenly in view as it leant forward into the moonlight.

'Jack!' I hissed. He tugged the line inch by inch against the strain, wrapping it round his fingers for purchase. The line led straight as a bar into the hole in the ice. Drips squeezed out of it and slid down into the water or dropped on the ice. 'Almost got him,' Jack said. He heaved the line with both hands, leant towards the hole. Where the fish line disappeared in the black water, I caught a glimpse of splicing. I had tied off the line in the eye of the hook and spliced the loose end back on itself for one hand's breadth.

'A hand's breadth, Jack,' I said. 'You're a hand's breadth away.'

'They'll pass within a hundred feet of us.' Nick stared over his shoulder. 'For Christ's love, Jack, give it up, or we're caught.'

The excitement of catching the fish overwhelmed me, and I knew Jack wouldn't give it up. I didn't want him to. He said, 'How long?'

'Ten deep breaths.'

Jack slid to the hole on his knees. He stretched himself out in full moonlight. He plunged his arm into the hole, but instead of pulling out the pike, the water seemed to jump over him. I glimpsed the gaping mouth of the fish, I saw the ribbed roof of its mouth, I saw its rows of backward-pointing teeth, I saw one black eye in its silver scales. Jack's hand, reaching out to grasp, was grasped instead by the fish's mouth, and the fish slid back down and Jack after it. He lay across the hole, his arm pulled down in the water to the armpit, his head on the other side of the hole holding him up. The riders were almost on us. Jack froze, his arm jerking from side to side beneath him and drops of water splashing and sliding over the ice. I closed my eyes. The sound of hoofbeats came closer, thudding, and harness jingling, and the horses snorting at the sight of the castle and the scent of warm stables and hay. Their long shadows sweeping over us flickered the moonlight on my eyelids.

The sound faded.

I sat up. The drawbridge was down, the horses' hooves drummed loudly across the timbers, the riders disappeared behind the castle walls. Briefly I heard the calls of ostlers and squires and all the scurry and flurry of a great organisation, then the drawbridge rose and everything was silent and still.

'Did you see them?' Nick whispered. 'Did you see them?'

'Jack!' I slid across the ice. Jack sat by the hole with his elbows resting on his knees, cradling his arm in his lap. The ice creaked beneath us but I didn't think. All I saw was his face as pale as the moon, and I thought he had lost his hand. 'Jack?'

Nick slid out. 'You with us, Jack?'

'Jack, please,' I said gently. Jack put up his face to be kissed. I kissed him. I cried over him. He licked my tears. Nick kissed me. He put his arms round us both.

'It's all right,' he whispered. 'I'll look after you, I'll look after you both.'

Jack held up his cut hand. 'Did you see?'

'I saw,' I said.

He tried to impress me by showing me his hand. 'Live bait,' he said. He sounded shaken but so proud of his injuries that I could have hit him.

'Let's get home,' I said.

He grinned and squeezed me. 'Boy caught by fish.'

The moment Jack touched the shutter and tried to climb through the window, the door opened, a candle was held up, and Cristina's huge angry face pushed into the circle of light like a storm. 'Get down. Get away from there. Come here. Where have you boys been? I was worried sick!' She gave Jack a slap, and I knew exactly why, wiping the infuriating cocky smile off his face. Jack looked so shamefaced I could have laughed, but I knew better than to give myself away. I slipped towards the yard wall, and in a moment I would be gone. 'You,' Cristina said. 'You. C'mere.'

I ran.

'You come here right this instant,' came Cristina's voice, 'or I'll talk to your mother, that I will.'

I stopped. How could she know where my mother was? Cristina couldn't see me in the dark, but the power of her personality was undeniable. I touched the wall, I actually touched it. One big jump and I would be free of her.

'Come, come, my dear.' Cristina stepped forward, carrying the candlelight across the yard, and I saw she wore a bleached linen nightshift and an embroidered woollen cap. 'Come inside. Milk and bread for you.' She held out her hand. Her hand was not soft, as I had expected, but rough with hard work. And warm, her hand was so warm. It took mine as though swallowing it into her warmth, and I did not want to be free.

Jack said, 'Mother, it was all my fault—'

She gave him a slap round the head that made Nick and me flinch. 'That's because I love you,' she told Jack, 'and don't you forget it.' She noticed his hand. 'What's this?'

'Something wonderful happened tonight, didn't it, Alice?' Nick said. I remembered Jack's kiss but I supposed Nick remembered the knights and their pale cloaks flapping in the moonlight. I kept my mouth shut.

'A fish caught me,' Jack said. For each of us the something wonderful was a little different. Then Jack winked at me over his mother's head examining his hand, and I knew he remembered the kiss.

Cristina led him inside. 'Who bandaged this?'

I held up one finger. 'Me.'

'Shut the door, there's a good girl, keep the heat in.' She sat Jack at the table, a real bench at a real table made of shaped, smoothed timbers. I looked around in awe. The bench rocked a little on the stone floor, a small dog growled at me over its bone in the straw, then wagged and returned to the fire. Cristina unwrapped the bandage I had torn from the hem of my smock, examined the cuts. 'Bound up in the blood, that's good,' she said.

'I rinsed it to spread the blood first,' I said.

'I thought you were dangling it in the water to call the fish back for another go,' Jack said.

'Yes. I was.'

'You two,' Cristina chided us, binding up the bandage exactly as it had been. 'I don't know, Jack, I really don't. You tried to stop him, didn't you, Nick?'

'Yes, Mother,' Nick said.

'You're a good boy.' She tied off the knot briskly. 'Jack, you're white as this nightshirt of mine. Go to bed.' She pulled a curtain across the corner near the fire, hiding the two straw mattresses – the boys actually slept behind a curtain of their own, in their own beds. Across the back of the room I saw that another curtain, decorated with needlework, could be drawn to hide the large wooden bed of Cristina and her absent husband, though at the cost of cutting down the heat from the fire.

'Will we be allowed to see her again?' Jack said suddenly. He pulled me forward like a small rebellious possession.

'Go to bed. You're in enough trouble already.'

Jack said recklessly, 'You can't send her away. She hasn't got anywhere to go. She'll freeze to death outside if you do.'

'Her? She isn't the sort.' Cristina gave me a dry glance. 'You'd freeze, Jack. But not her.' She clapped her hands and the boys lay down. She said something soothing then closed the curtain, turned to me appraisingly. Jack's voice came from behind the curtain: 'Her name is Alice.'

'Yes, boy, I know.'

I couldn't tell from her eyes what Cristina felt about what she saw. Her gaze travelled down me, then she frowned at my knees revealed by the torn hem. When I tried to explain about the bandage, she placed her plump finger to my lips, glanced at the curtain behind which the boys lay, doubtless with their ears flapping as wide as barn doors, and I saw her come to a decision. Not just about me, but about herself too. She had decided something big.

I pretended to be meek. Cristina took my elbow and I allowed myself to be led to the other side of the fire, which was a whole other room. It was lower and so rather smoky, as there is no means of ridding a house of smoke other than a hole in the roof covered with a raised tile. The dark greasy walls were hung with cooking implements, knives and saucepans and other vessels, no doubt with their own names, which I did not know. The old servant, Agnes, had wadded her night straw in one corner and lay asleep, snoring. I saw her hook nose and one clawed hand clasping her blanket. It was a comfortable life.

Cristina pushed my shoulder, sitting me on the three-legged stool between the scratched, scored, hornbeam work table and the fire. She went to a side room and I saw her scoop milk from a bowl into a wooden mug. My eyes closed and I listened to the crackle of the fire, and my body drank in the heat of the flames. 'This evening's milking.' Cristina held out the mug. I cupped it in my hands and drank the milk in one, already a little rancid. She held out half a stick of yeasty white loaf and watched me eat it.

'Slow down, slow down.' She sat on the stool opposite me. 'You're little Alice Lacknail, aren't you? Mary of Swanton's girl.'

I didn't know my mother's name, or where she had come from. We all called her Mother, even our father did, and all that mattered was that she lived with us in the forest and had a baby every year.

'You look like a little bird,' Cristina said sadly. She reached forward and moved a curl of hair from my eye. 'There. Now I can see you properly.'

'You've known about me for a long time.' It wasn't a question, but I did wonder how long she'd known.

'Your hair touched Christ's blood. My boys have few secrets from me, far fewer than they think. Boys are thoughtless. They whisper between themselves, or talk in their sleep. Sometimes they even confide in me.'

'You knew Nick almost drowned me in the river?'

'I knew you before that, my dear. I'd seen you in the barn, your shadowy figure round-eyed as an owl, watching us.' I was mortified. She added, 'And Yvon Piggott can't keep his mouth shut about anything. You see, dear, I knew your mother long ago.'

I wrinkled my nose. A free woman of Cristina's standing, wife of a freemason, a woman with two rooms in her house, and barns, and rents, knew my mother?

35

Cristina sighed. She fetched me an apple from the barrel in the side room, then saw I was still hungry and fetched two. 'Nowadays people call me Mistress Cristina the mason's wife, or Alfred Mason's wife. I've come a long way in the world. I didn't always live like this. When I was your age, I was Cristina of Swanton. I am your mother's cousin.' I was too fascinated by the implications of her confession to remember the apples. One dropped from my hand to the floor, rolled. I snatched it up. Cristina said: 'I was born *nativa*, like you.'

That was impossible. 'But you're free.'

'Eat your apples. Yes, I am now free. My boys would never imagine their own mother was once like you.' She chuckled. 'But I am.'

I ate the first apple. It was tiny and delicious.

'Alice, my dear, I was lucky. I gained my freedom by marrying Alfred Mason.' I looked at her blankly. I still didn't understand. 'If you marry a free man you get your freedom. It's the law. You know that of course.'

'No.'

'You plan it with one or other of my boys.'

'No!'

'Jack's the one, isn't he? It's plain as a pikestaff to me. I saw it at once.'

'No, I swear, Mistress Cristina.'

She grinned sceptically. 'I don't blame you. I, too, was quick and clever and determined, and I got my man, after we had paid a fine to the abbot whose property I was. But freedom is a harsh task mistress, as you know, Alice.'

So she knew I had run away from home. She knew everything. I nodded calmly, but I was terrified she would send me back. 'Yes, Mistress Cristina.'

'Freedom is freedom to starve. For years Alfred struggled, and we starved. We were so unhappy. I could not control my temper, I was not myself, I hated him. Unhappiness changed us both into people we would previously have despised. Alfred's work was shoddy, he drank, he lay with women. But then something happened.'

I had an idea. 'Your son Jack was born? He changed everything?'

She looked thoughtful. 'No, not my son Jack. Everything changed after Nick's birth . . . after my boy Nick arrived. Alfred pulled himself together. His work improved, he has not been without employment for one day. But he cannot stay in one place, just as once he could not look at only one woman, so he is working in Canterbury now. His drinking ceased and he has never touched a drop, not even weak beer. Not since I gave him his sons.'

She was proud of her boys. 'I was so sure they were twins!' I gossiped, giving myself time to eat the second apple before I was thrown out. 'Nick doesn't look a day younger than Jack.'

Cristina said firmly, 'Nick looks at least nine months younger to me.'

'I suppose he looks very like his father.'

'Yes,' Cristina said after a moment. 'Yes, he does.'

I nibbled round the second apple core to make it last longer. 'You must have such hopes for them. Jack will follow in his father's footsteps and take the oath to be a mason.'

'That is his father's plan. The secrets of construction are passed from father to son, it is hereditary. There are even women masons, from masonic families where the only child is a girl. But I don't know what will happen.' I thought she would go further, but she bit her lip.

'And Nick too? He'll be a mason?'

'The same as my Jack. That is the custom in Kent, and in this part of the world. Offspring share equally.' She hesitated. 'But I don't know what will happen. I just don't know. They are at a difficult age.'

Hearing her doubt, a strange feeling stole over me. Everything was not what it appeared. I popped the apple core in my mouth, stalk and all. A window shutter banged and I heard the wind outside, then the flutter of a bird. After the warmth of this fire the cold outside would be almost insupportable. I shivered despite the heat of the flames, feeling nearly too hot down my right arm. A spark burnt my bare knee. The shutter banged again and a little bird whirred up into the rafters, lost to sight.

'When you were a slave,' I whispered, 'how did you make Alfred marry you?'

'Nothing could *make* him marry me. Alfred loved me. He still loves me. Love is all it is.' Cristina smiled, brushed my hair tenderly where it had curled over my eyes again, put her fingers to her nose as though inhaling the scent of Christ's blood. This moment was terribly real to us both. I felt so close to this wonderful woman who had lived as I did, once, that whatever happened next, whether she sent me out into the cold or let me sleep till morning in the barn, seemed unimportant. 'Alice, my dear, I bedded Alfred and let him into my heart. It is the hardest thing in the world. We have made each other happier and more unhappy than any other couple, but he has never loved any other woman but me.' She pushed on her thighs and stood. 'If I love my boys, I can't send you out.'

I sat motionless by the fire while Cristina rummaged in a plain wooden chest. 'Agnes is worn down, this winter weather will see her to God.' She heaved out an old dress, shook it, and held it in front of me. 'Twelve inches too long. You'll grow into it in a year, if you live. Use it as a blanket tonight and sew it up at first light, before you start your tasks.'

'My tasks?' I knew nothing of household tasks.

'I'll show you in the morning. I'm not doing this only out of the kindness of my heart, my dear. I'm putting you where I can keep an eye on you.' She reached out to touch my hair again, then drew back sadly. 'You are exactly as I remember her. You have your mother's chestnut hair.' I was confused. My mother's hair was the colour of soot with dirt.

Mistress Cristina dropped the mat of woven straw that had covered the chest on to the floor. 'Sleep there. Tend to poor Agnes if she wakes. Remember, nothing happens in this house without my knowing it, and I'll throw you out if you displease me, snow or not.' I saw the white flakes sifting between the shutters and marvelled at my good fortune. She watched as I moved the mat beside the fire and lay my head on my hands in the rosy firelight, and closed my eyes in bliss. I slid into sleep as though it was a slippery slope, down, down, the entrance to another world.

'Jack is in love with you,' Cristina said. 'So is Nick.'

Why do we not change ourselves? Why are we always who we are?

Why are we here? Why now?

If God is perfect, why am I born to sin?

If God is perfect, why did He make the world of dirt?

I did not sleep, or if I slept I dreamt I lay awake on the straw mat by the fire, listening to the old woman snoring, dying. The bird fluttered from the beams on to my hand, a tiny rosy robin redbreast, and she – or he, I cannot tell – nestled between my hands while the crackling fire died to a silent shimmering glow. *Jack is in love with you.* I was so delighted I'd hardly heard the second part of her sentence, forgot whatever it was. I suppose you could say my heart sang within me. That Cristina did not believe in my innocence did not matter at all. One woman is a wife, they say, but two are a conspiracy. It was enough that she saw herself in me. And when I woke in the morning the fire was out, my hands were empty and cold, and the old woman Agnes lay silent, dead.

I sewed my dress, and I thought, *Jack loves me.*

We sewed poor Agnes in her shroud, but I thought, *Jack loves me.*

We carted her to the churchyard and Jack and Nick dug three feet into the frosty earth, and we dropped her down, and I watched them work to fill her in, Jack wielding the shovel right-handed, Nick with his left. I watched the sweat on Jack's forehead, I watched his sweat darken his hair, I watched him wipe his shining face with the back of his wrist as he covered her with soil. I brought him clean water to drink, and he drank and grinned at me as he worked and I thought, *Jack loves me.*

I learned my tasks, I learned my home. Up before cock-crow even in the height of summer, up much earlier than that during harvest, up from my mat in the dead of night in winter to rake out the hearth and relight it from saved embers, the fire was never out. The cow to milk, and the goat. The eggs to collect. The butter to churn, the cheese to store away from mice – the house rent was paid to the abbot in eggs and hens and cheese, and the land rent in quarters of barley, and a pig to be sent with Yvon Piggott's yearly drove to Canterbury, a cartload of faggots for the abbot's hearth, and two cartloads of cheaper bavins for the monks' fire. A master mason was well paid, and Alfred Mason had invested his money wisely, changing his silver shillings into woodlands and fields and a quarry by the Medway River, so that even his money worked instead of resting in his pouch for a thief's grasping fingers.

Fetching water from the well in the corner of the yard, I was for a moment out of sight from the house. Jack kissed me as I turned so I almost dropped the buckets, and he put his hands over mine so that I put the buckets down, and kissed me again, and I knew that what he felt and what I felt was love. I wanted everything of him, I wanted to talk. I asked, 'Who was King Lovernios?'

That made him pay attention. He peered curiously into my eyes. 'How do you know about King Lovernios?'

'The first time we met—'

He remembered. 'You terrified us.' His fingertip touched the tiny scar between my eyebrows. 'When you are angry or upset or ferocious, Alice, your eyebrows draw together in a straight black line and hide your scar.' He cared enough to notice my moods, he had noticed my eyebrows were black, he thought about me. He whispered, 'Lovernios was the last proper King of Kent before the Romans conquered our land. He owned London when it was a holy place, a Druid nemeton, a ring of trees, a sacred grove. Half of the great circle was on the head side of the River Thames, and half on the foot, and on certain nights of the full moon the circle was completed by sacrifices.' I listened but I didn't care what Jack said, only that he said it to me. I wanted him only to talk to me, look at me, touch me.

I said anything. 'Christian sacrifices?'

'Before Christian,' he muttered. 'Kings were priests in those days,' and he kissed me again, careless of whether or not his mother could see us, so that I pulled away and skipped into the house and had to return later for the buckets. He had left them waiting, filled ready for me.

Whatever I gave, I got much more in return. I had a home, I had hope. I had more than I had ever dreamt possible, as though I had stepped into a kind of heaven while still on earth. And the boys brought their learning home, even the new way of counting numbers stolen from the Evil Ones by the Templars during the Crusade, so I got an education too. Everything my young men knew, I knew.

Jack and I found places we could go. You remember our favourite was the low arch at the western end of the stone bridge. It was silted with reeds by then and we had to bend over to get inside, but in the middle we could stand up and we talked and giggled, but we had to be careful because the arch by magic magnified every utterance. Jack kissed me and caressed me and I warmed my hands inside his shirt, and he slipped his hands on to my breasts, and you can

38

imagine how close and secret we felt, and I would have done anything for him. We both knew it was obvious to everyone what we were doing but we were so absorbed in each other's company and in being in love that we couldn't think of anyone else, only each other. Everyone else was shadows. Only Jack was real to me and only I was real to Jack. Only love was real. I smoothed my dress and put back my hair, we came out into the sunlight. Nick sat on the the riverbank, fishing. He looked startled. 'What were you two doing in there?'

Jack and I exploded with laughter. Nick gave an uncertain smile, then kissed me affectionately. He was cooler by nature, and sometimes I did not think he liked me at all. I returned his smile warmly and he looked happy, even slipped his hand into mine as we walked, so that I walked with Jack holding my hand on the one side and Nick on the other.

Alfred their father always returned home in the autumn, his outside work on the abbey finished for the year with the first frost, his winter work renovating the interior yet to begin. He was a tall, severe, grey man, his hair cropped to a tight grey fuzz, his hands large and grey as though stone dust leaked through his skin from his blood. Although he embraced Mistress Cristina, even as his arms went round her his eyes noticed me, and the corners crinkled, and his glance took in all of me before returning to his buxom wife and her upturned face of wrinkles, her gap-toothed mouth. She led him to the table and sat him, snapped her dry fingers for me to bring him meat, and I brought him watered wine too but he refused it angrily, and so I knew that what Yvon Piggot had told me was true. I fetched water from the well and he drank until he coughed. The stone dust had dried his lungs. Cristina beckoned his sons into his presence, but Alfred could not speak until his cough released him. He drew a breath.

'The Frenchman, William of Sens, Master Mason of the building of Canterbury Cathedral, has died leaving plenty of work to be completed.'

'Here is a great opportunity for you!' Cristina burst out. Her eyes glowed with ambition for her husband, plans for him, and thinking of the extra money and prestige too no doubt. 'The archbishop is bound to put you in his place. What an honour!'

But Alfred shook his head. 'It does not work like that. The man to be Master Mason must be experienced in the French ways of building. The archbishop knows I have never studied in France. William the Englishman, so called by the French who raise the most beautiful cathedrals, and who learnt his craft in France, will take charge.'

'But you're the master of the Chapter of Masons,' she objected. 'You can block his election somehow, can't you?'

'It is a condition of the masonic fraternity that we accept all masons of whatever nationality as brothers. The Pope has blessed us with a Bull overriding all national borders, so masons travel freely by virtue of papal authority whatever objection is made by kings, fraternities, guilds.'

Cristina didn't give up. 'Surely there are forgeries. Even forged Bulls.'

'Disappointment makes your tongue foolish.' Alfred stopped his wife's complaints with a formidable frown and I realised he was firmly in charge. Men always were, or thought they were, and she knelt obediently at his elbow. He explained, 'William has been entrusted with the tokens and passes which allow his transfer between one Lodge and another. He knows the secret signs and passwords to ensure truth not forgery. I must welcome him.'

She tried flattery. 'But you are too important to ignore.'

'Exactly.' Alfred nodded immediately. I decided that flattery was a lesson I would not forget. 'A cathedral is too big a job for one man to supervise everything. William has agreed to appoint me his foreman of works. I know the best local work gangs and how to make the most of them. The best quarry masons to get stone, the best hewers, the best axemen, the best chisellers. Which layers and setters will argue and must be kept apart. The best cutters, the best shapers, I know them all. Lifetime of experience, man and boy.'

His voice droned on. He would rise no higher in his profession, he would never build a cathedral out of his own heart, and I watched Cristina's expression. What would she do? The boys watched their father, not her. Her face struggled, then she made second best of it. 'I'm so pleased for you, husband.' She kissed his cheek, and Alfred coughed.

He was still coughing when I brought his supper of milk, bread, meat and peas to the head of the table. Like all men of his age, Alfred had lost his teeth and mashed his food to a soup. I wiped his chin as he ate, a wifely duty, but Cristina was still upset with him. So I heard everything. He was asking Jack how the stone bridge over the Little Stour fared.

Jack replied efficiently, 'The arches stand well and curve smoothly, Father, but the pointing is crumbling between the stones.' He glanced at me, he'd noticed the condition of the bridge even while he was kissing me. I narrowed my eyes and he knew exactly what I was thinking, grinned and paid close attention to his food. He thought there was more than me in his life. I would remedy that.

'Crumbling? How deep, son?'

'Not deep, Father.'

I cleared away Alfred's bread. 'I did poor work on that bridge,' he decided honestly, and I warmed to him. 'I worked during the frost, so the mortar was bound to flake. But I . . . When a man is old, there are things he wishes had happened differently. One day I will remedy that matter of the bridge, if God lets me live.' I knew Alfred meant in a practical manner, not by paying for a gilded chantry and purchasing prayers to be said for his soul in the church. Alfred was an interesting man, and as I bent to poker the fire I wondered if he would look at the backs of my legs.

'Alice!' Cristina said sharply. 'Attend to the fire later.'

Within a few days Alfred returned to Canterbury, and everything between us was as it had been before. I fetched all day, and carried all day, and did this Alice, and that Alice, and I thought about Jack without a pause. Whatever I was doing, sweeping, milking, I imagined Jack with me in a thousand ways, the sun in his hair, or raindrops, or that dazzled light in his eyes, and how he would look at me, and how we would talk together in low voices about whatever moved us. And what actually happened was, he met me by the bridge and kissed me and touched my legs as he kissed me. But we had to get home before it was dark. As we walked, Jack said in that low voice I loved to hear, 'Nick likes you.'

I hadn't thought about Nick. 'I like him.'

'Do you? He thinks you don't.'

I cuddled Jack's arm by way of an answer. He chuckled. There was always that about Jack. Whatever I said, whatever I didn't say, he understood. It was him I loved. We parted behind the barn as usual so that we would not arrive back together. I would wait for the time it would take me to walk the path to the church, then fetch the buckets I had left ready by the well and return all innocent, my high colour explained by the weight of the buckets. We were so clever that Mistress Cristina never suspected anything. I was about to fetch them when I heard a low whistling along the path, saw plodding shadows with a taller shadow rising behind them, then the crack of a stick. A pig squealed. I let out my breath. 'Oh, it's only you, Yvon.'

'What do you mean it's *only* me?' Yvon said suspiciously. He thought a lot of himself in his own odd way. He eyed me dirtily. 'Working inside now, I hear, you,' he said, and nodded at the stone house.

'That's right, Yvon.'

40

He said something I could hardly believe. 'Lucky boys.' He eyed me from top to bottom and I knew exactly what he meant.

I hit him harder than he thought I could. 'How dare you talk about Mistress Cristina's sons like that! How dare you talk about *me* like that!'

'Me, I don't blame you!' Yvon protested, upset. 'Bitch of a bitch like you, it's your only way to get on in the world. Clever old Mistress Cristina to use you that way, *I* think.'

I smiled, put my face close to his smarting cheek, said, 'Go screw your pigs.'

He wasn't offended, I suppose he often got this advice and often took it. He tapped his nose wisely. 'Anyway, you're wrong. They aren't Mistress Cristina's sons.'

I needed to get away, I would be late, but I heard myself say, 'What's got into you, Yvon?'

'Not both of them aren't, anyways. They're both her *husband's* sons, if you get my meaning.'

'I'm going now, Yvon.'

'Me, I was the monk-warden's urchin afore I was strong enough to help my old man with the hogs.' Yvon tapped the shitty backsides proudly. 'I knew what I knew. And what I didn't know, I heard tell. And what I didn't hear told, I heard whispered.' Monks are famous gossips. I waited stonily. Yvon's face fell and he gave in. 'The Garwynton miller. Your fine Nick is the miller's daughter's son.'

I laughed. 'So what?'

Yvon was offended. 'I thought it'd mean something to you, that's all.'

'Good night, Yvon.' I closed the gate behind me and hurried across the yard, hurried inside with the buckets. I was late, but I smiled prettily, and forgot what I had been told. I am always too busy.

I am always too busy thinking of Jack.

It's afternoon and I'm out of the house the moment Mistress Cristina closes her eyes and opens her mouth for her nap as she always does – she hates my disturbance and makes sure I'm busy with an errand. Today to Mistress Emma's house, something to give her, I don't care what, afterwards I will come by Jack at the bridge. Nick runs after me past the church. Having seen me 'by chance', he walks beside me, talking, pointing out this and that. The frost has killed the leaves and they whirl round us on the wind as dry and crisp as leaves of gold. Nick catches one in his fist, presents it to me, feels my hand is cold and insists on holding it, warming it. I do not care about my hand. Now he speaks of whatever he thinks will amuse me, I forget what, I'm in a hurry, I'm hurrying, I can't wait, make some excuse, leave him standing in the lane with the leaves blowing round his head. Finish my errand, dying of impatience, with Mistress Emma the roofer's wife in Ulrington. Curtsy politely as I back away from her door and run, run, come running along the footpath by the Nailbourne to the Little Stour and the bridge, and Jack takes me in his arms. And with a gasp because he is so beautiful I see myself as Jack sees me, I glimpse my blue eyes through my fine curls of chestnut hair, see how small-boned and delicate I am, my breasts rising with quick breaths, yet something wary and taut like a hunted wild animal about me, my wide eyes and wide lips almost overfilling my pale, elfin face, but my body in his arms just as tall and skinny as thirteen years old can be, and with a gasp I say, 'I can't wait!'

Jack can't wait. He fills himself with me, we're beneath the bridge, fills himself with my mouth, the arch of my legs, sinks into my soul on the hard-packed earth, summer-dry. We're terrified, we can't stop, we want the moment to last for ever. The dry heads of the bulrushes rattle in the entrance as the wind or whatever moves them, and Jack cries my name over and over until it is meaningless, except for my body in his arms, all of me in his arms, I am his.

'Alice.'

I lay with my hair over my face. 'Alice,' he repeated. I put my hair back, or Jack did. I sat up, or Jack sat me up. We were dusty and brushed each other down. We did everything together. We went out and sat on the riverbank together. We held our hands in each other's hands.

'You felt the same thing,' he murmured. 'I love you.'

'I love you, Jack.'

'That's exactly it,' he said. 'Something's happened. It's love. Isn't it strange?'

'It's wonderful.'

He lay shielding his eyes from the sun. Then he said, 'She wants you to teach me about sex.'

I stared. It was all I could do. I felt the earth had opened beneath me and dropped me down. '*She?*'

He shrugged as though it was obvious. 'Cristina. Your mistress. My mother.'

I held his hands earnestly. I looked deep into his eyes.

'I'll always tell you the truth,' Jack said, sitting up. 'I'll never lie to you. To her – *not to me* – you are a girl of no importance. Surely that's obvious to you.'

I laughed. My laughter died. Yvon had said Mistress Cristina was using me. I gazed at Jack seriously. He kissed my nose, licked it where it was dripping. 'Don't cry,' he said. 'I love you. That's the difference. That's what she doesn't understand.'

'*I* don't understand! How could she be so cruel?' Then I saw. Cristina *had* once been like me. Once, but no longer. She had forgotten what it was like.

'In her scheme of things, Alice, you're the apple. She controls you, employs you, *owns* you, you teach me all I need to know to make a good husband, and then I go off and make a good marriage to a girl I don't know.'

I gasped enviously. 'Margaret de la Ley?'

He made a face. 'Richer.'

My voice choked. 'And as for me?'

'Farewell.'

My throat swelled into my mouth. I couldn't stop myself. Tears leaked into my eyes, overflowed. 'She makes me feel like . . . like a girl who wears red.' A harlot, but I was too upset to say the word. Then I was so angry that I did say it. I shouted it.

'You aren't,' Jack said. 'Because I love you.' He gave up my hands, hugged me in both his arms, lifted me off the ground. He lost his balance, his feet came up, we rolled back in the grass, laughing, me on top of him looking down at him. I sat on his chest, dropped my long hair over his face, rubbed his nose with my nose. Just the two of us there inside the shadows of my hair. 'Ow,' he whispered. 'Your hot, hard little nose!'

'It's your nose too, if you really love me.'

'My mother means no harm.'

'She's determined, jealous, ruthless.' I had learnt these words.

'But she means well.'

'I hate her.'

'You mustn't.' He swept his hands through my hair, making the sun flash. 'I know what you're thinking. Don't try and love me more to take revenge on her, or take me more from her than you already have.'

'Do you think I would?'

'Anyone would. Especially you.' Only Jack would make me everyone, then special, then forgive me. 'You mustn't hate her, you must bide with her or it will come between us. It's all gone wrong for her, Alice, don't you see?'

42

I closed my eyes, pressed my face against his, my lips moved against his skin. 'How can I see?'

He sat up but did not let me go. 'She does not understand love between a man and a woman. How could she? My father loves her, I'm sure, but all she ever cared about was her freedom and the children he gave her. Mother's love. We are her life. She'll do anything for Nick and me. Spoil us rotten. Keep us from our father. Make sure we read and write and count, because that's the way to get on in the world now, as clerks attending some great man or cleric, or as novices.'

'Jack, you were born to be a mason.'

'I know it,' Jack said.

I kissed his hands. His fingers were longer than his father's. 'You know you'll be good at it.'

'If I love you, I will be.' He plucked a few strands of grass and wove them between his fingertips. 'If I love you.'

'You'll be the finest mason who ever lived if you love me as much as I love you!' I stopped, horrified. We were in love, we were speaking like this, but our lives were falling apart. I was an incident. Jack would marry a girl who brought with her a dowry, money, land; he would be a fool if he did not. He read my thoughts.

'I'm no fool. My mother's plan fails because I love you. Love is all it in between you and me, Alice, but it's everything. She'll never understand that. Because she doesn't believe in love.' He held up the grass ring he had woven between his fingers. 'That's us.'

I was so excited I just stared at it. Yes, two women are a conspiracy, but a boy and a girl in love are a greater conspiracy. 'But she'll see.'

He slipped off the clog from my left foot, slid the ring over my fourth toe where it would always be there, hidden.

I plucked some grass and twined it while the sun set, took off his boot, and we exchanged rings. That's us.

I felt sorry for Nick because he had nothing and Jack had everything. Nick did not love me. He did not know love. I contrived to push one or two of the village girls his way, Ellen Cowherd with her pretty smile and lisping Matilda Lukedale, but obviously I have no idea what makes other girls attractive because he ignored them both. Jack had never ignored me even when we were children. I was happy and I wanted to make everyone else happy, so I decided to do my sister Elviva a favour. I imagined Nick falling in love with her and us all together, all happy as Jack and me. Or perhaps a guilty something of my heart remained in that lean-to in the woods, calling me back.

Coming silently through the fallen leaves – I never lost my woodland stealth – I saw my little sister Noelle, who had been a baby, running outside cuddling a knot of smooth wood she called her baby. She talked to it, checked its bottom was clean and scolded its head, then saw me. She stopped, standing still, grimy, dark, part of the forest like a small dirty tree, the whites of her eyes like blossoms, a lovely little woodland nymph who reminded me of someone, I could not think who. I went to pick her up but she shrank back, held up her wooden baby as though to ward me off, then peeped round it. Noelle really was the sweetest, most vibrant little creature, but she did not remember me.

I smiled, but she looked in awe at my woollen dress.

I called to her softly, 'Where is your sister Elviva, little one?'

Like all children, Noelle loved to show off her knowledge. 'I know where she is! She's in Heaven, mistress.'

Elviva was dead. I could not go on. I'd have tousled Noelle's sooty hair but she flinched away, and a feeling of loss washed over me. I turned on my heel and left her staring after me, cuddling her knot-baby and fingering the mole on her cheek, wondering who I was, until we lost sight of each other. I never saw Noelle again, alive.

But God promises us that we never die. In fact there is more. The monk-teacher Paulus in his cell had laid his hand, alone, on Jack's knee, *more*, and whispered through his corrupt blackened teeth into Jack's ear: 'Those who say they will die first and then rise, Jack, are in error. If they do not receive the resurrection while they live, when they die they will receive nothing.' Jack told me because Paulus's taking such a risk impressed him – the Rule of St Augustine's strictly forbids a monk to be alone with a child even for a moment. Brother Paulus would be flogged by his brother monks and monk-priests if word leaked out, so Jack had believed him and kept silent for the same reason. Except to me. Jack tells me everything. Jack removed the monk's hand and asked, 'Then tell me, Father, what must I do to receive the resurrection while I live?' Paulus slid his hand back. 'The resurrection arose for Our Lord Jesus through His pain and suffering, His humility and His sacrifice. As it is for the Son of Man, so it is for a man.' Nick had called Jack away then, and presumably Nick had had the same conversation with Brother Paulus. Pain and suffering, humility and sacrifice. But Nick tells me nothing.

All I know is that Pevynges Wood, once all my world, was shrinking. The trees were smaller, and I strode across roots I would once have jumped over. Branches grew lower, too, and several times I crouched to find my way back to the path. I recognised the clearing behind Three Oaks From One Root, and then a figure sitting between two of the trees moved. 'Nick!' I covered my heart, gasped. 'Don't frighten me like that. I wondered who you were.'

'I saw you,' Nick said. For a moment his remark made no sense to me, then I thought he meant the shabby lean-to, and would think less of me for it. Then I saw the pain in his eyes. It was terrible pain.

'Nick, what's wrong? What is it? Shall I get help?' I saw no blood or broken bone, but he held himself as though injured.

'It's you,' Nick said. 'I love you.'

I said furiously, 'For Heaven's sake, I thought you were hurt!' Then I burst out laughing. It was the first time I had ever known Nick play a joke. 'Oh Nick, you're such an idiot!'

He sat there looking in such terrible pain. 'I love you, I love you.'

I laughed, 'Well, congratulations, that's the first I've heard of it. You don't even like me,' I provoked him. 'Not enough to show affection.'

He gripped my wrist lightly. He was much stronger physically than Jack, I realised. I could have pulled away easily, but I was afraid he might grip me tighter. He was as strong as three of me. If Jack touched me, I found myself in his arms, but Nick was shy and I could not relax.

'Nick, whatever is the matter with you?'

'You must be blind.' Nick looked up at me yearningly. He did not realise he was hurting my wrist and I didn't want to tell him because I could tell that whatever he felt about me was genuine. I bit my lip from discomfort but he took it as rejection. He let me go.

I did not rub my wrist in case that insulted him. I sat beside him so that he did not have to look at me, but he felt the touch of my hip and turned to me earnestly.

'I'm so ashamed,' he said.

I was baffled. 'Ashamed?'

'I saw you with Jack. I saw Jack pull you, pull him, both of you under the arch, and I heard . . . I heard. I couldn't help myself. I know I shouldn't have listened.'

'You listened?'

Nick said simply, 'I thought my heart would break.'

I remembered the bulrushes rattling in the entrance. 'You spied on us too? You *watched*?'

'You don't love him, Alice.' I could not speak for anger. 'It's not love,' he said urgently. 'Love isn't pure, it's just bodies. Only love for God is pure.'

'All that matters is I love Jack and Jack loves me. If you can't understand that, I pity you!'

'Why Jack? What's different? Why not me?'

'Because I just do.'

'Alice.' Nick put his lips against mine. 'There. Doesn't that feel the same?'

I looked at him steadily. I was quite different from him. I saw everything differently from him, felt everything differently from him. We sat together a world apart.

He said, 'Remember, my mother owns you.'

I stood up. I brushed the bark from my dress, jumped down on to the path, and as I walked away I threw over my shoulder, 'She isn't your mother. You're the miller's daughter's son.'

I was appalled by what I had said in anger, and confessed everything to Jack. Jack laughed. 'Oh, that. I've heard that before. There's always whispers in a village. Gilbert Woolton spread it around after we stoned him. Maud Lukedale told Nick, she can't keep anything to herself. She'll have her tongue cut out one day.'

Maud Lukedale told Nick but he hadn't talked about it even to Jack, let alone me. He had kept the information inside himself for years, twisting it tighter like a piece of string.

'What did Nick say?'

'Say? Nothing. He pretended not to hear. He went white as a sheet. I didn't say anything.'

'I wish I could cut my tongue out.' I made a face. 'I didn't mean to hurt him.'

'You haven't got a spiteful bone in your body. He'll get over it,' Jack said cheerfully. 'Knowing you know probably hurts him most, if he wants to bed you as badly as I do.' I knew that look in his eye.

'Ssh!' I looked round for Mistress Cristina's loving watchfulness but she was somewhere else for once, and Jack hoisted me on the table, but I squealed and got on top of him and drew my pleasure from him as well as his from me, and we cried out as quickly as rabbits. This is love when you are fourteen and not married, the love the Church calls the sin of incontinence.

We sought Nick out in the barn. Jack said merrily, 'What's this about you being the miller's grandson? I don't believe it, do you?'

Nick pitched straw into the loft. He ignored us. His body worked back and forth with a regular rhythm. I watched the muscles bulge and quiver in his arms and shoulders and thighs as he swung up the long pitchfork and the heaps of straw. Straw motes swirled, every knothole sent sunlight streaming across the barn and around his toiling figure. As I came close, so close that I felt the draught of the pitchfork, I saw the straw speckling Nick's gleaming skin, already blotched and reddened with irritation from the sharp stalks. He had worked too hard and too long to breathe only through his nose, and his open mouth gulped the dusty air. The veins rose on his arms from the strain. He glanced at me. He worked as long as he could, then spoke past me to Jack.

'Everyone knows.'

Jack chewed a straw. 'There's nothing to it. It's just an insult.' Everyone had to take their grain to the abbot's miller and no other for grinding. The abbot took his cut and so did the miller. In effect the miller was a tax collector, so he always cheated. Even if he didn't, everyone believed he did. Millers were always being accused and insulted. 'The Garwynton miller, wasn't it? Old Alured? He hasn't even got a daughter.'

'He hasn't now,' Nick said. He struggled to control his breathing. 'She died. She was a beautiful single girl, as beautiful as Alice. She gave birth to me and she died of shame.'

Jack said nothing. There was nothing he could say confronted by the pain like an open wound in Nick's voice, loss, despair, anger. Nick would never know what his mother was like. He had only the kindness of his adopted parents to remember, nothing of the mystery of himself. Even I had so much more than Nick.

'Nick, I'm sorry.'

He gave me a wounded look. 'You meant to hurt me and you did, Alice.'

'I only meant it for one moment.'

'You can't unsay it.'

'It isn't true anyway,' Jack shrugged. 'Anyway, so what if it is?'

'I've lost everything I ever had,' Nick said. 'Don't you see, I'm not who I thought I am. I'm nobody. Alice loves you because of who you are, Jack. You *know* who you are. She'll marry you, she's clever and determined, and you'll inherit the house and everything, and so will her children. My best wishes to you both.' Nick hefted the pitchfork, turned his back to us, and continued his relentless work.

Jack grinned at me, raised his eyebrows and shoulders. Nick was obviously not to be consoled. Then Jack ran his hands back through his sun-streaked hair, and the gesture was such pure Jack that I slipped my arm through his elbow. Jack never gave up. 'Listen, Nick,' he said. 'You're taking this all wrong. Even if the worst comes to the worst, my mother loves you and so does my father—'

'You see? *Your* mother, *your* father.'

'Then ask Cristina the truth of it.'

Nick pitched and swung, pitched and swung. 'I can't.' He stopped, looked at us appealingly. 'I can't bear to hear it from her. I don't want to have to believe it's true.'

What I could say or do to ease Nick after the awful thing I had done? I took his head gently between my hands. For the first time he looked me in the eyes. I kissed him on the lips, tasted his straw and sweat, the bitterness of grief in his saliva.

Nick jerked back with an oath. 'I'm sorry, I'm so sorry, I do love you!'

He never referred to it again. Whatever Nick felt about me, he hid it inside himself with a coolness and strength I admired. These days, when only the best and worst of monks practise self-denial, and men and boys talk openly of the Garden of Eden a woman carries between her legs, of walking her garden path, of entering Heaven on earth, Nick treated me with perfect courtesy, and I liked him and trusted him. Admired him. But did not love him. Soon I forgot whatever he once felt about me and our lives rushed on, for everyone knows life's span is seventy-two years, divided into twelve ages like the year into months, and though we youngsters had rushed through the drought of March we had yet to reach the strong sun and showers of April.

Alfred, on the other hand, ended his September (the ninth age of Man, when a wise man stores up his goods) and came into the October of his life. I was shocked at the change in him. Canterbury Cathedral took all his strength, and like the cathedral, Alfred's life was almost complete. Before he re-started his spring work on the choir roof he returned to complete the little stone bridge whose shoddy pointwork had nagged his mind all these years. I wondered why. It was only a shabby, cheaply-made bridge, not a confession unmade or a guilt unshriven. I helped him down the muddy track, his large grey hand quivering on my shoulder, and he looked round him curiously at the peasants ploughing and grafting in the fields as though he had never seen them before, villagers setting vineyards on the sun-side slopes, digging ditches, setting hedges along the ditches, repairing the fences against the wild deer, row after row of bent-over toiling figures planting madder and sowing linseed and woad seed, and the growing crops pushing through the fields in brilliant stripes of colour as though the earth was weaving a garment. Pilgrims trailed past us on their way to St Thomas's shrine in Canterbury, tossed their offerings into the monk's little stone hut, crossed the bridge. Jack and Nick went ahead with the pointing trowels and a cart of sand and lime and I don't know what, strange inventions in tool boxes of polished oak, but Alfred hung back for a moment. Old men like being with young girls, they remember the heat of their youth with the peace of old age, and he confided in me where he commanded Jack and Nick without explanation. He nodded at the bridge. 'I've always wanted to set this right. You see stone bridges ten a farthing now, but once this was something.' I, too, nodded wisely, as though I cared.

Alfred tutted over the flaking mortar, rubbed it between his fingers. 'Good mortar makes a join stronger than stone, yet allows the stones to move just a little without cracking. Stones grow in summer, and shrink in winter.'

'Are stones alive, sir?' I asked.

'Yes, they are alive, Alice.' Alfred called for his tools, unrolled the sacking in which they were wrapped, took out an instrument like a fish line with a heavy lead pointer on the end and let the line over the parapet. The pointer swung just above the water, then settled a little away from the stone. 'Out of plumb by a hand's breadth,' Jack said, but Alfred said it was only half that, of no consequence. 'The flow of water pushes the bridge, makes it lean. A fish can pull a bridge over.' Jack and Nick had heard this before, and nodded. The wide world was marvellous. 'I've seen a shoal of eels use a bridge to cross from one side of a river to the other,' Alfred said, then rapped his stick on the stone. 'Come on, you louts!' Jack and Nick jumped to it. 'I'll show you how to mix mortar. The trick is to add a little soap . . .'

I hung behind, watching. I saw why Alfred had come back. He was taking the boys away from Cristina, teaching them all he knew. Soon everything would change, and without Jack, the life I had known would not exist. I tried to imagine the house quiet. I imagined loneliness. It was all too easy. I returned to the house and found that Mistress Cristina, too, was sad, and we worked together to prepare the men's midday meal without needing to speak, two women of one mind. It was still Lent so only fish was allowed, but everyone knows that any animal living in water is fish, and Mistress Cristina had obtained a fat barnacle goose from the estuary – a small boat comes almost as far as Garwynton. Barnacle geese are fish, the Church teaches us, because the geese breed from a worm in a shell on trees in the sea. We lifted the last cuts of meat – I should say fish – from the carcass, pounded them in vinegar and wrapped them with peas and bread in one end of a pastry, and honey and Sandwich almonds in the other, to make a pasty. We slid the pasties in the oven and when they were brown, Mistress Cristina snoring by this time, I wrapped them in muslin and lay them in the basket which I hung over my arm. At the bridge I found that Jack, rather than erect scaffolding, worked from planks hung on ropes from the parapet, chiselling out damaged stones, wielding a pointing trowel and a small wooden smoothing peg with skilful strokes while Nick mixed mortar. Jack saw me, waved and climbed up – he loves his food. Alfred, who had instructed and interfered rather than laboured, divided his pasty with the monk in the toll hut and the two old men muttered and yawned. Nick and Jack and I jumped down

47

on to the riverbank and I sat with my chin between my knees watching them eat like starving men. The sun was high and hot after winter, beating down on my head and my eyelids, and I dozed.

A priest's ministration changes bread into the flesh of Christ, and a piece of manure transforms itself instinctively into flies. A fly buzzed, settled on my lip. I brushed it away sleepily, and heard Nick talking. Talking about me.

'I don't love her, Jack. I swear it.'

Jack's easy-going tone replied, 'I know what you feel for her, Nick, and I don't blame you.'

I was fascinated. Had I been snoring? I snored lightly. After a moment Nick's voice came again. 'I cannot. Man cannot love God and woman at the same time.'

I could pretend no longer. I opened my eyes, shaded them against the sun. Nick crouched by the water, dabbling with his fingers.

'God made woman too,' I interrupted.

Jack chuckled. 'God made Alice, that's for sure.'

But Nick said earnestly, 'Jesus Christ is the Son of Man, not woman. God did not choose a woman. Women are not in His image.'

Jack glanced at me. He pointed out to Nick, 'Jesus was a Jew.'

'So is God,' I said.

'That's not true.' Nick flicked drops of water from his fingers and stood. 'God is the supreme head of the Roman Church and the Pope speaks His will. All other religions are false.'

'God made Eve,' Jack said, 'so God must be like a woman too.'

But Nick raised his hands at this blasphemy, not amused but horrified. 'Stop it!' He put his hands to his head. 'You're wrong. Wrong. God made women from the dust of Adam's rib, not His own likeness. Women are an inferior part of man, only rib and cleft and teats. They can come to God only through man, through a priest. Pain, suffering, humility, sacrifice, these are the truths. Without those we learn nothing, our lives are worthless.'

Jack looked startled. 'I think you've been talking too long with Brother Paulus, old friend.'

'Brother Paulus is a wise man. A monk's vocation is the quest of God. Not *for* God, *of* God.'

'What does that mean?' Jack yawned.

'Forgetting the world. By the world forgot.' Nick turned to me so solemnly that I thought his words were beautiful, but he looked straight past me and I heard the clop of hooves approaching the bridge above us, and we all shielded our eyes from the sun. A Knight Templar rode a white horse towards the bridge, the same man I had seen those years ago by Three Oaks From One Root, but today in the sun the splayed Cross of Christ's Blood glared on his chest almost too red to look at and his armour flashed barbs of light. Geoffrey de Prudome, bow-shouldered, with grey in the moustache and eyes hooded beneath heavy eyebrows, looked watchfully from side to side of the road. Meat grease clung to the warrior's lips and beard. Alone of Christians, a Templar was forbidden to observe fasts, lest his strength fail him. Behind him rode three horsemen in black like Benedictine monks but wearing swords over their robes from ankle to armpit, and daggers almost as long as swords on the other hip, and they spurred their black horses forward after their master.

'They're his sergeants,' Nick whispered. 'Look at his shoulders. A knight carries an enormous burden of honour on his shoulders. Without the Knights Templar the Christian City of God, Jerusalem, would be wailing and suffering under the Evil Ones.'

Jack said, 'The Devil?'

'Muslims. They follow a false prophet and St Bernard's Rule shows us it is the duty of Christians to kill them. The killing of an Evil One is not the sin of murder but the blessing of malecide. To destroy evil is to do God's work. How can anything else be the truth? Ours is the one true God.'

'There's not much evil round here,' Jack said. 'Humphrey the priest lies with Widow Gore—'

'He does not. Repeating a rumour is as bad as starting it.'

'Brother Paulus—'

'Stories,' Nick said. 'You don't know how much they hurt him. The wickedness of stories. There's evil, Jack. Believing scandal and rumour.'

Jack reached out his hand to Nick's shoulder. 'I understand why you should think this way, old friend, but . . .'

Their voices faded as I shrank back from the sunlight into the shadows of the bridge. A little dust spilled over the parapet, and I had the oddest feeling, seeing the knight's helmet riding above the stones, turning from side to side, that he was looking for me. I crouched among the bulrushes at the entrance to the arch, then ducked inside as the hoofbeats stopped above my head. He remembered me. He looked for me still. I heard him speak to the monk, then the heavy thud of hoofbeats resumed and was gone. Jack and Nick were looking at me.

I was embarrassed. 'He frightened me.'

'The knight? How could he frighten you?'

'He was looking for me,' I sulked, because I knew Nick wouldn't believe me. He laughed for the first time in weeks. As always, laughter made him most serious. He touched my head with his fingertips and fell silent, and I knew he remembered my hair blowing over the Cross of Christ's Blood when we were children.

I whispered, 'Where does Christ's blood come from?'

'The holy blood? The same place as pieces of the true Cross,' Jack said, 'and the crown of thorns, phials of the Virgin's milk, the drips collected from Christ's wound by the Roman soldier. Workshops.'

'That's all true,' Nick nodded, then lowered his voice. I followed his eyes across the fields to the figure of the knight riding towards the church. 'Brother Paulus knows. God speaks to us in signs, just as Jesus spoke in parables. Monks and priests stand between us and God and so more is revealed to them than to us. And all monks are in awe of the Templars, monks who fight as well as pray. You know the Temple the Templars are raising in Jerusalem. Brother Paulus says that beneath the Temple—'

'We've heard the story of Hiram who was sacrificed,' Jack said.

'It's true the Templar masons uncovered the winding stair to Solomon's Sanctum Sanctorum, and this led them down to Bir Arruah, the Well of Souls, and to many tombs. Jesus Christ is, as you know, sometimes called the first freemason.'

Jack glanced at me. 'Jesus said he would destroy the Temple of Herod and rebuild it in three days,' he explained.

'When the Templar masons drove the foundations of the new Temple across the foundations of the old, they broke into a tunnel to a cave and fell down. There the Templars found the tomb of Joseph.'

'Joseph, Jesus's stepfather?'

'No, Joseph the Arimathean, the merchant and Jesus's friend. They were visitors together to our land. Joseph of Arimathea was a dissenting counsellor, St Luke tells us, of the Sanhedrin Council that sentenced Jesus to death. It was he who begged Pilate for Jesus's body and placed it in his own tomb.'

I flicked the flies buzzing at my lips. The knight passed by the church, and we watched his figure drop slowly from sight behind the hill. I asked, 'Did the masons or the Templars find anything at all in the tomb of Joseph?'

'Yes. They found the body of Christ wrapped in a linen shroud.'

'How could that be?' I whispered. I had never read or heard the Bible, of course, the Book is not for the common people, but everyone knows for certain that Jesus was resurrected to eternal life as Christ, to return and save us at the end of time. If He is still here, how can He return?

But Jack understood. 'I see what Paulus meant. If we do not receive the resurrection while we live, when we die we will receive nothing. It's a subtle way of saying Jesus remained alive in His bodily form after the resurrection. It explains why the Templars, who follow St Paul, like him don't believe in the crucifixion.'

'Jesus's earthly remains may have been placed in the tomb years later,' Nick said.

'They're just bones by now,' I said.

'No!' Nick was excited. 'The body of Christ cannot rot, it is pure spirit in earthly form, as real as the moment He was hammered to the Cross. The Jews escaped from Egypt and embalmed their kings in the Egyptian manner – Jesus was of the royal line of David – withdrawing the blood into large jars, or holy grails, that were stored beside the body. St John deliberately tells us that Nicodemus wrapped the body in embalming spices, a hundred pounds of myrrh and aloes, to preserve it. *Necessitas non habet legum.* All we have to do is believe. *Credo quia impossibile est,* faith is stronger than reason. We celebrate His sacrifice with the sacraments of the Church. Templars spirited the body and the holy blood, the *sang réal* in the Holy Grail, to a secret place only they know where. And each precious drop of His blood that leaks through the shroud or is unstoppered from the grail anoints a Poor Fellow-Soldier of Christ and the Temple of Solomon, and colours the cross that the Templar wears with such pain and suffering, humility and sacrifice, in hope of the resurrection in our lifetime.'

Nick said nothing more and we listened without moving, our eyes half closed, to the lap of the river passing through the arches. What a speech! There was no doubting the intensity of Nick's passion for God; his face was flushed, his fingers moved as though still dabbling in the water. It still seems incredible to me that in those days we could talk of such matters without fear of being struck down by lightning or burnt as heretics. A hundred years later our words would have been sacrilegious blasphemy, heretical, we would have been excommunicated or burnt. Even ten years later we would have risked our lives and our immortal souls. But these were days of peace when we were young and Jerusalem was ours, when heretics did not see themselves as heretics and witches did not know they were witches. St Paul himself, who tolerated heretics, had been killed for heresy, and soon our Church would open our eyes to heretics, witches, infidels and demons, detestable crimes and evil deeds among us, abominable works horrible to think of and terrible to hear, striking us with great astonishment and causing us to tremble with violent horror. Peace breeds talk, we would learn, and talk breeds doubt, and blasphemy is the child of doubt and the father of heresy. In peace the divine mystery of the sacraments of the Church is violated by thoughtless chatter, and the power of the Pope flouted by wagging tongues and new Christian ideas and beliefs which he is helpless to prevent.

Those days were ending.

But that's not how I remember that day, as an ending. Every end is a new beginning. My life, my existence, is full of new beginnings, not of endings.

After three days the weather broke and the rain fell in the afternoon. The pointwork was completed the day before and the stones looked smooth and all of a piece when I brought the pasties down at midday. Jack, Nick and Alfred outlined the pointing in oily red paint during the early afternoon so that the blocks stood out neat and square in appearance if not in fact – that was the purpose of the decoration, to make ragged seem neat to satisfy fashionable taste. I helped them pack up before the threatening rain arrived. The rain fell sooner than we thought and we sheltered in the toll-monk's empty hut, listening to the rain pouring on the roof.

'I have something to say to my boys, Alice.' Alfred pushed me out, then handed his cloak out to me as an afterthought, and I stood shivering in the downpour. I know my place. But after a while I peered through a crack in the door, caught snatches of his voice. 'Masons were once monks . . . masons are still organised in chapters just as monks are. Our masters are elected just as abbots and priors are in monasteries . . . our monastery is our Lodge. Sometimes the Lodge is called the Ark, or Arch, after the Arch of the Covenant. There is a Lodge on every building site. Matters are discussed by the brothers and decisions taken by vote . . .'

I blinked rain from my eyes. Alfred opened one of his polished wooden boxes, unfolded a muslin cloth from the object inside and held it reverently to Jack and Nick. I pressed my eye hard to the crack, breathing through one nostril, and glimpsed in Alfred's grey hands a strange circle of shiny metal marked round its edge with the Arabic numbers of the Evil Ones, and an arrow that turned like a wheel to point at the numbers. Alfred showed Jack and Nick how to squint past the sight pin to line the point of the arrow against the numbers. I pulled back and rubbed my nose, blinking, then returned my eye to the hole. Rainwater pattered from the roof on to my shoulders.

'Is it an astrolabe?' Jack asked. An astrolabe was an invention of the Evil Ones, used for strange purposes and rites.

'Called a skirret by us masons.' Alfred laid the device across Jack's hands. 'You hold it flat for lateral angles, or on its side for vertical.' Jack turned it curiously. 'Properly used from three places, it will reveal distances and heights to you. It is the all-seeing eye in the triangle.'

'Does it see by magic?' Nick asked.

'No. It sees not by magic but by geometry. What is G for?'

'God,' Nick said.

'More than that.' Alfred turned impatiently to Jack. 'Why will you be made a mason?'

'For the sake of the letter G,' Jack said.

'What does it signify?'

'Geometry.'

'Why geometry?'

'Because geometry is the root and foundation of all arts and sciences.'

'Also God,' Nick said. 'The Grand Geometrician of the Universe.'

'I've been watching you work, Jack.' Alfred returned the astrolabe to the box, closed the lid, pegged the hasp. He glanced at the door but did not sense me. 'You have a feel for the life in the stone, you. But you work with an open-hearted ease that does not suit the seriousness and hardness of stone. We will train that out of you. You too, Nick. You too shall be a mason.'

'Stone is soft, not hard,' Jack said. 'The shape is in the stone. It works itself whatever way it will. I fail if I do not let the stone be what it wants to be.'

Alfred stared at him. 'Do you see it too?'

'Yes, Father. I feel it. I feel what the stone wants to be.' Jack would not have spoken these soft words of his love for stone in front of me for fear I would laugh. But because of his sincerity he made me love him very much. My feeling overcame me. I pushed the door and went inside with the rain pouring down my face.

Alfred ignored me, finished what he was saying. 'You are old and strong enough to be lawful 'prentice boys. At the end of seven years you will have earned the privilege of compasses, square, level and plumb-rule. God the

51

Almighty Architect will record your every word and action. I have spoken in Lodge with the Chapter of Masons in Canterbury. It is arranged that you will start with me at the cathedral from the spring commencement.'

I gripped Jack's hand.

'I won't,' Jack said. Alfred looked surprised, then his face darkened. 'No, Father,' Jack said. 'I won't go alone.'

'Nick shall go with you. Are you defying me?'

'I won't go without Alice,' Jack said.

'You'll do as you're told,' Alfred shouted. 'I am your father. You'll serve your seven years and learn obedience, and then you'll think of marriage, and of exacting obedience in your own turn, from your wife!' He saw Jack's determination. 'Four years, son. I'll not give my permission—'

'Mother will have me enter the abbey as a novice monk,' Jack said.

'Good God, the celibate life is not for you, boy.'

'Or I'll go with Sir Alexander Gloucester as his clerk.' I wondered if Jack might actually do it. These were Mistress Cristina's dreams for him.

Alfred said tersely, 'You'll be a mason.'

'And I won't marry Margaret de la Ley.'

Alfred looked at me, bedraggled, soaked creature that I was, my dress weighing a ton and my wet hair in rat's tails over my eyes. Drips running down my nose. I sniffed defiantly. Then I felt the ring on my toe. Jack was pressing his foot over mine, reminding me, and I knew he would win because he had something, and his father did not.

'I'll marry *her*,' Jack said.

Alfred reached forward and lifted the hair from my eyes. He held the dark chestnut locks on his fingers, then pushed them back over my parting. He looked both interested and sad. Remembering, now that his handsome old face was withered and his chest racked by a cough, what he would have done with a girl like me, when he was young.

'Oh, Jack,' he sighed. 'Oh, Jack.'

Of course my father had never married my mother, so I had no one to tell me what was expected of a wife. At first it seemed sad that my love for Jack and his for me should be brought to earth with a contract of mere words, but I was used to being sold. First I was baptised at the red-painted font, then Humphrey the priest who lay with Widow Gore intoned to the kneeling people. I listened captivated as the holy water trickled over the scar between my eyes. 'This is the baptism of Alice a woman of our parish, which is the baptism of such as are of riper years.' That made me frown, and Jack struggled not to laugh. Meanwhile Father Humphrey mumbled the words and rushed through them, so that I was hardly sure of some of them, and I forget whether he said 'man' or 'woman'.

'There was a man of the Pharisees' – I hear the old parson mumbling as though it was yesterday – 'named Nicodemus, a ruler of the Jews. Nicodemus came to Jesus by night and said, Rabbi, we know that thou art a teacher come from God, for no one can do these miracles that thou doest, except God be with them. Jesus answered, Except a man be born again, he cannot see the Kingdom of God. Nicodemus saith unto him, How can a woman be born when she is old? Can she enter the second time into her mother's womb, and be born? Jesus answered, Except a woman be born of water and of the Spirit, she cannot enter into the Kingdom of God. That which is born of the flesh is flesh, and that which is born of the Spirit is spirit. Marvel not that I say unto thee, Ye must be born again. The wind bloweth where it listeth, and thou hearest the sound thereof, but thou canst not tell whence it cometh, and whither it goeth: so is every one that is born of the Spirit.'

We prayed beneath the blue vault of the church roof, and then I was married at the church door, both freed and married in the same breath. I looked at the demon mating with the woman in the shadows, and knew I would live in sin no longer, and turned to kiss my husband. But something terrible happened. Alfred gave a low groan and leant his shoulder lightly against the doorway of the little wooden church, and then his shoulder slipped down the doorway until he sat on the step, grey-faced, gasping, his right hand clutching his left elbow as though he was trying to hold himself up; and then he toppled slowly over until he lay on the green grass looking up at the blue sky.

Cristina screamed. Everyone pushed forward. Jack pushed them away. 'Give him air. Let him breathe.' But even I could see Alfred could not breathe. I dropped my flowers and knelt beside him, but Nick pushed me back and took my place, cradled Alfred's head in his lap. He bent down until their foreheads touched. The blue reflection left Alfred's eyes as Nick's shadow hid the sky.

Nick whispered, 'Are you my father?'

I heard Nick clearly. I was the only one who did. Nick whispered again, fiercely, to the dying man, 'Are you my father? Is Mother my mother?'

Alfred struggled in Nick's arms to breathe. His throat made a sound like a child's rattle. He was past speech, his hand slipped from Nick's shoulder, and Nick went as pale as a dead man.

That day at the church was a baptism, a marriage, and a death. Another new beginning.

The moment Alfred's heart broke, Cristina ceased to be a freewoman and reverted to the status of serf, property of the abbot. It must have been a cruel blow to my indomitable taskmistress to find herself below me, her daughter-in-law, in social class. But she had suffered worse, and prevailed. Alfred was richer than we knew, but *she* knew. By *gavelkind*, Kentish ancestral law, half her husband's estate passed to her. The day Alfred was put in the ground, she purchased her freedom – the abbot's price almost more than she could afford, naturally – and took in a poor girl to replace me as servant and company.

Alfred's will treated Nick as equal with Jack. But he was bound to do this anyway, since Kentish law recognises all children accepted as sons as equal, and Nick's grief and suspicion flowered rather than relented. That same day Nick faced Widow Cristina, who waited pale as death – even a woman who does not love her spouse must grieve his loss – at the head of the table in the chair so recently occupied by her husband. She told Nick to sit but he would not. He asked her the question we all dreaded.

'Am I your son?'

Cristina's mouth was thin and implacable as a trap. Her eyes glinted. 'Of course you are,' she said. 'How dare you suggest . . . how dare you.'

Nick shouted at her. His voice rose. Jack and I shouted at him, pulled him back. Only Cristina remained calm. Her eyes barely flicked at Jack when he spoke.

'People talk in the village,' he said.

'Talk,' Cristina sneered. Her body was rigid, her hands laid like white claws on the table, and I realised she was as furious as Nick, all the shame she had kept inside her all these years bubbling to the surface. 'Why should I say yes or no? What is the advantage in dishonour?'

'Dishonour!' I said.

'Yes, dishonour!' Cristina's voice crackled with hatred. 'Why should I humiliate myself by letting the truth be known in the village? Why should I? Should I best honour my husband's memory by repeating tattle-tales as if they were true?' Her lips tightened over her toothless gums. 'I tell you this. I would rather live proudly by lies than let truth dishonour all I have achieved in my life!'

Jack and Nick spoke but she swatted their complaints like flies. 'Listen to me! Listen to me. Alfred was feckless and weak. He married me because I was strong. Who carried the burden of his infidelities? *I* did, I, his wife. I bound him to me with his bastard son. I stopped his drinking. I made him work. I made him pull down our wooden hovel and build this house in stone. I made him make his name and I dared him to lose it. I will not change it now.' She smiled, demanding our approval for her achievements. She had cared only about keeping Alfred and her comfortable life, never about Nick at all. And now Alfred was gone.

'You witch,' Nick said. 'I pray you die.'

I knelt beside her. Only her eyes moved warily. I covered her cold hand with my own, warm. 'Widow Cristina,' I said respectfully. 'Think of Nick. Think how cruel this is to him. You cannot leave him in agony like this. Acknowledge him, love him, forgive him. Whatever happened, whatever went wrong all those years ago, *he* did nothing wrong.'

Cristina spat. 'Acknowledge, love, forgive!' She jerked her hand from mine, she would not be underneath anyone. She gripped my wrist, her brittle nails sank into the back of my hand as her grip tightened. She said spitefully, 'Why should I care? He is not *my* son. He gets half of the sons' share of the money as if he is my real son, he should count himself lucky. All I care about is my Jack, and so should you.'

Her spittle peppered my face. I shall always remember it, sour and hot.

We could hear the new serving girl sobbing in the kitchen, terrified.

Jack said, 'I'm getting out of this house.'

Widow Cristina did not move from the table. She said, 'Wait.' But we followed Jack.

We heard her hobbling after us. 'Jack. Wait. I have spoken with Sir Alexander. There is a position.'

Jack said over his shoulder, 'We are due in Canterbury, to start at the cathedral.'

Her cries faded behind us.

We walked all day in a horrified daze. The three of us stopped by a tree on the Canterbury road and none of us had spoken. Something had happened that none of us understood. Jack whispered, 'What makes evil happen in the world? What made her into the woman she is?'

Nick said in an empty voice, 'I did.'

We did not go back to Abbot's Littlebourne, not until Jack built the church. But that was years later. By then we had started many new beginnings, the three of us.

First there was Canterbury, the town walls rising above the flatlands, the few church towers and brightly-coloured banners showing over the battlements dwarfed in turn by the mighty tower and pinnacles of the cathedral. Alfred had lived frugally, and we came through the narrow overhung streets to his small stone house by the cathedral close expecting more, but I was overjoyed. I made the little place my own house, swept, cleaned the glass windows – the first I had seen – with vinegar, as the old woman next door showed me, and bought candles from market and all the food we could eat. Jack ordered a bed from the carpenter and a mattress from the downer. Nick took the attic for himself, lived frugally and alone. By law the two apprentices ate their midday meal in the masons' Lodge, eating a small supper with me in the evening, saying little. Jack and I were so happy together that I could not tell whether Nick was happy or sad, and in truth I thought little about it, I was so full of my new house. Apprentices' lives were hard but we were not poor. Alfred had sensibly willed his rights in the quarry to Jack and Nick, and his various holdings of land were farmed by tenants who, unusually, paid their rents in cash not kind because Alfred had kept no large household of servants or sojourners to feed.

In the years to come I would be mistress of many different small houses, rooms, attics, occasionally even a hovel, but that was my first house, and there I made my first home with my husband and our best friend, the best friend who, it seemed to us, would always be with us. The three of us. Jack and Alice and Nick. In happiness it seems the moment of happiness will last for ever and the future will be the same as the past. In my happiness I forgot unhappiness. In my happiness I forgot that Nick had once said he loved me. In my happiness I forgot Nick saying emptily, 'I did.' I became blind. For four years I was stupid, ignorant, besotted by love. All I thought about was Jack and the child we desired. I was with Nick but hardly saw him, fed him but hardly noticed him; he was as familiar as a piece of furniture and I thought about him not at all, except to push the occasional Canterbury girl in his direction.

By the winter of the fifth year the last work on the cathedral was finished, the contracts ended. The vast network of whispers, nods and winks that binds masons like blood brothers swung into operation. As the rattle of hammers and chisels dwindled day by day, the cathedral bells rang out loud and clear over the city, calling pilgrims to hurry past the pits where ordeals of fire, water and manure tested the innocence of criminals, past the gallows of the Prior of Christ Church, to hurry to worship among the brilliant gilt chantings, roundels and tapestries that filled the nave. Canterbury rents fell, shopkeepers and stallholders went out of business as the family gangs of masons took the tallies and passwords of their Lodge to wherever new work was found, Lincoln Cathedral with its round arches damaged by an earthquake, castle walls at Newcastle and Belfast, any number of French cathedrals and monasteries, the Campanile at Pisa. The finest and most experienced masons travelled to work under Grand Master Bénezét on the bridge at Avignon. Jack looked envious, remembering his father's tiny bridge, one of the first built in stone since Roman times. Now, twenty years later, stone bridges were all the rage in France. Bridges were the most complex, arduous and difficult – and dangerous – branch of masonic discipline, and only masons belonging to specially skilled fraternities undertook such work.

Jack and Nick were freed of their apprenticeship but continued to job under their master, William English, on small work in the close. Then word came of work at Dover Castle under Maurice. 'The pay is fourpence a day,' Jack said excitedly, 'a quarter more than a carpenter receives. The contract lasts until frost, with a half-pound loaf and five pints of wine a day, fish on half the days of the month, meat the rest.' The chance was too good to miss and Jack, being Jack, rushed off at once to the inn to buy a mule for our journey. But Nick sat without moving on the window seat. Outside my house the busy street hurried and rippled and smeared itself in a thousand colours beyond the glass, the busy, bustling sight as familiar as the furniture, my window, my table, Nick. It was his stillness that made me notice him.

'I'm not going with you, Alice,' Nick said.

I sat on the window seat facing him. I was incredulous. I talked.

'Sssh.' Nick shook his head. 'It's all decided. Jack knows, he understands. I never did have to explain things to him.' I felt foolish for missing so much. 'Months ago I sold my half of the quarry to him. Changed my holdings into gold.'

'You make me feel terrible,' I told Nick. 'Is this my fault?'

'Of course it's your fault.'

I tried to dismiss him. 'Don't be silly. What will you do? Where will you seek work? We've all been so happy together.'

55

He said simply, 'I have spent four years in Hell being near you. Never touching you. Never showing what I feel. Didn't you know?'

'God forgive me, how could I?' I tried to take his hands. He crossed his arms to prevent me. I sat numbly.

'Believe me, Alice. I'm going not because I do not love you, but because I do. I love you as much as Jack does, more. Much more. I burn for you. I lie on my mattress alone all night and I imagine you beside me in every detail. You obsess me. You torment me.'

'I do not mean to.'

'Jack has you. I do not. I cannot bear such pain, Alice. I won't seek work as a mason, I might meet you. I can hardly bear to be alive. Say you love me. Can you say it?'

I swallowed. I did not love him. I loved Jack. 'Don't talk like this,' I said, and smiled.

Nick spoke from his heart. 'I feel your warmth without touching you. I inhale you without breathing. I know I shall do something bad if I stay. Jack is my best friend and I love you, Alice, and I would rather die than come between you.' Sitting there with the colours of the street shifting down one side of his face, shadowed by the light coming into the dark room, Nick moved and for a moment his eyes flashed me a dazzled look, and he seemed so like Jack that I almost reached out to him.

I clasped my hands in my lap. 'What will you do?' I laughed. 'Take orders as a monk, renounce the world, do something stupid? I'd never forgive myself, Nick.' I grinned cheerfully but he did not. He took every word to heart. I prayed for Jack to return home so I could share this awful conversation.

'I am to be a monk. I shall take the oath of the finest order of monks, Alice. A Poor Fellow-Soldier of Christ and the Temple of Solomon. It's all settled.'

'Surely you can't. You're – ordinary!'

That did make him smile. 'I'll do God's work, do you see? They can't deny me. St Bernard's Rule for entry says, "If any secular knight, or other man, wishes to leave the mass of perdition and to abandon this century, do not deny him entry. For thus said St Paul: Approve the spirit if it comes from God. Assemble the brothers in chapter and let him show his wish and his will before all." That's what I'm doing, Alice. Travelling to the Temple in London to show my wish and my will before all. A life of service.'

I said incredulously, 'You will be a Templar?'

He turned to the light of the window and his face was radiant, innocent. 'Not a knight wearing the white robes with the Cross of Christ's Blood, no, that honour is beyond me. A knight is of noble birth or very wealthy. But I have enough money to be the poorest of the poor, and that is all I crave. I shall renounce all my money and property to the Templars. I shall freeze when it is cold and burn when it is hot, Alice. I shall fight for Christ. The Templars show us the way to the resurrection through pain and suffering, humility and sacrifice. It is the only way.' He grasped my hands eagerly. A wave had washed over him, overwhelmed him, he had deliberately allowed it to take over his love for me. He needed a nice fat girl and a dose of common sense.

I saw no sign of Jack through the window. Give away his money! I said desperately, 'You don't know what you're talking about.'

Nick knew. He had rehearsed it. 'I will speak these words to the Master. "Sire, I come before God, before you and the brothers, without debts, without illness, a free man. I beg and require you in the name of God and Our Lady to accord me to your company and the benefits of the house, as one who will henceforth always be its servant and slave."'

I didn't doubt his ardour, but I said sceptically, 'What do they promise in return?'

'Bread and water, hardship and work, wounds and death, and the certainty of Heaven. Forgetting the world, by the world forgot. Only Jesus Christ will be my friend in the dark watches of the night.'

'Glory?'

'How can there be glory, except in Heaven?'

'You'll have to take the oath of celibacy.'

'Yes!' he said exultantly. 'Chastity! I shall remain a virgin, as all Templars are. I will never know a woman, Alice. The brothers even have their own cemeteries, without female corpses.'

I jumped to my feet, crossed the room to the table, put my hands in my hair to try and think, crossed back again.

Nick said, 'No one compares to you. If I can't have you, I won't have anybody.'

'For goodness sake, don't do this because of me,' I said. But I saw his face, his eyes, his earnestness, his radiance, his belief and faith in purity and innocence and the justice of his cause and what he would become, and knew I was too late. Renunciation. In his mind it was done. Nick had renounced earthly love and would fight in God's army wherever evil was found. It was so romantic.

I cried myself to sleep that night, Jack holding me in his arms, and we knew we were alone. Nick was gone. I woke from a dream of him riding in shimmering armour on a white horse, the strange black and white gonfalon of the Templars bannering above his helmet, a sword shining in his left hand and the Cross of Christ's Blood on his left breast, Evil Ones falling back on every side. Probably it was an image not far removed from Nick's own hopes and aspirations.

'Don't worry about him, he'll sort himself out,' Jack yawned, and that was the end of it.

Just the two of us, Jack and me.

And Dover Castle.

We did not hear from Nick again. *The world forgetting, by the world forgot.* In Dover we often met pilgrims and sometimes lodged them. We watched from the wall protecting the quays as the tax-exempt Templar ships loaded wool and cloth and pilgrims in the port, *Baucent* sailing with pilgrims to La Rochelle to begin their journey overland through France to the Mediterranean – the Evil Ones occupied southern Spain and blocked the straits of Gibraltar. Templar ships sailing from the safety of Collioure or Marseilles would carry the pilgrims to the Holy Land. Templar knights would guard the pilgrim convoys to Jerusalem from roadside bandits and Evil Ones. Templar treasurers at the Temple in Jerusalem would redeem the pilgrims' thief-proof coded promissory notes issued in return for deposits of gold at the Temple in London or the Temple in Paris – less a handling charge. Sometimes in the evening Jack and I watched the Templar ships returning to Dover, unloading weary pilgrims, spices, porcelain, glass, colourful dyes, the Muslim fabric called muslin, sometimes books and strange artefacts. When I thought of Nick, he seemed like part of another life. The year ended and I almost forgot him, there was so much else to do, and then Jack bid for and was granted the Master Mason's contract building the round Templar church at Temple Waltham, and the coincidence put us in mind of Nick. We looked for him there next summer but never saw him; and each year passed more quickly as I grew older, and still I was a wife without child.

To be married is to be a prisoner. I am the slave of my husband however free I am in law. And he is the slave of his work. It calls him hither and thither, we are dragged wherever the masonic whisper of employment reaches him, always arriving in this new place or that new place, which is always the same as the old place, the same hours, the same hammers, the same dust, the same

57

risk of injury or falling. For the woman it is worse. With no family I have no work to fulfil me and too much time on my hands, so that I came to envy my little servant her constant tasks and dismissed her. Yet I am bound by time and each new line on my face, and I look with yearning glances at my neighbours' children playing. Here the children shout in French. Jack worked that summer at Saintes Church overlooking the bridge, and a tall man dressed in white robes walked up from the bridge and watched Jack at his business. On his left breast I saw he wore the outline of a bridge superimposed with a red cross, the sign of the *Frères Pontifes*, the bridge-building fraternity blessed by the Pope. The old Roman bridge across the sparkling water was visibly crumbling and the fraternity struggled to save the arches before they settled beyond repair. One arch had given out a few days back, killing some men.

Jack worked without looking up, but I knew he'd noticed the *frère*, or brother. Like most craftsmen, Jack's speed was amazing, and he was not the sort to miss a chance to show off. As we watched, his swift hands wielded various patterns of hammer, from blunt to broad to sharp, and the rock fell apart to reveal a precisely designed block, and I realised that the rock had always wanted to be this shape, each angle seventy-five degrees which is the masonic golden mean, expressing tension and purpose and beauty to the eye. Such was Jack's skill that even the stone chips flew off in orderly curves away from his eyes, and I watched him with pride and love rising in my breast, excited by the observer's rapt concentration, sharing his fascination. Two quick strikes from Jack's broad chisel and the trapezoid (I have picked up a little geometry) became a pointed V as if by magic – some peasants make the sign of the Evil Eye with their first and last fingers, seeing the Devil's work in such skill. Jack rested the V on its point, then upturned it quickly so that it stood without wobbling on its two short legs, perfectly formed. I was looking at a keystone, the shaped point at the tip of a lancet arch. The stranger gazed at the gap where the arch would fit in the church wall, observed the weight of wall that would be built above it, which the arch must bear, then looked back at the keystone. 'Where did you learn the pointed arch, mason?'

Jack spat on his hands. 'Rebuilt Lincoln Cathedral for a season, master, after it fell down.'

'What are the three pillars of the earth?'

Jack responded easily to the catechism. 'The three pillars are beauty, strength, and wisdom. Beauty to adorn. Strength to support. Wisdom to contrive.'

The stranger nodded at the church wall. 'How does the pointed arch support such weight?'

'It spreads the strain more easily than a round arch, master, but requires more skill.' Jack could not hide his enthusiasm. I stepped forward, scenting work. Jack would get a higher price if he did not sound so keen. I cleared my throat warningly but he rushed on as he always does. 'The pointed arch reduces the side thrust on the walls. Thus the gaps between windows may be thinner and pillars slimmer, and the church grows larger and lighter.'

'Even so—'

'I'll place a relieving arch of rough construction, hidden in the wall above, to spread the weight still further.'

The stranger looked at him thoughtfully, then examined other pieces of work. I tried to catch Jack's eye, but he was looking at that old bridge so intently that I stepped between him and the sight of it as quickly as I would have stepped between him and another woman.

The tall man came to a decision. 'It is not your skill in decoration that interests me but your instinct for structure.'

Jack considered his words carefully. 'Geometry makes a building stand.' He explained something very complicated very simply. 'When the proportions look right, the building does not want to fall down.'

The tall man said, 'Perhaps you've heard of me. My name is Isenbert. I am ingeniator of this bridge.' Ingeniator meant contriver, deviser, engineer.

'I'm Jack. I've heard of you,' Jack said pleasantly. 'You studied under Bénezèt. You advised him on the mathematics of Avignon.'

'Then you have heard of the *Frères Pontifes*.'

'I heard the Saint-Cloud bridge was not put up by you and the masons are cursed and the bridge is falling down.'

'Indeed, the work of the brothers is highly appreciated. By vocation I am Master of the School. My skill is in mathematics,' he tapped his forehead, 'calculations, the runes of algebra, not the handiwork of masonry.'

'Good handy masons are rare in these times of trouble, sir,' I said, wanting in on any negotiations before anyone started talking about money and Jack gave away everything for a carpenter's miserable threepence a day and half loaf before I could stop him.

The tall man bowed irritably, but a strong woman is accepted as an equal by most men. He started to speak.

'Alice my wife, she is,' Jack said proudly. He's lovely.

I spat on my hand and curtsied. 'Honour it is to meet you, master,' I said in the French I had picked up. Mostly we English refuse to speak it, and apparently many of the French can't understand it either. They are as many nations as we, though we often share the same king.

Isenbert bowed for the second time and started again. 'You see, there is as much geometry in a bridge as in a cathedral, since a bridge is in effect one wall standing up alone, not four walls bracing each other, with all the support and comfort that implies.'

'I never thought of it like that,' Jack said. He squeezed me.

Isenbert gestured at the river and the bridge. 'And there are other problems . . .'

'You can't even see your foundations,' Jack said. 'Whether they're right or wrong, they're hidden under twenty feet of water and mud.'

I knew Jack had got the job. I said quickly, 'My Jack won't work for less than five pence a day. Parisian pence,' I added quickly – they were worth more.

'He would have to abide by the rules of our order, and our pay scales and benefits, which are generous. Messes of meat to the value of four sous a day—'

'Parisian.' Four sous for food! The *Frères Pontifes* lived as richly as monks.

'Parisian sous, agreed. But no second meal from mid-September to the end of Lent.' The *Frères* were a religious order dedicated to St Jacques du Haut Pas, strict on such matters. 'And no work on saints' days.'

'Agreed,' I said reluctantly, though that would cut down on the money. Most weeks had at least one saint's day as well as the Sabbath.

Jack looked from one to the other of us. He grinned.

'And right of promotion within the order,' I insisted. I haggled like this about voting rights, the size of portions, whether or not offal was called meat for as long as you may imagine.

Isenbert said finally, 'Agreed,' and the tallies were marked and exchanged. Within the week Jack put on the white robe marked with the bridge and the cross in red cloth, and for a moment as he went out into the sunlight he reminded me of someone, and I realised I must have been thinking of Nick.

I had made Jack a success, he said, pinching me, so it was all *my* fault, he said, that I was a prisoner at Saintes for a year. In truth all I wanted was our baby, but Jack never took my afflictions seriously. I was stifled and lonely in the lovely chattering town, I could take pleasure in nothing. When the bridge repairs were finished, Jack followed the work to Rochelle, and I followed Jack. For two years he worked rebuilding Roman work on the Pont St Sauveur. I watched the seagulls whirling above the toiling workmen like a cloud of noisy white crosses, and they would snatch Brie from the men's platters if they got the chance. I made my home in one of the houses on the bridge where I could look down on Jack at work, see who he talked to, see if he talked to any women. The girl who sold mussels had breasts that overhung her tray, they swung as she walked, all the men watched her, and I ran down to stick close to Jack when she was about. There was a harlot with earrings and I was sure he smiled at her. When he bent over his work, ignoring her, I supposed he had seen me watching. Next time I would be more careful, leave my door open a crack, or observe him from the shadows. But he would be more careful too . . .

Oh God, what had I become? I watched a naughty little boy called Durand selling apples, stealing crumbs from the masons' tables. The men adopted him, tousled his golden hair, called him Durand le Petty-pom, Durand the little apple.

Every man and every woman wants immortality, a son, a daughter, to give meaning to their life. I had nothing. I rushed to the other side of my house, opened my window to the river breeze and cried like a seagull. I wanted to be heard. I tore my dress, accidentally scored my breast with a fingernail. I had realised that I shared Widow Cristina's fate: she had only believed herself barren, but I really was. My body could not conceive, I was trapped. My monthly courses were a cruel deceit, my womb was dry and empty, I was guilty. Like Widow Cristina, I blamed myself for my husband's imagined infidelities, I imagined him wrapped in love's sweating embrace with bodies lusher than mine, hated imagining it yet strangely wanted to. Jack's secret child. I need never know. Because I do love Jack. Because I want him to be happy. I love him so much.

The door clicked closed behind me, the latch dropped down. I turned slowly. Jack had caught me pulling my hair. I dropped my hands, embarrassed. My fingers twisted nervously at the folds of my dress; they had a life of their own, I could not stop them. Tears welled in my eyes. Jack dropped the peg through the latch, locking the door, and grinned. 'You're drunk,' he said cheerfully.

'I'm not drunk!'

'Then you should be.' He hefted a skin of wine from behind his back. Every Frenchman drinks at least eight pints of wine a day, but we do not. Jack poured a couple of mugs, held one out. 'Drink.'

'I don't drink and neither do you.'

'Then we should.' The wine was strong and sweet. He made me drink a little more, though not as much as himself. He lifted my foot and pulled off my leather boot – they are reasonable at the market. He did the last thing I expected. He licked my toe. I giggled.

'Have a good cry,' he said.

'You don't go with other women, do you?' I said.

'Only the beautiful ones.'

'There are no beautiful women in Rochelle,' I told him.

'How would I know?' he said. 'I've never looked.'

He licked between my toes, but I twisted his ears to stop his tongue. He ignored me, flicked the wet tip from side to side, and I felt something move. My toe still wore the green grass ring he had woven for me when we were children. It had long ago dried to straw, dark yellow, and more grimy than I myself would like to lick.

'Old gold,' he said. 'You know why I'm reminding you, don't you?'

'Yes, I know,' I said. 'Because you love me.'

'So why are you crying?'

'Jack, I want to go home.'

'I don't want to stay here,' he said.

'But I know you want to work at Avignon . . .'

'Nothing's worth an unhappy wife.'

I gasped, 'Stop it, you're tickling.'

'Then we'll go home,' he said.

I said, 'Don't stop!'

Doesn't everything always work out for the best when you are in love? The Channel was calm and the sun shone, and in Dover we joined a company of jovial pilgrims setting out next morning for Canterbury. Their talk was of little but the price of tolls and the fall of Jerusalem, and what was the best vintage of grape, and how to test whether the innkeeper's beer was good or not – spill a drop on the bench, sit on it, and if it sticks to your arse it's not ready. We were neither robbed nor delayed, except by tolls and innkeepers. I walked beside Jack, my arm through his. He was happy in my company. We would have a baby, he gave money to the wayside shrines. Everything was for the best. 'Looks like rain,' one dour pilgrim said. We parted from them before Canterbury and came to Abbot's Littlebourne across the bridge. We remembered it so large, but now it seemed so small, so homespun. Its red paint – strange how I remember the smallest details – had long ago run, which Jack said was because it rained in the afternoon after we painted it, and we remembered how it had rained. The village had not changed, the people had not changed. Yvon Piggott drove his hogs along the path, waved his stick in welcome. Widow Cristina's stone house had not changed. But we were amazed, as we rounded the corner in sight of the church, to see that there was no church. The wooden structure had been struck by lightning, half burnt, half collapsed. Now summer thunder rumbled again, as if reminding us of its occasional power. Clouds had gathered in the west, but the sun still shone.

Widow Cristina lay in her bed. We saw at once that she was going to God, her face was grey as lead. 'I've been dying for years,' she scoffed, 'since the day you left, Jack. And you, Alice.' She embraced us both, weeping, we felt her whole body trembling through the blanket. 'And Nick.'

'Have you word of him?' Jack asked.

Cristina stopped breathing as though she had already passed on. 'You mean you do not know?'

Jack glanced at me. 'We know he joined the Templars.'

'Nick is dead. He was killed! Thousands were lost in the great battles around Jerusalem. They died bravely, fighting to their last breath to the glory of God.'

A shadow crossed the glass that had replaced the shutters since our time, and we listened to the rain begin.

'Dead since April,' Widow Cristina muttered, falling into sleep.

Jack was summoned by the chaplain of the church on some business or other, but I could not sit still. I walked through the rain to Pevynges Wood and stood gazing at the broken lean-to, leaf mould, dripping rain. I called but there was no reply. My family was gone, dead as though they had never been.

After supper Jack and I sat up alone, drinking wine. 'Do I have a happy wife now?' he asked, and I kissed him. He was all I had. I could not help thinking of Nick lying dead, picked open by birds, on some battlefield I would probably never hear of. Lightning flashed and we counted, then thunder banged so loud that dust drifted down from the rafters, making the fire crackle. Jack leant against me, spread his cloak over my shoulders. He prodded the flames with a stick, then the windows stood out with flickers of lightning and we cuddled tight, counting. Thunder crashed, the rain redoubled, sounding like footsteps splashing on the path.

'Closer next time,' Jack said.

61

Lightning flashed, and a knock came on the door, then we heard nothing for the thunder.

Jack frowned.

'It was just the tree,' I said. A tree had grown up near the door and with Widow Cristina ill the servant girl had not thought to trim the branches. She did nothing she was not told. She would have to go.

But Jack went to the door.

The knock came again, one, two, three.

'Don't open it!' I said.

Jack lifted the oak bar that secured the door.

The door flew open. We stood with sheeting rain blowing around us from the dark. There was nothing outside, only the sound of the noisy rain and the storm. I gasped with relief, helped Jack push the door against the wind. 'You've blown the fire out,' I said. Jack slipped, soaking his knees on the step. We would laugh about this later. Then the lightning flashed.

I screamed.

I saw the ragged bearded figure of the man standing on the path. The raindrops ran down his hair and beard, he gleamed with rain. His feet were bare. He raised his hands to cover his ears, his mouth a silent, open O. Pain. Suffering. His eyes were black from the night, dazzled by the lightning. The tendons stood out on his arms and legs. He crouched forward as though bearing the weight of the thunder on his back.

Jack said, 'Good Christ forgive us.'

I screamed from the doorway, 'Help him, Jack!'

Jack splashed down the step, reached out, and the man fell against Jack's arms.

Then the man pushed Jack away, struggled towards the doorway, to me.

His eyes stared up at me from his filthy face.

I whispered, 'You can't be.'

Nick fell inside.

Two

The Bridge

Alice's tale

London Bridge, 3 February 1832

Are you there? Can you hear me? Can you hear me scream?

Where are you, Alice? Are you here tonight?

Do you feel me? Do you touch me? Touch me. Caress me. Aaah.

What of your story? Tell me of the storm, what happened next. Was Nick alive? Were you really so jealous of Jack's skill with stone that you felt his job was more important to him than his love for you?

His job was less important. He showed that!

Ow, you scratched me. Come back.

Jack gave up his work on the Pont St Sauveur for me. You saw that. Because he loves me!

Loves?

Watch with me here. Listen, listen. Move from the darkness to the moonlight. Look down.

I see the moonlight on the water.

Do you see me? Dark as night. Do you see my eyes? Lift me, hold me. Close. Aaah.

But what of Nick?

Listen, listen, I must tell. Not of a man, yet, but of the stronger sex. Women bear more pain than you, we are built for pain, born for pain, designed for pain. God gave us our shape for a purpose, as surely and as carefully as He made each hill and river. We know pain will catch us one day, we carry it in our loins. You men . . . men are children. You risk injury at work or in war or by accident or disease, but you tell yourself, not me, it won't happen to me. Your strength is on the surface, in your muscles, your stupid show of pride, your ignorant bravery. You never believe the worst will take you. But, sometimes, it does.

And a woman?

We believe in pain. We believe in love.

What was it Nick said? Pain, suffering, humility, sacrifice. Are you talking about Nick? Did he live? What had happened to him in the Holy Land?

You have forgotten my sister Noelle.

The little girl in the forest, who looked like you? The quiet one? I didn't think she was important.

Everyone is important. And sometimes pain is unendurable.

Noelle's tale

The Temple, London
The Festival of St Peter and St Paul,
29 June 1190

I can see her now. To Noelle, these are the last moments of her life.

She's sixteen years old, a candlelit figure crouched on the winding stair, one knee bent. The hem of her cheap carry-marry smock lifts in the draught, showing her perfect white skin blackened with bruises. She raises the candle in its heavy gold candlestick above her head so its glow does not blind her sight, her chestnut hair gleams with the flame as she stares below her. The base of the candlestick is speckled with dark liquid, blood, and a few bloody strands of hair. Beneath her feet the winding stair falls twisting and turning, round and round, into the shadows from which she has climbed, the darkness down there.

Does anything move down there?

What do I hear? The same as her, nothing, no shouts from the Great Hall or huge vaulted rooms, no alarm, only her gasping breaths; now the tap of her clogs as she climbs again. She lifts each foot high, the steps are very steep. The candlestick is heavy, slippery, hard to hold; she clamps both hands round its stem. The stair winds up like a huge stone screw in the tower above her. She is climbing the Dovecote Tower. It goes nowhere. She has nowhere to go.

She's running away.

She climbs with her pale, luminous face turned upward, terrified of the drop below her – she has no head for heights, no more than I. The candlelight glows on her arms and legs as thin as sticks, her hair, her face again. Was I really so beautiful? She has eyebrows almost as straight and black as mine, but no scar between them; she has my wide eyes, my nose, perhaps my generous mouth if she smiled, and of course she has that pretty mole on her cheek exactly where it looks most perfect; she does not yet have those faint lines and dryness in her complexion and tendency to weight with which God afflicts every woman a little past her middle twenties, as I was then; but overall she is almost as beautiful as I was.

I feel as though I am watching myself, made innocent again, young again. I am seeing through her eyes the fate that almost overtook me. Almost. That day at Three Oaks From One Root perhaps, or later when I hid beneath the bridge. My instincts had been right, I *was* looked for.

But it was Noelle who was found.

Feel her from the inside. Imagine yourself inside the head of Noelle, my poor dear sister, underfed, terrified, exhausted. Look out through her eyes, feel the cold stone, the steep steps pushing you back, feel your fear, be afraid of falling, and know you are about to die.

She climbs to the stone landing matted with straw. No one comes up here but the kitchener and his snotty, foul-mouthed lad with the birdcages. The walls of the donjon, the Dovecote Tower, are four feet thick even at this height above the ground – Noelle glimpses the moonlit Thames through the arrow slit, a silvery worm below her that wriggles past the City into the distance, throws a silver net of channels and ditches over the black marshes of Southwark. Freedom.

Freedom, as far away as the moon.

Robin lives in Southwark with his father. They, too, might as well live on the moon. The Temple is huge, its walls are thick enough to keep out an army of Saracens.

And to keep a girl inside.

She cannot throw herself from the arrow slit, she can see even her skinny shoulders will not fit through, however hard she tries; and hunger has not made her head smaller.

A ladder made of wooden slats angles into the darkness above her. The ladder creaks when she touches it.

Far below, a door bangs open, bangs closed. A shout, then more shouts follow like echoes up the winding stair. She is missed. The chase, the chase. More doors slamming. The brethren sleep in long dormitories like monks, each brother lying in his own cubicle curtained off with red muslin for privacy without secrecy, modesty yet chastity, for muslin lets through the lightest whisper or sigh. They sleep alert, they wake alert.

Noelle fills her mouth with spittle. Hate fills her. She hawks white spit down the winding stair.

Somewhere down there doors bang and dogs bark, the hunting hounds called talbots probably jumping over the long tables, skidding on the rushes in their excitement. More calls, oaths. A call, 'To arms!' Another call, 'Steady, steady.' The men do not know where to look for her. Then a strange distorted shadow rises up the curved wall of the winding stair and Noelle's heart jumps into her mouth, but it is only a small cat fleeing past her, terrified, though not terrified enough to drop the mouse squealing between its teeth. The cat vanishes sinuously into a hole in the wall, gone.

Noelle grips the ladder in one hand, the candlestick in the other, climbs. On the second rung she pauses to kick off her clogs, wood slips on wood. She curls her toes over the rungs and climbs one-handed. Stops again on the fifth rung, panting, her arm trembling from the weight of the gold candlestick. She can't hold it, yet she's afraid of the dark. She leans forward against the rungs, reaches her other hand behind the ladder and pulls out the candle, lets the candlestick drop. The candle is as thick as her upper arm, white wax, heavy as a leg of pork. Until she was brought here in the cart from Temple Moat at the age of twelve she'd thought only the Church could afford wax. The wax candle alone cost enough to feed her for a year; the wealth implied by the gold candlestick is incomprehensible.

Below her the candlestick strikes the landing with a dull thud, then tumbles down the winding stair with a sound like clanging bells.

She climbs with a will. It doesn't matter now if the ladder breaks; if she falls she breaks her back or her neck or her head, she dies sooner or later. She hears the scratch of claws on the winding stair, then furious barking breaks out round the foot of the ladder. She's high in the darkness above the dogs, they see her candle flame but cannot climb the ladder. The ladder shakes as they jump and fall back but she clings on, spitting, then climbs further.

Her head bangs on wood, rough wood. She's reached the ceiling hatch to the *volière*, the bird loft. She leans back, pushes, but it's too heavy. Splinters jab her hand like quills, bringing tears to her eyes. She climbs another step, bends her head forward, pushes up with her shoulders. The hatch lifts. Then sticks. She climbs another step, straightens her legs, pushes with all her strength and the ladder creaks, bending. The rung bites under her bare toes. The candle flame feels like a hot breath against her face. Her hair crackles, stinks.

She gasps, 'Aaah!'

The hatch flies up, falls back on its hinges. As she scrambles up, the dogs yelp, fall silent. Her foot slips between the last rung and the hatchway, her smock catches a nail, rips noisily from hip to knee. Noelle's bruised thigh shows a fresh, agonising line of blood. She bends over, squeezing the pain, then realises how silly she is. In a few moments nothing will hurt and she will be dead.

The deep, calm voice of a man calls up from below. 'Child.'

She shouts down, shouts at him, screams. 'You won't hurt me any more, you can't hurt me any more!'

She can hardly see him. A shadow among shadows down there. He has no candle. The ladder creaks as he puts his weight on the first rung. 'You won't kill yourself, child.' The ladder creaks again, the second rung. 'You know what will happen.'

Noelle trembles. She knows. But she knows what will happen if she lives.

The third rung creaks. 'Be still, *mon bête à bon Dieu.*' His ladybird. This is Geoffrey de Prudome's pet name for her. 'You will fall into Hell,' he says, climbing another step, and now his heavily-accented voice shows compassion. 'Perdition. It is the abyss, the bottomless pit. You don't want that, do you, child? The inferno.'

The fifth rung. Her lover looks up, only his eyes showing, everything else is hair and dirt. Blood trickles from his hair, she glimpses the flash of flesh pink bone where she struck him with the candlestick. His cheek is split from ear to mouth.

She says, 'I hurt you.'

He roars at her like a wild animal, like a lion.

She throws down the heavy candle, it strikes his arm, scatters stars of burning wax across the straw below. She slams down the hatch. The dogs yelp, she hears the crack of the ladder breaking, he has jumped down. She hears his boots stamp the burning straw, the dogs snarling and howling, then he calls to them from the winding stair. The scratch of claws. Silence.

Far below, calls for buckets, water.

Noelle realises she is not in darkness. She turns, and her eyes fill with moonlight.

The *volière* brims with slatted moonlight. The light and shadows stream from the slats of the *volet*, the special hinged shutter set in the end wall. During daylight the birds fly out to freedom through the *volet* and at night they return to roost, knowing nothing of the kitchener and his nets and knives and noble recipes. As Noelle limps forward, the moonlight ripples over her body like pale fingers. Here is her death. She pushes her hands against the foul-smelling wood.

The *volet* swings open. There is nothing beyond here but air, where only birds can fly. She can go no further in this world than here. In a few moments she'll jump.

She's numb with fear. 'God, forgive me!' The doves disturbed by her cries flutter round her, flash white in the moonlight, then stream past her like an exhalation of breath into the night air. Their tiny claws and beaks tangle in her hair, their wings brush her cheeks.

She almost tumbles out by accident, but instinctively her hands grab the frame.

The peg that had secured the *volet* falls, turning over and over into the dark. She hears it strike the courtyard below.

Noelle pulls herself back into the safety of the *volière*, utters a cry of despair. If she falls by accident, her freed immortal soul will rise like a dove to Heaven. If she jumps deliberately to her death, it is suicide, third of the three greatest sins, and her soul will fall beyond the comfort of the Church. Like the damned who die unbaptised or excommunicate, prayers will not be said for her, her body will not be buried in consecrated ground, her soul will plummet through the earth to the pit of Hell and demons will rip her flesh, claw her with hooks, burn her in the furnace of living death for eternity.

Every Christian knows these facts are true.

How beautiful the night is.

From the top of the tower Noelle sees like a bird. The Festival of St Peter and St Paul is over. The King's new law permits fires and candles in London after the evening bell, but by this hour nothing remains of the festival bonfires but glowing mounds of embers. Beyond the River Fleet the City lies quietly under the warm midsummer moon, a jumble of castles and church towers and houses and hovels cradled together within the gargantuan embrace of the ancient Roman wall.

The Temple is a city within the City, inside the boundary but deliberately outside the City's Roman fortifications and jurisdiction. The new battlements and gaunt defensive towers of the Temple turn inland at the marshes where the Fleet joins the Thames, follow Crocker's Lane to Fleet Street. There the Temple wall turns west past the Great Gateway to Temple Bar, overlooks the Strand as far as Aldwych, angles back to the Thames shore and the Temple's own wharves and quays.

The Temple is filled with buildings spread out in the moonlight around the Dovecote Tower. A town for the Order to live without women, without children, without love, except love for God. Rows of stables, armouries, storehouses, smithies, forges, workrooms, brewery and bakery and abattoir: a monastery dedicated to war. Fields and courtyards for soldiers to practise war, butts for archers, straw target dummies painted with round black eyes and red lips like Evil Ones. Monks' cloisters and chapter rooms, refectories and dormitories, chapels and chantries, all exist for the purpose of war. Even the new circular church, oddly ornate in fresh white stone, is for the blessing of war. Without war, without Evil Ones, these men cannot exist.

Noelle sniffs smoke. A faint smoky mist drifts past her, she hears the faint crackle of fire. She is trapped. The first smoky red fingers of flame poke through the floor. If she jumps she dies of her own free will, and condemns herself to eternal suffering. But if she endures burning to death, she goes to Heaven.

She hears men shouting on the winding stair, the rattle of buckets, the slosh of water. They are fighting the fire. Whatever happens, she has very few minutes left.

Beyond the river wall of the Temple, black with shadow, lies the Thames like a silver sword. A cockerel crows, mistaking the moon for the sun.

She closes her eyes, remembers Robin's voice, remembers his *urgency*, hardly older than she is, and as poor, and even dirtier. 'Run away, Noelle. Run away with me.' Robin slept on the floor of his father's sty with pigs for company – doubtless lying asleep there now, unaware of her agony and death. Each working day in summer – dead pork spoils in a day – Robin herded his father's live meat across London Bridge into the City. If the bridge was broken he hired a boat, bribing a ferryman double guild rates to take such a messy cargo. Sometimes he carried a clutch of chickens roped to his back, always a basket or two of eggs, and haggled a sale to the butchers of Cheapside. Noelle often accompanied Hugh the cellarer to Cheapside. Someone had to hold the donkey or it would be stolen, its panniers ransacked in a flash, and Hugh was a thin, knowing man who liked to bargain for hours with stallholders for his cut. At his command Noelle waited head down by the donkey and ignored the crowds bustling around her. Her spirit was broken, she saw nothing, heard nothing. One morning someone tapped her shoulder and she turned to see a large brown hen's egg almost touching her nose. The egg was held by a hand, and the hand belonged to a boy as thin as she was but much taller. 'Go on, take it!' he said. 'You look like you need it more than I do.'

She shook her head. He touched the egg to the tip of her nose. Noelle blinked, then caught it, stared after the boy weaving through the crowd. He turned and waved. 'I'm Robin – Robin the swineherd, of Southwark!' Without taking her eyes off where he had disappeared in the crowd, she pierced the egg with her thumbnail, sucked it dry, then ate the empty shell.

After that day she looked for him every time. She raised her head, she was alert now, she had a reason. Robin tossed an egg over the crowd and she caught it one-handed . . .

A cockerel crows, mistaking the moon for the sun. Noelle remembers the taste of the egg perfectly, as though she still eats it even now. She thinks, I remember . . .

'Run away, Noelle,' Robin said urgently. 'Run away with me.'

'He'd kill me.'

'Who?'

'You know who.'

She remembered Robin taking her hands in his. 'You can't suffer like this. You can't let him do this to you. Don't you understand? The only reason you let him do it is because you know nothing else.'

'No, he swears he is *éprise* with me. Smithin He's like a father to me. He'll give me a gown of wool for my own, and a gold chain, and shoes bejewelled with the three portals of St Paul's Cathedral, and keep me safe.'

'If?'

'If I do as he says, that's all.'

'You're infatuated with him because he's important, notices you, owns you. His attention flatters you and you think more of yourself because of it. That's not love.'

But she remembered saying, 'Yes, it is.'

Noelle's head jerks. She is back in the *volière*.

How was she so wrong, trusting, innocent, stupid? If the God I believe in lives, how is there so much evil in the world? If I had eyes that saw everything, how much would I see?

Her toes curl over the edge of the *volet*. Bats whizz and whirr in the night air below her, snatching invisible moths. She teeters.

'I believe.' Her lips move, reciting Latin words she does not understand but whose sound comforts her. 'I believe in God the Father Almighty, Maker of Heaven and Earth, and in Jesus Christ His only Son our Lord, who was conceived by the Holy Ghost, born of the Virgin Mary, suffered under Pontius Pilate, was crucified, dead, and buried, He descended into Hell. The third day He rose again from the dead, He ascended into Heaven, and sitteth at the right hand of God the Father Almighty.'

The smoke thins. Banging noises from below. They're bringing up a second ladder. Her hands, her legs shake, only a moment left. 'From thence He shall come to judge the quick and the dead . . .'

The moon slides behind a cloud, darkness falls.

Her frail, faithful voice recites in the dark, 'I believe in the Holy Ghost, the Holy Catholic Church, the Communion of Saints, the Forgiveness of sins, the Resurrection of the body, and life everlasting. Amen.'

The hatch bangs open behind her, the moon comes out of the cloud, slanted light streams across a steep thatched roof below her. The kitchen, a tall circular building like an upended funnel, with shutters round the top to let out the cooking smoke, is kept apart from the Dovecote Tower by a narrow passage against fire. Fire is frequent in London but thatch is cheap.

71

Noelle wonders if she can jump. She will die, the gap is too wide, she will smash herself on the stones of the courtyard. But she tells herself, *I can jump and live*. If she dies trying, at least it is not the sin of suicide.

She thinks of Robin. Much the same way as I think of Jack, I suppose. And Jack thinks of me, I hope. She imagines being alive with Robin. Being in love. The life she would have lived.

Footsteps in the *volière*, and a deep voice says, 'Stop. Child. You don't know what you are doing.'

Noelle jumps.

She falls through the air screaming, arms windmilling, legs running, her smock pulled over her head by the wind of her fall. A fearful crash. Her body bounces down the steep kitchen roof, rolls, slides. Her legs slide over the edge, she clings on, then lets go.

She lands on her feet, sits on her bottom, sprawls in the straw and hay and manure of the yard. The straw rustles with mice busy about their nocturnal tasks. A horse whinnies softly from the stable, thirsty, hoping she will fetch water.

Noelle sits up, holds her feet with her hands as though feeling them for the first time. She's alive.

A head shows in the *volet* high above. Did she jump so far? The head pulls back, disappears. The tower is ominously silent behind its thick walls. Boots must be pounding on the stairs, doors banging in the hall, but there is no sound of this furious activity outside. Yet.

'Noelle, hurry,' she whispers. She picks herself up, limps from the yard. Where to go? Every bone aches. She crosses the tiltyard, ducks beneath the rail, keeps to the shadow behind a barn. She runs across the moonlight to a warehouse, scents spices. Slips between two buildings. The ground is lower here, damp, it's been easier for her to run downhill. Beyond the warehouses a track covered with straw leads to the river gate.

The gate is closed.

She hides behind a cart, then a pile of sacks. Any moment this place will be like an ants' nest. She hears a trickle of water. The kitchen drains into the latrines, the water has to go somewhere. Think, think. A conduit angles round the strange white church, carries the waste to a ditch, the ditch must go downhill. It must be here.

She finds it by its smell. In winter it is a stream, but now little more than a foul-smelling trickle flows between the steep, deep-dug banks.

Now she hears shouts, muffled, distant. She splashes along the ditch. The ditch must lead to the river. Mud splashes her lip, tastes foul. A plank bridge crosses the ditch; she hides underneath as a couple of men run over. They're complaining, they don't know what's going on. Someone calls, 'It's a fire.' But someone else calls that it's not a fire, it's a drill. The two men turn back cursing to fetch their weapons.

Noelle crawls along the channel to the river wall. How does the water get out? There must be a way beneath the wall. London has not been attacked from the river for hundreds of years. While London Bridge stands – and a short, massive length of Roman wall joins the bridge with the Tower of London – no enemy can sail past the City. The Temple is still under construction, but no one seriously believes the Evil Ones will sail past London up the Thames.

The river wall is the Temple's weakest point.

Something echoes. The ditch enters a short tunnel beneath the wall. A heavy iron grille blocks the tunnel from side to side.

But not underneath, or rains and rubbish and sewage would foul the obstruction and back the flood up into the warehouses. Probably this has already happened, the lower bars are deliberately bent outwards. Noelle

72

crawls, then wriggles beneath the iron spikes. The mud stinks worse than the latrine.

She slides forward on to a muddy bank. All around her are wooden pilings, rough boards over her head. She is beneath the wharves. A ship's hull is beached in front of her.

Southwark. Freedom. She must cross the river to Southwark.

But she can't swim. She's afraid of drowning. But she imagines being caught.

She crawls left, along the mudbanks and refuse and broken pots and bottles under the jetties. The river laps closer, rises to high tide. Now she splashes, slows, forces herself to move quietly. She must be past the Temple's wharves, the wood is green and slimy here, decrepit, moonlight pours through in strange shapes. Footsteps halt above her head. Noelle turns to stone, her shape camouflaged by moonbeams. Someone spits on her. 'A girl broke into the Temple.' The other man says, 'A thief?' The first man grunts, 'They're all thieves.' The Temple is served by certain women who undertake tasks too disgusting or too low for men to bear. For some reason Noelle does not know, the butterer is always a woman. She knows the women can be worse than men. They are shut away at sunset. Women who live without men are frightening creatures, they turn half into men, as coarse as men, as brutal, sometimes wearing hair on their chins. The strongest women, she knows, turn on the weakest of their sex more savagely and spitefully than the worst of men.

The footsteps move away. Noelle creeps forward.

The wharves end in moonlight over the River Fleet. She keeps to the marshes, moves crouching along the muddy channels between the reed beds. Now the water is deeper, the tide flowing sluggishly into the mouth of the Fleet, pushing at her gently as she wades across, slowly turning the paddles of the Templar's mill. A shout, she is seen. Too late the moon goes behind a cloud. She pulls at the grasses of the far bank but she can see no steps on to the rickety boardwalks above her. She splashes along the mudbanks of the broad Thames – there is Southwark, on the far side!—then climbs the rotten river steps of the Prior of Okebourne. She senses rather than sees his dark mansion, almost falls over a boat. It is overturned, chained to the wall to save it from thieves. Further on is another, not chained, but too heavy to move. She finds other boats on the shore, but each with the sculls removed, or mast taken away, or its bung withdrawn so that it will sink. She crosses the rickety bridge over the City moat and the walls of London rise above her. She runs along the wharves and docks.

A French voice shouts, 'Stop, thief!'

That's clever. Noelle is both the stolen property and the thief, a serf of Kent, officially a foreigner in London. She runs along the foreshore and the moon comes out again, showing her the way but also revealing her position to watchers. Here is Fish Landing, now Queen's Landing, the Roman wall fallen down to reveal Haddock Lane, and the mongrels kept by common folk lunge at her out of the stinking shambles, pulled up on their hind legs by their chains so they stand taller than she does. The sound of their barking marks her trail.

'Stop, thief!' A commotion of barking dogs, running feet, shouts, then the hue and cry is taken up in a nearby churchyard with growing excitement. 'Thief! Stop, thief!' Someone's running, perhaps a real thief. The shouts go the wrong way, and Noelle runs for her life along Thames Street, into the deep shadows between the tangle of houses and the huge ruined wall.

The street appears empty of life, but she knows this is an illusion. Noelle is a country girl but she knows the City; Geoffrey de Prudome comes to London twice a year while Temple Moat is cleaned. She knows that in London eyes are always watching her, however empty the street seems.

She pulls her hair over her face and keeps to the shadows.

The unseen eyes belong to thieves, scavengers and whores, free people. Freedom means freedom to fail, and all they care about is money. Freedom has none of the benefits of slavery, the right to work, food, a roof over their heads. These people have nothing but freedom, and so no honest man or woman ventures out in London after dark. Will they let her go as one of their own, or give her up for money?

The dark figures draw back. She's one of them. Free.

Noelle crosses the Walbrook footbridge. The shouts, which had been distant, come close. There are houses all round her, but no lights show in windows. Last year thirty Jews were murdered in one night and no one interfered. Some of the gangs report to the highest citizens of London, who are their leaders.

Hoofbeats. Noelle crouches in terror, but the sound passes behind the buildings towards Eastcheap.

She clenches her fists. She is exhausted. 'You won't hurt me any more,' she whispers over and over, 'you can't hurt me any more.'

But she knows he can.

A gravel roadway, one of the first she has seen, slopes downhill from her left. This is Bridge Street, leading her down to the river. She crosses herself at the image of St Christopher in the churchyard of St Margaret Towards-the-Bridge. The air stinks of yesterday's fish. Ahead of her the river shines like a mirror of the moon.

Running men spill from Eastcheap, jostle each other in the road. There's a fight, knives flash, rival gangs. Some poor woman in Crooked Lane is beaten, her hood torn from her head. Hoofbeats again, someone holds up a fiery flambeau. Geoffrey de Prudome pushes the men back with his sword, looks down on the woman from his warhorse, then shakes his head. 'She is not her.' He presses his hands together in prayer for her forgiveness, the moonlight glinting on his helmet. 'Forgive me, mother.' The woman curtsies, she actually curtsies, her eyes fixed adoringly on the cross on his left breast, coloured black on white by the moonlight. 'Go home safely, mother.'

Noelle sees him take the flambeau and ride alone into Bridge Street. His eyes darken, becoming orange in the firelight like an animal's. The woman's shrieks are lost under the sound of heavy male laughter and he turns away, despising the men for their weakness.

Noelle crouches between the stone church of St Magnus Martyr and its wooden chapel. It is consecrated ground and the gravestones are hard beneath her hands and knees, mostly covering drowned bodies retrieved from the river. Many are nameless, but God knows His own. She finds her fingers wet with dew, licks them thirstily.

She stops, her tongue still touching her fingertip.

Sir Geoffrey is close to her. He puts back his head and sniffs the air. His horse whickers softly, knowing perfectly well she is there.

Noelle slips into the shadows between the chapel and the church, bangs her hip on a headstone, muffles her cry with the back of her hand.

Sir Geoffrey spurs forward to Thames Street, white with stones broken from the Roman wall, sends a man running as far as the Vicus Sancti Martin Orgar. 'No one, my lord,' the man calls, and men deploy into Billingsgate. Their calls return faintly, 'No one, lord.'

Sir Geoffrey stares into the dark to his right, then to his left. Three years ago, two, only two, Knights Templar returned alive from the Battle of the Sermon on the Mount and the loss to Christianity of Jerusalem to the Evil Ones; only two men, Giles de Ridefort, Grand Master of France, and this man, Geoffrey de Prudome, Grand Master of England. A Templar never disobeys an order, never retreats, never surrenders, and if overwhelmed is killed by the Evil Ones on the field of battle or soon after, because the Temple never pays gold ransom. But these two men returned. What price did they pay? Noelle wonders what the Evil Ones would value more highly than gold.

It's whispered the two men took oaths to Islam, the religion of the Evil Ones, and renounced their oaths as soon as they were free.

Now Geoffrey de Prudome looks straight at her, and does not see her.

She hears him mutter to himself, '*Oc, où est tu, mon bête à bon Dieu?*'

Oc, the French word for yes.

She remembers . . . his private chamber, the fingers of his right hand moving in her hair, he feels her beauty. *Oc*. Beauty he can hold no more than a beautiful butterfly. He cannot touch her, only bruise her. Yet her femininity, she knows, makes him feel as though he can do anything. *Oc*. Even love her . . .

He strides forward, and Noelle can no longer bear to stay still. She runs behind the chapel on to the Fishwharf, gasps at the brightness of the water. The broad Thames, ablaze with the moon, casts up its radiance against the underside of the old wooden bridge so that the whole structure seems to glow from beneath, rippling with silver lines like the river.

Beside the old bridge, the stone foundations for a new bridge stand a few yards upstream like a row of stepping stones for giants. A few of the arches look complete, striding across the bright water like the tops of church windows towards Southwark. But the rest is water.

She'll cross the old bridge.

She climbs from the wharf to London Shore, stops, horrified. The entrance to the old elm bridge, the London Bridge that has served London for a thousand years in one form or another, is barricaded. A small shrine is placed against the boards so that no one will defile the crossing by theft or by attempting to pass over.

She looks behind her. She stands in full moonlight, in plain view. It is only a matter of time before she is seen.

Noelle kneels and genuflects to the Virgin, not wanting to give insult where none is intended, for she means to cross, then leans forward and peers between the planks. The wooden superstructure was rebuilt only a few years ago, after fire destroyed the City from London Bridge to St Paul's Cathedral, but the timber foundations deep beneath the water are Roman. They have finally given way, and from this angle she sees the rickety roadway leans like a drunkard, dips and loops under the weight of piles of rubble, enormous oak cranes, counterbalances, barrows and carts bearing great lumps of stone to be lowered on to the new bridge. But the building work already has a derelict air, moss shows between the stones, and the once-smooth curve of a new stone arch stands like a broken tooth. The old bridge is exhausted, but the new one has yet to be born.

Again she glances behind her. Sir Geoffrey has only to turn his head to see her.

She has no farthing for a ferryman; anyway ferrymen are all sticklers, father and son, for the stringent terms and conditions of their guild. None work before dawn.

Noelle must cross the bridge.

She pulls carefully at one of the planks, inches it aside, slides her shoulder through the gap. To her horror, a nail squeals, and the whole rickety fence falls away from her in a cloud of dust.

Noelle runs across the planks on to the bridge. Sir Geoffrey shouts behind her. She runs with big, slow footsteps, holds down her hair with her arms, slithers on the heaps of gravel. The stones jab her bare feet. She's so afraid that she can't breathe, runs without breathing. The bridge railing stops, gives access to the giant footsteps of the new bridge below. She glimpses the moon in the water. The bridge dips away from her.

Her bare feet skid. She slips. Her hips slide over the edge. There's nothing beneath her.

The edge rakes her ribs, tears her breasts. She tries to cry out but the wind is knocked from her lungs. Her body fills with pain, but her hands grab instinctively at a beam.

She doesn't fall.

She hangs by her hands above the moon, stares between her swinging legs. The last of the tide flows beneath her, draws silver lines around the foundations of the bridge. She looks up. Sir Geoffrey gazes down at her.

Then he kneels, and his gloved hand reaches down to her. She looks from her hand to his eyes.

His fingers beckon her. Take hold. He leans down.

Her hand slips from the beam. She swings by one hand.

His fingers jerk impatiently.

Noelle stares up at him.

She lets go. The water strikes her at once, sweeps over her head, fills her mouth, her nose, rushes noisily into her ears. She gasps for breath, the cold river pours into her lungs, fills her belly like an enormous dead weight. She struggles against the water. The tide carries her upstream against the flow of the river, her struggles weaken. Something made of stone bumps her softly, she is deep beneath an arch of the new bridge. The moon grows above her, it is the light. Her fingers stretch out towards the brilliant light, and she sees her mother dressed in white light, brilliant, her arms outstretched.

She thinks, my mother never wore clothes like these.

Mother wears a white headpiece, and a halo like the Virgin Mary. The halo is the source of the light. She holds a child in her arms, a child's body with a woman's face, and the source of the light becomes the child. The child grows smaller, not larger, grows into a small, round-eyed monkey, a lizard, a fish, a tadpole and the moon. 'No, don't go!' Noelle cries. Her body struggles with the last of its strength, but she cannot lift the weight of a bubble.

Her hands and feet sink inertly into soft mud, the tide turns her over, bubbles trail from her mouth towards the dim moon. She remembers Robin and his urgency and his plans and she feels everything going away, numbly receding from her after the point of light, the life she will never know, bright sunlight and smoke from the cooking fire and the laughter of her children who will never be born turning to darkness, fading away. Her face swells, her eyes and tongue stick out, her body writhes in a parody of life in its death agony, weed gently wraps her legs and neck and holds her without moving.

'She's gone.'

He stares into the water. A man brings his cloak, places it on his shoulders. The tide carried away her splash at once. He waits for as long as he can hold his breath but she does not come up.

But still he waits. As long as he can. Then exhales.

He turns away. 'She's dead.'

He walks from the bridge. His man follows him. 'Who was she, lord?'

He frowns. He remembers only his names for her, not her real name. He remembers the feel of her body but not her face.

'She was no one.'

Nothing moves.

Silence.

Darkness. Her heart quivers for the last time then she feels nothing, nothing at all. She turns inside herself, accepting death.

The body of Noelle Lacknail lies motionless on the bottom of the river, wrapped in weed. Her hands float limply above her head, her eyes stare upwards. Sadness fills her, and loneliness.

Nothing hurts her now, not her cut feet, not her scratched thigh, not her bruised ribs, not hate, not love. The splinters which she remembers in her hands do not pain her. She lies without feeling, without movement, without life.

She wants to leave her body, but the light is gone.

She cries out but makes no sound.

Slowly the dull, shimmering moon passes above her staring eyes. The ebb tide begins to move past her, begins to rush downstream, tugs at her. The weed is pulled with the current, slowly flapping and swirling, wrapping itself round her, covering her left eye. The tide eases, stops. Slack water lies on her like glass, hard, smooth, impenetrable, she cannot scratch it. She tries to blink the weed from her left eye. She screams. Nothing. Her body is meat.

The river loses its darkness, becomes brown like thick soup. Sunrise.

The tide returns, tugs her the other way in the weed, buries her deeper beneath the rising water. Her body sways gently in the rush.

She screams and screams. No bubbles rise from her watery grave.

The underside of a boat crosses the river's surface high above her, drawing an arrow of bright ripples. Later it crosses back the other way.

The tide falls, rolls her over. She sees mud blowing gently along the bottom of the river. Something moves in the mud, a flounder or plaice perhaps. Southwark plaice are a famous delicacy. Then a fish like a trout, but blue on top, a shad, investigates her first from one side then the other. She knows shad are delicious to eat, caught by the thousand in nets at Shadwell. Its tail quivers beneath her right eye and her head jerks from time to time as it nibbles her lips or tongue.

The shad flees and an eel ripples sinuously past her, as long as her arm had been. It turns back towards her body, its mouth opens, becomes huge, bites. Her right eye goes dark.

Noelle lies in the dark.

The Graveyard, Abbot's Littlebourne
30 June 1190

At the exact moment, as I later learn, that the eel eats my sister's eye, midday on the last day of June, here I am. No, not up there with those sweating, sweltering idiots hammering on the church roof. Down here in the graveyard, beautiful, sulking, scowling, my fists on my hips, frowning like a thunderstorm, do you see me now? Wearing my special green woollen dress, my Rochelle dress trimmed with linen and lace and a green woollen belt, a green girl on the green churchyard grass with my hair carefully combed and braided over my shoulders, staring up at the men working high up on the skeleton of bare rafters, tapping my foot with impatience. Does Jack notice the trouble I've taken with my appearance, notice my dress, remember the day? Does he even care? What do you think he calls down?

'Alice, Alice, lovely as a palace!'

Jack's keeping the lads going, he knows he's getting the best work out of such a hot day; they'll rest through the heat of afternoon then start again in the cool evening. His raillery makes the men work harder, the tiling hammers pound together as a team. Jack's being competitive, he can't resist drawing attention to what his oldest friend does not have and does not want, a wife. Nick works his tiling hammer with a steady rhythm, clout-clout, clout-clout. He's shaved his beard but it reveals little more than before of his carefully expressionless face. His eyes are without reflection, keeping his thoughts and feelings inside him.

After all he's gone through, does Nick love me, still, just a little, as when we were children? Tending a tiny warm coal of love somewhere deep inside himself? Love that can never do any good because of his oath of celibacy, and because I love Jack. But do you think that curiosity for what a man might hide inside himself gives a woman my age, married for ten years, locked in the routine of my childless days, a touch more life?

I'm shielding my eyes from the sun as I watch them work, busy with all this busy business of living, sunlight, long grass, clouds in the sky, rattling hammers, and I have no idea, none at all, that Noelle is dead. I did not feel her loss in my sleep last night; lying in Jack's arms, my dreams were undisturbed. I feel nothing different in my heart today. I still do not know. God does not speak to me. I felt nothing when Mabel died, or Elviva died, I can't even remember when they went exactly. There's only now, my own selfish life rushing forward (do I not sound a little like Widow Cristina?) and I'm in a fine temper and thinking only of myself. I'll be sorry – later.

But for now there's Jack up there, and me down here, and beside my tapping foot the midday meal is spoiling in its basket, hours of preparation wasted, the bread already stale and flies buzzing at the meat. He's going to catch the sharp side of my tongue when he comes down and he knows it. Being Jack, who after his good fortune in being born down Cristina's birth canal and no other (unlike Nick), and has had everything in his life handed to him on a plate (usually by me), Jack decides he might as well be hung for a sheep as a lamb. He leaps nimbly as a sprite along the steep untiled rafters, he knows I have no head for heights, I can't bear to watch. But I have to watch as though I don't care. If I scream he wins. He knows that too. Ah, my husband. I won't give in.

He slips, and I squeak.

Jack puts his tongue between his lips, grins down like a long-legged demon, and I could kill him. He swings his legs comfortably over the ridge pole forty feet above the ground, strums an invisible lute and sings down to me, 'Alice, Alice, tell us please, what dainty mess, for us to bless, have you brought for us to eat? A lovely piece of cheese, and a nice fat lump of meat?'

'I'll bash your bunion with an onion if you don't shut your throat!' I called up. The men laughed and Jack nearly fell off the ridge pole laughing.

Clout-clout. Nick worked on, thin and hard as a nail, pegging tiles between his spread legs, shifting another six inches, clout-clout. I think he felt sorry for me, Jack had gone too far. He called down, 'We won't be long.'

One of the older Tyler men or uncles, four generations of them toiling on the roof, put Nick down on Jack's behalf. 'Before you go down you'll ask permission of your master mason first, Sir Apprentice.' The men didn't like Nick, they always supported Jack.

Nick glanced at them, and they fell silent. They were always a little afraid of him.

He bowed his head, in prayer, or hiding anger. I thought it was wrong that cheap workmen should heap humiliation on a man who had suffered so much.

I lifted my fingers towards them in the rude gesture you understand, and carried my basket to the churchyard oak to wait. Jack slid down the ladder and grabbed my elbow. 'Don't insult my men.'

'It was you I was insulting,' I said. 'You know why. Nick's twice the man of any of that lot. And talking of insults, don't insult me with your doggerel.'

He laughed and pecked my lips. I tried to bite him. He chuckled and ran back up the ladder, unforgiven.

All round the great tree, which had escaped the lightning flash that destroyed the church, the wooden crosses of village folk were planted, mildewed, mossy, rotting. Widow Cristina's imperishable stone cross (though already a little mossy) stood in the warm consecrated earth nearer the church, where more important people lay buried so they need not walk as far as the others on Resurrection Day. The sun on her name put me in mind of her. Cristina had lived long enough to understand, despite her failing mind, that Nick had returned alive, somehow, miraculously, from the Holy Land. Whatever had happened to him there, or during the perils and adventures of his journey home, he never talked of it to us. Like a man coming out of darkness, he returned alone. Had travelled alone to the Temple in London, renounced his oath to the Templars in the circular church in the faces of his brothers, the Poor Fellow-Soldiers of Christ. Drew his sword, broke it, threw it down. Threw down his dagger and his mace. His helmet. Spurs. Tore off the white tabard with the Cross of Christ's Blood on the left breast and threw it down, stood before them naked except for his loincloth and his robe. The Templars never let their own go, but they let Nick go, and so he came to us. Jack told me what Nick had told him: a Templar could renounce his oath to join another order, and so Jack had arranged for his oldest friend to join the *Frères Pontifes*, the Order of Saint Jacques du Haut Pas. Such favours are neither cheap nor easy but not impossible, so Nick was deeply in Jack's debt. But he remained silent, quiet, filled with pain.

I thought I was the one person Nick might talk to, but he clamped tight.

Did he tell Widow Cristina before she died? If so she took his secret to her grave. I knew something very big, very . . . *personal*, had happened to Nick. What little I knew of his story didn't make sense, and as you know, that is irresistible. Renounced his *white* tabard with the Cross of Holy Blood? Nick had been a man-at-arms, at most a sergeant with his own horse, he had worn brown or black. But the morning after the storm I walked back along the road. No reason, curiosity. His bare footprints pointed towards me in the mud, interrupted where brambles were pulled into the road and he had stumbled among them. The monk at the bridge, drunk out of his mind after dark and probably terrified of the storm, had seen no one. And in truth there was no reason for Nick to have come this way. But I found a white cloak bundled into the lowest arch beneath the bridge. Ah, curiosity, this is where it leads me.

I unfolded the white cloak. Soaked with rainwater, the thick wool was almost too heavy to lift. Inside, where it would touch the left breast, was the dripping, rain-smeared imprint of a red cross.

Cristina had known she lay on her deathbed, she'd seen the *caladrius*, a bird which stood on the bedstead, and it had turned its head away from her, which meant she would die. Within a week of Nick's return three years ago, she had called me to her. 'Leave the drapes open. No more secrets.' She gripped my hand sadly. I owed her so much. 'There have been too many secrets in my life, Alice. There are always too many stories to be told, always more than we know. Sometimes I think we don't live life, we just glimpse it rushing past and it's gone. Before we know it, everything's happened and that's the end. Nothing matters.'

But we saw Nick sitting half-naked, shivering by the fire, still filthy, haunted, hardly half a dozen words past his lips since his return. I said, 'You're wrong, Widow Cristina. Everything matters. Everything's important.'

Whether she took my words to heart or not, she said nothing then. But before she died she called Nick to her, told him to close the drape behind him, and what she said I did not hear. Did she finally tell him that though Alfred was his father, he truly was the miller's daughter's son? Did she finally tell him his mother was Heylewise? I'm sure of it.

What did Nick tell her in return? He was in there for an hour, two hours, three, I strained after the sound of his low voice whispering but I couldn't make out the words. Then Widow Cristina cried out, and Nick drew the curtain.

He said, 'She's dead.' I stared at her blackened face. Cristina had choked on her spittle, obviously. Her body started to smell almost immediately in the hot weather after the storm. Nick knelt beside her in prayer.

It seemed so long ago.

'. . . Sir Apprentice.' That mocking call to Nick from the workmen, and my sharp words with Jack. The tree, overhanging, rustling, its leaves moist from the nutrition of graveyard soil. Nick's hammer, clout-clout, busy with his work on the steep roof, but I had the feeling he was watching me as though I emitted an invisible scent.

I was still angry with Jack. I dropped down beneath the tree, listened to the bees droning to the parson's hive – Humphrey had died years ago, his son Maurice was parson now. The rattle of hammers was more distant here. I patted my burning cheeks. Jack had not noticed my dress, though it had been a gift from him, not woven by me like my others, and I was upset. The wool was hot and I lifted my knees to cool my legs. He'd forgotten the day and that was even more upsetting. If it had been anyone else it wouldn't have mattered. I wore the dress to please him. No one ignores me except my husband. No one hurts me except him.

I picked an apple from the basket, opened my mouth, bit it, and a fleck moved in the corner of my eye. I rubbed the place then realised I saw something moving not in my eye but in the distance. So small I hardly saw it when I looked there directly, a dot moving on the road from Canterbury.

So I saw the stranger first.

None of the workmen noticed him, high above me though they were with a view from here to the sea, busy with their work. I chewed, my first thought that he was a pilgrim returning alone from St Thomas's shrine. I took a second mouthful of apple. The man did not walk, he rode on horseback. A rich man, therefore. But rich men do not travel alone.

The trees of Pevynges Wood hid him for a while. I chewed, took another bite, then the distant figure reappeared by Three Oaks From One Root. Now I saw he wore black robes, a Benedictine monk. But everyone knows St Benedict's Rule forbids his monks to ride horses. Neither are they permitted to undertake pilgrimage. What I saw was doubly impossible.

If the Black Monk was not a pilgrim, he must be travelling to our village – a village belonging to an Augustinian abbot, remember – for a purpose. But what purpose? And what of his horse? I grunted, seeing now that it was not a horse but a donkey. The Black Monks are famous for applying such fine distinctions to their advantage. Obedient to St Benedict to the letter, they ride anything *except* a horse, donkeys, mules, even goats, and I have often seen sandalled, white-footed, black-robed monks carried across puddles by strong men, and once a fat monk carried by a woman. I laughed, finished the apple. A Black Monk riding alone? A man who eats thirteen courses a day and drinks a gallon of wine, and pays a boy to get up at night to perform his prayers for him doesn't get much sympathy from ordinary folk. But still, this man travelled alone.

So the reason for his journey was urgent.

By now my interest was thoroughly aroused. I watched him drop from sight in the sunken lane through the fields of Downham, then reappear on the dusty track close to the church. His long legs almost trailed on the road; either the donkey was strong or the man not so heavy as his height and bulky robes suggested. They had come much further than just from Canterbury, both were weary, caked with dust. But the most remarkable event was yet to come. The donkey stopped at the churchyard gate, the monk swung his legs down, left the donkey drinking from the ditch and chewing the grass, opened the churchyard gate and walked, stiffly, straight towards me. 'What village is this?'

Most people would simply say it was our village. 'Abbot's Littlebourne, this is.'

'God be thanked.' His face was made of bone, but his eyes were vivid. He eyed the beer pitcher so I offered him a sip and he tilted it back and gulped, his Adam's apple bobbing like a ball in his gullet. He gasped, wiped his face with his sleeve, lifted the pitcher again. I put my hand over it. 'That's my husband's beer.'

'I'm thirsty.'

I grabbed the pitcher before he drank it all. I exclaimed, 'What brings you here on such a long journey, and in such a hurry?' He wondered how I knew so I told him what I told you, and he looked at me with respect. 'I seek a man called Jack Mason.'

'You've drunk his beer,' I said. 'That's him on the church roof. He'll be down in a minute. Wait in the shade if you want.' The monk sat on the grass by my basket, opened it, rummaged inside, pulled out a pasty. I glowered at him.

He returned my look, picked a crumb from his lip and ate it. 'I'm hungry. Who are you?'

'Jack Mason's wife, and that's Jack Mason's pasty.'

'Eel. Delicious. In London my housekeeper,' he said obliquely, 'makes me eat nothing but mutton.' I knew a monk's housekeeper often performed the functions of a wife, a *lecherwite*, which either means a lecher's wife or a lecherous wife, depending if it's a man or woman talking. Whichever it is, it's more than a

81

housekeeper. The monk ate through the eel to the cooked apple, picked a clove from his tooth stumps. 'My name is Peter Colechurch.' He bit down on the clove, sighed peacefully as the spice flooded his mouth. No doubt the sweet apple twinged his stumps and the clove soothed them. He saw my doubt that he could really be who he said he was. He added, 'Yes, I am Peter Colechurch, Bridge Master and Ingeniator. I see your husband has almost completed this church.'

I smelt work. 'Jack!' I yelled.

This skinny-bony black crow of a man who thieved my Jack's dinner was the great Peter Colechurch, the builder of London Bridge. Jack had spoken of him like a god, but he was human. His breath smelt of cloves, his robes of donkey sweat, boils erupted where his robe had rubbed his neck. The sun had burned his bald tonsure scarlet, which was going to hurt him tonight. Twenty-five years ago and perhaps a little more, about the year I was born, Peter Colechurch rebuilt London Bridge after a fire. London Bridge was always built in elm, which does not rot in water. He must have been a young man then, but the bridge was still new. I wondered what brought him to Abbot's Littlebourne now. I saw Jack and Nick climb down the ladder and cross towards the tree. 'I'm in trouble with Alice,' Jack said cheerfully. He knows my mood when my scar does not show between my eyes.

Nick said calmly, 'It's her birthday.'

'What?'

'It's the last day of June.'

'God help me,' Jack said. He saw why I had gone to all the bother of wearing this dress, ran forward. 'Alice, I'm sorry.' Then he saw the monk dozing behind the tree. 'Who's this?'

'He's eaten your dinner,' I said.

Jack looked angry, then cheerful again. 'No, yours,' he said, and snatched my pasty (though I make mine smaller) from the basket. He took a mouthful and watched the monk snore. Nick whispered, 'Many returns and much happiness, Alice.' He took his pasty and sat a little away from us on the grass, in the sun. He wore only breeches and I saw his neck and shoulder blades were blistered by the hot rays, but that was his business. I watched him kneel in front of one of the little wooden crosses, his mother's, as fresh and new as though she had been planted yesterday. He had painted it white. The argument over the manner of her long-ago death, whether it was murder, or accident, or suicide, which I am sure it was, which no doubt had seemed so important to Parson Humphrey at the time, was so long forgotten that Maurice knew nothing of it. Nick had dug up her bones from the Garwynton woods and carried her here, laid her skull (the most important part, being the abode of the soul), and her mouldy green spine, her ribs, hips and leg bones to rest in consecrated ground, and the parson's office was said over her remains: 'I am the resurrection and the life, saith the Lord: she that believeth in me, though she were dead, yet shall she live: and whosoever liveth and believeth in me shall never die.' And then the parson's blessing, and her soul had risen at last to Heaven.

The monk snorted, snored loudly. I called Jack to me in a low voice, whispered.

'Peter Colechurch?' Jack returned my whispers, understanding at once. We're such a team. I couldn't let the monk see him like this, sunburnt, almost naked, his hair standing up like a half-raked stook of hay. I unfolded his robe and hung it over his shoulders, made sure the symbol of the cross and bridge showed plainly, then swept off the pastry crumbs he dropped as he ate. 'Be dignified, be respectful,' I warned. 'Let me handle any talk of money.'

Jack finished, belched. 'How shall we wake him?'

I tripped over the monk's foot. 'I'm sorry, I didn't mean to wake you.'

The monk rubbed his foot, then saw Jack and stood. 'Thank God!' he said. 'You really are *le Maître Jacques le Mazon*, pupil of the great Isenbert de Saintes, Ingeniator and Master of the School?'

Jack looked confused by the monk's enthusiasm. 'I've worked for Isenbert, yes.'

'You knew the ingeniator personally? His formulae? His spells?'

Now Jack was mystified. 'I know him well enough, yes.'

'Jack knows *le Grand Maître* very well,' I said. 'Jack is a brother of his school.' I pulled Jack from the shade so the cross and bridge showed clearly in the sun.

Peter Colechurch lifted his eyes from the bridge-builders' symbol to Littlebourne Church, and it was his turn to look mystified. 'Why does a brother of the *Frères Pontifes* work on a very minor church in a village of no importance?'

Jack said, 'My wife is happy here. There's nothing of greater importance to me than that.'

The monk looked surprised. One would hardly expect him to comprehend, let alone agree, with such a statement. He may even have thought Jack was joking, but we never joke. He said, 'But a church, my son, is not a bridge.'

'A church is a bridge between this world and the next,' Jack said. I shot him a warning glance. It is a bad idea to lecture monks who, after all, have their own ideas on religion which are much better than ours because monks and priests are more virtuous and closer to God than we are.

But Peter was more worldly than I had thought. 'Even so, Jack, a church is not physically a bridge.'

'Both are a crossing from one side to the other,' Jack said firmly.

Peter nodded, and I realised Jack had passed a test. 'How long has this church taken you to build?'

'Three years.'

'Only three years!' Seven was the usual reckoning.

'The old Roman road lies underneath, so the walls required little foundation work. In fact the floor of the nave *is* the old road.' Jack was sounding too enthusiastic, as usual, but the monk smiled as if remembering his own youth, and I realised he had been Jack's age during the great rebuilding of the wooden London Bridge. 'For the walls we dug up road blocks, those which hadn't already been used to build houses, and larger blocks I shipped almost as far as Garwynton by boat from my own quarry. The abbot permitted us to fell some of his oaks for roof beams. A lead roof is too expensive, too easily stolen, and slips in hot weather, so the Kilner family fired tiles from the local clay pits at Tegham, the Tylers and Teggs are fixing them, and the abbot has promised local people rewards in Heaven in return for free work.' The churchwarden yawned sleepily beneath the bell over the west door, nodding against the warm stone as the sun moved round the building. Jack went on, 'I'm fully paid up and tallied with the Society of Masons, and so licensed to work on churches as well as bridges. Besides, there's already a bridge here. My father built it.' He pointed down to the little bridge over the stream. Easy now, I thought. He's hooked.

Peter Colechurch said, 'Not in London, there isn't.'

I didn't breathe. This was the crucial moment. I could almost taste Jack's excitement.

Jack said, 'I know you're building a new bridge of stone in London.'

Peter Colechurch shook his head. 'I am building the greatest bridge in the world,' he said.

'I've heard there are difficulties,' Jack said.

'Difficulties!' Peter raised his eyes to Heaven. 'I would call them more than difficulties. Insuperable difficulties. Impossibilities.'

I said, 'But you built the new wooden bridge only a few years ago.'

Jack glanced at me. 'It's falling down.' He turned back to the monk. 'Isn't that so?'

'Yes. So is the stone one, as far as we have got, for reasons we don't understand.'

'It's not surprising. Nearly everything about bridges is not understood.' Jack repeated what his father had told him. 'A bridge-builder finds how a bridge wants to grow. God allows His work to take on natural shapes, so for a bridge-builder to impose human ideas of symmetry on God's work is the sin of pride. You must find the patterns and rhythms of nature, the earth, the shape God has put in the stone. How many arches are you using? How long?'

'Twenty arches, nineteen of them of stone. The river is about twelve hundred feet wide at high tide.'

I noticed Jack look at the small size of the monk's feet, but he nodded. 'No one has built large stone bridges since Roman times. A few small bridges thrown over streams, like my father's Stone Bridge here. There's Castleton Bow Bridge in Yorkshire. The Bishop of Durham's bridge at Elvet even has houses on it. But all large stone bridges stand on Roman shoulders, Saintes, Rochelle, the Paris bridges, nearly all the *Frères Pontifes'* skill is in rebuilding Roman work. Except Bénezèt, and he's busy at Avignon.'

'Unfortunately the Romans built no stone bridge in London.' Peter Colechurch reached into his long black sleeve, pulled out something tightly rolled. 'I am offering you a position.'

Jack glanced at me. Would I go? His father had been willing to work away from his wife, but Jack was not. My power, therefore, was absolute.

'My Jack doesn't take just any old work,' I said sharply.

The monk handed over the tightly rolled scroll. 'It is a letter from the King.'

This time I met Jack's eye. He turned it over and over in his hands, then unrolled the King's words reverently.

The document was written in Latin. Jack frowned, translated. '"Richard, by the Grace of God, King of England, &c., to his beloved and faithful Petro Capellano de Colechurch, greeting."' He saw the awe on my face. 'The King doesn't actually write this or even speak it, Alice, he just tells a clerk roughly what he wants.' But I thought the words were so long and bombastic and authoritative that they sounded just like a king should.

'The King really writes to you?' I asked the monk.

'I am also the chaplain of St Mary Colechurch in London,' Peter said with a modesty that I already knew did not suit him.

'I see, Father.' Jack struggled with an almost endless sentence from the King's clerk, drew breath at each third comma. '"Considering in how short a time the bridges of Saintes and Rochelle, by divine providence and the careful diligence of our faithful Clerk, Isenbert, Master of the School at Saintes, a man distinguished both for his worth and learning, have been constructed, we have entreated, admonished, and even urged him, by the advice of our venerable father in Christ, Baldwin, Archbishop of Canterbury, and others, that, not only for your advantage, but also for the general good, he will come and use the same diligence in building your bridge; for we trust in God that the London Bridge so necessary to the Mayor and Citizens and all those passing over it, will, with God's assistance, by means of the industry of Isenbert, be quickly completed. Witnessed ourself at Westminster, on the 18th day of April in the first year of our reign."' Jack showed me the florid signature.

The monk added, 'Signed just before he left the country for the Holy Land.'

Nick said, 'Outremer.' I jumped, he moved so quietly. Outremer is the Templars' name for the Holy Land.

Jack rolled the scroll carefully, handed it back to the monk. 'Why show this to me?'

'Isenbert is dead.'

Jack bowed his head. I know he had liked and respected the architect. He said practically, 'Then find someone else.'

'I have,' Peter Colechurch said. 'The perfect man.'

'Me!' Jack said. 'Me! By God, me!' He hugged me. 'I mean us!' He looked at me anxiously. 'It's the opportunity of a lifetime.'

Nick poked the fire, and the flames lit up our eyes. 'I know,' I said.

'London Bridge!' Jack said. 'The *Frères Pontifes* are hardly known in Britain. This is our chance.' Then he said, 'Alice, if you won't go, I won't.'

'Suppose I won't?' He looked horrified. I relented. 'I know you've already said yes.'

'My God, yes!'

'We have to go,' I agreed for his sake. I was sure I could have negotiated a better deal than the shilling a day Jack had accepted, but there would be plenty of opportunities to make money on the side, and we'd get a house rent free, a serving girl, a large mess of food (enough for four) at dinner and supper, and we were guaranteed conger eel twice a month and a swan at Christmas, and four pewter plates, dishes, and saucers, with pewter mugs for ale and cups for wine. I would have held out for silver. But that was by the by. The monk, the King's letter, the sheer scale of the project flattered my husband's vanity beyond restraint. Our vanity. We would be citizens of London. By London Bridge I would buy shoes with points and buckles, cloth of gold, and for my table the spoons that were now so fashionable and impressive. I was excited for Jack, but the thought of living in London excited me a good deal more than it did him. I knew all he would care about was the bridge. I made a small show of reluctance, but not too much. 'This little church is almost finished, and what would we do for money then anyway?'

'I still won't go if you don't,' Jack said. 'Both of you. You too, Nick. It's all arranged. You'll be my assistant.'

I said impulsively, 'London is the centre of the world!'

Nick said, 'No, Jerusalem is.' I had forgotten he had seen Jerusalem too.

'Tell me about London!' I said.

Nick said, 'Jerusalem is the City of God. London is the City of Hell.'

I stared at him. He smiled.

'Old Teggs can finish off the chancel roof,' Jack said impatiently. 'We could leave tomorrow. Peter must return to London tomorrow, we could accompany him, the road is dangerous.'

'Not if Nick is with us,' I said. 'Isn't that right, Nick?'

'I've got a sword,' Jack said. But I thought Nick without a sword might be more useful than Jack with one. Nick just smiled and poked the fire. As he leant forward his shirt stretched tight across his shoulders and watery, bloody stains showed where his blisters broke. He must have been in agony.

'Margaret de la Ley had white skin,' I said. 'Her mother treated it with butter.' I went to fetch some.

'Don't interfere,' Jack grinned. 'Sunburn's a self-inflicted injury. Isn't that right, Nick?'

'London is three days away,' Nick said. He got up and packed what he would take in a small sack, lay alone on his mat in the dark.

I sat beside Jack watching the fire, and he stroked my legs, and we made love in the little stone house for the last time. I cried out with laughter, he always makes me laugh when he tickles me at that particular moment, and I gripped him as tight as I could, biting his neck. 'Alice, Alice,' he murmured. 'Your storms are darker, but your sunshine is brighter than any other girl's.'

'We're both ambitious,' I whispered. London Bridge would make us wealthy if he played his pieces right. Once again good fortune had fallen clean as a plucked bird into Jack's lap. He tickled, and I can't help being noisy, and afterwards I supposed Nick must have been unable to shut the sounds of us out, lying behind his thin curtain, chaste. Lonely. Better than us.

We set off early, and I thought I would come back in the winter when I supposed there would be no work on the bridge, and I kissed my shy, blushing servant girl Rosie (she couldn't have been more than ten years old, as fat and sweet as a little angel) and embraced her mother, and as I rode away looking over my shoulder I never thought it would be the last time I saw my little house.

We had hardly left the village before my mare threw a shoe.

Jack had seen some men shoeing a colt between poles at the smith's so he and Nick walked my mare back. Peter Colechurch handed me the reins of his donkey and went behind an oak to relieve his bowels after breakfast. The flies already buzzed about my face and distantly I heard the clout of tilers working on the church roof, without Jack not so fast as yesterday. Another rhythm took over, deeper, heavier, the sound of horsemen riding fast. Dust rose over the brow of the hill ahead of us, where we would have been by now, and out of the dust rode a white horseman wearing a red cross, sergeants and other men riding behind him, foam on the horses' mouths and throats. Above the men's heads fluttered the Templar banner, Baucent, a solid ebony-black square like night above a solid white square. I pulled the donkey behind the tree. Peter Colechurch said, 'What?' But I could not explain my fear, and anyway the horsemen turned away at the fork in the road by Fishpool, raced out of sight between the trees towards Temple Moat. Slowly the sound of them died. I never saw them again.

But I knew I had seen Geoffrey de Prudome.

So why did I feel that something dark had almost touched me? Everyone knows that monsters exist, the griffin, the *manticora*, the *glaistig* whose kiss sucks dreams through the lips of a sleeping girl, and finally her life and her soul if she does not wake; the boa-dragon is often seen in our countryside, they drink the blood of cows and become so strong they eat the herd; the *caladrius* that foretells death (which Widow Cristina saw just before she died). But Geoffrey de Prudome, though a great man, was only a man, and everyone knows that men are not monsters.

'I had meant to be alone,' Peter said, glaring at me. They're such prudes, his wasn't the first bare male arse I'd seen. I blamed the wilful jack donkey for pulling me, jerked it back on the path. The sight of the horsemen had disturbed me, but still I didn't think of Noelle. Life is a mystery, and so are we. Why do we think as we do, why are we not more clever? Our thoughts and passions rush boiling from our hearts, then the soul of reason whose grey spirit fills our heads restrains us, cools our blood with good sense, and sense, being good, comes from God. Yet if my thoughts come from God, how can they be imperfect? How can I make mistakes? If I were perfect I would not now be wiping the monk's turd from my shoe. I know, being a woman, I am not made in the image of God but only from Adam's rib, but I have noticed that men are no more perfect than we are, even, I suspect, when they live apart from us, in pursuit of virtue. For if men live without women in monasteries, how can they still be capable of sin and require absolution, as they do? So it seems to me, therefore, that my thoughts are my own. But where am I? *Who* am I? Where do my thoughts come from? Is it from my heart, or my hands, or from my eyes, as it feels? Yet a blind woman thinks. Why are my hands not the same, with each thumb on the left? What is the purpose of it? I inhabit my body, but where am I?

The monk returned and would not look at me. Jack rode my mare from the smith's, Nick walking beside him. A Templar never rides a female horse and neither, it seemed, would Nick. Perhaps a touch of the oath he had renounced stuck to him still, in the back of his mind where he was not aware of it. Men are as strange creatures as we women, though they do not admit it, and more sensitive, and more easily hurt. 'Why aren't you riding?' I asked.

Nick shrugged, swung on to his own stallion, and spurred forward. I felt better, and climbed daintily into my side-saddle, settled my satin-slippered feet comfortably on the broad wooden shelf, and clicked my tongue.

Jack rode beside the monk. 'Tell me of London Bridge.'

Peter Colechurch sighed. 'The Romans built London Bridge of elm and oak. It decayed and was rebuilt, fell down and was rebuilt, washed away and rebuilt, burnt and rebuilt, the Vikings broke it down with longships and grapnels, but it was rebuilt. Always on the original foundations.'

Jack asked, 'How deep is the water?'

'Deep.'

'So no one has ever seen the foundations?'

I could see Peter did not want to answer. He had rebuilt the bridge only twenty-five years ago and it was already in trouble, or the King would not be taking every bale of wool to pay for a new one – though some said he skimmed the cream off the wool tax to pay for his Crusade to reconquer Jerusalem. We came to a crossroads and the monk prayed at the cross, then Jack asked the question again as we continued.

The jack donkey kept nuzzling my mare. I pulled her behind the two men to get some peace, heard the monk saying merely, 'Fifty years ago my grandfather, Geoffrey, in those days Ingeniator and Bridge Master, rebuilt two wooden arches, then after a fire he rebuilt the whole bridge for two hundred and fifty pounds. Work was quick and cheap in those days, and a more ramshackle contrivance you cannot imagine.'

Jack said, 'He did not examine the foundations?'

'When I was elected Bridge Master – the position is, of course, hereditary – I already knew that a complete rebuilding was necessary and carried it out, in elm.'

Jack said, 'But you didn't examine the foundations either?'

'They were under the water!' Peter prayed to one of the shrines to the Virgin or saints that inhabit and protect every woodland glade. Fields only happen near villages, but sometimes children ran out of this or that lean-to in the woods and begged for alms. I had done the same myself, many times, and knew all the tricks. I kept my whip handy; a yelp from one light-fingered child is a lesson to all.

Jack said, 'So the foundations of the old bridge have given way where you can't get at them, and you have to build a complete new bridge.'

'In stone, which will not burn and lasts for ever.'

'So, you want to make your mark.'

'I am the last of my line.'

'You will be successful providing your foundations are good,' Jack said. 'What is the trouble you are having, exactly?'

'You will see,' Peter Colechurch said. 'You will see.' His donkey hee-hawed plaintively for my mare's company.

Jack dropped back. He spoke quietly to Nick. 'God knows what more we will find that has gone wrong.'

'In London,' Nick said, 'everything is wrong.'

On the third afternoon, after dinner at the Pope's Head in Valle Dei and prayers at St Thomas's Pool, a mess of paths and tracks with thieves and pilgrims jostling one another on every side, we rode down from the cooling breeze of Bleak Heath into the marshland that surrounds London. It was late and the heat rose over us, dense, dank, intolerable. Ahead of us London stood on London, its second image hovering upside down in the shimmering mirage so that I could hardly tell which was more real, the London above the river or the London below. I called to Nick excitedly, recognising St Paul's Cathedral among the towers by its huge spire, a cone of beams and rafters still unfinished, pointing like a skeletal finger to God. Jack slapped himself as midges swarmed in whining clouds from the waterways crisscrossing the marshes, and Nick told me it was high tide. He handed me a muslin veil to hang from my cap. Through its misty gauze I saw men, women, children setting traps and nets, fins slicing the scummy water, and more long nets strung on poles to catch the little birds fluttering above. A filthy lipless corpse grinned from a gallows, crows clinging expertly to its cheeks. I decided to be cheerful. 'Will we reach London today?'

Peter looked back. The only way to keep his jack donkey off my mare was for him to ride well ahead, and in his black robes he looked more than ever like a crow with his beaky nose, potbelly, gleaming eyes. 'Aye, Mistress Alice, we will, but we won't cross the river tonight. St Martin's Eve. It wouldn't be proper.' Our life on earth is a forest of saints' days through which we creep like little animals towards Heaven.

I wrinkled my nose. 'What's that smell?'

Nick said, 'London.'

Huts, then houses, then streets sprang up around us. The houses and people closed about us in a solid mass. London was huge, a huge dark warren of thousands of souls massed on top, and underneath, and beside one another and around us in huge stinking crowds. Londoners hated us at once, blocked our way with their bodies, swarmed at our horses, shrieking at us to buy the finest wine in the Borough, buy the best beer, buy ointment for sores, best offers, cheapest prices, bolts of cloth, knives, cold roast chickens and hot roast chickens sweating on spits, roast beef dripping yellow fat, wet fish, dry fish, salt and smoked fish, anything living or dead. Children, children everywhere, dirty and savage, with sweet childish faces polished like apples, offering their bodies, their mothers shoving at them eagerly when they were shy. 'Herrings, nice oily herrings!' We turned from the market into a lane between churches, women's prisons – we heard the harpies' shrieks, saw the cocking stool and cesspit for the extraction of their confessions – barred cells for men (I saw a monk's shaved head, he spat at me) and then we were swept forward with the crowd beside a long wall without openings or doors. 'So this is London!' I said.

'No, this is the Borough of Southwark in London.' Nick scraped the wall with his knuckles, licked them. 'Across the river is the City. Different laws.'

'What's this wall for?'

'St Thomas's Walk? Our martyred archbishop built it to make City people walk further.'

'Why?'

'So they do not reach their pleasures so quickly. Behind here is the Liberty of the Clink.' He glanced round as someone shouted out, 'Hello!'

I said, 'The Clink?'

'A prison for priests, whores, procuresses, sodomists, unlucky honest men, cheats and jugglers. All this land is for the profit of the Bishop of Winchester, and the Liberty is a sanctuary for criminals from the City. The bishop owns . . . owns everything that you will see.'

'Ow!' My head banged an open shutter, ramshackle houses now leant forward on every side. Land is so precious here that houses are built on two or even three storeys, and men and women on horseback must ride down London lanes in single file, or get their heads knocked off. Nick reined his stallion in behind me, its hooves plopping and skidding in the foul brown gutter. I rode between stairways, upstairs rooms, overhanging bedrooms and dormitories, thatched eaves that scratched my shoulders, dark hovels, crooked attics, glimpsed rooms with children laughing, a woman screaming, a man gnawing a pig's trotter on a bed, a girl pissing in a pot. 'What a place!' Jack called back. Pigs jerked their chains outside the butcher's stall, the stench of offal poured from a pudding mill between the shambles and the river, steaming pudding barrels lined the street full of guts and hearts, livers, lungs, strings of testicles like knotted rope, ladled out to be eaten piping hot or left to set cold. I looked, startled, into the open window of an upstairs parlour where a family of five, two girls and a boy, sat straight-backed round a table eating primly, Mother stern and Father smiling, his knife halfway to his mouth, none of them aware of our heads bobbing past the window. Sometimes I think we see almost nothing of everything that is all around us.

My mare stopped, held back by the crush of people pushing past. 'City folk,' Nick said. 'They're all thieves.'

'But they're dressed so smartly.'

'That's how.'

I grew worried because I couldn't see Jack. Nick nodded with his head, pointing a short cut between the buildings to catch up. Someone called out, 'It's not you, Nick! God damn my soul.' We turned towards the river. Gulls whirled over us, a yellow beak snatched my veil and it was fought over, dipping and trailing, in the brilliant sunset sky, finally falling to earth but I could not see it, and I realised how dark it was beneath these steep roofs. The sweet stench of the place, food, manure, urine, filled my nose until I tasted it. I turned. 'Nick, who was that?'

'What?'

'Calling out.'

'How should I know?'

'That's the second time.'

He laughed. 'These people think they know everybody.' He rode alongside, caught the bridle of my mare, led me forward beneath the taverns' flags and banners hung out from poles as advertisements, their names not written but drawn in pictures for the illiterate to recognise their pleasure, the Red Rose, the Cock, the Maidenhead, the Bleeding Heart, the Virgin, the Lock and Key. I blushed. I had not considered myself a prude, as you know. 'Don't look,' Nick said, 'and you won't see.' The pornographic banners slid over my head and shoulders, rippling.

Jack dismounted ahead of me but the monk stayed on his donkey. 'This tavern is the Angel and is respectable as any,' he called. 'I shall seek shelter at the Priory of St Mary Overie.' He eyed a man selling dripping, steaming hunks of roast beef off the tip of a knife. 'Sell your horses. I shall see you at London Bridge two hours after dawn, by the bell.'

'Very well,' Jack said.

Nick ordered me down and I hung my little bag of things from my wrist, slid from my saddle, soiled my pretty shoes at once on the hard cobbles. Jack and Nick led the horses beneath a low arch with a room built over it, called by masons a *haut-pas*, a bare-breasted girl sitting in the window there, and she smiled down at me and put her elbows on her knees. Jack and Nick were negotiating with a fat woman in the yard. I ducked beneath the arch after them but two children fell out of the shadows, shouting, fighting, the elder lad pulling the youngster's curly hair so that he shrieked like a gull, and I couldn't get past. 'Stop it!' I shouted at them, then shouted for Jack when they knocked against me. 'Jack!' It was a trap. I felt someone behind me, saw a hairy hand slide down and grip my bag. I screamed, and the lads pushed me. A knife flashed at my eye.

'Quiet or I'll slit you,' a low voice behind, whiskers against my neck, stinking breath. 'Give it to me.' The hairy fingers jerked, twisted, but my bag was looped to my wrist by a cord. *'Give it to me.'*

'Alice?' Jack called, turning slowly. 'What's keeping you?'

I stared at the blade of the knife, its nicked edge, the cheap metal stained with meat or fruit. I screamed.

Nick ducked back under the archway. He walked at a steady pace. He knew what was going on. The lads drew knives, savage as cats, circled him. 'We'll cut you, we'll cut you, we'll kill you!' Then they shouted, 'Now, Pa, quick, quick!' The hairy hand jerked my wrist and I prayed for the cord to break but it would not. 'Don't hurt me,' I whispered. 'I'll take it off for you, I'll take it off.' I tried to swoon, fell to my knees. The lads sprang like dogs at Nick, I heard a childish scream, the smallest lad ran away past me, his vicious little face contorted, unrepentant, tears of pain running from his eyes for the loss of his knife, which Nick now held. The elder brother, same face, same expression, held his elbow, his broken elbow. Nick had broken the lad's arm, I did not see how, and now Nick held two knives by their blades, and still he came forward at the same steady walk. I sobbed, I was so frightened. I was pitched forward on my face, the hairy man stabbed at Nick. Nick took the man's hand in his own, I saw him turn it back on itself, I heard the gristle crunch. The knife fell, clattered. The man cursed, tried to heave himself up on tiptoe but still the bones in his hand broke, I heard them snapping. Nick relaxed, pushed two fingers into the man's nostrils, lifted him against the wall.

Jack ran to me. 'Alice! Alice, are you all right?' I was so terrified that I did not know what to do. I nodded like a doll and let him pick me up. 'Devils!' Jack shouted at the man. Nick said nothing. He looked at the man, then looked at me. I realised he would do anything, anything I wanted.

'Let him go,' I said.

Nick let the man drop like a bundle of rags, kicked him away. I looked at Nick cautiously. I had never seen men fight like that, or imagined it was possible. I rather liked it.

'You could have killed him,' I said.

The hairy man stared at us from the shadows, hands pressed to his face. I wanted to go over to him and kick at him for making me so frightened. He hobbled away and I shouted after him, 'Go away!' Blood dripped down his hands, he looked pathetic. I felt sorry for him. 'Nick, you hurt him.'

'I could have,' Nick said.

Jack told me, 'Alice, my God, my love, that scum hurt *you*. He might have killed you.' He sounded so shaken.

I still looked at Nick. I put one hand on my hip, wanting to know what he was thinking.

'Least said soonest mended,' Jack said. 'Best get inside.'

But I held back. 'Would he have killed me, Nick?'

'No. He was afraid. Desperate, probably. Most people are.' Nick dropped the knives in the gutter and piss and filth covered them.

I asked, 'How would you have done it differently, Nick? Tell me.'

'I would have cut your throat then cut the cord.'

I laughed. Someone brought a candle, a large woman with black hair and black eyes, foreign skin. Fat, but her dark flesh looked hard as a conger eel's, and her teeth as sharp. She eyed me. 'What, no trouble?'

Nick said, 'She tripped and fell.'

'Not safe on the streets these days.' The woman beckoned us through a doorway. 'Mistress Tarmantelle, me. Welcome to the Angel. Only the best people here. You're upstairs.'

Nick pushed past men and girls on an outside landing, cleared our way to a room inhabited by more men and women of various sorts. They looked at me with contempt for not being as low as they. I made a space in the corner.

'The bishop's calling has opened his mind to foreign lands,' Nick said. 'Mistress Tarmantelle seems a good sort, and the Angel does have a good reputation.'

Jack found a piece of curtain to close us off from the grunts and groans and sighs, the sounds of flesh, cries of possession and delight, weary bumping. There was no broom to sweep the floor. Nick lay on guard outside the curtain.

Jack whispered, 'This place is a stew-house, Alice!'

A babble of shrieks and cries rose outside the windowless room. I closed my eyes tight, covered my ears with my hands. It was best to get to sleep quickly in the City of Hell.

I woke. For a moment there was no sound. My hands were still clamped over my ears. What had woken me? Nick pulled the curtain aside cheerfully. 'I found a man to take the horses.' He rattled a pouch of money, grinned. I blinked at the level sunlight pouring through the open doorway, then stood yawning and picked the straw from the clothes I had slept in. The room was empty, as though my nightmares had never been and I had merely dreamt those people existed but now I had woken and everything was fine.

'It's dawn? Where is everybody?'

'The dawn bell rang a while ago. In London nobody sleeps. They've crossed back to the City to their houses, their wives and children, and work.' I draped my skirts decorously round the pot and relieved myself inside their concealment.

'Is Mistress Tarmantelle really owned by the bishop?' I asked. Jack emptied the pot into the yard.

'Everyone's owned by someone,' Nick said. So I had not imagined her, or anything else I thought I had heard. I watched Nick and Jack swing the saddlebags on their shoulders, followed them on to the outside landing, stood between them. Sunlight struck across the mossy thatch roofs slanted around and below the balcony. I thought we'd see London Bridge but the Bishop of Winchester's Palace and the Priory of St Mary Overie hid it.

Nick said, 'Every soul in the Liberty belongs to the bishop. Every brothel and hovel is his, or the Mayor of London's, or belongs to his aldermen. Or to their wives.'

'Their wives! Why?'

'For the sake of respectability. They are respectable men.'

I said, 'If the bishop sent all these people to prison, there would be no profit here, and no evil.'

'There's no evil here, only people,' Nick said. 'The bishop depends on their activities, profits, rents, fines. If he sends them to prison, he loses. In fact he does imprison them, because he owns the prison. These poor creatures pay to be locked up, food, visits, the smallest kindness, then pay to be unlocked. It's enormously profitable.'

'You seem to support them.' Jack sounded odd. I realised that he speaks with a Kent accent. So do I. We must change, or for ever be outsiders not citizens of London.

'How else can these people live,' Nick said, 'except in the way they do?'

I blasphemed like a Londoner. 'Then the bishop is an evil man, because he creates what he absolves!'

Nick said, 'Of course. That's always the way it works. You might as well blame a man for the shape of his nose or the colour of his eyes.'

'Don't talk like this here, Alice,' Jack said uncomfortably. 'This is our home now.'

Yes, London would be our home until London Bridge was finished. That would take years, perhaps many years. For a moment my heart was bleak, I was overwhelmed. Then I smiled and pointed out a peaceful scene, monks netting fish from ponds in the bishop's park, the sun gleaming on their tonsured heads. But Jack pointed beyond them. 'What's there, Nick?'

Nick said shortly, 'That's Gravel Lane. The gravel stops it sinking into the marsh.'

'No, beyond the lane.'

I saw sheep pastures and water mills, ships unloading corn for grinding, a lake for waterfowl, a round church. A Templar church. Outside, in the early-morning sun, I made out the marble effigies of dead knights standing with their white marble hands clasped on the hilts of white marble swords, white marble armour and white marble cloaks shining, looking for all the world ready to jump back to life at the Pope's call.

'Is that the Temple?' I asked.

Nick laughed at my naivety – after all, that's what I once was, a *naif*, and I suppose I'm too old now really to change. 'No, Alice, that's Temple Paris.' He pointed west along the river, away from the sun – though I noticed that by an amazing coincidence the sun, and us, and Temple Paris Church, and the direction of Nick's pointing finger all made a perfectly straight line – and he pointed out the white battlements on the far side of the Thames, just where the river curves from Westminster. 'That is the Temple.'

A perfectly straight line.

Above the battlements rose a white tower with four bartizan turrets, one jutting from each corner, and white and black banners hung from their spires. It was the most overawing sight. Nick said, 'That's the Dovecote Tower.' Below I saw a large circular church, the petals of its rose-roof (because it looks like an upturned rose) rising to a central point, foreign-looking, almost Arabic. Nick followed my eyes. 'The crowning point is called the Thorn. It's symbolic of the Crown of Thorns, Christ's rejection by His people, His suffering.'

This was the first time Nick had let slip anything of his time with the Templars, anything at all. The sun streamed our shadows away from us, past the monks, past Temple Paris, towards the Temple a mile away.

Jack yawned, the sun pale in his hair, and I realised he had hardly listened to us. His mind was on the bridge. 'Come on, Alice,' he said, trying to make me feel his enthusiasm for his project, 'or we'll be late at London Bridge.' He put his arm round my shoulders and pulled me away from Nick, downstairs into the foul yard, then the stinking street. Still Nick stared at the Temple, then jumped down after us.

Pigs had been let out overnight to feed on the garbage and sewage in the street and anything that even people could not eat. There was no one about except begging children and we pushed between pigs and mongrels and scrawny chickens, cats winding between our legs or leaping beside us along the tops of walls. A few men lay drunk, their clothes stolen, and I believe one was dead. Jack said angrily, 'Surely there is some means of punishing these people, of keeping them off the streets?'

'Punishment?' Nick rolled his vowels like a Londoner, I realised, sounding slightly French. Templar discipline had even taught him how to speak. 'The bishop has had a furca dug under some of the cells beneath his palace.'

I asked, 'A furca?'

'An oubliette, Alice. A deep, deep hole.'

I was surprised Nick knew so much about London – but of course he must have lived at the Temple for two years or more. 'How long are criminals imprisoned in a furca?'

'For ever. It's where you put people to forget them.'

I was not sure whether to believe him. I smiled nervously. 'It sounds a dreadful punishment.'

'No. How can you punish people who don't respect punishment?'

'Punish them worse,' Jack said. Lord, we lilted Kentish like country cousins, we'd be robbed in no time. I could tell Jack wasn't looking at the prison or even thinking about it. He pressed forward eagerly into Borough High Street, holding my hand in his elbow, patting my fingers excitedly. All he cared about was his first sight of London Bridge. From the moment he said yes and exchanged contracts with the monk, Jack would be paid his shilling a day and we would be rich. If I can't make one shilling do the work of two, and four messes of meat make eight, and a house into a home, my name isn't Alice Lacknail, Jack Mason's wife. I leant against Jack and smiled to make him look at me. But he pointed.

'Look!'

We saw not one London Bridge but two.

Everything was a mess. It was a building site.

We walked from the shadows into the breathless heat of the riverbank, the Thames a glassy mirror holding London upside down as real and sharp as London above it. The small figure of Peter Colechurch stood outlined between the two bridges as though he was pulled both ways, he did not know which demanded his attention more, the old elm bridge visibly dying, the new bridge stuck half-born.

He saw us, waved. He liked Jack. 'You slept?' he called, well-rested.

'He didn't sleep at all,' Nick said. From my husband's shrug I knew Nick was right, but I wondered how he knew.

The monk opened a gate in the high wooden fence. 'Here's the Bridge House Yard.' He led us between piles of stone and timbers to the Bridge Foot and the brink of the filthy brimming water. Half a hand higher and this land flooded. 'Well, what do you think?' Peter asked proudly. 'Impressive, is it not?'

'It's worse than I thought,' Jack said. 'Much worse. Is the tide always this high?'

The old bridge lay a few feet downstream of the new. Water lapped the roadway of the old bridge and I really thought it would fall any moment. The wooden platforms looped and staggered broken-backed towards the north shore, the Bridge Head, under the weight of stores and equipment dumped on them. In places the railings had given way. I could almost hear the wood creaking.

'You can't keep those stones and cranes on the old bridge,' Jack said. 'Take the burden off, reopen a passage to foot traffic, make some money.'

Peter cleared his throat, came to a decision. 'We make more money from the ferrymen.' He thought Jack would understand.

'They pay you to keep the bridge closed,' Nick nodded.

Peter laid his scrawny hands over his round little belly, probably full of St Mary's roast swan and white loaf. He said uncomfortably, 'Our project has four founding fathers, Jack, including myself. They are all rich London merchants. William d'Almain, the German, you have heard of.' I had not. 'His brother Henry FitzAilwyne is Mayor of London – the post is hereditary, his son will follow him. And of course there is Serle Mercer. They say every bolt of good cloth in London has passed under his hand. But the richest is Benedict

Boatwright, son of Benedict Shipwright, Master of the Guild of Ferrymen. These gentlemen find it convenient that the old bridge remain closed.'

Nick grinned. 'I told you,' he whispered to me. 'In London—'

'Everything is wrong.' I rolled my vowels, asked the monk, 'How much do the ferrymen pay to maintain this state of affairs?'

Nick tipped me a wink. 'You watch, Jack'll soon get the hang of London politics.'

But Jack did not. 'I suggest we build the new bridge forward on its own arches from each shore, carrying its own burden of materials, and meet in the middle instead of trying to accomplish all at once, piecemeal, from the old bridge, and accomplishing . . .' his eyes roamed along the half-finished piers and starlings, the enormous gaps where the ebb tide was beginning to swirl downstream, 'accomplishing nothing.'

Peter sounded more uncomfortable than ever at all this talk of accomplishment. 'We'll see. The King's letter has hurried matters. But he has gone on Crusade . . .'

Jack turned to me. 'Alice, you saw this was the way we rebuilt the Rochelle bridge, working from the structure itself.'

Nick said, 'The ferrymen will want to make a contribution to your fee, Jack.'

Jack asked the monk, 'How long exactly have you been working on this bridge?'

'Nearly fifteen years.'

'Fifteen years! How can it possibly take so long?' Jack looked appalled. To his experienced eye the new bridge was little more than lumps of rubble sticking out of the water joined by a few weak, round arches. Several showed gaps yawning between the stones. One arch ended jaggedly in mid-leap, it had already collapsed.

A figure clambered on to the old bridge, catching my eye by scrambling over the shrine that forbade entrance. I thought he was a young man, sixteen or seventeen years old perhaps. Visibly distraught, he leant over the railings looking so intently at the water that I thought he might jump.

Jack asked the monk, 'What are your dimensions for the stone bridge?'

I heard the young man shouting down into the water, his shouts fading as he went from one side of the old bridge to the other. 'Noelle . . . Noelle . . .'

'That's my sister's name,' I said. Nick nodded, listened to the monk.

'Over a thousand feet long, Jack, as you know. About twenty-five feet wide.'

'*About?*' Jack looked frustrated. Masons measured length and established the proportions of their work with a pole about the height of three men, though the length of a pole differed in every city. The Roman measurements of foot and stride, called a yard, also differed because people's feet were different in length. Jack had already noticed Peter had quite small feet, so his numbers would be much too high. I knew Jack himself used the tailor's foot, sometimes called the English foot, a standard length taken from the foot of Algar's statue in St Paul's Cathedral.

'I shall measure everything from the beginning,' Jack said. 'The breadth and depth of the river. Where is hard bed, where soft. Then I will know what to do.'

A skiff pulled from the north shore, a man stood in the bow with his hands on his hips. 'Ah, here is Master Boatwright.' Peter sounded relieved.

Boatwright was a big man wearing jewels and velvet, so he stank like the river on such a hot day. He cursed the waterman, tossed him a penny, stepped ashore and swaggered to us. His red face made Jack look quite pale by comparison.

'This is Jack Mason, Isenbert's pupil,' Peter said.

94

Boatwright spat on his hand, clasped Jack's. 'Knows his stuff?'

'I don't doubt it,' the monk said. He didn't like Boatwright.

'One of us, is he?'

'He says it may be possible to reopen the old bridge.'

Boatwright spat on Jack's shoe. 'My pardon, Master Mason.' He rubbed his own filthy shoe over the spittle, making it ten times worse. 'Anything I can do for you?'

Jack cleaned his shoe. 'Such as?' Jack, I thought, this is the time to go along with this horrid man and raise your price!

'Got to be something,' Boatwright said.

Nick said, 'Jack, there's our quarry – *your* quarry,' he corrected himself, and I remembered Nick had sold his half.

'What use is that?' Jack said.

'We get our ragstone from Reigate,' Boatwright said. 'Eighteen miles by cart up muddy tracks, no load more than half a ton, and broken wheels as often as not. How far's yours?'

'Rochester. Thirty miles.'

'But that's no distance at all by boat,' Nick said persuasively. 'Ship it down the River Medway, up the Thames, the tide does all the work. No carts, no breakdowns. And a barge carries ten tons.' He added, 'One of your barges, no doubt, Master Boatwright.' Why hadn't I thought of that? My God, I exulted, we really are going to be rich, not just in my dreams. I imagined the shops and stalls of London, and myself wearing shoes two feet long.

Boatwright was a hard-headed businessman. He said sceptically, 'How much d'you charge for your stone, Jack Mason?'

Jack named a fairly high price. 'Twopence halfpenny a foot. Rough-cut by the hewers but unworked. Your men load and sail your boat, your risk.'

Boatwright said, 'Well, Master Mason, the Bridge House Estate will pay you five pence a foot. What d'you say to that?' He clapped Jack's shoulder.

'But that's double my asking price,' Jack said.

Boatwright laughed jovially with his mouth but not his eyes. 'Deal?'

I pressed my hands together in prayer. Still Jack did not answer. 'Yes!' I said. 'He says yes.'

Boatwright would not look at me, but Jack said, 'I always ask my wife's advice.' He nodded sharply. Yes.

'Deal it is.' Boatwright spat on it, clasped hands, clambered into his skiff. He called back, 'And no more nonsense about reopening the old bridge!'

Nick watched him go, then told Jack, 'You're rich.'

Jack looked at me angrily. 'Next time I'll talk for myself. Don't make me look a henpecked fool.'

'You're a lucky fool,' Nick said, but tears filled my eyes because Jack was right. I shouldn't have interfered. But Nick misunderstood my expression. 'You're right to be angry, Alice. You tried to help him,' he said. He didn't understand they weren't tears of anger but love. Once again Jack had been so lucky.

'And all he has to do,' Nick said, 'is not open the old bridge.'

Peter whistled and a waterman sculled alongside, held the boat as we climbed aboard. 'We can see the work best from the river, between the two bridges.' The waterman pushed off and the boat slid forward over the interval of smooth glassy water between the old work and the new. Jack lowered a plumbline over the side, ordered the boat closer to a huge half-finished pier of the stone bridge. 'There's eddies there, lord,' the waterman warned. Jack let the string slide through his fingers until the weight touched bottom. 'Twelve feet. Is this dry at low tide?'

'Aye, dry here, lord.' The boat turned peacefully, drifting closer to the pier.

Jack pulled up the line. 'Sixteen feet. Waterman?'

'At low tide the shore ends about here, lord, and the water begins. You're a gentleman of Kent, if I'm not mistaken, lord.'

'We're Londoners,' I said. I did not want to be robbed as soon as we set foot on dry land.

'A tidal range of about sixteen feet, twice a day,' Jack muttered. 'That's a great weight of water. How fast does it flow?' The boat swung in the eddies that the bridge pier towed behind it as though the stone itself was on the move, forging upstream, rather than the water flowing down past it. In the shimmering lane of air and swirls of glassy water sliding between the two bridges a great sense of dislocation rose over me and I clutched the side of the boat.

'How fast? Faster than I walks or rows, lord, and faster down than up. Sometimes it can be very bad. The river's alive, it is alive, lord. Ask the wind and the rain and the moon.'

I didn't believe a word of his nonsense. 'The moon? The wind?'

'Aye, lady, the moon drives the tides. Get the wind blowing behind the tide, and there's nothing left of Southwark but rooftops. Get heavy rain, the river swells like a woman with child, pours down against the tide and wind coming up.' He spat. 'That's when watermen drown.'

If he drowned, his body would like as not never be recovered from such deep, turbulent waters. To feed his family he risked not only his life at his dangerous trade, but also his immortal soul. 'Can you swim, man?'

'Not I, lady.'

'Why not?'

'Best to sink quick than slow.'

Jack lowered the plumb. 'Forty-two feet!' He tasted the tip. 'Mud.' He tried again. Only twenty-three feet, gravel. 'The river bottom is all hills and valleys. If only I could see it . . .' Eddies sucked the boat into the vortex of spinning water behind the bridge pier, the bow dipped, dank, weedy stones rose over us. 'Look out!' I cried. I really thought we would be dashed and Jack granted his wish in the most dreadful way. But the waterman twisted his oar skilfully and the boat bobbed towards the foaming ramp of water filling the next arch. I watched the brown slope of water slide towards us, massive, imponderable, breaking slowly into waves that leapt and jostled around us. Just when it seemed it must overwhelm us, the waterman turned away, worked forward into calmer water.

Jack said, 'Twenty-eight feet.'

The waterman called, 'Aye, we're past the top of the flood by the length of my leg or more, lord. Well into the ebb tide.' The taste of the river was on my lips, and I realised my dress was wet, splashed, cool. I splashed myself again.

'Thirty-three feet, mud and weed . . .'

I heard footsteps running on wood, turned with a start. The old wooden bridge was rising out of the water as the tide fell, revealing green pilings like the mouldy broken teeth of a corpse. The young man I saw earlier leant over the railing, an iron grapnel and rope over his shoulder. 'Have you seen anything?' he cried out to our boat. The waterman shook his head.

'What does he hope to find?' I asked.

The young man scrambled down on to a weedy timber platform revealed by the falling tide. He took a flat plank, and beat it on the surface of the water with loud claps.

Peter said, 'The poor lad is demented by grief.'

'Forty-one, weed and gravel . . .'

'We often see 'em,' the waterman said. 'Out of their minds, most of 'em. Lost a loved one in the river.'

96

'But why is he carrying a grapnel?' Neither the waterman nor the monk answered. I asked, 'Why is he clapping the water?'

'To call to her soul, so that her body rises,' said the waterman. 'I've seen it happen after three, four days. The body rises to the surface and floats, begging to be caught, moaning, then sinks again.'

I said, 'He must have loved her very much.'

'They all do. That's why they're there.'

'Who was she?'

Suddenly I knew. I felt it in my heart. I wished I had never spoken.

'Some poor girl who killed herself, lady. A Templar saw her drop but could not save her. The good man gave a shilling for prayers to be said for her soul, her damned soul, in the chapel of St Magnus Martyr. That chaplain would pray to the Devil for a shilling.'

'Her name was Noelle,' I said.

'Aye, Noelle Lacknail.'

And that is how I learned my sister Noelle was dead.

I stood beside Robin on the wooden bridge. We looked at the water roaring beneath us. 'How long has it been?'

'Five days!' he said. I could not in all honesty remember Noelle very much, her name, her mole, something about her. For ever a child. When I thought about her face she turned into me. Robin and I stared at our reflections rippling below. The tide had fallen ten or fifteen feet, revealing a mass of broken, dripping timbers. The old bridge trembled, sinking a little, no longer held up by the water. The ebb lost its force, and trickling noises from the timbers became loud.

'Did you love her?'

'Yes.' Robin Swinert was exhausted, dark circles under his eyes.

'Did she love you, Robin?' I could see he was at least ten years younger than I was. He would be bright as a button tomorrow. Or the day after. Or the day after that.

'Yes, she loves me, she does!' he asserted vigorously, and I heard all London in his mouth. 'She's not dead, she's not!'

I touched his shoulder. 'Remember her as she was.'

'Sometimes they come back,' he whispered. 'When the belly swells with rot and decay, sometimes the soul strives to lift up the body towards the light.'

'Would you really want to see her?'

'To save her.'

At Saintes I saw the body of a drowned man heaved from the river by a rope round its ankle, dropped on the stones swollen, bloated, discoloured, more a creature from Hell than a man. 'Remember Noelle as she was,' I repeated.

He cried, 'Poor little Noelle, the unhappiest creature ever born!'

I tried to remain calm. 'If you love her, grieve for her as you loved her when she was alive, not as she is now she's dead.'

'She's not dead until she is buried in consecrated ground, her soul cannot rise.' He spoke the truth, I couldn't deny it. He went on rapidly, 'Maybe the tide has carried her down to the sea, maybe it has carried her up to Westminster. But I feel . . . I *know* she's here, somewhere near the bridge. I've tried catching her with the grapnel,' I shuddered, seeing the long hooks, 'I've tried beating the water so that the noise may dislodge her from wherever she lies. I paid for a drummer to row on the river.' We both nodded, everyone knows that when the drummer passes over the dead body the drum will not sound. 'That did not work, the drum beat the dirge loud and clear. I stuffed a pound loaf of bread with quicksilver, which is the spirit of life, threw it in the river. All the old women selling quicksilver swore the soul will struggle to reach the quicksilver in

97

the bread, and pull the body after it from the bottom of the river, they had seen it happen. But nothing happened.' He groaned. 'With the last of my money I hired a ferryman to row me back and forth, and I called her name over and over into the water, Noelle, Noelle, and I . . .' This was awful.

The tide died away to nothing at all. The river lay around us, flat, shimmering, speckled with islands near the shore. I felt a cold touch on my arm, a stone buttress of the new bridge moved its shadow across me, the sun swinging its light a little further round our earth.

'Robin,' I said as gently as I could, 'you cannot help Noelle. She is doubly damned. She killed herself.'

'She didn't kill herself.' He pointed beyond his left hand, where the railing broke. 'She fell. Or she was killed.'

I kept my peace.

He put his mouth close to my ear. 'She was killed by the knight Geoffrey de Prudome, Grand Master of the Templars.'

I stared at him, amazed not by the accusation but by the coincidence. He had picked on the very name I knew. 'But de Prudome . . .' I shivered, and moved back into the sunlight. 'But he gave a shilling for prayers to be said for her soul.'

'For *his* soul, his guilty soul! The Templars are Muslims, they worship the Evil One. He comes to them in the form of a severed head, everyone knows this.' Robin's voice rose in the stifling glassy air. 'They are drunkards, rapists, sodomites, meat-eaters in Holy Lent, moneylenders, usurers worse than the Jews, heretics worse than the Cathar heretics whose children they hunt and kill and eat, translators and spoilers of the Bible whose holy pages they tear and abuse in secret ceremonies—'

'Stop!' I said, frightened.

'*She* told me.' He leant forward on the railing, rested his forehead on his wrists. 'With them everything good becomes corrupt. Even love. Geoffrey de Prudome hurt Noelle. He destroyed her.'

It wounded me to say this. 'Yes, so she killed herself.'

'She would *never*. You didn't know her at all, did you? You'd know she was tough. She loved me. She was trying to get to me.'

'How do you know?'

'I live in Southwark. She was trying to get across to me.'

I touched his face, turned him towards me. He really was rather a handsome young man, he reminded me a little of Jack when Jack was young, vibrant, urgent, unformed.

'You'll do well,' I murmured. 'You'll find some other girl to love. We're all the same, you know.'

He looked at me searchingly, and I knew he was trying to see Noelle in me. 'No,' he said. 'You're wrong. Everyone is . . .' he fumbled for a Latin word, a holy word he must have heard in church. 'Unique. We're all unique. You're wrong.'

But he kissed my hands, and I could feel he liked me. Trusted me.

It was past midday. We parted, he towards the south shore of the bridge, me to the north. Then he turned, and his tiny figure in the distance called back, 'If you're right, and her soul is damned, then mine shall be too. At least I shall be with her.'

I watched him until I could see him no longer, then walked to the Bridge Head. Nick leant against a headstone in the graveyard of St Magnus Martyr, arms crossed, watching me. 'You waited for me?' I asked, surprised.

'The others went on ahead hours ago. Someone has to show you the way.' I kept forgetting Nick knew London, and listened to the chant of prayers from the chapel, prayers for my sister's damned soul.

'Noelle would never kill herself,' I said.

'My mother did.'

I looked at Nick properly. 'But you buried her in consecrated ground.'

'But still,' he said, 'she did kill herself. Jack's mother told me before she died. Round and round in the millwheel. It must have taken her a long time to drown. She wanted to die, and die, and die. She wanted to know.' He leant in the hot sun watching me with his dazzled eyes, dark blue, his father's eyes.

'Give me a shilling,' I said. That was a lot of money. Nick reached into his breeches, flicked a coin casually from his thumb to my hand. I took it into the chapel, knelt before the chaplain, held it on my outstretched palm in offering. 'I need prayers said for my sister.'

The fat, seedy chaplain took the shilling, bit it, could hardly believe his luck twice in one week. 'Yes, a shilling buys prayers that fly straight to the ear of God. A good choice.'

I held out any old coins I could find in addition. 'But I want the shilling the Templar gave you back,' I said. 'I'll pay you for it.'

The chaplain snatched my money, perhaps another ninepence in all, and laughed all over his filthy face. His belly bumped with mirth. He would give nothing back. I knew my request was outrageous. Jack would have laughed too, embarrassed, a prayer said was a prayer paid for, no refunds, everyone knew that. But I neither looked away nor dropped my hand. The chaplain stopped laughing. He looked angry. By now Jack would be exhausted by my persistence. He'd say apologetically, 'Alice, you can't . . .' Jack would have to take the chaplain's side.

Nick stood behind the chaplain. He put his lips against the chaplain's ear. He whispered, 'Give it to her.'

I held the Templar's filthy shilling in my hand, stood on the riverbank, threw it away in the sparkling water.

I wondered what Nick had said, exactly, to the chaplain to make him relinquish Geoffrey de Prudome's money. Perhaps it was not what Nick said but how he said it. For all I know he twisted the chaplain's arm behind his back where I couldn't see. Perhaps he had known the man in London before. Twice in the last twenty-four hours Nick had saved me, once from distress, once from death. I was grateful. But I did not like it that there was something about him I did not know. And what was I to make of Robin's wild accusations against the Templars, most respected of any organisation in the world, below the Vatican?

Nothing. Robin was just a young man in love, demented by his grief, striking out in love and grief. But still, I had instinctively feared the Templar Grand Master, and now I feared his generosity. Why? I do not know. A feeling. There are so many things the mind does not know that the heart feels. I was glad I had thrown away his shilling.

But that made me think more about Nick.

Nick took my arm because the streets of London are dangerous, walked me up Bridge Street. He turned left and told me this was Langburn Street, its name punned to Lombard Street by Londoners because of all the Italians from Lombardy who lend money here now no Jew dares show his face. Headless pillars and fragments of massive ancient wall overhanging the tiny modern churches showed where the Roman forum once stood. In a churchyard richly-dressed merchants weighed huge bales of wool, many times the weight of a man, ready for shipping. Nick's hand guided me along the Poultry, the largest, loudest market of fowls ever seen, chickens, ducks, geese, guineas, their feet protected by tar boots for their long walk from the country. What was missing? I saw no manure, none at all. 'Sewn up in the gut to increase their weight,' Nick said. The cries of the stallholders and the cries of the birds rose above us like Babel between the teetering thatch taverns. Butchers' stalls were hung with birds in every state of dress and undress, great coops of pigeons, peacocks, snipe, pheasant, partridge, quail, even a swan, and a beautiful sad kingfisher fit for the plate of a king. Strung on poles were delicate wicker cages for songbirds, blackbirds, thrushes, starlings, magpies, crows, and strange brilliant birds I did not recognise adding their foreign shrieks to the din. Sacks of feathers of every colour, soft down for beds, long, gorgeous plumes for the decoration of clothes. Beaches of eggs like pebbles piled in straw, eggs of every shape and shade and size, robins' eggs tiny and speckled light red, starlings' pale blue, chickens' eggs white and brown, and pails of water to test their freshness, cracked or rotten going cheap.

St Mary Colechurch, where Peter Colechurch was chaplain, was built above our heads over the Mitre tavern. Jack called us from the steps. 'Look at this!' We followed him upstairs into the gloomy loft of the church, across creaking boards to the daylight pouring through a window in the end wall, where Peter waited beside a model on a table, and suddenly I felt like a bird flying high in the air, looking down on the river and the London Bridge that was to be. I was looking into the future.

'But it has houses on it!' I said.

'Shops too,' Peter said. 'They'll help pay for it. Even a chapel to St Thomas.' The model was perfectly made, the wood gilded with gold leaf to make it look finer. I moved my eyes close, counting nineteen smooth, round arches regularly spaced, and towards the southern shore an opening spanned by a drawbridge. Peter's finger raised it, he pushed a tiny matchwood ship beneath, lowered the drawbridge again with his fingertip. Little boys all their lives.

'It won't stand,' Jack said. 'Round arches won't bear the weight.'

'But you are the master of pointed arches,' Peter said smoothly. 'If I'm not mistaken.'

Now everything was plain to me. This was why Jack's skill was so essential; only pointed arches would do. Peter had lost at least one round arch already.

'I'll build from the riverbed up,' Jack decided. I realised why he had been so quiet during our journey. Making plans. 'First, I'll drain the river dry.'

'That's impossible,' Peter Colechurch said at once. 'Only God does that.'

Jack pointed at the model downstream of the bridge. 'I'll dig a canal from Rotherhithe,' his finger followed the marshes behind Southwark, cut behind the curve of the river to Patrick's Island, 'to here.'

'No, it's impossible, it can't be done,' Peter said.

Jack said, 'King Canute did. He dug it, sailed his ships along it, and conquered England. All we have to do is find his canal, dig it out. Then I'll build two dams with the soil we dredge from the canal, drain the water in between, and make the Thames dry land.'

'It can't be done,' Peter repeated, alarmed, and I knew why. Nick knew too.

But Jack was blind. He rushed on, 'Building proper foundations will be easy in the dry. The work will take one-third the time. Five years. Less.'

There was an uncomfortable silence. The monk looked at Nick.

Nick said, 'You're wrong, Jack.'

'What do you know about it?' Jack said. He coloured, but Nick was calm.

'Jack, Jack,' he shrugged. 'Peter's right. It can't be done.'

'I can do it, Nick!' Jack was furious. 'Whose side are you on?'

Nick said, 'You can't, because Benedict Boatwright and the Mayor would never allow it.'

'So what? I'll save the lives of two or three hundred men who will probably be drowned if we work from boats.'

But Nick said gently, 'Jack, haven't you learnt anything about London yet?'

100

Peter said, 'Do you want people walking across the drained riverbed for free? Where's the money in that, Jack? We might as well not have a bridge at all.'

Jack's proud scheme came crashing down. Red-faced, he pushed Nick. 'Where's your support, Nick?'

Nick did not budge. He looked amiable. 'What's that got to do with it? The monk's right. You want to build the bridge successfully, don't you?'

'No thanks to you.' Jack patted the bridge-and-cross symbol on his chest. 'Brothers, remember?'

'You're an idiot, Jack,' Nick said. 'What do you think, Alice?'

I dared not say a word. Jack felt betrayed by his best friend.

'Sirs, be gentle,' Peter warned them. 'This is holy ground.'

'Alice?' Nick said.

I said diplomatically, 'Jack, if there's no river, there's no bridge, and if there's no work, there's no livelihood, we cannot live.'

Jack said angrily, 'Then I shall do as Alice says.' He would not look at Nick. I held Jack's hand to calm him, understanding his frustration; he was a man of dreams just as Nick had been, once. Something had happened to Nick. I hoped it would not happen to Jack.

Jack sighed. His good nature reasserted itself. 'Wherever the riverbed seems firm I shall drive timber piles at low water, as the Romans did. When they are as firm as I can make them, working from boats, I'll lay timber planks, and within them build up huge starlings of rubble like stone boats, and on top of them the stone foundations of the bridge piers will be built.'

'And the arches?' Peter asked.

Jack spoke with his old enthusiasm. 'A simple lancet arch, though strong, is too narrow. I propose an equilateral arch, produced by two curves, each with a radius equal to the span and meeting in a point at the top. The haunches will be ribbed for strength.' He had forgotten he held my hand, let go, and from the background I listened to the men talk and plan. Jack put his boxes of instruments under his arm and left the room with barely a glance at me, returning to London Bridge. 'I've taken a room at the Mitre,' he called over his shoulder.

Nick said, 'Alice, I've offended your husband.'

'He'll get over it.' But I thought that Jack, despite his understandable outburst of disappointment, had been almost frightened of Nick. Perhaps not frightened. Respectful. Careful.

'Without your support through thick and thin, Alice, he'd be no one.'

That was a remarkable thought. I reproved him. 'Nick!' He grinned, but it was the sort of grin that made me realise Nick was still angry. Jack forgot and forgave, not Nick. But then Nick smiled again, not blaming me for my husband's bad temper. We went downstairs and he pushed through the crowd for me. The Mitre was full of pilgrims starting their journey to St Thomas's shrine in Canterbury.

'Thomas was born a few houses that way,' Nick pointed sideways, 'and he was baptised in St Mary Colechurch,' he pointed upwards, where we had come from.

A decent plain girl opened a door and I looked round the room, which was indeed respectable, and as bare and boring as a stone cell. She said nothing. Nick left, he must perform the surveying tasks Jack set him. I was alone.

I sat on the bed, which was large enough for twelve, and dusty. No sound came through the thick walls supporting the weight of the church above. There was a fireplace but the room would be cold as death in winter.

I laid out my few small things around the room.

I sat on the bed again.

I ran back to London Bridge.

All summer was a fury of activity, before the winter rains began and then the frosts. But at first there was a lull while stores were ordered and soundings made of the river, the areas of clay and gravel mapped out. Because gravel beds made solid foundations and clay and heavy mud doubled the work, the arches would not be set at equal intervals. 'I had in mind spans of twenty-eight feet, Jack, perfectly symmetrical, standing on piers twenty feet in width,' Peter Colechurch said.

But Jack shook his head over the plans of plaster and charcoal. 'No, this is the way God wants the bridge. Some arches will be only fifteen feet wide, others more than double that.' A new model was made. The piers supporting the arches might be only eighteen feet wide, or more than twenty-six feet – not as it pleased Jack but as it had pleased God to make the shape of the riverbed. The gigantic starlings supporting the piers would be exposed only at low tide, and were even wider. These were shaped, as Jack said, like sharp-ended boats to cut through the rush of water up and down, four times a day in all. The starling near the centre of the bridge, which would have the Bridge Chapel of St Thomas of Canterbury built into it, would be almost two hundred feet long. The huge scale of the work came home to me. I watched the mason's lodge erected on the first pier at Bridge Foot, already completed by Peter Colechurch on the Surrey shore, and nagged Jack to build us a timber house in a corner of the yard. A home of my own. But Jack sailed to the Medway River with Benedict Boatwright and Nick, who was trusted by Boatwright, to make arrangements at the quarry, and I was left alone at the Mitre with the plain mute girl and the lifeless stone walls of my prison. I hated the inn, watched from the bridge for Jack's return.

The Thames estuary is full of sandbanks and pirates and desperately rough in an easterly, the wind that blew now. I stood on a bridge pier with the wind gusting in my eyes, trying not to think of Noelle, gradually forgetting her, but still Jack did not return. Then the *Benedictus* came sweeping upriver laden with stone blocks, and from the hut on the stern, looking very frail and seasick, Jack produced my little serving girl Rosie.

'Rosie!' I embraced her on the steps, squeezed her tight. 'Rosie, Rosie, my sweet!'

'Come on, Jack!' Nick called, and Boatwright beckoned. 'Come and have a drink.'

I had not realised how lonely I had been with only male company, and as the colour came back into her cheeks, Rosie did indeed look like a sweet, rosy-cheeked as though coloured by rosewater and sweet red apples, her eyes as blue as speedwells. 'Oh, Mistress Alice,' was all she could say as we waited for the men to return from the tavern. 'The sea was so rough and I was afraid I would die!' Then we laughed together, her teeth like tiny pearls moving between her plump red lips. She set herself to work at once cleaning the horrid room.

'I've returned the lease on our house in Littlebourne to the abbot,' Jack told me that evening. I had nowhere to go back to, the bridge was our life now. I wondered where Nick was and asked Rosie. She had not seen him. 'Nick?' Jack laughed. 'Where do you think?'

'I have no idea.' I made a face. 'He's not still drinking with Benedict Boatwright?'

'Nick can look after himself.' Obviously he and Nick had made up. Jack drew the curtain down the side of the bed to sleep. 'Ask him in the morning what he got up to.' As though thinking of what Nick got up to heated his blood, Jack asked me to stroke him, and when I touched him I felt how hard he needed me after five days of male company on a boat. *He* had taken no vow of chastity, like Nick. I let him have his way, it doesn't take a moment, then lay afterwards as I like to do, this is *my* time, imagining a tiny perfect replica of a man like the infant Jesus in paintings, who has a baby's body but a man's face, Jack's face, the face of the man I love, swimming upstream towards my womb.

But nothing happened, as it never had, and perhaps never would.

In the morning Nick lay asleep on the floor outside our curtain, and I forgot to ask him where he had been. The one thing I was sure of, it was not with a woman. Gambling, probably. I forgot it. The rhythm of the piledrivers, the rhythm that would become so much a part of our lives, began.

'I want a proper house,' I told Jack, but Jack was too busy. I watched him adoringly. He was so selfish, but selfish is what *I* do best. After all, he gets all of me in return. I'd get my way in the end.

Day after day I watched the tide-carpenters hammer wooden piles into the invisible riverbed from heavy barges called shouts. A large piledriver was bolted through the deck, a team of tidemen wound the winch with all their strength, raised a stone block dangerously high to the top of the crane. The tide-carpenter whistled, the stone plummeted with a crash on to the massive elm pile below, rammed it another quarter-inch into the riverbed. This thumping pulse started at dawn every day but the Sabbath and holy days, and did not end, except for breakdowns, or the loss of a man, or the dinner half-hour, until sunset. The Guild of Carpenters began new piles at high tide, trees standing thirty feet high as they were planted in position, then hammered down as the water fell until almost nothing of them showed at low tide, only the top few inches. The starlings looked like boats full of water.

One day I heard a splash, then silence. The young man who had jumped from the old bridge made no effort to swim. Robin's pale, upturned face was swept beneath me by the tide, the river filled his eyes, then the brown water flowed over him entire, and his clutching hand shrank beneath me, slowly, white, fading, gone.

Suicide. Robin's soul had joined Noelle's.

Even Rosie looked stricken, though she had not known him, and I realised I was seeing my own expression reflected in her face.

'I want a proper *home*,' I told Jack. I couldn't stand the Mitre any more, and even the irrepressible Rosie was miserable. Jack took rooms above the Bridge House in Southwark. We lived over stores of I don't know what, but Jack did, timber nails used in the starlings, door nails, plank nails – twelve thousand of them, Jack counted them in his sleep. Irons for driving the piles, weys of valuable lead, mortar and timbers of every quality from the cheapest deal boards to precious heart lathes to huge oak timbers stacked across the yard, he knew them all. People treated Jack with respect. He had money, status, recognition for his skill, a loving wife. But his work consumed him. I forget what Nick was doing at this time. He never ate dinner with us these days. One morning I noticed how smooth his mattress was, cold, the blanket neatly folded. Sometimes I thought about Nick because Jack was never there during the day, whereas Nick often sat in the carpenters' lodge, I heard him laughing, drinking. People say 'drink like a carpenter' as often as they say 'drink like a Templar', it's just a common saying. Probably he was with Richard Fairless, a tide-carpenter, a shifty, needful man who took on odd jobs. They were often together. Anyway, I had Rosie, always young Rosie to keep me too busy to think, baking, or boiling, or we would buy oysters from Oystergate, Shoe Lane for shoes (I got my wish, with gold points!) salted fish from Stockfishmonger Row and fresh fish from Fishwharf, meat from Stinking Lane or the Stocks Market on Cornhill whose rents help the building of London Bridge, offal from Pudding Lane, warm winter furs from the Steelyard . . . I'm in Heaven.

Workmen swarmed over the Roman river wall of the City, tearing it down, filling the starlings of London Bridge with huge quantities of rubble, Roman headstones, statues, broken arms and legs and hands, more rubble, gravel, lumps of chalk, anything that could be found, until the filled starlings stood like a row of rocky islands across the river, except for a wider gap in the middle. At Bridge Head and Bridge Foot the masons strengthened the piers Peter Colechurch had begun, then the first pointed arches appeared, striding out from both the south shore and the north towards the empty middle.

I watched the tide sweeping through the broad central gap, smelt the wet spray of the river. It was the first time I had thought of Noelle for months. Or Robin. Oh, God!

'I want a proper house,' I told Jack. In winter the draughty Bridge House was unbearable.

Winter came and the masons were laid off, as always. The carpenters continued their work for threepence a day and a fire, their hands wrapped in rags against the cold. Jack took half a dozen and had them build a wooden house for us at Bridge Foot. From its upstairs window, looking across the river towards the City, I saw something amazing. The Thames was freezing. This miracle had happened before, but it was a rare sign, and no one knew what it meant. Gradually the ice spread upstream of the bridge until the river was white. A few brave souls ventured on the ice, but then someone was drowned and the others withdrew. The weather warmed, but the ice did not thaw for days. Then great cracks appeared, and the melting slush was washed away downstream.

My house at Bridge Foot was almost as cold as the Bridge House, and it was near the corner where the carpenters drank beer, and Nick drank with them. Then during the summer the mason's lodge was rebuilt on the bridge amid the huts and stores and ramshackle dwellings which moved forward as the arches were completed.

'Jack!' I insisted. 'I want a proper house.' As you know I had demanded this many times, but this time he did not turn away busy or allow himself to be called away. He expected this.

'I've not been looking after you properly, Alice.' My lip trembled. It is a strange thing about love, how it overwhelms you when you least expect it. Jack gripped my hand. By chance we stood on London Shore, ferrymen busy plying their trade beneath us to the Surrey side. Jack led me on to the bridge above their heads. Already the watermen had given names to the passages through the arches, called locks, for the way the water dropped as it swept through. The sixth arch was called King's Lock, the seventh Queen's. The last arch completed so far was the eighth, St Mary's. Here the roadway ended abruptly in the air, nothing beyond our feet but the river swirling past the enormous starling below us that would one day be the foundation of the chapel, and beyond that the broad watery gap to the arches marching from the Surrey shore. Jack showed me the mason's lodge built out from the east side of the bridge, overhanging the brown flood.

On the top of it was my house.

'When the masons build the final lodge,' he promised, 'all this will be yours. Ours. The downstairs as well as the upstairs. It's your home, Alice.'

I was so relieved I kissed him with my open mouth, even at my age, especially at my age. The downstairs was large enough for fifty men to eat breakfast, dinner, conduct chapter meetings. The stairs were in a turret in the corner, and I climbed to the upper floor. Its length was divided into rooms by thin walls. From experience I knew that the heat rising from the men sleeping below would provide sufficient warmth to heat us, and our cooked food, of course, would come from the masons' Kitchener of the Bridge. Emotion swept over me like a wave, the pure ecstasy of possession of a place that was my own home. The walls rose around me like a wave. Jack tried to catch me, I felt my body slipping through his arms, I fainted.

I heard Jack. His laugh. Holding me in his arms. He was telling someone I had fainted. 'She fainted from delight! From sheer pleasure!'

But Rosie's voice came dimly, 'There's something wrong, master.' Her touch felt slippery on my legs. 'She's bleeding.'

I heard myself groan, embarrassed. 'I have a cramp. I need a pot. Something.'

'She needs to relieve herself,' my husband said. He was telling Rosie to fetch something but Rosie would not go. Blood slid from me, loose, hot, innocent. I felt her fingers.

Rosie said, 'Master, she's miscarrying her baby.'

'She can't have a baby,' my husband said. He laid my shoulders against the wall. He did not know what to do. He was helpless. Through my groans I saw the fear on his face. I smiled for him, to give him strength. 'She's barren, she can't,' he told Rosie. I felt something tiny slide out of me. Poor Rosie! She stared at the thing in her hand, her small hand, her short plump fingers dripping with blood, and what she held was no larger than her hand. No larger than the palm of her hand. She screamed.

She thought she held a tiny monster, part fish, part reptile, lifeless. Had it been a little smaller I might not have noticed passing the thing, a blood clot gone in the bucket, thrown away, I might never have known. Rosie screamed and screamed. She had never seen a stillbirth, her mother had sheltered her from such sights, but I had come across calves dropped half-formed, and once tried to eat a fertilised egg. I knew what I saw.

'Rosie, Rosie,' I said. I held her hand, I kissed her cheek. I suffered nothing worse than a little weakness from loss of blood. 'Rosie, it's all right. It's not a monster.' I heard Jack being sick. God, I must look after all of them. 'It's not a monster, Rosie. It's a human being. Pray for it.' It had no sex, Rosie's speedwell-blue eyes stared and I thought she would scream again. I took off my headscarf and laid the thing inside. Then I lifted Rosie's hands in my own and pressed them together. 'Pray for it, Rosie. Thank you, God, for . . .'

Jack wiped his lips. 'My God,' he said, shaken. 'You're thanking God for that?' He sounded revolted.

I took Rosie's shawl, held it between my legs until I was clean, stood. 'Don't you understand, Jack?' He didn't, men are so helpless at female business. He didn't want to know. 'It's a good sign, it's good news, not bad. It means I can have a baby.'

'My God,' he said, 'that wasn't a baby. That was a monster.'

I wrapped its little body reverently in the scarf. Most women, I knew, would have let the thing be taken away, chucked in the river, but the memory of Noelle's fate overhung me. I would not take it to the chaplain of St Magnus Martyr but instead carried my pathetic little burden to St Mary Colechurch, and there Peter Colechurch, who was in his way an honest man – as honest as he could be – took it from me and said a prayer. He could not baptise it for it was not alive, could not bless it for it was not Christian. But he blessed it for what it might have become.

Jack knelt beside me.

I'd almost had one. I could have another. I could.

It's amazing, nothing puts a man off for long. He'd seen me bleeding like a pig, and my body and what came out of it had revolted him to the point of making him sick, but in a week he was knocking at my poor you-know-what again. It's strange, this business of love. Jack loves me, he's tender, careful, cares for me, but he's also indomitable. He's got to have what he wants and he won't stop until he's had it. But I was more afraid than I admitted of bleeding again so I lived strictly by Church rules, sleeping in my clothes and not allowing him to touch me in case I submitted. My first monthly course was entirely normal, but still I thought it best to live by the Church's teaching – which is the best way to get with child, the conception has God's approval. And though I prayed to get pregnant, I contained myself on the Wednesday and Friday of the week, and Saturday and the Sabbath of course, and lived by all the other restrictions of holy days and fast days and Whitsun and everything else that rightfully restrains us for our own good. It wasn't hard for me. Jack was never home until the dead of night anyway.

The bridge works moved forward, and a new temporary masonic lodge was built on the Chapel Pier. Now I had a proper home all to myself, the downstairs as well. Half our long house, the portion over St Mary's arch, was given over to Benedict Boatwright. Other houses were springing up between dusty sites all along the bridge, but all I cared about was my own home. I had the downstairs converted into two rooms, with glass in the windows, and we (or rather I, Jack being so busy) slept upstairs with another glass window which revealed between my feet, as I awoke, a perfect sunlit view of the City past St Paul's to the Temple, and all the boats already busy on the great blue river. I put Rosie in the attic, the roof so steep and pointed that she could stand up in the middle.

One day, quite suddenly, the building site outside my door turned into a street. Though far from finished – some of the central arches were formed from beams of wood – and distinctly rickety in places, the Mayor, aldermen of London and Bridge Warden (Peter Colechurch, of course) decided opening the bridge would bring them more profit than ferries, and Benedict Boatwright was overruled. He looked suspiciously cheerful. 'He's been paid off, of course,' Nick said, unsurprised.

'Paid off?'

'The City looks after its own. Money will be found for Peter's chapel, too.' I'd noticed Boatwright's clothes were finer than before, and he rode a horse across the bridge. 'You watch, Alice.' Nick had an instinct for how London worked. 'The bridge will make more trade, no tolls for going over or pontage charges for boats passing beneath, yet. So prices will drop. More goods will be sold, profits will rise, trade will increase.'

'I see.'

'Because of more trade, more people will need to use the bridge. There's no other bridge on the river and there never will be. So after a while the increased trade will need boats.' He must be right, I had already noticed the river as busy as ever despite the bridge. 'After a while the bridge will be so crowded that tolls and pontage will be levied, small at first, then larger. But for the moment the Bridge House Estate receives an income of hundreds of pounds a year from lands and markets all over London. Each shop being built on the bridge pays a rent of fifteen shillings a year, going up. Within a year there'll be over a hundred shops, you'll see. And the Mayor, for a fee, naturally, has given permission for a market to be held in the Square.'

'The Square?'

He pointed outside my door, where Rosie sat, the gravelled area without houses or shops. 'Here. Between your house and the chapel.'

Where the chapel would be. I saw a few workmen digging rubble from the huge pointed buttress built on its artificial island; Peter's chapel would go down as well as up. 'A market, a chapel, an opportunity,' Nick said. 'If I were you I should turn the downstairs of this house into shops. All London will pass across London Bridge.'

I looked at Nick, interested in him. We had known each other for so long. I had known him as a boy. But as a man Nick was completely unknown to me.

I like to think I know everything about men, nothing about them surprises me much. But he surprised me. I flattered him to draw him out of his self-imposed shell. 'You know everything, don't you, Nick?'

'Yes,' he said honestly. 'That's my curse.'

'Oh!' I said. The wind was knocked from my sails.

'You think *you* know everything, don't you, Alice?' Nick stared at me steadily. 'You women always do. You know, you even sound like a Londoner.'

'I'll take that as a compliment.' My transformation was deliberate, speech, clothes, an assertive London manner. I could swear as foully as Richard Fairless, God's-this and God's-that, I knew the price of everything, and I had not been robbed once.

'You still owe me that shilling,' Nick said quietly.

I could not think what he was talking about. He grinned, and left.

It was evening before I remembered. Noelle's shilling. He gave it to me, I had never returned it. The river took it. But he still remembered the debt though it was years ago. I laughed and Rosie, sewing by the window in the last of the light, glanced at me. I fell silent. Nick took this seriously. Nick took everything seriously. Jack joked, Nick never. When Nick laughed, it was not because something was funny but because it was important. Even his silences were important. He remembered the debt. Inside himself, Nick was still the miller's daughter's son, he still remembered Mistress Cristina, and Nick and Jack together, and Nick and Jack and me together, and Jack and me together, and suddenly I was quite sure of this: Nick remembered everything. All my faint adult memories of childhood – Nick almost drowning me, Nick saying *Why Jack? What's different? Why not me?* Nick's terrible pain, his innocent *I love you, I love you* and my laughing rejection of him – these memories were cut deep, deep into Nick's heart. They were still alive.

I shivered, cool spring weather. I wished Jack would come home.

The tide-carpenter's whistle blew in the dusk and the piledriver ramming the final sections of the Drawbridge Pier, the last to be completed, abruptly ceased its heavy thumps. Beneath the timbers of my house the rush of the ebb tide died away. In two hours the flood tide would begin its rush the other way, accompanying our sleep, colouring our dreams with its increasing roar. We would hardly hear it, so used were we to its sound, and by dawn the river would be falling again. If only Jack was home.

I swept my Flanders cloak over my shoulders, stepped to the door. Rosie no longer had light to sew, she had fallen asleep over her poised needle. I woke her to send her to her bed. 'Mistress,' she whispered, her eyes pale in the dark, 'you're not going outside alone – not in your condition?'

I whispered, chuckling, 'We are not certain of my condition.'

But Rosie would not let me out alone. Her feet scampered, she fetched her shawl and headscarves for us both, followed me outside. She carried a piece of wood in case we were attacked, and we tied our scarves well forward so we did not show young or old. Past the Chapel Pier shops enclosed us on every side. The road was narrow – the shops paid rent, the road did not. Two men passing with arms outstretched would touch the shop fronts on each side. All shut up at sunset, but upstairs cheerful candlelit windows cast yellow gleams against the houses opposite, and we heard families going about their business behind the thin wooden walls. I walked confidently. 'Doesn't the fresh wood smell lovely?' Boatwright's skilled carpenters had built them. Rosie looked nervous. Today was Friday and the teams of masons, carpenters and labourers were all paid tomorrow, so Jack would be going over the accounts at the Bridge House, probably with Boatwright. It was a task Jack often told me he hated and I knew he did not like Boatwright. He was always kept late on Fridays. That was why I would fetch him.

107

I crossed the walkway spanning the gap where the drawbridge would hang, the massive oak winches and capstans and brass weights already mounted on each side. The wooden towers that would be the cranes for the lifting gear – and also houses – rose half-finished into the night sky.

Rosie turned, thinking she heard a footstep no doubt, then hurried forward. 'Mistress Alice!' Afraid to be left alone. I took her hand.

More houses, the road between them very dark. A *haut-pas*, a third storey joining the attics on each side of the road, crossed above our heads. People would shelter here during rain, and while they shelter people buy anything that catches their eye. I do. These shop rents would cost more.

Another open space, then Tom Bedell's hut. A dog growled, some sort of black mastiff breed with a ginger chest. The chain dragged taut. Tom was Keeper of the Dogs, like his father before him on the wooden bridge. The dogs kept vermin off the bridge, including human vermin. Tom recognised me and called out from his doorway, so drunk he could not stand. One of the dogs licked his hair. Beyond the hut a stone castle was under construction, a pale heap in the dark. We passed through the echoing arch, and in a few moments came to the posts that marked the end of the bridge. Nearby a fire flamed in an iron basket on a pole, sending up filthy smoke, revealing the bridge's entrance to travellers. None were about, the last pilgrims safely shut in their inns and hostels.

To my left stood the Bridge House. We came to the west gate. Candlelight showed as the door opened and three men sauntered into the stone yard yawning, scratching. I'd meet Jack here saying it was by chance, he'd walk me home, I'd have him to myself, we'd talk, we'd be together. But then I lost sight of them in the darkness, the piles of stone and timber. Suddenly their voices came from an unexpected direction, the south gate. I heard Boatwright's jolly laugh, one of Jack's jokes.

'Let's go back,' Rosie whispered. She tugged me, her hand slipped from mine.

The watchman showed the three men through the gate into Southwark, closed it, locked it. His dog barked.

The three men crossed St Olave's Street, stopped in front of a tavern's lighted windows. There was Jack's silhouette. There was Nick. Why were they not coming home?

Nick turned and looked at me in the darkness. He looked straight at me. I saw his eyes.

Nick threw his arm round Jack's shoulder, took Boatwright's elbow, and instead of walking on to the bridge, the three men went the other way, into Southwark.

'Mistress, don't.' Rosie tugged my sleeve.

I followed the men as though they drew me forward with invisible ropes, I could not stop myself, Rosie could not stop me. My infallible curiosity, my curse. The Borough High Street, all taverns. Nothing left of the market but rooting pigs and stinking rubbish.

The shadows moved into the darkness along St Thomas's Wall. I followed the three men into the Liberty.

Why was Jack with them? What had happened to me?

Rosie's teeth chattered. I remembered her, wrapped her in a wing of my cloak for warmth. She felt so warm and soft, but she clutched her hard stick tight, and I kissed her forehead to reassure her. She whispered, 'Where are we?'

'I don't know,' I lied. We were near the sign of the Angel.

Mistress Tarmantelle's. The three men changed shape as they turned and went into that long, narrow yard. I couldn't believe Jack was going with them. The opening door lit his face. Jack. Nick hung back, Jack went ahead of him. Nick put his arm on Boatwright's shoulder, they followed Jack inside.

I waited in the dark. There was a window but it was too high to reach, its glass too rippled to see through.

Rosie began to cry.

More men coming, shouts, curses. I led Rosie up the steps on to the balcony. She tripped. I reached out, fumbled in the dark for the door that was somewhere here. At last I pushed, not pulled. It opened, puffed smoke and stench around us, and we slipped inside and closed it before we were noticed.

We stood on a filthy wooden gallery, smoke swirled past us towards the roof, firelight flickered, banners hung from poles over the room below. Between the banners I glimpsed tables, legs, the tops of heads, a breasty maid carrying a flagon of beer over each elbow, dumping them from her wobbling arms on to the tables. I recognised Boatwright's shoulders by his hair, then his velvet-clad thighs appeared, wine-red, as he sat directly below me, then his velvet arms thumped the table for service. Nick clapped Boatwright's shoulder, pushed through the crowd, met Richard Fairless who stood at once, eager, swaying, drunk. Beer froth clung to his mouth, he'd been waiting for Nick. Nick shoved a girl at Fairless, pushed forward alone towards Mistress Tarmantelle, the crowd swirled, moved on. Now beneath me I recognised Jack's head, the firelight in his hair. God, Jack, no. He sat legs apart, relaxed. Boatwright grabbed the busty girl, she screamed, she screamed with laughter, put her big white arm round his neck and showed him a good look. He squeezed her, she smacked him reprovingly. Jack's finger beckoned, he spoke to a girl wearing red shoes, she kissed the top of his head with her hair over his face. I could not believe what I was seeing. My husband. Everything that was mine. The girl in red took his hand and moved it towards her. The banner was in the way, I could not see where she put his hand. *'Don't look, Mistress Alice!'* Rosie sounded so angry with me. I had failed Jack. I must have failed him. I could not look, I could not look away. I had failed my husband. The harlot stroked Jack's hair, *my* hair, hair that I adored. Rosie tugged me angrily. 'Come away, come away.' I felt myself slide, I really thought I would faint again. The boards swayed close to my eyes, I held my tummy. I remembered how revolted Jack had been by our half-formed baby that had slipped out of my body. Now I heard Jack laughing, saw the harlot's scarlet lips moving, the colour of blood. He turned his face away from the stench of her. My Jack. I was sick. My vomit trickled across the boards. I hoped it dripped down on them.

'Come, come, go!' Rosie begged. She was crying her eyes out, poor little creature, no more than a child. 'Please, mistress. Please.'

The girl slid off Jack's lap, an urchin brought him a plate of roast beef. Thumping footsteps, close. Rosie gave a terrified chirp. Richard Fairless came upstairs towing the girl behind him. Did they share these girls? I smelt Fairless's beer and sweat, saw his fingers wrinkled and hardened by work and sun and the river. Rosie turned my head away, made a show of fanning my face, hid me. I was a bundle of clothes, any old whore overcome by the heat. I stared below me with my eye against the boards, I could not help myself. I felt as dazed as a child witnessing Hell. At the far end of the room Mistress Tarmantelle, the bishop's whore, watched beadily over her business from her throne, and talked behind her hand to Nick.

And Nick, comfortable, at his ease, looked at me. I was sure he did. He didn't take his eyes from the shadows above the banners where I was hidden. He bowed to Mistress Tarmantelle and she to him. Nick came forward below me, he stood behind a girl, he looked up at me, he drank his wine with one hand, with his other hand he squeezed her big arse as though testing the freshness of the meat. He shook his head, moved on, staring at me.

Below me Jack ate his plate of beef. He rubbed salt between his palms to season it.

Rosie pulled me, the door opened somehow, she pulled me into the dark, down the steps, outside into the yard. I slipped on the foul stones, fell against the wall. Above me the girl in the window above the archway went about her disgusting business with her mouth and breasts. 'Come, mistress,' Rosie begged me in floods of tears. 'We'll be home in no time.'

Something moved in the arch. Here I had almost died. A shadow crossed the stones, slid up the wall. Someone was coming. I pushed her. 'Run, Rosie, run!'

The man put out his arm, stopped her. Light outlined him, he held a candle behind his back. He carried her forward into the light from the window above him. It was Nick. He held the candle in front of him, so that his face was illuminated from above and below. He glanced at Rosie, the candle flames moving in her terrified eyes, but I think he hardly saw her. He let her go, gently.

I called, 'It's all right, Rosie. Run home. Go to sleep. I'll see you in the morning.'

Rosie dithered, terrified to go, terrified to stay.

'It's all right,' Nick said calmly. 'No one will stop you.' He didn't care about her. He stepped past her, hardly noticed her, forgot her as soon as she was behind him.

Rosie ran.

I glanced upwards, distracted, as the girl above us cried out in simulated passion. I hated her.

Nick came close to me. I stood back against the wall. He looked so sad. The candle flame between us stood straight and pure, the air was perfectly still in the sheltered yard. 'Oh!' the girl cried, muffled, and this time Nick's dazzled gaze did flicker. He hated her too.

He told me sadly, 'You don't understand us at all, do you?'

'I don't want to understand you!'

'You don't know me. You don't know your husband. All you ever think about is yourself, Alice. Loving Alice. Kissing Alice. Fucking Alice. A nice warm home for Alice.'

'No!'

'All I've ever done is love you, Alice.'

'No. I don't love you.'

'You don't know what love is. You aren't lonely, you don't look around you, you don't see. You don't see us. Two hundred and seventy-three good men died building London Bridge. I knew them all. Every single man. But you. Blind. Selfish. You, you, you, Alice. Shopping. Cooking your husband's supper. Lying in your husband's bed. That's all it is to you.'

'It's all I want. Let me go.' But Nick was not holding me. He put out his hands, palm open, only his thumb curled round the candle. I was free to go. But I was not.

'Here.' He handed me the candle. 'This will light your way home.'

I must call for help. No one would hear, or care. Nick pressed his fingertip to my lips, gentle as a butterfly's wing. The wall touched me on each side. I was in the corner. I could plunge the burning candle into his eyes but I could never really do that, in fact. I had known Nick almost all my life. Whatever he felt, he was genuine. He either said nothing, or he told the truth. He was telling the truth now, as he saw it.

'I love you.' He touched my cloak and it opened. He touched my dress and the straps slipped from my shoulders. He looked at my breasts with his eyes so like Jack's.

I whispered, 'That isn't love.'

'Pain and suffering, submission and sacrifice. It's love.' He lifted my dress and penetrated me and I screamed into his hand. 'This is love, my love.' If only he didn't have Jack's eyes, their father's eyes. 'I love you, Alice. How long is it since anyone said that to you?'

I murmured, 'Don't hurt me.'

'I won't hurt you.' He lifted my knees on each side of him, working himself deeper. I endured him limply, my head turned to one side towards the candle flame. 'Alice, I love you. I'm mad for you. I repent nothing.' He was trying to reach my heart. 'Do anything for you. Commit any sin for you. Burn in Hell for you. Here I am.' He closed his eyes. 'Here I am.'

He snarled in his throat. Shuddered. Shivered.

He put me down carefully. Released me gently. Replaced my shoulder straps. Closed my cloak.

'Remember, Alice. I love you.' He kissed my forehead. I was the guilty one. He had simply done what men do. We didn't understand them.

I whispered, 'Suppose I am with child?'

He grunted, amused. 'I hope so. Will you tell Jack whose it is or shall I?'

I understood. Blackmail, he was blackmailing my emotions. Of course if I was a man I'd do the same thing, I couldn't blame him. Jack would have killed him, possibly would kill me, and at the very least Jack would always wonder if my baby was really his. I blamed myself, I was so sorry for Nick, I had caused this. He was right. I had been blind.

He kissed my lips, took the candle in his hand, looked into my eyes. 'That's the end of it.'

It wasn't the end of it. It was the beginning. He'd started and he'd be back. I gazed at the girl in the lighted window. She lay with someone else. Do they say they love her? Probably. I don't know. Nick's right, I don't know them. No, this is what I think, I think they come back to her and back again and treat her with more contempt each time until they hate her, they hate her because they need her.

'No one will harm you, Alice.' Nick turned and walked quietly away, and I watched his candle flame bob into the dark until it was too small to see.

'That wasn't love, Nick,' I called after him. 'Whatever you're feeling, it isn't love.'

I put my hands to my face. I wanted to cry aloud until dawn. But I couldn't let Jack find me here. A door slammed, someone pissed against the wall. I walked calmly into the street and walked back to Southwark looking neither to the right nor the left, not listening to what I heard. You see, something in me trusted Nick. You must despise me by now, but that's what I felt. I knew, *knew* he wouldn't lie to me, and I knew I wouldn't be harmed, and I walked safely on to London Bridge and reached my home, and there I shut the door, bolted it, leant back against it. Then remembered Jack would be home, unbolted it again.

I heard Rosie shivering in the dark. Her chattering teeth tried to ask, did anything happen, did anything happen?

'No.'

She understood. 'But you are already with child.'

I screamed at her, 'Go away! Go upstairs! Go to your room and sleep!'

She cried and ran away. Tomorrow I must show her somehow that I was sorry. I put my hands in my hair. I pulled my hair.

Later Jack came home, fumbled around me in the dark, and I thought of the girl in the red boots and where she had put his hand that I had not seen.

111

He got into bed beside me and he said, 'Alice? You awake?' I did not reply, and he went to sleep.

Long ago before he left to go to the Templars, Nick had told me, '*I shall do something bad if I stay.*' A warning, and he always told the truth. '*Jack is my best friend and I love you, Alice, and I would rather die than come between you.*' And so he had gone away. But he had not died. He had come back.

And now something very bad had happened. Something much worse than I could imagine. I did not know how to deal with it.

I must tell Jack.

I could not tell Jack.

Jack had been there at the Angel. Oh God, my Jack, my husband. I lay beside his sleeping body with my eyes wide open in the dark. Beneath the window the river trickled, then rushed, then roared through the arches, then was still again. Daylight grew. The sun came up, I held St Paul's Cathedral between my feet. Jack woke, left me sleeping as he thought. Rosie put out his breakfast bread and beer downstairs. Jack never talked in the mornings. Outside, the bridge came to life. He grunted, went out, the door closed.

Rosie and I did not say a word all day. Boats slid busily about the bridge. The tide rushed, then roared, then was silent, and the boats came out again, and later the sun set.

We sat in the shadows. We both knew I had to tell Jack.

But . . . could I tell Jack?

How much was Jack part of what was wrong?

What wrong had I actually seen Jack do? All men go to taverns. All men like to see bright, lively girls. A girl had kissed him, taken his hand, but what had he done? Nothing, as far as I saw. The worst thing I actually saw was Jack eat beef not fish though it was Friday.

Jack was not home until late. He swept off his cloak as usual, then took one look at me by lanternlight. 'Good God, Alice, are you ill? You look dreadful.'

I wrung my hands. I couldn't say a word.

'Rosie,' Jack said, 'take my wife up to her bed at once, make her a pot of hot spiced ale.'

Rosie shouted, 'Nick kissed her!'

I burst into tears.

Jack laughed. He ran his hands back through his hair. 'What's this about?' he said reasonably. 'Why shouldn't he? He's known her long enough.'

I shook my head. Rosie muttered, 'It was more than a kiss.'

'Nonsense. You wouldn't.' Jack took my chin. 'What happened, Alice? What have you done?'

I couldn't meet his eyes. I was afraid he would think I was dirty. If I told him, he'd always be imagining another man's cock in his wife's holy of holies, he'd never want to touch me in the same place again, he'd never listen.

'Look at me,' he said.

I blinked at him. My eyelashes stuck to my eyes, making my tears even worse.

Jack scratched his cheek. 'Whatever has got into you two?' I could see him running over the dates of festivals in his mind. 'This isn't one of your little games, is it?'

'I didn't mean it to happen,' I said. I slipped to my knees and I put my arms round his legs. 'I didn't want it, Jack. I didn't want him.' I shut my eyes tight. My sobs were wrenched out of me. I couldn't hold myself back.

'Holy Mary, Mother of God,' Jack said. 'You're lying. You low slut. You whore. *Nick?* Where was this?'

112

I couldn't reply.

Rosie said, 'The Angel.'

Jack pulled me up by my hair. I squealed. 'I want to hear you,' he said.

'Jack, Jack, don't,' I wept.

'*You were at the Angel?*'

'Yes!' I shouted. 'I was at the Angel! I followed you!'

He looked baffled. 'That's an awful place. That's no place for a woman.'

'I saw you!' I shrieked. 'I saw you!' He slapped me for my own good. I shrieked at him, he shouted that I was hysterical. I threw something. He grabbed my arm, I shrieked, he pulled my arms behind my back. If only God hadn't made them stronger than us.

'Alice,' Jack said quietly, reasonably. 'You'll hurt yourself. Stop. I'm letting you go.' I was silent, acquiescent. He let go carefully.

I turned on him, shrieked at him. 'I saw you there! What were you doing there?'

'It's none of your business. I was drinking beer and eating a pickled herring.'

'*You liar!*' I shrieked. 'I saw you and you were eating *roast beef*!'

Jack looked angry, then he laughed. His smile touched his eyes, the same old Jack. He put out his arms and hugged me. 'What are we arguing about?' he murmured. I cuddled into his warmth.

Rosie said, 'He raped her.'

Jack looked at me seriously. He sighed. He wanted this to go away. He turned my face, examined my arms. No bruises, no scratches, no broken bones, and I was alive. 'It didn't really happen, did it? It's just your time of the month.'

'It happened,' Rosie said.

'If it happened, you didn't put up any resistance, did you, Alice? I can see you didn't.'

'I was afraid to.' I felt my face wrinkle up like an old woman's or a baby's. I felt so helpless. 'He – he made me hold a candle.'

Jack said, 'A candle. He made you hold a candle. How frightening.'

All I could say was, 'Yes.'

Jack turned to Rosie. 'Did you see this, Rosie?'

'No,' Rosie said. 'I was afraid.'

'Did he threaten you, too?'

Rosie looked very frightened now. 'No. Mistress Alice told me to run away.'

'How convenient. Did you?'

'Master Nick said no one would stop me.'

'That's not a threat, it's reassurance,' Jack said dismissively. 'Did he threaten you, Alice?' I shook my head. 'Did he say he would harm you?'

'Jack, this wasn't how it was . . . not how it felt.' He made a sharp, impatient gesture. I admitted, 'No, he didn't hurt me, and he said no one would harm me.' I was crying again.

'You're obviously upset.' Jack wiped my eyes with his sleeve. 'There must have been a misunderstanding. Listen, I'll have a word with Nick.'

'No, don't!'

He asked gently, 'Why not?'

I couldn't tell him, I simply could not. I should never have said a word, kept silent, head down, mouth shut, denied everything, even to myself. It never happened. 'He'll lie,' I mumbled. 'He'll lie to you. Tell you things.'

'When have you ever known Nick lie, Alice?' Jack stroked my hair. He was worried about me. 'We're talking about Nick, remember? I'm sure there's some obvious explanation for what happened, if anything happened. I'll find out everything, all right?' He fetched his cloak, went to the door. 'You go to bed now. Try and sleep.'

I called after him, 'I'm not lying.'

He smiled with his whole face, pure Jack. 'See you in the morning.'

Jack shook me. His hand shook my shoulder, would not let me sleep. I rolled over, murmuring, groped for him. Nothing. I opened my eyes to broad daylight. The bed was empty. Rosie knelt beside it, shaking me. It was her hand, not Jack's. 'I've been trying and trying!' she wept.

I pressed my fingers to my temples, pulled my palms down my cheeks. 'Oh. Rosie. It's light.'

She whispered, 'Master Jack's not home. He never came home last night.'

I struggled to remember last night. I had been so tired, not sleeping the night before, that it felt like a dream. 'He's been drinking with Nick,' I said. That's how Jack would do it, friendly, relaxed, good-natured, persistent but not offensive, finding out the truth over a tankard or two of ale perhaps. 'Probably sleeping it off.'

Rosie gripped my hands. 'You didn't imagine it, mistress. It really happened. All of it.'

'I don't think we should take it any further,' I decided. 'I think we should forget it.' I felt better after my long sleep, saw things more sensibly. 'What good would it do to make a fuss? And after all,' I chided Rosie's large, round, reproving, speedwell-blue eyes, 'a woman can't get pregnant twice when she is already pregnant.'

'But you told Master Jack,' Rosie said.

'I think Nick is feeling very ashamed of himself by now, don't you? He's broken his sacred oath of chastity, he must confess it to his priest, and his penances will be very heavy. He'll have to apologise to me, and he'll be so embarrassed. And really, no harm has been done. It's Nick I feel sorry for. He simply . . . burst. It was my fault for wearing my Flanders cloak, it makes me look too shapely. I'll get rid of it.'

'But you didn't tell Master Jack you're pregnant,' Rosie said. 'Now, when he hears, he's bound to think it's Nick's baby. That it *might* be. He'll always wonder.'

'It obviously isn't Nick's. The date of birth will be a month early.' I smiled in pleasurable anticipation.

'Only a month,' Rosie said. 'The baby might be a month late. Margaret Woolton's baby was born only a day short of seven weeks late.'

'Stop it, Rosie.' I kissed her. 'Really, you're making mountains out of molehills.'

She whispered, 'But still, Master Jack hasn't come home.'

I knew Jack would already be at work, he had probably stumbled straight from the Angel to the Bridge House. Doubtless he had a headache. I opened a window and lowered a bucket on a long rope to the river, splashed cold water over my face to bring up my complexion, smoothed the dress I had slept in, and swept my cloak over my shoulders as I went down the stair turret to the road. I know I'd said I wouldn't wear my Flanders cloak but it's so warm, and the morning was clear, cold autumn with a touch of frost.

Already a man was out selling expensive roeskin gloves from a tray. I felt at once they were calfskin, he would be fined for his deception if he was caught. A taverner – he wore a taverner's fur-trimmed gown – sold hot wine over his counter to passers-by, attracting such a crowd I had to push through them. The bright sun made the roadway seem quite dark beneath the overhanging buildings but the smell of travellers and horse shit and hot wine was warm and welcoming. Already, pushed and pulled between the shops, I felt how London Bridge was a special place quite apart and different from the land. A bridge is a different, closer, friendlier thoroughfare than any on dry ground. I saw

114

strangers talking as they held back to let carts pass, pilgrims gathered devoutly round a woman selling souvenirs and badges to St Thomas before St Thomas's Chapel was even built, praying and paying and talking excitedly. And all the while, beneath all this busy life, the river sliding beneath us, gathering its power for the next rush of the tide.

Jack was not among the masons working on the chapel. I went to the drawbridge where Richard Fairless came down a ladder. He eyed me and looked away, stuck his hammer through his belt, plainly so uncomfortable to see me that I asked him, 'Have you seen Master Jack?'

He spat the nails in his mouth into his hand. 'Don't ask me, ask him.' He pointed at Nick. I didn't want to talk to Nick but he saw us, dismissed the team he was leading to start some work or other, and came to me. He wiped the stone dust off his hands, took my elbow and spoke to me quietly by the parapet.

'Alice. Forgive me. I can hardly believe what I did. What I did to you. What we did. I didn't mean it . . . oh, God, forgive me, I *did* mean it, I do love you, I do. Forgive me and it'll never, ever happen again.' His words tumbled over one another, low, urgent, sincere. 'Alice, I'll do anything you ask. I've damned my soul by touching you with my foul flesh, Alice, instead of simply loving you as I always have done, with my heart. My soul is damned to Hell because I love you. I've not slept the last two nights. Since the moment I left you, remorse overwhelmed me. I've been on my knees, praying, praying.' The knees of his breeches were dusty. 'Praying for God's forgiveness . . . praying for your forgiveness, Alice. Praying that God will make me suffer for the dreadful thing I've done.'

I watched the tide swirl upstream against the river. We had known one another for so long. Jack had obviously decided this abject apology was sufficient, at least for the moment. Maybe Nick had offered money, to endow a chantry for prayers perhaps, to assuage his crime and mollify Jack. And where, in fact, would Jack find another assistant who carried out his instructions as skilfully and carefully and faithfully as Nick?

'If Jack forgives you,' I said, 'I do.'

'Thank God.' Nick kissed my hand. 'Bless you, Alice. Let's go and find him. I'll beg him on my knees for his forgiveness.'

I stopped. 'What? You mean you haven't seen Jack yet?'

'No. He's late at work today. I thought he was with you.'

'No.' I searched Nick's eyes, he looked as confused as I was. I said, 'Jack came to see you last night, didn't he? At the Angel, I supposed.'

Nick frowned. 'No, I wasn't at the Angel.'

'Where in goodness' name were you, Nick?'

He pointed to the City. 'On my knees in St Magnus Martyr, at prayer, the chaplain will—'

'Then where is Jack? Jack went into Southwark to look for you at the Angel!' I sounded alarmed, I could hear it rising in my voice.

Nick put his hand on my arm. 'Richard Fairless!' he called. 'I'll ask him, Alice, he always knows, don't worry.'

Fairless stopped hammering, came over. 'Master?'

'You, did you see Master Jack at the Angel last night?'

The carpenter spat a nail. 'No, master, for sure he never came to the Angel last night.'

'You must have seen him,' I said.

'No, mistress.' Richard was adamant. 'If he set off, he never arrived.'

'You're a fool, upstairs with some woman no doubt,' Nick said irritably. He called out to men working on the pier below us. 'Anselm Westminster, have you seen Master Jack? You, William Gloverson? Bartholomew Southwark, Mark

Laguerre, have you seen Master Jack? Thomas Stoner! John Chiseller! Robert Sharp! You men!' They all shook their heads.

Nick turned to me. 'And you're sure he's not at home?'

'No, he left last night, late, he has not returned!'

'Run back, check every room,' Nick ordered. 'He may have fallen asleep in another room if he was . . . did not want to be with you, or was too drunk to know his way. If he's not there, find me at the Stone Gate.'

I ran back home, cried out to Rosie to search the rooms. No Jack. *Did not want to be with you.* I swallowed. *I* was not the one at fault. But I felt as if I was.

I ran to Nick at the Stone Gate. 'He's not there.' Nick shouted to the men working on the huge thick walls, their white dusty faces looked down. 'Master Jack there? Seen him, Dick Darenth? You, Alexander Crowder? Edward Wright, Daniel Shadwell, George Green, don't gape, you seen Master Jack?'

Shaken heads, and their dismal calls, 'No, sir, not we.'

Nick dragged out Tom Bedell, who slept with his dogs in the hut.

'No, sir,' Tom yawned. 'Never saw Master Jack, except I saw him come on to the bridge quite late, after dark, with his lantern, going home.'

'Didn't see him again?'

'No, sir, he never got off the bridge again, not at this end.'

'Tom doesn't know anything,' I cried, 'he's always drunk!' The dogs barked.

'Now then, mistress,' Tom said, offended. 'No call to be insulting a man.'

Again Nick laid his hand quietly on my arm. I calmed myself.

'My dogs bark, see,' Tom said. 'I'd know.'

Nick shrugged, then turned back to me. 'I shall have to inquire at the Angel. I had hoped never to go back there.'

I watched him walk into Southwark, then ran after him. 'I'm coming with you.'

'It would be better if you didn't.'

'It's not that I don't trust you,' I said.

His hurt expression acknowledged the blow. I walked beside him. Strange how I feel safe with Nick, even walking these streets where the worst things happen. After a while in silence he said, 'I am sorry, Alice. I'm sorry for everything that's happened. I'm sure this little alarm will turn out to be nothing.'

We came beneath the sign. He knocked at the door of the Angel and after a while a cocksure lad opened it. 'Come back later when we open.'

He shut the door but Nick kicked it open. This was better. 'You! Master Jack here sleeping it off?'

'Never seen him, no, who's he?' The lad eyed me shiftily.

'You can tell me,' Nick said.

The lad tried not to look frightened. 'No, sir, Master Nick, not here last night.'

Nick pushed past impatiently and I followed him in. The room I had seen from above was now dull and drab, lifeless, boring. We moved between the overturned stools and spilt beer, found Mistress Tarmantelle sleeping like a bitch beneath the counter. She yawned, propped her elbows on the split wood. 'Jack. No, him, he wasn't here. I'd remember him. I'll ask Mary the virgin.' She called out.

This was awful. 'Jack didn't . . . doesn't go with her sort,' I said.

'Whatever you says,' the procuress shrugged amiably. 'That's what they all say. *Mary!*'

'What, God rot you!' shrieked a girl from the balcony. I recognised the tattered face of the girl who performed in the window.

116

'You bitch, you see Jack last night without telling me?' Mistress Tarmantelle roared.

'No, not last night!'

I staggered from the room. I had to leave. I sat down on the steps outside. Nick put my head between my knees.

'Alice, Alice,' he said gently. 'I'll take you home. I expect you'll find Jack waiting there asking what all the fuss is about.'

Jack was not waiting at home. Jack was nowhere. Jack had vanished from the face of the earth. Rosie and I were the last people to see him *alive*. There it was. That word. By evening it was on everyone's lips. *Alive*.

'Jack's still alive,' I said. But I heard Nick had sent Thomas Stoner, Robert Sharp, Dick Darenth and Daniel Shadwell, who were good men, to look in Southwark alleys and yards for . . . Jack not alive. For his body, stabbed or strangled. Jack might be dead. There was a chance he was dead. I waited with Nick and Rosie in the little downstairs room at the front of my house, with its view through the gap in the houses opposite of St Paul's Cathedral and its gold cross glinting atop that thin, tall, incredible spire against the sunset, the sun striking brilliantly through my window. Then the sun dropped and it grew dark so quickly, and Thomas Stoner, Robert Sharp, Dick Darenth and Daniel Shadwell came back shaking their heads.

'Don't give up, Alice.' Nick held my hands. The doleful chaplain of St Magnus Martyr confirmed he had seen Nick there praying. He had seen nothing of Jack. Nick said, 'There's a chance he's still alive.'

But we did not find Jack alive the next day, or the next.

I went to the parapet, and looked at the river sliding below.

They say a death without a body is the worst sort of bereavement. I had nothing to show me Jack was dead. He was gone, not dead. He might come back any moment, any knock on the door, I jump up, it might be him, he fell in the river, was swept downstream to France, he had no money, he could not get back. Or a French family nursed him back to health. Or pirates picked him up in the Thames estuary until he escaped. Or he fell from the bridge and banged his head and lost all sense of his memory, and was living as someone else. But none of that happened.

I remembered Robin Swinert grieving for Noelle. Calling for her from the bridge, calling. Nick led me back home. He was so kind, sat with me and Rosie during the evenings. He blamed himself for Jack's death. He even said, 'If only I *had* been at the Angel, this might never have happened.' He glanced at me in the candlelight. Jack's eyes. I groaned, feeling my grief come fully out of me for the first time. Jack was dead. But I couldn't believe it.

'What do you think happened to him, Nick?'

He shook his head. 'I think he fell in the river. He was tired. Perhaps angry. The water was cold. I think he was swept away and drowned very quickly.'

'Then he's down there still.' I rocked, groaning.

'Don't think of it,' Nick said.

In the morning I heard the drummer. The drum beat mournfully as the boat crisscrossed the river, missed a stroke. A grapnel was cast in the water, hooked, the men heaved, but it was only part of an old boat. I paid children to beat on the surface of the river with planks, I had a loaf stuffed with quicksilver and towed behind the drummer's boat . . . the drum missed, the hook was cast, and up rose a ghastly slopping body with the knife still through its neck. 'Jesus, Jesus, no!' I cried. But at last the men ascertained by the number of ribs sticking through the flesh that it was not Jack, it had been a woman, dead for months, waiting to be found on the bottom of the river. The sheriff's man had her wrapped in a sail to be buried in consecrated ground.

The coroner of Bridge Ward in the Parish of St Magnus Martyr – the bridge is under the City's jurisdiction – visited me. He was a rough, kindly man, a butcher by trade, I had often bought a forerib of beef or an ox tongue from him, and he asked if I wished Nick to be present. I did. Nick would understand what had to be said.

'Widow Alice,' the butcher said formally, 'we do now presume your husband is dead of a death by mischance. The most diligent inquiries have been made, and at the inquest the jurors have reached a verdict of death by said mischance.' They believed Jack had fallen off the bridge. There was no evidence of violence or an argument that might lead to suicide. Nick caught my eye, put his finger to his lips. He had not told the inquest anything of the events of that night. *Suicide*. Jack had been going to speak to Nick on a purely technical matter concerning the bridge.

'Best kept quiet,' Nick told me later. 'I said it for you, or they might have reached a verdict of self-murder. Don't let on.'

My God, no. I tried to remember. Had Jack been so very upset by my words that he might have killed himself? Men are obsessed with possessive feelings for their wives, I know, and I realised I had behaved in exactly the wrong way. I whispered, 'I should *never* have told him. Do you think he was really upset? I feel as though I killed him.'

'Perhaps so,' Nick said, and I felt his arms round me just like Jack's. 'It's not your fault.' But just saying it made me feel it was.

Jack was dead and there was nothing I could do about it.

A few days later – time is vague during grief – someone broke my window. I sent Rosie for Nick, and learnt he had been appointed Master Mason for the remaining work on the bridge – the Stone Gate and the chapel, mostly. Nick at once sent the bridge glazier to repair the damage. I paid the man and for the first time I thought about money, the shilling a day which had naturally ceased at the moment of Jack's death. The messes of food also stopped. And because Jack had borrowed to buy the copyhold of our house, I must now pay the Bridge House Estate sixpence a week, including interest, and it was due. But I had plenty of money.

I looked for Jack's money purse but he was wearing it when he died. No matter, I'd twenty shillings saved. I joked with Rosie about taking in washing, or buying old clothes from the rag market on Cornhill, and set off to the Bridge House. Being the quarter day when accounts fall due, the bridge was busy. Something struck me on the head and I lay in the crowd blinking my eyes on the gravel, trying to make sense of what had happened while rough hands searched me and were gone. A kindly man helped me back to my house. Rosie bathed my head and sent for Nick.

'You're tough,' he said, examining my head. 'Your long hair saved you.'

'Yes, I suppose so.' I didn't feel tough. Jack was gone.

'You'll live, Alice. But you must be more careful.' Nick was concerned. I suppose I was turning into a bit of a problem. 'How much did they get?'

I was confused. 'Oh!' I felt for my purse.

Nick asked gently, 'How much?'

'The next quarter's payment. Six shillings.'

He sighed. 'Well, it doesn't matter. At least you're safe.' He brushed my hair from my eyes with his fingertips. 'Is it all right between us now, Alice?'

I nodded. I knew what he still felt for me but I didn't feel it for him. Nevertheless, Nick had behaved with perfect courtesy. I was using his love for my own purpose, of course, but what else could I do? It is hard for a woman to survive in a man's world on her own. That's what men are for, to be used.

'Do you think he loves me?' I asked Rosie one evening.

'He raped you!'

'But I was wearing my beautiful cloak. And Jack was right, I didn't resist.'

'Nick isn't Jack.'

Because I must pay for all our food now, every morning Rosie and I went to the shops and stalls by the City wharves to buy a fresh fish for dinner. Some men noticed us and the more we tried to ignore them, the more they swore at us. I don't know who they were. Neither Rosie nor I knew what we had done. We turned back to the bridge without buying anything, and someone jostled me painfully in the ribs. I saw Dick Darenth working on the chapel wall. 'Have you seen Master Nick?'

Dick took one look at me, bless him. 'I'll fetch him, Widow. I saw him knocking at your door earlier, but you were out.'

Nick did not arrive. We waited for him all morning. Then in the afternoon he arrived in a hurry. 'I came as soon as I could. What's wrong now?'

I felt ashamed to make a fuss about the men who had sworn at me.

'They're workmen, that's what workmen do!' Nick dismissed my fears at once. 'Something more important has happened. This is serious, Alice. A writ has arrived from the Abbot's Littlebourne and Temple Moat manorial court. A writ has been taken out against you by the Knights Templar to recover stolen goods.'

My eyes widened. 'What stolen goods?'

'Yourself, Alice.' He unfolded a thick piece of paper dark with Latin writing. 'You were born *nativi*, a serf. The abbot sold your father and his services to the Grand Master of Temple Moat. Thus he also sold you, being your father's daughter.'

'Yes, I know all this, but—'

'You married Jack and became legally free. But now Jack is dead.'

Tears slid down my face. This is how it hits me, suddenly.

Nick took a piece of rag from his belt, held it while I blew my nose, brushed my lip where a piece of snot had landed. Jack's eyes. I stared at him, fascinated, uneasy, complex. Nick thrust the rag matter-of-factly back through his belt as though everything was simple. 'Now Jack is dead, you have reverted to the status of serf, the property of Geoffrey de Prudome, Grand Master of Temple Moat Preceptory in the County of Kent.'

'But that's just a piece of paper, isn't it?'

'An important piece of paper. You can appeal against a manorial claim like this to the King, but King Richard is on Crusade and Prince John is in charge of the *Curia Regis*, the King's Court. Appeals are slow, extremely expensive, and fail.'

'This can't be right.'

'All legal and posted above board in the manor.'

'But I live in London.'

'If you live in the City for a year and a day you are a free citizen of the City of London. But you've not lived in the City for a year and a day, Alice. London Bridge is in the City but after you lived in the Mitre Inn, you broke your residence by living in the Bridge House, which is in the Borough of Southwark. Under feudal law you are defined as a feloness. You have stolen yourself.'

'What am I to do?' Then I remembered what Widow Cristina had done. 'Yes,' I said eagerly. 'Can't I pay a fine? Buy myself back?'

'That occurred to me. I wrote a plea to the Grand Master some days ago, which is why I did not wish to broach this matter until I had received his reply. He doesn't know or care who you are, of course. This afternoon I received a note from the Preceptory Treasurer, who deals with these affairs, that you may purchase your freedom for a small fine.'

119

'Thank God! How much?'

'One hundred shillings.'

One hundred!

'But that's a fortune.'

'No. You see, you'd buy freedom not only for yourself but also for any children you may have one day. You'd be buying your descendants' freedom in perpetuity from any hereditary obligation to do labour services – should you marry someone unfree, as most men are.'

'I must pay it!' I cried, and felt a hot flush rise from my tummy to my forehead, which broke out in a perspiration. Nick looked at me closely.

'Is it really so urgent?'

'I am with child!'

He looked from my eyes to my belly and back again. 'It does not show.'

'I – I caught less than two months ago.'

He looked thoughtful. I reddened. Did he think it was his? 'Then the child will be born a serf.'

'Nick, please. I can't go back to Abbot's Littlebourne and Temple Moat. I can't. I've nowhere.'

'*Nick, please*?' he mimicked. He looked interested. 'What do you mean?'

I licked my dry lips, afraid of offending him. 'Isn't there something you can do?'

'What, Alice? A nunnery? And you with child?'

I took a deep breath. 'Can't you lend me a hundred shillings? You've got Jack's job, you've got a shilling a day, you earn a hundred shillings in four months. You could easily borrow that much against your pay. The Italians of Lombard Street, the Jews in Cheapside . . .'

Nick crossed the room, deep in thought. 'But you would never pay such an enormous sum back.'

I said wretchedly, 'There must be a way.'

He paced, thinking, then came back again. He knelt in front of me. 'There is a way. I know how we can save ourselves a hundred shillings, Alice. Only one way.'

And so I married the man who raped me, who thought he was the father of my child.

I was a free woman again, and a wife again, and would be a mother. I should be happy. But Rosie irritated me like a grain of sand. She thought me foolish, and . . . this word again. Blind.

As though I could not see what was so blindingly obvious.

I knew I did not love Nick. I knew it. But I needed him, and he was confident, and strong, and masterful.

Rosie was so difficult and obstinate about my sensible arrangement with Nick that I thought of dismissing her, sending her back to Abbot's Littlebourne, anything to get rid of her nagging tongue, her whispered, baseless accusations that I could not quite rid from my mind. How did the Templar Grand Master know Jack had died? I didn't know, what did it matter? Who told him? Rosie whispered. The wind? A little bird? How convenient it was, she whispered, that Nick was so very helpful. Rosie, I demanded, would it make you happier if Nick had deserted us to the jostling crowd, and swearing louts, and crime? Or if he had paid a hundred shillings for my freedom and thrust us all into penury? No, this way, by marrying a free man, at one stroke I achieve freedom and freedom from debt. But I don't trust him, she whispered. She thought I should not trust my own husband, to whom I had sworn the sacred oaths of obedience and fidelity! Besides, what did she, a little thing barely eighteen years old and never known a man, know of the hardness of this world? All the world,

Rosie whispered, crosses London Bridge. 'Don't trust him, Mistress Alice,' she said. 'I've seen them. Men, they're all the same. I can't walk along the bridge without someone giving me a squeeze like an orange.'

'You flirt. Get to your room.' On my finger I wore the ring Nick had given me when we were married – not of silver, as usual, but a ring of tiny rubies like drops of blood, rubies whose redness commemorates the circumcision of Jesus, for when He was circumcised, just such a ring of His holy flesh was cut from His holy body. I stopped Rosie at the stair turret, clawed my nails angrily into the back of her hand, so that her eyes filled. 'They aren't all the same, Rosie. They're not. Jack wasn't the same.'

'Wasn't he?' Rosie said tearfully. She got so lonely in her room, no window, only the gulls whirling beyond the shutter. 'I bet he was at heart.'

'No. No, Rosie, he wasn't like that. Not my Jack.'

'Why?'

'Because he had me.' As soon as I said it I realised it was true.

Rosie said, 'So that's what love is.'

I wore Jack's straw ring still round my toe, and no doubt it was inseparable from my flesh by now. But then Nick came in, and I didn't want to be seen listening to my serving girl's prattle. 'Go!' I banished her to her little room, she must come out only to work and not to talk. Not one word.

But in bed that night I thought, yes, that's what love is.

I stiffened as Nick moved. He propped himself on one elbow beside me, examining me by moonlight. I turned my head away as though sleepily. He was very virile. He knew that as soon as he touched me I would submit to my duty. But he liked my initial resistance. Of course Church law had not permitted us sexual relations immediately after our marriage, nor for three days and nights. Sleeping beside a man had put me in mind of Jack again, and I did not want that. I knew my life had to move forward. But Jack and I had had a thousand signs whereby we knew each other's thoughts and desires and emotions as clearly as though we spoke aloud, the way Jack had turned over, or touched my pillow, or snuggled. That was gone, everything now was silent. It was as though I had fallen deaf, as though my body had lost all sense of touch. But Nick was gentle, considerate, firm, and I lay, as I said, with my head slightly to one side whatever he did until he had finished. Until this evening, when he had asked me to stroke him in a way, as it happened, I used to caress my dear Jack. I could not bring myself to do it.

'My love,' Nick whispered. 'You must do as I tell you.'

I shook my head. I could not.

'I am your husband now, Alice. Do not think any more of Jack.'

He was right. But I could not. I searched for any excuse. 'It's the baby.'

Nick said, 'My baby.'

I lay with my head on one side, my submissive posture.

Nick said, 'My baby, Alice.'

I whispered, 'Jack's baby.'

He slid his leg across mine, crouched lightly on my thighs, his manhood and his face above me in the moonlight.

'Jack never told me. He would have told me such important news, don't you think?' Nick laid the palms of his hands lightly over my tummy, which by now was slightly swollen even when I lay down, and larger when I stood.

I whispered, 'Jack never knew.'

'Jack was married to you for more than ten years without begetting a child.' Abruptly Nick knelt between my knees, touched me with three fingers like a midwife. 'Ah. There is the truth. There. My emission is as potent as fire. I give flame to lifeless wood. I lay with you once and gave you life. My life.'

121

It is best to say nothing to a man when he is so fired with his own spirit. My head turned to one side. My eyes closed.

Nick lifted me under my armpits, his strength was enormous. He looked up at me, held me over him. He smiled in the moonlight, knowing what would make me struggle. To my horror he pressed me lightly against the wall, lifted my knees on each side of him, and while he possessed me, you know where I was. Not here. I was back against the wall of the Angel. Nick knew what I was thinking. It excited him. He spoke in a low, deep, rapid voice while he had me, so fast and so deep that I remembered what he said more clearly afterwards than at the time, and his words were pure Nick.

'Kissing Alice, Alice, don't you think this, *this*, fucking Alice, this is what I dreamt of all my life, imagined you with me beneath the bridge, imagined you in the woods, imagined you in the bare Temple dormitory, imagined you with me lying on the freezing sand beneath the burning moon of the Holy Land, can't you imagine how this is all I dreamt?'

I scratched him like a cat. Deep blood welled from his back, I felt skin hanging under my fingernails.

Nick laughed.

'My God, Nick,' I whispered now, my head turned away. 'Whatever must have happened to you in the Holy Land?'

He propped himself on one elbow, examined me.

'Outremer,' he murmured. 'One day I will tell you, Alice. And every word I will tell you is true. And you will wish you had never heard it.'

Each night my husband lay with me in his strength and pride, but his embraces were increasingly uncomfortable for me because of my baby. Fierce protective feeling rose up in me, I was no longer so submissive. I sat on the side of my fine bed combing my hair or making a business of tying my ribbons until I heard his snores. Only then did I lie beside Nick, and often I lay awake for hours, uncomfortable, sad, sleepless, unfulfilled, thinking of my baby. Jack's baby inside me. Imagining how happy I would have been with Jack. I could not get comfortable lying on my left side, or my right side, or lying flat on my back, and I could not possibly lie on my tummy. Probably by now my baby had decided whether to be a boy or a girl, blond like Jack, chestnut like me. Would he, she, grow up with my eyes, my blue eyes gleaming through chestnut curls? Actually I had cut my hair short now, the wooden bridge houses encourage vermin, lice especially, and at the wharves ships are always unloading spiders, mice, beetles with their cargoes, so that London lice and insects and mice and the cats to catch them are the strongest in the world. I hear them sliding and scuttling behind the wainscotting in the dark of night, when even London Bridge is quiet and still, if the tide is slack. As it is now. Low tide.

Reflections from the water far below my window rippled quietly across my ceiling, and I lay watching them, sleepless. Nick's eyes opened.

It was a cold night after Christmas. I remember that clearly.

He sat up, turning slowly. I closed my eyes, made my breath gentle, sleeping, I did not want him. He leant over me, his face against mine as though staring into me.

His fingers. He unbuttoned my throat, my neck, my chest. Stuck out his tongue, licked my nipples. His tongue was rough as a cat's, he was like a cat at the milk, or rather, waiting for the milk, of course my body would not really have milk to give until my baby was born.

My nipples stood up painfully.

Nick grunted. He rolled out of bed, pulled off his filthy shirt. The reflections rippled across my scratches on his back, which had healed badly even after these

122

months. Each cut was thickly encrusted with scabs. His shoulder blades were hairy. He shrugged on a new shirt, white. Pulled on his black leather boots. His cloak. Stopped, listening, held his breath. I breathed lightly, regularly. I heard the trickle of the tide begin to flood. Then his footsteps moved across the boards to the door, the drop-latch clicked softly, the door creaked. The latch clicked shut.

I was alone.

Nick was often out in the evenings. Perhaps he went to the Angel with Robert Sharp, Thomas Stoner, Alex Slay, Richard Fairless, William Gloverson, Dick Darenth and Alexander Crowder and all the others. I never dared follow him, as I had Jack, which I had regretted so bitterly ever since. I didn't care where Nick went, I didn't want to know. I wanted my own life, my own baby.

But going out in the dead of night is not going out to the tavern. Whatever it is, it's different.

I sat up, swung my legs to the floor, pushed myself forward with a grunt. The boards were rough and cold. I pulled on red velvet slipper-shoes over my night-socks (lambswool, Nick is not mean with money) and went to the door. My cloak lay in a chest beside the door, safe from moth. I hung it from my shoulders, pinched it over my tummy to keep warm, lifted the latch and looked over the landing. This narrow corridor serves the stair turret, closed off by a door on my right, and separates the night room from the day room, not used as much as my ordinary rough room below. I opened the door. This is my room, very pretty and smart. I can't help loving possessions. I would have lost my lovely room if I had not married Nick. I moved between the delicate Flanders chairs with a feeling of pride impossible to explain, a unicorn's horn Jack had bought from a Baltic trader, a folding table from Saintes, a lovely tapestry that must be the work of nuns, Christ walking on the water with the sun rising behind His head so it was His halo, His finger upraised either in blessing or to point at the sun.

The window shimmered black and silver, opaque. I opened its warped panes and suddenly the night was clear, the river winding eastward shining like a tapestry of silver threads beneath the rising moon, the brilliant crescent moon balanced on one horn in a sky the colour of ink, the moon pulling the river after it, and now I heard the river's steady gathering chuckle, rising. The water lapped round the great weedy starlings, the rising water swirled upstream around them, sent silver lines rippling over the Chapel Pier and its arch.

I saw no sign of Nick, unless the man standing in shadow by the parapet was him.

St Thomas's Chapel stood some fifty feet from me, half-finished, unroofed, but its jagged stone walls were already higher than my head. The moon touched its walls with silver and ebony, ebony black that the Templars used to trade in Jerusalem with the Evil Ones, exchanging it for walrus tusks, Cornish tin, Combe Martin silver. By rights, I knew, the masons' lodge should have stood in the chapel's place, since wherever possible the Lodge always faces to the north-east, where the sun rises in midsummer. But I now realised Nick had built the chapel somewhat to the north of midstream, as though it was the Lodge as well as a holy place. Like the *Frères Pontifes* or the Templars, the masons often endow their own chapels, which they call arks.

The moon appeared to fly through the rags of cloud that the wind moved past its face, and it seemed to me by the same trick of the eye that London Bridge also moved forward, like a great ship forging downstream against the flow of the rising water. I clutched the windowsill, the sensation of movement was so strong.

A cat screeched, I heard the rattle of elmwood shingles from my roof, and I had a powerful superstition that I should close the window. There was nothing for me to see here. I should get back to bed. Yes, I should get back to my bed right now, yawning, and sleep . . . sleep . . .

I heard voices. Men's voices, deep and harmonious, but soft, like a dirge. Not a light showed except a spark of flame near the south end of the bridge, and shadows walking behind it from Southwark, a column of men. It was their voices I heard.

> London Bridge is broken down,
> Dance o'er, my lady lee;
> London Bridge is broken down,
> With a grey lady.

The figure of a girl carried the flame over her head. She danced lightly in front of the men as they sang, coming slowly across the bridge.

> How shall we build it up again?
> Dance o'er, my lady lee;
> How shall we build it up again?
> With a grey lady.

They were too far away between the dark, silent houses for me to recognise the girl, but there was something familiar about her. Her ankles flashed beneath her dress.

> Build it up with silver and gold,
> Dance o'er, my lady lee;
> But silver and gold will be stole away,
> By a grey lady.

The wind caught the flame, and I glimpsed her red dress, her red shoes, her uplifted, tattered, ecstatic face. She was smiling.

> Build it up with wood and clay,
> Dance o'er, my lady lee;
> But wood and clay will wash away,
> With a grey lady.

I stared. I did not dare draw back from the window as they came to the chapel. Two men walked at the girl's elbows, Dick Darenth one side and Richard Fairless the other. Wine trickled from her smile. I knew her. She was the girl in the window, Mary, the girl from the sign of the Angel. The men sang their low, deep melody.

> Build it up with stone so strong,
> Dance o'er, my lady lee;
> Huzzah! Twill last for ages long,
> With a grey lady!

The girl twirled on her toes, then the man by the parapet kissed her and struck her face casually, caught her fiery torch as she fell inert, and the two men picked her up by her elbows before she touched the stones. They carried her into the chapel, they disappeared, and it was as if I had never seen them.

The moon, the tide. Nothing had changed. I had dreamt everything I saw, and then I knew I was dreaming now, because something impossible happened, as though (as in a dream) everything that looked solid was not solid.

The shapes of the men walked from the solid stone arch on to the starling that supported the pier and the arch and the chapel. They walked from the solid wall.

They were real. I was not sure if the man who led them was Nick or not. Whoever he was, he stood on the bow of the starling, the rush of the river flowing upstream inches beneath the heels of his black boots, breaking into foam like a silvery bow wave on each side of him. The foam splashed and sparkled in the moonlight. His shadow stretched from him to the pointed buttress of the pier that would stand against the flow of water as the river rose.

Another man appeared, much older, moving slowly, dressed in the long black robes of a Benedictine monk. Peter Colechurch? Perhaps. Was William Almain there, Henry FitzAilwyne the Mayor of London, Roger his son who would be the next Mayor? Was Benedict Boatwright there, even Serle Mercer? Perhaps. But this was a dream. Except that it did not feel like a dream. I pinched myself, as you are supposed to do, and did not wake. I was awake.

Three men carried the girl from the solid stone. She had recovered her senses and struggled, but silently. She had no voice, no face. She had lost her red shoes and her red dress was replaced by black. Over her head a white sack had been tied with a white rope.

The men who had crossed the bridge filed from the solid stone on to the starling, a dark shoving mass of them with the tide rushing past on each side of them.

Their voices began the chant. I thought it was Latin. '*Deus. Ingeniator. Rex Mundi. Amen.*'

A single voice called out, 'Master, how shall we build the bridge?'

The shadowed man replied, 'Make the bridge strong.' The arch echoed his words, distorted his voice. Nick? Perhaps.

'*Deus. Ingeniator. Rex Mundi. Amen.*'

Another man stepped forward. 'Master, shall we build the bridge by ordinary means?' Richard Fairless's high, thin voice!

'Give the bridge strength.'

'*Deus. Ingeniator. Rex Mundi. Amen.*'

'Master, shall we spatter the bridge with the blood of little children?'

The choir chanted, '*Deus. Ingeniator. Rex Mundi. Amen.*'

The three men raised the struggling girl over their heads. 'Here's a prisoner we have got!' They put her down. The girl stood swaying, wondering what was happening, the sack twisting on her shoulders as her head turned inside trying to see.

The shadowed man walked to her. He undid the rope, pulled off the sack. I saw her grinning, hopeful face in the moonlight. She had done her job.

The shadowed man spoke to her. 'There is no rescue. There is no escape. There is no hope. There is no death. Pain, suffering, humility, sacrifice.' I saw the sharp edge of a mason's pointing trowel flash, his arm swept across her, he cut her throat.

The shadowed man turned her so that the sacrificial blood splashed fully on the stones, trickled down the dark weed that stained the buttress. Her struggles weakened. The Benedictine blessed her. One by one the men filed past her body, reached into her throat, pulled bloody fingermarks down the stone.

The monk and the men and the shadowed man returned to the stones, were gone.

The starling was deserted but for the body of the girl. The tide lapped over the stone, the waters swirled around her body, her hands floated up, her face turned over as the water lifted her, I watched her swept away, sinking, fading, gone in a few moments.

I heard a child's sweet, pure, high voice singing a hymn as faintly as though far away or deep underground. I could hardly hear the words but I recognised the rhythm of the rhyme.

> Sur le Pont d'Avignon
> L'on y danse, l'on y danse,
> Sur le Pont d'Avignon,
> L'on y danse tout en rond.

The hymn ended. From the dark doorway of the chapel a pretty child ran, white smock flapping, a silver coin flashing in his fingers as he ran joyously away across the bridge, and I watched until he was gone safely from sight.

I closed the window.

I returned to my bed. What had I seen? A menacing ritual, or a piece of theatre? Had the girl really died? How had they made it appear so? Had they somehow substituted the girl, by a trick of the eye amid the flickering moonlight on the rushing water, for a sack of straw and a bucket of pig's blood? Had the straw body been weighted with stones so that it would sink?

I knew what I had seen.

I knew that if I went to the Angel – and not for a cartload of silver would I do this, but if I *did* – I knew I would not see the girl in the window.

I took off my cloak and lay down on my bed.

My eyes opened. I had slept. The tide roared like thunder, like distant thunder, but my whole house shakes at full flood. The little painted plaster Jesus standing on the clothes chest falls over sometimes. Perhaps that was what woke me now. I sat up, blinking, trying to see Him, and the door clicked closed. Nick was in the room. I glimpsed his shadow outlined by moonlight, then his moonlit hand appeared and set the little Jesus upright. His weight settled on the bed.

'You're awake, Alice.'

'I couldn't sleep.'

'What woke you?'

'I thought I heard a little boy singing.'

He pulled off his boots. 'Singing?'

'Nothing. A childish rhyme. *Sur le Pont d'Avignon.*' I smiled. 'Couldn't you sleep either? Did you hear him?'

Nick turned his face towards me, half moonlight. 'You heard wrong, Alice. It is not *sur le Pont*. It is *sous le Pont. Sous.* Under. The *beaux messieurs*, the masons, dance *under* the bridge, not on it.'

I whispered, 'I didn't see anything.'

'You never do, do you, Alice? You never do.' He leant towards me, spoke softly. 'Jack would have done the same, the very same that you saw.'

'The joke with the straw dummy and the pig's blood?'

'Now you are lying to me, Alice.' He took off his blood-spattered shirt, hissed as a scab on his back peeled off with it. Fresh blood, his own, from the scratch I had made, trickled down his spine. He lay down beside me, his hands behind his head, watching me sit there.

I said, 'She didn't really die, did she. Did she?'

'She is not dead, Alice.'

I was so relieved that I lay down beside him. 'Do you want me to look at your back?'

'No.'

'All right.'

126

He touched the mound of my belly, felt the child there, then put his arm round me and pulled me on to my right side against him, my head resting on his naked chest. 'You mustn't be afraid of me, Alice. Everything you think is bad you blame on me, everything good you put on Jack's memory. By now you think Jack was perfect, no doubt.'

'I still love him though he's dead.'

'Jack told you of these initiation ceremonies long ago. Before he took the oath of secrecy. He told you more than he should have. Hiram the Mason, the ingeniator of Solomon's Temple. Hiram's terrible death, the completion sacrifice. The winding stair the Templars discovered. The Sanctum Sanctorum, the Sacred Lodge. The Well of Souls. The Tomb of Christ. *Necessitas non habet legum.*'

I remembered, I remembered Nick's translation from all those years ago, the three of us crouched under the bridge barely more than children, and I repeated it now, when I could not be very far away from giving birth to my own child. 'All we have to do is believe.'

'Yes. *Credo quia impossibile est.*'

'Faith is stronger than reason.'

'Yes. But reason must also be part of faith. Reason is the roof and walls. Faith fills out the inside, just as songs and prayers fill a church.'

I said sleepily, 'Walls and roof! Said like a true mason.'

'I'm still a Templar, Alice.'

I jerked awake, tried to sit up, but his grip was firm. His chest was warm under my ear and the side of my face.

'But you can't be still a Templar, Nick.'

'I never relinquished my oath. I am a Master Mason and a Templar, both.'

My eyes moved, trying to make sense of what I heard. 'But you renounced your oath in the faces of the Poor Fellow-Soldiers of Christ, threw down your dagger, broke your sword . . . you told me.'

'I lied.'

Nick never lies.

'Are you lying now, or then?'

'Alice, Alice. I lied back then. You would not have believed the truth. What I really did was much worse.' He picked a piece of velvet thread from my leg, he knew I had worn my shoes. He knew for sure I had watched. 'Do you know the truth when you hear it, Alice? Do you believe a tunnel connects London Bridge with St Paul's Cathedral?'

My head rose and fell slightly with his breathing. The moonlight made a forest of the hairs on his chest. I raised myself enough to see his eyes. 'Do you believe it, Nick?'

He said casually, 'Of course I don't believe it. It's a ridiculous idea, how could it possibly be true? It would fill with water, or the weight of the river would crush it. Anyway, someone would know, wouldn't they?'

'Obviously someone does know,' I said, 'or you would not have heard it.'

'You're much cleverer than Jack, you know. He never did deserve you, Alice. Not one inch of you.'

I struggled against him, but he held my head effortlessly against his chest. 'Careful, careful, we don't want another miscarriage, do we?'

Nick was so much stronger than I was. 'You're hurting me!' I said.

'No, Alice, I'm not hurting you. I can't hurt you. Only Jack could hurt you, I know that. He ate one plate of roast beef on a Friday and you were as wounded as though he'd stabbed you through the heart. I don't think there is anything I could do that would really hurt you. Because you don't love me.'

I lay still. 'But *you* love *me*, don't you?'

'Yes, Alice. I love you. You hurt me.' He said sadly, 'You've always hurt me. I'll love you until the end of time. Until the sun ceases to spin round the earth.' He stroked my belly.

I whispered, 'Who is *Deus*?'

'I knew you heard.'

'It was a completion sacrifice, wasn't it?'

He sighed. '*Deus* is the Latin word for God.'

'God? I heard *Deus, Ingeniator, Rex Mundi. Amen.*'

'*Deus* is also the French word for two. Deuce. The Devil. The second, the opposer. In southern France the Cathar heretics of the Langue d'Oc believe God did not make the world.'

'Who did?' Then I understood. The ingeniator.

'*Deus*, the Devil. Contriver, deviser, engineer, architect. Ingeniator. Rex Mundi, the Lord of the World.'

'The *Devil* made the world?'

'Look around you!'

I shivered. 'Do you believe this?'

'All Templars know this is true, Alice. What else makes sense? How can God, *En Soph*, who is perfect, create imperfection? Think, Alice. Pain. Suffering. Manure. Death. Bereavement. How can God illuminate the death of a child? How can Light create Darkness?'

I didn't know.

'You have to understand this, Alice.' Nick's ribs rose and fell gently as he spoke, my ear muffled against his chest heard the boom of his voice inside him. 'God is perfect. Endless. Boundless. The Aged of the Aged. Impossible to comprehend or describe in words. Light, pure Light, the Shekinah. Blinding Light, too bright to see. You don't know the Bible of course. Moses in, not *on*, the Mount could not see God except by means of the cloud, Exodus 24, verse 18, *and Moses went into the midst of the cloud*, which is translated *by means* of the cloud. The cloud was a garment.'

'Translated? How can you know this?'

'Believe me. Moses wove for God the garment he saw Him by. The luminous shroud Moses wore to endure the Light that streams from the Lord of Light.'

'You read this in Exodus?'

'It's true. It's the truth. God gave to Moses, *in* the Mount, the book of moral truths by which all mysteries are to be revealed.'

'But I thought the Jews wrote the Bible.'

'I'm talking of the Holy Kabbalah, the Word of God. Moses's stone tablets blinded all who looked upon them. He broke them, as you know, but even the shattered pieces were too brilliant to look on for more than a moment. Even the Sages of Tanna, the group of the holiest rabbis, could bear to glimpse only single letters which they assembled as *Sephers*, or ciphers, meaning Books. The Book of the Palace. Book of the Chariot. Book of Brilliance. Book of Splendour. For these slim texts the rabbis gave their eyes.'

He took a deep breath. I heard the rush of air in his lungs, then he spoke again.

'But the first man to fully decipher the Word was Rabbi Simon ben-Yohai, a man already blind, a follower of Christ, known as the Lamp of Israel for his powerful preaching. To the Romans this was rabble-rousing. They imprisoned him in a cave beneath the Temple in Jerusalem for twelve years. The Jewish rebellion that Jesus would not lead had failed. The Romans destroyed the Temple but not the caves. They looted the sacred Menorah, the seven-branched candlestick, and the Temple treasure, but they did not recognise the Word. Rabbi Elias smuggled the divine precepts past the guards

128

and his son Rabbi Eliezer wrote them as the *Zohar*, a system of books written in Midrash form – a sort of running commentary to accompany readings of Scripture. These rabbis believed that the scriptures – the Testaments of our Bible – are like a garden, that it was their duty as scholars to tend the garden. They believed the Bible had four levels of meaning: *Peshat*, the literal, simple meaning you understand when you hear it; *Remex*, the homiletic 'hint' for the educated comprehension of a priest; *Derash*, the meaning under the Law; and *Zod*, the secret interpretation which requires *peshers*, or keys, to decipher the hidden meaning. There are ten levels of this secret interpretation, the ten holiest Books, the *Sepherot*. The first *Sepher* is the simplest. For example, it tells us that when Jesus was "tempted by Satan" He was in fact having political discussions with Judas Iscariot, and when he "ascended to Heaven" He went to a monastery – we are even told which monastery, and why. Jesus Himself says, in Mark 4 verse 11, "For those outside, everything is in parables," but then he reassures his apostles, "To you is given the secret of the Kingdom of God." The second *Sepher* of the Kaballah continues the process at a deeper level. The tenth *Sepher* contains the most sacred, deepest, most profound meanings. These scrolls were never copied, are long lost beneath the desert. The wisdom of the *Sepherot* was transmitted only by word of mouth. Died as Jews died. Reborn with each child. Scattered as the Jews were scattered.'

'But this is not our Bible.'

'No. Kabbalah means "tradition" in Hebrew. The Word was oral tradition, from father to son, for more than a thousand years.'

'But?'

'A few years ago, in Barcelona, wealthy – *very* wealthy – Spanish Jews were threatened, and still are, by the advance of the Almohads, Evil Ones, religious fanatics, through southern Spain. Those Jews are so rich they can afford books. Beautiful books that take a scribe a year to write. Precious books encrusted with jewels. The man with the most books of all, naturally, is the richest of all: Rabbi Judah ben-Barzillai. The library of this collector is – was – huge. Over many years, scribes working among the library's airy colonnades distilled the traditions of the Kaballah from the memories of old men. The ten Books, the *Sepherot*, were illuminated, ornamented, jewelled by the finest jewellers. The scribes had no idea what they were writing, just coded numbers; and the keys to the codes were jealously guarded and kept separate from the books. But by now Seville, Granada, Cordoba have fallen to the Evil Ones, they're marching towards Toledo, it's probably only a matter of time before Barcelona is overrun. Imagine the fear! The crowds wild with fear. The library of Judah ben-Barzillai was ransacked by the mob, burnt, scattered, lost. Some books found their way into the hands of the Evil Ones. Others were taken north, turned up in Provence and the Langue d'Oc.'

I exclaimed, 'The Cathar heretics of the Langue d'Oc who believe God did not make the world!' I saw the connection. 'But you Templars persecute the Cathars, don't you?'

'We are the servants of the Pope. We cannot disobey. Disobedience is our only heresy. But some Templars do not believe in the Crucifixion, any more than the Cathars do. The Cathars of the Langue d'Oc claim, rightly – many of them are from Templar families – that their beliefs are closer to Christ and the first Christians than the beliefs of the Church of Rome are. One good man, or a few good men, can save us all. Like St Paul, like we Templars, the Cathars believe that we are made of body, soul, and spirit. The spirit remains in Heaven, the human soul is trapped in a mortal body.' Then I knew that what Robin Swinert had said was true. The Templars were tainted by contact with the Evil Ones. Perhaps some of his other accusations were also true.

'You have spoken with Evil Ones?'

'Alice, Arab traders have met ragged but immensely wealthy men from the east, from a land called Vedantia, who all believe matter has no existence independent of mental perception.' Nick tapped his chest. 'Soul and spirit can only be reunited through knowledge. Until then the soul is condemned to wander, to migrate to another mortal body when the first one dies. We seek knowledge. Faith is not enough. *We must have knowledge.*'

'That is a rejection of the Christian faith.'

'Perhaps. The Cathars reject Christianity because they believe Jesus was just a man, a very wise man, a very knowledgeable man, his soul very close to his spirit, very close to God because of that, but just a man. Jesus, of the royal line of David, belonged to a sect called the Essenes. The Essenes of the Qumran Monastery believed that souls were immortal, they descended from the pure air to be chained in bodies. Who can say, yet, that they were wrong? So Cathars believe in neither the Incarnation nor the Resurrection. Some Templars, especially those from the remote, mountainous region of the Langue d'Oc, the land of Yes, now also share that disbelief. But most Templars do believe in the Resurrection, I know. We believe in it as passionately as any other Christian. Passionately. Without the Resurrection, Christianity has no meaning.'

I struggled to understand. 'But surely God did make the world. The Bible says so.'

'No, Alice. No, no. The Bible says God made Heaven and Earth. That's true. The stars are perfect. The sun could not be bettered. The earth has rivers, seas, fresh air. It is perfectly constructed. Each river is perfect, each hill is perfect. It is the Garden of Eden. But, after Adam and Eve, there is this world full of evil. There is us.'

'*Us?*'

'Life, Alice. The mistake. Knowledge. Imperfection. The world.' He stroked my tummy gently. 'Accept it.'

I'm afraid. I don't want to know. The moon's disappeared long before it's due to set, I don't know why. The more I hear Nick speaking in the dark, the more I'm unsure of the life I had with Jack, of the world I live in. Are all my memories wrong? Do I miss so much? For all Nick's talk of spirits and faith, I can't get that picture of the poor girl out of my mind, her blood splashing across the stones, the men dipping their fingers in her throat. *Jack would have done the same.* Jack would have cut her, splashed her blood? Nick knows what I'm thinking, my unspoken question.

'Jack went to the Angel, didn't he?' His answer came out of the dark, deep, sounding so like Jack. Their father's voice. 'How little you knew about your husband, Alice. He liked the girls to kiss him and stroke him just the way . . . the way that you know so well, Alice.'

'Don't. Please don't.'

'Please? Shall I continue, then? Did you know Jack was baptised into the Order of African Architects by King Richard? The order was founded by the King in the year of our arrival in London. You haven't heard of it? Some call us the Master Builders. A mixture of masonry, Christianity, alchemy, chivalry. Jack didn't tell you this?'

I shook my head.

'I am telling you the truth, Alice.'

That was the trouble. I knew he was telling the truth and I was afraid of it. I didn't want to hear it. I covered my ears.

Nick said, 'I've read the Bible.'

'You can't! You're not a priest!'

'Ah, I knew you could hear me. The Templars have translated the Bible

130

into English, did you not know? No, of course you did not. It's our secret. One of many.'

I was appalled. English is not a sacred language. The Truth of God made ordinary, in the same language I ask for a pound of peas or a nice piece of tripe? I shook my head. Suppose such work were copied, available to anyone able to read? Who will believe the truth if they can understand it, if the mystery is stripped away? I remembered with longing the mumbling Latin in the parish church and not having to think, only believe.

'Listen to me, Alice. It is important that we understand the Bible. *Our* Bible. The Bible is for the common people, not just priests and theologians. We can make up our own minds. In the Bible every noun is a symbol, every verb describes interplay, there is new knowledge in every verse. The Kaballah, along with its most profound Books, the ten *Sepherot*, helps us understand our Bible. The Kabbalah is the Word, the key to everything that is hidden by the clouds of the mind of Man.'

I said, 'Surely the Bible should remain hidden. It was never meant for ordinary people.' The thought of having the holy words of Our Lord Jesus Christ read to me in English frightened me. Who knows what chaos will happen if butchers, bakers, louts and wives like myself carry the Bible in our hands to bolster whatever misguided view we fall to, and believe we hear authorised in the Bible?

'Only through knowledge can we find our way back to God,' Nick said simply. 'I have learnt this, Alice: we are surrounded by marvels. Are *we* not marvellous? In the sky, the skin of Heaven, we see stars and planets' – I couldn't, the sky was solid black cloud, no sign showing of the dawn – 'and we see comets and constellations whose movements and patterns we feel, but cannot prove, contain strange conjunctions and profound mysteries that influence our lives. How is it possible that the planet Mars stops its progress with the other planets across the sky and alone reverses its course? How can that be? What is He trying to show us? We are sleepwalkers in this vile, filthy world made by the Lord of the World, we know almost nothing. So it is with the skin, made by God, which covers the body of the Son of Man, the stars and planets of the skin. Why am I as I am? What does it mean?'

'Perhaps it doesn't mean anything.'

'There is a reason for everything, Alice! Why is the moon exactly the same size as the sun? The Evil Ones have proved that it is, they have observed eclipses, the fit is perfect! Why are there only seven planets to be seen spinning round the earth, not including our sun and moon, when the Kaballah tells us there are nine – and ten, as everyone knows, is the sacred number of God? Why is Man born with two hands, their design reversed, so that each thumb points to the other? It cannot be explained rationally. Why do we live and die? The form of the body depicts a Tetragrammaton, the sacred name of God. Why? What are we to learn from it? How do we improve ourselves, what choices can we make? The Muslim sect of Karmathi asserts that the name of Allah, not God, is to be found in the human body – standing an *Alif*, kneeling a *Lam*, and so on. Very well. *What does it all mean?*'

Nick's anguish was genuine. His voice groaned in his chest. He really wanted to know these answers. For the first time I felt, a little, that I could love him. That I could love such a questing man, a man for whom such questions mattered. Even I mattered to him. Even I who was not really capable of loving him deeply in return. Not as deeply as, perhaps, he deserved.

Jack had never asked these questions. Jack had simply loved me.

'Look at me, Nick,' I said. I lifted my head but he could not see me and I could not see him, it was so dark. I fumbled for the candlestick but touched the plaster Jesus instead, felt Him wobble, grabbed Him, murmured an *Ave* in

Latin for my disrespect. The window was grey, but not with dawn. I went to it, stared at the rippled glass. Then I threw the window wide. The world was soft and grey. Snowflakes as great as feathers whirled gently past me on to the rooftops around me and the bridge. Tom Bedell was a grey lump keeping the watch, his black dogs scampering silently round him with grey backs and heads, and nothing else moved but the grey falling snow and the sliding black river.

'Have you seen it, Nick?' But he was asleep.

The draught was cold down the right side of my face and my ear. I closed the window, dawn could not be long away. I lit the candle, stopped as I caught sight of my face in the little tin mirror. I'd picked it up for a penny in Cheapside and it always makes me look like a goblin. This morning my face was red down one side, flaked with white like snow.

I touched my cheek with my fingertip. My cheek felt slippery.

My fingertip came away red, dark red. I rubbed it with my thumb and the slipperiness turned sticky. Blood.

I reached up to my face where I had lain against Nick, pulled away a white flake. Not snow. Skin.

Nick's skin. Pieces of Nick's skin, soft and fine, some still with the hairs of his chest clinging to them, stuck to his blood on my face.

I held the candle above my husband's sleeping form on the bed. He lay on his back. On Nick's chest the pattern of my face was printed in shiny red flesh, as though the top layer of his skin which had peeled away was no more substantial or permanent than a thin page of paper.

'She *did* die, didn't she, Nick?' I whispered.

I was more than afraid. I was terrified. I was so terrified that I was numb with shock, I was actually calm. I knew what I had to do.

I had to get away.

Yet I admired Nick, and I think I loved him a little, just a little. He was strong. But he was dangerous. He was very dangerous. If I stayed with him, I would believe in him. I would believe in him because he believed in himself and I was married to him. My personality was being overwhelmed. But there was more than that. It was simply the practical consideration that Nick was ill. I could not look after him. I could not be ill, I dare not. My baby, Jack's baby, would be born within the next month or less, and the thought of Nick's skin, the loose, sliding feel of it under my finger when I touched him as he lay there asleep, simply the feel of the skin slipping off him under the gentle caress of my fingertip was more than a little disgusting. By candlelight I stared at the shiny pink line I had drawn across his flesh and the loose luminous curl of his skin hanging from my finger. I was sorry for him, but I had to think of my baby.

I was the guilty one. I'd married Nick for the worst of reasons, all of them the worst reasons, and now I was backing out.

It grew light. Nick woke. He sat up beside me. He looked at me, he said nothing. He put on his clothes, carefully. Carefully. He knew he was ill with whatever illness, skin disease, plague, whatever it was. Perhaps the symptom was worse than the illness; but there was a distinct smell of rotting meat. And then he kissed my lips.

He went out and I heard his footsteps thud downstairs. Did he know what I was thinking? Could he read my secret thoughts? The door slammed. The snow had stopped, everything outside was soundless. I watched from the upstairs window. Nick crossed below me to the tavern counter, drank a pint of ale, bought eel chopped in a little wooden bowl, ate it with quick stabs of his knife. He looked round him with his feet deep in the snow, then cut a quarter of bread from the baker's loaf and swallowed it as he walked from sight between the long line of houses.

132

I thought the houses of London Bridge looked like cakes, as though the snow was sugar. Their smoke rose in straight lines into the still air, except over the northern end of the bridge where the houses were not yet complete. I could no longer see Nick.

I threw off the cover, clambered awkwardly out of bed. 'Rosie!'

Rosie came downstairs and stared at me silently, difficult girl.

I said breathlessly, 'I'm running away, Rosie!'

I did not know what her reaction would be. She had never liked Nick, never trusted him. But she had a roof over her head.

Such a smile broke over her pretty little face that I kissed her snub nose, hugged her. Then an anxious look came into her round blue eyes. 'You'll let me come with you, won't you, mistress?'

'Let you? I need you! I need your help, Rosie. We must pack everything we possibly can. We'll need a boy with a cart.' Rosie knew a boy in Thames Street, she would send for him. 'Warm clothes, Rosie. I still have fourteen shillings of my own. We'll buy hot pies in the Borough. If we hurry we can sleep tonight at the Pope's Head at Vaudey.' I clapped my hands. 'Hurry!'

She ran to the stairs, then hesitated. 'Where will we go tomorrow, mistress?'

I made a vague gesture. I didn't care about tomorrow, I just wanted to get away from here. Through the window I saw the blood-spattered stones of the pier washed clean by the tide as though it had never happened. 'I don't know. Away. Anywhere. Abbot's Littlebourne.'

'That's the first place he'll look, mistress. He won't give up. And you in your condition.' She opened the door, letting in a freezing draught. 'And it's snowing.'

She was right. The snow was starting again, driven in lazy swirls by a freaky, uncomfortable wind, and the sky was the colour of lead. 'There's a fire in Southwark,' Rosie added. 'Another bakehouse I suppose.' She looked worried. 'Suppose we get lost? Suppose you start to have your baby?'

Yes, yes, she was right, but I said, 'Did you hear the voices last night, Rosie?'

'I didn't hear nothing last night,' Rosie said. 'I pulled my blanket over my head, and my bolster over my blanket, and I put my fingers in my ears.'

'My husband's ill,' I said.

'He's unhappy, mistress. He's *angry*. But I was wrong, he does love you, in his way. Have you seen the pain in his eyes? The terrible pain?'

We were talking about Nick again, losing our momentum. In a few minutes I would decide to stay another day, let the weather improve, choose a better time, make preparations. I smacked Rosie's backside, chivvied her to the stairs. 'Quick, Rosie! Hurry! Winter days are short!'

Too short. Deciding to leave my Flanders chairs was agony. What would I do without a man to look after me? I was mad. I might die in the snow. But I knew I was doing the right thing.

Rosie wrapped up the precious woollen blankets in another blanket and staggered past me. I realised I had been standing at the window, staring at the snow, lost in a daydream.

'He's going to come after us,' Rosie whispered. 'He's going to come after you, and he's going to catch you, and he's going to bring you back. You know that, mistress.' She looked over her shoulder as she carried the blankets to the door.

'I should never have married him,' I said.

Hurriedly Rosie warmed a hot broth for dinner to heat us on our way, wrapped oatcakes in a cloth. To save time I sent her to fetch the urchin with the cart, packed up the rest of my clothes in a canvas. The chest was too heavy for me to drag downstairs. I clasped my hands over my belly and sat for a while

133

to settle my breathing, then glimpsed a cart approaching through the whirling snow outside. When I went down, the wind almost pulled the door from my hand. The boy was as miserable and thin as his donkey, clutched his rags round him. I gave him the broth I could not stomach and a torn blanket to hang over his shoulders. 'You aren't going out in this, mistress?'

The cart was hardly more than a barrow and the donkey was half dead. I told him, 'I'll give you a shilling for both. You pick them up at the Pope's Head at Vaudey tomorrow.' I knew the Pope's Head rented horses. 'Hop off home, quick! Get to a warm fire.'

'Two shillings,' the boy said, mopping the last of his broth. 'I know women like you.'

'Do you?'

'Running for your lives.'

'Eighteen pence.'

He judged my cloak consideringly. 'Done.'

Rosie clipped his ear. 'And you'll help load it.' But still, it took longer than we had thought, then the boy ran away clutching his money happily. I said goodbye to my house, my home. The wind wailed through the arches beneath us. Snow blew off the roofs, adding to the snow already falling. As I came out, I saw the figure of a boy toiling through the snow towards us, his head bent against the wind, and I thought it was our urchin come back again. I swore at him angrily, then saw it was the cocksure lad from the Angel. But I hardly recognised him, black with soot down one side, limping. He called through the snow, 'Mistress Alice on London Bridge?'

'That's me.' I pulled him into the doorway. He flinched, his hand was soft with blisters. His clothes stank of fire. The lad was exhausted.

'Fire, mistress. A terrible fire at the Angel.' I vaguely remembered smoke blowing over Southwark. 'I'm Dickie Swinert. The Angel's gone. Mistress Tarmantelle's head's burnt to a cinder. Fire started first thing this morning, no one knows how, all asleep, we were.' He coughed. 'Richard Fairless needs to talk to you.'

'Fairless?' I had no love for the shifty carpenter. 'Let him come and talk to me then. Another day. I'm busy.'

The lad coughed, sighed. 'He can't come. He's burnt. He's dying, mistress. Dying. For God's love, mistress. He's asking for you over and over and we can't stand it, he's crisped like a pork chop, he won't last the day. Put us out of our misery, for God's love.'

A dying man's wish. Even if it was a trap, I had no choice. I pulled the door shut against the wind, my cloak flapped open, and the lad looked at my belly with interest. 'Any minute, is it?' Now his job was done he sat cockily on the cart while Rosie led the donkey and I walked beside it. I held on to the shaft as the wind blew, my feet slipping on the ice. We came to the end of the bridge, clear of houses, and felt the full force of the gale. I pulled Rosie's shoulder. 'You stay in there, Rosie.' I pointed at the Bear Tavern. 'There's a fire, and a window where you can watch the donkey.' She nodded, too blown by the wind to resist. I beckoned the lad. He slipped off the cart, pulled down his cap against the snow. I thought he seemed honest enough. He walked ahead of me into the Liberty, and I followed him.

I recognised where the Angel had been by its long narrow yard, clear of debris. Everything else was gone. A skeleton of blackened timbers smoked in the snow, a few flames flickered, lumps of burning thatch like Christmas bonfires. The room above the arch was gone except for one roof beam blazing brightly in the wind that roared. We picked our way forward between bodies like joints of cooked meat, still too hot for the snow to settle on them, gleaming and dripping. Fire and flesh, the only patches of colour in the snow and darkness. Somebody kicked the dogs away, someone screamed, another smoking body was poked with poles from the ruins, half a dozen women ran forward, then all turned back except one.

'Poor bitches.' The lad pulled me through a doorway into a hut. The children were pushed back in the corner and the body of a man lay across a bale of straw. His legs were gone below the knee, the charred thigh stumps stuck forward, black bones. I could not recognise his face. I thought he was dead, but then his eyes moved. The dying man gripped my arm with sudden force, pulled me down.

'It's her, Richard,' the lad said gently, then something in him broke and he cuffed the shivering children, he was probably their eldest brother. The little ones argued back at him and a family row started, then a woman stormed in and smacked about her with her hands as big as hams. 'Priest's coming!' she said angrily.

The man who pulled me down tried to speak but his lips were burnt off, I could not make sense of him. Then he spoke between his teeth with Richard Fairless's high, thin voice, and I recognised him by the grooves worn in his teeth by carpenter's nails.

'I'm a dead man.' He pulled my face close to his stinking breath, it stank of smoke. 'I'm a dead man. Nick killed me.' His tongue worked between his teeth, trying to utter the sounds.

I whispered, 'Do you mean Nick started the fire?'

His claw tightened on my wrist, dragged me closer. He whispered in my ear. 'Nick killed Master Jack.'

'You're lying.'

His eyes glared at me unblinkingly, without eyelids.

I licked my lips. I whispered, 'Nick did this to you?'

'Listen, you, wife. Nick met Master Jack on the bridge. Argued. Nick thrust his knife into Master Jack's heart.' I could barely make sense of the slurred words.

I covered my mouth. I felt my heart beating, I felt the weight in my belly. 'Are you telling the truth?'

'I am dying.'

I had to know: 'Did Nick push Jack's body in the river?'

Fairless gave a low, formless moan, I think it was of unutterable agony. He stared so stiffly I thought he was dead, then his tongue moved again. 'No, wife, Master Jack, he don't go in the river. Knife wound, it's murder. If he's pulled out, who does the finger point to?'

I swallowed. 'The man who benefits most by Jack's death.'

Fairless cried, 'Sweet Jesus make my pain stop!'

'But Nick said he was on his knees all night in St Magnus Martyr. The chaplain said so.'

'They'll say anything.'

'All of you swore you never saw Nick. You swore.'

'Nick was here at the Angel with us. Arrived late. Bloody dust on his knees.'

'Swear it, your dying oath.'

'I swear this.'

'How do you know it was Master Jack's blood?'

'Master Jack? Only a matter of time before he got it, that one. All us knew it. That fool.'

'And the dust on Nick's knees?'

'From where he buried Master Jack.'

I shuddered. 'Where?'

Fairless twisted me with that horrid claw. 'Revenge. I've got my cock up

135

Nick's arse now, haven't I? Revenge, he's killed me!' Fairless gave a terrible cry. 'Dick Darenth! Robbie Sharp! Dan Shadwell! God help me!' He lifted himself up, the flesh falling off him. He stopped. Fell back like a piece of wood.

The priest, a fat novice from St Mary Overie, came in.

'You're too late,' I said.

He descended awkwardly on his knees. 'I shall pray for his soul.'

'You're too late,' I repeated. 'He is already in Hell.'

The hut creaked as the wind blew it. I listened to the low Latin incantations then staggered outside, leant back against the wall. Strangely enough, I still felt calm. I knew Jack was dead. He had not slipped in the river and been swept away and drowned God knows where, or fallen in with pirates or lost his memory or been taken up by some family in France. He would never come back. My dear husband was dead, murdered by my husband, and buried somewhere on London Bridge.

I held my hands over my tummy, trying to feel warm and strong. A piece of thatch roof whirled past me on the icy wind, blazing, burst into a shower of sparks against a wall, and the sparks blew away so brightly that I realised how dark it was. Someone ran forward with a bucket of snow, doused the embers. No one else was out. The cold bodies were crescents of windblown snow, like pieces of the moon thrown down along the bare, windy street.

My cloak flapped, slapping my legs. I made myself walk forward. I recognised Mistress Tarmantelle's headless body by her plump snowy legs, stepped across her with no more feeling than stepping over the carcass of a pig on a butcher's floor, and walked back to St Thomas's Wall.

I had to think what to do. I couldn't run away now. The storm made it impossible, but what I mean is, I couldn't run away from what I knew. I had made excuses for myself and for Nick but I couldn't now. *Nick killed Master Jack. Met Master Jack on the bridge. Argued. Nick thrust his knife into Jack's heart. Nick killed Master Jack.*

I had sent Jack out on the bridge that night. I had let Jack go.

Nick would hang. But the story of my rape would come out, I would be blamed, everything I had done that seemed so right at the time would seem so wrong. And Nick would be tortured beneath the bishop's palace until he confessed, for the salvation of his soul, and then he would hang.

'I hate you, Nick,' I whispered as I walked. 'I hate you. I hate you.'

I came into the Borough High Street, into the full force of the wind by the bridge. My cloak bannered, I really thought I would be pulled over, then I came into the shelter of the Bear at Bridge Foot. The little cart was in a corner of the yard, Rosie shivering miserably beside it. She had been afraid it would be stolen.

'We can't go anywhere in this.' I beckoned her. 'We'll walk the cart as far as the Tabard Inn.' Rosie nodded, she knew the place opposite St Margaret's Church. We came out of the yard, bent our heads against the wind. 'My Jack is dead, Rosie. Fairless knew for certain. They lied. Every single one of them lied for Nick.'

But Rosie said, 'Jack's still alive in there, mistress.' She patted my tummy, her little cold face smiled. My baby, Jack's baby. Another problem, even the best things happen at the worst time. I couldn't think any more now. Whatever I did would be whatever was best for my baby.

I said wretchedly, 'I'll decide what to do tomorrow.'

Nick spoke behind us. 'What you'll decide to do is nothing.'

Rosie screamed, we both screamed like little girls, and I tried to run, which was ridiculous. Nick grabbed my elbow, swung me against the parapet of the bridge, which Jack had built rather low, there had been accidents already, he'd intended to have it raised when there was time, but for a moment my feet came off the ground and I really thought I would go over. Each arch stuck out a tongue of brown foam flooding into the dark. The snow-covered houses above stretched out, peaceful and luminously pale.

Nick snatched me back, I realised how terribly hard the stone was and fell to the ground. I felt my baby touch my ribs, something inside me gave way. 'Oh. Oh,' I said. I thought my knee was broken. Nick dragged my arm but I struggled and tried to scratch him. He laughed and pulled Rosie round, I saw he held her hair. He jerked her and she shrieked, writhing.

'Stop,' I said. 'Stop, Nick.'

He nodded. 'Pax?'

How I hated him. *Pax*, Jack's word. Rosie shrieked again. I nodded.

He let go of her hair, gripped her arm. 'If you try anything, Alice,' he said, 'I shall break her arm and it will be your fault.'

I nodded.

'Run, miss,' Rosie sobbed.

Nick called towards the Stone Gate. 'Tom Bedell! Come here!'

A dog came from the doorway, then Tom Bedell's tousled face appeared beneath the builders' scaffolding. I ran towards him, felt warm water pour down my legs. 'Tom! For God's pity, help us!'

There was a low wrenching sound and Rosie howled. I stopped as though struck. Her arm hung in two different directions from Nick's hand, like a broken straw. I saw the bruises starting already and her face was frozen in pain.

'Tom,' Nick called. 'Come over here, man, would you.'

'Yes, master.' Tom put on his cap, wrapped himself in a blanket and waddled over.

'Bring our cart, would you, Tom, right now,' Nick said. 'My lady's maid has foolishly broken her arm. Wife,' he called to me. 'You'll want to help your silly girl, won't you?'

I went to Rosie, threw one side of my cloak round her. Rosie looked at her arm. 'He's broke it,' she sobbed. 'He's broke my arm, mistress.'

Nick took my elbow smoothly. 'That's better.' He walked us back to my house which I had thought I would never see again. Tom followed with the donkey and cart. Nick opened the door and pushed us inside, into total darkness. I heard him paying Tom off, then I heard him toss the goods wrapped in blankets and canvas through the door, the slap of his hand on the donkey's rump, the clop of the donkey trotting away and the fading clatter of the cart. The donkey would know its way home, the urchin would not have to go out to Vaudey, and he was eighteen pence richer.

What was Nick going to do?

Nick came inside. He closed the door. He lit a candle and held it up to our faces, then lit the hearth.

Rosie's teeth chattered with fear and pain. I said, 'You broke her arm, Nick.'

He tossed a stick from the fire. 'Splint it.'

Rosie whimpered during my rough work. I made a sling for her arm and she began to cry with the agony. I stroked her forehead soothingly.

'Get rid of her,' Nick said. 'Send her upstairs.'

I kissed Rosie's forehead. 'You go to your room now, Rosie. I'll be all right.' Rosie went towards the stair.

Nick watched me. Then his eyes narrowed. He took two rapid strides towards me, so fast and so strong that I instinctively pulled away from him. He clenched his fist on my cloak, staring into my eyes.

'You hate me, Alice.' His gaze dropped down my front to the floor, the wet patch spreading between my boots.

137

From the step, Rosie gasped, 'Your waters is broke, mistress!'

Nick opened my cloak. He pressed the palm of his hand to my belly. He smiled. 'You still owe me a shilling, Alice. Very well. A blood shilling.'

'You like blood, don't you, Nick?'

'In the Holy Land I have pressed my mouth to the wounds of the crucified. I have drunk the blood that flowed from their wounds, from the whiplashes, from the nails hammered through their ankles and wrists. The Templars have calculated the exact number of lashes Christ suffered, on His back and on His chest, until He was one great open wound. I have seen His bloody footsteps on the Via Dolorosa and seen how His eyes and His beard ran with blood, His jaw distended, His mouth open, His tongue swollen with blood. His stomach was pulled in to His spine as if He had no more intestines. I know for a fact He was tied so tightly to the Cross that the blood spurted from His fingernails.'

'You disgust me and I hate you.'

He said sadly, 'Blood is atonement, Alice. The blood sacrifice is atonement. It is the gift of life between humans and God. Leviticus tells us that only if this penalty is paid can sinful man hope to be forgiven and come again into God's presence. Life is strength. Strength is Gevurah.'

'Gevurah.'

'The fifth *Sepher* of the Word. Gevurah, the fifth Book, the Book of Strength, the raging inferno of the Lord.'

I sat weakly. He reached in his belt, flicked a shilling to Rosie. 'Fetch a midwife.'

Rosie looked tearfully at me. I nodded.

Nick stopped her with the back of his hand. 'Don't be long. I believe the pangs of birth are very painful.' He lit a lantern, closed the horn window, gave her the handle. 'Don't let your mistress suffer. Don't be one minute late in your return.'

He opened the door and Rosie hurried into the storm. Nick slammed the door, then turned back to me gently. 'Let's go upstairs to your pretty room. I know you'll be more comfortable there. We have a while to wait.' He put his arm round my shoulder, guided me to the stair.

I burst out, 'I know you killed Jack!'

'I know you know, Alice. I should have taken more care with Master Carpenter Fairless.' He carried the candle after me up the stair, lit the fire. I coughed, it makes so much smoke, but on such a windy night – it blew against my house like a great mouth, and even between breaths the river shook us from below – the smoke drifted away through the chinks and gaps in the wooden walls, visibly swirling in the draughts. Nick pulled up my favourite chair, too big to pass through the door and assembled, like the table, inside the room by the carpenter. Nick dropped a rug carelessly over my lap. We watched the fire. While he watched I felt the first cramp build slowly inside me. I tried to give no sign of it. My back arched in spite of myself. I gave a low cry. He looked at me, nodding, then returned his attention to the fire.

The wind roared, the door slammed below. Footsteps on the stairs, then Rosie, half dead from cold and pain, almost fell into the room. 'There's no one! No midwife will come out on such a night.'

Nick said casually. 'Get out. Stay in your room until I call for you.'

'But . . .' Rosie looked at me frantically.

I said, 'Do as your master says, Rosie.'

She bobbed, cradling her arm, and I heard her run up to the attic, crying. Nick stared at the fire.

I felt my back arch. My teeth pressed together. I saw my knuckles drain white on the arms of my chair. The worst of the tension passed, but I kept the anger in me, stared at Nick with the same intensity he stared at the fire.

'Nick, damn you. You told Mistress Cristina. You told her what you did in the Holy Land before she died, didn't you?'

'Yes, I did tell her.'

'Tell me.'

Nick came to me, touched his hand to my forehead, felt the sweat there. 'Poor Alice, you need someone, don't you? You know I love you.' It is the oddest feeling being told this at such a moment by such a man. It was as if Nick was not harsh or cruel, as if he was not Jack's murderer. He was the boy I grew up with whom I never loved, that's all. The miller's daughter's son.

'Tell me what happened, Nick. Tell me what happened in Outremer, the Holy Land.' The tension left my muscles. I breathed out through my mouth. I was very thirsty but I was afraid to ask for water, and he didn't think of it. He sat on a stool, looked earnestly at me. Jack's eyes, dazzled, sincere, yearning. But something more there, more than innocence, deeper than truth. Something wise.

My sweat made me shiver. I was completely vulnerable. Completely in his power.

'I can make you love me, Alice,' Nick whispered. 'When you know what happened to me, you'll understand. You will love me.'

'Tell me as though I am you,' I said. I groaned, tensing. 'I do want to understand. I want to understand the monster you are.'

Nick said, 'I'm not the monster I am the victim.' He took a deep breath, and the storm rattled the house.

Tell me as though I am you.

'Killing Jack . . .'

Nick's tale

Christmas Day, 1200

Killing Jack . . . I first thought of killing Jack long, long ago, in Canterbury, Alice. Thought it somewhere inside my innocent heart, boyish heart, young man's heart, honest heart, foolish heart, must have done. I know and you know (we are both human beings, different only in sex) that it feels as if each of us is born with two brains though only one speaks, and the other whispers but we hear nothing except in our dreams, those hidden night thoughts and impulses that form our actions as powerfully as the consciousness that we think we are. We are more than we know. Somewhere inside me, I thought of killing Jack. I should have.

Perhaps much earlier, much younger, I should have drowned my effortless, beautiful brother that first day you came between us, us chasing you across the fields, not tried to drown *you*. But I was no jealous that it was Jack who got you. The wine the truth is that I loved Jack. Jack who did everything first. Jack who first wiped the mud from your face and was first to say, 'But you're lovely.' I should have drowned him and had you. But I didn't. Later I should have killed him when he made peace with you. *Pax.* Because from then on, after you arrived, I had no chance with Jack.

But I could have had just you and me.

Kissing Alice. Not Jack kissing you. Me.

Loving Alice. Not *Jack* loving you beneath the arch of our father's bridge. No. Me. In my dreams, my night thoughts, it's *me*.

I should have killed him long ago.

It was you who drove me into the arms of God, Alice. Look at you that day, there with me in Jack's house in Canterbury.

I love you.

There in that room in the shadow of Canterbury Cathedral, there's me sitting still as death on the window seat, you pacing up and down. All I see is Alice. Beautiful Alice. Perfect Alice. Even your imperfections are beautiful, the scar between your eyes is perfect, even the way you play the innocent, *I* can't tell if you're lying or not, it's perfect. I think you want to touch my body but I can't be sure. You claim you don't want to obsess me or torment me but you *do*, and I think you want to. Your smile – you keep smiling at me, laughing at me – your smile is lovely, perfect, utterly cruel. Your eyes are loving, yet completely cold. And the warmth of your body fills the room but I dare not touch you.

If Jack had returned home then, perhaps I would have killed him. I was in such agony.

Then killed you.

Killed myself.

But you see, Alice, I didn't think any of these things. Not consciously. I was young, wholly ignorant of myself. I hadn't learnt to live, I knew nothing of life. I thought everything was possible except being with you. I thought it was possible to forget you, to submerge myself in another life, a dedicated life. To become another person. To live without you. Like a priest, I would grow balls of stone. I would never think of you again. *The world forgetting, by the world forgot.*

141

Riding away from Canterbury that night I *know* I'll never see you again, never think of you again, and I know I am doing everything that is right and true and honourable. This is my life from now on. I ride to London, I sell my horse, I sell everything but the clothes I stand up in, and I beg admittance at the Gate of the Temple. A bearded man in white orders me brought into the yard, asks me quietly what is my wish of the Order of Poor Fellow-Soldiers of Christ and the Temple of Solomon.

I throw every penny on the stones at the feet of the holy warrior. 'To be the poorest of the poor, sire!'

'And if it is cold, pilgrim?'

'To freeze, sire.'

'And if hot, pilgrim?'

'To burn, sire.'

'What do you most need, pilgrim?'

'God's love, sire, and to fight for Jesus Christ Our Lord.'

'And what do you most crave, pilgrim?'

'Sire, I crave the Day of Resurrection of Our Lord and the road to Heaven.'

'Pilgrim, pilgrim, for those who believe in the Resurrection the way is pain, suffering, humility, sacrifice.'

I cry out on my knees, 'Yes, lord, give it to me!'

He takes my clean-shaven chin in his hand, he looks at me steadily. 'The path is harder and longer than you think. Strike me!' He holds out his arms as though defenceless. 'Strike, pilgrim.'

I strike at him, an untutored blow, but with all my great strength. He catches my fist gently, easily. I cannot pull away.

'You are left-handed, pilgrim?'

'Always, sire.'

'We always have a use for left-handed men.' Thoughtful. 'Are you free-born? Are you free of debt? Are you free of disease? Are you ready to die?' When I nod, nod, nod, nod, he turns his head towards a building like a barn, and I realise the silver and gold I threw down is gone. 'There, pilgrim. Ask of the draper.'

In the barn, scratchy brown clothes like hair are pulled over my head, I'm hurried barefoot past workshops, hammers ringing on anvils, to the white Templar church. Nothing is said. I'm pushed on my knees with my face against the stone floor – the first stone floor I've seen in a church. The door booms closed. When I dare look round me I see two or three others like me, crouched as I am. Darkness falls, none of us moves or speaks, no one comes. I whisper, 'Is there food?'

No one answers. One of the brown shadows moves slightly. 'Only prayer.'

My knees crack with the pain of kneeling. 'Who are you?'

'Peter. Sssh. It's a beating if you're heard.'

'I'm not afraid of a beating. I want to be hurt. I want to feel pain until I'm close to God.'

'They beat you until the blood runs down your back, pilgrim. And you'll feel close enough to God after three days without food or water.' Peter turns his head a little, a strapping, evenly proportioned lad, and I make out his split, dry lips.

'How long have you been in here?' I whisper.

'A day and two nights.'

Three days and three nights without food or water, kneeling in prayer!

I pray. I'm strong enough. I can suffer and prevail.

Our whispers utter the Templar prayer. *Non nobis Domine*. Our prayers fill the Templar church like the hiss of rain. *Non nobis, non nobis Domine*. One

142

of the young men faints, kneeling immobile, wakes and prays again. Later I hear him weeping. Dawn lights the stained windows like rainbows above us. The man who had wept crawls from the church, and I know I'll not see him again.

'Strength,' Peter whispers. By daylight I see his lips cracked and blistered. 'Pain, suffering, humility, sacrifice, *strength*.' He stares up at the figure of Jesus crucified above the altar. Sunlight swings across Him and we see His tears shining in His eyes. Peter whispers, 'Water.'

He crawls towards Jesus, falls exhausted at His feet. Peter's body is emaciated, his tongue grotesquely swollen by thirst. Night falls. I crawl forward, knees cracking. Together we lick the moisture that beads the cold stones. We pray to the gigantic Christ in the shadows above us, the holy blood dripping from His wounds. We touch His feet with our mouths, and He sustains us.

I realise something deeply important about which I never felt the slightest curiosity before. I whisper, 'Why is a Templar church round?'

'Because a circle has no end and no beginning,' Peter whispers in a voice as dry as sand. 'Every point of a circle is its end, equally every point is its beginning. A circle by its nature is the Alpha and Omega. Our Lord teaches us, "I am the Alpha and the Omega, the Beginning and the End." Our Lord Jesus Christ is to be found at every point of this building. However small. However large.'

We kneel praying, our heads between our wrists. Peter falls on his side. He rolls over, his eyes stare, his tongue moves helplessly between his lips. He's been here so much longer than I have. His mouth opens and I find spit to give him, I dribble my spittle into his mouth, he drinks me, and his eyes begin to blink, he puts his arms weakly round my neck. I have never felt so close and so dear to anyone in my whole life. Not you. Not anyone. My comrade. My brother.

Later Peter's time ends. I hear him carried away, he cannot walk. For me an eternity of thirst begins, I know I'm forgotten, day after day passes and night after night, but He sustains me, and the brothers come to me, and I am lifted between them. I feel their warmth, their woollen robes, their beards against my body as they carry me forward from the church to a great hall set with tables. The heavy hunting dogs called talbots prowl for bones in the rushes, sniff me hungrily, leave me alone. In a plain silver dish is plain bread. In a plain silver goblet is spring water.

I drink it down, it is refilled.

I drink again. It's refilled to the brim.

I eat. I drink. I sleep.

I awake on a hard bed between red muslin curtains, poke my head out and see a huge dormitory of at least another hundred hard beds, all neatly curtained off from each other. Another head pokes out. It is Peter. He smiles. 'You passed your first test, pilgrim.'

We're taken down, drink spring water, eat white bread.

Brother Peter is the fourth or fifth son of a wealthy lord. Both of us scratch at our unmerciful brown smocks, woven of horsehair, and we are sent into the yard where a hundred other brown, unmerciful smocks are moving in unison, perfectly together, the most amazing sight, more like a dance than fighting. Everyone knows knights fight one another, they do not fight together. But the Templars fight as one. These young trainees step forward with wooden swords and perform identical movements, left foot forward together, parry together, thrust together, like a single organism. There is no noise, no shouts, no insults and no abuse, no swearing. We join the line, we become part of the movement.

143

And suddenly I realise that *this* is what makes the Templars such a formidable fighting force. We fight as one. We are brother pilgrims ascending through difficulties and tests closer to God. Each of us is a part of an organism. A team. We will never be alone.

In fact we are never allowed to be alone. Even in the latrines we squat on the poles in rows together, a hundred at a time, we void our bowels together at the same clap of the hands and at no other moment except at the special dispensation of the sergeant, or the *magister*, or the *domine*, who rule our lives according to the sacred Rule of St Bernard down to the smallest, most private detail.

We run and fight and worship until we are exhausted, every day.

We are shown the horses, fierce black steeds that kick and bite everyone who does not ride them. They are trained to savagery and only their rider is their master. The riders mount in unison, spur together, wheel and turn together in fierce obedience, in perfect formation. Each line is straight, each curve is smooth. Obedience. Worship. Always hungry.

We circle, canter, gallop, drag the reins to halt in front of the sergeant. A perfect line. Dust and steam from the horses rises into the air of the Temple.

One man is not good enough. We know we will never see him again.

'Disobedience,' the sergeant says, 'that's the only Templar heresy.'

But obedience is hard, our numbers dwindle. Most men cannot endure Templar discipline and self-effacement, miss the grandiosity and show of fighting for their houses, families, lands, King, glory. We celibate comrades train only to fight for the Order, for the Pope who is our father, whose wish is our command. Our submission is to victory, to God, to worship. Without the Templars, Jerusalem will fall to the Evil Ones, and our God who overcame Baal will be shown to be less than the god of the Evil Ones. We warrior pilgrims have no reason for our existence other than to retain the holy ground of the Temple of Solomon in Christian hands by Christian force of arms, or else endure eternal shame.

Never have I felt so close to God. So sure and certain of God. All I have to do is submit everything I am, cease to exist as a man, become a Templar, a fighting machine for God's glory and His victory.

The trumpet rouses us before dawn, we fight and drill and train all day, in groups of three now, the perfect trinity of comradeship, with steel swords, razor-edged, almost as tall as ourselves. We fight on horseback laden with armour twice our own weight, carrying lances eighteen feet long. Few of us remain now, injuries are common, dreadful, unavoidable. After supper even Peter, who is as strong and quick as I am, and of the same build and stamina, drops into his bed without a single conscious thought.

But Peter, like me, is tormented by nightmares.

This is when you come to me, Alice. You come to me fully alive with all the vivid reality of a young man's imagination, *here*, you *are* real, perfect, seductive, dressed only in muslin, and I am helpless. Helpless. You are not only attainable, you are as lustful as I am. I resist you valiantly and awaken dripping. But it was only a dream. But then I see, by the light of the candles of virtue that burn all night in the dormitory, my cock standing up like a flagpole. How I hate myself. I'm demeaned. I think of you in no other way but this, the merely bodily. What happens is . . . *sinful*. No illusions, no clothes, there's only the essence of you. Temptation irresistible, shame unbearable. The chaplain listens to my confession, treats me with contempt, punishes me severely, I disgust him. I disgust myself. But still I cannot erase my own nature, cannot even imagine you as a real female person, like a mother or a sister. I spent all my life trying to treat you like a sister, and I never had a mother that I knew.

I am an animal, you are a goddess. I cannot bear to face my own true animal inner self any more than Peter can.

From now on we pilgrims, we few good men who have passed the trials that beset us on the road to Heaven, will be brothers. We shine. Peter, high-born of a wealthy family, closer to the King in the social hierarchy and thus to God, will assume the white mantle of a Knight Templar and the Cross of the Holy Blood. My gift and free-born standing suffices for the black robes of a man-at-arms. The initiation ceremony is held in the church before the congregation of all the brothers after the hours of prayer. Our little pilgrim group, encircled, exhausted by vigil, lack of sleep, prayer, hunger, thirst, finally wears nothing but cotton undergarments gathered by belts. It's a cold night, the stones gleam with frost, stars glimmer in the stained glass. The doors are closed, no outsiders are permitted in chapter. At the centre of the circle of brothers stands Geoffrey de Prudome, Grand Master of the Temple in England. For a moment I have the oddest feeling that his massive, fatherly, bearded figure draped in priestly white robes, the candles shimmering on the rosy cross on his left breast, might recognise me from so many years ago. But of course he does not.

At the appointed moment I step forward and show my wish and my will before all. 'Master, I have come before God, before you and the brothers, and I beg and require you in the name of God and Our Lady to accord to me your company and the benefits of the house, as one who shall always be its servant and slave.'

The Master speaks to us all. 'Every brother who is professed in the holy service must and shall, through fear of the flames of Hell, give total obedience to his Master.'

We speak. 'Aye, Master.'

'You must give up your free will.'

'Aye, Master.'

'I promise bread and water, and hardship, and work, and the poor robe of the house.' Our stewards place our new robes upon us. 'We live as one and die as one.' The prayers begin, the junior stewards file out, silence falls. The Master comes towards us pilgrim brothers in his white robes and I never saw a more glorious sight. The chaplains wear pale green and I understand it now, pale green is the colour of death, they are the pale riders. They give Holy Communion and our dry tongues lap the blood and flesh of Our Lord, His sweetness floods us. We fall on our knees at the feet of the Master. He touches our heads. 'Come, brothers.' The Master leads us to the wall, the curving wall of the circular church, the Alpha and the Omega. From the solid stone he opens a tiny barred window no larger than my hand. 'See. Learn.'

For a moment I see nothing but darkness, then make out the cell chiselled into the thickness of the wall, the ragged skeleton that hangs from its chains, white-haired, its bony jaws broken where its tongue has been roughly ripped out in life. I turn to the Master.

'Master, who is he?'

'Brother, he is death. The penalty of disobedience to the order.' So it was true. The Grand Master of Ireland had been bricked up in the wall for whispering the Templar secret outside the Order, the winding stair of Solomon found below the order's new Temple in Jerusalem, and the discovery of the caves beneath.

The Master pulls aside a curtain, steps open, a winding stair leads down beneath the church. We follow him down, round and round. The roof of the crypt is vaulted, of course, imitating the crypts and caverns of Solomon's Temple. Huge candles burn in heavy silver sticks round the walls, making the white cloaks glow.

'Let the Reception Ceremony begin.' The Master's steward unlatches the heavy Agnus Dei clasp that secures his Master's cloak. The cloak is folded, then the Master's white tabard is pulled reverently over his head. His body is unwashed, of course, hairy, filthy. He wears only a greasy cotton loincloth knotted on one hip. The steward frees the loincloth and places it on the tabard and cloak.

The Master speaks without covering himself. 'Christ is not the true God, but a mere man.'

The brothers respond devoutly. 'Amen.'

I look at Peter. We utter, 'Amen.'

The steward pulls me forward, takes my clothes. 'Brother, your proper response is to kiss the Master on the lips.'

Naked, I kiss the Master on the lips, our beards touching.

Peter also kisses the Master.

The other brothers under reception kiss the Master.

I lick my lips. No one shivers. The air is quite warm from the candles.

The Master says, 'We believe in the great omnipotent God who created Heaven and Earth, not in the Crucifixion.'

'Amen.'

The steward takes me forward. 'Brother, your proper response is to kiss the Master on the navel.'

I bend forward and kiss the Master on the navel. Peter crouches and kisses the Master. The other brothers under reception kiss the Master in their turn.

The Master says, 'We believe in the Quest of God through the pursuit of morality and spirituality and through perfection of the individual soul in the desert. Pain, suffering, humility, sacrifice, strength.'

'Amen.'

The steward whispers, 'Brother, your proper response is to kiss the Master on his third eye, the Master's All-Seeing Eye.'

The Master turns. I crouch between his buttocks. The stink is foul. I kiss him between his cheeks, taste his hairs and slimy flesh. My stomach rises in my throat, then settles. My lips, my tongue clean him. The steward raises me to my feet, my Master embraces me.

A plain silver cross is held up in front of me, close to my lips. I kiss it.

My steward says, 'Brother, your proper response is to spit three times.'

My cross is held up to me. I spit on it.

Held up.

I spit on my cross.

Held up. I spit on my cross for the third time. I'm shaking all over.

'Brother, there is much you must understand.' My Master takes me by the elbow to what I had thought was an altar – the crypt is consecrated ground. But this altar is bare except for a bulky object covered by a white cloth. 'Remove the cloth.'

I lean forward, pull away the cloth. The Master seizes me by my hips behind. I exclaim, am thrust forward. The object is a head, a human head, worked in priceless white ivory and ebony, soundlessly screaming. Screaming. Each tendon, each muscle, each vein stands proud. The eyes stare in agony, blind. I cry out as I am pierced like a woman. I shriek. The Master holds me down, my knees on each side of him, working himself deeper in the most disgusting act known to man. 'It is the Head of Baphomet,' the Master cries out. 'Baphomet, Son of Deus.' I endure limply, my head against the Head, clinging to its screaming face.

'Brother, hear me.' The Master leans his elbows on my back, whispers. 'It pleased Deus, Lord of the World, *Rex Mundi*, to take the form of King Hiram of Sidon and Tyre. All his life, the King, a faithful disciple, loved from a distance a certain princess, the Rose of Armenia, a woman of surpassing beauty married to another. Their love was never consummated in their lifetime, but he swore to love her even in the afterlife, after death. And, tragically, she did die. On the night of her death, a changed man, He enters her tomb where she is laid out on a cross of roses, wild roses, perfumed roses, thorns, rose petals. He lies with her, having in death what the King could not have in life, and fills her with His seed. Nine months later the King returns to her mouldering skeleton and finds the Head of Baphomet lying between her legs, freshly born.' The Master grunts, finishes, slides from me. 'Life. Life from death. Life after death. Life without a woman.'

I slip from the altar to my knees. The Master looks at me with interest. There is one part of me which never can and never does lie.

The Master meets my eyes, pulls Brother Peter to me. It is I, poor Brother Nicholas, whom the Master has put first. Not the wealthiest, not even a knight, but he has seen something in me. I am the strongest and perhaps the darkest, the one with most, and he has seen it.

The Master puts his lips against my ear. 'Brother Nicholas, show your brother the story of the Lord of Sidon, the Rosy Cross, and the Head of Baphomet, as I showed you.'

And so I do as I am commanded. We are the sons of Baphomet. But I promise you this, Alice. It is not Peter's body I see but yours. You. You I love. You I feel. And in the release of love, the first I have ever endured, you may be sure it is your name I cry out. But quietly. Quietly. Under my breath, so no one hears.

The roaring wind, the smoking fire. You sit there so calmly, Alice, your belly like a hill beneath your cloak, your knees apart like a whore. Every so often you grow tense, more frequently now your knuckles whiten on the arms of the chair, and you arch your spine. Then relax, but not for quite so long, until the pain comes again.

But always, always, Alice, your eyes watch me steadily. As though, as I unfold my story, you are watching a dangerous wild animal. Which I am. I am a Templar. A lion in the desert.

Now, Alice, I hear you whisper. 'I understand all this, Nick. But if you Templars do not believe in the Crucifixion, or in the incarnation of Our Lord as Jesus Christ, then you are simply Cathars, how can you believe in the Resurrection? But you said that most Templars do believe in the Resurrection, passionately. Passionately. Your very words. You said so.'

Ah, did I not tell her once how clever she is? Alice, my quick, clever one, what made you marry that fool Jack?

'No, my Alice,' I reassure her, 'you see, I am describing events and beliefs not as they are, but as they were more than ten years ago, when I saw what I saw. The Templars do now await the Resurrection, believe me. Passionately. While we live.' I add modestly, and fearfully, 'I played a large part in this change. The central role in fact. It is my story.' The wind blows the fire with a roar, shaking the house, and I know someone is standing behind me. I know it. I am watched.

I turn slowly. There is no one.

From upstairs I hear the sobs of your unimportant serving bitch whose name I forget. You arch your back slowly, Alice, and I feel your pain. Your terrible pain.

I remember pain now. I remember fear. I lick my lips, look behind me. No one.

'And so, Alice, I come near to the Battle of the Sermon on the Mount, when everyone, all of us, finally lost our faith in Christianity and in God.'

Bear in mind that when a messenger returns to our country from the Holy Land with news, let us say, of one hundred Templars on the march, or twenty Templars killed by Evil Ones, he speaks only of the knights. The real casualties

147

are much higher, but no one else matters. The knights are the shining example to the ranks below. A knight of the Temple, like those of the Hospitallers or Malta, or Freemasons, or Master Builders, or Rosicrucians, is of the eleventh age and degree of his order. A Master Mason, for example, is of the seventh age, an esquire the ninth. As a man-at-arms of the Temple, with two black horses, I am of the tenth age and degree.

But the knight is the one who matters. The shining figurehead. If you hear of a Knight Templar killed by the Evil Ones, certainly his ten men-at-arms have been killed too, and the foot soldiers attached to his guard killed, and the half-breed *poulains* who are his escort of light cavalry also killed. A Knight Templar may not refuse battle however great the odds against him, however certain death may be.

I am fortunate in my timing. My induction to the Templars was swift not only because of my left-handedness (in battle we fight two to each horse, a sword to right *and* left and cloaks flying on each side, which is how the legend of our winged horses arose) but also because in the year 1184, some months before my prostration at the Temple, the Patriarch of Jerusalem had been sent to Paris and London by King Baldwin of Jerusalem to plead for a new Crusade against Saladin, leader of the hordes of the Evil Ones. The battles for the Holy Land rage constantly back and forth and our old King Henry, as part of his penance for his murder of St Thomas at Canterbury, has pledged to maintain two hundred knights, fully armoured and supported, in the field of battle for one year. All I knew of this at the time was a thousand rumours. The Temple is simply a gigantic barracks, a hive, and even washerwomen do not gossip as busily as soldiers. Anyone with ears hears the armourers and smiths busy with their forges and hammers, anyone with eyes sees warhorses brought in day after day from the shire preceptories, grain and livestock from Temple manors and country houses. The storehouses issue huge leather tents coloured according to rank, and ships sailing upriver now moor three deep along the Temple wharves. Such a great enterprise takes time to assemble, but in early spring of 1187 the ships begin to board their cargoes.

I, of course, am part of Brother Peter's guard. Everyone knows that if strength and skill were what counted most, I would be a knight. I fight as hard as my betters, but I am not one of them and I never will be. Then by chance outside a tavern I meet Gilbert Woolton, now a wool merchant on Cornhill, dressed as gaudily as a merchant too. The awkward boy is grown into a man who can't see a fire without fanning the flames, and we drink a few cups of wine and I get rid of him, and a few days later a man I pass in the street points to me and whispers behind my back to his friend. The miller's daughter's bastard.

It's started again.

The brethren give no sign they know, but of course they do. They're waiting. Am I really an impostor? Breeding tells. Everything will be harder for me now, any failure will show that they are right, that I am low-born and a bastard, that the whispers are true. The miller's daughter's bastard. So I must be better than all of them. Never slip. Never fail.

But Geoffrey de Prudome, the Grand Master, is different. I know nothing of the degree of his birth or how he will die, no more than I know of myself. But there is something that holds me in his gaze. A special interest. Something fatherly, but not kind. He will tread me down if I fall. But there is something about the way he looks at me . . . He knows I will not fail. This feeling he gives me is more than good leadership from him, he is more than encouraging me, using my loyalty. He knows he is like me. He senses me like an animal scents another of its own kind. I see it in his eyes, and I am on my knees, alone, in prayer, in the church, when his shadow falls across me. The Grand Master demands more than obedience. He expects no mercy and will give none. He expects much more.

And I do not mean only this, his finger to his lips, then the kiss of his lips on my cheek, his hand pulling my shoulder, tugging me to the winding stair behind the curtain. We go down and here is the crypt. He smiles, we remember this, he pushes me to the altar. But what I expect, and what you expect, Alice, the act of sodomy that binds this man and myself, does not happen. He pulls the altar, and the plinth of solid stone scrapes as it rotates like an arm swinging round a shoulder, and steps form from the floor and slide down, round and round, the blocks of stone dropping into place below us, some smoothly, some rattling. A winding stair dropping down into the shadows.

A winding stair. Of course.

I begin to understand now. He plucks a heavy candle from the wall, puts his foot upon the step, then turns and looks up at me. 'No harm will befall you from me, Brother.'

I call down, 'Master, you have built a replica of the Sanctum Sanctorum of King Solomon below your church?'

'The Sacred Lodge. You are correct. This church was blessed and consecrated by Heraclius the Patriarch of Jerusalem himself, on his visit to London two years ago.'

I follow the Master's shoulders down to a small stone cellar, its walls hung with bright tapestries giving it a strangely sumptuous, almost effeminate look, more like a grand lady's bedroom than a plain Templar cell. And London cellars are always damp. But here the air smells fresh, clean, dry.

'But the Patriarch was not shown down here, Master?'

'Of course not!' The Master leans back against a tapestry, splays his arms and legs against the woven circle, telling me something. I realise it is a map. Maps are important to us because it is our duty to protect pilgrims on the road, and there are many roads. The Order learnt geometric mapping from the Evil Ones – Christian maps are always of a flat world – and Templar maps of cities and fortifications are always circular. The Master's right knee bisects the Sepulchre and Golgotha is marked with a Templar cross. His left arm is thrown across the Temple of Solomon, and his head is one of the city gates. It is a map of Jerusalem, and Jerusalem is the centre of the world, the Bible says so. Then I look round and see the next tapestry is of the whole world, with London at the top left and Jerusalem marked far down at the bottom right-hand corner. It's a Templar 'Golden Line' map. If an ordinary flat map is mutilated to fit over a globe (which the Evil Ones believe is the true shape of the world) the map becomes a lie, and Scotland is larger than England, and from the Pillars of Hercules to the Holy Land seems but a day's sail, and the ride from Acre to Jerusalem is twice as long in fact as the map makes it. Men easily die by such errors. The Golden Line shows distances in true proportion, and thus, as far as the mapmakers and mathematicians of the Order can calculate it, by God's will London, Paris, Rome and Jerusalem lie in a straight line that may be drawn with a ruler: the Golden Line.

I look around me in awe. All these tapestries are maps, mounted on wood like doors set over the walls. I see London (with the Temple at its centre, I recognise the Dovecote Tower), Paris with its bridges and its huge Temple, the country towns of England and France showing the positions of Templar forts, all of them joined by straight lines measured at precise angles, making a complex pattern. We are particular. We know what we defend.

I am looking at knowledge. Knowledge is priceless. Knowledge is power. The Order keeps everything it knows to itself.

'Only Templars know of this room?'

'Of course.' The Master speaks without moving. 'This is the New Temple.

149

Before your time our Temple was a mile to the north, in Holborn. But then we discovered this. This . . . place. Originally a Saxon well, no doubt. Saxon farmers lived here long ago, long forgotten, their wells and wattle houses covered over, filled in, nobody remembered them. Twenty-five years ago a Red Knight riding by dismounted and knelt here to drink at a pool, and as he looked past his cupped hands he saw down deep into the water, and the surface gave way, and he fell down.'

I look round me. 'This must have been a very large, deep well.'

The Master says softly, 'This is only the start of it.'

I kneel in front of him. 'There's more, Master?'

'By legend a tunnel leads to London Bridge.' The Master is hot beneath his robes, hot against my mouth. He plants the candle in the wall, kisses my lips. This is the only truth we care about. This moment of, not of love . . . this short moment of warmth in a terrible male loneliness. Not love, we can never know love. Kinship before death. For a moment not to be alone.

I whisper, 'But London Bridge is built of wood.'

'The crossing is more ancient than any bridge.'

I have some vague idea of pagan ceremonies, groves of trees, Druids. Long ago, before the Romans.

The Grand Master touches my hair tenderly. He knows. He knows all this. This secret must be handed down with all the other hidden knowledge and arcana of our order, from Grand Master to Grand Master.

I try to imagine Solomon's Temple in Jerusalem, the winding stair and the Sanctum Sanctorum and the caves and vaults and tunnels supposedly found by Templar masons below Mount Zion.

I whisper, 'You have built a complete replica here? Even the Well of Souls? The tunnels?'

'By legend a tunnel leads from here to Jerusalem.' Without laughing the Master tousles my hair, and I know he is stark staring mad. If there was a tunnel, why should we make the dangerous Channel crossing, and ride across France, and take ship again to the Holy Land?

He whispers, 'The road to the City of God is hard. Unbelievably hard.'

I put my lips against his ear. 'Is it true that masons building our Temple in Jerusalem broke into a tunnel and fell down, and there in a cave found the body of Christ lying wrapped in a linen shroud?'

The Master closes his eyes. 'Who except a Templar could know the truth of such a story?'

I whisper, 'A mason could.'

The wind thunders, the tide shakes the house. You groan, Alice. I know, I feel your pain. Your unendurable pain. I call for the serving bitch but she's too frightened to come. 'What's her name?'

'Rosie,' you whisper.

I bellow, 'Rosie, come down here and help your mistress to her room!'

Here she is, plump little thing, terrified and whimpering, cradling her broken arm. Yet when I snarl at her I see a flash of defiance in her eyes. But all she cares for, even above her own pain, is her mistress.

You, Alice. We lay you on your bed. Little Rosie tries to get me to leave but I send her out, you've got hours to wait. You haven't heard anything yet.

Our Templar forces disembark at our mighty fortress at Acre, one of the chariot cities of King Solomon, and we breathe the hot, dusty, perfumed wind of the Holy Land for the first time. Almost at once we're swept off our feet, plans change. We must march to Jerusalem. No, we must march to Tyre. The truce with Saladin is broken; no, peace endures. The trumpets

150

call us to arms, we are stood down. Peter knows a little more than I. 'Guy de Lusignan is now King of Jerusalem. He's a weakling who follows the advice of whoever spoke to him last. Fortunately the Templar Grand Master of France, Gerard de Ridfort, has him well in charge. A Christian warlord has attacked a rich convoy of Muslim traders and Saladin has declared the truce between the armies null and void.'

'What armies?'

'His army of a hundred thousand men. And ours.'

'Ours?'

Peter grins. 'Us.' He pats my shoulder. 'Templar odds!'

The trumpets blow, and we march through Armageddon and the lands of the Bible to Jerusalem, and for the first and last time I see the Temple built by our order in Jerusalem. It is immense, longer and broader than an arrow can fly even from a Balearic bow, a wonderful and intricate building resting on piers supporting an endless complication of arches and vaults. The stables have stalls for ten thousand horses, each with its groom. The rest is a magnificent palace with gardens and fountains, halls and courtyards, chapels and antechambers, vestibules, granaries and cloisters.

On the last day of April two hundred Templar knights attack a raiding force of seven thousand Muslims, and are killed. King Guy, prodded by Grand Masters de Ridfort and de Prudome, orders all fighting men in his kingdom to gather at Acre. We will take the fight to Saladin. And so we march back again to Acre. The Patriarch, Heraclius, remains ill in Jerusalem but gives into our care the True Cross, found by priests in the wall of the Church of Holy Sepulchre, and the Bishop of Acre rides out to receive the sacred relic and carries it ahead of us to symbolise our coming victory.

But in war nobody knows anything.

On the first day of July, thirty miles to the east of us, Saladin crosses round the southern end of the Sea of Galilee. King Raymond of Tiberias is with us. King Guy hesitates. Will we march, will we not? Almost at once intelligencers bring good news. Saladin has made a serious mistake, sent half his forces into the hills, half to besiege Tiberias on the sea's western shore. At night, incredibly, word comes that Tiberias has already fallen to the Evil Ones. Only the citadel holds out. What to do? King Raymond is for wait and see, King Guy for marching at once. Even behind the thick stone walls of the castle the heat is stifling. Peter has been told King Raymond is afraid of the desert, of the heat in the height of summer, no wells, no water, he wants us to await reinforcements from Antioch. Grand Master de Ridfort overrules him, Galilee is the centre of Our Lord's ministry, he insists the duty of our Order to our Pope obliges us to march at once. King Guy agrees, then changes his mind, then late at night changes it back again. We march!

At dawn the trumpets sound and we march through Cana, where Jesus performed His first miracle of the water into wine and some say He married Mary Magdalene, and come in the evening to Sephoris. Here we are almost in sight of Nazareth. There is water here and grass for the thousands of horses, but next day the trumpets sound again, and we march into the face of the sun. The heat is intense. Someone is struck by an arrow. More arrows fly, but whichever way we charge, there is only the desert. The rays of the sun make each suit of armour burn like an oven, the sand rubs into the joints, we have no water. Everywhere is uphill, I hear screams as the stragglers are cut down. We charge back, too late. Now we are harassed on the right flank, now the left. The desert shimmers and blazes, full of movement, the heat ripples make a thousand men into ten thousand. An arrow strikes the man beside me. He struggles, eyes wide with fear, slides away from me, rolls down the barren hill. At once the thorny trees of the desert come alive with shadows rushing at

151

his prone shining body, curved swords flash. We charge. There is no one. Two more men down. We see the enemy everywhere, and now the sun is falling behind us, and our shadows rise ahead of us up the rocky slopes that tower over us.

Night is falling.

'This is not fighting,' Peter says. 'They are cowards.' He gives the last sip of water to his horse. A scout races back, there's a village ahead of us, Hattin. Then smoke rises, all roofs are burnt, all wells poisoned. King Raymond spurs ahead, uphill, he knows of a secret well, the Well of Lubieh where Christ drank. We are half mad with thirst.

The well is dry.

Here, on this barren rocky shelf, below the two summits known as the Horns of Hattin, Christ spoke to the multitudes. King Guy's red tent is erected at the place. Far below us we glimpse the sparkling, fresh, moonlit waters of the Sea of Galilee. O Lord, our temptation. Men maddened by thirst run forward into the dark, we hear their screams as they are cut down.

Night is the time for fear.

All night there are screams and alarms, trumpets blow. To arms! Stand down. To arms, this way! Terrible shrieks. The Templars stand firm, but where is the enemy? What use is bravery against cowards? All around us fires spring up, we are surrounded, smoke blows over us from the burning bushes, we lick the tears from each other's faces.

Peter whispers, 'Are you ready to die, Nicholas?'

'Yes.'

He grips his sword tight, his cloak as white as the moon. 'So am I, with honour.'

Above Galilee the sun rises like a god. Saladin has brought his huge army together, we are surrounded. Our war is over. We are dead men. Our hearts beat, we breathe, our eyes move, but we are dead. The circle tightens. Panic begins, just a few peasants at first, foot soldiers, but it spreads like fire. Men singly then in groups then whole companies throw down their weapons, armour, run downhill not to fight but to drink. We try to save them but are driven back. The air fills with arrows, screams, confusion everywhere. I sweep my sword around me, cut into flesh. Who am I fighting? My horse crumples. Peter's hand, I am pulled up behind him. I see the flags and banners of Saladin's royal pavilion but we are driven back on King Guy's red tent. The hiss of arrows like a breaking wave. The clang of swords again. We are exhausted, my hands and legs and face are numb, my heart thunders. Our armour drags us down, the points of our swords trail on the ground, the horse falls on top of us. Darkness.

And now the horror.

The horror in this divine place is worse than you can imagine.

I see this with my own eyes. I see the Bishop of Acre running, dragging the True Cross behind him. He drops the Cross and runs free. A small bearded man cuts at him but the bishop keeps running. No blood comes from him. Every word I tell you is true. Dark forms gather round the bishop, cutting and slashing at him, but still he runs. Not until the bishop is struck through the head does he fall, close enough for his dying spittle to spray my face. His body is raised up on the curved swords, his ecclesiastical vestments are torn away to reveal chain mail. The bishop wore armour. The bishop himself had not trusted God. Among the men lying around me I hear a groan go up as if our misery could rise to Heaven. If even our bishops have no faith in God to save them, what hope is there for us?

Our God has forsaken us.

And so catastrophe overtakes us. I see King Guy's red tent totter and fall.

King Guy and Gerard de Ridfort and Geoffrey de Prudome and various warlords stand exhausted, surrounded, then drop slowly to their knees. Their swords slide into the dust. We are all prisoners.

And here is more horror.

I am afraid, but I am also greedy. Facing the certainty of death, terrified, but greedy to live.

Do you see the day? Here is the sight and stink of the day. Muslims busy stripping armour, clothes, weapons from the bodies of the dead. They cut and disjoint the limbs and scatter the pieces over the field of battle, crack open heads. I see throats split, eyes gouged out, stomachs disembowelled, ribs smashed, skin flayed, foreheads pierced, souls flown, their ghosts crushed. Under the pitiless afternoon sun the bodies lie like stones among the stones. Behind us where we kneel tied by chains and ropes, below the steps of the royal pavilion, Saladin hands a gold cup of rosewater glistening with snow to King Guy, and promises him, 'A king does not kill a king.'

We are dying of thirst. King Guy drinks, then passes the cup to the warlord beside him. Saladin says quietly, 'My gift of hospitality was to you, not the man beside you.' He has that man's head struck off with a sword, and the blood spatters King Guy from head to toe.

But King Guy will not be harmed, I know. A Muslim may not harm a guest to whom he has offered hospitality. It is their law.

I see the True Cross dragged in the dust, beaten with sticks. Saladin swears he will nail the True Cross in the doorway of the mosque in Damascus to be kicked by the bare feet of the Muslim faithful.

De Ridfort walks from the royal pavilion on to the top step, a resplendent figure clothed in the dusty, blood-spattered white robes of our order. Silence falls. He cries out, 'I am a Muslim!'

Saladin has the True Cross brought forward. 'Swear it '

'I am a Muslim, I swear it!' We stare at de Ridfort in confusion, our backs beaten by rods if we move. Is de Ridfort trying to save us? Are our lives to be spared? Will God now in the face of this dreadful blasphemy strike down the Evil Ones with His lightning and His angels, as He did the prophets of Baal?

De Prudome steps forward. He reaches out, lays his hand on the True Cross. 'I am a Muslim. I swear it.'

In the front rank a Knight Templar, Brother de Blanchefort, has his chains struck off. He rubs his bruised wrists and ankles, staggers forward, then stands tall, a magnificent sight. He calls out for news of his son, also a Templar. 'Bernard? By God's sweet mercy, does anyone have word of my son?' The sun strikes off the silver Agnus Dei, the amulet of the Lamb of God that de Blanchefort wears at his throat, his white cloak swirls in the desert wind. He is dragged forward, thrown to his knees, sodomised, beheaded.

The blood spurts from his kneeling body. The Evil Ones dance and shout, the sun flashing on their swords as they torment us with the dripping head of our brother. The kneeling body, forgotten, topples forward on its neck in headless prayer. The wrath of the Lord does not come. The sun shines towards evening, throwing long shadows now. I see de Ridfort and de Prudome watching calmly. Another knight is dragged forward, brutally sodomised. Saladin knows us well. But as the sword is raised to behead the victim, he commands, 'Stop.'

He beckons.

Accompanying Saladin's army are fifty Sufi novices, young students of the Koran training for the priesthood, not for war. They are brought forward and given swords which they handle nervously. One boy drops his sword, the blade makes a high tinkling sound against a rock, and such is the silence and the tension that suddenly everyone laughs. Even us Templars. A great roar of

153

deep male laughter rises up from both victors and defeated. Saladin, smiling his gentlemanly smile, his face and hands covered with boils from some foul disease, tells the novices, 'You know what to do.'

These children do not know anything but books and prayer. We watch the knights dragged forward, appalled. This is the greatest shame and humiliation imaginable, and still God does not strike the Evil Ones down. He does nothing. The most brutish soldiers are chosen to sodomise the kneeling Christian figures, lots are drawn. Peter cannot bear to watch, he hides his face between his elbows. 'You lost this battle because of your lust for the vice of sodomy,' Saladin calls to us. 'You violated your own faith and law. You do not deserve your God.' The little novices hack clumsily at the necks, hardly knowing the blunt side of a blade from the sharp, four or five to each knight, advice shouted at them from all sides, and we wait our turn, rank after rank of us, dying of thirst, deserted by our God, in the desert red with blood and sunset.

Peter whispers, 'They are not killing the men-at-arms, only the knights.'

'It'll be my turn tomorrow, Peter.' A terrible scream splits the air.

'You've always wanted to be a knight, haven't you?' he whispers. 'You should have been one.'

'Me? I'm the miller's daughter's bastard.'

'You're a survivor, Brother Nicholas.'

Here is an interesting fact you will not have thought of, Alice. Saladin, except in his wildest dreams, no doubt, did not really believe he would capture so many prisoners. Chains are heavy to carry. He does not have enough of them, so for those of us at the back, ropes suffice. The butchery ceases at sunset and we kneel shivering under the stars. We know what will happen to us at dawn.

Peter speaks in a hopeless voice. 'Why does God not punish the Evil Ones with His divine wrath? Why has He deserted us? What must we do? The Holy Christian realm of the East has lost so much that it will never rise again, we are dead. The Evil Ones will make a mosque of holy Mary's convent, and since the theft pleases her Son, who should weep at this, we stand no chance of victory. Anyone who fights the Evil Ones is mad, for Jesus Christ does not fight them any more. The Muslims have conquered us, they will conquer the Holy Land, Jerusalem will fall. They will grind us down knowing that our God, who was awake, sleeps now, and Muhammad grows more powerful. Truly this is the Devil's world!'

My fingertips pull a knife from my boot. I grip the handle between my teeth, slice at the rope binding my wrists. Blood drips down my hands.

He whispers, 'What are you doing?'

'Escaping.'

'They won't kill the men-at-arms, they only care about the knights.'

I cut his ropes.

'No,' Peter says. 'No, I won't run away.'

The wounded man on my other side has died. Beyond his body the chains begin. I turn back to Peter. In an hour the moon will rise and illuminate every movement. Brother Peter changes shape, a pale shadow, and I realise he has taken off his white cloak and white tabard. He thrusts the bundle of harsh wool into my hands. 'Give me your black clothes,' he whispers. 'They won't kill me if I stay, but they'll kill you if they catch you.'

The first glow of the moon on the horizon. I stare at him. The tears shine in Peter's parched eyes, God knows where he got them from.

'I'm afraid,' he whispers. 'I'm terribly afraid.'

Who will benefit most from his cowardice? When they've killed the knights, they'll kill the men-at-arms for sure. I say, 'You're right. They'll spare the men-at-arms.' I wriggle quickly out of my clothes, give them to him.

I pull the white tabard over my head, and don the white robe of a Knight Templar.

I kiss Brother Peter's cheek, then hold the knife under my robe as I back away through the dust and dark. I need a horse. The first thing I think of is a horse. The first thing any man on foot thinks of is a horse, it's what the Evil Ones will expect of any man escaping. The horses will be guarded. There are men sleeping everywhere around me, the air has the curiously spiced scent of men who eat different food from us. They are exhausted by battle and do not stir. A horse's hoof chinks against a stone, here is a line of Arab steeds. It's very tempting, but I have made my plan. A man stands up in front of me, I cover his mouth and slide my knife into his heart, move smoothly forward over his falling body, cut the rope that secures the horses, slip away. The horses do not yet realise they are free, but when they do they will instinctively run downhill. I climb uphill. Behind a boulder at a hundred paces I find a stone, throw it back. It clatters, strikes a spark from a rock among the horses, and every shadow jumps to life. The horses pull free, tossing their heads, then the leader gallops noisily downhill and the herd follows him like a dark stain in the night.

I climb quietly. Up here the moon has risen and I keep to the shadows high on the southern Horn of Hattin. Moonlight strikes across the plain below me, the shadowy confusion of a camp of thirty-three thousand men, or sixty-six thousand or ninety-nine thousand, I know not, and more thousands of dead bodies – and suddenly I hear screams, cantering horses and the horse boys chasing them on scampering feet, cursing. Gradually quiet returns. I settle behind a boulder on the peak and watch while below me the moonlight falls to the Sea of Galilee, and through the long night touches its water with silver, and a man dying of thirst never saw a more beautiful or tormenting sight.

The wind knocks the window open, fills your bedroom, blows out the candle, I feel snowflakes swirling against my face, a rattling noise as the little plaster Jesus on your clothes chest is knocked over. 'It's all right, Alice, don't worry.' You scream again, whether from pain or fear I do not know. What can a man know of the pain of childbirth?

I know. I understand. I know pain.

Unendurable pain.

I reach into the dark, push the window closed, drop the bar across it so this cannot happen again. Poke the fire, light the candle from a tongue of flame, set the little Jesus upright. You reach out for Him.

'Give Him to me.' Your spine bends, one leg straightens, the sweat breaks over your face. 'Give Him to me!'

I hold Him out to you, then move the little statue so it is my hand you take. You grip my hand. I hardly think you realise. Writhe, Alice, writhe. Your grip tightens, you cry out in your agony. You can't be this strong, you're breaking my fingers. My skin parts, my blood wells up rich and red from my flesh between your fingers.

Your pain eases, releases you until next time. But you do not let me go.

'Tell me,' you whisper. 'Tell me. I want to know it all.'

I stare at my blood. Hold the candle close to the blood, staring, seeing the red gleam of my face in my reflection. I remember.

I remember.

I see everything. They kill the rest of us at dawn. When the knights are finished they chop down the sergeants and then they butcher the men-at-arms, working in rows, hurrying impatiently now, and I stare down through the infernal rippling heat from my eyrie on the Horn of Hattin, as high above them as an eagle. I cannot tell which was Peter whom I loved, by whose loss of faith I am alive, all I see is meat and fear. Meat and fear and shit is all we are, all love is. The lower ranks are butchered perfunctorily, the army is busy packing up, losing its shape and reforming, men pushing and shoving everywhere, shouting orders. The boys who had let the horses go are beheaded, and then the great mass of the Saladin's army, kettledrums pounding, drains away from the plateau like water from the back of your hand.

I can't stop thinking about water. Everything I think of turns to water. The plateau is quiet now, the bodies of the dead no larger than drops of blood. No water. No movement, only vultures.

From this height, a thousand feet above Galilee, I discern the faint blue line of the Mediterranean far to the west. The dust of Saladin's army blows over it towards Acre. Our sleeping God will not help us and Acre will fall, the town at once, the immense Templar fortress a little later. So I cannot go to the west. To the east, between me and the lake, Tiberias burns. Anyway there will be people everywhere along the shores of the lake, fishermen, farmers, villagers. The lure of water, the certainty of capture.

So I go south. I walk downhill. I walk downhill all day, dust blows from my bare feet, I've lost my boots, there's not a cloud in the sky, the sun burns my head. The waterless ruin of the Temple of the Moon casts no shadow. On my right the land drops, I see flashes of silver thread winding among trees. Water. I run, limping. The silver thread grows to a sluggish stream, olive trees, sharp thorny bushes. I plunge through them into the water, plunge my burning face into the water, open my mouth like a fish, gulp down the cool silver bubbles.

I put my head above the water, stop still. I'm watched. Not a Jew. Dark-skinned, dark eyes, a dark red cloak with ochre stripes, good quality, very pretty shoes. A Muslim. His donkey hitched to a tree, sleeping. The man gives an embarrassed tittering laugh, perhaps he's waiting for someone. He smiles, calls something to me that I don't understand. I nod, put my fingers above water, wave my hand as though I know him. There must be a Muslim convoy somewhere near here, in the trees perhaps. I think I hear children playing, a child's mother shouting angrily. Someone may come any moment.

I stand up and the man stares at my emerging white robes and red cross as though the Devil himself has stood up in the shallow waters. His mouth opens as I wade forward, he turns to run, a spiny bush stops him, he turns. I draw my knife and smile my sympathy for his predicament. His last sight in the world.

His body is much smaller than mine, his goat-hair cloak hangs only to my knees. His shoes are mortally tight but I squeeze my feet into them, straddle his donkey, and whack it like a madman with his stick. My toes almost touch the sand, but the donkey trots with a will.

When I am sure I am clear of pursuit I search the saddlebag. A type of very hard bread, half a dozen yellow eggs, a sort of spicy cake. On the other side hangs a skin of water. Although my belly sloshes I have a dread of running out of water. I cram the eggs into my mouth, hard-boiled, drink. Later, as the donkey jogs forward wearily, I eat the cake and finish the water. When the stars come out I lead the donkey carefully between bulrushes, kneel at a wide river. It is the River Jordan. I drink my fill and refill the water bladder.

In the day I hide and sleep. In the night I travel. The donkey is lame with my weight so mostly I lead it, but on the third night it will go no further. I tether it to a bush, sling the water bladder over my shoulder, and walk. The moonlit nights wane, utterly dark now, so I wander through the wastes of Endor and Belvoir during the day, hide behind the trees in the valley of Jezreel, refill my water bladder as I wade the river, and crouch behind the back wall of an inn at the sound of voices. News. Acre is fallen. The cities of Nablus, Jaffa, Toron, Sidon, Beirut, Ascalon. All are fallen.

Jerusalem falls.

Our God sleeps.

I have nowhere to go but west, across the desert of rock and dust towards the sea. Along the roadside, Christians have been nailed to crosses in mockery of the Crucifixion. Yes, truly this is the Devil's world. The sun rises like a fiery furnace, the night freezes. The sand slides backwards as I climb forwards, then pushes me forward as I descend. At least I have my water bladder, heavy though it is. Thorns tear my cloak, filth stains it any old colour, I wrap it round my head to keep off the burning sun, wrap it round my body against the freezing night, stagger and stumble, fall exhausted and get up and struggle forward. It's easier now, suddenly my water-bladder weighs almost nothing. I run forward through the night as though in a dream.

The water bladder flops against my side, split. Every drop has drained away long ago.

The sun rises behind me, and I walk after my shadow as I do every morning. But this morning there is the sound of bells. It is the sound of the Abbot's Littlebourne church bell summoning us to prayer. A goat stands on a rock, then jumps away with the sound of jangling bells as I approach, I follow it and the brow of the hill drops away to reveal, to my eyes blinking through the chinks in my robe, a dry riverbed and a strange pattern of dark boulders overhung by palm trees.

I lift my right foot then my left foot, I pull myself forward. More bells. A whole herd of bells, goats, dark-skinned children, women with hidden faces, the scent of spice. Nobody touches me. A hand claps and around me the circle of watchers parts like the sea. The gap reveals a tall man wearing long black robes, long black beard, his sharp, cruel eyes shadowed by a hook nose, his hard, cruel lips turned down at the corners like a falcon's.

I realise the dark boulders are tents. Leather tents. Tents and camels. Goats and children. But no water. I sway.

Another single clap of his hands. A silver cup flashing in the sun is passed to the man. He holds the cup out to me and I grasp it in both hands, and gulp pure water.

He says some words. I shake my head. The cup is refilled.

He claps his chest and says, '*Muhammad. Šayk Muhammad.*'

He wants my name. I clap my chest. 'Nicholas.'

The background gabble of gossip stops as though cut by a knife. The sheik snaps his fingers, and my battered robe is unwound from under the goat-hair cloak and here I stand, the scarlet Cross of the Holy Blood blazoned on my tabard from hip to shoulder, surrounded by Evil Ones and about to die. I have lost my sword and knife and boots. I have only my pride.

But nobody moves. I do not die. I cannot die. I have deceived them, but Sheik Muhammad has given me his hospitality and he is bound by its rules. I am his guest, not his enemy. But then he jerks his head and the cup is snatched from me. Sheik Muhammad takes it, looks me in the eye, spits into the water, returns the fouled cup to me with his own hand.

I raise the cup and drink. I drink his spittle deep and hold the drained cup out to him.

Sheik Muhammad looks at the faces of his people, then takes the cup. A Christian has drunk from it, he throws it down, will not take it back even though it is gold.

'I see you are a man of honour, Sheik Muhammad.'

Sheik Muhammad's lips move at the corners. He smiles with a mouth of

157

teeth like yellow saws. Then he laughs. He braces his hands on his hips and laughs.

'Welcome!'

I have met someone worse than I am.

I am drawn into a tent, cool dim shadows beneath the leather, and collapse on sumptuous rugs surrounded by women, too weak to resist their soft, scented hands washing my face or take offence at their whispers and giggling. The tent flap blows in the wind, throwing a shaft of sunlight inside, and my last memory before sleep is of them staring at my eyes, my blue eyes.

It is a moment of peace for you, Alice, between the bouts of pain. You lie quietly, exhausted. The fire flickers on the sweat that beads your face. In a few minutes your next labour will begin but for now everything is clear to you. You realise you hold my hand, my red hand not your little statue. You struggle, but I tighten my grip.

'Call Rosie to attend me,' you whisper. 'Please. Please.'

'Later, my love.'

There is so much more for you to understand.

The sheik's hospitality has bound him. There is nothing, by the oaths of his people and religion, that he may do to harm me. I am his guest until the sun rises tomorrow, I must be treated like a gentleman, must behave like one, and must be allowed to depart in peace. I awaken at sunset, drink water, yawn, stretch. No one stops me leaving the tent, I am ignored as I strut round the camp. Sheik Muhammad is a rich man, his white camels are groomed and fat with water, his hawks shuffle on their rods eyeing me with their concentrated gaze as though I am their prey. The desert light fails as if a candle is blown out, a mouse squeals as the birds are fed. Now I smell smoke, see the flames of a fire sending sparks among the stars, inhale the mouthwatering odour of roasting mutton. A feast.

A boy is sent to lead me between the tents, past the dogs and women and children furthest from the fire, past the lesser men and then between the warriors seated on rugs. A Templar has no mercy and expects none; I walk among them unscathed but I feel their hatred like a burn. The chieftains recline on the best side of the fire, in the wide mouth of Sheik Muhammad's tent. From the centre the sheik beckons like a genial old thief, beaming, and I wonder how I ever thought him cruel or forceful or powerful. 'Come, come.' He slaps the place of honour beside him and I squat like a foreigner. I tell him my story and admit the victory of his religion over mine. A babble of talk breaks out. They want me to know that Jerusalem is fallen, every Christian citizen sold for ransom, the power of the Templar Brotherhood in the Holy Land broken.

But I am alive, the guest of Sheik Muhammad of the Karmathion nation.

Sheik Muhammad watches me. He watches me as though seeing inside me.

A sweet drink is brought by a crouching girl who bows her head, kneeling, and offers me the cup she holds. All I see of her is her eyes above her filmy green veil, her slim form almost concealed by flowing clothes finer than any I have seen before, light as air. Such beauty could not bring poison. I drink the cup, it is thrown away because my lips have defiled it. The sheik spears choice cuts of mutton from the steaming cauldron, feeds me from his own knife, which is then thrown away. I offer him steaming hunks of liver and pieces of guts such as we Templars eat in the desert. There are bowls of rice flavoured with saffron, fabulously expensive, dishes of turmeric eggs and the eyes and testicles of various animals that give us wisdom and strength. The sheik tells me, 'You see how poorly we live in the desert.'

I pick a strand of fillet from between my teeth. Everyone knows these people are all thieves. He is a king of thieves; but he has his pride. 'Your hospitality does you credit, Sheik Muhammad.'

'The finest saffron from Africa.' He cannot resist bragging of his possessions, all he has bargained or looted or stolen as he moves from place to place. 'Eagle eggs from the mountains. Silk, satin, muslin. Peppers and spices from lands that lie months below the horizon of the world.' He claps and now lesser guests are permitted to reach into the cauldron. 'We Karmathis are traders, Sir Nicholas. Doubtless your masons use our metalwork, tools and devices – dividers, triangles, gauges, astrolabes, wind-roses, hexalpha and pentalpha, the five-pointed star which is the seal of Solomon and the shield of David. Did you not know? They are all manufactured by our Karmathion guilds of craftsmen.' He wants me to believe he's no thief – or at least that he's a clever one. 'We have spies and informers everywhere. We know you much better than you know us, Sir Nicholas. The guilds and orders and societies that bind your Christian nations in mutual interest are modelled on ours, even your Pope follows our example with his licensed companies of craftsmen who pass freely across borders, as we do. I speak English, French, Spanish. I was recently in Spain.' His voice rises. 'Your Christianity will not prevail, you know. We are taking the cities of Spain from you and the Holy Land too. It is Allah's will. You drinkers of fermented spirit have made a mere prophet into your God. You worship the wrong God, this is a proven fact.' The sheik lectures me angrily, and his words mean little to me at the time, but as you know, I forget nothing. 'The name Allah is to be found in the human body – standing, an *Alif* . . .' He goes on and on with much more in like vein, but I am too distracted to reply. The girl in the green veil has dark sweeping eyebrows like yours, Alice, which almost meet between her eyes. She will not look away from me. I lick my dry lips, she brings me sherbet water. I glance at the cauldron and she fetches meat.

I hear the silence.

'Ah, she pleases you.'

I jerk my eyes away from her. 'A woman? I have not noticed her.'

He knows I lie. 'Have not, or cannot?'

'My order is celibate, as you know.'

'Yes, I do know.' He smiles. I am beginning to know his smile. 'She's yours tonight. My youngest daughter. Laila.' The sheik looks at me straight in the eyes, no longer genial or entertaining. He means what he says. 'Laila.'

In God's name, Alice, her eyebrows.

'No.'

But he knows I mean yes. I shake my head, but he knows I mean yes.

Sheik Muhammad begins to frighten me. Beneath the veneer of manners with which we converse, he hates me implacably. To him I am a pagan. Perhaps he senses I am worse than pagan, I doubt my belief. I am almost an atheist, a man who believes in nothing, a man to whom the world itself is Hell.

He smiles that smile. 'My dear Sir Nicholas, you cannot refuse my hospitality, any more than I can refuse to be hospitable.' The shiek's greasy hands are rinsed in rosewater, he claps and observes with satisfaction the women and children and dogs rush forward to gobble his leftovers, a ragged swarm plucking scraps from the cauldron, dribbling juices down their faces, fighting to the blood over lumps of gristle and bone. 'Most interesting, is it not?'

Hunger? I've been hungry all my life. 'I don't know what you mean, Sheik Muhammad.'

'Temptation, Sir Nicholas. Temptation.'

It is on the tip of my tongue to admit I am no knight, I'm the miller's daughter's bastard, no one. On the tip of my tongue, but no further. I cannot bring myself to admit the truth.

'I am obliged to resist temptation, Sheik Muhammad.'

'As are we all, Sir Nicholas.'

The lad who led me earlier returns, as pretty as the girl, I imagine, though I did not see her veiled face, but he has her, your, strong dark eyebrows, Alice. Probably he is her brother or cousin. The Evil Ones take many wives, the children of powerful men are half their tribe. The boy leads me back to my tent, bows respectfully, waits. I feel I am observed, the only light flickers from a wick floating in a pot of rancid oil, the leather drapes and rugs seem full of moving shadows. It is only the wind. I dismiss him but still he waits, then abruptly leaves. Hours pass. I lie on the low divan prepared for me. I do not sleep. Or if I sleep, I do not dream.

The night wind gusts, the drapes flap heavily, the flame blows out, a hand from the dark touches my face. The spicy scent of Laila's perfume, roses on Laila's breath, the caress of Laila's clothes as light as air. I feel her filmy veil, feel its greenness. It slides into my hands, I crush it like petals, strain my eyes to see her, but there is only the feel of her beauty above me, the feel of her robes parting, the feel of her beautiful legs straddling my body. Her beautiful lips close my mouth and her beautiful breasts hang against my hands and it is as I told you, Alice. It is always you I see, you I feel, you I love, whatever happens, your name I whisper. Alice, Alice, Alice, my love.

I do not sleep. Or if I sleep, it is a nightmare.

The wind blows the drapes and she is gone. Only her veil remains, crushed in my hand. I push it quickly under my belt as the tent flap opens, a flame rustles, grows, drawn out in the night wind, its glow revealing Sheik Muhammad's face behind it, and now I know it is the cruellest and most powerful and forceful face I have ever seen. His eyes look at me like stones, so that I reach instinctively for my sword which is not there.

'Be calm, Sir Nicholas.' He comes forward quietly. 'I mean you no harm, though we are enemies. I have sworn the oath of hospitality and I keep my oaths. No harm will befall you except by your own hand.'

I say bravely, 'Then I am safe.'

'Did you enjoy her?'

I must lie, dawn cannot be far off, he won't find out the truth until I'm gone. 'She is very beautiful but I did not touch her.'

He smiles. 'Of course you did not touch her, Sir Nicholas. Because of your oath, I knew you would not. You are a man of honour.'

'Yes.'

The sheik squats, sinks the holder in the sand between the rugs, observes me across the flame. The tent is all smoke and darkness except for his face, an occasional movement of his hands as he speaks.

'I have a gift for you, Sir Nicholas. At dawn, not long, I will give you a fine horse and safe conduct to the coast, a day's ride. The port of Caesarea belongs to us, you cannot go there even in disguise. But nearby you'll find the fishing village of Bat Yam and there you may find a boat. Perhaps even someone you know.'

My enemy is giving me my life. I dare say nothing. What does he want in return?

I start to thank him but he flicks his fingers in a gesture of dismissal. 'That is nothing. I do not reward those who deceive me. I care nothing for you, Sir Nicholas, whether you live or die. To give me your life would be too poor a gift. But I have in mind for you, my enemy, a gift which is priceless. And I know you will agree.'

He reaches behind him, knowing someone waits there in the darkness, and now I see them, his men filling the tent around us, their shoulders against the sloping leather walls.

160

Sheik Muhammad holds out a book to me. Its cover is the softest leather I have ever touched, brown as dried blood. Over its surface, designs and symbols are inlaid as finely as spiders' webs.

I stare into it. Lift the cover. Turn the pages. I don't know what it is, but I sense its importance.

I whisper, 'What is it?'

'Knowledge, Sir Nicholas. That's all. Christian knowledge. Make of it what you will.'

You, Alice, despite your pain, your agony, or because of it, you understand at once. Knowledge. Knowledge, that replaces faith.

Knowledge, the most dangerous gift. Sheik Muhammad, educated and a thief, knowing that knowledge corrupts and that absolute knowledge corrupts absolutely, is taking his revenge.

But it's only a book! Words can't harm us.

You remember what I told you earlier, I see it come into your eyes. You cry out, 'Sheik Muhammad gave you a – the – Kabbalah?'

Ah, my clever wife. I wipe the sweaty hair from your forehead. 'The Holy Kabbalah that Moses brought down from the Mount, containing the ten Books, the ten Sepherot of the Word of God.'

You bite at your lips in your agony, Alice, you strain to bring my child to the moment of birth, but you do not take your eyes from my own. 'The sheik traded with Muslim Moors in Spain. He claimed he had even been to Spain. He got the book from the library of Rabbi Judah ben-Barzillai, didn't he? After it was ransacked, looted, the books scattered?'

'The book was a trinket to the sheik, Alice. He does not believe in the Bible. But he knows it is a priceless prize to us Christians. Us Templars.'

I watch you lie quietly for a moment.

Then you whisper, 'Why?'

I stare at the pages, then raise my eyes to the sheik's level gaze.

'But these are only numbers!'

He smiles. 'No, it's not the Devil's Bible. Unless you make it so. The Word of your God was not translated as words but as numbers. The rabbis of Tanna believed the Word, as words, would blind them. The secret interpretations of ben-Yohai are ciphers. Numbers are precise, they are the truth that cannot lie. Logic can be applied to them. Words change their meaning with time and exegesis and language but numbers and values do not. You have heard of our science, *al-jabr*?'

'Algebra?' I shrug. 'Some French mathematicians use it, bridge-builders, cathedral masons mostly. The knowledge was translated from Arabic' – I do not call him an Evil One to his face – 'into Latin about forty years ago.' I know William English, who finished Canterbury Cathedral, had seen Robert of Chester's translation in the archbishop's library and been allowed to handle it, though I do not believe he could read.

'Algebraic computation is our Arab science of restoration to normal, *'ilm al-jabr wa'l-mukabala*, reuniting like with like. Those who study the Kabbalah, wiser men than I, see that your Scriptures and Bible are an enormous library of symbols that can be precisely interpreted to express their true meaning.' The sheik tells me of the devices of interpretation, *Peshat, Remex, Derash* and *Zod*, and the ten *Sepherot*, the keys to the ciphers. 'All this is in the Kaballah.'

Again I stare at the meaningless pages . . . and suddenly, by staring, I glimpse a pattern. It dissolves before I can fix on it. Yet as I concentrate, another design forms on the page, a repetition of numerals that must mean something. It slips away from me. A ship in fog, a face in the dark.

161

Then, for a moment, clear.

'Aboth,' I say, not knowing what the word means. Then I see it. 'The Book of Aboth, chapter four, verse 29. "Against thy will thou becomest an embryo, and against thy will thou art born—"' I slam the book closed, shaking.

The sheik says quietly, 'Do you accept my hospitality?' The threat behind his words need not be spoken aloud. If I do not accept his gift, I am a dead man.

'Yes. I accept your hospitality, I accept your book.'

He touches the tooled leather with his fingertips. 'Knowledge. Knowledge is tempting, is it not? Now, know this. The Kabbalah is divided into the Gematria, the Notaricon, and the Temura. Gematria gives each letter in a word a numerical value, so "And, lo, three men" in the Genesis of your Bible reveals that in fact the three men were angels, and their names were Michael, Gabriel, and Raphael, because the numerical total of these three names is the same, 701. Do you see it?'

I glimpse the pattern. 'I think I see it.'

'Notaricon is a sentence made from the letters of a word. Thus Bereshith in your Genesis becomes "In the beginning God saw that Israel would accept the Law".'

I whisper, 'What shall I do with this book?'

'You will know when the time comes. Temura is permutation. The alphabet is bent in half and transposed. Some of the ways of doing this are very complex and reveal great truths.'

'Sheik Muhammad, is this book a force for good or for evil?'

He laughs, he finds my question too simple. 'Who made your heaven and earth, Christian?'

I swallow. 'God.'

'Who made the world, Templar?'

I whisper, 'The Devil.'

He opens the tent flap and orange sandy light pours into the tent, the sun rising. 'It is dawn, my friend. Time for you to make haste. Quickly, go!'

I call after him. 'Sheik Muhammad.'

He turns.

I hold out the book. 'Are the answers to everything in here?'

He smiles. 'Yes, Christian. They are.'

I am pushed and pulled outside. The people gather, the sheik claps his hands and two boys run towards us pulling a white horse that prances nervously. He scolds the boys, turns the horse so it is not frightened of its shadow, and a thin bearded man kneels for me to mount from his back. Two ferocious-looking bandits ride up beside me.

'I need no guard!'

'Your safe conduct,' the sheik says smoothly, 'and to ensure the safe return of my best horse. It's a dangerous land, the Holy Land. Farewell, my friend.' For an instant, as though I had opened the book in my saddlebag, I see inside his head. He means 'friend' in the same way the hunted is the friend of the hunter, the vanquished is the friend of the victor, and in the hot sun I shiver as though coming down with a fever. I kick my horse forward, but a dry, cawing voice calls to me, following me through the crowd.

'You thief, aren't you going to give it back to me?'

I look around, but it is me she calls to, no other. The crowd parts, and an old woman pushes through, limping, her hood pulled across the lower part of her face. 'I don't know you, woman.'

She calls up, 'Give me my best veil you took, you thief!'

With a stab I remember the green veil tucked behind my belt. 'Who is this?

162

Who is she?' How can she know of Laila's veil? Laughter. Everyone jostling around the horses. The old woman reaches out a clawed hand.

'Give it to me!'

To Sheik Muhammad I call out, 'I don't know her!'

He smiles. 'She is the woman who came to your tent last night, Christian. The temptation you resisted.'

The woman snatches at my belt, plucks out the green veil. Her other hand drops her hood. She reveals her white hair, her raddled face.

I shout, 'She's lying!'

The crone presses the veil tenderly to her loathsome skin. 'Alice, Alice, Alice, my love.' She almost prances in the cruelty of her joy, mimicking my English endearments she will never understand. 'Alice, Alice, Alice, my love!'

The sheik slaps my horse, and I ride like a madman into the desert. I deserve what he has done to me. There is no morality in the world, nothing good.

'Look at me, Alice. Look at me.'

I take off my cloak, untie my surcoat, pull off my shirt, stand naked beside your bed. Do you see me? I see your pain, but do you see mine? Your eyes are closed, you gasp for breath like a bellows. Then for a moment your unborn child releases you, your eyes open. You touch my chest with your fingertip. Your lightest caress draws a bloody line down me now, my skin parts at your touch like the surface of boiled milk, as if revealing the thing consuming me, all that is hidden inside me.

'The old woman the sheik gave you,' you whisper. 'That you thought was a beautiful girl—'

'That I dreamt was you, Alice.'

'She was diseased, wasn't she?'

Are you afraid, Alice? You do not have my disease, your skin is firm, but you are in too much pain to care.

'That wasn't the worst thing the sheik did, Alice.'

You groan. I reach under the rough blanket, touch the bloody hair between your legs. Your body opens under my fingers. Soon, soon. The gift of life. The miracle. I pull out my red fingers, twist your face towards me.

'Listen, Alice, I must tell you. He gave me the Book. The Book the sheik gave me . . .'

All day I ride as though the Devil rides behind me, the wind from the sea blowing over my face, my cloak tugging me, the ciphers of the Holy Kabbalah banging heavily in the saddlebags. Ahead of me the sky rises from a dark blue line, the Mediterranean. The sheik's guards ride alongside me, fine horsemen, I cannot turn aside even if I want to. If I lose the path, they guide me back to it. The horses come to the crest of a stony hill, the desert falls away, and below me is the sea.

The sun sets in my face. The fishing boats of Bat Yam are drawn up on the beach, but one remains tied at the ramshackle wooden jetty. We ride between the drying nets and fires for smoking fish, children running beside us. Three men wearing white stand by the boat at the end of the jetty, I see the Cross of the Holy Blood that they wear. My guards stop, the bridle of my horse is held, I dismount, then as I walk to the jetty the saddlebag is thrown to me. Not a word is said. They watch, then they ride away.

I walk on to the jetty alone.

Now I am close I see that the three men negotiating terms with the captain of the boat are filthy, travel-stained, their cloaks torn and greasy. The man nearest me hears my footsteps, turns suddenly with his hand on his sword: Sir Geoffrey de Prudome. With him is Giles de Ridfort, eyes staring like a madman's – like my own, perhaps. The two men have been arguing, their faces are still red with disagreement just when they should be pulling together.

'Brother Nicholas.' My Master, with more grey in his beard, shows no surprise at seeing me. 'If I should meet anyone unexpectedly in such circumstances, I should expect him to be you.' He embraces me. 'And wearing the Cross of a knight. That, too, I should have expected.' He laughs, then stares into my eyes. 'I confirm you in your new rank. How did you survive?' He finds something in my gaze that makes him uneasy. 'Later. Tell me later. We must sail before dark.' He calls to the third man, who negotiates with the captain of the vessel. 'Oc, my dear Bernard, just give him all the gold you have.' Now I know the third Templar is Bernard de Blanchefort, very young but the grandson of Bertrand, sixth Grand Master of France; his son, also Bernard, was the first man Saladin executed. Does young Bernard know the manner of his father's death? I watch him hand a pouch of money to the captain, who weighs it in his palm. The captain nods and ties it round his waist. If he falls over it will drag him to the bottom of the sea, but he will die rich.

We jump down into the open boat, but de Ridfort stays on the jetty. 'I will not come. My duty is here. I shall ride to the castle at Acre, I shall fight to my last breath. Go to the Pope, tell all the kings and princes of Christendom what has befallen us. Raise a mighty army, and return!'

My Master responds to this tirade angrily. 'Jerusalem and the Holy Land are lost to us for ever! Don't be a fool! There is no hope for us here.' Hearing this, de Ridfort shakes his head violently, he will not accept defeat.

At the captain's command the moorings are cast off, boys scamper, the oddly-shaped sail is raised, the ropes creak, then I hear the splash of spray as the boat turns in to the waves.

My Master shouts back, 'There's no hope for the Brotherhood in this godforsaken land! It's lost. Lost.' But the dwindling figure on the jetty turns from us with a gesture of contempt, walks back to the shadow that is now the land . . . and then there is nothing but the sea and the sound of the waves in the dark.

Where do we sail? I do not care. To Cyprus, or to France? It does not matter. I sleep, and dream I send the saddlebag spinning into the sea. I wake, dawn light pours into my eyes, and the saddlebag remains in my lap where I have clutched it all night. I throw it into the sea . . . but first I take out the Book, tie it safely round my waist with a rope. My Master, leaning back against the hull, his cloak pulled over his head against the spray, watches me with interest but says nothing. I remember him laying his hand on the True Cross. *I am a Muslim. I swear it.*

The midday sun is sharp, the black shadow of the sail swings back and forth across us. I say, 'I heard what you swore.'

He shrugs. 'A Templar cannot be forced to swear an oath.'

'You did. Of your own free will, you did.'

My Master smiles, twists his forefinger and middle finger together. 'I lied for my God.'

He touches the Book at my waist, he wants to know, but I crawl away from him. We were both prepared to pay any price to be what we are: alive.

I curl up in the bow, the spray sheeting each side of me into the blue water. De Blanchefort, my own age or younger, with dark eyes and pale beard, of noble blood but no more or less a knight than I, sits beside me and soon he is Bernard and I am *Nicholas* in his strange French accent. He speaks the language of the Oc, the land of Yes in southern France, so called because to them *oc* not *oeil* or *oui* means yes. Most Templars are French – so many that the Evil Ones call us *Franj* – and France, as always, is the prize of Europe.

We murmur, casting glances at my Master, who sleeps. Finally Bernard admits the truth: he escaped death not through any feat of bravery but because he relieved himself behind a bush during the night of our retreat, and got lost. At dawn, alone as I, he escaped by dressing as a Muslim and various humiliations. Finally, with tears in his eyes, he admits the whole truth. The grandson of Bernard de Blanchfort, the Master who by legend discovered the Sanctum Sanctorum and the tomb of Christ beneath Solomon's Temple, escaped by slipping through the lines of the Evil Ones wearing a woman's clothes, hiding his beard behind a veil! And so he is alive.

He touches my face earnestly. 'Is my father truly dead?'

'Yes. *Oc*. I saw him die.'

'On the field of battle?'

'No. After.'

'But with honour?'

Bernard has told me the truth and I treat him the same way. 'He called out your name, for news of you. No word came. He prayed and the Evil Ones sodomised and beheaded him.'

Bernard closes his eyes. 'We are betrayed by bishops who do not believe, and yet the Pope declares us honest Christians with Cathar beliefs to be heretics. It is not God that is corrupt and has forsaken us, it is our Church.' *Us*. Bernard is a Cathar Christian. He believes he knows Jesus and the road to Heaven as well as the Pope, believes even the lowest peasant is an individual with personal responsibility for his actions and rights as well as duties. 'The Pope knows he's lost the Holy Land. He's free to turn his fury against us to his own advantage, distract the energies of ambitious men and priests. It will suit his purposes. There will be civil war, and the Pope will win.'

'Is it true you Cathars do not believe in the Resurrection?'

My Master's deep voice interrupts. 'Bernard believes.' His eyes are open, he crawls towards us along the heaving timbers of the hull's curve, the boat is so heeled over by the wind. 'You do believe, don't you, Bernard?' My Master places his hand on my shoulder, lightly, but with all the formidable strength of his personality. 'You see, there's something very important you should understand. Bernard is a Cathar, but he is also a Templar.'

Bernard says, 'I have seen the body of Christ.' He repeats it. 'I have seen the body of Christ.'

My Master looks at me steadily, unsurprised. He knows.

I'm dizzy, seasick, the whole world seems to move, not just the boat. I murmur, 'But only the Church may change bread and wine into the flesh and blood of Jesus Christ. The Mass is the only resurrection we are permitted before Judgement Day.' My voice trails away, snatched by the wind that pushes our little boat. I whisper, 'The legends are true?'

'*Oc*. While my grandfather was Master, masons digging the foundation of our Jerusalem Temple found His tomb. It's true.'

'Your grandfather saw Him with his own eyes?' I lick the salt taste of the sea from my lips, then realise the magnitude of our loss. Jerusalem is fallen. His body is gone from our reach.

'Be calm, Nicholas. *Oc*, I myself have seen Him. The earthly manifestation of God. The body that God inhabited and will again, at the Resurrection.'

'But how did you *know* it was Him?'

Bernard looks at me simply. 'You will know. You are a Templar knight. You wear the Holy Cross and the Holy Blood. You have the right to see Him.'

I don't know what to say. I really do not. I am merely a human, a sinner. I do not need, Alice, to catalogue my sins again to you, the desire to sin born into me even as a child, as much a part of me as my blood and bones, my secret desire to kill Jack because I love you, my fear of drowning so that having you slipped

165

from my grasp, every downward step that fear and lust has since driven me to, including the sin of sodomy, which by perverting nature is rebellion against God . . . and I have the right to see Him? I say, stupidly, 'In Jerusalem?'

The Master answers in his deep voice. 'The body of Christ is our greatest treasure and secret, moved to a place of safety many years ago.'

'Where?'

'Safe.'

The captain tacks his boat from side to side against the wind, night falls, the moon rises. I can't sleep. The knot that secures the Book to my waist digs into my stomach, and when I ease it, the rope slips undone, the Book drops into my hands. I look around me through half-closed eyes. The others sleep, the boy on the steering oar is hidden by the sail.

The Book falls open in my lap, and I read by moonlight.

I have told you already, Alice, a little of what it contains. There is much more. There is more than my mind can hold. How can I read by moonlight? Yet I do, the page is clear. Here are the ten *Sephers* or ciphers which are the foundation of the Kabbalah, the Grace. The numbers seem to move with the rocking of the boat, open themselves to my eyes like an index. First, the nature of God. Second, the creation of the universe. Third, the relationship between angels and man. Fourth, our destiny. Fifth . . . there is so much more.

The pages turn under my hands, the paper flutters as though finding its own place. Here is Keter, the Crown, first *Sepher* of the Tree of Life. Not only the Bible is the Book's source, the real world is, even the seemingly random waves of the sea around me have meaning, organisation, and there is a reason for the wind. The divine truth is hidden within creation, in the earth. Suddenly I know this is true. More than know. Feel. Comprehend.

I blink, and the numbers move. Am I seeing merely a clever *trompe l'oeil*, a trick of the eye such as women delight in weaving into their embroidery? Yet I know what I see is true. I turn the pages forward and glimpse the second *Sepher*, the second level of understanding called Hockmah, Wisdom, and for a brief instant everything I think I know is turned on its head, I am erased. Wisdom, a wasteland, a place of riches. A *palace* of riches. Something not to be approached without awe or attained without submission. I think I see . . . I think I see . . . I feel as though my brain will burst.

My eyes turn up, my head lolls. The pages flutter back to Keter, the first *Sepher*.

My Master is awake, watching me. I see his eyes gleam.

I continue to read by moonlight. I cannot stop. Whose wedding did Jesus attend at Cana? His own. Where did Jesus walk on the water? At a place called Qumran on the Dead Sea, when He walked along a jetty to baptise Gentiles not Jews. And more. Much more.

And this is only the start of the first level of understanding.

My mind reels. Is all that I have learnt true, or merely fact? If truth differs from fact, which is the heresy?

The Book is taken from my hands. My Master reads. He is older than I am, wiser. He shudders as he reads, and the pages turn. My eyes close but I cannot sleep. The moon sets, darkness is total, I cannot tell if he still reads, but I hear the pages flutter. Daylight comes and he sleeps, exhausted, dark beneath the eyes, the wind lifting the pages of the Book against the weight of his hands. I slide the Book from his lap. He wakes, holds on.

'You can't keep this to yourself, Brother Nicholas. Our every belief is vindicated.'

I tie the Book to my waist, crawl forward to the bow.

'You can't keep it to yourself!' he calls.

All day the wind from the deserts of Africa blows stronger, we taste sand as well as salt on our lips. The sun shines in a halo, and my friend Bernard reads the Book. The world is stranger than we ever imagined, and the truth more and deeper and more marvellous than we dared dream. But is it really truth, or is it a lie? How can we know? Is the Book a force for evil, or for good? A gift from an enemy. But many of the gifts of the Evil Ones, numbers, algebra, geometrical devices, astronomy, translations from the Greek sages lost to us, have done nothing but good even though learning sows confusion and casts doubt.

I remember the sheik's warning. *No harm will befall you except by your own hand.*

As I turn the page it cuts my finger, and I bleed.

Bernard, like me, cannot read beyond the first *Sepher*, falls into an exhausted sleep. I snatch back the Book before he can hold on to it, tie it again at my waist. A blue wave rises beside us, breaks into white foam, drives our little vessel forward. The sail is lowered until only a scrap shows, then taken down altogether at sunset, and all night the gale moans around the bare mast. We sense the waves rising to peaks, water pours aboard, we hear the thunder of surf, the captain tries to put about. The steering oar cracks, ropes snap, the mast goes. There is a terrific crash and rocks break through the bottom of the boat, we are spilt into the foam and breaking waves, scrape our hands on rocks and barnacles. The captain drags me down as he drowns, I kick his belly, stick my fingers in his eyes, and the air trapped in my clothes and the Book whirl me up. Hands grip my arms, I am dragged on to the smooth sand of a beach.

Dawn lights just the three of us. I whisper, 'Where are we?'

'This is the Langue d'Oc. We are not so far from home.' Bernard finds a village. He knows this place, is known, and returns with three horses. The marshland and vineyards behind the beach quickly give way to parched hills, then green mountains rise above us. The hot sun dries our cloaks but leaves them heavy with salt. In the distance the mountaintops hovering above the horizon are white, like a line of clouds. 'The Pyrenees. We shall not go that far.' Bernard's voice echoes as we follow a foresters' track along a wooded valley, a stream which he calls the Sals foams beside us. He played here often as a child, holding back the Muslim hordes with taunts and a wooden sword. I cannot imagine Muslims here. But he gives me a haunted look. 'Four hundred years ago the Muslims controlled all this land.' He adds grimly, 'And may do so again.'

Yes. This is the change that has come over us. We have lost Jerusalem. We are not invincible.

Bernard points through the treetops to a bare rocky mountain on our right. 'Cardou.' His accent is so strong that for a moment I think he says Corps Dieu, but he is already pointing left. 'There on the other side is Château Blanchefort.' I glimpse something white, then the steepness of the hill hides the building. At the crossroads in Serres the villagers do not welcome us and one old man spits. We cross the river on a stone bridge and soon I see Blanchefort clearly on its bare hilltop, no village around it, more like an eyrie or an observation post than a dwelling. We follow the steep track out of the valley and arrive at the castle, built of rock as white as its name. We are not expected, of course. News of the terrible defeat has arrived and the place is empty, benches and tables overturned, the kitchen fires cold. An old hunting dog creeps whining across the empty great hall to greet Bernard. Looking out of the narrow slitted windows towards Cardou with its strange triangular cliffs, to my left the village of Peyrolles with its church shining in the last of the sun, and the Château d'Arques similarly prominent beyond the flank of Cardou, seem for a moment to my mind to form a great triangle whose purpose I can only guess. As you know, we Templars site our houses with the utmost precision. But I blink and the moment is gone, the valleys fill with evening shadows and only the pattern

167

of the hilltops stands out, then winks into darkness with the setting of the sun until only Cardou remains.

Without turning I say, 'He's here, isn't He? This is where you hid Him.'

My Master says, 'He's ours. He's ours to the Resurrection. The body was brought here years ago, just a body like any other man's.'

I realise the scale of it. Such an ambitious undertaking could never be kept completely secret. 'So all the legends, all the rumours, all the stories about the Holy Grail—'

'They're all true,' Bernard says. 'The most precious object in Christendom belongs to us.'

'The source of our power, our strength,' my Master says. 'Even our Pope doesn't know, not for certain.'

The sun lingers on the rounded summit of Cardou.

Bernard says in his gentle voice, 'My grandfather started the work but my father, who was born before his father took the Templar oath – we Templar families are careful in such matters – bought the land and finished the buildings whose placing both reveals and guards our secret.' He looks bitterly at the empty hall. 'Did.'

Now I see only the deep blue afterglow of the sky above the black world.

Bernard whispers, 'Pain, suffering, humility, sacrifice, strength. We must be strong.'

My Master orders, 'Show him.'

You don't hear me, do you, Alice? Not a word. I'm telling you of these great truths that are the underpinnings of our world, but you're too bound up in the business of life to hear – or at least, to know that you hear. Ah, my Alice, how I wish I could put an end to your agony. Your chin presses your chest, the blanket falls from your opened thighs, you grunt like an animal, pushing, pressing, groaning. You swear at me, shout at me, curse me. A girl in labour lies about nothing. How you hate me!

Not much longer now.

We ride our horses in single file downhill through the dark woods, Bernard illuminated by the burning torch he holds above his head to light our way. We cross the river, come to the foresters' track, then Bernard finds a path that goes nowhere. Soon it is very steep, twisting back and forth up the slopes of Cardou. Gravel slides from the horses' hooves and falls rattling into the darkness below. We can go no further on horseback.

Bernard tethers the horses to the last tree and we continue on foot. I ask, 'Are the villagers never curious?'

'They're superstitious and believe in demons. They believe in Asmodeus, Baphomet in his earthly form, architect of Solomon's Temple.'

'And other demons.' My Master's voice recites out of the dark. 'The seven princes of evil. Samael and his staff of demons. Zaafiel his deputy. Zamiel. Qasfiel. Ragziel. Abriel. Meshulhiel. This is the secret knowledge of demons deciphered by Rabbi Sherira and Rabbi Hai, so they could ascend the ladder of prophecy.' I realise my Master has read into the second *Sepher* of the Book at least, and hurry forward after Bernard.

'Let's turn back.'

He says gently, 'You know you cannot.'

Bernard's right. We can't stop. Even the Order of Templars cannot stop, we have become the prisoners of our fabled possession.

Bernard climbs. 'We Cathars are Gnostics, Nicholas.' He holds up the flame, it roars as it blows in the night wind. 'That means we are Christians who believe in *gnosis*. Knowledge. We are very close to Christ.' Does he mean literally, or close followers? Perhaps both. 'We are followers of St Paul. St Paul was a Pharisee as well as a Roman citizen. The Pharisees, like the Essenes, disliked the rites of the Jerusalem Temple and believed that our own bodies are the true Temple. We are responsible for our actions, we are all capable of the resurrection in our own lifetime by our own individual efforts, we do not need the chanting of priests or the sacraments of the Church to improve us or tell us what is good and what is evil.'

'No wonder the Pope hates you. No sacraments. No priests. No Church.'

The huge pale triangle of the cliff I had noticed earlier on Cardou glimmers above us. There's no food even for goats up here, nothing but rock and shale. My feet slither, I hang on, Bernard takes my elbow. The knot that binds the Book to me hurts but I dare not retie it in the dark for fear of losing it.

Bernard says, 'St Paul, the first Christian, believed in the resurrection of the soul after death.'

'Yes, on Judgement Day.'

'No. That's the Pope. St Paul's Christians, Christ's Christians who are the foundation but not the fabric of the Roman Church, believe in the resurrection of *everyone*'s soul after death. No waiting till the end of time. The constant improvement of the soul by good works. The moral imperative, the upward ascent of the soul by its own efforts to achieve the closeness of God.' *Of*. Immediately I heard the echo of my schooling with Brother Paulus. *The quest of God*. Not *for* God. *Of* God.

Bernard had more company in his beliefs than he knew.

Still we climb. I sense the windy space below us, the swish of wings, but see nothing. Then suddenly I understand, grasp Bernard's shoulder.

'My God, Bernard, you believe Jesus will return before Judgement Day!'

He turns with a smile. 'Yes. Is it not the most marvellous certainty?'

The light of the flame moves over my Master's face, gleams in his eyes. He is staring at the Book tied to my waist. Knowledge. He wants it with all his heart and soul. He knows, thinks he knows, he can use knowledge, not be used by it. He raises his eyes to mine. 'That is why we are His guardians. It is the Templars' most sacred duty is keep Him safe, that the Resurrection may come while we live, and we shall be ready kneeling and girded for war at His side, His servants and His apostles.'

I'm awed by his ambition, but see the sense of it. The Resurrection, the Templars, the Messiah.

'Suppose some goatherd finds the place?' I ask. 'Or Muslims overrun this land, as they did before?'

Bernard points upward at the pale triangle. 'Chains hold back tons of rock, a single blow—'

'No!' my Master says. 'The Temple of God would be lost to us for ever.'

Bernard ducks beneath an overhanging boulder, reaches up. He finds something, winds a mechanism, but the boulder is too heavy to move. Instead, the path drops down on one side to reveal a ramp into the hillside, and the way between the rocks is blocked by the most incongruous sight I can imagine.

A door into the mountain.

Bernard takes an iron key and unlocks the door. He takes another key and a second lock thuds open. I look up, acutely aware of the tons of chained rock hovering above us. He pulls on the door, it does not move. 'Help. Help me.' We all pull. Slowly the door, studded with brass or gold, swings outwards, and reveals . . . nothing.

Bernard calls some men's names, but no one replies.

The guards have run away; Jerusalem is fallen, our God has forsaken us, this place has lost whatever magic it once had in the hearts of the men of this region. I doubt we will truly find the body of Christ inside.

And yet . . . I have started the Book. All I know is that I do not know.

Bernard reaches his blazing torch forward into the dark, a flambeau in a wall-holder bursts into flame, spits fiery sparks of pitch, then burns steadily. He hands it to my Master, sets another aflame for me. We pull the door closed behind us. There is barely room to stand.

We follow the tunnel upwards at an angle. At intervals brass flambeaux are set in the walls. The rough rock gives way to smooth black marble, glints of gold, the headroom increases. I hold the flame high.

I see masonic symbols etched in gold into the marble. Theodolites, astrolabes, dividers, beautifully worked. The All-Seeing Eye. I walk forward on echoing footsteps as the roof angles away above me. Gold steps lead up to a screen of gold worked with twelve gold pillars, gold cherubs, angels, trumpets, and in one corner the savage, mournful figure of the demon Asmodeus, a chain round its neck, imprisoned by an angel.

I climb the steps.

Here is a double door. I sense its weight, solid gold. One side of it is ajar. There is a chamber beyond. I turn slightly, squeeze through without touching the gold.

I am inside the Temple of God. I am entering the Tabernacle.

Clouds of smoke rise from the flambeaux burning along the walls. It is as I have read in the Bible, in Exodus. The Menorah, the seven-branched candlestick of hammered gold, stands on its ordained table. Here is the altar of burnt offering; here the altar of incense; here the mercy seat where the blood of the sacrifice is to be sprinkled. Only by prayer, sacrifice and blood can a man or woman come to God. The Lord dwells among His people. He is here.

I pass through the final doorway.

At once the flame is redoubled, fiercely bright. The ceiling is the Shekinah, the visible manifestation of the Divine Majesty in the Temple of Solomon, a golden glory of reflected light like a sunrise. In the centre of this circular room, the Arch of the Covenant, round as a Templar church, stands an altar of pure white marble topped by a gold casket as long as a man.

On each side of the casket, in solid gold letters of Latin or Hebrew, I cannot tell, is written: ARAM MENAHT MENOU.

I cannot see inside the casket. I climb the white marble steps.

Inside, wrapped in a linen shroud, lies His earthly body.

Believe me. I recognise His face. I know Him. His blood seeps through the weave, I see the outline of His face as clear as though He is alive, only sleeping. The crown of thorns bleeds. His large, lidded eyes, small understanding mouth, His suffering, His humility and strength, all are as I imagined them, worked deep as wounds through the fabric from inside. Blood drips from the wound in His side, from the bloody nail holes in His wrists and ankles.

I touch the cloth.

Warm. 'My God,' I whisper, 'why have you forsaken me?'

My Master whispers, 'Do you doubt what you see?'

No. I shake my head. I cannot speak. I know what I see.

He whispers, 'Give me the Book.'

I shake my head. No. His hands grapple at my waist, I push him away. He shouts, 'The Bible tells us it belongs here. The Arch of the Covenant in the Tabernacle of the Lord. The tablets of the Law, the Word, carried in the desert for forty years.' He draws his sword. 'Only by blood and sacrifice can sinners ever come to live with the Holy One—' We are fighting.

'Gentlemen!' Bernard shouts. 'Not here!'

We fall back.

I put my hands to my head. 'We must be mad.'

At the head of the earthly body are the golden Holy Grails containing the

170

holy blood and internal organs removed by Nicodemus. But His body still bleeds. From this holy blood we are anointed.

It's all true.

My Master speaks decisively. 'One good man – a few good men – can save us all.' He smiles, and for the first time I realise his teeth are rotten. 'We can't leave Him. Jerusalem is fallen and everything that was safe is in danger. Lord, help us!'

Scream, Alice.

The blood gushes from you, I see my child's head jammed between your legs, neither in nor out in the moment of birth. My fingers slide over its wet hair, I cannot pull, it will not come. In your agony you grab my hands, try to pull yourself up, or back, I do not know. My skin slides from my hands into your hands. I am bones and veins and fingernails, I cry out in my agony just as you do.

Cold rain falling from the cold grey sky.

The clouds hide the mountains on our left. Each mountain torrent has washed the road away and we manhandle the cart across the slippery stones. I forget ever being warm or dry, my life is walking beside the solid wooden wheels of the cart as they turn, my feet in the mud, my hands turning the muddy wheels, pushing with my shoulders. I am made of mud. Another torrent, icy cold, the water sprays, and the rain falls, the cart bumps, the mud splashes and smears. I cannot see, I cannot hear. Bernard, too, is exhausted, and my Master rides the cart, and once it almost overturns in a stream, and we hear the coffin slide under the tarpaulin that hides it, hear it strain against the ropes that hold it and bang heavily against the side of the cart.

Bernard and I stare at one another, wide-eyed.

Another Templar refugee who also by a miracle survived the rout, Godfrey de Charney of the ancient Normandy family, follows the tracks left by the cart, joins us. He's wild-eyed, mad, strong, and we need every ounce of strength.

At night we make camp as far as we can from anywhere, a forest glade, the bank of a stream, where we will not be seen. Somehow we make fire, a great bonfire of any old deadwood and branches we can hack down, and sleep like the dead, but always my Master comes to me and puts his hand where you know, Alice, and strokes me and caresses me in the way you know, then puts his mouth to my waist and looks up at me with the whites of his eyes and says, 'Give me the Book.'

I will not.

We've lost the Shroud. Thieves, or children. De Charney is gone, perhaps it was him, but we still have the prize, and the knowledge, and we will find the strength somehow.

During daylight we stop at no village, rattle between the hovels with drawn swords, and the cart bumps down the muddy track on to the great broad plain that leads to Bordeaux. There are always Templar ships at Bordeaux, the wine is profitable.

In the night my Master whispers, 'Give me the Book.'

But I will not.

The clouds evaporate, the sun beats down, burns our heads, blisters our necks, the dust clogs our throats. At my Master's command I am pushing the body of Jesus Christ to . . . to I know not where. Safety. Bordeaux. And from there, where? I do not know. I do not know what I am doing. I push the wheel and it turns, I lift with all my strength and stumble forward, but why? Do I do right or wrong? Is this good I do, or evil? I follow my Master's orders in every matter except the Book, but am I doing evil or good? Do I have a choice? My mind goes round. Should I give Him to the Pope? Should I give Him to the

171

Archbishop of Canterbury? To that farmer watching us from the shade of the tree, drinking his wine? Shall I call out in the village square, 'I carry the body of Jesus Christ, He is yours, take Him, He belongs to all of us'?

I do none of these things. I push the wheel, I put one foot in front of the other, I live.

And at night my Master comes to me again. 'Give me the Book.'

I hear Sheik Muhammad's voice. *No harm will befall you except by your own hand.*

I endure my Master's attentions. He seeks love, as I do.

O God! Help me. If only I didn't know so much. If only I could unlearn what I have learnt, unknow what I have known.

If only I was a child again.

My finger still bleeds, dripping, where the page cut it.

The Templar ship *Baucent* lies at Bordeaux. There are rats on the wharf, creatures like mice but black, and very much larger, vicious, the first I have seen so far from the Holy Land. My Master commandeers the vessel, the prize is manhandled into the hold by labourers who know nothing but the cost of bread and beer and women, the ship sails into the storms of Biscay regardless of the weather. My Master smiles at the wind and the waves. He knows we are safe.

But I do not feel safe. I feel that every wave, as it rises beneath us, may reveal the edge of the world, and fling us down to Heaven or Hell.

And now the sea is calm. I know we're being deceived. I can smell the storm coming.

My Master will not put in at Dover. Men are ordered into the longboat, bent to the oars, tow us laboriously round North Foreland into the Thames. 'Now the wind will blow from the east,' my Master says, and the wind does blow from the east. But is it God's wind, or the Devil's? It blows us upriver, the rising tide sweeps us round the Isle of Dogs, the old wooden drawbridge is raised on ramshackle London Bridge and we slide through on the last of the tide and the last of the light, and moor beneath the walls of the Temple.

And the wind turns, and blows from the west.

All evening we're busy. Torches are lit, flames smoke in the rising wind, and as the torchlit procession enters the round church I feel the first kiss of the rain. The gold sepulchre is lifted on to its altar in the centre of the church, and my Master draws his sword and shouts, 'Truly this is the Temple of God!'

The Knights Templar draw their swords and we roar our approval.

But then I shout, 'No!'

Nobody hears me, or cares. The great circle presses forward to kiss the gold, to pledge their allegiance, every forehead is pressed in prayer and religious devotion to the hilt of a sword.

'No!' I shout. But no to what? I do not know.

I drop my sword. It clatters.

I face the circle of my brothers, the Poor Fellow-Soldiers of Christ, beef fat gleaming on their lips, their bellies full of beef and wine. I throw down my knife, pull off my tabard with the Cross of His Blood on the left breast, throw it down, stand naked but for my loincloth and white robe. And the Book which is tied by rough rope round my waist.

I pull the knot free, send the Book sliding across the floor to my Master's feet.

My Master picks it up. Already the gold sepulchre is being carried to the winding stair, will be carried down, I know not where. The soft scrape of the pallbearers' feet sounds very loud. I hear the gentle hiss of rain on the roof vault high above.

My Master calls out to me. 'You are a man, Nicholas. You cannot deny

your nature. You can try but you cannot. You are what you are, no other.'
He holds the Book tight to his chest.

I walk past him to the great door.

He calls after me, 'What do you search for, Nicholas?'

I run. I run into the rain. Here are stable lads, here a horse, I'm in the saddle, the gate opens on to Fleet Street and I ride, I ride faster through the rain, London Bridge flashes beneath me, the storm pulls out my cloak behind me and the lightning flickers and the wind blows and I swear I fly, I swear it.

What do you search for, Nicholas?

And so, in the storm, I come home to the bridge my father built. Dismount. I've even lost my boots.

Here it is, the arch. Kissing Alice.

I stand under the arch, take off my robe, let the stream take it. I have returned to the place where I started.

I walk through the dark and rain, brambles scratch me, then lightning lights my way. Here's the house. The door opens.

It's you.

I fall inside.

Three
Durand

Alice's tale

London Bridge, 4 February 1832

Quickly, quickly, run to me, comfort me. Over here, do you see me now?
Hurry, quick!
  Alice?
Touch me. Your hands are warm. Warm me, stroke me. Do you hear me?
  Why did you run away last night?
I could not bear to tell you more.
  Did you believe Nick's terrible story that he told?
Every word.
  But surely—
I know now that every word is true. Every word.
  And that he told Widow Cristina too?
Yes, on her deathbed he told her, behind closed drapes. And then he
strangled her.
  *I hardly see you in the dark. I sleep all day, I wake all night. I can't work
for thinking of you, can't draw, can't hold a pen, thinking of you. Are you a
dream, Alice?*
Young man, tell me your name.
  Frank Laguerre. A picture artist for the Morning Herald, *when I can. And I'm
thirty-one years old.*
What brought you on to London Bridge that first night? Look at me. Was
it to die? Look into my eyes, don't be afraid. Thirty-one is a sad age to die.
Cling on to life.
  Tell me of you. Did you have your baby?
Yes. Yes, I gave birth to my son. My sweet son.
  *Is that the end? What happened to Nick? Did he redeem himself? Did he learn to
love you?*
Nick was evil. He could no more love me than a fish loves a hook.
  Are there tears in your eyes? How can that be? How can you weep?
I remember the moment of my death.

London Bridge, Boxing Day, 1200

This is all I was. This push. This agony. This unendurable agony. I heard my throat screaming as though I was someone else, I was pushing my insides out, and then I felt my baby rush out of me, the marvel of him, his head, his shoulders, his hips, his fingers and toes, perfect, a boy. Into my husband's hands.

I slumped back with my eyes closed, unaware of almost everything, muttering wearily. 'Jack, he's here. The boy you wanted.' Fine gold hair, Jack's hair. 'He even has your hair.' I smiled despite my exhaustion, half asleep, half awake, half dreaming, and suddenly I remembered vividly, as though you have somehow reminded me of it, Jack, the bright memory of the naughty little boy Durand selling apples to the workmen on the Pont St Sauveur, cadging leftovers from their tables, and they adopted him, tousled his gold hair, called him Durand le Petty-pom. Durand the little apple.

I knew what name I wanted for our son.

My eyes blinked. My son Durand's face was red as an apple from crying. I couldn't help smiling. He'll have your smile, Jack.

'Jack?' Nick said. '*Jack?* Jack's dead.'

And I remembered everything. The Horns of Hattin, Sheik Muhammad, the Book. The completion sacrifice, Nick splashing the blood of the girl on the stones of London Bridge.

Nick had thrust his dagger into my Jack's heart and buried him somewhere on the bridge. But where?

Nick bellowed upstairs for Rosie. I heard the door creak and my faithful girl crept in, her broken arm in the sling I had made for her. Her round face was fishbelly white, scaly with dried tears and distress. She avoided Nick's gaze, crossed to me, meek and terrified. She squeezed my hand. 'Oh, Mistress Alice,' she whispered. 'He's *so* beautiful.' She set about my bloodstained blankets, and the afterbirth must be dealt with.

'Leave her,' Nick said. 'Look after my son.'

Rosie said, 'He isn't your son!'

But Nick was tired, the only person he listened to was himself. His hands looked like skinned venison, he was dark beneath the eyes. Telling his story was a kind of birth to him, he was as exhausted as I was. 'Just do as you're told,' he muttered.

I nodded to her. So Rosie held my son before I did, laid him in her lap by the fire and wrapped him warm, wiped his face, all with one hand, awkwardly. I wanted to see everything, hold everything of my baby, but I was too drained even to sit up. Nick left the room, I heard his footsteps go downstairs. He must be hungry, probably he was finding meat in the house, it keeps at this time of year. Suddenly the fire was brighter, Rosie must have added fresh logs, I had dozed and she was shaking my shoulder. I shivered, the blood that coated my legs was very cold. '. . . Alice, Mistress Alice.'

At once I turned my head to my baby, placed in a basket near the fire, but not too close, no spark would land on him. 'When is it?'

'No hour, mistress.'

Midnight! 'But it can't be.'

'You were in labour for a night and a day until this evening. Doubtless you didn't see the day, in straits as you were.'

All I remembered was Nick's story. The body of Christ bleeding in its sepulchre, His soul separated from His spirit until the Resurrection, was more real to me than the events of today. 'Did . . . you hear what my husband told me?'

'Mistress? Upstairs, I was.' Rosie touched her arm, made a face. 'I don't think it'll set straight.'

'But you must have heard something.'

'Not me, not a word. The storm's stopped its awful wind, but it's still snowing. Pretty, it is.' She smiled, seeing my gaze had not left my son once while we spoke. 'Shall I fetch him to you?'

'Yes, Rosie, quickly!'

She laid the warm bundle in my arms. I smelled Durand, inhaled the scent of his hair. Touched his tiny fingernails. 'He's so ugly! He's so lovely I could eat him.'

Rosie was eager. She would want a baby of her own, one day, and would want to leave my service. 'He's got your eyebrows, mistress. And your husband Jack's eyes, and his smile too, I'll wager.' She burst into tears.

Misery washed over me, but then I remembered how Rosie had patted my tummy full of child and told me, 'Jack's still alive in there, mistress.' It was true. Jack and I, the happiness we'd had together, lived on in our Durand. Our happiness was not all gone. I must fight, and fight, and fight for every day. I touched my thumb to Durand's snub nose, stroked his forehead. Rosie was right about his eyebrows. They were dark under his blond curls. His mouth suckled my breast, his tiny leg kicked in time to his sucking.

I heard footsteps start upstairs, then they came faster and faster, pounding on the landing. The door banged open. Nick's eyes were alert, suspicious. He held back the door with his fist, and I saw he wore gloves. 'What did she say? It's not my son? *What* did she say?'

Rosie cradled her broken arm, too terrified to speak. Then she cried out, 'I'm sorry, mistress! I'm sorry!'

I handed the baby up to her. 'Place him in his basket by the fire, would you, Rosie.'

She performed the task. Nick let the door slam, stood close to me. A thread of blood oozed from one fingertip of his gloves, swung, dropped somewhere I did not see.

I said clearly, 'Durand is not your son. He's Jack's.'

Nick clenched his hands, I heard the blood squeezing from his gloves but I dared not take my eyes off his own. He swore. 'You filthy disgusting liar! You're trying to take my own, true, legitimate son away from me.' His eyes widened. 'My God, my God, you still love Jack!'

I screamed, '*Of course I still love Jack!*'

Nick stared at me as though I had struck him in the heart. His mouth opened, then closed. 'Yes. Of course. It's obvious,' he said quietly. 'I would have done anything for you, Alice,' he added. 'I *did* do anything for you.'

I hissed, 'But you never thought of me, only yourself.'

Nick leaned over me and put his gloved hands on each side of my head on the bolster, looked at the baby asleep at Rosie's feet by the fire, then looked again down at me. 'Alice,' he breathed. 'Tell me you're lying.'

Rosie spoke up. 'She's not lying.'

Nick burst out, 'Jack was sterile as a mule!'

I said, 'No, I had been pregnant before and suffered a miscarriage.'

'Liar! Who did you tell? No one!'

'It was no one's business but our own.'

'I knew,' Rosie said in a tiny, terrified voice. 'I was there. I saw.'

'Damn you, Alice,' Nick muttered. 'He never deserved you. Damn you both.'

'My mistress told me she had caught with child before you raped her,' Rosie said defiantly. 'We were talking of it before she went out, that very night.'

'Rosie, be quiet.' I looked up at Nick. 'It's true.'

Nick knew it was true. Durand was not his son, he was Jack's. Jack's victory. I saw the realisation in Nick's eyes, I saw his bitterness and the jealousy that had driven him all his life.

He stood upright slowly. 'Well,' he said calmly, 'it doesn't matter any more. It's all in the past. You mustn't blame yourself, my dear.' What was he talking about? 'I know the protracted agony and labour of birth often throws women's minds into a state of despair and confusion. Isn't that so, Rosie?'

Rosie was perplexed. 'I've heard it said so, master.'

'Very well. I shall sit with my wife and son tonight. Go to your room and get your sleep. Off you go.'

'Yes, master.' Rosie hesitated, but I could not see her expression for Nick's shoulder hid it. I saw her hand adjust the position of the basket near the fire, then heard her go meekly to the door.

'Don't go, Rosie!' I called.

'*Go!*' Nick said.

I said, 'Nick, don't.'

He pushed Rosie out, closed the door. I heard the latch drop. The sound of Rosie's footsteps climbed out of hearing in the stair turret. Nick slid the wooden peg through the latch, locking it down. He came back to me and so deep was the pain in his eyes, worse than any I have experienced, that I felt sorry for him. Sorry for everything bad that had happened; but he had made it happen.

'I don't love you, Nick,' I said. 'I never have. I never will, whatever you do.'

Nick put his hands round my throat.

I said quickly: 'What did you learn in the Book?'

His hands tightened, squeezed off my air. I tried to say, *Nick, don't*, but I couldn't, and even momentary suffocation was a frightening feeling. He was threatening me. *Nick, don't*. He whispered in my ear, 'The Book says that after Jesus was crucified, dead, and buried, He descended into Hell. Well, He has. I brought Him here, Alice. I brought Him here and, Son of God or not, He's my prisoner.'

I lay still, keeping him calm, then I really had to breathe. I tried to push his hands away. Nick pressed down on his thumbs, hurting my voice, the hard lump of my Adam's apple, pushing it into my spine, really hurting me now. He put his mouth close to my face. 'I should have let you drown.'

I jerked away. He redoubled his strength. 'I learnt that there's *nothing*, Alice. In the Holy Land I learnt that after you die there's *nothing*, no God, no Heaven, no Resurrection, no right, no wrong, no joy, no penitence, no glory, no hope, and the Devil made the world, and Hell is *nothing*. I paid the highest price for a worthless thing. *We don't matter*.' My legs kicked, so he lay on me, he gouged his thumbs into my throat. My voice splintered. I grabbed his wrists but they were like iron rods. I couldn't move, I couldn't think, I panicked, I went mad, I writhed, I arched, wriggled like a fish, but I could not shift his weight bearing down on me. I stopped. He grunted, using all his strength now. How much time had passed? My lungs, my face swelled, my mouth hung open, I felt I would burst, my tongue filled my mouth. I heard a horse clop by in the street below, I remembered a horse thief strangling near Three Oaks From One Root, the gallows' rope had not broken his neck. Strangling is a long and hard death. A girl with nimble fingers may embroider her name many times over in the time it takes to strangle. My fingers were numb. I tried to scratch but my hands lost their strength, fell away. I forgot who Nick was, the room faded, I felt drunk. Now I understood. My childhood was more real than the present moment. Three Oaks From One Root . . . the immense forest, glorious in the spring, the excitement, the bridge, a child's voice calling, 'You hit her, Jack!' Jack's voice saying, 'Of course I hit her,' and the other child calling, 'Did you kill her? Did you kill her?'

I stared up. A strange sensation of peace washed over me. My arms, my hands fell back on the bed. My red velvet slipper fell from my foot and dropped, turning slowly over and over, on to the floorboards. My head drooped to one side, I saw my baby lying in his basket. I would never see him grow up, and I tried to reach out to him, comfort him. Dimly I felt my body tremble, and then I felt nothing at all.

Nick waited, lips drawn back from his teeth, no doubt from the effort, still squeezing. I suppose he could not believe I could hold my breath for so long. I tried to close my eyes to trick him into believing I was dead but I could not, my eyelids were fixed open, rigid. Now he held me with one hand only, peered into my eyes, first one, then the other. Then his other hand came into my field of view, reached up to wipe the sweat from his forehead, but his forehead wrinkled and the skin came away on the back of his glove. He shook it away with an expression of disgust, the only disgust he had shown. My body moved, he was no longer kneeling on my chest, I heard something tap as one of my arms, dislodged, slipped off the side of the bed, probably my knuckles knocking against the floor. Both his hands passed in front of my gaze, he must have released my throat completely. He bent down, put his ear near my mouth.

No. I was not breathing. He took my hand, pulled off the ruby ring he'd given me when we were married, the ring of tiny rubies like drops of blood.

'You're dead, you bitch.'

I wasn't dead.

I stared at the ceiling. Neither I nor the ceiling moved. I have never been able to hold my eyes open so long without blinking. My new ability almost frightened me, yet it was saving my life. If Nick saw me move, he would finish what he had started, make certain of me. I heard him open the window but felt no cold air. Why not? Why had he opened the window? There was only the river below.

If he threw me out, I would fall to a death by drowning. An accidental fall in a state of despair and confusion.

Nick bent over me to pick me up, grunted as he slid his arms beneath my knees and shoulders. My head lolled back as he lifted me from the bed, showed me the room upside down, my baby sleeping by the fire, and I thought my heart would break with terror and love. I glimpsed myself in my cheap little tin mirror, face blackened, tongue bulging between my lips, chestnut hair uncombed and stiff, arms out like a pathetic starfish. I was no longer beautiful, I was an ugly corpse. I hated that, I hated Nick with a terrible passion. My windpipe showed the livid bruises imprinted by his thumbs.

He had destroyed me.

I saw the reflection of the grass ring Jack had woven for me on the river bank so long ago. Nick had never noticed it, a thing of no value. I still wore it on my toe.

Nick's head reappeared above me, calm, businesslike, used to death, as he carried me to the window. Then he, too, noticed the bruises. He swore. A woman does not strangle herself before drowning. He thought for a moment then dropped me back on the bed. My head hung over the edge. I heard him leave the room, my eyes stared at the little plaster Jesus standing on the clothes chest.

Jesus, help me, I whispered. But I could not whisper.

181

I shouted for help, but I couldn't shout.

I could not catch my breath. I inhaled a deep breath, but my lungs didn't move. My situation infuriated me. If Nick had tried to attack me in my present state of mind he'd have found me as strong as he was. He came back carrying a wall tapestry torn from my front room – now nothing would keep out the draught from the patchy wooden wall. I was so angry with him I shouted and swore at him, but no sound came. The little Jesus disappeared as Nick covered me with the tapestry, then I saw nothing but glimpses of firelight as he rolled my body in the material and hefted me over his shoulder.

A man innocently carrying a roll of cloth.

Snatches of his booted heels walking. Stairs. The muffled thud of the front door. Snow, the heels of Nick's boots walking on London Bridge. Where to? He had to hide me where my dead body, as he believed it, would not be found.

My feelings of anger slowly gave way to terror. Sheer, blind, immobilising terror.

He would bury me alive.

Nick, don't.

Where was I? From the dim snow I was carried into a place of complete darkness. A door banged closed. A scratching sound, a flint. No movement. Was he lighting a candle? Then I heard his footsteps on a stone stair. Going up, or down? Where was this? I must be on the bridge, but where?

Was this the same place he buried Jack?

O my God, help me.

Nick, don't.

The last step. Nick took a few paces, stopped. Dropped me. I heard my head crack, and I think one of my arms or legs must have broken, the floor was *hard*. I heard him go away, return with a shovel or pickaxe, I don't know, I heard the sound of its blade inserted into the edge of something hard, a flagstone perhaps, something heavy. Nick grunted with the effort. I heard the stone or whatever scrape aside. Then the sound of him digging.

Nick was digging my grave.

I wept. I shouted. I shrieked. Nothing.

Nick, don't.

He worked steadily. I heard the soft rattle of pebbles and rocks and chalk, his breathing. He stopped, then the implement clattered as he put it beside the hole, his breath puffed as he pulled himself out. I heard him slap the dust from his knees: that was what he had forgotten to do last time, with Jack.

Nick took hold of an end of the tapestry and dragged me smoothly across the floor.

I begged him for mercy. I was so terrified that I could not think or feel, all I wanted was mercy.

He held one end of the tapestry, unrolled me into the hole he had dug. I glimpsed candlelight and shadows above me, a stone vault perhaps, then I dropped down and landed on my head and my body flopped over me. A tiny pebble in front of my eye looked huge. It moved slightly as Nick thrust down on one of my mortified legs, still red with the birth blood of the son I had given Jack, which must have been sticking out of the hole.

Nick made a satisfied sound.

A shovelful of pebbles cascaded down on me, dust stuck to my eye. Another shovelful pattered down, then another as he worked to fill in the hole. Earth and darkness pressed in on me, there was a distant thud as the stone was replaced above me, and then there was nothing but the silence of the grave.

Rosie sat in the room at the top of the house. She did not think of it as *her* room since it was piled from its narrow floor to its steeply-pitched roof with domestic debris, the household clutter and thousand bits and pieces that Mistress Alice, who knew her mind and had strong opinions about what she wanted on view in her house, no longer wanted to see downstairs. Alice (Rosie, who was shy but not subservient, did not think of her as Mistress in her own thoughts) had a magpie's eye for trinkets and bits of jewellery, haggled for any old knickknackery and gimcrackery for the joy of bringing a new trophy home. Rosie loved these impulsive tours to Cheapside and the riverside where anything could be found and bought and brought home, but they were hard work: Alice never carried more than her purse and Rosie tottered behind her laden down with whatever caught Alice's eye – she had no taste, no restraint – cheap bright cutlery, horrid plates, a garish pewter crucifix, beads, a ghastly plaster Jesus luridly painted, a woollen dress much too small for her, a bolt of linen, once even a stack of six spindly Flemish chairs that would break at a breath.

And Alice never threw anything away. When she tired of what she loved she sent the old rubbish up here, to the attic. Rosie lived among her mistress's discarded but fiercely-loved junk without a bed or room for one. Rosie's home was a palliasse of straw crammed in one corner with its edges turned up between the wall and a discarded deal chest, and barely enough headroom to sit up even where the roof sloped highest. From there a narrow warren led between dusty boxes of no value whatsoever, which threatened to overbalance any moment, a broken chair and old buckets with half a gilt flagpole perched on top of them, almost blocking the hole in the wall that was the top of the stair turret. The turret was topped by a small cupola, a hollow onion shape that from the outside looked strangely Eastern. Several houses on the bridge had them, as though the builders had travelled to Muslim lands.

Rosie was nineteen, so Alice was almost old enough to be her mother. In spite of her faults, or because of them, Alice was the most exciting woman Rosie had ever met – though Rosie had never been with a man. Like most mistresses, Alice did not allow romances, and after nearly ten years, Rosie no longer really wanted them. The baker's boy often eyed her and licked his finger suggestively, but she was content to be a young maid growing into an old maid.

In this strange, alluring, cluttered, lonely room not of her own choice or creation, freezing in winter and boiling in summer, Rosie shivered on her patch of straw, cradled her broken arm, and listened for more sounds from below.

What happened?

Now, Master Jack had definitely not been perfect, Rosie had seen *that* much better than Alice had, and forgiven less. Jack had liked girls, even squeezed her own buttocks once, and he had drunk more at the Angel than he should. And he'd trusted his friends uncritically. He had trusted Nick. He'd not taken Alice's side against Nick. But Rosie had liked Jack and she had certainly never, ever, been frightened of him.

Master Nick frightened her a lot.

Knowing so little of what Alice and Master Nick had talked about frightened Rosie even more. Nick was bad. He knew more than he said, Rosie could see it in his eyes. He knew a lot more about Master Jack's disappearance than he admitted, and Alice knew the truth about him. What had Master Nick told Alice? Rosie couldn't imagine. She had spent the last two nights in pain and suspense, banished upstairs, sometimes creeping down the stair turret to hear the low murmur of Nick's voice, and Alice's groans and screams, and she had sat on the stairs, her elbow on her knee rocking her broken arm, forbidden to help, and she had thought, this is what Hell is like. This is Hell.

Then Master Nick had called upstairs when the birth was over, and Rosie had crept down and seen the beautiful baby, and tried to cheer Alice up. But

Alice had looked awful, worse even than a woman her age should after a night and a day in childbed; a darkness in her eyes. And Rosie, exhausted and protective, was outspoken. But then Nick had been a good husband and offered to sit the night with his wife and the baby. That was all very well for him; but there was all the cleaning and clearing up to do, all the things husbands never thought about. Then Alice had called out, 'Don't go, Rosie!' But Nick had said, '*Go!*'

Tom Bedell's dismal hour-bell rang again in the street. 'Falling snow and icy cold, the third hour after midnight, and the tide dropping fast.'

Rosie crept from her straw bed to the stair turret. Silence. She peered down, and her shoulder dislodged a broom that clattered downstairs. That got the baby crying. Rosie listened, frozen, to his cries drifting up from the room below and no one comforting him.

She went down. The door was ajar. A freezing draught came through, she heard the flames of the fire blowing, and the baby would not stop its high, newborn cry.

'Mistress?' Rosie knocked, opened the door meekly, prepared to be shouted at.

The room was empty of life except for the baby. The window was opened wide. Rosie rushed forward, braced her good arm on the sill, leant out. She saw nothing below but the tide.

The baby's cries distracted her. She backed away from the window, then picked him up, murmured soothingly. Durand's face was pink, he clenched his tiny fists. Rosie stared at the open window. It seemed so wrong to close it. While it was open Alice might reappear at any moment, and everything remain unchanged.

Perhaps she had gone into the front room. Rosie knew that hadn't happened, but she couldn't think. She ought to check the rooms just to make sure. Anything was better than looking at the window.

She heard footsteps on the stairs, rushed out. 'Master, master, she's gone, the window's open, she's fallen!'

Nick came up the stairs. 'What are you talking about? I've been downstairs, finding something to eat.'

She stared at the snow on his boots.

Nick pushed her into the room. 'Keep quiet.' He went to the window. 'She didn't fall. She jumped.'

The third greatest sin, self-murder. Rosie whispered, 'Alice would never kill herself in the river, sir, not after the way her poor sister Noelle went in.'

But Nick had the answer. 'Doubtless that has weighed on her mind all this time. And the last year of Alice's life was dreadful – the tragic death of her husband, her own increasing madness, her wild accusations against me. And finally the sadness and strain of childbirth pushed her mind over the edge. I warned you! You know how oddly she has been behaving. Her visits to the Liberty like a common whore, her attempt to run away.'

He was twisting everything. Rosie said, 'I'm not daft, sir.'

Nick stopped. His face was muffled, his hands were gloved. He strode to the window, reached out, pulled it closed. The crescent of snowflakes that had drifted inside began to melt.

'What's your name?'

'Rosie, master.'

'There's been a tragic accident. If you say a word to anyone, Rosie, I'll kill the baby, and then I'll kill you. Is that clear?'

'Yes, master.'

'Now get out.'

*   *   *

184

I screamed.

I lay in the darkness of my grave.

I screamed again. I lay silent.

No other place is so silent and still.

I lay in the silence and stillness awake, aware, conscious. Only one thing explained the situation in which I found myself.

I was dead.

I tried to laugh but I could laugh no more than I could scream. They say the person who dies is the last one to know it – or if they don't, they should. It's true.

Death is hard. It's hard to accept. I'd thought I'd see the face of God and His angels. But I saw nothing. I'd hoped to see Heaven but there was nothing. I was trapped in my dead body in this world just as much as I had been trapped in it when I was alive.

Then I heard a sound.

Any sound was the most beautiful sound I had ever heard. A faint, muffled rustling, but undeniably real. It grew louder, the sound of tiny pebbles dislodged, pieces of dust and soil. The noise was insignificant yet now seemed hugely loud, as though I rubbed my fingertips close to my ear, now burrowing inside my ear.

I was hearing the sound of worms devouring me.

Silence at last.

My body was ceasing to exist. Soon, after an unpleasant interval of decay, nothing would be left of me but dry white bones huddled where I was buried, I know not where, hidden, secret, an unremembered crime.

Rosie crouched in the attic. She cuddled the baby to her soft dry breasts, stroked the blond curls from his forehead. 'No, I won't let him touch you,' she cooed, then she heard a footstep on the stair, clasped Durand to her. *There's been a tragic accident . . . if you say a word to anyone, Rosie, I'll kill the baby, and then I'll kill you.* Quickly she hid the baby under a blanket. But the footstep was not repeated. Then occasionally a floorboard squeaked in the rooms downstairs as Nick prowled round Alice's home, lifting items of her furniture, her bits and pieces, her rugs, her clothes, her pointless little ornaments, as though itemising Alice's life; as if by possessing her possessions, and living in her house, and owning everything she had loved, he acquired by her death what she had never given him in life: herself.

He'd won.

Rosie heard the Bridge Ward coroner, the butcher, arrive that first morning, sweeping the snow from his hat, and then she heard his footsteps with Nick's in the room below, heard them talking. 'Tragedy . . .' Nick was distraught, tearful, sad, the liar. The coroner agreed the situation was straightforward, the death tragic, the balance of Alice's mind disturbed. 'Never recovered from the death of her first husband, if you ask me, Master Mason.'

'She never loved him,' came Nick's voice. 'It was me she loved.'

'Still, a tragic business.' The creak of the door opening, street sounds. 'Farewell, Master. This won't go any further unless and until we find the body.'

'My friend, do you think . . . ?'

The butcher's reply was almost lost under the rumble of a cart. 'Sometimes the river likes to give up its dead, sometimes it don't . . .'

Rosie paced the attic nervously. At the top of the end wall was the gap in the boards where sometimes doves and pigeons, which had escaped from dovecotes long ago, fluttered for the crumbs she left. As well as smaller fry like Robin Redbreast and Philip Sparrow, kites, storks, jackdaws and owls also nested on

185

London Bridge and often windows were broken by small boys stoning them, even the stained glass windows of the chapel.

Until Alice's baby arrived, these birds were Rosie's only companionship, some so tame they allowed her to hold them, and pecked food from her lips. Now Rosie stood on tiptoe, peeping every five seconds over her shoulder to check the baby was all right, and stared through the gap at the river below. The business of beating the water with boards and trawling for the corpse was in full swing, Master Nick putting on a show of grief. He would not work, and the masons on the chapel roof and the Stone Gate, still grieving over the loss of their brothers in the fire at the Angel, downed tools to show respect and comradeship in this further loss. Nick wore the formal white headband of the Master Masons and white robes of the *Frères Pontifes* with its cross of red dye, its second, smaller crossbar shaped like a bridge. The Brethren of London Bridge, as they called themselves, forgathered beside Nick on the great central pier of the bridge, the water rushing past them on each side in smooth aqueous slopes, a silent congregation staring down as if to see the corpse revealed in the depths. Rosie had heard tell that masons believed the bones of a corpse made a bridge stronger. 'Alice didn't jump,' Rosie whispered. 'I don't know what you did, Master Nick, and I never will, but I know I saw snow on your boots.'

Rosie sat down beside the baby. She had never had to think for herself. When Ma died, Master Jack had brought her to London almost at once, and then there was Alice. Alice was used to getting her way but Rosie was not. The baker's boy had only to look at her and she blushed. Now she had a baby to look after, someone who depended on her utterly. Someone she could not let down.

Rosie knew nothing about babies. She had never expected to have one of her own. Was the baby cold? She wrapped him in an old green woollen dress Alice couldn't bear to cut into rags. Rosie thought she remembered an old woman saying newborn babes couldn't shiver. Now Durand flushed a strong pink colour; did that mean he was too hot? He opened his deep blue eyes a fraction, made a smell, and cried. How he cried! He had a way of squeezing his little fists and mouthing that made his meaning crystal clear. He wanted milk, right now. Could babies drink cows' milk? It was difficult to imagine beer hurting them, but water might. Could the baby eat bread if the crust was taken off? Durand howled with hunger, and he showed not a single tooth.

Rosie thought, I've got to do the right thing. He's more important than I am. Alice's baby. He's my duty to my mistress and I mustn't let her down. What shall I do?

What shall I do?

There was a knock on the street door. She hesitated. The knock came again. She wedged the baby in the corner with a straw bolster in case he rolled away somehow – she had no idea if he could – and ran down. A large dirty woman dressed in rags, a tattered red hat perched on her head and ice across her broad shoulders, stood on the step. 'Heard tell there's a birth.'

Rosie remembered the midwives who would not come out in the storm. 'You're too late! The mother's dead.' The woman turned away with a shrug, and Rosie noticed the rags swinging from the woman's heavy breasts. She had an idea.

'Do you do milk?'

'Not now. My sister keeps herself in milk, aye. The babe lives, do it?' The midwife spat on her palm.

'Yes, he needs milk!'

'How much you got?'

'What?'

'Can you afford milk, girl?'

Rosie shook her head miserably. 'I don't have money.' Milk was life, but the thought of asking Nick for money terrified her; she never wanted him to see or hear or think of the baby. She thought of Nick's red, remorseless face, she saw Alice's baby swinging by its heels from his gloved hand, saw Durand flung out like a little stone into the river. Rosie knew she was right: he would do it. Baby Durand was the one item of Alice's life Nick could not control. Jack's baby.

Rosie knew she must never let Nick think about him.

The big woman snorted, 'No money, no milk.' She plodded away through the crowds pushing across the bridge. Two boys threw a leather ball, throwing and catching it with quick flicks of their hands. Rosie stared at them, then remembered the shilling Nick had flicked to her, and she had caught it one-handed. Had she given it back? She left the door hanging open, ran forward after the woman in the red hat, saw it bobbing among the heads of the crowd towards Southwark, pulled the forgotten shilling from the sling supporting her broken arm. 'Stop!'

The woman stopped.

Rosie held up the coin. 'Is it enough?'

The midwife grinned. 'For a shilling,' she said, 'my sister squirts cream.'

Rosie tightened her grip. 'When I see her. When the baby feeds. The whole course.'

The woman narrowed her eyes, then bellowed with laughter. 'Done!'

Rosie remembered the open door, ran back to Alice's house. At once she heard voices, men's voices. All she thought of was the baby. She rushed inside. Two of them hulking by the table. She pushed one lout and he slipped on the snow he'd trodden inside, she snatched up the besom and screamed at them, struck the second lout across the shoulders. He dropped the candleholder he'd picked up. Another fell out of his coat. He swore at her and she screamed at him, hit him again, the handle split into a sharp point. He drew a knife. She jerked the pointed handle at his face, screaming at him, 'I'll put it in your eye!'

She would.

The man could not back away; the wall was behind him. He put up his hands defensively, slid his shoulders along the boards, then ran out alone through the door. The lout who had fallen crawled after him on all fours, complaining bravely, then hopped up and knocked his way out of sight through the crowd.

No one had helped her. Rosie slammed the door and leant back against it. No one was going to help her, ever. All right. She heard the baby cry upstairs. She put down the besom where she could find it to repair later. She climbed the stairs quickly but without haste. In the attic she picked up the baby, kissed him. She trembled all over, she had never felt so excited. She could look after him. Durand tasted of baby, he mouthed her lips as though they were breasts. She must change him at least once a day, she would have washing to do. She had been wrong to take him out of the basket, he felt enclosed, warm, safe in there. But for the moment she wrapped him in her arms.

'Baby, baby,' she whispered, pushing her way between the boxes and junk and last year's cobwebs. 'Here's your home.'

Later the knock on the street door came and Rosie went down quickly. The wet nurse waiting on the step wore the dirty white tassels that advertised her profession. Rosie led her upstairs. The nurse found the situation entirely natural, bustled to the crying child, muttered about the cold as she parted her rags to reveal a battered brown nipple, and Rosie watched Durand latch on. He squeezed the breast as he drank and kicked his leg. 'They all do that,' the nurse grinned. 'Just a baby, you know.'

Rosie was besotted. She was sure no other baby had ever done it so beautifully.

'He isn't yours, is he?' the woman chattered, pleased by Rosie's innocence. 'I'm Meg. He doesn't look like you. You haven't got his eyebrows. And look at his eyes!'

'No, he isn't mine. Meg, how long does he have to have milk?'

'What about the expense? But I'd say a Christmas baby likes a sip until Easter.'

'If you come twice a day, Meg, not too early, not too late, I'll pay you a penny a week until Easter. And I need you to tell me how to look after a baby.'

'I can't tell you that, love,' Meg said bleakly. 'I lost all mine, every one.'

'Then what am I to do?'

'You'll just have to work it out like the rest of us, my love,' Meg told her, and transferred the infant to the full side. 'Instinct. Instinct, that's all there is to it.'

Am I dreaming?

Am I mad?

How many days have passed? Months? Years? Sometimes I think – nonsense, how can I think, my thoughts are dust – sometimes I think . . . sometimes I think I hear voices.

Voices.

No, not voices, I have nothing to hear with, any more than I have anything to think with – where do my thoughts come from? But then, where did they ever come from? I'm simply *me*, I simply am.

I simply am.

The voices, not-voices, are no more than a background hiss, like the sound of a distant fire or falling water or the wind in the leaves. Ah, summer. I remember summer. The brilliant green leaves. The glory of green, of being alive. Of being a leaf, green in the warm sun. Is this me? There are no trees on London Bridge. But there's moss that clings to the stones. Flowers, too, no doubt, tended by the women. I remember one house being built on the bridge even has a flat roof, which by now must mean a roof garden four storeys above the street. For a short, dim moment I feel . . . I feel I may be there. The warmth. The green. Spreading myself. The pleasure of . . . of being.

It's gone. Darkness. Who am I? I'm Alice! Alice! Alice!

Where am I?

Bones, who knows where. Bones on London Bridge. I can't cross to the other side. Is there another side? Or is there simply everywhere?

Help me.

God, help me!

I'm so alone, can't you hear me, I'm so alone *I can't bear it.*

I scream. It's the primal scream of pure pain. Every dying animal knows it. Unendurable pain. Unendurable loss. It's my scream from the heart – if I had a heart – of *God, help me.*

And something moves. I can feel it. A pinprick of light moving beneath me, above me, on every side of me, and I know I am seeing a vision, something true. The truth rises around me like the sunrise, it is the glory of God I see, the *Shekinah.*

Where have I heard that word? I don't know it.

I reach out my arms.

And something happens.

The sound of a baby crying.

It's the sound of a baby crying and I'm shrinking, dwindling, falling away,

188

gone. The light is gone. Everywhere around me are strange shapes like me, felt rather than seen, rushing forward towards the enemy. Huge red dishes rotate slowly, we rush between them, there it is! I find its shape, hang on. Intense pleasure floods through me, exhaustion overcomes me, I die.

I die, and I begin again.

Is it years? Minutes? Moments? A lifetime?

Night again. Nick closed the door of the Bridge House, locked it, crossed the builders' yard to the west gate. The tide-carpenter assembled his team of night workers, checking their lanterns, tools and ropes – it was a dangerous job, more than three hundred men had been killed so far building and maintaining London Bridge. Still the work was not complete. A barge had knocked away timbers from one of the starlings and the piles must be repaired before the rising tide wore away the unprotected stone. Maintenance of the bridge was a never-ending task, kept them almost as busy as construction. Any moment now, Nick knew, they would hear his footsteps. The men would stop, fall silent, draw back. Let him through.

The carpenters heard Nick's footsteps, knew them, recognised their steady tread, recognised the muffler that covered his face except for his eyes, his broad-brimmed hat, his gloved hands. Their talk fell silent and the circle of lanterns drew back to let him through. But he stopped, looked around him at their dim, reflected faces. He smiled. Shall I tell them God is dead? Shall I tell them there's nothing, everything they believe in is a lie? God's dead, we don't matter, everything your religion has taught you is a cruel deceit for the living of priests?

There's no God. There's no love. There's no Heaven. *We do not matter*. That's what I have learnt. There's only the world the Devil makes, there's only us.

The tide-carpenter, a large, frightened man, Nick saw through him, stepped forward as though he had never known fear, knuckled his forehead respectfully. His hands were white, scarred by his dangerous work. 'God bless, Master, a fine evening, and the tide on the turn.'

Nick said, 'Then what are you waiting for?' The men scattered to their work.

He walked. A boy ran ahead to open the west gate for him. The usual crowd of itinerants waited there hungry for work, thin, useless. Someone wished him good evening, a man fat with employment bowed, pressed a gift into Nick's gloved hand, he wanted to buy an apprenticeship for his son. The thin men fell behind but the fat man beckoned someone and followed, used to success. He had eaten a lamb chop for supper, Nick smelt it in his belly and breath, smelt the fool's eagerness, his ambition for his boy.

Nick stopped at the posts that marked the entrance to the bridge, ignored the crowds jostling past him.

The bridge was huge, the people were insignificant. The strength of the bridge, the sheer size and weight of stone and the geometry that held it together filled him with contempt for the people who used it, who made their little lives on the mighty structure. They never looked around them, they were ants. Nick walked on to the bridge. The Stone Gate was finished and beyond it the roadway narrowed into a gut between the shop fronts. Upstairs rooms and *haut-pas* crisscrossed the stinking passage little higher than the head of a man on horseback. By Will Ladler's kitchen, two carts had met and locked wheels, and in the confusion people stole bowls of Ladler's steaming meat soup from the counter, and now the ox harness tangled, and the drivers whipped each other and fought. Nick grinned beneath his muffler. Even at this hour people pushed past the carts, cursing them, or laid bets on the outcome, or

189

pressed forward between the signs and vendors and shop counters as busily and hungrily as ants, unaware of Nick moving with them. Flames and candles and lanterns lit their faces, smoke swirled around them. By now Nick saw so many houses that the gaps and alleyways between them were closing up, no wider than a man, and the backs of the houses were pushed out from the sides of the bridge, braced over the river's rush on angled timbers, and the roofs had extra floors built on top. London Bridge was London's busiest and most expensive street by far, so narrow that the walls were shiny at waist and shoulder height with human grease and dirt, scored by iron-shod wheels and hubs, and the trapped stink of horse manure and ox manure and sheep manure and piss and humans made the air thick. But clean river wind blew over the Square by St Thomas's Chapel in midstream, and the man who wanted a place for his son came up behind Nick and reached out for his shoulder.

Nick turned before he was touched.

'Look here,' the fat man blustered. 'I've offered you money. What more do you want?'

Nick looked from the father to the son. The boy was about fourteen, pale, smooth-skinned, long dark lashes, dark eyebrows, dark chestnut hair. He would do whatever his father said. He sent glances at Nick, defiant and easy.

Nick said, 'Show me your hands.'

Soft white hands. Those long delicate fingers never worked stone.

Nick said, 'The Brethren start early, send him to me at first light. I may have a position for him. It will not be cheap.'

The man hugged his son proudly. 'I never buy cheap, Master. Teach the boy some discipline, make a man of him, that's all I ask.' Nick watched them go. Then he opened the door to his house.

Alice's house. Her property had come to him, naturally, as her husband. But even after these years it still felt like hers. Strange, because she was long dead. The particular smell of it, wood, cooked food, warmth . . . he never could quite forget her. He heard footsteps scuttle furtively on the stairs, grinned. They thought he didn't think of them, those two, Rosie the wench and the skinny boy, Durand. They were afraid of him. Good. A single candle glowed on the table, its flame wavering, then burned steadily as Nick closed the door. A shadow moved behind the illumination. An assassin!

Nick pounced on him in three quick paces, arm upraised.

It was only the skinny boy, crouching to ward of the blow. Durand was about seven years old, painfully thin, bright-eyed, blond curls, Nick hated to look at him. 'What are you up to?' he demanded suspiciously.

Durand said, 'Nothing, sir, not me.' Rosie had taught him not to meet Nick's eyes, but Durand did. His gaze was bright, straightforward, curious. 'A messenger came.'

Was he lying? Everyone lied, all the time. Then Nick noticed the sheet of thick paper rolled on the table, sealed with red wax, tied off with a ribbon. 'Get out.' The boy scampered to the stairs, looked over his shoulder.

As soon as he was gone, Nick forgot him. The wax that bound the letter was in the style of the Agnus Dei, the Templar seal. The Brothers of Christ kept their far-flung properties and banking activities in order with a postal system larger than the King's. King John was attended by only seven illiterate messengers and more often than not they got lost; the Templars' reached to Mecca. Nick sat looking at the roll of paper, undid the ribbon awkwardly with his gloved fingers, broke the seal. The letter from the new Preceptor of Castle Moat was written in *atbash*, the Templar code that kept their transactions secret. These days nobody trusted anybody. It was rumoured King John had repudiated Christianity and embraced the Muslim faith.

190

Nick clenched his hand round a piece of charcoal, worked to decipher the code.

Geoffrey de Prudome, Grand Master of England, was dead. The new Preceptor wrote of a tragic accident: one night the Master, suffering a cold, had ordered himself tied in leather doused in brandy as a remedy, but the boy knotting the string had held the candle too close, and the flame ignited the spirit. The Master had lingered for nine days in the most horrid agony, every inch of skin burnt off his body, each vein and muscle revealed, a naked man.

Nick read between the lines. De Prudome had deliberately killed himself, deliberately burnt himself alive. What made a man seek the release of such a terrible death? Suffering? Despair? Remorse? Awe? A furious anger?

Defeat?

Fear?

Nick took the candle, touched the flame to the letter. He held the letter by the corner until it was ashes. He dropped the ashes and stamped them under his boot.

The bridge was silent by this hour. Except that London Bridge was never really silent. Footsteps always passed by from somewhere to somewhere. Tom Bedell's dogs barked in the distance, and somewhere close a mouse rustled in the wall.

Nick took the candle and went upstairs to his room. Alice's room. It had changed little. He stood at the window. The high tide lay round the bridge like a full belly, brimmed over the starlings, lapped the top curves of the arches so the bridge looked like a row of caves spanning the river. An oarsman unhooked his lamp to get beneath, slid through. The great lantern atop the huge arrow-like spire of St Paul's Cathedral burned its reflection deep into the water, so the light seemed to glimmer upwards from the bottom of the river to the top of the cathedral.

Nick sat on the bed. He leant forward, took the garish plaster Jesus off the clothes chest, lifted the lid.

Her clothes.

He lifted them out. Long ago he'd been about to throw them away. But as he had lifted them up to throw them out, he'd seen something neatly folded in the bottom of the chest that stopped him dead, something white, very dirty, travel-stained, blood on it, and mud, but as sharply creased as though freshly laundered by the weight of her clothes that had concealed it.

His Templar robe.

He had told Alice he'd renounced the Templars, but she had found his robe. He couldn't imagine how, what had led her to the hiding place, the arch beneath his father's bridge, Kissing Alice. Why had she kept it? Sentiment? Nick couldn't imagine a single reason. Did she think it made a difference? Did she think he might idly wish for it back one day and she'd say, 'You know, I happened to find that old thing and keep it. I put it in the bottom of my clothes chest while we travelled to London and built London Bridge, just in case you needed it one day.'

She had kept it, that was all. Here, where he would never have looked for it if she were alive.

Nick touched the robe with his gloved fingers, and it opened at once, its inside revealing the rain-smeared imprint of the red Cross of the Holy Blood. Not stale brown blood, red. Red as if still fresh, spilt today. Gleaming as if still wet. Nick watched his reflection in it.

He shuddered, and a terrible empty feeling of loss swept over him. He knew more than he had ever dreamt, but it was nothing. Everything he touched slipped out of his tightening grasp. He remembered the monk Peter

191

Colechurch, ingeniator of London Bridge, dead of extreme old age this last eighteen months, buried in the chapel; remembered overhearing almost Peter's first words to Jack and Alice, there by the sunlit, leaf-dappled church Jack built at Abbot's Littlebourne: *But a church, my son, is not a bridge.* Peter was wrong, and Jack, even that fool Jack in his blind, ignorant faith had known it, and said it: *A church is a bridge between this world and the next. Both are a crossing from one side to the other.*

Nick gripped the robe tight, but it slipped out of his grasp and he stared at it on the floor.

That sunlit, leaf-dappled day. He remembered the sunlight, the swish of the wind in the leaves, then it slipped away from him.

Nick remembered Alice. She had been wearing a green dress. He remembered her putting one hand on her hip. Time had made his memory of her faceless, she could have been anybody. She had some special mannerism that he forgot, something he had loved. Some expression with her eyes . . . no, it was gone.

Nick knew what God had said to Moses. He knew what Moses had repeated, exactly, word for word, to the Seventy Elders, the seventy rabbis initiated into the mysteries of the Word in the Covenant. But he could not remember Alice's face. Could not remember loving her. That emotion, that feeling of fullness and completion and adoration that he mistily recalled, he could no longer feel. Could no longer feel love. But he remembered destroying her. He remembered hating her. Destroying what he most loved. Destroying love. He remembered the feel of her Adam's apple hard under his thumbs. He remembered her eyes. Her staring dead eyes.

He remembered everything of that.

Nick kicked the robe away from him. He unwound the muffler from his face. The pain felt like the worst sunburn he had ever experienced. He dropped the sodden wool on the floor, pulled off his gloves as carefully as he could. He whimpered, then peeled off his clothes one by one, adding them to the bloody bundle on the floor, and when he was finished he opened the window and dropped them into the river. By morning he would be dressed again. He sat on the bed, alone, a naked man. Yes, that was true. Hell is where we are.

First thing in the morning the knock came on the door downstairs, and then the door opened. That was cheeky. The fat man's boy stood framed by the dawn light, then came in. Nick, well dressed, shut the door behind the youth, then walked round him in the shadows. New tools in a soft pouch at his belt, a chisel that had never known a hammer's touch. The young man endured the examination with one hand on his hip, amused, contemptuous, smiling. Those eyebrows, long lashes, those long fingers. Those eyes. Nick spoke throatily. 'What's your name, boy?'

'Alan.'

That was enough. Even the name was almost the same. 'You remind me of someone.'

Alan chuckled eagerly. 'That's what they all say.'

Flesh.

Who am I? But you see, I always know who I am. I'm Alice. I am the body and the worm. I'm the germ that kills, I'm the living blood. I die, I die, I die, and I live. Nothing has changed, nothing changes. I am what I have always been since . . . no, I don't suppose since the beginning of time. Since the beginning of life. But I have no memory of what I was before I was Alice, any more than you do.

But I'm learning.

I am the sperm and the egg.

And I am born again. I feel it. From warmth I am squeezed and pushed into a vast, hard, cold place. I feel myself breathe. I feel fragments of straw and wood shavings prick my tiny shivering body. My body moves instinctively, wriggles of its own volition to cuddle into the warmth of its brothers and sisters. Something warm and delicious touches its mouth. Milk.

Thirst.

I can feel thirsty again!

Without warning Durand asked, 'Rosie, how did my mother die?'

Rosie had known this question would come, and she knew what she must say, but nothing prepared her for the look in Durand's eyes.

'There was a tragic accident.'

There's been a tragic accident . . . if you say a word to anyone, Rosie, I'll kill the baby, and then I'll kill you.

'What accident?'

'There was an open window.'

Durand had irresistible eyes, Jack's eyes, bright blue, dazzled. He'd knocked a window in the attic's end wall where Rosie leant out to feed the birds, and it was open on such a hot day, letting in the cooling breeze and the sounds of the river below, the calls of watermen, the creak of oars and sails, the shriek of gulls round something in the water. Durand was good with his hands, he had long, sensitive fingers – hardly a boy's fingers, twelve years old, but he did not live a boy's life, hurrying, scurrying, terrified, at his father's beck and call. His back and the backs of his legs were beaten to blood for his shortcomings, lateness, earliness, the master's food too hot, or too cold, the wine too stale or too new. The masons believed Durand was the master's son; Nick let them, it suited him, he bragged about it, the lie proved his manhood. All masons knew that the Templars had sired so many illegitimate children that their cavalry brigades, the *poulains* who were always half-breeds by local women, flowed entirely from Templar loins. The men appreciated a man who knew what to do with a woman, forgave such a man almost any fault, even hypocrisy, and the rumours of darker sins were forgotten, so the Templars' stained reputation had improved along with their enormous fortune. When the Pope declared the crusade against the Cathar heresy, the Templars had turned on their own people with fire and sword, and been richly rewarded. By now the holiness, devotion and moral commitment of God's soldiers was doubted by no one who mattered, and over the years Nick let the men see that he was a demanding father, made the boy live up to him, no leeway, no favours. The men appreciated that too.

In the house, when the door was shut, Nick's brutality was such that Rosie feared for Durand's life. She suspected his arse was as striped as his back and legs, but he was too grown up and too proud to let her look. Like Jack, there was something foolish about Durand; he would not creep, hide himself away, show fear, submit. Would not look down. Attracted punishment. Rosie couldn't understand it. She had learnt to be so meek, efficient, quiet that Nick probably hardly saw her, never thought about her, never forced her to sleep with him. Probably he almost forgot her name. But Durand . . . She had tried to teach him sense, to be sensible. But Durand was different.

Durand was not like her, and he was not like Nick.

Rosie had seen Jack work with stone.

Durand's fingers almost caressed wood, pulled out the shape that was in the grain. Rosie knew, everyone did, that God shaped everything on the earth ready for its eventual use, grew the curve of a boat's stem or keel inside the curve of an oak branch; everything had a reason and a purpose. A good workman instinctively felt the spoon match the bowl, the bowl match the table, the table match the room. Durand had inherited his father's talent for seeing the pattern inside whatever he touched, nothing was wasted. Over the years almost all Alice's clutter had been put to good use, the attic door matched the window, the two chairs slid naturally into place at the table. Even the little bird table in the window was at the perfect height for Rosie's elbows to lean on, and a broken wicker basket had turned into a pretty little birdcage with a cupola on top like the stair turret. Rosie had looked at that dusty old basket for years and not seen a birdcage, but Durand had. She realised that he had not removed his blue gaze from her, not blinked. Persistent, like his mother. He knelt, took Rosie's hands in his.

'Nick is not your father,' Rosie confessed. 'Your father was a man named Jack, Nick's best friend. They both loved the same girl.'

'Yes, I know,' Durand nodded. 'She was my mother.' Rosie stared. He shrugged. 'Taunts. The children in the street.' *The children,* not the *other* children. Durand did not think he was a child, he'd learnt to grow up so quickly that he made Rosie sad. 'They know. Children always do.'

'Jack disappeared and Nick moved in, married your mother. But Nick didn't know how to love her.'

'My mother didn't kill herself.'

Rosie squeezed his hands. 'That's all I know, Durand.'

Durand thought about what she had told him. The masons ordered their messes of meat from a certain butcher; the coroner prayed in St Thomas's Chapel, in his own stall near Nick and Alan's. Something rustled in the wall.

'There isn't any justice, is there?' The dam broke, Durand's eyes filled with tears. Rosie clasped him to her gratefully. At last he cried like a child. 'There isn't any justice.'

Motes of dust as big as pebbles, stones as big as boulders, splinters of wood as long as lances. I slip between them, stop, start, my eyes look round fearfully, a mouse is always fearful, predators are everywhere. A large white-whiskered mouse bites me, I'm in the wrong place. I'm running, running! Huge dark tunnels, flashes of brilliant sunlight, holes and gaps and chinks in the walls, tunnels barbed with brilliant spikes of the sun. Where am I? There, a glimpse of the river!

The river. I have seen the lovely river for the first time since my death. Black and white like a charcoal sketch, these eyes are not good at distance though everything close is sharp as a pin. The mouse sniffs for danger, the glorious scent of the day and the river, its sensitive nose revealing the layers of wet and mud and weed and food I never sensed before. Life. Life, the world, richer and more detailed than I ever imagined. Than I ever had the senses to imagine. These ears hear a pin drop.

The mouse stops motionless, wary, fearful, at a huge whirling shrieking sound. Its body shivers, sensing deadly danger, though I know it's only seagulls squabbling over something in the river. Don't be afraid, little mouse. But a mouse is always afraid, always running, now pausing still as a piece of wood, eyes watchful, always on the lookout for an opportunity: there's a thin gap above me.

The mouse races upward. The claws that once seemed so small I now realise are large and strong, stabbing and clinging for holds in the lathes and crumbly clay daub, pulling the mouse effortlessly up a tall shaft that seems to rise as high as Heaven. Where am I?

I'm in the wall.

Vast, deep voices. The mouse stops, danger, danger. Whiskers twitching. A gap in the boards.

A sunlit room beyond.

A human foot, its big toe larger than my body. The toenail with dirt beneath it, the shoe with a wooden sole, massive leather straps tying it to the foot and ankle. At night the mouse might come out to nibble those straps and know no more of the world of humans than I once knew of the world of mice.

The mouse stands back on its haunches, wipes the dirt and dust smells from its whiskers with rapid strokes of its forepaws, sniffs.

Humans. Danger.

Looks up. A white leg, a dress, an apron, a girl. Who is she? The curve of her bosom almost hides her face from down here. Her head turns.

Rosie. She's Rosie.

I cry out, or would if I had a voice. Thank God, Rosie's alive. She's thinner, older, more tired than she was, and I don't recognise that dress. How long has passed?

Is that awful dress *my* dress? That awful threadbare ragged thing all that's left of my beautiful green Rochelle dress? Doesn't Rosie know how important that dress is to me, how much it meant to Jack and me?

No, how could she?

What's happened to all my beautiful things? Why didn't they look after them, treasure them as I did, keep them just as they were?

Oh God, how many years have I missed?

The world's gone on without me. I'm dead and I never mattered.

Rosie moves her fingers, the mouse jerks back to the hole. Rosie draws breath. Her mouth opens, her Adam's apple bobs, she speaks.

'There was a tragic accident.'

Who's she talking to? I can't see. The mouse creeps forward. Loaves of bread scattered on the floorboards. No, they're breadcrumbs! Tasty breadcrumbs!

The floorboards race beneath me. I'm under a chair. Rosie's been feeding bread to the birds, never noticed these crumbs dropping. The mouse feeds hungrily. I can't see Rosie!

I hear her draw breath again. There's her foot, the bones spreading out, flesh compressing as it takes her weight, toes flexing, the ankle shifting slightly under the strain.

'There was an open window.'

If only I could shout! Yes, Rosie, but he wanted you to think that!

'Your father was a man named Jack, Nick's best friend. They both loved the same girl.'

Yes, she was me. Alice! I was Alice!

Another voice. 'My mother.'

Oh my God. Jack's voice.

No: lighter. Jack when he was a boy. My Jack as I first remember him, that I first fell in love with. Who are you?

'My mother didn't kill herself.'

He's right. Listen to me, I was strangled to death, Nick strangled me to death, a ghastly death.

Rosie sits, squeezes a pair of hands in her own. 'That's all I know, Durand.'

My God, my son. She's speaking to my son. Let me see my son Durand. That's all I ask.

The mouse turns the delicious dry fragment of stale bread in its paws, nibbles hungrily. Look up! But all I see is stale bread.

A gull squawks in the window, the mouse flees, I glimpse knees in torn blue britches. Durand kneeling between Rosie's feet. Then the hole in the wall, darkness.

His voice booms desolately, 'There isn't any justice, is there? There isn't any justice.'

Durand. I have not seen my son, but I have heard him. I know he lives.

The mouse runs down inside the wall.

I've heard my son and Rosie talking. Yet they didn't use my name once. And Rosie always used to say 'Mistress Alice' so respectfully. My memory has faded away from them, their time rushes forward. Alice is far behind them. I am the dead.

Faster and faster the mouse runs. Holes, gaps, tunnels, darkness, light, a pile of rubbish beside the street. A huge cartwheel rumbles past, dust showering from its iron rim. Shoes and boots and hooves thumping by. Danger, danger. The mouse's nose twitching, fearful. The wide road in front, danger behind.

If only I could sleep. Life is constant panic, constant fear, constant worry, for a few breadcrumbs.

The mouse snatches up a piece of straw. She's pregnant, the need for a nest, a quiet safe place to rear her young, fills her. Get across! A clear space, run, run!

Impact. I am whirled into the sky. The danger was not behind but above, a bird has my body. The mouse squeals, I've heard this sound before, this terminal squeal of loss, the sound of death. The rooftops of London Bridge turn below me, almost entirely covered now with houses, smoking chimneys even on such a hot day, no sound but the rush of air. The beak lifts me, bites down, breaks my bones. The moment of pain turns to darkness.

I know this darkness.

It was Saturday, so Durand came downstairs.

He was thirteen years old by a month, the coldest month of the year. His blond hair lay tangled over his shoulders, but his face and hands were clean, his clothes a mass of patches, but neatly sewn. His bare feet slid noiselessly past the steps that squeaked, knowing each one. The lowest steps, most used, were the worst and he braced his hands on the wall to take his weight, stepped on the sides. He glanced up. Rosie watched him from the top of the turret, her round face anxious for him. She hated Saturdays.

Durand opened the door. The room was empty.

Each Saturday Nick came home and met Alan in this room, they talked, ate a meal, usually from a cookshop, pottage from Will Ladler's or a couple of John Swinert's roast chops which they shredded with their knives, and plenty of wine in silver hanaps – mugs with handles – sent from the Bear Inn. The two men got full of meat and wine and Rosie hid Durand upstairs, listening. She didn't want him to see them. Then in the small hours when it was safest the two of them crept downstairs, cleared up the bones from the floor, ate them, drank anything left over, and slipped back to the attic before they were found.

But tonight Nick wanted Durand to cook. Alan had yawned, 'No, I like my food.' But Nick insisted. 'He's old enough. You'll see.' That secret grin between the two men. Nick wanted peacock and he wanted the boy to serve it and wait at table. He wanted Alan to see Durand serve and wait, his humiliation. Durand growing up – he would soon be taller than Rosie – fascinated Nick. Did he see himself in the boy? Rosie remembered Littlebourne gossip, how Cristina had taken Nick, the baby found in a basket, into her house in revenge for her husband's suspected infidelities. And now Nick was an adult at the height of his powers. Did he think or hope Durand was like him, somewhere inside himself? That Durand *could be made* like him?

Cristina had come to love Nick, and while her husband was alive had brought him up like her own son. But Nick didn't know what love was. Rosie had heard Brother Wasce, the chaplain of St Thomas's Chapel, tell the story from the Bible how the son was punished for the sins of the father, and his son after him, and his son after him, for the original crime of which they had no knowledge. The Bible's terrible and just punishment terrified Rosie. Nick had beaten Durand almost to death once.

She didn't want him to go down tonight.

Durand called up, 'Stop worrying.' He knew she wouldn't.

'Sssh!' Rosie said. 'Come back, I'll do it.'

'It's all right. They aren't back yet.' Now that villages and landowners were no longer compelled to build and maintain their own bridges, the Brethren of London Bridge were responsible for the upkeep of many other bridges, including the bridge over the River Lea at Stratford-atte-Bow, swept away by floods. Bow was marshland and Nick's new stone bridge simply sank into the mud. The problem occupied Nick and Alan Frater until the first frosts and a proper job was planned for next year. Meanwhile the wooden piles were being driven deep, winter work. To return from Bow was an easy row down to the mouth of the Lea, but from there, round the Isle of Dogs and the long pull up the Thames past Shadwell, the journey depended on the tide; and Durand had seen what Rosie had not, the flood tide would not flow until sunset. The Master and his assistant could not possibly return until well into the evening.

Rosie called, 'I'll come down.'

Durand said, 'No, stay up there.'

The kitchen at the back of the wooden house, overhanging the river because of the risk of fire, was little more than a hearth. First thing this morning Durand, taking the coins left by Nick, every farthing to be accounted for, had walked to Cheapside alone, without Rosie. He bought a peacock, had it killed but not drawn. He carried it home with all its beautiful finery of feathers intact, slit it from throat to tail on the table, and skinned it as carefully as a master cook. He'd folded the coat of feathers and kept it, and now he carried the naked bird, covered by a sheet so it was not coveted and stolen, along the bridge to Mistress Jane's cookshop at Bridge Foot. Her husband Henry Baker illegally stuffed his pasties with rabbit, goose and guts (illegal because they spoiled in a few hours) and sold high old beef as venison, as everyone who lived on London Bridge knew, but his trade was with travellers and his shop front was always steaming, cheerful, crammed. Being pay day Durand saw a bittern and a heron already cooking, a hundred hens turning in roasting, trickling, gleaming rows, a cluster of tiny larks like fists, a whole pig smoking and crackling, and his mouth watered uncontrollably. He handed over Nick's five pence for Mistress Jane's baste, fire and trouble, and ran into the street before he was sick with hunger. 'You boy!' Jane called him back, dredged up crackling from the bottom of the trough, dropped it in his hand. 'Put on a bit of fat, boy!' she beamed, her face as red and dripping as her beef.

A lifetime of roasting had given her furnace fingers; Durand tossed the steaming crispy pieces from hand to hand as he walked, gobbling hungrily. Dogs barked, Tom Bedell sat white-haired on a stool in the gatekeeper's door of the Stone Gate, his son Jonathan standing beside him mute and hostile. Durand looked at them squarely, they had never liked him, so he hated them. Durand thought Tom knew more than he said about the past. He knew Tom never would say; the old man was frightened now that Brother Wasce and Brother Boatwright had retired as Bridge Masters and Nick and Brother Alan were elected by the Brethren in their turn. The hereditary employment handed down from father to son in perpetuity, gatekeepers, tide-carpenters, clerks of works, were no longer secure. Safe jobs were no longer rights but privileges, and dismissal was devastating.

'What are you looking at, runt?' Jonathan called. He bunched his fists.

Durand called, 'What are you frightened of?' But he didn't want to fight. He knew he would never know the truth about the open window. Thirteen

197

years was a lifetime, time for everything to be covered up, forgotten; by now there wasn't any truth to be had, only belief and self-interest.

'Get away, get off, you!' Jonathan shouted.

'Yes,' old Tom said vaguely. 'Clear the way, you youngsters.' A cart lurched by, knocking Durand aside, a mouse scuttled in a pile of rubbish. A black and white dog yipped beside him as he walked, jumping on its back legs as high as his hands for the crackling. Durand bit the last piece in half and the dog caught it, lost interest in him and raced off.

He leant his elbows on the parapet by the Red Cock, looked over the dark river. He was crying. He couldn't stop himself. He was so full of anger that he was crying with it, scraping his fists on the stone, hurting himself. *She didn't kill herself.* He didn't know that. He simply had faith. The flood tide was flowing fast and no more boats dared shoot the bridge. He wiped his eyes, shivering. No one noticed him or paid him the slightest attention, a weeping boy. A lantern moved steadily upstream, alone, then the four oars worked hard in the glow of illumination to pull the boat to the Fishwharf steps. Nick's boat. Durand ran back home. Rosie had lit the fire and smoky tallow candles and the vinter's boy had brought over a pitcher of wine. 'I'll do it!' Durand grabbed the pitcher.

'You didn't do it!' Rosie cried. 'They're coming, they're coming. There's no wax candles. Get upstairs, quick, they'll blame me, you'll be safe.'

Durand took her shoulders in his hands. 'Rosie! I'll do it.' He kissed her forehead. 'I will do it.'

'Let's run away,' she said hopelessly.

Rosie always said this. For the first time Durand replied. 'Run away where?' he asked gently. 'Where's safe?' He wiped her nose on the back of his hand. 'Where is safe?'

'Anywhere but here.'

Durand said, 'This is our home, Rosie.' He said it so seriously that she smiled, him being a boy less than half her age. 'I'll handle everything, Rosie. Don't worry. Go on, upstairs!' He patted her bottom to set her on her way.

Rosie coloured, amazed. 'You, cheeky!'

Durand grinned. 'Not as cheeky as you,' he said, eyeing her. He swept back his blond hair. Then he was busy with the wine, fetched the heavy silver hanaps, set the wine pitcher by the fire to warm, bread, snatched up a broad platter, ran to the side door by the stair turret. He stopped, realising Rosie watched him. 'What?'

'You aren't a child any more, are you?' she said, then answered herself. 'No, you're not. I'm afraid, Durand. Don't forget me like that again. Always think of me. I always think of you.'

'I know.' They heard footsteps. 'I'll be careful, I will, I promise,' Durand smiled.

My God, I see so much of Jack in him. Yet he's more than Jack; he's me, too. I'd have said 'What?' impatiently just like that. And frowned my eyebrows like him. And Jack would have promised to be careful. But Jack would've been certain nothing bad would happen to him, and he'd have smiled with his whole face.

There's something wary, withheld, about Durand's smile. Something Nick. Durand already knows what I know and what Nick knows and what Jack never really learnt: bad things happen.

Durand ran out of the side door and a robin redbreast fluttered, startled, from the candlelit windowsill. He ran between the lighted houses to the Bridge Foot, claimed the cooked peacock, covered it, ran back with it. He heard

Rosie crying on the stairs, hesitated, listening. Nick and Alan were in the house. 'Rosie, Rosie, why didn't you stay upstairs?' he whispered. He knew the answer of course. She was still trying to protect him though he was old enough to look after himself. He slipped quietly into the kitchen, put the cooked bird on the table. A saucepan had been knocked off its nail, Rosie had started the black sauce, a ginger root and sage leaves had fallen on the floor. Nick, muffled, caped, stood by the fire holding his silver hanap full of wine that he had poured himself.

'I'm cold, damn your blood,' Nick said. 'Cold, and I come home to cold wine.' Durand thought Nick would throw the wine over him. But he just stared at him furiously.

Then he laughed. He'd strike a woman down, but not Durand. He cared nothing about Rosie but he hated Durand. He hated Durand's eyes, hated the colour of his hair, hated him standing *that* way, that mannerism of his hands lightly touching his belt. Nick hated Durand with a passion young men keep for love. But Nick was old. His hair stuck white and staring beneath his mason's black cap, he was grey around the eyes with stone dust, his eyelashes were white, he had the seamed and veined eyes of a man of seventy.

He was fifty years old.

'I won't hurt you,' Nick said. 'You're no servant.' He reached up his thick gloves to Durand's face, touched the scratched work leather to Durand's lips, the corners of his eyes, his chin. 'I know what you are. You're an outsider.' He parted his coat around his mouth – his neck was supposed to be ulcerated by scrofula, King's Evil, but Durand had never seen it – and drank his wine noisily. Then he held out the hanap. 'Fill it up.'

Durand bowed but thought his own thoughts. He went to the fire in the front room and poured wine from the pitcher. Alan Frater, seated on the fire bench, still thickly clothed against the cold journey, his pallid, fleshy face heavy with good living, watched the boy's movements with interest.

'So you're his next project.' Alan saved 'Master' for his public duties, domineering the masons under him, deferential to Nick.

Durand muttered, 'I don't know, sir.' Rosie always told him 'I don't know' was safe.

Alan laughed. He looked soft but he was hard, and he was ambitious. Weight had shrunk his mouth to a pout. 'I mean, you *are* his son, aren't you?'

Durand muttered something, shook his head. He moved the pitcher closer to the fire. Alan gestured for a refill. 'I can't say I approve. You seem such a poor sort.'

Durand realised, he's envious! It seemd extraordinary to him that Alan Frater, third son of George Viner, a wealthy vintner and City alderman, elected a mason by the Brethren after only four years' apprenticeship – five or seven years was normal for poorer folk – elected a Master Freestone Mason two years later and one of the Bridge Masters just a few months ago, should be envious of *him*. Alan, who'd had his eye on a career in the Church, had risen very high very fast in the masons. But he wasn't secure. Without Nick's support the elder Master Freestone Masons, solid reliable types like Martin or Geoffrey, who led family gangs well established in the London Bridge Lodge, would have won more votes.

Alan owed everything to Nick. He was clever but lazy, not popular with the men. But Nick had chosen him. Durand wondered why.

'Because he's mine.' Nick spoke behind him as though he heard the boy's thoughts. 'Because if I die before the end of the world, boy, Alan will know what I know.' Alan grinned, and Nick added with contempt, 'He's not the

199

only one.' Then he smiled, and pressed his muffled lips to the top of Alan's head. 'You're no one without me, are you, friend?'

Alan glanced at Durand. 'Master,' he protested, 'not in front of the boy, don't.' Nick chuckled. He enjoys Alan's humiliation, Durand realised. The two men behaved more like enemies than friends. Nick planted a kiss on Alan's forehead. 'Don't, Master, he's watching.'

'Watching?' Nick drew his dagger. 'I'll put out his eyes for you.' Nick's joking manner was going too far. Alan was alarmed and tearful. Nick snatched Durand's hair, held the point of the dagger to his face. He had never done this to Rosie, only beat her. Durand felt the iron blade lie cold and flat on his skin beneath his eye. The cold seemed to spread through his body. He had never felt so frightened in his life.

'Well, Alan?' Nick asked. 'Shall I? Just one eye. This one. He'll still be able to work.'

The point slid up, pricked Durand's eyelid. Nick would.

'I don't mind,' Alan said. 'Go ahead. It's not my eye.'

'Alan doesn't believe I'll do it.' Nick put his head close to Durand's. 'But you do, don't you, Jack's son?'

Durand said, 'Yes.'

Nick promised, 'And after I've done you, I'll do Alan.'

Alan said, 'Enough, Master. I'm hungry. Let's eat.'

Nick pulled Durand's hair tight.

'He'll do it!' Durand said.

'Master, stop the game, you've made your point,' Alan said.

Nick said, 'Beg me.'

Alan jumped to his feet. 'I'm going outside! You do what you like with the brat.'

Nick waited. Alan's face quivered. He believed Nick now. He knew he would be next. 'Master, I beg you. Please.'

Nick let Durand go. Alan gave a roar of rage and humiliation and flew at the boy, kicking him, slapping at his head and shoulders. A chair went over, broke, would not stand up. Nick laughed. 'You really thought I'd do it!' he chuckled at Alan, shaking his head. 'You really did.'

Durand escaped to the kitchen.

He touched his eyelid, licked blood from his finger. He could hardly believe he could still see. When he rubbed his legs he saw bruises starting through his tattered blue breeches. He heard Alan roaring and weeping, threatening to leave. He couldn't hear what Nick said.

He wondered if Rosie was still crying.

He scooped up the long-handled saucepan she'd dropped, slopped in plenty of wine vinegar, grated the ginger into it with the side of a knife, and chopped the sage. He made breadcrumbs of black rye bread and added the dark mixture to the sauce heating in the pan, then opened his breeches and pissed into it, careful not to stand too close to the fire. The black sauce boiled in no time and he left it to thicken. He found the peacock's coat of feathers where he had left it earlier, dressed the cooked bird in its finery, still warm, and carried it through on the platter with the sauce.

He took wine and four-day-old trencher bread to the men and crouched by the fire. He watched them eat. Alan was shaking, still shivering from the sweat that had broken over him, but drunk enough not to care. Durand watched him pull a leg off the bird, wipe it in the sauce poured over his trencher, tug at the meat with his gums. Neither man had teeth. Alan belched for more wine. Nick ate carefully but indifferently, aware of Durand watching him. The longer Durand watched, the more he realised Nick was lonely. Alone. He had no one. Nick glanced at him. Alan rested his head on one hand, still eating. Nick was alone even if surrounded by people. Alan's mouth slowed. A wingbone fell from his mouth and he woke with a grunt, then slumped forward with his head on his arms on the table.

Nick glanced at the fire. 'Why?' He knew what Durand had done. '*Why?*' Durand froze. He said in a high voice, 'What?'

'The sauce. Your piss. Why?' Nick wiped his trencher clean with a cut of meat from his knife, ate it. 'Hatred? Fear? Contempt? Why?' Then he threw Durand a thighbone, and answered his own question. 'Why not?'

Durand gnawed the bone. The truth was obvious. He had done it for Rosie. Nick couldn't see that.

'Why? Why not?' Nick turned to the sleeping man. 'Why shouldn't I cut off his ear?' Durand tugged hungrily at the succulent thigh meat. He had even white teeth, a youngster's teeth. Nick reached forward, lifted Alan's ear lightly, sliced it off. He put it on his tongue and chewed it as easily as a slice of bread, then swallowed. His cup was empty.

Blood trickled down Alan's cheek towards his mouth, then followed the fold in his skin towards his chin. Alan moved, dreaming. His fingers travelled to where his ear had been and he woke, grinning sleepily. 'I fell asleep.' He stared at the blood on his fingers. His eyes widened. He stared at the knife in Nick's hand, then clapped his hand to his ear, found nothing but blood. He jumped up, moaning. Nick steadied the table.

Alan pressed a napkin to his head. He staggered to the mirror but there wasn't one.

'Upstairs,' Nick said.

Alan stumbled across the chair he had knocked over before. He rushed to the stairs.

Nick watched Durand thoughtfully. 'Still eating. You really are hungry. Starving.' He dangled the handle of the empty hanap from his finger. 'More wine.'

Durand listened to the cries of the injured man in the room upstairs.

Nick said sharply, 'More wine, Durand.'

Durand realised, that's the first time Nick has called me by my name. Ever.

He slipped the bone in his belt for later, poured wine from the pitcher into the hanap. Nick held out Alan's hanap to be filled, pushed it towards Durand. 'Now drink it.'

Durand wrapped both hands round the heavy silver hanap. He drank.

'What would I have done in your place?' Nick said thoughtfully. He looked round the house as though seeing it for the first time. 'Exactly what you've done.'

Durand said, 'What choice do I have?'

'You could have run away. I did. I ran away from the woman I loved and I was elected to the Templars.' He stared into Durand's eyes. 'I see. To you I'm only one man without sons. When I die, you calculate that this house, your mother's, will be yours. You'll have everything you ever wanted. You'll rule the roost where you once suffered under my discipline.'

Durand felt the wine fill his belly with warmth. He smiled. Nick nodded at the confirmation. 'Yes. That's what I'd have done.' He stopped talking, listened. Put down his hanap, twisted in his chair to look behind him.

He looked for so long, and so intently, that Durand asked, slurred, 'What's it?'

'Nothing.' But still Nick stared intently, at the wall, the corner, the chair, a wooden box, a couple of pairs of mud-stained boots. There were gaps between the timber slats where draughts blew into the smoky room, making the fire mutter. 'It's nothing.' He turned back to Durand. 'There is a point, Durand,

201

which each man and each woman passes in the upward struggle of our lives towards Heaven. It is the point at which belief becomes knowledge. I know what I believe is true. *I know*. I *know* that one day, perhaps one day soon, Jesus Christ will awaken and heal our wounds, and He will fill our hearts with joy, and He will soothe our pain, and He will lead us to Jerusalem.'

Durand knew he must say something. 'Everyone knows this is true,' he said.

Nick refilled Durand's hanap to the brim with wine. A few drops spilt.

Nick said, 'Some of us are closer to the heart of the truth than others.'

The wine furred Durand's thoughts. 'Truth?'

'Divinity.'

'I don't know about these things,' Durand slurred. 'They're for priests.'

'Truth is for everyone,' Nick said. 'It doesn't have to pass through a priest.'

Durand stared. Nick said the words lightly, yet they were blasphemy. The Cathar heretics, hundreds of thousands of them, had been burnt alive in their towns for believing such words. Whole cities had been burnt by the Templars. Cathar and Catholic were slaughtered indiscriminately as they huddled together, men and women and children and babes in arms: God knew His own.

'Yes,' Nick said. 'God knows His own.'

Durand gazed fuddled at his wine. 'If you say so.'

'I do say so, for it is true. I *know* it is true. We have sure and certain knowledge.'

Durand blinked sleepily. 'How so?'

Nick stood. He finished his wine, rested his gloved hand on Durand's head. 'I shall show you, Durand. I think a boy like you would be interested. There is much I could show you.' He kissed the top of Durand's head just as he had Alan's. 'Come to chapel with me tomorrow.' A bell tolled distantly. 'Today, Durand, today. It's the Sabbath already.'

He took the wax candle and went upstairs. Durand heard his footsteps cross the boards above his head, heard Alan whining and sobbing gratefully to see his master, his fawning welcome and tearful complaints.

Durand knew he was full of wine. He held his mouth, crossed the kitchen, threw open the back window, pushed his finger in his throat and vomited, heard his vomit drop through the dark and splash in the invisible river below. He vomited until his stomach retched dry.

He touched the window frame, then pulled himself forward on the high sill. It would be an awful struggle to fall out even for a fit adolescent boy. For a woman exhausted by labour, impossible. No tragic accident, no suicide.

Durand thought about Nick. His head was clear of wine. He thought the unthinkable thoughts.

'*Did you kill my mother?*' he whispered.

He lay down by the embers of the fire, thinking.

Durand carried the peacock bones up to Rosie. About two years ago she had suddenly decided, for no reason that he could see, that they must not sleep together, moved Durand's straw mat into one corner and kept hers in the other. She had hung a blanket round it for a curtain. He flapped it aside. She was still awake, as he had known she would be. It was a clear, freezing night, with just enough starlight to glimpse her face like a pale moon. He pulled his mattress beside hers.

'What d'you think you're doing?' Rosie said.

Durand squatted, shared the bones with her. He said, 'He hit you, didn't he?'

Rosie sounded surprised. 'Yes, you were late.'

'He cut off Alan's ear.'

'Stop it, don't!' But Rosie was too hungry for her jaws to stop gnawing the bone.

'He did. And then he . . .' Durand realised she wouldn't believe him. 'Anyway, I pissed in the sauce. For you.'

She giggled. 'Is that why you aren't eating?'

'He gave me his own food.' Rosie's jaws stopped chewing. Durand added, 'And wine.'

Rosie put down the bones. She touched his face with her greasy hands. 'In God's name, are you all right? He didn't touch you?'

'No? Why should he? He patted my hair.' Durand decided not to mention the kiss or the game about his eye. He tore a bone off the carcass and picked at it to reassure her, waited until Rosie started eating again.

Durand said, 'Did he kill my mother?'

She dropped the bones and tried to hug him. 'No, Durand, don't say that. Sssh.'

Durand flinched away. 'What should I say? Nothing? Like you've always said nothing?'

Rosie was as silent as he had accused her of being. Then she said, 'It was all my fault.'

'What happened?'

'I told Nick you aren't his son. I didn't mean to but I did. I was so angry.' Two silver lines trickled down Rosie's face. 'Now you're angry too. I wished I could die. But there was you.' She gripped his greasy hands earnestly with her greasy hands, told him about Jack's disappearance and the fire at the Angel. 'You're never going to forgive me, are you?'

Durand put his arms round her. 'You aren't to blame.'

'It's my fault and I'm frightened.' She pressed her face against his shoulder. Durand kissed the top of her head, the boy comforting the woman.

'I'm not frightened,' he said. 'I'm curious.'

'Come, come.' Nick pulled Durand to his side in front of everyone. By Nick's command he was freshly outfitted in a blue coat trimmed with silver thread, a hard blue hat and lacquered shoes – like fishmongers, the tailors and shoemakers and hatmakers of London Bridge did not sleep if there was a penny to be turned, though on the Sabbath they worked behind closed doors. Durand looked round him as the well-dressed procession came together across the Square in its slow dance of hierarchy and privilege. He recognised most of the masonic brethren by sight and they in turn noted his new clothes, and Nick's hand resting paternally on his shoulder. Such hints were full of meaning. They were tight-lipped men breathing frost down their nostrils, stone dust hardened in every line of their grey faces. Then Hugh Child acknowledged Durand with the smallest nod, and Chale Souch bowed his head slightly. Richard Beke was an old man who had worked on Canterbury Cathedral as well as London Bridge. Nick told them the Lord Mayor worshipped at St Paul's Cathedral today, 'Keeping the Bishop of London and the clergy hot on our side, brothers.' He whispered to Durand, 'The bishop is a Frenchman.' Nick's breath smelt of spices. 'We'll need Sainte Mère de l'Église with us if the French King Louis is invited to London to replace King John.'

Durand was excited by the feeling of power and machination he sensed around him. He had known nothing. 'Could that really happen?'

Nick nodded to half a dozen City aldermen as thickly wrapped against the cold as he was. 'This young man is my son, Durand. I am commencing his education.' He turned Durand's head towards a man dismounting. 'That's Serle Mercer, boy. Remember him and never remind him of his low birth.

He'll be Lord Mayor next year.' He pointed to an ugly man Durand had seen before, fabulously dressed. 'Solomon de Basing. That family are all immensely rich, London traders since the dawn of time.'

'So he'll be Lord Mayor one day?'

The boy learnt quickly. 'Yes, if he can get Serle Mercer out, but Mercer knows the ropes. He has his hand in the present Mayor's glove. They were both behind building London Bridge.'

Durand thought, everyone knows everyone but they're not friends. Rosie would never have understood.

Nick said, 'There's William Hardell and there with the limp, that's James Alderman.'

'Future Lord Mayors.'

'Not if I'm backing Serle Mercer.' The procession broke up to let a rough crowd from Southwark across the Square, men and children with shovels, granted special dispensation by the bishop to work on the Sabbath. Nick nodded towards the White Tower where the banner of Sir Robert FitzWalter flew, Marshal of the Army of God and the Holy Church against the King. 'Everyone wants God on their side.' He said Baynard's Castle, FitzWalter's home, had been ransacked by the mob at King John's command and its barbican gate set afire, so London's defences were being hurriedly repaired and the ditch round the City walls dug deeper. 'King John has revoked London's rights and liberties, including the rank of Lord Mayor, which he wants to replace with sheriff and portreeve as before – appointed by him, naturally. The Lord Mayor will not give way. The King is a fool and may besiege London. King John was excommunicated and declared himself a Muslim, but now he's back in the fold and has had himself elected to the Knights Templar. He wears the Holy Cross as a soldier of the Church, subject only to Pope Innocent.'

Durand frowned. Nick had been a Templar and never renounced his oath. He asked, 'But you're a Templar, and you support the Lord Mayor and the Bishop of London, and yet the Templars also support King John?'

'Obviously. We're on the winning side whichever side wins.' He bent down. 'You have a talent for this, Durand.'

Durand nodded. He knew it. Rosie had said he had a talent for working with his hands. Working with his brain was more exciting.

'Men can be cut and shaped just like wood,' Nick whispered. 'They carry their destiny carved within them.'

'By God.'

'Or by the Devil.'

The procession moved forward into the chapel at the midstream point where the river ran fastest and deepest round the gigantic pier on which it stood – Durand noticed for the first time that this artificial island was far larger than the others. Aldermen in finery headed well-dressed citizens, followed by the less well-dressed, and ragged, shuffling folk brought up the rear under the watchful eye of two sour-faced clerks guarding the door. A bowing, smiling clerk preceded Nick and Durand to the Bridge Masters' stall, another clerk welcomed the aldermen and settled them in their own stall – it was crucial for a church to attract wealthy patrons and the immensely profitable endowments for prayers to be said for their souls. The masonic brethren, wearing the white coifs of their profession round their heads, solid citizens though not wealthy men, took their place standing behind the aldermen. The stalls had high backs to preserve these men of substance at the front from the stink and thieving fingers and prying eyes of the poor at the back. St Thomas's, the Bridge Chapel, was the local church for the thousands of people who lived on London Bridge; there was no hope of accommodating them all. Women and children were pressed noisily in the doorway, old folk on the single stone bench with their backs to the wall, shouting like the deaf. At the last minute Alan Frater pushed through, wearing a rag tied round his face as though for toothache, covering where his ear had been. He bowed to the chaplain and then to Nick, and the monk-chaplain Brother Wasce looked at Nick, then began the service.

Good God, Durand thought, the priest looked to Nick for permission to begin!

Durand had never sat in St Thomas's before, let alone seen a service from the front. Brother Wasce had long white snotty hairs sticking from his nose and waxy ones from his ears, his hands black with dried blood from his last roast. Beneath his black robe he wore a Templar chaplain's well-known dirty green smock. A mason's baby son was baptised, shrieking, in the black marble font and from so close Durand saw the bowl's rim engraved with mysterious symbols, the sun and moon, stars, and the Greek signs for alpha and omega, the beginning and the end. Young boys brought books forward. Brother Wasce opened the breviary bound in white leather and began the chant, and the choir sang responses from the books called grails. Everyone knelt, except James Alderman on his stiff leg. Nick whispered, 'Watch.' The linen cloths were removed from the crucifix and the glory of Christ's sacrifice was revealed on the altar. 'Pain, humility, sacrifice,' Nick whispered. 'Remember. Remember.' He was talking to Durand but Alan, swaying with pain, said, 'Yes, Master.'

Brother Wasce pulled on white gloves and blessed the body and blood of Christ on the silver pence board and in the silver cup. By now, after an hour's preaching, the low, midday sun had swung round the simple pointed windows into afternoon, and arches of sunlight rose up the far wall and the apse. A hundred church bells tolled. The service ended, and Durand stood up.

Nick pulled him down. 'Wait.'

Durand was disappointed. Like all boys he always wanted to be first out of church with the important people, but Nick sat yawning and Serle Mercer and Salomon de Basing remained deep in prayer. Finally Durand noticed that only James Alderman and William Hardell had actually gone out, with a few others he did not know. The chapel fell silent as the noisy poor offered up their miserable bent coins and left as joyously as if they had attended a party.

'Brother Geoffrey, Brother Martin. If you please.' Nick's voice echoed. He pointed at the door, the busy street rushing past, and the door was closed. 'Durand, you will say nothing of whatever you may see in the Lodge.'

'Yes, sir. I won't.'

'Swear it on your heart, boy.'

All children knew this ritual. 'Cross my heart,' Durand crossed his fingers then thumped his chest, 'hope to die,' he dropped his head on one side like a hanging man, then clenched his fist and stuck his finger in it, 'stick a needle in my eye. I swear it.'

'Good,' Nick said, and some of the masons chuckled, wondering if the boy knew Nick took the oath literally. A masonic oath meant every word. Nick took Durand's shoulder, pulled him to the circular bell turret on the south side. For a moment Durand heard street cries through the slits in the wall, then the sounds faded above them as they descended the winding stair. Brother Wasce came last, as meek as though down here a monk and priest was no more than an ordinary man.

Durand had never been down to the undercroft, but he knew it existed – the windows could be seen from boats on the river. The Lodge was about sixty feet long, its floor of large alternating slabs of black and white marble. Pointed windows started above head height and arched to a vaulted stone roof, more heavily constructed than the chapel above. The windows let in little more than slits of light as the sun slid towards the west. We must be below water level at high tide, Durand thought. He could hear the rising water rushing past the walls behind the nine brethren as they spread out round the sides. A circle.

Brother Wasce sneezed.

There was a rustle as three younger men carried forward a rolled tapestry or rug. Durand stood on tiptoe to see round the shoulders in front of him. The three young brothers lay down the rug then pushed it as one, and the rug unrolled as deep blue and circular as the night sky. Durand crouched, peered round knees, stroked the dense knots. Such work was unobtainable in this country. Jerusalem work. He saw past the surface into the pattern, far into it; it was real, three-dimensional, not like a flat picture. Round the circular edge twelve words like the points of a wind compass were woven in golden orbits, like the orbits of the planets across the heavens, but in elliptical oblongs, not circles. Durand was shocked by the blasphemy: everyone knew that God had made the heavens and they were perfect, the orbit of each planet precisely circular round the earth He had created as their centrepiece, and an ellipse was not perfect. Could the masons have made a mistake, simply not noticed? No, their buildings stood or fell by precise measurement, their lives depended on geometry. Everyone here must know that the ellipse was a deliberate blasphemy on consecrated Christian ground. Only Muslims believed the orbits of the planets were not perfectly round.

Durand shivered nervously, but the names were too tempting. He twisted his head to read them but was disappointed to find each one meaningless: Agla, Ehje, Jehovah, Elohim, El, Gibbor, Eloah, Sabaoth, Isebaoth, Schaddai, Adonai, Makom.

He whispered, 'Why are those words there?'

Brother Hugh, who had first acknowledged him, whispered without turning. 'Boy, those are revealed to us at this level as the twelve names of God.'

'This level?' Durand murmured. He wondered if there were more levels.

Five gold triangles pointed towards the centre of the night sky or diagram – Durand was not sure which the rug was, it seemed so real. Each tip was bisected by an arc as though to draw attention to the precision of its angle. Round the centre, an all-seeing golden eye in a golden triangle, was a golden square with each side ornately woven with a single letter to make the name AGLA.

'Each name is filled with meaning,' Brother Hugh whispered. '*Atar Gibor Loham Adonai!* Thou Art Mighty For Ever, O Lord.'

Nick called out in a loud voice. 'Brother Alan.'

Alan replied formally, 'I be here, Master.'

Nick called, 'Step forward, Brother.' He led the brothers in prayer. 'First pray we to the great saints who lead us in brotherhood, St John the Baptist, St John the Evangelist, St Thomas the Architect, and St George. We pray to the Quatuor Coronati, the Four Crowned Martyrs.' Alan walked carefully from the murmuring voices to the centre of the rug. He swayed, touched the bandage round his head. Durand thought, he still doesn't believe Nick really did that. Part of Alan still believes that when he unwraps the bandage he'll find his ear there as usual, as if nothing had happened.

Nick intoned, 'Pray we now to God Almight, and to His sweet Mother Mary bright, that we now keep these Articles here . . .' A small box was brought forward and its contents taken out, the type of mallet called a Hiram, the twenty-four inch gauge symbolising the twenty-four hours of the day, silver compasses.

Brother Wasce blessed them. 'God the Almighty Architect records every word and action.' Now that it grew dark, candles were lit.

Alan said, 'Brother Geoffrey, call forth your son that I may examine him with the catechism.'

206

Two brothers pulled forward a young man of about eighteen from the shadows. His shirt was torn to show he had borne arms. Alan spoke. 'What be you named, Brother?'

'Samuel be my name.'

Alan spoke the question. 'What form do your Lodge be, Brother?'

'In form, an oblong square.'

'How long, Brother?'

'In length, from East to West, and from West to East.' Durand wondered if by east to west Samuel meant the River Thames, which flowed westward on the rising tide and eastward on the ebb. He could hear the river loudly now, probably swirling above the level of his head beyond the walls.

Alan spoke more loudly. 'And how wide do it be, Brother?'

'In width, between North and South.'

'And how high, Brother?'

'From the World to Heaven.'

'And how deep, Brother?'

'From the surface of the World to its Centre.'

Durand listened to the oath-taking. Surrounded by this circle of shadowed faces, it was impossible not to feel the power of the ceremony, and easy to understand how a mason could never prosper in his trade unless he was elected a brother. All great buildings and bridges and palaces and important inns and houses in London were built of stone and these men controlled the work. The City and Corporation of London was itself like a great guild, almost a prison defended behind its high walls and London Bridge, with nine gates in all. The Great Stone Gate, drawbridge and portcullis of London Bridge shut Southwark out of the City, and could stop any ship sailing upriver. It made sense for the masons to elect honorary brothers to their fraternity, influential aldermen like de Basing and Mercer and Boatwright who knew nothing of stone but much of men and politics.

Brother Samuel knelt, admitted to the first age of the first degree of the fraternity. His father lifted him up, embraced him, rubbed his shoulders proudly, embraced him again. The men retired to the far end of the Lodge where a table had been set out with wine, bread and roast meat. Durand gulped with hunger at the sight of the mouthwatering food, then felt Nick's glove on his elbow.

'You can't tell me you're not interested,' Nick said. 'There's much more I can show you. You'd never believe what's beneath this floor.'

'I think I would believe you, Master.'

'Good. Am I talking to myself? I mean, you do clearly understand what I am offering you? All you do not have, Durand. The company of powerful men as you grow up. Money, influence, respect. A place in the world. If, Durand, *if* you work hard and live by the rules. Look at you now, no one. A dirty child in clean clothes. I take them back, you're no one again.'

Durand said, 'I want more!' He bowed his head. 'I am for ever in your debt, Master. I know it.'

'This is only the beginning.' Nick made a dismissive gesture. 'This is nothing.' His eyes turned angrily towards the men talking, eating, drinking, laughing round the table as though he had so much more to tell. He wished them dead. Durand could see it. Out of the way. Then Nick turned back to Durand, his fury perfectly contained within him. The muffler crinkled in a smile. 'Just you and me, Durand. You'll learn to be friends. I'll bring you up as my own son, I'll tell you everything. Everything. You'll know who you are. No more hunger, no more doubts. I'll show you.'

'Master, what do you want in return?'

Nick took Durand's chin. 'You're an interesting boy.' He bent to the level of Durand's eyes, peered into them. 'There are things a father will show his son that he would trust to no one else.' He followed Durand's gaze to the table. Most of the men had gone but Alan, pale and in pain, still talked to Geoffrey and Martin. They left broken white loaves and a rib of beef standing on the table. The beef fat steamed appetisingly in the cold air of the crypt. 'No, I won't feed you today,' Nick decided. 'Temptation is the best teacher.'

His mouth twisted, he stared, and Durand thought he would say more, but then Nick waved him away. 'Go home, boy.' From the winding stair Durand looked back. Nick had not moved. He stared at the floor cloth of London Bridge Lodge, the intricately-woven rug that contained the emblems of its legitimacy. Then suddenly Nick swung on his heel, stared behind him where the ragstone blocks of the wall met the marble floor. He crouched, peered under the table. What did he see?

Durand saw nothing there.

He ran back up to the chapel, full of people, breath and warm bodies and sound, voices raised in hymn, then slipped outside into the cold night. Braziers flared in the Square where a man showed off an atrocious half-formed human called a monkey. Durand stared. The monkey was dressed as a boy in breeches, a short cape, pointed shoes with bells on that jingled miserably. The little creature looked at him with large, brown, thoughtful eyes and for a moment Durand felt, ridiculously, that God had not created men entire and perfect from the first instant but worked towards men through lower levels of inferior creatures. But God could not stumble, He was perfect, He had made Adam in His image. The monkey scratched its chin with its hairy fingers. *Men can be cut and shaped just like wood*, Nick had whispered in Durand's ear. *They carry their destiny carved within them*. Durand had said, *By God*. But Nick had replied, *Or by the Devil*. Now Durand understood what Nick meant. Nick knew that God made Man but the Devil made men. That was what he had really been saying. And he had said it with the total certainty of a priest talking of God. Nick more than believed, more than had faith; he *knew*.

Durand pushed back through the crowd, circled behind them so he would not have to pay the monkey man's urchin, opened the side door and climbed the stair turret to the attic. Rosie stood at the little window looking down at the crowd in the firelit Square. She didn't turn. 'Are you still curious?'

'Nothing happened.' Durand took off his blue hat trimmed with silver thread and threw it in the corner. 'Nick says King John may attack London! He says the King himself was behind the fire at Baynard's Castle.'

'How interesting,' she shrugged.

Durand said impatiently, 'If only you could have seen what I saw. I saw Serle Mercer there, one of the richest men in London, and Nick says he'll be Lord Mayor next year.'

Rosie picked up the hat. She rubbed it with her arm. 'I'd better look after this. It isn't yours.'

'It will be. Nick's going to show me everything. He's going to give me an education.'

'Education isn't everything.'

'Yes, it is. It's who you know that matters.'

She said quietly, 'It's who you are that matters, Durand.'

Rosie could be difficult. 'Anyway,' he said, 'I haven't said I will, exactly. Nick's lonely. He's realised he hasn't got anyone, no family, no son of his own, no one to follow in his footsteps. But there's me.'

'Is this what he's told you or what you think? It's just a carrot he's holding out to make you do what he wants.'

'I don't think there's any advantage in thinking the worst of people, even if you do!'

Rosie murmured, 'I don't think the worst of you. Don't make me.'

Durand stood beside her at the window. They watched the crowd dispersing in the shadows, the monkey man packing up. 'I have to do it,' Durand said.

'I know it seems like that at your age.'

'It's the only chance I've got to get on.'

'Durand, don't be so stupid! Nick's still taking his revenge on your father and your mother, can't you see? He was obsessed by them alive, he's obsessed by them dead. He wants to *be* you. You're all that's left of—' She stopped.

He said, 'Left? Of what?'

'Of Nick's youth.' She touched Durand's curly blond hair in that faintly critical way she had, as though his curls weren't quite good enough. She could be infuriating. 'You remind him of when he was young. He needs you, Durand. You don't need him.'

'Why can't you see how wrong you are?' Durand tried to explain it to her simply. 'You're just a serving girl. My mother and father were someone. I'll never be anyone without Nick. I don't have to like him, and I don't have to listen to you. I have to get forward any way I can, that's all.'

Rosie cried. He hated it when she cried. She probably did it to manipulate him. Nick would have known for sure. He'd have known what to do.

Durand pulled Rosie's shoulder to make her look at him but she jerked away. She was really upset. 'You should be looking for a nice girl,' she wept. 'He isn't going to live for ever.'

Winter, as always, lasted until the end of February, and was followed as always by the drought of March. The fierce spring sun and cloudless skies softened the rough wasteland of winter ice that built up in the sluggish waters upstream of the bridge, and now the melting slippery mass was on the move, but the arches were so blocked up with floes and slush that the tide could not fall. Durand stopped in the Square, seeing the ice almost touching the arch tops on one side, a fall of ten or twelve feet on the other. Gangs of carpenters worked from the starlings with axes to break the ice jam, shoved the floes under the arches or locks as best they could to let the pressure of water force the ice through. Ice-water blew past them in fountains from the icy slopes. Shore Lock was only eight feet wide between the starlings, Gut Lock even narrower, and Long Entry was a roaring tunnel where a man with outstretched arms could touch each side as he was swept through. A brazier had been lit on Chapel Pier where shifts of soaked and numbed men huddled in steaming clothes. It was considered honourable among carpenters to jump from starling to starling to show their bravery, springing from floe to floe if necessary in the wider arches, and Durand saw one man urged by his companions to jump St Mary's Lock to join them at the brazier. 'Come on, Ydris, come on!' The man Ydris held his heavy leather apron in one hand, jumped, fell short, was swept down. Someone thought they saw him but he was gone. The carpenters waited for him to come up, scratching their armpits, until the tide-carpenter arrived and set them back to work.

'What a waste of a life,' Durand murmured.

'The man was a fool,' Jonathan Bedell said. The gatekeeper's son held his father's two grey wolfhounds on short leashes.

'You'd know all about it,' Durand said. 'Being a fool yourself.'

Jonathan's face tightened. He was big, his dogs looked fierce, and he had a reputation to uphold. 'What?'

'A deaf fool,' Durand said.

'What's got into you?' Jonathan was used to people backing out of his way. He let the dogs pull forward. 'Watch it, you,' he grinned. 'Be good if you want to keep your balls.'

'You got no balls,' Durand said. The fight had been a long time coming, but he could feel it coming now and he wanted it. He knew he could win. Jonathan had no knife at his belt, but he had his fists, and he had the dogs. Durand knew he had to get Jonathan away from those dogs. 'Dogs do it all for you, do they?'

Jonathan was very red. 'All I got to do is let them go. They'll tear your throat out.'

Someone passing by said helpfully, 'I'll hold them dogs for you. Fair play.' A large dusty hand wrapped the leashes round a fist worn and scarred by years of work, jerked the dogs back. Chale Souch's grey face looked down at Durand. 'You sure you want to do this, boy?'

Durand bunched his fists. 'I said I'm not frightened of him.'

'Rosie's bastard!' Jonathan swore.

So that was what they said about him. Durand went as pale as though he had been struck in the face. Jonathan had gone too far for him to pull back. 'I'm just doing my job, Master Souch,' he said. 'Keep out of this.'

'It's your father's job,' Souch said. The masons behind Souch murmured agreement. 'He should give you a touch of care.'

A crowd gathered. 'Just boys fighting,' a woman called to her friend in disgust. 'Not even a bloody nose. It's all over.'

Durand flew at Jonathan. The bigger boy fell back, then struck out. Durand felt numb. He flailed forward. Jonathan stepped back, tripped over someone's foot. Durand caught Jonathan off balance, pushed him. Jonathan's feet came off the ground, his arm went over the low parapet, the rest of him almost followed. The crowd gave a shout of excitement. The disgusted woman shouted, 'My hat on the littl'un!'

Chale Souch said, 'Two shillings on Durand le Mason.' That was a fortune. The crowd pushed forward.

Martin Stoner called, 'Three pence speaks for Durand!'

Geoffrey Masterson raised his voice. 'Another three pence for Durand.' The crowd chanted, 'Durand! Durand!' They had never heard of him, squires from Kent, a wife of Gloucester, a farmer driving pigs. A carter sold standing room on his empty cart for a better view. Jonathan had no friends who would run for the only man who could help him, his father.

A man wearing a taverner's fur-trimmed gown held up a frothing jug. 'For the winner! Come buy, come one, come all, come buy, best ale!' A fight always made the crowd hungry and thirsty. A pork crackling seller ran up with his pan and brazier, a girl sold buttons. The ale sellers Harry Fleet and Thomas Hyde sent up children with ale mugs to hawk them round the crowd, and the taverner's children spilt them if they could.

Jonathan fell to his knees and hands beside the parapet. Durand kicked him, hurting his toes, his shoes were cheap fabric. He remembered the soles were wood, stamped down on Jonathan's hand. Jonathan screamed. Durand gasped with joy and relief. He kicked again, not seeing where the blow landed for the blood stinging his eyes, but heard Jonathan grunt. The dogs yelped and snarled, excited by the smell of sweat and violence.

'A mutton chop for the young mason if he wins!' the mutton chop seller called out over his greasy counter. 'Fat mutton chops for a cold day, buy quick, buy hot!'

Jonathan crawled forward, grabbed for Durand's knees. Durand kicked him, got on Jonathan's back, shoved, rolled him over. He put his knees on Jonathan's elbows, squatted on his chest. 'Yield,' Jonathan said. He tried to protect his face but his elbows were trapped. 'I yield.' His mouth was too bruised to say it loud enough. Durand raised his fists and brought them down on the bleeding face. Tom Bedell's white hair came forward between the houses but Durand saw Nick take the old man's elbow, engage him casually in conversation.

210

'You've got him, boy,' Chale Souch said softly. 'If you kill him no one will see anything.'

Durand looked up. All he saw were faces that he knew, Chale Souch and Geoffrey Masterson and Martin Stoner beside him, and young Tom Darenth, Hugh Child and Frere Child and Samuel Masterson wearing his tools strapped on his back, called to work on Rochester Bridge.

Durand looked at the face beneath him. Jonathan tried to say something but his front teeth were loose and all he could do was swallow. He closed his eyes. The bones ached deeply in Durand's numb hands. He leant forward, exhausted, his mouth against Jonathan's ear, whispered, *'Who am I?'*

Jonathan retched then swallowed, his breath hot and bloody in Durand's ear. 'You're Jack's son. Jack and Alice Mason's son. My father knows it.'

'You do not have to feel guilty,' Durand whispered, 'for what your father does not say.'

'I do,' Jonathan said.

Durand slid from him. Souch tied the dogs to a rail, patted Durand's back. 'Well done.'

'You'll do, boy,' Geoffrey Masterson said, the quiet man's highest praise. Suddenly, it seemed to Durand, everyone was going, hurrying about their interrupted business. Men he did not know nodded to him, squeezed his shoulder as they dispersed. The mutton chop seller packed up his tray, ignored him. Durand limped across. 'I heard your offer '

The man shrugged busily. 'Fresh out, brat.' Durand sighed, walked past the man, then grabbed his hair from behind, twisted, reached past him and selected a fat chop from the tray, pushed him away. The seller glared but would not now dare complain. Peter Taverner saw what happened and handed over the pitcher of beer. Durand, victorious, leant back against the parapet eating with one hand, drinking with the other, ignoring the people pushing past him.

Nick stood in front of him. He rested his gloved hands on Durand's shoulders.

'Well done, my boy,' he said. 'I'm proud of you. There's more I have to show you.' But he went no further then.

Durand finished eating, licked his fingers, went upstairs.

Rosie would not look at him. 'I saw what you did to Jonathan Bedell,' she said, busy with nothing important. 'Didn't you see his mother? Mary Bedell was crying.'

'Good,' Durand said. 'The word will get around and people will respect me. They'll know who I am.'

'Yes, they all know who and what you are. I hope you're proud of yourself.'

'Yes,' Durand said. 'I am.'

Durand sat in the chair with his feet on the table, the back of his head against the wooden wall. The drought of March had given way to fitful April showers, the drought of May to the drought of June. The wood felt hot. When the house was built however long ago it was, the timbers had not been properly seasoned and each year the planks dried and split a little more. The July sun stuck hot fingers of light through each knothole, making the room seem dark, marking the table and floor with circles of sunlight like blinding coins. Durand thought, a fortune in coins. He refilled his silver hanap and decided they looked like eyes. Hundreds of eyes.

In the crotch pocket of his breeches was a small sharp knife called a bydawe, taken from the kitchen.

He knew he was drunk and that this was wise. The wine had not fuddled his brain as usual but made his thoughts stand out clearer than before. He remembered being drunk last night, out with Nick and Alan.

Nick had taken him to the Liberty as if by accident, getting lost. 'I've heard tell about these places, Durand.' Nick pointed at the signs hanging over the street. 'A picture of a hanap of ale means ale is sold. If a girl is shown serving it, you can have the girl as well.' Nick laughed his muffled, phlegmy laugh. 'So I've heard tell. *I* wouldn't know.'

They walked beneath the sign of a red cockerel crowing. Durand asked, 'Do they sell chickens?' trying to be witty.

But Nick chuckled, 'My boy, there is much you must learn. Everyone knows a red cock is the symbol of deflowered virginity, which may be purchased there.'

They came to a place obviously newly built, the girl on the sign serving beer, called the Angel. The name sounded vaguely familiar to Durand but he couldn't remember where he'd heard it. Inside smelt of sweet beer. A pretty girl showing breasts like half-moons served Durand with a hanap of beer twice the size of any he had seen before.

'Good portions here,' Nick said, following Durand's eyes. 'You want her?'

Durand shook his head and knew at once every man in the room could see he had never been with a woman before.

Nick pretended not to notice. 'Try her,' he urged.

Durand drank his beer but Nick pushed the giggling girl at him. She really was lovely, golden, her skin was flawless, her face so beautiful he hardly saw her, just desired her. She took him by the hand and led him upstairs, along a gallery. 'You're look so divine,' Durand told her. 'You're too beautiful to be here.'

'Nobody never said that to me before,' the girl yawned, bored. She pinched him. 'Wake up, cock-sparrow, you're dreaming.' Lice crawled like black dandruff in her golden hair, her teeth were yellow fangs. Two men came out of a room and a man and a woman went in. Durand knew what women did to men but not what men could do to men. He didn't think love had ever come to this place. Then the girl closed her lips and smiled, perfect again. Durand shook his head and ran downstairs. 'You'll be back,' she called. 'You always are.'

Alan was there, sitting close against Nick, two men together. He smiled, knowing he gave Nick something that Durand did not.

Sometime in the night the two men and the boy, drunk, staggered back to London Bridge, through the passage in the Stone Gate called the Conduit where Tom Bedell greeted them, bowed his creaking bones, and lit their way home personally with his lantern though that was not necessary, it being the full moon. Durand, stumbling against Nick's shoulder, felt sick with drink. Nick told Alan to help. Alan, as drunk as Durand, smelt of spices. They came to the house and Durand remembered Rosie asleep in her rags on her ragged straw in the fourth-floor attic, but the stair turret seemed to whirl dizzily round and round. He dropped down where he stood on the ground floor. 'Leave him, Alan,' Nick said.

Durand woke sometime when the night seemed deepest and darkest. The tide roared more loudly than usual in the waterfalls under the arches, the windows thrown wide on such a hot night to admit the noise and wet Thamesy smell, and the house shook with a faint persistent vibration. He looked for beer to drink but there wasn't any. He found wine, drank from the pitcher, but the bad taste stayed in his mouth.

Durand set foot on the stairs, and they squeaked. He remembered to put his feet on the sides as he always used to do, went up silently. He heard a muffled voice, someone moving furniture, a rhythm like a song whose words he could not hear. He stopped on the first-floor landing and listened to the thin wooden walls creak steadily as though they were alive. The bedroom door

212

was wide open, casting a shaft of moonlight. A shadow moved across it then the moonlight reappeared. He heard the scuff of bare feet on the boards.

Alan's voice came: 'Oh God.' Durand had never heard such pain in a voice, such hunger. Eagerness.

Durand watched through the doorway. He put the back of his arm over his mouth and backed away. His shoulders hit the wall behind him. He stared, then turned and ran upstairs where Rosie lay. He lay down beside her, pulled her into his arms. She murmured, 'Did you have a bad dream? It's all right, Durand . . . it's all right . . .' He hugged Rosie's warmth to him. Then, as she slept, snoring, he lay awake. He began to realise how much she had tried to keep from him, how much she had tried to protect him, to hide him. But he had grown up.

The sun rose, and now Durand sat with his feet on the table, drinking, drunk, watching the sunlight pour through the walls, feeling the heat of it. He thought about what he had seen last night. He could not get it out of his mind, worse than anything he could have imagined. Nick's voice called downstairs. 'What day is it?'

Durand drank, refilled the hanap. The pitcher was empty. He shook it.

Nick's voice called again, 'What day, Durand?'

Durand called, 'The eleventh day of July.'

'Ah.' Nick's voice sounded pleased. 'The Festival of the Translation of St Benet.'

Durand thought about what he had seen. He remembered walking upstairs drunk as a Templar, he remembered standing in the doorway. He remembered Alan kneeling on the bed, naked, the moon on his face, his back and buttocks in shadow. He remembered Nick crouched behind Alan, his face against the buttocks, like a man being born from a man.

Durand remembered Nick looking round. He remembered that look gleaming in Nick's eyes. The look was love, yearning, desperate love, and the terror of death. Then Nick stood up erect and gleaming behind Alan, the whole of his body raw gleaming flesh. No patch of Nick's skin remained, he was red skinned muscle and pale knobs of spine, knuckles, knees, elbows, nothing more. The muscles jerked, the bones and tendons moved, Nick's erect flesh entered the kneeling man who could not see him, and Alan repeated the cry Durand remembered.

Nick had twisted, grinned at Durand, his red gums showing through his skinned face. He knew Durand watched, knew Durand could not look away. Nick's smile opened and his tongue licked out, pointed like the tongue of a demon. Durand raised his arm and staggered away.

He had not imagined it. He remembered it.

Nick came downstairs. Despite the heat he wore a heavy cape, knee-boots, thick woollen clothes as though he was cold. Durand realised that all he really saw of Nick was his eyes. The eyes blinked awkwardly, softened. Nick reached out his gloved hand tenderly, covered Durand's hand on the arm of the chair. 'Don't despair, Durand.'

'I'm not,' Durand said. 'I'm drunk.' He scratched himself, touching the little knife against his belly.

'There's always hope,' Nick said simply. 'Live for it. Live in hope. I do.'

Durand frowned. 'Hope of what?'

'Life,' Nick said quietly. 'Live in hope of life, Durand. Pray for it. Work for it.'

'Amen.' Durand finished his wine unsteadily. He wished Nick would just go out and stop talking. Rochester Bridge was still under repair and he wished Nick would go there and leave him and Rosie alone. He needed to think. Rosie would never believe him.

213

He could not get what he had seen last night out of his mind. He could see it now, alive in his mind, he knew he would never forget it as long as he lived. He flinched as Nick's gloved hand patted his arm. 'Amen, indeed, Durand.' He picked Durand up effortlessly by his arm, set him on his feet. His strength was enormous. 'I told you there's more I have to show you, my boy. St Benet's Day is as good a time as any other.'

He pulled Durand stumbling after him into the street, the hot, smoky wind blowing over London Bridge. The roadway was even busier than usual with people pushing forward, probably going to the festival, and Nick let the rush sweep him across the Square to the chapel. He pulled Durand after him by the shoulder into the doorway. 'Be sober, boy. You'll need your wits about you.'

'Yes, Master.'

Nick said, 'Believe everything you see.' He opened the door and pulled Durand inside.

At the far end of the echoing chapel Brother Wasce, sunlight pouring from the stained windows illuminating his weekday vestments in rippling colours, read from the ordinal. He looked up at them, then paid no further attention whatsoever. Nick led Durand down the winding stair to the undercroft. The high tide was just starting its ebb and the sail of a boat passed along the row of windows above their heads. Nick's boots tapped on the marble floor to the Lodge altar. He laid his gloved hand on the cloth.

'Durand, there's an invariable rule which is the essence of a church. The greatest treasure is always hidden in the most sacred place.'

'That makes sense,' Durand muttered. His head was starting to hurt and he was thirsty.

Nick pushed at the altar. Slowly it began to move, the marble plinth sliding smoothly over the marble flagstones below. The heavy purple vestment of gold-trimmed velvet draped over the altar blew outward in a draught from below, then from under the fluttering gold-tasselled hem, marble steps appeared one by one as the altar swung aside, leading down.

Nick held out a candle in invitation.

Durand carried the weighty ornate silver candlestick in both hands, it was so heavy. He started clumsily down the steps. After a moment he was afraid the wine would make him fall, took deep breaths. The marble steps turned to stone and he found himself standing on a plain stone floor below the earth, deep but narrow. The masons had dug under the pier into the bed of the river.

Durand raised the candle, illuminated the darkness around him. The walls of the subriverine stone cellar were decorated with night-blue celestial tapestries woven with the golden sun and silver moon in all her phases as she whirled about the earth. He saw the seven planets and their signs, their orbits worked in silver thread. Elliptical orbits, the blasphemous masonic belief he had noted before. And at the centre of the orbits stood the sun with his flames flaring round his face like golden hair. Down here the earth was not the centre of God's universe.

'That's impossible,' Durand said. It contradicted what he knew to be true, what his eyes could see, what his body could feel: he was the centre. And now he realised that there were not seven planets woven around the sun, he counted ten. And beyond the planets he saw patterns of stars woven in every shade of red and blue, and some glittered as though they were real.

Durand murmured, 'What is this place?'

'The Sacred Lodge, Durand, revealed only to initiates of senior degree.'

Durand raised the candle high. 'There must be a thousand stars.'

'I have counted three thousand stars, Durand. As many as the eye can see.'

'But it's not true,' Durand murmured. 'It's all wrong, isn't it? We're God's children, *we're* the centre of the universe, not the sun.'

Nick shrugged, a shadowy figure. For the first time Durand realised that the altar had swung back into place at the top of the steps.

Nick said sadly, 'Perhaps the more we know, the more we realise we do not know.'

Durand looked around him in awe. 'Do you really believe that?'

'No.' Nick touched the all-seeing eye on its golden tripod. 'I believe in knowledge.'

Durand tried to count the stars, gave up. 'Is this what you wanted to show me? That I'm nobody?'

'No, Durand. The opposite. That you are somebody. That you matter as much as you feel you do. That's what I'm going to show you, Durand, that's why I've brought you here. I'm going to prove your importance to you.' His voice rose and Durand touched the knife lying against his belly. Nick chuckled as though he knew all about that. 'You'll see,' he said, and pushed his gloved hands into the tapestries. They parted, blew out around him, and Nick walked from sight between them. 'Come, Durand. If you dare.'

Durand hesitated. He knows he's got me, he thought. He knows I'll follow.

He followed. The drapes billowed around him, closed behind him, and he felt a strangely intense disappointment. All he saw in front of him was a wall. He looked down, saw nothing below him but steps. He knew at once that what he saw was impossible.

The stone steps dropped down out of sight, went winding steeply down like a huge augur or screw driven deep into the earth, growing smaller towards a vanishing point. Nick's head appeared several circuits below, then his eyes looked up. He knew what Durand would do.

Durand followed Nick. The lower he went, the further the point receded below him, leading him down. 'Each step is a foot in height,' he whispered. His legs ached, his head pounded from the wine, but he had never felt more sober. 'One hundred.' Round and round, down and down. The walls were compacted gravel, boulders, streaming wet and foul in places. 'Two hundred.' The gravel gave way to hard white chalk. Durand counted three hundred steps.

Suddenly it made perfect sense to him. How wide do it be, Brother? *From the World to Heaven.* And how deep, Brother? *From the surface of the World to its Centre.*

Nick spoke behind him, from an alcove. 'Stop.'

Durand stopped. He stared down. 'How much further does it go?'

'As far as you wish, Durand.'

'How did you dig this?'

'By magic.'

'Tell me the truth.'

'It was already here. It has been here since the beginning of the world.'

Nick turned, and Durand saw that the alcove was a start of a corridor that curved from sight. He followed Nick's flapping cloak into the draught that blew along the corridor. The chalk walls were ancient, worn smooth and dirty by time and shoulders, the floor scooped by many feet. In places sharp corners and projecting boulders had been recently and expertly chiselled away, fresh white work. Durand tried to catch up, stumbled. His mouth was dry as dust with thirst, he would have licked the walls for moisture but they felt as dry as bone. He rubbed the chalk dust from his fingertips. He called, 'Where are we?'

Nick walked without looking back.

Durand called, 'Master, where are we?'

Nick stopped. 'Beneath the City of Hell.'

Durand caught him up. 'Let's go back.'

'There's no turning back,' Nick said. 'That's what I have learnt.'

Durand watched him walk on, then followed. Entrances branched left and right. Nick stopped so suddenly that Durand bumped into him. Nick gripped his shoulder, leant close. Blood trickled from the corners of Nick's eyes.

'Durand, do you know what you will see?'

'No, Master.'

'You will know when you see it.'

He pushed Durand up the steps ahead of him, but Durand hung back, and it seemed to him that Nick was more eager than he was to go forward. Then as Nick climbed the steps, Durand walked beside him looking up at Nick's shrouded face, his staring eyes, Nick's whole body leaning forward in his eagerness.

'Look!' Nick said.

Durand glanced at the chamber that opened up ahead of them. The glow made the candle flame seem black, mere burning soot. He was afraid.

'Gold,' Nick said. 'This is the Sanctum Sanctorum we Templars have built. Look at the gold. Pure solid gold, for Heaven is made of gold.' He opened the golden screen, and light poured out around him. Durand watched in awe. He saw through Nick's cloak and hat and breeches and boots, saw through the glowing nimbus to Nick as he once was, a young man, handsome, his life before him, saw Nick's scrubbed skin and combed hair, fingernails, toenails, his even white teeth and all he did not now have, as though the light had made age an illusion and there was no reason for Time to run forward. Nick raised his arms towards the light. 'It is the Shekinah. Glory!'

He pulled Durand forward. Durand stumbled up white marble steps, fell to his knees beside an altar of white marble draped with chains. Nick pulled him up. 'Look.'

Light poured from the body laid out on the altar.

Durand stared at Nick. He saw through him and there was still something beautiful inside Nick, somewhere inside there was still a child. The articulation of Nick's bones was beautiful, the pumping of his heart was miraculous. Even the pumping of the tiny particles of blood in his veins and stomach was beautiful and miraculous, and Durand stared at him in wonder and innocence and awe.

Nick grabbed Durand's head, twisted him round. 'Look! See Him! He is the prize! Here is all we have fought for, suffered for, endured penance for, died for. *Look!*'

'I won't.' But he thought Nick would break his neck. 'I won't.' Durand squeezed his eyes shut but light blazed up from the body, and the image, the unforgettable indelible image was stamped through his eyelids as bright as though he stared with open eyes. Durand shrieked, fell back.

He lay with his eyes tight shut.

Nick was right. Durand knew what he saw. He saw like a blind man, without even opening his eyes. In his mind's eye he reached out and touched the ropes, the chains, the tight bandages and wrappings that bound the sleeping, unshrouded figure. Durand reached out and touched His eyes, touched the Crown of Thorns, touched His bleeding side, His beard, His hair braided for the tomb, he touched His gentle mouth, felt His humility and His strength, the awful majesty of His strength, His goodness, His patience, and Durand knew he saw the truth.

'The Arch of the Covenant,' Nick murmured. 'The body of Christ is His covenant. His covenant with man, His promise to us all. He will save us. He is the promise and the prize.' He looked eagerly at Durand.

'My God,' Durand whispered. 'You Templars, what have you done?'

Nick didn't understand. He smiled. 'We are His servants. He will awaken in our lifetimes. We know this.'

Durand tried to sit up. He was blind. All he saw was the luminous image burning – still burning – into his eyes. He whispered, 'Do you believe that you deserve Him?'

'Yes,' Nick said. 'Look at all the good men have done in His name. Look at all the blood that has been spilt.'

Durand thought of the chains and ropes that bound the sleeping figure. 'He's your prisoner not your saviour, you've made Him prisoner of your beliefs.'

'We don't have beliefs,' Nick said. 'We *know.*'

Durand stared at the image in his eyes. He thought: suppose He wakes? Suppose I shout and He wakes, and His chains fall off, and He tells me *with perfect certainty* that I am right and Nick is wrong? Suppose He tells me Nick is right, and I am wrong?

What difference does it make? Either way, I lose my life because I cease to think for myself.

Durand blinked. Slowly the candle flame reappeared in front of his eyes. He crawled to his feet. Dimly he saw Nick, cloaked, hooded, on his knees at the altar praying. Durand realised that the worst prayed as well as the best. He limped past the golden screen and glittering troves of he knew not what else, marvels no doubt, relics, treasures beyond price. Darkness was all around him now and for a moment he was filled with longing for the light that he had missed, for all he had not seen, which was almost everything, he supposed. He ran, sheltering the pallid candle flame behind his hand, stumbling from wall to wall, streaking his shoulders with dry chalk dust, and suddenly the simplest and most amazing thought occurred to him: *I'm not thirsty.*

It was true. He faltered, looked back. He need never be thirsty again in his whole life, or experience hunger, or worry, or sadness, or moments of small satisfaction snatched from the busy business of living. He could turn back, and like Nick and the Templars and the masonic Brethren of London Bridge appoint himself servant of the Body, and believe so deeply that belief became truth, and truth became fact. And perhaps the Resurrection would come in his lifetime.

But then Durand thought of what little he knew about Jesus, which was only from chapel services and Rosie's warm whispered bedtime stories of the Christ child, and he thought for the second time: if God exists, and I have seen He does, and if He is more marvellous than I can imagine, and I have seen He is, then, in real life, what difference does it make?

He asked himself for the third time: *What difference does it make?*

Durand ran. He had to get Rosie, had to get away from here. The candle flame blew, burnt his hand. 'Ouch!' He heard his cry echo from other rooms or caves down here, ran with his head down so he would not see the maze. Get Rosie, he thought, get far away. The flame singed the hairs growing on his upper lip. The walls banged his shoulders, he stumbled but did not slow down.

Far behind him Nick's voice called his name, echoing.

Durand skidded. The corridor ended in a platform, the winding staircase rose above him and fell away below. He did not look back, climbed. One step, two. The steps were very steep, the weight of the candlestick tried to push him backwards. 'Fifty-one,' he muttered, 'fifty-two.'

Nick's voice cried out below. 'Durand!'

Durand twisted the candle out of the holder. He let the heavy candlestick fall into the darkness winding beneath him as he climbed. It fell, clanged, fell free, went clanging downward until he could hear it no more. He gasped for breath. One hundred steps, he started counting over. 'Seven. Eight. Nine . . .' His legs ached and he pushed with one hand on his knee, finding it easier to climb the steps near the outer edge. Gravel showered down where his shoulder banged the wall. Two hundred.

217

'Durand!'

Nick must be fifty years old; how could he climb so fast? Durand glimpsed a line of light turning above him, shining through the starry curtains at the top of the winding stair. He threw down the candle and climbed towards the light, hands reaching up through the darkness, but the specks seemed no closer. 'Two hundred and ninety six—' The curtains parted in front of his hands and Durand fell forward into the Lodge chamber. The candles in each corner had almost burnt down. He gasped for air, then wriggled forward to the steps leading up.

'You can't go back,' Nick called from the darkness behind him. 'You can't go. You can't choose.'

Durand climbed three steps, crouched. The altar in the undercroft barred his way. Was it locked? He braced his shoulders, heaved. Nothing. He heard Nick's climbing footsteps.

Durand pushed to one side. The altar held him down like a trap. He turned, shoved backwards.

'Durand, my son, stop!' Nick shouted.

Durand pushed with all his strength and suddenly, easily, the slab slid out of the way. He clambered into the dim grey daylight of the undercroft. A gloved hand reached out of the hole behind him and grabbed his ankle.

Durand shrieked. His hands slid across the marble floor as he was pulled back. He grabbed the altar but it moved, swinging towards him.

'Durand,' Nick appealed from below. He held the ankle effortlessly. 'You can be like me.'

Durand screamed. He kicked out, catching Nick's muffled face.

Nick cursed, slipped back. The altar closed over him.

Durand crawled across the floor. He picked himself up, ran to the stair in the corner. Someone ran down, knocked into him, then more people came flooding down, almost falling over him. Durand, swept back, struggled forward. Voices shouted and screamed. A girl had lost her child. 'God, help us!' a man cried. 'God help us all!' I've gone mad, Durand thought. This is madness. More people half fell down the steps, an old woman held up by her daughter. Children, the boys frightened, not letting go of their mothers, the girls clinging to their fathers. Durand seized a boy alone. 'What's happening?'

'It's the fire.'

A woman knocked into Durand, swore at him. He grabbed the boy. 'What fire?'

'It's got worse. My dad can't stop it.'

Durand pushed through the people falling down. Upstairs the chapel was a solid mass of people pushing and shoving, the crowd inside pushed by the crowd outside. A girl held her baby above her head. She was squeezed so tight she could not breathe but the baby bawled lustily. Men grunted and swore, the women flattened between their powerful bodies or slipping under their feet. 'Get out of here,' Durand cried, 'run away from here, get away from the fire, not into church!'

'God save our souls,' shouted one man, and others took up the cry. 'God save our souls!'

Nick called, 'Durand, come back.' His pursuit was relentless, obsessed. He forced two people apart, his gloved hand snatched between them, caught Durand's coat. It tore. Durand lunged forward, pushed someone down, crawled over the shoulders of the people in front of him. He felt his knees knock their heads. 'I'm sorry, I'm sorry.' Their hands snatched at him, they fought and cursed and wailed for mercy. Durand could smell the smoke coming through the door and all he could think of was Nick behind him and Rosie in front, Rosie somewhere in the crowd in front. She'd be terrified. She didn't

218

even like going to the shops she was so shy. He imagined her terrified face among all these rough, angry, terrified faces.

The worst thought of all occurred to Durand. She didn't know he wasn't at home.

The people parted and Durand fell down into the street. Legs and feet tripped over him, fell on him. He could hardly breathe, he could not make sense of the chaos. He struggled to his feet, climbed on to the parapet of the Square, clung to a sign for balance. Now he saw.

Smoke poured along the bridge from end to end. Someone shouted that the fire had started in Southwark. If that was so then sparks had been blown on to the north end of the bridge. He saw flames and smoke right to the walls of the City. The crowds who had come to watch the Southwark fire from the vantage point of the bridge were now trapped.

'My God,' Durand whispered. He could not hear himself now for the roar of flames leaping along the wooden houses, or the shouts of the people by him, their mouths opening and closing silently. The crowd parted, a burning dog ran between them, some man wrapped it in his coat. An old and rather beautiful woman put up her hand for help. Durand dragged her on to the parapet. 'Thank you. I can't swim a stroke,' she told him, 'thank God.' She jumped before he could stop her, and Durand watched horrified as the river swept her down. He tried to close his eyes. The ebb tide foamed through the arches but fishermen tried to bring their boats alongside the starlings where survivors huddled from the flames. The people along the edges fell into the water. A boat pulled in skilfully, using an eddy of the flow, the crowd pushed aboard, the boat overturned and they were all gone.

Durand looked up. The doors and roof of the chapel were burning. He could hear the screams of the trapped people. He heard his name called, stared up into the smoke.

'Durand!'

The voice called from above him. Rosie's arms waved from the attic window. It was too small for her to get through, the bird table was in the way. She beat at it with her white arms but Durand had built it well. He glimpsed her pale, round, terrified face in the darkness of the room.

He jumped down off the parapet. The whole ground floor of the house was on fire, its heat blocking the roadway. The gravel crackled loudly as the stones split. A man tried to run by and his hair and hat caught fire. His wife screamed but she did not know what to do. A woman taking buckets from the team lifting them from the river doused him with water, spat on her hands, returned to her task. A burning man threw his boy in the river. Durand could not bear to see what he was seeing, he heard the shrieks of the people burnt alive in the chapel rise like a flock of gulls.

'Durand, jump!' Rosie shrieked. She saw boats in the river and maybe he would be picked up. He realised all she cared about was him, all she had ever cared about. Rosie had no other life.

Durand roared. The house across the road was only just beginning to burn. He dashed through the doorway, banged his head on the low lintel, found himself blundering through a dark room, half looted, a shop. No stair turret, only cheap boards angled up the wall. He tripped, ran upstairs. Heat and smoke blew past him, showing the way up the next flight. The rail gave way but he pulled himself through a narrow opening into an attic. Set one storey lower than his house, this attic had a flat roof. There must be a way up. He couldn't see one. He ran to the window looking towards St Paul's, boats circling, one crew rowing frantically as their boat was sucked beneath the bridge. Durand broke the window with his elbow. Most houses had a back rail overhanging the river for the relief of nature's calls, sometimes open, sometimes with a modest shed of clapboard nailed round it – like this. He stepped out on to the little balcony made by the latrine's top, ran up steps to the flat roof of the house. Smoke and sparks blew over him, and he heard the voice of the fire. The fire said, 'Durand.'

Durand was going to die. He knew it.

He struggled forward across the roof. Sparks had settled and it was burning, tinder-dry after the hot weather, tarred with pitch to keep the rain out. It burnt with stinking black smoke, clung stickily to his shoes. He came to the edge over the street, stared across the gap. The houses all overhung the road, ten or twelve feet narrowing to a jump no wider than the height of a man.

But his house was one storey higher, its roof steeply angled.

Rosie ran to the narrow street window. She'd never get through. Six feet apart. She stared at him through the glass. Durand looked down. Below her the house was a mass of flame. He knew both of them had only seconds to live.

The fire said, 'Durand.'

'Durand!' Nick shouted. He strode downt he steps from the burning chapel. His cloak was burning, his boots smoked where they touched the road. He held up his arms. 'Durand, come back! You'll die for nothing.'

Durand backed away from the edge of the roof. The pitch was slippery and sticky at the same time. He ran forward sliding and stumbling, jumped the gap. He glimpsed the road, thought he was falling, then his hands caught the steeply sloping gable above Rosie's window. His legs kicked in the flames now licking from the window below.

He dragged himself on to the slope of the roof above her, swung one leg across the apex.

The roof was wood tiles. He tried to lift them, broke his nails, remembered the knife in his breeches. He stuck the blade between two tiles and worked them apart, then pulled at the sides of the hole to widen it. A haze of smoke drifted out then Rosie's arms stuck up. 'Quick!' He hauled, and she came up coughing and spluttering.

'Where have you been?' she scolded him at once. 'You're filthy. Look at you! I've been worried sick.'

Durand kissed her. 'You've got eyes the colour of those little blue flowers that grow out of the moss.'

She looked both pleased and annoyed. 'What are we going to do?'

'I don't know.'

'Durand,' Nick said. Only the gap between the houses separated them. Nick held out his gloved hands. 'Jump, I'll catch you.'

Durand pushed Rosie behind him, backed away along the apex of the roof. Their feet skidded down each side. From here he saw the whole of London Bridge burning. Only the Stone Gate stood above the smoke. Beside him St Thomas's Chapel roared with flame. The roof leads melted and poured fire on the congregation below, the windows trickled down the blackened walls.

'Jump!' Nick said. 'I can save you. You know that. You *know* it.'

Nick looked round as the flat roof burst into flame around him. There was only the way forward. He tensed to leap. A bird, a rook or a crow in panic of the fire, fluttered at his head and he struck out wildly. But the crow came back, ragged wings flapping, pecked at his eyes. Nick's hand knocked the bird down, it swooped from sight between the burning houses.

Nick jumped the gap with burning breeches, burning boots. He slithered on the steep angle, then caught his hands on the apex, dragged himself up to Rosie and Durand.

'My God,' Durand whispered. 'Look at you.'

Nick stood. His gloves were burning. He saw, felt, nothing wrong. Rosie screamed. Nick's muffler slipped from his face. His fleshless lower jaw, shattered by Durand's kick, hung from its hinge on one side. He pulled his tongue in. 'Ah, yes,' he said. 'Durand.'

Durand drew his knife. He looked round. There was nothing behind Rosie, the roof ended in a small cockerel-shaped wind vane for good luck and beyond that there was only the long drop to the river, small boats circling in the eddies down there, a few heads bobbing, drowning in water black with ash.

Nick reached out his clawed hands. 'Come. You don't have a choice, Durand.'

Durand shouted, 'I do have a choice!'

Nick looked at him blankly. 'What? Leave her! Come with me, quickly, quickly!' He took a step, grasped.

'Don't,' Durand said. He lunged with the knife. It slipped through the front of Nick's cloak and met no resistance, only bones. The force pushed Nick back, they skidded backwards as though Nick weighed only a few pounds. Durand drew away with a cry of disgust. Flame poured up from the roof around Nick, the rafters charred, tumbled down into the intense heat. Something whirled up from below, a white cloak, caught round Nick's legs, blew upwards in the rising heat. Nick's bony fingers caressed the white wool, the red cross.

'The resurrection,' he marvelled. 'It *is* the resurrection in my lifetime.' His burning body wrapped itself in the burning cloak, reached out to Durand. 'Come with me. There's still time.'

Durand looked at Rosie. 'No.'

Nick's lidless eyes turned on Rosie with a look of pure hatred. 'You!' he said. 'You're the one who didn't matter, damn you to Hell.'

The rafters collapsed beneath Nick. He hung on by his blackening bones, then reached up. 'Help me, Durand.'

Durand held Rosie's hands.

'Remember what I showed you,' Nick shrieked. 'You can't choose. *You can't choose!*'

Durand looked away. The rafters collapsed. Nick fell like a candle. His shrieks faded into the roar of the fire.

Sparks shot up. The house swayed.

Durand gripped Rosie tight. His head itched. He pulled her past the weather vane, the heat blew like a dragon's breath on their backs. 'Swim!'

And they jumped as far out as they could together.

'Three thousand people died, husband,' Rosie remembered. They joined the others throwing flowers from the bridge into the water. She remembered smiling at how he had looked on that first day after the fire: his hair burnt off, his baldness making him look older. And there was something even older about him, too, something in his eyes. Not a child's eyes. Was the change just the fire, or something more? What had happened to Durand with Nick earlier that morning, before the fire? Durand had never answered, but his eyes were webbed with wrinkles, and his hair, when it began to grow, grew shock-white. Now Rosie slipped her arm through his, watching the petals, each one a life, turn gently on the full tide and drift away. 'We'll never forget them.'

Durand said, 'The fire spread from Southwark, across the bridge, into the City. Some say it was more than three thousand deaths.' He listened to the calls of the flower sellers. Someone always made money on the bridge. 'We knew hardly any of them.'

Rosie tugged him, tried to change his mood. 'The great fire of London Bridge will never be forgotten, anyway.'

Durand looked around him at the busy morning bustle across the Square, the crowding people, the chanting voices from the chapel and cries of glove sellers, hot-apple sellers, the shriek of gulls, new houses packed wall to wall with smoking chimneys, carts jamming the narrow roadway as usual. Fresh white gravel had been laid, already matted with manure. Everything was the same. 'They've forgotten already,' Durand said. 'We'll be forgotten too.'

She lifted the basket where their baby lay, touched his nose with her own. 'You won't forget us, littl'un, will you, baby, no you won't.' Durand said nothing. Those wrinkled eyes, as though he saw more than he said, saw everything so clearly that for a moment she followed his gaze – but she saw nothing special at all. She wanted to explain to him what she felt, vague though it was. She had faith. 'Our love will be remembered.' She meant the baby, love going forward. 'Love can live for ever. Don't be sad.'

He laughed. 'I'm not sad! I'm happy.'

Rosie was thirty-nine years old. She would never have another baby. She had put on weight comfortably, her eyes were the same speedwell blue, and she was as maternal as she had always been. 'Yes,' she said, 'I'm happy too.'

Again Durand said nothing, and again she followed his gaze: the toe of his boot, the first he had made, scratched through the new gravel to the black layer of charcoal beneath. The old roadway had not been taken up, only covered over.

Rosie shook him, she wanted him to pay attention to her. 'There's something I've always wondered. When we jumped from the roof into the river, how did you know I could swim?'

Durand said, 'I didn't.'

'Well,' she said, 'I couldn't.'

As they'd surfaced, spluttering, an eel boat caught them almost at once and pulled them up in its nets. They saw the fire already dying down along the bridge, the wooden houses consumed so quickly that nothing remained of them above the stone arches but a frail tangle of smoking timbers, and by morning even the embers were cold except in the chapel, where the walls still stood, and the burning roof had collapsed on to the trapped bodies of so many people. More lives were lost in the chapel, praying for salvation, than in any other single place, though the undercroft was intact. Down there some men – those who could nerve themselves to do violence to sacred property – had saved themselves by breaking the windows and clinging to boats.

Men digging through the ruins of the fallen roof found beneath it a layer of blackened bones beyond counting or identification, fused into the chapel floor in a solid mass with the burnt timbers. No one knew how many people had died in their houses but it was very many. New people were anxious to take up leases on London's busiest street – the rising heat had left the structure of the bridge as strong as ever – and carpenters were touting their skills before dark.

Durand had sifted through the blackened timbers. He never found Nick's bones. Most of the ruined house had collapsed into the cellar dug into the bridge pier beneath. There was nothing left of the house, *his* house. The formal documents stored in the chapel were all burnt, but copies tallied with the Brethren in the Bridge House survived, and his mind was already busy with plans. He could rebuild the house. He had the skill or could learn it, and he could do his own work better than any jobbing carpenter botching for a fee. Durand wondered how he would afford to pay for the wood. The nails would cost most. By making his own wooden pegs he could save on the expense. Rosie had watched him think. She had nothing left in the world but what she stood up in. 'So,' she cut gently into his thoughts, 'you're going to rebuild your mother's house?'

Durand shrugged. *Your mother's house.* Rosie had known his mother, he had not. He had no mental image of her, she'd died a lifetime ago. All he knew of her was an absence, ancient history. But that had set him thinking about Rosie. When night came they sheltered beneath a few boards on the bridge, one of the thousand tiny encampments of survivors like themselves, listening to the river rush below like passing time in its slow rhythm of ebb and flow. And Durand said, 'I've been thinking.'

'I've been thinking' was a phrase of Durand's that Rosie would find very familiar in the coming months. 'What about?'

'We'll get married,' Durand said.

Now that its arrival came too late, rain fell. Their fire went out and they sat holding a piece of dripping canvas over their heads.

Rosie said, 'But you don't love me.'

'Yes, I do. I need you.'

'But I don't love you.'

Durand chuckled. 'You do. We aren't related. Yet what would you do without me?'

They sat in silence listening to the rain. Then Rosie said, 'What do you see in the dark?'

Durand sat with his eyes tight shut. 'No more than you.'

'Yes, you do. You do see. There's something about you, Durand.'

I see a sleeping, unshrouded figure. I see like a blind man. I cannot close my eyes on what I see.

She leant towards him, whispering. 'Where did you go with Nick?'

'Nowhere. It was just a dream.'

'What did Nick mean? He said you can't choose. He said you didn't have a choice.'

'He meant I couldn't choose you.'

'But you have.'

Durand kissed her cheek. 'Exactly.'

Rosie listened to the rain trickle, and the tide rush, and she felt dawn coming. 'I'll marry you,' she said, 'but we won't do you-know-what.'

Durand made her wait. 'Actually, you're quite pretty even though you are old enough to be my mother.'

Rosie sat in silence. Then she said, 'I'm not *that* old.'

Dawn was the coldest hour of the night. Durand put his arm round Rosie to keep her warm. They rested their burned, itchy scalps together. Durand said, 'I've been thinking, Rosie.'

She sighed. 'Yes, Durand.'

'I could be a shoemaker,' he said. 'I'm good with my hands. I could pay for the house by making shoes. People always need shoes. In good times they buy new shoes, in bad times they have their old shoes repaired. And there's no shortage of passing trade on the bridge . . .'

'You and your ideas.' Rosie had begun to laugh. 'Whoever heard of a cobbler called Mason?'

Now they stood by the parapet in the Square, by their new house, watching the flowers flow beneath the bridge. There were fewer this year, and when next St Benet's Day came, Durand suspected there would be none at all. Lives and memories were short, and time rushed forward. He took his baby from Rosie's basket, named Henry after the new King like half the babies in the kingdom, and kissed his snub nose. 'Don't wake him,' Rosie warned. 'He hates being woken from his nap. He's just like you.'

Durand looked over his son's sleeping face to the chapel. St Thomas's had been rebuilt over the undamaged undercroft using the same walls as before, with a few new stones added where heat had crumbled the original masonry, and the roof rose to a point in the middle. It looked slightly Eastern, like a Templar church. Durand had never gone inside it since that day; he and Rosie worshipped in St Magnus at the Bridge Head or St Mary Overie at Bridge Foot. He looked over the edge as the stonework of the Chapel Pier opened and figures trooped from the concealed door barely above the level of the water, fishermen and eel catchers climbing into their boats moored to iron rings set in the stone. Mass had been said in the chapel so by law they were now allowed to sell their fish to fishmongers, and their oars sent the flowers swirling as they pulled for shore. 'Yes,' Durand repeated, 'I'm happy.'

Rosie shivered, for there was something unnerving about a second claim of happiness so soon after the first. She followed Durand's eyes to a fat figure waddling slowly across the Square. Alan wore the black monk-like robes of the Brethren of London Bridge. He ignored them as though they were not there, went into the chapel, and they did not see him come out again. Serle Mercer, elected Lord Mayor for the second time, rode by on a horse, left his page holding the reins by the chapel steps, went inside. Geoffrey Masterson and Martin Stoner, past Masters of the Bridge, arrived with Benedict Boatwright. Chale Souch's son Michael went into the chapel – his father had been killed in the fire – followed by Geoffrey's son Samuel, now wearing the chased silver ring of a senior degree. Durand would not look at them any more than they would look at him. Instead he turned away, gave baby Henry back to Rosie and fell into conversation with his firm friend Jonathan Bedell, nothing important, the price of leather, a new bridge regulation concerning the weight of carts, the fine weather. Rosie liked Jonathan, he had a heart of oak. His new young wife Rebecca, barely fourteen years old and already great with child, saw Rosie, smiled and waved. Bored by the men's conversation, Becky bustled across to coo over baby Hal. The two women made baby talk.

Rosie looked up, and Becky's voice faded into the background hubbub. This is it, Rosie thought. This is the golden moment in our lives. Things will never be better, this is all we have, we'll never need more than this. We'll watch our son grow, we'll hope and dream and struggle all our lives, grow richer or poorer by our own efforts, make our own luck, grow old, cold, die worthy of Heaven if we can. Durand made the right choice. He chose love. Rosie turned her face to the sun, felt its golden warmth, and thought, yes, Durand's right. This is all there is.

'Yes,' she said, 'I'm happy.'

A harsh cry interrupted her, but it was only a crow perched on a rooftop.

Rosie blinked and remembered what she had been talking about, fell back in conversation with Becky, and above them the crow swooped from sight between the houses.

He married her! Well, I don't know that I approve. Rosie's certainly not who I expected. I always, always imagined my son marrying . . . you know what I mean . . . someone more like me. A girl with a bit more spark and flash than dear Rosie, someone . . . *better*. Not that I'm saying a word against her.

Do I sound like an envious old woman?

I mustn't. I don't feel old. I feel . . . I feel the same as I always did, always the same person however much my body changed, whether I was little Alice Lacknail hiding in the woods, young Alice kissing Jack heart and soul beneath the arch, Jack's wife riding for the first time to the Angel in Southwark, Mistress Alice of Jack's house on London Bridge – always the same Alice, the same me.

The same soul.

What a glorious mystery life is, layer after layer of life and purpose, more than we ever knew, more than we ever imagined, more than we ever had the minds to know. We sensed it as dimly as a stone senses the sun. I don't know much, but I know life has a purpose. I don't know what it is, but I know it includes me as much as you.

I know . . . I'm struggling for words. I know, I *feel*, it's an ascent. It's a

224

journey going forward, reaching upward, but I don't know why. Because . . . because something happened to me, and you know what it is. And yet I am not changed. I am the crow; London Bridge turns beneath me crammed with life and houses and gates and there is a busy queue at the King's Weighbridge where carts and panniers are weighed and taxed before being allowed to cross, the crow's eyes see it all. Here is the rooftop where the crow likes to perch and survey its domain (he is, as it happens, a male bird) in the organised and busy routine of its life that I have no control over, none at all. It is the crow, I am the soul. The crow is an exquisitely made piece of life who has struggled from the egg designed for it with all its instincts and tasks implanted ready within it. Only a crow, with hardly a moment for leisure in the search for food and the lust for survival, yet sometimes I think even its tiny brain senses . . . senses something more.

Senses me. Longs for me. A crow knows fear. It knows death comes.

How shall I bear to live for ever without hands, without voice, a mere observer? How many more times shall I endure death, helpless, and be reborn?

Yes, but you saw what happened, didn't you? You saw the crow flutter on burning wings at Nick's head to spoil his jump between the rooftops, peck at Nick's eyes in the extremity of its panic and fear of fire. Its mind blank with fear, and so for a moment with all my strength I imposed my will, my as you know formidable will, upon the living brain of the bird which my insubstantial soul inhabits. And something real happened. You saw it. You might say the crow was only following its own nature, in its blind panic it would have struck out anyway. Perhaps. But I know what I know. I was there.

By the most enormous effort, I exerted a tiny influence.

I mattered.

And you've noticed this: Nick knew it, didn't he? Several times during the last years of his life I saw him turn as though he sensed me. A mouse perhaps. I don't think he knew it was me, but I think he was beginning strongly to sense that there was more to our lives than even he knew. And Nick, don't forget, was a man who'd read at least two or three of the ten *Sepherot*, the ten Books of sacred knowledge. Perhaps he'd even read as far as the fifth Book, Gevurah, Strength, the raging inferno of the Lord. Strength, the Deceiver.

Yes, I think, by his look, Nick had read some of that.

Nick's dead now. He's gone. I don't know what happened to him, my poor bird swooped between the flames in its agony, shot into clear air over the river. Landed on a mudbank, almost died. Poor raggedy-feathered crow. How I love you.

And then, as the tide rises, the crow flaps towards the riverbank and the City, and I cease to exist. I cannot cross the water.

Long ago Nick buried my bones on the bridge, and not on consecrated ground either – at least, not on ground regarded by God as consecrated. I can go no further, the City is behind a glass wall through which I may see but not enter. I hate this moment: the crow flaps forward and suddenly there is nothing but this wrench into the dark, to my bones, to Alice's bones somewhere in the dark. Mercifully dry by this time. My flesh has decayed and only my skeleton remains, wrapped more or less in its old bit of tapestry. I am again the prisoner of my old body's bones and of my desolation, of pure, ghastly loneliness, longing for the light and the life.

Perhaps the crow will return soon; otherwise I shall not be reborn until its death.

Are there others like me?

My bones cannot call out. My world is earth and dark and silence. But I have time, time not exactly to think, to *feel*. To need. To love. To remember.

225

To remember love and my life with Jack.

Does love end when we die? No. Has Jack's soul gone onward? I don't think so. Even when I was alive I had thought he was buried on London Bridge. And it made sense too. Nick couldn't allow the murdered body to be found, the search for the murderer would begin. I remembered the dust on Nick's knees.

Nick had more than buried Jack's body on the bridge; he had *hidden* it. Hidden the body where the bones would never be found, just as he had hidden Alice's poor body. But where? In the same place as her?

No, too romantic.

I don't sense him here. I don't even know where *here* is. Beneath the roadway? In one of the piers or arches? Perhaps, but I remember steps, a room, the hard floor that broke my arm when I was dropped. Rubble beneath the stone floor. A cellar. I'm trying to remember the buildings that had been under construction at the time, unoccupied. The Stone Gate, sooty though it is now, was only half finished in those days. The chapel was incomplete. And any number of houses were being knocked up, mostly at the northern end, near the Bridge Head. Those over the arches had hanging cellars at the rear, made of wood, but houses over piers invariably had the cellars dug beneath them for storage or lodgings. The houses were all burnt and have been rebuilt now, but of course the stone pits were intact.

So whatever had been buried beneath any of these places is still there.

Jack, for instance.

My bones too, perhaps.

Oh God, what a sad, yearning, restless creature I am, filled with love, and yet at the same time worn down by loss too, this cruel loss of everything I once held dear in my life, it's all going, slipping away, never to be recaptured. How are my family, my Durand, and Rosie, and my grandson young Hal? Come back, sweet crow. They say a skilful crow may live for much longer than twenty years. Come back to your river and your home on the bridge.

And suddenly, it must be one day, I burst into the sunlight again, sight and sounds and the rush of air in wings, London Bridge like a bright carnival thrown across the muddy water swinging beneath the crow's wings. More crows have taken over this territory, it must fight for its place on the rooftops, and mobs of gulls swirl between the sky and the busy river. The crow swoops across the Square from time to time, but all I glimpse is crowds and traffic, and my changed house now has a flat-roofed fourth storey and larger windows too, I think, and I don't care for the look except that my son Durand made them. The crow settles nearer the Stone Gate than I had hoped and goes about its business: a boiled and peeling human head stuck on a pole, and now another, and another, wings fluttering about them, beaks fighting for strips of flesh which is tarred and distasteful, but the heads are soft inside. I no longer think of these severed heads as man's cruelty to man, merely as nature. It's the nature of men and women to destroy themselves.

And here, through the archway below, walks Rosie. I hardly recognise her. Grey in her hair and broad waddling hips! What's happened? How has she aged so quickly? And yet she looks happy, and beside her scampers a boy with a serious face on his lively body, his hand almost lost in his mother's. This must be Henry, darling little Hal, my grandson. The baby in him's gone, Hal's ten at least, his eyes dazzled by the sun as he comes from the shadow of the arch. And here comes Durand to greet them, hands hard with work and hair shaved to a white stubble against the lice that are everywhere these days because of the swarming docks and the ships unloading from foreign lands. Durand puts his hand on his son's head, embraces his wife. She's not so meek with him as she was with me, scolds him for lateness. Durand laughs. Stay, crow, let me see more!

But the crow flaps upward on its grisly task, and they are gone.

With all my might I try to turn back from the awful heads and see my bright, living family once more. The crow's eye glimpses the squashed body of a mouse in the road, swoops down hungrily. The stone from a child's slingshot strikes the crow beneath the wing; it is a trap. The crow moves feebly on the roadway, a hand picks it up, breaks the neck. Here it is again. The crow melts into me in its agony. This awful moment of death.

The dark.

But I saw them. My life goes on. I love them so. My family, my family.

There is time to think in the dark. All I think about is my family who have come from Jack's love for me and mine for him, my family who go forward through time, my, our, immortality. But then my thoughts turn more and more to Jack, and the most remarkable, most obvious thought occurs to me.

If Jack is buried here, like me, is he . . . like me?

Is Jack, like me, aware of himself?

Is Jack looking for me?

I must find him.

I am the sperm and the egg.

I am not alone.

I come not from the shell but the womb. I sleep, I open my eyes. Who am I? My brothers and sisters are mice.

I exert my will and the tiny mouse turns aside, actually turns aside from its hunt for food, and begins to run.

I have begun my search for Jack.

Four
Jack

Alice's tale

London Bridge, 5 February 1832

Alice, Alice, are you there?

Quick, it's raining, I hate the wet. Run to me here. The shelter, over here! You're late.

Did I splash you? Let me caress you.

Aaah, that feels good. I don't need you, mind. My other side, just there. Ah.

I didn't know there had ever been a fire on London Bridge. Three thousand people killed? It seems incredible.

St Benet's Day, 11 July 1213. Look it up.

I do believe you, Alice. About everything.

Of course you do, dear Frank. There's no other explanation for what you're hearing, unless you're mad.

Do you think Nick, had he lived, would have succeeded in making Durand like himself?

No! Durand saved himself by his own efforts! You saw that. He turned down what Nick offered him, refused to be deceived by Nick's promises.

But Durand did not believe what he saw, did he?

Durand believed utterly. I think he saw Him until his dying day. Durand simply preferred to choose. My son believed in God, not in religion. He knew what he had seen, but he lived his own life in his own way. And a busy, hardworking, good life it was too. His son Hal married Becky's daughter Ann, their children were Mary and Richard, who married Liza, one of Will Ladler's granddaughters, whose mother had married Sam Swinert. Then, having achieved all this in his life, Durand turned his mind to God a few days before he died, an old man mute with a stroke, his son and grandchildren at his bedside, and at the proper time was buried ashore at St Mary Overie.

Even Durand can't have believed in the staircase that led to the centre of the world. How was the delusion performed?

Durand saw what was real.

Show me.

In good time.

But Durand never told Hal or his grandchildren what he had seen?

Would they believe him, unless he showed them too?

I see. No.

Durand had seen what truth did to Nick. He saw it burnt into his own eyes. What loving father would do that to his children?

So you searched for Jack. Did you find him?

Listen to me, listen, hold me tight. I searched. There was something I should have remembered.

What's that, Alice?

Love lives for ever, but hate never dies.

The Liberty, New Year's Day 1270

A life ends; another is born.

'You can't do that here,' Richard whispered to Liza who stood behind him. 'It's wrong. And you'll freeze.'

Nursing mothers were not allowed in St Mary Overie Church so, being Liza, she'd smuggled Tom in under her cape. Tom was a good baby, strong and red, with hair gold like the sunrise, but he needed the breast and then he would need a burp. He was like his mother, determined, and he would not take no for an answer. 'He wants it,' Liza whispered.

'God help us,' Richard muttered. He kept between her and the watchful clerks who prowled through the congregation, a touch on the shoulder for the oldster, Jonathan Bedell, snoring on the stone wall bench during his old friend's funeral, a sharp word for Spinster Tailor who allowed her dog to piss on the wall. A child said, 'Mummy, I'm hungry.' Someone farted, Southwark riffraff.

The priest stood over the withered body of Durand Mason in its casket, the bereaved family facing him. Hal, Richard's father, was head of the family now. They all felt older, except little Tom, who did not think yet but simply was. The priest began.

'I am the resurrection and the life, saith the Lord: he that believeth in me, though he were dead, yet shall he live: and whosoever liveth and believeth in me shall never die.'

'Ouch,' Liza whispered. The priest looked at Richard.

'I know that my Redeemer liveth, and that He shall stand at the latter day upon the earth. And though after my skin worms destroy this body, yet in my flesh shall I see God: whom I shall see for myself, and mine eyes shall behold, and not another.'

Richard glanced back. His wife's cape moved rhythmically, Tom was busy sucking. His blue eyes peeped out, his tiny fist clasped the cape. He slipped from the nipple, grinned at his father. He was a happy child. Richard returned the grin, then looked upward to distract himself from the pleasurable curve of Liza's breast. St Mary Overie had been rebuilt in the amazing new style after the fire and the roof vaulted upwards, supported, it seemed, only by air and the winter sunlight streaming between the arcades. He thought about Liza's breast.

'Let us eat and drink, for tomorrow we die. We brought nothing into this world, and it is certain we can carry nothing out. The Lord gave, and the Lord hath taken away; blessed be the name of the Lord.'

Tom burped. Richard coughed, and Liza began to giggle. To giggle in church was a terrible crime, and she too turned it into a cough. The priest intoned the *Dixi*, *custodiam* then the lengthy *Domine*, *refugium*, and the people's breath hung around them in the cold air. The priest turned to the lesson from the endless Epistle of St Paul. Everyone listened devoutly, scratching themselves, looking for friends. There were more than Richard had thought, and still arriving. He nodded to people he knew. He imagined sucking Liza's engorged nipple like his baby. He had a hard lump in his breeches and tried to turn his thoughts dutifully to death.

'What advantageth it me, if the dead rise not? Now is Christ risen from the dead. All flesh is not the same flesh; but there is one kind of flesh of men, another of beasts—'

'Beasts, not breasts,' Liza mouthed at Richard.

'—another of fishes, another of birds. There are also celestial bodies, and bodies terrestrial; but the glory of the terrestrial is one, and the glory of the celestial is another. There is one glory of the sun, and another glory of the moon, and another glory of the stars; for one star differeth from another star in glory. So also is the resurrection of the dead. O death, where is thy sting? O grave, where is thy victory?'

Hal turned his head towards Liza. He liked his daughter-in-law's determination, not her irreverence which Richard loved. She exhibited wilfulness. Age and work tolled Hal's youthful strength, his long limbs moved stiffly, his back began to stoop. At a stroke he had taken his father's place and become like him, though more serious, without Durand's wit. You never knew what Durand was thinking, but Hal did everything with thoroughness. He beckoned the sweaty gravediggers, frozen soil still clinging to their spades. 'Here is a penny extra for your work. Don't spend it in the tavern, do you understand?'

'Never, sir, not us,' the head gravedigger assured him. 'See you soon, sir.' None were as insolent to the living as those who handled the dead. These men were gravediggers like their fathers before them, their knowing manner as well as their trade passed down from father to son.

'A penny each!' Liza muttered, shifting Tom from left to right. 'And the soil's sandy and loose beneath the top layer, it wasn't *that* hard.' She felt maternal about her father-in-law since Mistress Ann had died and worried about him spending his money which would come to her and Richard one day. That day suddenly seemed much closer. She'd known Richard all her life, and when they were children on the bridge, their days seemed to last for ever, but now the years rushed by. 'If he'd given those pennies to me,' she confided, 'I'd have spent them on a nice cord of wood for the fire.'

Richard sighed. Liza was reminding him, again, how poor he was compared to his mean father, how small their house was compared to his father's, how small their fire. Durand, widowed for many years, had passed his old age in the *haut-pas* attic of the house he gave over to Hal and been happy, almost nostalgic, in such poor quarters. Durand made all his furniture beautifully, finer at carpentry than the trade he had chosen; even now beneath their cloaks both Hal and Richard wore shoemakers' belts stuck through with hammers pointed and flat, and punches of various sizes. Liza was an ambitious woman. She had found happiness with Richard but not contentment. The rub made their love more intense. 'But you don't need a nice hot fire,' she goaded him. 'You're always working!'

Richard said, 'At least in church give your tongue a rest, would you?'

Liza grinned. She loved to spark him up. She grinned at Tom so that Richard wouldn't know she did it deliberately. But of course Richard did know. She could tell he wanted to kiss her. He wanted to touch her nipple like the baby, too. But it was true; he did work too hard. The two men needed taking in hand, or one day Richard would grow old like Hal. She never wanted Richard to grow old.

'The value of money's fallen to nothing these days,' Hal muttered. 'Those gravediggers, my boy. See the look in their eyes? Think I'm mean.'

Richard's lips tightened nervously and he tried to intercept his wife's tongue, but Liza said pertly, '*You*, sir, mean? *You're* not mean, sir, you're generous. You treat your family, us, most generously.' That was a lie. 'Gravediggers just drink their money, what good does it do them?'

'Then I've encouraged their vice.'

Richard looked alarmed, the old man always took everything so seriously. Liza smiled. 'If I were rich I'd encourage virtue.' My God, Richard thought, here she is in church with her baby hanging off her right tit, preaching virtue to my father. And yet somehow, he knew, she'd get away with it.

Hal asked, 'Which virtue would you most encourage?'

'Your family, sir. A family is love. Love is the greatest virtue.'

'Paid accounts are the greatest virtue,' Hal said drily. Shoemaking was a fashion trade and making shoes was easy compared to getting paid. 'I'll do what I can.'

Liza winked at her husband. Durand was supposed to have been wealthier than he showed off; perhaps some of that would trickle down, if it hadn't been lost or stolen by priests and lawyers.

'It's baby Tom we think of, sir,' she thanked Hal. 'Perhaps I could do the talking to customers at the counter. That would give you more time.'

She would be good with the customers, Richard thought. Hal was dour at selling his brightly coloured wares. It would give both of them extra time for their skilled work in the back room, too. 'You know how she talks, Father,' he said. 'She could sell shoes to fish.'

'I don't know,' Hal muttered seriously. 'Fish don't wear shoes.'

Richard and Liza laughed, coughed.

The priest raised his voice, it sometimes seemed to him that people came into church simply to cough not to pray. 'Therefore, my beloved brethren, be ye steadfast, unmoveable, always abounding in the work of the Lord, forasmuch as ye know that your labour is not in vain in the Lord.'

The service moved to the graveside, the sun blurring hazily but still bitterly cold, and the mourners lowered the body into the consecrated earth beside Rosie's wooden cross. The priest and clerks began the chant. 'Man that is born of woman hath but a short time to live, and is full of misery . . .'

Richard looked round. 'Grandfather had more friends that we thought,' he murmured to Liza. Beyond the cheerful neighbours he had known all his life the crowd was growing, pushing forward, ordinary men and women paying to take time off work for their last respects, hurrying but sincere, some of them dropping little gifts as well as handfuls of soil into the grave. Richard recognised Jane Cook, the cookshop matriarch who looked a hundred years old, held up by her fourth husband. Many others he knew by sight, glovers, skinners and shoemakers from London Bridge, tanners from Bankside. Liza tucked the baby away, excited; arriving were solemn companies of men she did not know, brethren sent by City fraternities. She recognised them by their liveries: the Barrelmakers and the Cordwainers, the Leather-dressers and Curriers, Cutlers and Drapers, the Mercers, the Dyers' Guild and the Fishmongers' Company, the Society of Masons and now others whose signs were less familiar. 'What's this about?' Richard whispered to his father, but Hal shrugged, his nature dutiful rather than curious. One of the senior Brethren of London Bridge, Samuel Masterson, accompanied by the present Bridge Master, James St Magnus, bowed to the grave. The Vintners' Company and the City were represented by the wine importer John Adrian, this year's Lord Mayor, with Gregory de Rokesle behind him whom everyone tipped to be Lord Mayor in his turn, and people clustered round them asking favours.

'Did you see me touch the Lord Mayor's sleeve?' Liza whispered.

Hal disapproved. 'I don't know what they're doing here. We don't give ourselves airs and graces. My father avoided people like that in his lifetime.'

The Mayor paused by Hal. 'My commiserations, Mason,' he said, brisk as all City gentlemen. 'The end of an era.'

Hal knelt. 'Aye, my lord. But we were just poor shoemakers, lord, despite our name.'

'The man doesn't know what I'm talking about,' the Mayor chuckled to those fawning on him, but old Samuel Masterson beckoned, put his frail hand on Hal's shoulder.

'Your father was notable not for what he did, but for what he did not do. For what he knew and did not say. He was a gentleman.'

Hal bowed subserviently. 'Aye, my lord.' The older man turned away.

'What did he mean?' Liza whispered.

'His Worship the Mayor made a mistake,' Hal said. 'My father never knew gentlemen of such quality as these.'

'They came to the shop,' Liza said. 'He spoke to them as an equal, and they spoke to him with respect though he was only a shoemaker.'

'No, mistaken, you are,' Hal insisted. 'I seen them pass, that's all.' To live on London Bridge was to see the world pass.

'I think they were a little afraid of him,' Liza said.

Hal said, 'Enough, that is!'

Everyone bowed their heads for the collect. Liza whispered to her husband, 'But they were.'

Someone gave a low cry, seeing one of the black rats that had come into the country and bred in great numbers, moving from the wharves into graveyards and even on to London Bridge, until the apothecary's poison quelled them.

The priest and clerks chanted the collect. 'We meekly beseech thee, O Father, to raise us from the death of sin unto the life of righteousness; that, when we shall depart this life, we may rest in Him, as our hope is this our brother doth; and that, at the general Resurrection in the last day, we may be found acceptable in thy sight; and receive that blessing, which thy well-beloved Son shall then pronounce to all that love and fear thee, saying, Come, ye blessed children of my Father, receive the kingdom prepared for you from the beginning of the world.'

Silence fell, the service ended. The bath women, quietly working the back of the congregation throughout the proceedings, touted the more well-dressed worshippers to sample the pleasures of the Liberty. 'Is it over?' quavered Jonathan Bedell. Old tears trickled down his withered face. 'Cold weather,' he excused himself. But it was not now so cold, Richard saw the sun was a pearl and winter mist drifted between the rooftops overhanging the churchyard hedge. Hal took one of Jonathan's elbows and Liza, nestling baby Tom in her left arm beneath her cape, took the other side. She was related to Jonathan by marriage; Becky Bedell's younger sister Josephine had married into the Swinert family. Nearly everyone on the bridge was related to the Swinerts, both numerous and promiscuous; in fact, most bridge families were related to each other by now. Liza's brother Peter Swinert had combined his cookshop with Ladler's. Everyone had thought Liza would marry into the Ladler family, many of the Swinerts did, and vice versa too. But Richard and Liza had always been in love even as infants, they had an instinct. Richard saw his wife struggling and took the baby. They always argued, but they always did the right thing by each other.

They came past the Bridge House. Fog was rising off the river, and London Bridge rose broken-backed out of the fog. Few now remembered when the bridge was built but Richard supposed it was more than a hundred years ago, eternity. Time and Queen Eleanor had not been kind to the bridge; as a boy Richard remembered the City mob, which called itself the Commons, pelting the unpopular Queen with garbage as the royal barge struggled beneath the arches. In revenge the King granted her the revenues of the Bridge House Trust and she let it go to ruin. In summer the tumbledown bridge was strangely beautiful from the distance, its cracked arches and subsiding piers golden with London rocket sprouting from every split and patch of damp. Richard

235

remembered St Vincent's Feast two years ago and the high tide lapping the roadway, filling the cellars, then the enormous rush of water scouring at the rubble stabilising the starlings. Now the piers above them slumped, cracking the arches further, and each tide did more damage. Winter's cold had shrunk the bare grey stones and frost filled the cracks, he saw, splitting them deeper. A restless, angry, rootless feeling filled him. He realised it, too, was love.

'Surely something can be done,' he said.

'The City chose the wrong side in the civil war against the King,' Hal said. 'The punishment will take time to earn out. Now the King appoints the Bridge Master.'

'Don't make no difference!' Jonathan Bedell said loudly.

'And has done for the last thirty years,' Hal insisted. 'Of course it makes a difference.'

'Nay,' scoffed the old man. 'The money's the thing, don't you see? The Brethren and chaplains of the Chapel of St Thomas still get enough money, they're still there. What matters still happens.'

'But the bridge is falling down,' Richard said.

'London Bridge fell down since the day it was built,' Jonathan scoffed. He shook his head. 'Durand understood.' The two men had been friends with the thoroughness of those who had once been enemies. 'He understood. The Brethren of the Chapel and the Bridge get their money one way or another, through the Brethren of the Hospital of St Catherine by the Tower, or through the Brethren of the Poor Fellow-Soldiers of Christ and the Temple of Solomon.'

'Who are they?' Richard asked.

'The Templars.' Jonathan nodded upriver, they glimpsed the sooty towers of the Temple through gaps in the mist.

'But they're sodomites, perverts, drunkards,' Richard said.

'Aye, and they own half the country, and half of France too, and the Italians, and the Spaniards. And London Bridge.'

'Nonsense,' Hal said.

'And they make sure the revenues of the Bridge House Trust go where they matter. Even Queen Eleanor don't stand against them if they think it matters.'

'Nonsense,' Hal said. 'Things don't work that way.'

Out of the fog they passed by a woman looking furious and embarrassed in the cage, hoping they would not recognise her. But they did, she was Nell Ladler; everyone knew everyone else. Her views were well known too. She refused to attend prayers for the Pope, saying that since he could forgive sins he must be clean himself, therefore she need not pray for him. Hal ducked his head away from her to hear such dangerous views, but Jonathan laughed.

They settled the old man by his fireside in the Stone Gate, put his ginger cat on his lap. Liza squeezed Richard's hand as they came out, sad at Jonathan's decline. They had known him all their lives. 'His mind's going,' she said.

The ginger cat slipped round the window, sat with its tail coiled round it, preened its paws on the sill.

'Shoo!' Liza said. 'Go back to your master.'

'Cats know no master,' Hal said.

'Baby's wet,' Richard said, and handed him over.

They crossed the drawbridge that had been so recently and so often raised or lowered depending on which faction, the King's or de Montfort's, appeared to be winning. Liza pushed the baby back in Richard's arms.

'But he's dripping,' Richard complained.

'I'll be working on the counter in future,' she reminded him. 'You'll get used to it.' She pushed at the crowd with her elbows then they shrank into a doorway to let a cart past, followed up the clear space behind a pannier mule plodding steadily forward, its baskets knocking people aside. Where the houses met overhead, which was most of the way, there was no fog, only the stench, noise, gloom. Iron-shod carts made the buildings rattle. Liza moved past the chapel into the foggy Square. Strange that Durand had not chosen to be buried here, in the building he saw from his window every day of his life, and in his will had left sixpence for prayers to be said for his soul in St Mary Overie, not here. Mostly only important people were buried in the chapel, masons connected with the bridge and revered historical figures like Mercer and Boatwright and Colechurch, the builders of the bridge long ago. Liza had wondered if there was some connection between the Mason family and masons. Obviously not.

The family across the road had been lost, together with their house, in the fire and Durand had bought the ruin from the Bridge Master; Hal still had the precious document, the signature 'Alan Frater' across the bottom, witnessed 'Geoffrey Masterson, Martin Stoner'. The house that Durand had built from the ashes, slowly, over the years, was on each side of the road, joined at the fourth storey by a *haut-pas*. Durand had lived and traded on the east side and rented the west side, less fine, to an ale seller, then when Hal married Ann he had given it over to them. Now Richard and Liza lived there. Overall it was a pretty house of ornate stained wood and tiny leaded windows, the roadway running through the middle. From each side a stair turret rose to a cupola topped with a wind vane in the shape of a cockerel that was everywhere these days, the design approved by the Pope to remind everyone of the cockerel crowing three times for St Peter.

Liza looked round. The ginger cat followed them, its tail raised as it wove between the legs coming down around it, leapt nimbly on to the parapet. Again it sat, wound its striped tail round its haunches, licked fastidiously at one paw. 'It's taken a shine to you, Liza,' Richard said. The cat surveyed them with its yellow eyes.

'Beautiful eyes,' Liza said. She liked cats, being a little like one herself, and the cat arched its back for her as she approached. 'Go on. Home. Go now. Poor Jonathan.'

The cat curled against her, purring.

'A cat's home is where a cat is,' Hal said. 'We could do with one to keep the mice down.'

'It's Jonathan's cat,' Richard said. The cat looked at them looking at it, then blinked its yellow eyes once and leapt down, weaving, was gone.

A shabbily dressed man, blind, his face disfigured by some dreadful puckered wound, pushed forward through the crowd. 'Good ale and a warm fire at the Bear.' He pointed at his face. 'Got this for my King. Alfred Shadwell, I was.' He pushed out of sight, his voice faded among the crowd. 'Best ale, warmest fire at the Bear.'

Over Hal's door hung the sign of the Three Shoes, its circle design of three shoes supposed to be used by no other, though Otto Parson by St Magnus had a similar sign to steal trade, and his shoes were not as good. Today Hal's counter was shuttered, his father's death cost them half a day's business. Liza opened the door to the narrow workroom, fragrant with the dark, heavy scent of wood and leather, piled to the roof with skins and the wooden lasts on which shoes were formed. Richard had inherited something of his grandfather's skill with wood and made the lasts and then the wooden soles to which Hal hammered the leather or fabric uppers. They could not do the dyeing themselves, and both men had right palms as hard as iron from stitching needles through the thick leather. Behind this room was the counting-room, its back overhanging the river, sounding hollow. The narrow steps in the corner curled upwards into the turret, which was of a bartizan design to save space at ground level. Where had Grandfather learnt such refinements? Liza supposed he had copied it from the chapel.

They went upstairs into Hal's plain wainscotted rooms, but warm, with simple furniture well made. Hal had silver plate worth three pounds in money and this wealth was taken from the ornate carved chest and put on display. Stephen Ladler, plump and genial, laid out bowls of food from his cookshop, his smiling fat daughters scurrying after him. 'Ah, my dear Liza.' They were related half a dozen ways. Liza saw white bread on the large table, and oatmeal biscuits softened with small fancies from the river, shrimps and whelks artfully circled. Stephen clapped his hands as the guests filed upstairs, sent his girls for the hot pies, hot stews and pottage. The spotty boys from the Three Neats' Tongues arrived rolling barrels of ale and Lorraine wine. Hal worried about his guests getting the best view of his silver, balanced this against the risk of them stealing it. The front windows overhanging the busy street below were large to make the best of what little natural light seeped beneath the *haut-pas*, and chairs, tables and rugs could be lifted through them without trouble – the stairs were too narrow.

Liza snatched baby Tom from Richard's arms and changed him upstairs, brought him back in a basket so he would come to no harm. The room was full now, Hal in the most senior position with his back to the fire, closest family nearest him at his table. Liza didn't recognise half the people here. She wished she'd thought to open the window against the stink of flesh and food, and the room was almost too hot now. But she looked at Hal's face, saw his pride. This was hospitality, and he was providing it. One day her husband would do the same.

Hal tapped his knife handle on the table, then when silence fell – insofar as any house on London Bridge was ever silent – he raised his voice and welcomed his guests with St Paul's Christian greeting that they had heard so recently at the graveside.

'Eat and drink, for tomorrow we die.'

So here you are, my family. I know everything about you. You have no secrets from me.

And here I am, here at this exact moment, here on the rafter looking down at the tops of your heads below me. Don't you see the mouse? See the small grey shape a little to one side of the middle, near the knot in the wood. No?

And there's Liza. Isn't she gorgeous! Is she not a little like me?

Like the girl I once was.

Look at you down there busy with your little lives, the little you know of your lives, almost everything hidden from you, and you'll probably never look up and see the mouse, and if you do you'll never understand. I'm as alive as you, as all of you, more. I *am* you, and maybe one day you'll be me, if you see what I mean. Sometimes Hal puts out cheese with a lick of poison on it, but I'm well up on those tricks. The mouse follows its nature (was, of course, down there among the tables in good time when the food was set out) and now turns the crumbly wedge of pilfered crust between its paws, eating though its belly is full. A mouse need never go hungry on London Bridge.

You people gather beneath me, filling the crowded room, more pushing through the doors, and Arnald the currier gets squeezed too close to the fire and burns his breeches. You're imposing in appearance, Arnald, but not bright. In the evening, alone, you teach yourself to read by candlelight. I wish I could help you. You have such plans, but by the sound of your breath I don't think you have much longer to live.

God, all of you, your boring conversation, the price of salt herring, the weather, how pleasant to meet you again, all the disguises with which you humans cloak yourselves. I wish the party would get going. You lot, your polite smiling faces, your mostly fake commiserations – no one knew my son as well as I did. I know every lie you tell. And every sweet small truth and kindness, each gentle remembrance. I forget none of them.

I don't mind what you say, your words are just hot air blown by hot meat. The reality is that Durand is at peace in consecrated ground, and his soul's gone on – or so I believe. I wish I could have seen him laid to rest, but at the riverbank, as you know, I cease.

Laughter as well as greed, smiles in addition to sadness. I'm glad it's a happy funeral. They are the finest.

Look at you all. I know what you really think and feel. Here's Richard's aunt Kate Ladler, strict and prissy in black weeds: I know who you're sleeping with, because sometimes I'm there. And stiff Crispin Whyte, chantry priest from St Thomas's Chapel: I know what you get up to.

This is better. After the respectful condolences a big burst of laughter, the curtains are pulled back from the barrels of beer, everyone shoves forward. It's well known that these days wedding parties turn into riots – God knows I've seen enough of them. I love to see weddings, love to see love, to see the girl and her young man and imagine, *remember*, all her hopes and fears, and his, and see the people being foolish and wise and . . . human. Maybe it's the coming fashion for wakes to turn into riots too, these fashions change as quickly as hairstyles, the colour of breeches, the length of shoes. If I was Hal I'd keep my silver in the chest, locked. Knives now, they're at the meat, half of them ate nothing yesterday to economise and blow up today at Hal's expense. Ah, here's dear Betty Ladler drunk as a trout. Mary Swinert, Liza's sister, not as pretty, darker, but sweeter, talking to the baby. Dirk Wintle slips cuts from his knife into his narrow mouth and into his wide pouch, too, to keep him tomorrow. Sam Tully meekly fills his ample wife's ample platter, stuck with the women not the men, she has a voice like a shrike and at night, straddling his arse, her breasts and arms wobbling like blancmange, she stripes him with that small fierce brush as long as her arm. There's Dominick Siddall, the thief, he has something going with John Weigher or Wayer at the King's Weighbridge, to do with fixing the weight of corn, I think, and cheating on weys of old lead. I see Margery Batchelor, thin and dull-looking but the happiest, kindest woman you could meet, whom I saw write in her will by candlelight that she leaves her gold wedding ring to London Bridge. Many do, it's quite the fashion. Johannes and Johanna By-the-Way, who make shoemakers' and sailmakers' needles, and charge too much, have left twelve pence to London Bridge. On such small bequests are the mighty finances of the Bridge House Trust founded – though now keeping Queen Eleanor in men-at-arms and cloth of gold. She swears she'll give up this large income next Feast of St Giles for bridge maintenance. Ho, ho, do I believe her? *I* wouldn't.

The sight of you fills me with affection for you all, every single one of you in your own way. You're all my family, and my son's – now my grandson's – house creaks with the weight of you. I'm so happy, and so sad. I don't know where my journey takes me. Suddenly it all seems so far away and long ago when I was Alice, and so unimportant. Yet I am still Alice.

While I'm moping, not concentrating (I might be sniffling back tears, if only a mouse could cry) the mouse darts suddenly along the rafter. Whoa! This always catches me out, this sudden racing movement, the mouse following its instinct and the mysterious workings of its brain. Into the corner, down the wall, too fast to see!

Under, over, round the rush mats thrown across the floor. And here's baby

239

Tom, laid in his basket between Liza's legs beneath the table, safe from feet, sleeping.

The mouse stares into the round, pink, cherubic face of the human. How can he sleep in all this noise and movement, the voices of humans echoing like drums, the floor shaking with their thumping footsteps? Yet he does, and we all have. Nothing changes.

It's his time; but it's still my time too. I'll see him grow up, I'll see him marry, I'll see him die.

Tom's eyes start open, blue. Alice's eyes. No one will ever know. He will never hear of me.

The baby reaches his tiny hand in front of his wondering blue gaze towards the mouse. They all do. It's a gift which children lose, in a few years he would try to torture or kill me. But for now, that innocent gaze senses me. It's a precious moment, but it lasts only a moment.

You will never understand this aloneness, this sadness, until you are dead.

I let the mouse follow its nature, which is to run. Wooden houses are all nooks and crannies, hidden spaces and secret places, tunnels and paths huge to a mouse, nibbled corners to make new tricks, even the tiniest gaps have a chink to slip through. Each house is a maze, each maze connected with another, so that London Bridge is built up like a huge wooden web above its twenty stone arches.

Here's Hal's cellar, here are the stones, cracked and split in every direction by tide and frost. Each stone arch curves into the stone pier that supports it, each pier drops down through the middle of the starling and cutwaters that protect it and stands in the riverbed. There are a thousand ways through and ten thousand dead ends. The roadway has fresh gravel dumped on it every few years and is now a foot higher than in my time, making a depth of nearly three feet over the crown of each arch, the stone chips and wadded manure worked by a thousand scurrying generations into warrens of tunnels for mice, roaches, beetles and more creatures of the dark than I can imagine.

I have never stopped my search for Jack.

Thirty-five years. My obsession has driven tiny bodies to starvation, exhaustion, madness. Some are trapped in impossible spaces as the bridge moves – the bridge is always moving, expands, contracts, settles – and they, *I* (each little death is mine also) died of thirst or hunger or madness suffocating in the dark. Yet this, too, is in the nature of life. I never give up.

By now, with an animal's keen senses and other gifts, sometimes nose, or eyes, or wings, and creeping, wriggling, soaring, you'd think I've seen everything. But there's always something new. Dirt falls down to reveal a new crack that joins another, that leads to another.

It happens often.

Sometimes I think the bridge is alive. But it's just chance.

Such a chance happened a few days ago, towards the northern end of the bridge. Again, the mouse followed its own nature, which is food or sex as it is for all of us. A cart carrying a pesage of corn lost a wheel, the sacks spilled and split across the roadway, grain filled the gap as wide as your finger between the parapet and the gravel. Most gains stuck there, but a few tumbled down into channels worn by rainwater into the bridge, and one or two fat, rich grains ended up deep below the foundations of Widow Stainer's house.

And as the mouse nibbled, another iron-shod cart rumbled overhead, mud and stones rained down from the tunnel roof, and the floor cracked. There was something in the dark. It smelt of chalk rubble, not stone. But the mouse smelt a stone slab beneath it. Then more mud came down, and it ran away full of the fear in which a mouse constantly lives.

But with the cold weather everything is fixed, frozen solid now.

The mouse's belly is full of crumbs, but within an hour I know it'll be hungry again. The mouse remembers the grain, hopes for more before it's stolen by other mice. Hesitantly at first, distracted by other scents and the thoughts that flutter across its brain, the mouse begins its journey. It moves more purposefully now, deep in the stones across St Mary's Lock, the boats sliding beneath, for it's slack low water. Sometimes its ears hear the voices of fishermen talking, now some gentleman telling the waterman to scull faster. It means nothing to the mouse. Here's Queen's Lock, the stone more fissured than any man suspects, the mouse glimpses the water shining below. Here's King's Lock, and Widow Stainer's house at one side of it, partly over the pier. And so it has a deep cellar.

These houses were built about the time Jack disappeared, I remember.

Here's the mud that blocked the tunnel, stiff with cold but too deep in the bridge to freeze. The mouse digs with its forepaws, moves forward expertly, finds a grain. I exert my will, and the emotion of greed drives the mouse forward.

The mud stops. Here's the rubble.

The mouse's nose sniffs. The stone slab is down there beneath the rubble thrown on top of it. Perhaps, I suggest curiously, there's a cavity beneath, full of grain. Wondering, hopeful, the mouse digs eagerly. The small debris slides down between the larger stones, a hole opens up. The mouse tries to run backwards, slips down with the dust and soil and pebbles into the hole.

A space barely higher than a man's skull, but a cathedral to a mouse. A tiny barb of daylight strikes through a crack in the bridge arch.

A bone.

My God, a white bone. But it could be anybody. Many men were killed during the building of the bridge, hundreds of them, some buried beneath falling masonry, not all were found.

Jack, is it you?

No flesh remains. A few fragments of clothes. What was Jack wearing the last time I saw him? I can't remember, all I see is Jack's face, Jack's smiling reassurance that everything is all right. His clothes are rotted, their colour lost. His body lies thrown down on its back on the remains of his cloak. Is it Jack's cloak? Everyone wears a cloak. His bare ribs rise up, seeming as large as the ribs of a whale, his arm bones angled against them as though warding off a blow or clutching a wound to his chest as he died.

His finger bones hang down between his ribs. The injury to his flesh is gone, along with his flesh. Erased. But not to me. I imagine everything.

A money purse like Jack's has fallen into the pelvis.

The mouse searches for grain, leaps nimbly into one of the leg bones that lies in the dark like a tree trunk. The bones of the foot rise up like roots towards that tiny barb of day.

And here it is. Proof. There, round his fourth toe, the grass ring I wove for him when we were children.

I've found Jack's body. I'd cry if I had tears. Even the mouse senses something, lays its head sadly between its paws. They do sense us somehow, these little pieces of living machinery that are sometimes, for their brief span, the habitations of our souls.

Jack, Jack, where are you now? I love you, I love you, can you hear me?

The tide makes a sound like distant thunder now; the water must reach almost to here. The mouse backs away sensing danger, change. Beyond Jack's ring-toe – I remember we called them our ring-toes – a few pebbles are moving. Falling down. Then another entrance is revealed, tiny, narrower than the thumb of a human, and a mouse's head appears, ears flattened. Inches forward as though against its will.

241

Grey around the nose and mouth, old.

It limps slowly forward. One of its legs is twisted, drags behind it. It will fight for its territory, I should let my mouse run for its life. But something in the eyes stops me. Jack? Are you Jack?

He lies down. I nuzzle his mouth, lick his fur, the thread of blood that trickles from his twisted leg.

I stay with him. Being with him. He knows it's me. It grows dark then light, the tide roars and falls silent, and I endure Jack's death for the second time.

The mouse races through the maze of tunnels into the spring sunlight, don't stop, don't stop, images of birds, cats, dogs, pounding feet, noise, danger fill its little brain as it darts along. There's Liza at her counter, a customer's trying on a shoe. Here's a rolling wheel, here a plank wall, the top of each plank a narrow shelf. The mouse pauses, round at the back of the house now, above the river. A fish jumps below, a gull screams, swoops for the fish, children throw pebbles from the road at the gull, and the Keeper of the Dogs, Simon Bedell, scolds them, and then the dogs bark at the ginger cat they've driven from the Keeper's Lodge. Or perhaps the cat simply wanted to adopt a different family. Cats are like that. I know. I am one, sometimes.

The mouse darts nimbly up the wall towards the flat roof, and London Bridge opens into view below, a broad mass of life as always moving forward across the arches, packed solid with heads and hats and shoulders in each direction.

And this extraordinary thought occurs to me: does *everything* I see moving have a soul as I do? Are we all more interconnected, more *with* one another, than even I believed? I mean, not only Jack. Something much, much more than Jack and me. I'm glimpsing something, trying to grasp at something, an idea, a creation so huge that it's almost beyond my reach.

Have we been wrong to fear death?

Because *everything* is life. Perhaps there is no death.

Perhaps there is no such thing as death.

Perhaps we are all alive, always. I can't speak for the land, I know nothing of it. But everyone whose bones are on or at the bridge . . . *three thousand people died in the fire*. And how many untold others have died building the bridge, or of accidents, illness, or old age and are buried in the Bridge Chapel, or have died of drowning or suicide, during the three generations since the bridge was completed?

Oh my God.

What of Noelle?

Perhaps my sweet, dear sister Noelle, who fell from the bridge rather than submit to Grand Master de Prudome, is alive. She's alive too.

And her young man whose name I forget, his grief affected me very much at the time. Robin. That's it, I remember, Robin Swinert. My God, Liza's family; she was a Swinert before she married. Robin must have had brothers. And now I think of it, the name does ring another bell from somewhere . . . I can't think of it.

My mind's eye sees Robin Swinert jump from the old bridge and swept beneath the arches of the new, the water swirling over his pale face. Suicide. He'd deliberately damned his immortal soul for his body to sleep with Noelle on the riverbed. Young men and girls do this in their agony of love, I've seen it a dozen times.

Or do their souls fall straight through to Hell and eternal torment?

Where are we all going? What's the meaning of it?

Because there is a meaning. Of that I'm sure.

The mouse climbs through the angled spout that on rainy days spurts rainwater from the flat roof away from the sides of the building, so that the wooden walls will show less damp. The boards are simply tarred, Durand could not afford lead. The tar makes a pleasant rich smell, warming easily in the April sun. The mouse likes this place, hides behind the pots and tubs near the balustrade, listens to the traffic streaming in the tunnel below the *haut-pas*. Because Richard and Liza's house is joined to Hal's by the *haut-pas*, and because the backs of the houses overhang the river by ten or twelve feet each side, Liza's roof garden is a broad and pleasant expanse. In the evening she comes up here and busies herself planting seeds, herbs mostly, rosemary, cumin, fennel which is fragrant. Yellow honeysuckle winds itself round the balustrade, she has her little apple tree blossoming in a tub. Later Richard comes up and I like to see them kiss. Sometimes they sprawl where they can't be seen from below and he moves his hands in her skirt. There'll be another little Tom in no time if he keeps this up. Bees drone around them as they make love, and the mouse watches. It's a very private place, this, here in the centre of London.

The mouse nibbles moss that grows in the roof corners, and I must admit steals out in the dark to eat the choicest delicious shoots of Liza's herbs.

But the real attraction up here is baby Tom. He's a lad and a half already with his red face and strong, pudgy limbs. Liza carries him up with her now the days are warm enough, on Sundays puts his basket in the shade, and he lies sleeping, then wakes and kicks his blankets off, so she lays him on his side, talking to him while she plants the seeds, and he watches the sails of boats moving on the river. Tom's the son I never had – I never really saw my own son grow up, as you know, and though I see so much I can hardly bear to miss anything. He puts on weight and pleases me, he coughs and worries me. And in a way that is very real to me, Liza is my daughter too. I never had a little girl but I imagine her growing up like Liza. It's time to move Tom's basket into the shade, Liza. Sometimes she lays the basket on the bench, wedging it carefully so he cannot roll out. As soon as he walks she'll have to watch him like a hawk up here.

The cat which has adopted the family has found a way up over Robert Gander's roof and leaps lightly on to the rail that separates the two properties. Naturally, each time the cat appears, the other wildlife that inhabits this place, beetles, roaches, butterflies, keeps out of reach. The mouse makes itself scarce in a groove it has nibbled beneath one of the tubs, peeks from the entrance. The cat leaps down like ginger water flowing, prowls its quiescent kingdom. The tomcat has taken to Hal particularly, in the way that male cats are attracted to single men (just as it was to Jonathan Bedell), and Hal sometimes puts out food for it up here. The day of which I speak is a Sunday, the Sabbath, the congregation still in the chapel, I hear the chanting of the choir through the chapel windows, the arches of stained glass only fifty feet away. The cat leaps on to the bench, waiting. It opens its mouth and a mouse falls out. The cat catches it beneath its claw, torments the little creature, it being a sunny day. The chapel doors open, the cat watches, then kills the mouse and eats it. Hal climbs up still wearing his wool church breeches, sits on the bench yawning, the cat curls into his lap. Liza carries Tom's basket up, does a little weeding, goes down and returns with Hal's beer, cheese, bread, an onion. Richard calls her down on an errand. Some errand. *I* know what they get up to on Sunday afternoons. She leaves the sleeping baby in Hal's care. Hal spreads his legs to the sun, hot, feeds a piece of cheese to the cat. The cat purrs, curls into his lap.

Hal finishes, puts his head back, snores.

It's the hottest hour of the day and the mouse creeps through the deepest shadows, busy on its business. The cat stretches on Hal's chest, claws out, fangs showing. He pushes it off without waking. The cat slinks to the basket. It's time Hal woke up, the shadows are moving, the sun will fall on the baby's face. The cat preens its paws, then settles itself smoothly into the basket, its tail round it, the tip almost touching its nose.

The cat's lying on the baby.

Hal, wake up. The cat's asleep on baby Tom.

The mouse peeps from beneath the tub, afraid of the wide expanse of roof leading to Hal's outstretched feet. There must be something powerful enough to overcome the mouse's fear. There! The crumbs Hal dropped, flakes of cheese. The mouse goes forward, pulls back as Hal snorts. The mouse is terrified of gulls, crows, the open space. Run, little mouse, run!

Against its instincts the mouse darts across the roof. I exert my willpower. The mouse is drawn to the tempting pieces of crust and cheese on Hal's lap.

Greed overcomes caution, it pauses on his shoe, runs up his leg. Here's the strong rancid smell of Hal, bread, cheese, drops of fermenting beer sweet and sugary in his crotch. From this close his snores sound like a smith's bellows, the crumbs on his chest rising and falling, the hairs blowing in his nostrils.

From Hal's chest the mouse looks down into the baby's basket, the cat coiled asleep over Tom's face.

Tom's limbs are white. He does not move. The sun beats down.

Hal, wake up! Wake up, for God's mercy's sake!

The mouse turns in a circle, nips Hal's thumb. Nothing.

I'm hysterical. I can feel it. I'm watching Tom die. I'm screaming but making no sound. I can hear footsteps on the stairs but they seem to climb through treacle. I can hear the cheerful calls of the watermen to one another far below but nothing means anything. Tom's suffocating, perhaps already suffocated. His little body lies as still as plaster beneath the cat.

The mouse jumps down on the cat, and bites its ear.

Everything, the bridge, the sky, turns round the mouse as the cat rears up, lashes out. I seem to fly through the air. The mouse lands on its side on the roof, slides then cannot move. There's no shelter for it here, no hope.

The cat settles back on Tom's face.

The mouse tries to stand. Its back legs cannot.

Liza's hand appears, plucks up the cat. It claws her wrist, she lets go, but she screams, 'Tom!'

Hal wakes, grunting. 'What's happened?'

Tom gives a sleepy cry. Liza clutches him to her. 'Oh my God. Oh thank God.'

The ginger cat flows down from the bench like pure vengeance, takes three bounds; its yellow slitted eyes and fangs are everything the mouse sees, they bite at the mouse like swords. The mouse feels pain, then numbness.

This is the moment I know so well. Death. And life to come.

The cat torments the mouse with jabs of its claw. To me this suffering is incomprehensible evil, but the mouse accepts it as ordinary.

The mouse lies in its blood. I hear Liza's voice say, 'It was the most incredible thing I ever saw. A mouse attacking a cat.'

But Hal's ashamed he slept. 'Too much young beer with your lunch, more like,' he declares, not to be argued with.

The cat sinks its claw into the mouse's body, its splayed whiskers and fierce breath press close. For a moment its eyes, slitted, golden, seem to peer through the mouse's eyes and see into me.

The cat senses me. I'm sure it does. It wants to hurt me.

The cat sinks its claws into the mouse's eyes. I'm blind.

Liza says in a shaky, overwrought voice, 'I don't trust that cat. I won't have it here.'

I hear Hal say, 'It's a cat, Liza. Cats are cats.' Then he sighs. I hear the cat miaow as it's picked up, then Hal curses. It's clawed his wrist. I hear the sound as he breaks its neck. 'There. That make you any happier?' He liked that cat.

'Yes,' Liza says shakily. 'My baby nearly died. I'd never have forgiven myself.' Her voice grows louder, yet softer, she's come close to the mouse, kneeling perhaps. 'The mouse attacked the cat. I did see it. Poor little thing. It's dead.'

Not quite. This agony. This death. This life.

And I am born.

Sniffing other dogs' bottoms is important, though I've never liked it, but I've come to appreciate its virtues. It's an economical greeting that shows you at once who your friends are, your enemies, who's strange, who's new. Nothing natural is bad, animals are simply animals. We follow our natures. It's humans who have a choice, sometimes. Sometimes. Perhaps once or twice in your lives.

Your? Who am I? Did I ever really know? Yet I made my choices. As the saying goes, I made my bed and slept in it. It's such a long time since I was Alice, and I've learnt so much, but I begin to realise it's almost nothing. The more I live, the more life fills me with awe and humility. The sheer scale of it, the height and depth of it. Everything I never saw when I was Alice.

And why did I choose to fall in love with Jack? No, I didn't choose. No choice involved. It happened. I loved Jack and I didn't love the other boy, Nick. That's not choice, it's chance. I happened to be made my way. Jack was made his way. Glue. That's all.

Fate.

But if the world is fate and chance, we have no choice. I believe we do.

If only I could remember what I was before I was Alice. I can't.

Who was Jack before he was Jack? I don't know.

Were we lovers? Were we born to love?

We do have a choice. If Jack hadn't thrown the stone by Three Oaks From One Root, I might never have seen them again. (There we are, *them*, always the two of them.) If Jack had been held back from chasing after me by Francis Oxworth for only a few seconds longer, I might have been drowned by the time he found me. But look at it from the other side. I didn't have to let the boys catch me, but I did. I didn't have to push to move into Mistress Cristina's house, but I did. I could have said no to Jack, but I didn't. I chose. I chose, and I kept on choosing.

And I'm still choosing. The mouse attacked the cat.

I see Tom from time to time as he's growing up, and it's because of me. I think he would have died that day. I've changed something. And I watch over him, as best I can, with love. He'll marry someone and have children, and it will all be because of me, my choice. And those children will have children. Maybe the line will die out or flourish. It doesn't matter. Tom will make his own choices according to his nature. But I, *my love*, has made a difference, has made it possible.

At the moment of death that comes before life, when I return to my bones wherever they are in the dark, I exert myself. Once, like a child, I knew nothing. I was swept along, no more than a piece of blood or bone. As I learn more, I know more, I have more to be. I choose.

London Bridge is full of life, and more is conceived every second of the night, and surprisingly often during the day. *I am the sperm and the egg.*

I sleep in the warm red glow, and am born.

Most of the pups were tied in a bag and dropped off the bridge to drown,

245

poor souls. But Arnald the currier took one, a lapdog to accompany his master's last days. Arnald died in the winter and I hear the dog starved rather than leave his body. We are small, warm, faithful company for old people, small bodies with loud barks. Widow Stainer took one of us but when she came round to see Kate Ladler – Richard's Aunt Kate, you remember – she said it had died. *No*, I think, *not died.* She wanted to bury its little body in the chapel but Brother Chain, the senior chaplain, forbade it. The widow, a thin, shy sort, married for only a year half her lifetime ago, was distraught nearly out of her mind. Some people give such love to their dogs.

Love is what I want, too. I crave love.

Kate Ladler's the same, except different. All her life she was married to a man who cared for no one, and in her old age she loves men. She loves to attract them, poor old fellows, with rumours of her wealth (not true) and her fine black clothes and sad sighing stories of her loneliness since her husband passed on. As you can imagine, suitors cluster around her like flies on a turd, and their small gifts and respects, when quietly sold (she is in fact almost penniless) provide her living. She's seventy-eight if a day, too ardent to be a whore, she loves to be conquered. But she has more sense than to make it too easy, so she carries her snappy little white dog (with brown splodges) to keep hands off her and make sure she's in command and treated respectfully. How she roars with laughter when her little dog tugs at her lovers' breeches and shoes.

I have to admire her. But I do not like her. Yet is there something of Alice in her? Could Alice have grown old like her, obsessed by sensation like her? I deny it, but I know myself well enough to see it's possible. Aunt Kate's terrified of dying, poor thing. She clings to life, panting and clutching like this, with every ounce of her strength. There's hardly a man who creeps from her house at night (or, as I said, surprisingly often during the day) without scratches. And the little dog barking, as the rhyme puts it, to see such fun.

It's a sad life. Even in winter she likes to be seen in the street, carries her dog pressed between her bosoms, her shawl over it, her cape too, its little white head peeping out. There's Sam Tully, thin as his wife is fat, bowing and smirking nervously, he's been in Kate's bed I know, he cheats on his horrible wife yet is attracted to other women like her. If I was ever a man – this is the first time it's occurred to me – I should find it very strange. What would it feel like? A state of perpetual rage, urged hither and thither by the thing between my legs, by desires I could not control? Would I have the strength to be calm and kind? Would I fall in love with someone like me?

I notice part of the parapet has fallen down and there's no money to repair it – obviously Queen Eleanor decided not to give up her Bridge House income on the Feast of St Giles a few years ago after all. A single workman heaves the stones off the road and Kate admires the muscles on his shoulders, and the dog knows to bark. The man notices old Kate and ignores her. Life is cruel, too. She was beautiful when she was young.

There's Tom! He's growing up! Time passes so quickly when you have so much of it. He's already nine or ten. I recognise his eyes though, and his flushed cheeks. My, he looks strong, he smells so healthy, I'm proud of him. He's carrying skins for his father and Richard (I thought for a moment he was Hal) looks so proud of him too. Richard stops for the ritual word with Aunt Kate, she complains about her bones, the cold, prices risen so high, then says she can't complain. Meanwhile I discern Liza busy at the counter, a dog must make do with seeing black and white but she looks fine. No more children though? Surely she can't be too busy for more children. She loves her work and I can see she's good at it, though one man won't buy from a woman and demands that Hal come out front to serve him. Dear me, how much older Hal looks. He's been with Aunt Kate once, I was so embarrassed for him. Mostly he hides his loneliness, but in the old woman's bed he cried in her arms instead of doing what men do best. The dog caught my mood and whined, then the poor beast got a smack from Kate and was shut in the cupboard. She lives on emotion, and she's probably the only woman who really loves Hal a little. Spinster Tailor says *she* does, but she loves his money more. Hal won't talk to Kate now; gets rid of the customer, waves too quickly, ducks into his workroom. It's the first hint that perhaps he means to marry Spinster Tailor. Kate turns to Liza.

Here's Liza close, already showing white hairs in her curls, her hands and face browned like a workman's by the sun. Does her body contain a soul, as mine did? She scolds Tom for something. Her skin smells lovely, of shoe leather. She strokes the dog's head, scratches its ear, but it yaps at her. From the chapel belltower, which rises from the top of the stair turret, the bell clangs seven times, the seventh hour from dawn, and already the winter sun is setting. Kate is thrown into a frenzy of anticipation.

'My, is that the time already!'

'Stay for a cup of wine,' Liza says. 'Hal would like to see you.' Hal would not; but now I understand that Liza knows a little of Spinster Tailor and would like to know more from Kate who is the complete gossip.

But Kate says rapidly, 'Can't, didn't realise it was so late.'

'Already warmed and spiced.' Liza takes her elbow.

'No!'

Liza lets go, mystified, reluctant. 'All right. It must be very important.' She's so domineering.

'No, of course it's not important.' Kate pushes past. 'It's nothing. Goodbye.'

Liza must greet another customer, and Kate hurries across the Square clutching her little dog. She bows her head as she passes the chapel, reaches her home, rushes upstairs as fast as her bones will carry her. She pauses, wheezing, then continues to her bedchamber and lets the dog jump from her arms on to the bed. The dog puts its head between its paws, watching. Knows the routine.

Kate's chamber, as she calls it, contains almost all in the world Kate owns of value (her tenement is not hers but rented from the Bridge House for thirty-six shillings a year) and after a lifetime of scrimping and saving she has her dead husband's enormous bed to show for it, a polished mirror, a chest, a wardrobe with a door, a small table and a heavy chair. I rather approved of vanity when it was mine, but watching this handsome old lady go through the business with which we are all so familiar with tweezers, files, pumice then rouge to blossom her cheeks and nipples, blue woad to draw out the attractive veins in her breasts and powdered chalk to cover those in her legs, all the time peeping out of the window to check the street below, fills me with curiosity. What man could be worthy of such preparation? I pray it's not Hal. She's put on such a lot of weight since I knew her before. She pulls on her wig, pushes in the wooden teeth that cause her such discomfort, and before she can sit down the knock comes on the street door. The dog barks, is tucked under her arm.

Kate calls prissily from the window, 'Who is it?'

It's Crispin Whyte, the chantry priest! The brother is still thin and stiff as a broomstick, his greasy black garb hanging to the ground, his hair now as white as his name. Even more distinguished than before.

He calls up, 'I heard you were ill, Mistress Ladler.'

'Yes, terribly ill,' she flutters, in defiance of her flushed appearance.

'I shall visit you and pray for you.' He pushes at her door and it is, of course, open.

For his work as one of the bridge chaplains, appointed and paid for by the

Bridge Master, Brother Whyte receives two shillings and threepence each week from his Master, and his chantry prayers for the souls of various departed Lord Mayors must be worth twice as much – by now, as you see, the finances of London Bridge are far more complex than even Queen Eleanor can possibly comprehend – so Crispin is a man not of substance but of means. His looks, celibacy and reticence make him doubly alluring.

His footfalls climb upstairs. Kate is so nervous she can neither stand nor sit, clutches the dog against her. Whatever she means to say (she rehearses clumsy endearments), as he appears she blurts out the truth.

'It's been years!'

It's the moment for truth, obviously. Crispin lifts the hem of his garb to reveal the most striking erection standing from a nest of sticky white curls. Kate drops the dog on the chair. The two humans rush together, fall on to the bed with her dress up and all her work wasted and rouge on the bolster and she winds her fat legs and arms round his thin body as though utterly to consume him. The little dog stands whining on its back legs, paws against the sheet, excluded.

At last the two lie silent, exhausted. 'You still go to sleep afterwards,' Crispin whispers, 'just as you always did.' And I realise he's fond of her in his way, he wasn't completely using her.

Then he says, 'Kate?' He scrambles to his knees. 'Kate? Mistress Ladler? God help me!'

She's dead. I see it at once. The dog will starve. Kate's heart stopped in the moment of extreme passion, the expression fixed on her face is the grinning rictus of that agony. 'My God, my God,' Crispin mutters, pulls himself from her as limp as a sausage skin without sausage. He covers her face with his hands, looks in her face again, but this is the expression her body will carry into eternity, he can't change it. Her teeth fall into the back of her throat. Crispin closes his garb, runs to the door, then puts his hands to his head. He has to think.

He's in dire peril. To sin is one thing, to be found out another.

The dog barks, and Crispin stares at it guiltily. He's in such a state of mind I seem to hear his thoughts exactly. *My God, the dog saw us, saw me, the dog saw what happened.* A priest's whole life is based on sin and guilt, he believes animals are simply animals, without souls, that the only meaning in life is God and God's teachings. God sees the fall of every sparrow. Crispin is about to panic. *The dog saw me.* After all, it is not uncommon to hang dogs for their masters' misdeeds, just as a sinner may purchase forgiveness with a priest's prayers.

Crispin grabs the dog by its scruff. There is a window at the back of the house, the river below. *Drown the dog. Where's a bag? I was never here.*

He's not thinking straight. The dog barks at the open window at the front of the bedroom, the busy street below. Now Crispin remembers. *'Who is it?'* Kate's arch call, she knew perfectly well. Half a hundred people must have seen him. The dog whines, licks the hand that hurts it. Yes, Crispin thinks, I called because I'd heard she was ill. Yes, she was so ill she died. I can brazen it out.

He goes to the door, then remembers Kate's parted legs, goes back and closes them, arranges the blanket over her horrid gargoyle face, mutters a quick prayer and carries the dog downstairs. His arms are still trembling but he's calmer now. *Stroke me.* He remembers to stroke the dog. In the gloomy, firelit street, Crispin calls out to Kate's neighbour.

'I heard Mistress Kate was ill and found her in the extremity of sickness, dying.'

'Sick? She weren't sick!' the neighbour says.

'I heard her say she were terrible ill,' the glover's wife calls over her husband's counter. 'Did you give that wicked woman her last rites? Did you hear her wicked confession?'

'Yes, of course—'

'No, he didn't, that would've taken all day,' the neighbour says. He's a painter, his face splashed with dyes of white lead and red lead, his hands burnt raw by the cancers of his trade.

'Speak of the dead with respect,' Crispin says stiffly, 'for you are soon to join them.'

'As are we all,' agrees the glover's wife devoutly. '*Very* wicked, I suppose?'

'She died penitent.'

'You were in there long enough for me to eat my supper,' the painter says.

Crispin knows he must get away, and the dog must get away from Crispin. The bond between priests and cats is well known, but I have never known a priest keep a dog. The dog barks frantically, writhes in his arms. 'Here. It's yours.' Crispin pushes the dog into the painter's knobbly grasp.

'Nasty bitey thing,' the painter says. 'I won't have it.'

'They make me sneeze,' the glover's wife calls quickly. 'What about the stainer's widow? She's got no company.'

Painters and stainers know each other well, belong to the same brotherhood. The painter scratches his head. 'Well, I could try her, if she'll answer her door. She's a strange one.'

'That's settled then,' Crispin says, 'God be thanked.' He strides away briskly to make arrangements, and by the set of his back and the angle of his head I can almost hear him thinking, *The bitch, the bitch, the bitch, dying.* Then, *Got away with it, those fools.*

Of course he's right. But the painter and the glover's wife exchange knowing looks by the glow of the lantern, and I realise fools have more sense than clever men, and both know exactly what the priest did in Kate's bedchamber. Ah, bed, how that word reminds me of her, makes me so sad for her. She, too, was lonely

Rather than go to the trouble of carrying the dog, the painter ties it to a rope. He drags it along the street, knocks thunderously on a door. He waits. There is no answer to such a commanding summons. The painter curses, ties the rope to the latch, walks off into the dark.

The door opens quietly. A pale face looks down, a pale hand grasps the rope.

And so I return to Widow Stainer's house.

She picks the dog up, strokes it tenderly, kisses it, and the dog licks her eagerly. Dogs know the smell of someone who loves dogs. 'I can't,' she whispers sadly. 'I swore I'd never have another one. If only you lived longer. I can't bear it when you die.' But still she strokes the dog, then caresses her thumb behind its ear. 'You're Kate's dog, aren't you? What's happened to you? Naughty dog.'

A tradesman passing on his way home calls out of the dark, 'Kate's dead. Mistress Glover says she died abed – but not asleep.' He laughs crudely and walks on.

Widow Stainer shrinks back into her side of her house – she rents the other side to Spinster Tailor – then closes the door firmly.

The dog has found a home. I hate the terrible business of starving and illness, I want love and a long life for every creature, as always. 'Dear me,' the widow murmurs. She holds the dog in her thin uncomfortable lap by her pallid fire, hardly worth sleeping in front of. Why is she so worried? Dear me, she thinks, what shall I do? She says, 'Dear me, what shall I do?'

I see the reason for her concern. She already has a kitten for company.

A tiny large-eyed tabby kitten creeping on her stair, peeping through the wooden slats. The dog goes berserk, jumps barking from the widow's lap, races upstairs as fast as its fat little legs will carry it after the intruder. The kitten leaps unsteadily on to the handrail, teeters, the dog jumps against the slats as best it can, barking and growling, and the infuriating kitten balances on the newel post, gazing down in its infuriating way. The widow's pale hand appears and instead of picking the dog up, picks up the kitten.

She kisses its nose. The kitten does not take its eyes off the dog jumping at the widow's knees. Then it deliberately purrs and brushes its head against the widow's cheek, and the dog howls with rage. What am I to do? the widow wonders. 'Bad dog!' she says. 'What am I to do with you both?'

The dog tries to ignore the kitten, gnaws angrily at the step, then goes back to the fire. Puts its head between its paws, watches jealously. The widow sits, holding the kitten in one hand, and strokes the dog's head with her other hand. The dog feels calmer.

The widow smiles. 'You'll have to learn to get on, you two,' she chides. 'Yes you will, yes you will.'

It's not going to work. Every night the dog sleeps by what's left of the fire (and it wasn't very much to start with) and the kitten, growing rapidly into a cat, prowls the house. A cat catches more food than a dog. The cat has perfected its leap on to the newel post, curls its tail round its haunches, and licks its paws at the dog until the dog gives up. The dog goes and throws itself down by the fire. The cat jumps down; the dog jumps up. It begins to learn that the cat can jump faster than a dog can run. The dog stares into the embers, nose twitching, ears alert for the tiniest sound as the cat drops from the newel post, winds itself daintily behind the chair. The dog jumps up, the cat leaps back to the newel post.

At last the dog sleeps.

The cat sits on the floor, wanting the fire, licking its paws and pretending not to look at the dog. Then it comes close, soundlessly. Even the smell of a cat is infuriating. The dog twitches in its dreams. Chasing the cat, but only dreaming it. What idiots dogs are – I know exactly what the cat is feeling. I can almost hear it.

Alice?

Is that the cat's name? Strange, the same as my own name I remember from so long ago.

Alice, is it you?

I can't see the cat, only the dog's dreams, its eyes are closed. But I hear the soft pad of the cat's paws on the boards. I feel its shadow between the fire and the dog, and suddenly I'm afraid. I'm so afraid that it's a cat like the other, that tried to smother sleeping baby Tom (or rather, it was the cat's nature to curl itself in such a warm soft place), the same cat that put out the mouse's eyes for pleasure, playing (which was its nature to do), and I'm so afraid this cat will suddenly claw the dog's eyes.

The dog ceases twitching in its dream, its eyes open, it wakes and sees the cat. Instinctively the cat arches its back, hisses, tail erect, then leaps back to the newel post. The dog stares up, and the cat stares down.

All cats are not the same. I can't quite say what the difference is. This cat has the same slitted eyes, the same manner, the same claws – it's a cat. It will fight if cornered. But somehow I'm not afraid for the dog now.

The dog ceases growling, returns to its favoured place by the fire, sleeps. *I* trust the cat, but the dog does not.

The cat's paws, the sound of its fur moving, light as a breath of wind.

Alice, is it you?

Oh my God, my goodness, it's Jack.

Alice, my God, it's you? It's really you?

How do I know it's you, Jack? Where do you wear your ring?

My ring-toe! My darling, my love. The same place as you, the grass ring I wove for you . . .

It's Jack. It really is. He died and he's alive. He's so much stronger than I am. I'd cry for him if I had tears, I'd laugh for joy if I had breath.

I've found you, Alice. I searched for you always.

The dog wakes, and Jack is gone. The dog chases the cat and the cat jumps on to the newel post.

This has got to stop.

Widow Stainer had few illusions about herself. She was a plain sort, brown dress to the floor, oatmeal-coloured apron, and nobody noticed her on the rare occasions she went out. Her only vanity was the blue enamelled brooch she wore at her throat, her husband's work. She lived plainly, ate plainly, no meat, only fish on Fridays, and drank river water which she pulled up in a jug on a rope. No man would ever again love her.

But she had her animals. They were her life.

Widow Stainer opened her door and stepped into the street. She was terrified of robbery and had paid the boy opposite a penny to watch her house this afternoon. She no longer shared her dwelling with Spinster Tailor, for obvious reasons connected with today's celebration, and though the widow had nothing worth stealing she was afraid of her neatness being disturbed. Tugging the little dog after her on a piece of string, she closed the door carefully and locked it. The widow was not poor since her husband (so long ago that she hardly remembered him) had fallen at work from a ladder in St Paul's Cathedral, and so she had been granted a pension for life by the Stainers' Company, or until she remarried, which of course the brotherhood had constantly pressed her to do. There was no chance of that. But today she was going to a wedding.

Her lodger, Spinster Tailor, was marrying Hal Mason today.

Widow Stainer sniffed through her thin white nose. That woman would not be missed.

The widow's dog pittered and pattered beside her on its little legs, sniffing at every smell from King's Pier, past Hal and Richard Mason's house, to the Bridge Chapel. She attended chapel twice a day, briefly in case her door was forced, and the routine was always the same. If she looked back she knew what she would see, her cat accompanying them, sometimes on the rooftops, sometimes on the parapet, sometimes walking and leaping nearby as if on its way somewhere entirely different, the way cats did, but always keeping her, and the little dog, as if by accident, within sight.

Cat and dog were inseparable, slept curled together, ate from the same dish. The dog was greedy, the cat fastidious. Each remained exactly what it was, made no concessions. The dog chased other cats, the cat hissed at other dogs. 'Animals can't be friends,' Spinster Tailor had laid down the law definitely, 'they don't know how to. At most a dog feels a kind of fawning loyalty.'

Widow Stainer dared say, 'But they behave like friends, Agnes. They're always together. They sleep in front of the fire.'

'It happens all the time,' Spinster Tailor dismissed the widow's tentative wonderment unsentimentally. 'If animals are put together young enough, they go soft. That's all!'

Spinster Tailor was always right. She'd kept a dog until it died, so she knew everything about them. But Widow Stainer knew what she would see if she turned round. She would see her cat following her.

She stepped aside to let some rough men barge past, and the thought occurred to her that the cat was actually following the dog. She was distracted

251

by the sight of a fishmonger displaying a large porpoise caught in the Thames, forgot her reverie, hurried on. She could just remember her wonder as a child seeing a whale swim beneath London Bridge, the size and mystery of the beast. Men shot it with so many arrows that it beached itself somewhere upriver. But she remembered the surge of that endless curving shape sweeping through the arch beneath her.

She turned, and saw her cat followed her.

She smiled her small smile, picked up her dog, and went into the chapel. She couldn't get to her usual place near the front and for the first time she noticed the winding stair leading down to, she surmised, the crypt where smelly fishermen and others were supposed to worship, and lepers and people with contagious diseases were allowed to gather on the starling at low tide to witness the service through the water door. The cat wound itself round her legs, and the brief wedding service was conducted by Brother Whyte, as severe and devout of feature as Hal himself.

'Lord save us,' the widow murmured, seeing the bride.

Spinster Tailor had undergone a transformation. She'd never see her fortieth year again, but gone was every trace of the comfortable middle-aged maid Hal thought he'd chosen. She arrived peacocked in the height of fashion, wearing a man's tunic like one of the parti-coloured brigands of the Langue d'Oc. Hal simply stared at her, baffled and outclassed. Her female friends were dressed in the same fashion. Supposedly her family had once had money; doubtless Hal would receive the bill. She'd even plucked her eyebrows, a vanity the Church warned was punished in the afterlife by the Devil stabbing the hair holes for eternity with hot needles. She smiled at Richard and Liza, who had opposed the match, and who now looked horrified. But Hal was completely under her thumb. The priest, after prayers and singing and the offering of gifts to the altar, made them one flesh and stepped back. Spinster Tailor had ceased to exist and Mistress Agnes was born into matrimony, and her husband, fifteen years her senior, an old man, kissed at her averted red lips and received her cheek instead – at least in public.

Widow Stainer stood peacefully, her dog under her arm, her head bowed in prayer. She never saw the fixed faces of Richard and Liza, or heard their good wishes to Hal and Agnes like drops of ice, or noticed Tom looking up at his parents, wondering what had gone wrong. Widow Stainer smiled shyly to see everyone so happy, prayed for them and received Communion, and then she tucked her little dog under her arm and followed the wedding party dutifully to Hal's house.

Such celebrations are so loud that the guests do not hear thunder.

But *I* see. *I* notice everything. *I* hear Liza whisper furiously to Richard, 'Suppose that woman has children?'

Widow Stainer sits quietly on the bench in the corner, her dog in her lap, but *I* can see Richard hasn't thought of this nightmare. 'She's too old, surely.'

'It could happen.' It hasn't happened again for Liza. That's the first time I've heard her sound bitter. She dotes on Tom. The dog whines.

Richard shakes his head. 'No, I'm sure she doesn't want children.'

'That's right,' Liza says implacably. 'She wants to spend your father's money, and then spend his house, and *our* house which is in his name, and we'll all end up working to pay for her. What about Tom's birthright? What about *us*? What about *him*?'

The cat is shut outside the window. I don't know what to do.

I go over and over it. Of course Jack, like Richard, is infuriatingly calm. But I know just how Liza feels! Her family, her son, her dreams of everything she

252

has hoped and worked for are threatened. Reason doesn't come into it. Liza wants to fight tooth and nail. I would.

The cat and dog lie curled asleep together in front of Widow Stainer's fire. *Alice, relax. Hal's no fool.*

Of course Hal's a fool, he's a man. And there's no fool like an old fool. *You're talking about my great-grandson, you know.*

Jack, we've got to help them. There must be something we can do. *These family things have a way of working themselves out.*

I try not to sound so earnest. That's just it, Jack. They don't. *Oh, it'll be all right.*

I remember the last night of Jack's life, him walking off into the dark. Jack, it wasn't all right for you and me. You're still lazy. You don't think anything bad will happen.

It's not the same. Our young Tom, he's a handsome lad, isn't he?

Yes, he is. I realise our descendants are so very much more than our family, still so very much *us*.

I feel so desolate. You walked off into the night, Jack, and I never saw you again. You don't know what it was like for me. You'll never understand. It's a terrible world, Jack. Terrible things happen out of sight.

I feel so strongly that the dog whimpers in its sleep, its paws kick unhappily. The cat stirs into wakefulness, disturbing us, then slips back into sleep. I can feel Jack's sadness.

You know, Alice, when I died I didn't feel anything. I stared into Nick's face and I thought, yes, how inevitable this is. I understood how inevitably my life led me to what is happening. I can't change it, anything, me, you, us, without changing myself. What hurt was losing you.

You didn't lose me.

Never, Alice, never.

But he sounds so . . . accepting. Jack's still so lazy about the things that matter. I wish he'd *do* something! And like a blade between us, suddenly I remember Nick talking to me once about Jack. 'Without your support through thick and thin, Alice, he'd be no one.'

Jack catches my thought. It's like a revelation to him. But, being Jack, he accepts it. *Yes, Alice, I think that's true.*

I don't want it to be true. I hate the thought of it. Of Nick telling the truth, *knowing* the truth, being wise about anything. I want everything about Nick, everything he had been, to be a lie. Just me and Jack to be true.

Jack?

Yes?

I love you more than ever.

Of course you do. You're learning to be stronger all the time. Be strong enough to do nothing, Alice.

He's right of course. Ah, Jack, I still need you. Agnes Tailor married that old misery Hal for his money, of course she did, her own was almost gone. And it's true that women are always considered deceitful, usually by other women, often correctly, because we – I should say *they* – simply have to be. It's in the nature of the world. Men do, and women make do.

Agnes made do wonderfully. She made Hal happy. I would never have believed anything could have made him happy, but she took ten years off his shoulders and put a smile on his face. Good things happen, I don't know why, but they do.

It wasn't that way at first. I know for a fact – the cat was out hunting – that Liza lay with Richard on their scratchy straw bed and joked about killing Agnes. 'She was bending over at the water hatch in the floor, the tide running fast, tugging her bucket, all I had to do was push her, and . . .' I was alarmed to hear about this (I sense Jack even at a distance of some yards now, a constant background of emotion like the running of the tide) because I know that people, even good ordinary people, never really joke about such serious matters. Especially Liza, there's too much of me in her.

'It wouldn't work, her arse is too big to fit through the hole,' Richard pointed out, yawning. There's my Richard, common sense! But you're lazy, too.

Liza cuddled close, her lips moving against the hairs of his chest. 'I could arrange for the latrine rail to break. She's in there from prime to vespers sometimes. It's forty feet straight down.'

Richard still didn't take her seriously, lay back. I wish I could put my hands behind my head like that. 'Sssh, Tom will hear you.' He gave a warning glance at their sleeping son, eleven years old. Eleven is old enough to pretend to sleep.

But Liza obviously felt better now she'd said her piece. She chuckled, Jack told me, when Richard said, 'I'll just give her one of your pies, she'll choke to death.' The cat jumped on to another rooftop beneath the stars and their voices faded away.

But Tom, of course, had been listening, a strong, highly-coloured boy old enough for strong feelings. A few days later when Agnes told him to go up to the roof and water the herbs he burst out, 'You can't tell me what to do!'

'Yes I can,' Agnes said cheerfully. 'Off you go.'

Tom shouted in a hurt rage, 'It's my mother's garden not yours! She grows it not you!'

Agnes understood at once. All the resentment of her that had been hidden was now out in the open, thanks to the boy. She bent to Tom's height, observed his tears. 'Tom, I'm not your enemy. Can't we be friends? Please?'

'We all hate you!' Tom burst out, his face swollen bright red and sweaty and teary. 'My mother's going to kill you.' He bunched his fists.

Agnes laughed. She sat beside him and put back her head and laughed, defenceless. Tom lowered his hands uncertainly.

'You see,' she said, 'you don't believe I really do love your grandfather. But I do.'

Tom frowned. He couldn't imagine anyone loving his grandfather as much as he did. Grandfather Hal was sour and crotchety, but leather came to life in his hands. Tom's hands were learning the same skill and he admired Hal with an earnest passion. His father was, well, his father, but his grandfather was teaching him something no one else could.

Agnes took Tom's hands in hers. 'I would never do anything to hurt your grandfather. Have I made him unhappy? Does he seem sad to you? Does he complain about me?'

'No,' Tom admitted.

'Does he say, that Agnes, she cooked me a nasty piece of fish for supper last night, she's no good?'

'No,' Tom smiled. 'He doesn't.'

'I'll tell you a secret. Do you want to hear it?'

'Yes!' Tom said eagerly. 'I mean, I don't mind.'

'I'm showing him how to read.'

Tom's eyes went round. 'What, read words?' Tom could count to twelve like most boys, and he knew what some words looked like, such as 'shoe', but he saw Agnes meant reading words like speaking them. 'But he's too old.'

'If he's too old,' Agnes said, putting her finger against her chin, 'you must be too young.'

Tom bridled at the insult. 'Too young, not me!'

She straightened the collar of his jerkin. 'Come upstairs to me every day after your work and chores, and I'll show you how to read.' She added, 'If your father allows it.'

'It's not him,' Tom worried. 'It's mother.'

'She's already teaching you?'

'She can't, and I can count as well as her!'

'That's enough for now.' Agnes turned him, pointed him at the open door. 'Why don't you ask her to come with you? Not to learn to read. Just for her to listen to me showing you. Will you do that?'

Tom looked at her seriously. 'You're all right really.'

'Off you go now. Don't forget.' She noticed the cat for the first time. 'Shoo, puss! How did you get in here?' But she had some thin milk left over from the butter-making, put it down in a wooden platter, and watched Widow Stainer's cat lap it up.

The cat and the little dog lie curled asleep in front of the embers.

Admit it, Alice.

I won't admit it.

Admit it, Alice, I was right about Agnes.

Oh, you're always right about everything, Jack.

The feel of his warm chuckle, his pleasure. *Still the same old Alice.*

Less of the old, thank you.

We still don't know where he hid your bones.

He. I don't want to think of him, of Nick. Nick doesn't matter any more, Jack. He's gone.

He buried you on the bridge. You're as much a part of London Bridge as I am.

Masons believe bones give a bridge strength, don't they?

Now you know why.

The windows glow faintly with dawn, the embers are cold. We know the cat and the dog will awaken soon, the cat to hunt and the dog to creep on to the cover of the widow's bed. But London Bridge remains strangely silent, even though it's not the Sabbath. The grip of Eleanor, the Queen Mother, on the bridge finances is loosening. Gregory de Rokesle, seven times past Lord Mayor of London, has been appointed Bridge Master. But it's too late. The bridge is ruined. A man of immense prestige and influence like de Rokesle does what he can, and King Edward issues a royal warrant for the relief and reparation of the bridge, fearing its sudden collapse and, in his own words (the proclamation was read at the drawbridge) fearing the destruction of the innumerable people dwelling thereon. (The crier had to move hastily to the Great Stone Gate when the drawbridge creaked alarmingly and one of the massive brass lifting pulleys, weighing fifty-five pounds, fell from one of the towers into the crowd.) The King wants to show he cares for his people, but his appeal for charity read out in churches throughout his kingdom falls on deaf ears – or at least, nothing has happened yet. On windy days dust showers visibly from the arches, and with a running tide the whole structure cracks and groans. Londoners cope with this cheerfully, of course, are used to it, even tiles falling from the roofs of shifting houses.

De Rokesle has banned the market and introduced tolls. Tolls. The very word reminds me of Nick, Nick again, he *knew* it would happen. *Tolls and pontage will be levied, small at first, then larger.* Now it's true. By the Royal Grant of Tolls every person crossing the bridge pays one quarter-penny, every packhorse one halfpenny, every horseman one penny, and every boat passing beneath is charged pontage of one penny.

The little dog twitches as its dreams turn to nightmares, my mood has darkened. Jack?

Alice?

Do you think we'll be together for ever?

I think there is much more than this, Alice.

Do you think we're alone?

Surprised. *I'm sure we're not.*

Are very many more like us?

Everywhere.

How many?

Everyone there ever was. All the way back to the creation of the world five thousand years ago. More. It can't be, it must be. Everyone has a soul – don't they? I glimpse so many things I don't understand. The river rises and falls. It's not part of the world. I mean, it's not the same. We're in between. It's like a journey.

Nick took Durand down below the chapel and showed him something amazing.

What amazing?

I'm not sure. Durand came back with chalk on his hair and hands. Where did he get chalk from? London's built on clay, chalk's nowhere on the ground here, it's shipped in boats from the River Colne or the River Darenth.

Some masons believe there's chalk deep beneath London.

Durand never said a word. Even Rosie never knew.

There's so much we don't know. Almost everything. I never saw Nick kill you, and I never saw him bury you on the bridge, but he must have done.

He didn't take me far. Down stairs. The floor was smooth. Hard. He dragged me across it easily. Stone.

Marble. Alice, the undercroft of the chapel has stairs down, a marble floor, a big black and white check pattern. The chapel was still under construction at the time, wasn't it?

Nick buried me beneath the floor of the undercroft. I remember the scrape of the marble slab.

I know where my bones lie.

Alice? Don't cry.

I'm not crying. How can I?

The dog runs in its sleep, emits a desolate howl.

The warm feeling of Jack returns.

Alice, there's something more.

What more?

You saw Nick burnt alive, didn't you?

Yes, in the great fire. Three thousand people—

Where was Nick exactly?

On the rooftop of course. Everything below was on fire.

Alice, what happened to Nick's body?

He fell.

Where did Nick fall to?

Suddenly I see what he means. Oh my God, Jack, Nick's not there beneath Hal Mason's house. He's gone. He's gone, Jack.

I think of Hal and Agnes, Richard and Liza and dear young Tom, my family through time living over the charred remains of the house I had known in my life.

Alice, what exactly happened after the fire?

Teams of workmen cleared a path across the bridge. It took four days, everything was still smouldering. They just chucked it in the river, or smashed it up, or used the ash for hardcore.

They didn't find everyone, did they?

Jack, there were so many. The heat turned them to ash.

And Durand built his new house on top.

Nick is dead. Nick is gone, I keep telling myself. The dog pees, upset, on the widow's bed and receives a thrashing. The cat stays close but I'm in too much of a state to think of Jack, and when I do he's little comfort.

Nick's here, Alice. He's still here, somewhere.

The dog is taken out for a walk to the fishmonger's stall, it's Friday, fish day. Some nice little shad perhaps, of which the dog, begging, will receive flakes dropped from the table, and the cat the heads and tails and guts. This cat is never hungry and never catches mice. It follows us past Hal's house, Liza leaning on the counter beneath the sign, mouth wide, calling lustily for trade as usual. Is Nick here? The busy scene pushes past me, a cage of thrushes carried towards the Poultry, coops of chickens. Rooks are circling the heads spiked on the Great Stone Gate, a robin redbreast hops on the parapet, a crab waves its claws on the fishmonger's slab and eels writhe in a bucket.

I use all my strength. Jack?

The cat chases the robin off the parapet, bounds after the widow. It likes the fishmonger's stall. *Alice?*

If Nick is here, we'd never find him unless he wanted to be found.

He wants to be found.

The little dog looks so miserable and off colour that the widow picks it up, tucks it under her arm. She takes her time choosing a fish. Shad caught off London Bridge, or haburdens? Autumn, so fresh herring were on the slab, their eyes already drying as the morning sun burnt off the mist over the water.

Alice, he wants to be found, don't you see? He wants to do harm. It's all he can do. He's full of hate. Nothing but hatred, Alice.

No one's like that.

Everyone Nick tried to love betrayed him. I betrayed him, married you. You, his perfect Alice, betrayed him.

I never did. I didn't mean to.

Look at it through his eyes. Even the Templars betrayed him. Durand too.

Jack, you're frightening me.

Nick tried with all his heart, but he was never really a part of our family. Our family is all he can hurt. He needs revenge. He'll have it.

'Herring,' the widow decides, and points. The cat jumps on to the parapet, it does not like herring, a cheap fish.

Revenge.

The little dog is carried home. It refuses to beg beside the widow's chair, cannot stomach the leftovers, lies miserably at the window. Through the ripply glass the river, the boats, the churches and the living mass of London are inextricably blurred.

The cat cleans its paws, licks its fur patiently.

What aren't you telling me, Alice?

I remember the ginger cat. Not this harmless fat tabby, I remember the lean ginger tomcat with claws and fangs sleeping on Hal's chest, jumping on to the face of baby Tom in the basket, curling asleep there on the baby's face, almost smothering him.

But it was just a cat.

But I remember the cat peering into the mouse's eyes, sensing me. Sinking his claws into the mouse's eyes, hurting *me* in the only way he can.

Nick can hurt my family.

Nick almost killed baby Tom.

And for the first time I really understand this. Evil exists. Not everything happens by chance, like a roll of dice. We really only ever have one choice, to know, or not to know. He's here. He's somewhere on the bridge.

Alice, it's all right. Nothing will happen. It was just a cat.

You're lazy, Jack, and you're too confident for your own good. But perhaps you're right, Jack. I hope you are.

And it's true, I'm not afraid with him here. With Jack's company, for all his faults, I'm never afraid. I wish he could cuddle me and kiss me and hold me tight. I wish with all my soul we were human, with human arms and lips.

But the cat slips away to the rooftops or the gaps between the houses or wherever it pretend-hunts until the evening fire is lit, and the dog stays at the window.

The light begins to fail, the colours fade. The dog wakes with a start. A bird has flown thump into the glass. Poor thing, it lies stunned on the sill outside, a pigeon, the thinnest pigeon I ever saw, its feathers fluffed over its scrawny body crawling with fleas, its beak broken. The dog jumps up furiously, barking, but the widow is upstairs, and anyway this dog is always barking. The dog jumps at the glass, scrabbling with its paws – and one side of the window swings open and the dog slips out, the river sliding below, its claws scrabble on the sill. It drags itself back, whining, sorry for itself, licks its hurt claw, then blames the pigeon for its pain and fear.

Just like you.

What?

Only thinking of yourself. As always.

Oh God, it's not Jack. It's someone who doesn't love me.

Intense terror grips me. It's Nick, it's Nick. Jack, Jack, help me, come back, it's Nick!

Shut up. I'm not your precious Nick, you bitch.

Who are you?

The one you forgot, Alice. The one you forgot.

Noelle. She's Noelle.

Do you remember her, my sister? I've forgotten the others – no, I remember Elviva, and there were more. Noelle was special because everyone said she looked like me, which naturally attracted my attention. I remember the baby coughing in the wood smoke, see her growing up into the thin, enchanting girl Noelle became. She had a mole on her cheek, but she smiled with my face. And so Geoffrey de Prudome, obsessed, took her, not me.

Noelle, I never forgot you.

I'm so alone.

I begin to feel her pain.

She can't know that I bought the Templar's shilling, the blood-money he gave the chaplain to redeem his conscience. I hope Noelle's death lay hard on de Prudome's heart to the end of his days.

Noelle, I'm sorry.

She allows me a glimpse inside her, her misery and loss engulfs me. The furious heat of her anger, her despair. I have suffered nothing by comparison, no one can bear this. My good fortune was Noelle's damnation, and now I even have Jack back again.

But what of Robin? Were you not reunited?

Silence. The terrible desolation of her soul, I feel it.

Robin was swept away.

I cannot imagine Noelle's loneliness. I must have something to say. I'm sorry. I hate myself for that little word.

I'm sorry I was ever born, Alice.

Noelle, talk to me.

I try to be a stone, Alice. I felt him die. The tide took Robin from me, rolled him over, lifted his body over me, turning over and over, and pulled him away, I felt him go. I sensed the Light take him.

The Light?

The Light took him.

258

Once Nick told me the name that is given to the Light. I've forgotten it, I didn't want to believe him about anything. I wanted to erase every word that passed Nick's lips simply because he said it. I need to believe, if I can, that everything Nick ever said was a lie.

Shekinah. That's the word he used. Now I remember, something bright painted on ceilings, gold leaf perhaps, the visible manifestation of the Divine Majesty in the Temple of Solomon, a queen. Nick called it a glory of reflected light like a sunrise. But Nick lied about everything, didn't he? The Shekinah, and his crazy, terrible story about finding the earthly remains of Christ in a cave in the Langue d'Oc, his madness, his renunciation of the Templars, his hiding the Templar cloak and Blood Cross beneath the arch, all a lie – except that I found it there. Where's the truth? *London is the City of Hell.* But Nick had come back here. Why? Because I did. Because of me, he accepted it. Because of me, he embraced it.

What have I done? It *is* a moral world. It *is* a moral universe. Surely.

For a moment I am aware of the dog pushing its face round the side of the closed window, its claws clinging to the sill, mouth agape, trying to reach the pigeon.

Noelle senses my sadness. *Oh, Alice, don't you know the Light? I died and could not reach out. My bones lie deep in the riverbed, the bridge is on me. But the river swept Robin to the sea and he reached out and the Light took him.*

What is the Light, Noelle?

The Light is God.

I've not seen that. I know nothing of it.

Didn't you see our mother when you died?

I hardly knew her. I can hardly remember her. She was dirty.

I saw Mother with a shining halo and she held a baby with a grown-up face, a woman. Then the woman was a monkey, then something else, then a fish and a tadpole with a long tail. And then she was the moon.

It was the moment of your body's death and you dreamt, that's all.

What I see is true, Alice. There's no end to it.

What do you search for, Noelle?

She feels surprised. *The same as you. Love. Companionship on the journey. Hope. You have Jack. You're so lucky, Alice. You always were.*

Don't go! I try to reach out to her, but it is the moment of the pigeon's death. Her soul slips away from me like water between the fingers of a thirsty woman. You could no more hold her than I. For a moment I sense the deep river, weeds, mud, clay. *You're so lucky, Alice.* Then she is gone.

The widow comes down. 'Poor creature.' By candlelight she peers through the window at the pigeon's broken body on the sill, then pushes it off with a stick rather than touch the fleas.

But I feel it still: Noelle's love, her loneliness, her unendurable pain.

The dog curls miserably in front of the fire until the cat comes in. I could no longer bear to exist without Jack. And yet I cannot die, no more than Noelle.

The little dog shivers, sick.

I have so much more than Noelle ever had. Wherever she is now on the bridge, she has no one. She wants to believe, and who can blame her, that Robin whom she loved was taken to Heaven, which she calls the Light. By now she believes this so strongly that she *knows* it. London Bridge will not stand for ever – hardly an eyelid's blink in the scheme of Time, perhaps – and one day she will join him.

Perhaps she is right.

But I have Jack, I have my family, I even have the widow for kindness and

259

affection, and I have grown quite devoted to her. The little dog, quite recovered from its – or my – malaise, always pulls hardest near Liza's house, and wags if it is picked up and put on the counter. Liza wears a thick wool scarf and leather gloves against the cold, it's a terrible winter, the arches are blocked with ice (I'm sure I remember this happening before, but they don't, it seems marvellous to them that the river freezes upstream of the bridge). 'Richard skated as far as the ford at Westminster,' Liza blows white breath, her scarf is coated with frost beneath her nostrils, 'and the weir itself will freeze, he says.' She scratches the dog's tummy, which makes it kick its leg in ecstasy. 'Seems in better spirits now.' She knows the widow dotes on the dog.

'My mother used to call it an attack of the river mist,' the widow says tenderly. Smoke rises all over London as though the City steams. In the churchyard of St Paul's Cathedral the bishop's bonfire gleams where they burn heretics for the salvation of their souls. Trade on the bridge will be slow until the Southwark crowd returns from the burning and the brothels around the cathedral. The vintners are already gauging the dying of the St Paul's fire and heating the mulled wine, the taverners drawing back the curtains from their barrels of ale and swinging their fur-trimmed cloaks on to their shoulders. A few gentlemen throw pennies from the bridge on to the ice, encouraging the young louts skating on blades of beef bone to various feats of bravery and broken arms. Tom is counting Matthew Currier's tallies and calling to his father that they could buy their skins cheaper from the Duponts, another old bridge family. 'We've always bought from the Curriers,' comes Hal's voice from the back room.

Agnes says, 'Are Dupont's skins as good?'

Three months ago Liza would have given her youthful mother-in-law an angry stare for interfering, but Tom's reading lessons have brought them together, and now Liza can read a little too. It's a strange, almost useless gift since none of them can afford a book (Agnes writes out her own pages) and all shops are identified by their signs, and the owner's name is usually the same as his sign. 'Your father should have changed his name to Shoemaker or Last or Cobbler,' Agnes told Hal. 'You'd get more trade, people would know what to expect.' But Hal likes keeping the name Mason, it's become a family tradition.

'Dupont buys them from the same tanner on Bermond's Isle,' Tom says. 'I saw him.'

'We should buy direct from the tanner,' Agnes suggests.

'It's not done that way,' Hal says. 'Young Currier is family, Liza, your cousin.'

Tom yawns, begs to run the dog. To live for ever doesn't mean that every moment is not precious; running with Tom along London Bridge, the little dog yapping with delight, its ears flying, are among the happiest moments of my existence. We return panting. 'Look at your face, red as an apple,' Liza scolds Tom, proud of his health and strength. She wanted a little girl too but now accepts it is not to be. 'Be ready to help me at the counter, Tom, the crowd will be coming soon, we'll sell shoes for cash today.'

But the crowd does not come. Rather than pay a farthing to cross the bridge, the people are cutting short across the ice from Paul's Wharf or Blackfriars Stairs, and one fool launches his horse down the icy slope of the West Water Gate, between the boats frozen there, and gallops to Bankside with the hooves ringing like swords on the ice.

'Best to pray for a thaw,' Hal says.

But the thaw does not come. The frost sets harder into the bones of the bridge, making a bridge of ice, the arches festooned with icicles and very pretty.

The little dog wakes suddenly in the night, disturbed. The cat is already awake.

Alice?

What's wrong?

Do you not feel it?

No, but the little dog does, it jumps up excitedly, something's terribly wrong. A little soot falls on to the embers, putting them out, and suddenly the room is dark except for the glow of the window. There must be moon above the clouds. The window cracks, and warm fog rolls into the room. Warm fog? It's the thaw.

The dog barks, bustles forward officiously.

The thaw has come. The thaw has come so fast. This damp, dense, foggy air from the west is as warm as spring. Why isn't the widow awake? Why aren't the humans awake, can't they feel the ice melting? The frost, hard as cement, turns to water between the stones, the stones make a sound like grinding teeth beneath us. The dog's ears hear the high-pitched squeal of planche nails giving way. The tide-carpenter's wooden bulwarks against the pressure of the ice are being torn out.

The river is on the move.

Dogs are barking all over the bridge, the little dog hears pigeons fluttering beyond the window, disturbed from their nests on the inaccessible house backs overhanging the ice. Pale ice shadows sweep across the ceiling, reflections of the ice being swept into the arch below us.

The floor trembles beneath the dog's paws, then vibrates. Danger, danger! The cat leaps instinctively to the place of safety it remembers as a kitten, the newel post. The faithful dog scampers up to its mistress, barking. The widow sleeps on one side of her bed as though her husband still slept on the other side, her arm thrown across. She dreams, and smells of sleep. The dog's barks make her dream that it is not the middle of the night but the morning, when the little dog always barks. She wakes, then sits up in growing confusion. 'What's the matter?'

The dog leaps on to her bed, barking, tail wagging frantically. Its nose smells the dark, cold odour of shifting ice, the resinous scent of breaking wood, houses breaking up, and now the smell of human fear. Its ears hear the sound of running men in the street, shouts, calls, distant screams. The melting ice is forced by the rushing water into the arches, the floes overturn and jam together, sliding over each other, scraping and grinding against the cracked masonry.

Widow Stainer is still half asleep. She puts on her cape, then goes back for her shoes. 'Be quiet!' she says. 'I can't think.' She goes downstairs, to the door, then remembers the cat, picks it up. A joist falls from the ceiling like poor workmanship, then the others bend and splinter. The foundations are shifting.

Jack!

Don't worry, Alice, I'm here.

The widow has the cat tucked under one arm, the dog under the other. Her face is pale but in this mood she is indomitable. She lifts the latch with her elbow, almost falls into the street, is swept along by rushing people and carts stacked with household possessions, chests, tools, beds. Some man is even working to remove his door. The carts wobble, top heavy, across the gaps in the road. One cart stops, tilting, sinks to the hubs. The mule makes a dreadful screaming sound, dragged backwards between the shafts, but a resourceful man cuts the harness free with a sword. The cart drops down, the mule stands shaking like a shocked man. A crowd gathers. Someone says,

'The whole bridge is going. There's no way off the north side. Turn back to Southwark.'

Liza touches the widow's elbow. 'Come back to our house. The ebb tide hasn't reached its full force yet.'

'How long?'

'Not until prime.'

'Nothing will happen.' The widow will not leave, Liza will not leave her, so the two women stand watching. Liza takes the little dog. But for the roar of tide and ice the scene is surprisingly peaceful, the houses standing serene and insubstantial in the fog, men like shadows toiling below in the firelight. An iceberg drifts downstream with slow, imponderable force, grounds briefly on a mudbank, then the ice piling behind pushes it irresistibly forward. Its prow strikes the bridge gently at Queen's Lock. The houses rise up then slowly settle. Children run through the crowd, bumping, playing icebergs. The bells of St Mary Overie toll the hour of prime, joined by St Olave's, then St Thomas's Chapel on the bridge, St Magnus, bells chiming through the fog all over London.

The widow puts her hand to her throat. She's forgotten her blue enamelled brooch.

The iceberg slides through the bridge like a knife. A house moves improbably with it, then others pull forward, drop slowly into the rushing water. Ice flows across the river, funnelling into the breach. Even humans feel the bridge shake now. Another arch falls, blowing dust out of the fog. Queen's Lock is gone, and where Queen's Pier stood is a slope of racing ice.

'I'm sorry, I've forgotten my brooch,' the widow says. She walks towards her house, which is safe. Liza runs after her, then stops, almost dropping the dog as it writhes and yaps. The cat jumps out of Widow Stainer's arms, runs back along the roadway, tail up, jumping the cracks that appear in the roadway.

There is a crash, the roadway breaks, falls down, the river splashes up, the houses collide. In front of us everything moves sideways and is gone. It happens so suddenly that at first I don't realise Widow Stainer's house, too, is gone, and so is she. King's Pier is gone, only the stump sticking out like a broken tooth.

Jack?

The cat winds itself round Liza's ankles, which is something she dislikes, she has swollen ankles from standing at the counter every day.

It's all right, Alice.

My God, Jack, I thought you were gone!

You always did worry too much.

The level of the water is visibly lower now. Liza calls out the widow's name but there is no reply. The dog licks her chin. It knows what has happened, or perhaps it simply senses my knowledge. Pigeons flutter panic-stricken, mice come on to the road and run between the feet of humans.

Stones fall from King's Pier into the rush, the neat masonry drops away to reveal its filling of chalk rubble, ragstone and rocks from the old Roman walls of London, then a stone slab is lifted up by the spray. And the dog's poor vision sees, I *think* it sees, for one moment, exposed, Jack's bones.

Alice, remember I love you—

The brown water flows over the place.

Listen, listen, this is true, I swear: I saw dawn rise in the east.

Dawn always rises in the east, downriver. I mean, for the first time I *saw* the dawn. I really saw it. I felt it, felt it like a vision, like sure and certain knowledge. Not as a stairway to Heaven, not cupped hands, not the face of God. Not a dream like we would dream it. For a moment, the little dog saw not what we *think* we see, it saw what was real. For

262

an instant I think I saw beyond my personal existence to real, absolute reality. The glory.

Jack? Where are you, Jack?

No answer.

Jack?

Pigeons, bats, there were even bats on London Bridge, living in the roof spaces, their shapes flit through the fog, whizz flawlessly between the buildings that still stand behind us. And I think I hear Noelle's tiny voice.

The Light has taken him.

I remember that Noelle believes in the Light.

The cat winds itself round Liza's ankles, just a cat.

Jack?

Nothing. Jack has gone forward. His journey has continued without me.

The little dog howls.

Five arches gone. The northern end of the bridge open to the tide. I hear the hammers of the tide-carpenters at work night and day. Within a week they have a wooden footbridge going up and down at all angles, but usable, spanning what is left of the piers and buttresses. Most of the damage was from floating ice, so the stone beneath the low tide mark is considered sound. Now, too late, enormous amounts of money must be spent repairing the bridge where only a little maintenance would have once worked wonders. I don't care. Beneath Liza's window on St Mary's Pier, where the little dog lies listlessly on the window seat, heavy four-wheeled carts and sweating teams haul building materials from the Bridge House Yard, piledrivers and lengths of oak and elm for ramming, white Portland stone for facings and show and Coyston stone for cheapness. Boats filled with Medway ragstone and chalk pour tons of rubble to repair the starlings. The activity is endless, day and night. None of this matters.

Jack's gone.

I found Jack and now I've lost him for ever. I want to be no one.

The cat, no more than a cat, ordinary, vacant, sleeps against the little dog. The little dog sleeps too, shivering in its dreams. But I never sleep. I hear the ice. I feel the cold.

What am I to make of what happened? Was it meant to happen? Was I meant to lose Jack just when I had found him? Then where is the mercy, where is the love? Are Nick and the Templars right? God made Heaven and Earth, but the Devil made the world.

The Devil does not control the movement of the ice – does he? How much more is there that I do not know? Perhaps the Devil wants to be found, just like Jack said Nick wanted to be found. Wants us to know. I've seen no devils, but would I recognise one if he didn't have a red tail and pointed horns, like the seducer painted on the girl in old Abbot's Littlebourne church? Nick believed in the Devil, I remember him talking of all those demonic names, so many I've forgotten, Samael and Zaafiel, Qasfiel, Ragziel, others. Asmodeus the son of Deus, Baphomet in his earthly form, worshipped by the Templars, architect of the Temple of Solomon.

I remember everything Nick said.

I take Nick seriously now.

To the dog, all that's a long time ago, and summer comes. This dog is growing old. Its memories of Widow Stainer fade, although it would still jump up on its old bones and wag its tail as best it could if by some miracle she walked into the room, and sometimes it dreams of her now that it sleeps most of the day. Liza feeds the dog meat, and sometimes Tom carries it in a basket when he walks along London Bridge to the tanners', and I look around me through the dog's eyes. The arches are all repaired, sooty and dark already, but the yellow petals of London rocket have yet to take hold. The peeling heads of unsuccessful traitors adorn the Great Stone Gate, and the Keeper of the Dogs, Simon Bedell, looks as old and crotchety as I remember his father years ago. Jonathan Bedell must be long dead by now. I remember that Tom Bedell was the first. I can hardly recall what he looked like. Not much different, no doubt. Tom, my Tom, a strapping lad of fifteen, waves to people he knows, and he knows almost everyone. Crispin Whyte, the little dog manages a bark at the sight of his cassock. Widow Glover, Mark Stoner, somebody Fairless – did *he*, poor man, have a wife? He must have done, I never thought – and here are the Ladlers and the Swinerts, noisy as always. Does Noelle watch over her own loved one's family as I watch over mine? I hear nothing of her. Timothy Wayer is at the Weighbridge gauging cargoes, his two daughters in the doorway giggle at Tom. The twins are fifteen, always together, I think Tom's already decided to marry one or the other of them, Sophia or Elise. He'd like to marry both. Sophia is intelligent but Elise has warmth, they complement each other perfectly; to have both, a man would have everything. It always amazes me how quickly young men get erections – Tom hides it unsuccessfully behind the basket – at the sight of perfectly nice girls.

'Hello, Tom,' they call. My, what hot olive-brown eyes that Elise has.

Tom hurries by with a show of indifference, and behind him the giggling breaks out again.

The wheel is turning. Tom will marry and have children. I can feel it happening, turning, turning.

Winter is hard on the little dog, but winter has a fire. There's no respite from the heat of summer. The dog finds a piece of shadow on the roof and lies in it, panting. From a seed Liza has grown a small apple tree up here, it stands in a barrel and this year (making up for last year) bears rich clusters of fruit. The dappled shadow waves over the dog, and Liza sits sewing beneath the rustling leaves. Sails clap in the breeze, echoing against the house walls, as a boat tacks to the Custom wharf. Shouts as a rowboat shoots the bridge, the bang of the standing wave against the hull, huzzahs of their victory over the tide from the young men aboard, fools. Bees buzz drowsily around the apples. I have seen the King and courtiers rowed below us half a dozen times, rowed down to the royal hunting lodge on the island in Rotherhithe and rowed back again, late, laden down with heron and snipe. A bee circles Liza's head, she waves it away.

Then Liza sees a customer she recognises in the street, waves, calls down. The rumble of a cart drowns her voice. She draws breath and – these accidents happen – the bee settles for a moment on her tongue. I see it clearly. Deliberate, meant to happen. She opened her lips, the bee darted inside.

Liza clasps her hand to her throat, stung.

No, not Liza! Not my Liza!

I see it all, I cannot turn away, I must watch, I cannot cease.

Liza's mouth gapes wide. She drops down half in the shade, half in the sun. Her tongue swells, her windpipe closes. She struggles, her tongue protrudes from her mouth, her eyes stare at the sun. This little death. It's over now.

The dog limps to her, curls shivering against her body.

The bee flies from Liza's mouth, settles on her eye.

I'm here, Alice.

No, it's not Jack. It's Nick. It's just beginning.

Noelle's tale

The Bridge Chapel, Friday, 13 October 1307

Quiet as mice.

See what I have seen, I whisper.

Is Alice with us? No, Alice thinks only of her family. Alice does not see the truth. She does not believe.

But we know the truth. We meekly believe. We humbly submit. Pain, suffering, humility, sacrifice.

I, Noelle. I know what Durand saw all those years ago. I have been there too.

I have seen the Light.

Beneath the door we come, first one, then two, stealing into the silent chapel. Only a single candle burns, the vigil. Almost midnight; the human life of London Bridge does not interest us, but the busy tread of human feet is paused, so we pass freely. Along London Bridge more tiny shapes scurry from the walls of darkened houses, they hear my call, hurry along the borders of the street, across the deserted Square, scuttle quickly beneath the chapel door. Some comprehend only dimly; but they come.

We cross without a sound, like a carpet moving across the floor, to the winding stair.

Today, in France, at dawn, every single Knight Templar was arrested, and will be tortured until he confesses the truth about the order at his trial. The Templar order and all its branches in England, Ireland, Spain, Portugal, Italy, are cut off. Their Temples, Templar preceptories, Templar houses and all their lands are seized. Recognising the justice of the legal case against them, abandoned by the Pope, the Templars put up no resistance and cannot attempt to defend themselves in law. At first they will pretend to be confused, plead they do not understand the accusations against them. So the question will be put to them. They will be beaten, starved, racked, thumbscrewed, their teeth broken out and their fingernails torn off, their flesh bruised by hammers and scorched by flames, until they understand the question and give the answer. They will confess to sodomy, to heresy, to witchcraft, to the black arts, to spitting on the Cross, to worshipping Baphomet, to unspeakable crimes. All these confessions are true, for unspeakable evil does exist in the world, and justice must be seen to be done. The Templars will confess and their leaders will be burnt alive. Any Templar who recants his confession will be burnt alive. Many will die before they can be brought to trial and burnt, others will suffer lifelong imprisonment. They will suffer as they have made others suffer. As I have suffered. As I have suffered terribly. I pray that God will have mercy on their souls and that they scream in Hell until Judgement Day.

We flow down the winding stair like a shadow to the undercroft, cross the black and white marble floor to the second altar beneath another candle. A new wine-red cloth ends in silver tassels just above the floor. The tassels shimmer in the candlelight as we pass beneath. Here is a tiny cleft worked between the

265

marble slabs. Within a few minutes we are gone, every last one. The undercroft is empty.

Each one of us is almost nothing. Together we are a grey furry tide down the winding stair beneath the altar, down to a deep, narrow stone room hung with tapestries of midnight-blue and gold, worked with strange pagan designs.

Here is the Sacred Lodge of the Templars and the Brotherhood of Masons.

For years my poor revenge was to nibble the corners and musty folds of cloth, alone. One tiny spark of will. Almost nothing.

Now I am a thousand. I am important. I matter.

We flow beneath the tapestries and the winding stair falls away below us. I know it winds down for ever, for I have seen the truth.

Here is infinity and eternity. We need never stop.

Downwards we go. Some will not return; perhaps many.

Down, down. I remember the night I died. I remember that winding stair . . . I can't remember love. It's gone. Some things are more important.

We wear out these poor little bodies but I know what I must do, I know what must be done.

We pass corridors branching away from the steps; here is the one.

The King of France has seized the Templars' treasure, all he can lay hands on. But already there are rumours that the Templar fleets sailed yesterday, or last week, that only the old men remained to be caught. *Baucent* was sighted off the Isle of Wight, *Gonfalon* near Ireland. Some say the Templars are in Scotland fighting for Robert Bruce, others that they have fled to Norway, still others that *Baucent* and *Gonfalon*, flying the skull and crossbones of their maritime flag, will sail west from Ireland into the setting sun and not stop until they reach land, or ice, or fire, or the edge of the world – though of course the Templars, who have strayed far from Christianity, believe the world is round.

The Grand Master of the order will be burnt at the stake with his treasurer, Geoffrey de Charney, great-grandson of the Godfrey de Charney who by legend stole the burial shroud of Christ and fled with it to Normandy (but some say that in these hard times it has been bought by the bankers of Lombardy). And as the flames consume them, these old men will recant their confessions that they sold their souls to the Devil, committed bestiality, buggery, worshipped idols, denied the sacraments. But denying the accusations simply proves them true, for everyone knows the guilty always deny their crimes, and their protestations of innocence simply prove their guilt.

Then with his dying breaths the Grand Master will curse the King of France and the Pope to death; within a month the Pope will be dead, and six months later the King will die. It is the Devil's work.

How I hate the Devil!

I am a prisoner in my dreadful existence, irritable and melancholy as a cloistered nun, *aeiparthenos*, eternally virgin yet constantly demeaned by this tiny body, its fluids, sustenance, wastes. I believe in the pure Blessed Virgin Mary, I believe that Jesus had no brothers and sisters, I believe that Mary was without sin all her life. Christ passed through her body as light passes through a window. Nothing else matters but the worship of Him.

Some are falling behind, exhausted, but the rest of us race forward. Hurry, hurry!

Stop!

Now come forward with reverence.

We know what we see. Here is the greatest treasure the Templars left behind. The gold and jewels are nothing, made in the world. The altar of white marble does not matter, is corrupt, worldly, the work of men.

Here, draped in chains, is what men, devils, have made the prisoner of their beliefs.

Our noses touch His blood that drips constantly from the wound in His side, our teeth nibble faithfully at the bonds that bind His wrists, His ankles, the threads that sew closed His eyes, His nostrils, His lips, and at the massive links of iron chain that are thicker and heavier than our bodies.

We worship. We adore. We pray.

We await the Light.

In the corner is a book. Its cover is soft leather, brown as blood, its pages flutter; but I cannot read.

Five

Nick

Alice's tale

London Bridge, 6 February 1832

Alice, are you there? Alice?

You don't have to come, you can stay away, I don't need you. I suppose you have a girl.

I was engaged to be married.

Ah, that explains it. She changed her mind! Turned you down! So that's why you'd throw yourself off London Bridge. It's easy now they've knocked down the houses. In fact they were knocked down about seventy years ago, you'd never think they were here . . . Everything I know, gone. Everything I loved.

She died six days ago.

She isn't here, Frank. Don't look for her. I'm not her.

It was the cholera.

I only know the bridge. I'm sorry, Frank, forgive me. Stroke me. Do I make you feel better? What's the matter with your knee?

I fell over on the rubble. The bridge is barricaded, the demolition gets a little further each day. I bribed the Irish watchman with a sixpence to look the other way. Talk to me, please. Tell me about Liza.

There's no more to tell. Nick kills her.

But I thought she was so important!

Everyone is important. She is Tom's mother. She's buried over there, behind you, the St Mary Overie Church, now called Southwark Cathedral. There she is. Tom's important, but he died too, at a grand old age. His sons are important, and his daughters are important, and everything he did, everything he was. Is.

Did Liza go forward to the Light?

Everyone goes forward. Everyone changes and remains the same.

But not you. Poor Alice. Eternal life.

My bones are in the bridge. Do you call this a life, living on mice and scraps, starving for company?

So Nick came back. Taking his revenge.

His terrible revenge.

A ghost haunting ghosts.

You still don't understand, do you? We're people. It was as a person, alive, clothed in human flesh, that I fought him.

Did you win?

271

The Sacred Lodge, London Bridge
Tuesday, 15 June 1381

How I love you. I love you all.

Listen, I'll put it quickly and simply so you'll see these people, my family, more clearly than they ever saw themselves. As you've guessed, Tom married Sophia Wayer (elder of those beautiful twin sisters, you remember) in St Mary Overie Church on the Feast of St Ambrose in the spring of 1290, when they were both twenty years old (not a hasty courtship, *I* don't think Tom could make up his mind between the two girls), and so you see Richard watching his son married where long ago he himself had married Liza. (He never got over Liza's death, always spoke of her with the threat of tears.) Agnes, also widowed, stood half a pace behind him, her hair white, but she had been as good as a mother to Tom, and almost as good as Liza (though Richard would not admit it) at attracting customers to the counter.

John Wayer, drunk as ever, gave Sophia away and his other daughter, Elise (remember those olive-brown eyes, her cheeks heated as red as Tom's own?) wound spring flowers in her long sandy-golden hair and was the first, after the bride, to kiss the groom and weep. I know how she felt, I'd be the same. She was the passionate one, whereas Sophia was clever, quick and neat. I'm sure everyone felt Sophia would organise the shop, and organise Tom, and in due course organise their children better, and keep Tom's nose to the grindstone. He had a slightly wild streak, like Elise.

Now, Sophia was a good wife to Tom. Their first and only son was born on St Peter's Day, the twenty-ninth of June 1293, and Sophia's screams in labour (Elise attending her, that's my girl, not afraid of getting her hands wet) drifted through the thick walls of the Bridge Chapel while Brother Hom read the morning lesson, Ezekiel 3, verses 4 to 15, as always on this date, and the screams went on until the tribulations of Job were completed by the chanting priests. 'Never again,' Sophia gasped as her baby was handed to her.

'That's what they all say,' Elise murmured wisely, 'until it happens again, *I* don't know how.'

'Never again,' Sophia repeated. She meant it. She organised her life completely, though Tom (rather confusingly, if you ask me) chose to name his son Richard like his grandfather. Sophia had no more children. What Tom thought about it I don't know . . . but of course I do know, because *if* it happened that Tom, much as he loved his cool wife, bumped into her trusted, hot-hearted, hot-headed sister Elise who enfolded him in her thighs and breasts and rode him like a stallion on her bed behind the river window three storeys above the Weighbridge . . . *if* . . . then I would have, as they say, a bird's-eye view of both the *flagrante* and the *delicto*, wouldn't I?

Not that it's any of *my* business.

Except that they are my business. I know you all, you're all my family. I watch over you.

On the eleventh of July 1301, my darling Richard Mason (they called him Dickon), eight years old, left his school in Southwark and walked home for lunch which dear Sophia had already laid out on a plate as usual, bread, cheese, an onion in the middle, for her boy to eat behind the counter while she was busy

272

with the lunchtime trade. Then he would return to the St Mary Overie school for his afternoon lessons from Father Roger. She worked busily, keeping an eye out for him. But Dickon had stopped to play on the drawbridge, put his satchel over one shoulder, and swung from a beam. Something happened. A thousand people were passing, the bridge was thronged as usual at this hour, but no one saw quite what it was, a gull swept down, or a dog barked suddenly, or the wind blew . . . Dickon lost his grip, fell into the river, drowned. Sophia waited anxiously. It was a hot day and slowly the butter she had put by her son's bread softened, the cup of milk turned sour. I remember seeing Sophia staring back along the bridge. Staring while she dealt with customers. Her rising panic. I remember her running to the drawbridge where the crowd stood.

Richard's body was carried by the tide to Queenhithe, dropped on the sand there. The coroner's jury inspected the body, found no injury, suspected no one of the boy's death except the accident, and returned a verdict of mischance.

But *I* saw the poor little corpse, dried, dressed, his hair combed, carried back across London Bridge for burial at St Mary Overie. *I* saw the tiny gash on the forefinger of his right hand such as any boy may get in play . . . or from the beak of a bird. A gull perhaps.

Nothing else happened. Perhaps I was imagining it. Except that I have learnt that I imagine nothing. Everything is real.

Sophia walked beside the corpse of her son, staring. She worked at the counter listlessly, suddenly filled with life, stared back along the bridge as though expecting her son's running footsteps. I feel her pain. Such pain that I know evil is at the root of it. I know accidents don't happen. Choice happens, whether it's the cry of a gull or the bark of a dog or a gust of wind. It's all choice, somewhere, somehow. Why? I know the reason.

He's here. He'll hurt me any way he can.

Sophia faded away. I watched her. Her eyes grew larger, the bones appeared under her skin, her hair hung lank, brown, unwashed. No one could have been a better husband than Tom to her, more considerate, more caring, more loving of her. It was not enough. I knew she lived in such pain that she would die. I knew it takes a long time to die of a broken heart. It took nearly a year. I suffered almost as much as she did, I think. That, too, was meant to be. In fact that was Nick's point.

There's nothing I can do to assuage their pain, or mine. I'm helpless.

Tom buried his wife next to his son in the churchyard. He was inconsolable. Agnes died later in the year, from an infection of the blood, I believe she pricked herself with a needle, an accident. But I *know* what I know. She died quickly, only two or three days, but agonisingly. Nothing anyone could do.

Damn you, Nick. Stop.

But life isn't like that, is it? Life goes on, as they say. It was only a glance between Elise and Tom, I saw them pass in the street, but I know exactly what glances mean, and *I* knew how she meant to console him. The Church doesn't allow a man to marry the sister of his dead wife, but Tom would have married Elise if he could. He needed a wife, his house was too large even with the side west of the street let out to the Duponts, and he needed help with the business, and Elise, being a weigher's daughter, could count and do arithmetic. Then John Wayer died of drink, Elise lost her room, and what was more natural than she should move in as Tom's housekeeper? Keeper of his bed, that is. Elise knew how to make Tom happy, and soon no one remembered Sophia – or rather, in a way Elise had become Sophia as well, a broad-beamed, passionate Sophia, hot with life and love, half a dozen babies in half a dozen years, and twins in the seventh. By then Elise was almost forty years old, her cheerful, beaming face as round and red as an apple, her broad apron as white as goose feathers, her children waddling around her like goslings. I almost forget their names – James was the eldest.

Then there was Dick, then Sara – no, I think she was older than Dick – and William who everyone called Will (who came to a bad end I hear but do not know, twenty or thirty years later, I believe, on the end of a hemp rope at Tyburn gallows; our family doesn't talk of it but of course the Ladlers and the Swinerts do, though they have more than a skeleton or two in their own cupboard, if you ask me). Then there was Robert who squinted but was so strong, and Bartholomew who never did anything much with his life, worked in one cookshop or another, served in Southwark in the bishop's household, married and drifted away I know not where. The eldest twin was Elena, Tom's favourite because she was nimble and quick like he remembered Sophia, and last was Bess who made three bad marriages. These children had childhoods as happy as any I know; strange how their lives turned out so different, and they grew up so different each from the other too. Sara married the glover and had thirteen children, Dick took to the bottle and a soldier's life. Robert studied to be a monk and was eventually a prior in Essex, at Tiptree, I hear. He never married of course, but a hundred years later I saw a man cross London Bridge with exactly the same sort of squint and colour of eyes as long-ago celibate Robert – as though I had by chance seen some illegitimate grandson or great-grandson and glimpsed a love story about a long-dead man, a story that I shall never know. There are so many of them. James followed Tom's trade and took over the tools (the cult of the firstborn is by now well-established, following the royal example, despite our closeness to Kent) and, when the Duponts' lease ran out, took over the west side of the house too. He married Margaret Ladler (later Margaret's younger brother Humphrey married Elena) and then James was followed by seven sons, only two surviving him, and two daughters. The youngest, loveliest, was Catherine.

Catherine was clever and quick, so you know how much Tom thought of her. He was severely afflicted in the joints by a lifetime of hard work and weather, and young Catherine supported his elbow as they walked through the Conduit beneath the Stone Gate, beggars who had lost limbs or sight limping and hobbling beside them, hands outstretched if they had hands. The Keeper of the Dogs by this time was Edmund Bedell. The dogs, black mastiffs with chests as big as a man's, dragged on taut leashes, snapping and growling at the beggars. Edmund called out, 'Don't give 'em any money here, Tom, I'll never get rid of 'em.' Foam dripped from the dogs' mouths.

But Tom stopped by one fellow with stumps for legs. I saw it. The dog closest to him, excited, leapt up and tore at Catherine's face. The injuries inflicted by dogs are almost as bad as those inflicted by men, I saw her face drop ragged from her skull on to her breasts, her breasts drip blood from the claws of the beast. Tom took his knife to the dog's throat, it lay dying. But it was at me it looked, the black cat on the parapet. I saw into the beast's eyes. I saw no dog there, only evil. Nick. I was his victim. Not Catherine. He cared nothing for her, whether she lived or died. It was me he hurt.

Oh, Catherine. Our pain had hardly begun.

She survived.

Why does God tolerate our world? Why are we allowed? There's no more reason for us than there is reason for love. Give me peace, let there be just Heaven and earth. Let me rest.

I have no peace, I can't rest. I hate Nick, I never loved him. But I can be like him. I can be worse than him somehow.

I'll fight Nick. I'll hurt him. But I can't. He has nothing, loves no one, *is* nothing. Should I have scratched out the eyes of the poor dying dog in my revenge?

274

No, no!

Catherine endured. Many years later I saw her often, an old woman, her face a mask of scars. She terrified children. At night, kissing them goodnight, mothers whispered that the white-faced woman would take away children who had not been good. The children stoned her and she rarely came out. The Bible, I hear, in Exodus tells us plainly that thou shalt not suffer a witch to live. Now that the Bible is read in English such truths are commonplace, and learned professors and ignorant commoners both rise up against the kings who govern them and the Pope who cares for their souls. In fact there are two Popes, one in Avignon and the other in Rome, and it is heresy *not* to believe in witches, lenient judges are denounced as enemies of the people of God, and Bishop Oresme tells us that the earth is not fixed but wanders among the stars, and that there are universes beyond our own, so where is the truth? Slowly, and most painfully, Catherine lost her mind and was burnt to death with other women like herself in St Paul's churchyard.

And there are the rats. Some say they were brought on Templar ships from the Holy Land. The Bridge House Yard is a moving mass of rats, for years corn was stored on the bridge to keep it from them, but these days apothecary's poison no longer keeps them down and they swarm across the arches, their black fur writhing with fleas, kill the mice and invade the houses. James's son Perceval was bitten and he died; James's four other sons died of the plague that kills holy and unholy alike.

Then James sired two more sons, Arthur and George, when his wife Margaret was nearly forty, and he was the happiest man alive. Both were supposed to follow him into the trade. But the brothers fought like cat and dog as boys, and then fought as men. They fought over girls, customers, trade, ale, money, especially money, and Arthur never forgot an insult or remembered a favour. He believed his father hated him and no favour or gift from his father persuaded him otherwise. Being their eldest son, his father and mother gave him everything he could desire, gave way to him on everything, took Arthur's side against his younger brother, punished George for Arthur's sins. It was insufficient. Drunk at the Bear, his gambling debts unsettled, Arthur attacked George with the edge of his knife, was arrested by the Keeper of the Dogs but ran away. Given the temper of the times and the King a boy no older than himself, Arthur fell in with the rebels in Kent, I hear.

And so George inherited the shop only a few months later. His father died of guilt, it was said, not at his treatment of George who had so hard a time, but at losing Arthur.

The country was again at war with France so George prospered making boots. But wars must be paid for, so taxes were raised, and by the middle of this month in 1381 I saw the prisons burning in Southwark and the angry mob, led by a common tiler from Kent and a mad priest, Arthur among them, running towards the bridge. The drawbridge was raised against them and chained up by the Lord Mayor, but the ordinary people let it down again, welcomed the rebels into the City, and I saw the smoke spread along the Strand. The mob poured into the Temple – the gates had long ago been knocked down – in the popular belief that it contained a fabulous treasure. They found nothing but a few unarmed monks who called themselves the Brethren of St John and the Priory of Zion, tortured them to reveal the treasure, and beheaded them when they did not. But one witless old man, terrified by Jack Straw's threats and demented by the swinging axe – forty headless bodies lay around him in the circular church – promised to reveal the hidden treasure of the Templars. His interrogators broke his knees so he could not run away, dragged him down to the crypt. And there, they say, the old man operated a secret mechanism unused for seventy years. The altar swung aside, the floor dropped and made stairs going round and down – a winding stair leading, in the usual Templar fashion, to a second crypt below the first.

I remember Nick telling me of this place. Again, Nick had told the truth.

Listen, listen, I swear this is exactly as I overheard it from Hugh Sewell, an ordinary draper of London Bridge who was there with blood on his hands. When the rebels were being hunted down a few days later, and Wat the tiler's severed head was spiked on the Drawbridge Gate forty feet above the draper's shop, Jack Straw's head soon to be spiked beside it, Sewell lay shaking beside his wife in bed, and whispered what he had seen; they thought (like their doings in bed) that it was their secret.

'The walls was stone, that's all. There was mouldy hangings tacked to rotten wood there and here.'

My God, the maps of Jerusalem and the Golden Line in true proportion – and this fool did not know what he had seen!

'Most of the room was taken up with paper, that's all. A huge great pile of rotting paper higher'n my head.'

Codes, instructions, records, locations of the Templar treasures, all there had never been time to ship away, everything abandoned that Friday morning seventy-four years ago. If only one of those idiots had been able to read! Everything they dreamt of was within their grasp.

'Our lad Straw, him and Arthur Mason, they knew what to do with that stuff. Burnt it.'

So I begin to wonder, and I believe everything that seems incredible. This familiar world and even my own life, my own consciousness, Alice, me, begin to seem incredible. Once I thought I was made of Adam's rib, and perhaps that's also true. Yet also I'm simply the combination of sperm and egg, nothing more. And yet I know that I am who I am. How can this be? How can *you*?

Whatever the shape of my nose or my bones, the shade or texture of my skin or the colour of my eyes, sometimes I come down here to the undercroft beneath the Bridge Chapel where the bones lie of the body who was Alice – *and still is* – and I hear the tide rush, and watch the fishermen come in for their blessing from Brother Wodham, and sometimes I watch the masons, mostly elder men of position and influence, gather for their strange, harmless and faintly ridiculous rites.

But last night I saw Arthur run limping from the City, covered in blood, the rebels around him ridden down by the guard of Sir Robert Knollys. I saw Arthur beating on George's door with the butt of his broken axe, weeping with fear. 'Let me in! Let me in for God's mercy's sake!' And so last night I saw George open his door in reconciliation and Arthur pushed in. 'About time.' And last night I overheard Sewell whisper to his wife, and today I watch these fat, businesslike men kiss the rosy Templar cross – some educated men of the physical sciences call themselves Rosicrucians, followers of the Rosy Cross – and I hear them swear obedience to the Arch and the Lodge. I see Brother Wodham push at the altar, and it swings aside to reveal steps to a deep, narrow room beneath the undercroft. It is like the room Sewell and Nick described beneath the Temple, it is their Sacred Lodge. But here the tapestries are in good order, properly maintained and obviously repaired from the depredations of mice and other vermin.

Nick showed Durand here.

I think Nick showed Durand even more than here. Is there more?

I remember Nick telling me, *Knowledge is priceless. Knowledge is power. The order keeps everything it knows to itself.*

And still does. These men are Templars.

Nick claimed a tunnel led from the Temple to London Bridge. He claimed a tunnel followed the Golden Line joining London, Paris, Rome to the foundations of the Temple at Jerusalem, and that beneath the foundations masons had found tunnels dug from Solomon's Temple to Zion, and there found Christ sleeping. *The Lord dwells among His people.* What Christians call the indwelling God. Nick claimed to have brought His earthly body to the Temple, claimed de Prudome drew his sword and shouted, 'Truly this is the Temple of God!'

How can this be? How can evil and secrecy accomplish what goodness cannot?

Yet I believe him. Nick had struggled to be a good man, a good man doing good, and failed.

Yes, I do believe him.

In his despair he is a formidable enemy. Now I know him I see and hear him everywhere, the dog that barks, the crow that calls, the whisper of the wind in wings, the fall of a scrap of paper. Now I know that I have long been the same to him – almost all his life. The man I did not love. We are obsessed.

Are we different from anyone else? Humans seem formidably equipped to suffer, expect suffering, cope with suffering. I see it with my own eyes, more than I would believe possible. I am beside the mother who patiently comforts the death of her child. A child mourning the loss of its dog, I'm there. I've seen a man with four lovely children and a loving wife, and the plague came into his house, and all lay dead on the third morning. I am there

The prayers I hear whispered and begged in the Bridge Chapel. If only you knew. I'm there too.

And there's more. So much more.

How can this experience be leading me upward, how can my life possibly be a moral ascent leading me towards Heaven? It cannot improve me, it leads me down, I am trapped here in Hell which is where we live our lives.

And I see.

I see Arthur Mason – you remember the two brothers who fought, Arthur and George, then the day came when George saved Arthur's life, took him into his house, gave him wine and bread, his own bed to sleep in? Did I tell you that next morning Arthur drank more wine, ate bread and meat, then took more meat, more wine, until he was drunk and filled with jealousy for his young brother's house and happiness, and contempt for his trade and hard work? 'House should be mine,' I heard Arthur say. 'Father wanted me to have it, not you. I'm the eldest.' And there it might have ended in blows again; Arthur's dagger was quick as his temper and he was ruthless, there's a hatch in the floor where water was drawn up from the river, easy to dump George's body down with stones in its pockets where it might never be found. But that didn't happen. I think the future changes. Their mother Margaret, so recently widowed that her face was still gaunt with grief, saw what was coming and shouted from the stair.

'Stop!'

'It was him!' Arthur said. 'Whatever he tells you it's a lie.' He held out his arms. 'I love you, Mother. I've come back.'

'You're no good,' Margaret said. 'Your father and I did our best. You were born the wrong way out and you'll be wrong until the day you die.'

Arthur shouted, 'You wouldn't dare say that if Father was here!'

'God bless you, and get out of this house.' She turned her back on him.

George said, 'Mother, we can forgive him.'

Margaret's voice came implacably. 'I wouldn't forgive myself if we did.'

Arthur's lips trembled, and for a moment I really thought he would strike his mother between her shoulder blades. Then he strode from the house, slammed the door.

I saw him often after that. Arthur wouldn't leave the bridge, wouldn't leave them. He kept George in his eye. George prospered, and Arthur set up with some girl near Bridge Foot, then in one of the old hovels shattered and left derelict by the rebels, near the Stone Gate. He found a new girl who worked as a prostitute, so by her he made ends meet, and then he moved in with her little sister and lived off both of them. He was mostly drunk – their room stank like a pit – but when he was sober he was quite clever, generous with clothes too, and both girls as they grew up thought they could bring him round. Each worked six months of the year, being too visible with child for their trade during the other six months, and Arthur took their babies and tied them in sacks with stones, and dropped them from the bridge. I daresay their little souls would have damned him if they could, but there is no justice in the world. Had men caught him, no doubt they would have done the same to him, but they never did. He told the sisters he sold the babes to childless noblewomen, and then he was generous with clothes, and so they believed him. Then the young girl died and I heard the other one say, 'Now we can get wed, Arthur.'

'You're an ugly old bastard,' he said. 'Get out of here.'

'You got the Devil in you,' she swore, and he grinned. So did she. Something in us likes our men with a touch of the devil in them.

'This is what you want in *you*,' Arthur said, knelt, parted her legs which were scaly with yesterday's stains. She lay back thinking he wanted to have her. I'm not sure if he killed her, I never saw. But I never saw her again.

So Arthur took up with Moll, an ale-girl, one of Lizzie Brewer's daughters, most brewers are women. Arthur drank, and watched out for George. He blamed George for turning their mother against him, probably blamed George for everything that had gone wrong. Sometimes I saw Arthur sitting well back from his tumbledown doorway, in the shadows, drinking and watching the street go by, and George would go by, and I don't think he ever knew Arthur was there. But Arthur watched him with his eyes wide in the shadows, dazzled by the light, and George always walked by looking so fine. He had the family trait that one or other of my descendants, I forget which, called 'a touch of flourish'. Twenty years old, with curly blond hair and moustache, about to wed Jacqueline Dupont (three years older than he was, her second marriage, her first husband died of the plague, well-off), I call George a walking advertisement for his trade. He wore the long shoes called *poulaines*, beautiful work, so extravagant that they were barely within the law. Tight woollen leggings (he had good legs) led up to a short tunic, a little shorter each year. Once I saw George pause as if sensing the weight of Arthur's silent contempt from the shadows, but then new business hurried him away.

George used Jacqueline's money to take on a couple of old jobbing cobblers in the back room while he put on finishing touches at the counter and flattered the customers. Jacqueline (her mother was Alice Swinert) put on weight, she had a lovely, warm-hearted, buxom figure, cared only for her children, and left the trade to George downstairs. Her first daughter, Bonny, turned out with her mother's chestnut hair and George's curls. Then their son Clement had the wide blue eyes I know girls will fall for – *I* did, long ago (Jack, I still miss you). The third child, their second daughter, they would not name at first, the mite was not expected to live and names can be so painful, then they called her Lauretta because she was so small.

One night, from the rooftops, I saw something I did not understand at the time.

It was summer, fireflies everywhere, which are the unbaptised souls of dead infants, and the call of the Keeper of the Dogs for the darkest hour of the night. High tide, set flat calm about the bridge like a black mirror. And I saw Arthur walk from the Stone Gate to the chapel, stumbling sometimes as though unsure of his purpose. Once he lay down to sleep but almost immediately rose to his

278

feet and walked steadily forward. I thought he was drunk but he didn't sway like a drunk man. Then I thought he was sleepwalking, he seemed to struggle with himself, and yet somewhere inside himself some part of him wanted to do exactly as he was doing. As if by night he fulfilled a secret desire his mind would not admit by day.

He fell over the chapel step and lay there like a drunk man. A couple of men hurrying home ignored him.

Arthur rose smoothly to his feet and crossed to where I am sure he wanted to go. Crossed the Square. Stopped at George's door.

Arthur stayed there without moving while the fireflies drifted and whirled about him on the occasional breeze. Was he dreaming? Perhaps he had lost his mind. A bell clanged the hour, he raised his arm as though to bang on the door, then turned back. He stopped by the chapel steps looking for all the world like a man listening to a voice inside his head. There are many like him in time of wars and plagues, poor fellows, you see them living rough in doorways and shacks, unable to care for themselves or others; like, I now realise, my own father. For the first time I felt sorry for Arthur, the black sheep of my family, sorry to see him reduced to such a state. I watched him nod like a sleepy horse snuffling for its nosebag of oats which it knows is somewhere near its head. Arthur actually reached out his hands as if to grasp the prize that tormented his sleep. Then abruptly he returned to the alehouse, ducked under the blanket hung over the doorway, crawled into the greasy straw with Moll. Nine months later his son Nicholas was born and I dreaded that he, too, would be tied in a bag with stones; but Arthur sat peacefully cross-legged on the dirt floor, his tiny baby son curled pale, pink, vulnerable in his filthy hairy arms, and I saw Arthur put his mouth close and kiss, tenderly, the baby's head.

A month later I watched them asleep together, the tiny baby asleep in his huge father's strong, protective arms, Arthur twitching and grunting in his dreams. Moll pushed into the back room, a curl of hair over her face, a tankup of beer in her hand. 'You're going soft, you are,' she swore.

'I was soft before,' Arthur murmured, waking. 'I didn't know it, that's all.'

Moll looked alarmed. 'Bless me, you are,' she said. 'Give me my baby back.'

'You wake him,' Arthur said, 'I'll break your shoulders.'

'There's paying customers out front what need keeping in hand. They'll steal everything I got.'

Arthur looked at his baby. It moved in its sleep and he slipped the tip of his little finger between its lips as though giving it milk. Moll hesitated jealously, held out her hands. 'Here. I'll do it, you haven't got what it takes.'

Arthur thought about it. 'A baby needs its mother at this age,' he decided. He pulled down the top of her dress, pushed his son to the nipple.

'No, Arthur, I know you, don't, get out front with you,' Moll said. 'Stop looking at me.' She let her other breast out. 'I know what you're thinking,' she said eagerly. But she realised that for the first time she *didn't* know what Arthur was thinking; Arthur got quietly to his feet, covered her naked side and left through the river door, walked away along the parapet rather than pass through the front room, and she wouldn't see him again that night.

The baby changed everything. Arthur was a changed man. *I* know where he went. He went into the chapel and threw himself down on the echoing floor, his hands clasped over his head, a penitent.

A few nights later Moll came into the chapel. 'Lizzie said it was you. I didn't believe it.' She waited, then spoke again. 'Are you all right?' She knelt, tugged him. 'Arthur?' Her eyes filled with tears and she sounded afraid. 'What's got into you? Come back to me.'

'Did you leave my son alone in the house?'

279

'Of course I left it alone, what else?' She gasped as Arthur took her wrists in his hands, squeezed gently. He was easily strong enough to break her arms, and she knew he would.

'Look after my son.'

She looked into his eyes. No one looked away when Arthur wanted their attention. 'I will, Arthur.'

'You'll look after him, won't you, Moll? You'll bring him up.'

'Yes, Arthur, I will.'

Arthur said, 'And then, one day, when he's old enough, I'll come for him. Your job will be done and you can go back to being a whore or a slut or whatever you are. Unless I have a better use for you.'

'I only want a bit of love,' she said. Then she said obediently, 'Yes, Arthur.'

He patted her rump, in chapel too, a flash of the old Arthur. 'Off you go now, you saucy bitch.'

Moll looked back from the door. Arthur was prostrate in prayer. 'It won't last,' she told herself.

But it did last. One day, at dawn, a cold day, I saw Arthur stand on the drawbridge. He took a length of wood and touched his forehead with it. Then again. Again. The wood began to make a tapping sound on his forehead. Arthur's skin flushed. A crowd gathered as he banged the wood hard against his head, striking himself until the blood ran into his eyes. The blood dripped from his chin.

Then he stopped.

Arthur returned to the chapel, threw himself down, prayed.

The next day Arthur took a horsewhip to the drawbridge. You sometimes see such people there, they are called the flagellants. Priests try to stop them, the flagellant masters claim to intercede between God and Man, as priests do. That is the job of priests. But the common people believe that priests are sent by Rome to rule us, and charge us for every prayer, and for last rites, and charge more in a crisis, or for turning out at night, and pass round their silver offertory grails at every opportunity, and drink Communion wine from gold cups, and a woman or a child is not safe alone with a priest. That is why the common people, though they believe in God, believe far less in priests, and I hear the Priory of St Mary was burnt, and the bishop of somewhere imprisoned in his cathedral, and in one place only seven friars out of one hundred and sixty survived the plague, and the common people considered that seven too many. By contrast the people treat the flagellants with reverence, for the flagellant shows by his suffering, or hers – sometimes they dance in penitential circles together – that he or she is closer to God. They say it is God. They say they bleed for God. Their blood atones for human wickedness, they say.

Arthur whipped his body until the blood ran from his ribs.

The women wound garlands in their hair and screamed when they saw a priest as though they saw the Devil. People possessed by devils were brought to the flagellants, exorcised. The crowd shared in the exorcisms, sensing the presence of evil. Priests, too, began to perform exorcisms, seeing the people wanted them and would pay.

Arthur lay on the floor of the chapel. A hand touched the back of his head, the ringed fingers turned Arthur's bearded, bloodied face up, his lips still moving in prayer. Brother Darenth murmured, 'What can I do to help you, my son?'

An offer not of prayers but of real help.

Without opening his eyes Arthur said clearly, 'I am a raper of women and men. I am a killer of babies. I have beheaded priests and important men while they screamed for mercy and I dipped my hands in their blood.'

'Do you wish to confess?'

'No.' Arthur's eyes opened. 'I have tried to find love.'

'Have you found love?'

'Yes. I love my son.'

'Do you ask for sanctuary?'

Arthur sat up slowly. 'I ask for what is impossible.'

'Forgiveness is not impossible.'

'No,' Arthur said. 'I ask for shelter.'

'Such gifts are from the Bridge Masters,' Brother Darenth murmured. 'Master John Hoo, and Master Henry Yevele. Do you have money?'

'No. You know who I am.'

'Yes,' Brother Darenth murmured, then moved his fingers slowly in Arthur's matted hair. 'I know who you are. And you are welcome.'

Arthur was always to be seen in the chapel after that, sweeping the straw, his ragged, long-haired figure cleaning the silver candlesticks and grails with fine sand. He acquired a reputation as something of a holy man, a recluse. No task was too small or too dirty for him. When the bellrope broke he made the dangerous climb up the tower, clinging to the top of the swaying bell, and re-knotted the cord. The chapel was being rebuilt in the modern style at this time, very complex and ornate, the windows enlarged almost to the roof, glowing with saints' heads and heraldic shields.

The staircase to the undercroft was renewed and Arthur was often to be found down there, alone, working quietly, binding the chapel's service books or about some other business. As his skill and dedication grew, he covered the chant books in new red skin and ornamented their great brass clasps, even sewed the eight buttons with silk tassels. The cross was covered with fine linen cloth when not in use to keep it clean and pure, and he draped the altar with white samite.

He must have known about the altar right from the start.

There they are, the two brothers, the imposing bearded figure of Arthur standing watchfully on the chapel steps overlooking the Square. I remember it was a bright sunny day, Lammas Day, the first of August 1393. The crowd parted and George came into view between the sign of the roper's shop and the porridge pot, walking home from church across London Bridge, his open hands shepherding his two young daughters in front of him like geese (doesn't that remind me of someone else, Elise was it, who used to shepherd her children in exactly the same way, with exactly the same mannerisms? George never knew his grandmother but his cheerful face is as red as Tom's, long ago.) Beside George, not half a step behind, walked Jacqueline his wife, plump, plainly dressed, devout. Young Clement, seven years old, had his hand firmly held. Jacqueline was stricter than her husband and did not allow Clement to run ahead like the girls. She was afraid of losing him.

Within the year, I now know, all three children will not be alive.

The girls ran forward to look at the fashionable sugary confections in one of the new bow windows, later so popular on London Bridge because they project over the road and grab trade yet do not contravene the Master's regulations concerning the blocking of the highway. I heard the girls' trilling voices, Bonny was eight and Lauretta only five, but she was more my sort, pretty, scowling, wilful, determined. Their trilling voices and the dull, wet, sliding thunder of the river below.

'Please, Father! Please!' They asked Father because Mother would say no.

George laughed, reached into his roeskin pouch.

'No,' Mother said firmly. 'Husband, you'll spoil them.'

Clement, trapped by her hand, stared with wide eyes at the full quivers in the arrowsmith's. Once, the arrows had been made on the premises but these days they were turned out somewhere cheap and dirty in Southwark and only sold on the bridge. Mother let him go and someone pushed Clement to steal his belt or the clasp of his little cloak. He ran, caught his mother up, clung to her plain gown. George bought some sticky thing and the children took turns licking it. 'People will think we're rich,' Jacqueline scolded him.

'No one's watching us,' George said. 'No one cares.'

But Clement saw the man standing on the chapel steps watching them, tall, thin, bearded, clad in coarse cloth patiently darned. He watched them with eyes of dark blue. A passing straw cart sent yellow flecks flying in the wind and others blinked their eyes and turned away, but that commanding gaze did not flicker. 'Father, who is he?'

Father followed his eyes. 'No one. It's no one.'

Mother said, 'Don't talk to him.' They crossed the Square pretending not to notice Arthur. 'Don't look at him, Clement.' But Clement couldn't help looking, and then the girls stopped too.

'George Mason,' Arthur called across the heads of the crowd. 'Why don't you worship here at the chapel in your own parish as you should? Aren't we good enough for you?'

George was shamed into stopping. In truth he didn't know why he walked to St Mary Overie; his father had. There was some ruckus in the crowd, a fallen horse; he was grateful the shouting voices prevented him answering. He looked away, shepherded his family forward with his open hands. But Arthur stood in front of him.

'I've forgiven you, George. I've forgiven all of you.'

'Leave us alone.' George stepped forward, but Arthur did not step back. His emaciated figure had an intense ragged authority that left George looking merely plump and prosperous. George tried to make the best of it, a social meeting. 'This is my wife.'

'I know.' The eyes glanced at Jacqueline, returned to George.

George shepherded the children towards his doorway.

Arthur nodded at them as they passed. 'Bonny. Clement. Lauretta.' He knew their names. Bonny giggled, she was always the silly one.

In bed that night Jacqueline said, 'You'll have to get on with him. It's so embarrassing. He's your brother.'

'No, I won't get on with him, I'm not embarrassed by him, and I don't regard him as my brother.'

Jacqueline made the sound in her throat that says *men*. 'I thought he was rather handsome.'

'Don't be silly.'

'He's not my sort. Did you see the way he looked at me?'

George sighed irritably, he had to be up at dawn. 'They say he hasn't touched a woman for years. He lives like a priest.'

Jacqueline was interested. 'I can't believe that.'

George and Jacqueline turned over away from one another as though Arthur lay between them. Their marriage was not perfect. Both felt injured, both worked hard to make up. But *I* think, it was so easy for Arthur, wasn't it? It only took a few moments, but the damage hatred does takes weeks for love to repair.

Within the year, as I said, as Jacqueline fell pregnant for the fourth time, young Clement was killed by a table being winched up through Sergeant East's window in the Stone Gate. The rope broke, people shouted but the falling table struck the boy a glancing blow, killed him instantly. The rope was found frayed, chewed by rats perhaps. East, a gentleman, paid compensation to George and employed a novice priest to do penance.

A few months before the baby was born, Bonny fell asleep on Saturday evening and did not wake on Sunday morning. Dead of I know not what.

She stopped breathing. Death needs no reason, though humans always try to find one, and the coroner wrote in Coroners' Rolls that the child 'met a death that was her natural death', and George on his knees in St Mary Overie Church muttered that it was God's will.

'How can God *will* my little girl should die?' Jacqueline burst out. 'God is *good*.'

George didn't know how he could comfort her; he needed comforting himself. 'It happens,' he said doggedly. 'It's not for us to try to understand.'

'If we'd worshipped in the Bridge Chapel it wouldn't have happened,' Jacqueline decided, and nothing would persuade her otherwise. In its misery the mighty Church that we once knew splits into sects like a falling building splitting into separate stones, Lollard priests are burnt and excommunicated for living in poverty and preaching it, there are Bibles everywhere.

A month before the baby was due, Lauretta, small, determined Lauretta, my favourite, was gone. She followed some boys, all bridge boys, good boys, down through the undercroft of the chapel and out through the little door high in the wall, on to the massive starling of the Chapel Pier. Long ago a pond was dug in the starling and an iron grid laid over it, so that fish which swam in at high tide, when the starling was deep below the surface, could not escape as the tide fell. Watching the trapped fish fascinated the children as much as catching them, shad, smelts, eels often, salmon and pike occasionally, and sometimes their eager pointing fingers identified sea fish floundering in the brackish pool, plaice, haddock, a sole. The pilings were thickly encrusted with mussels and some of the children carried baskets to collect them, sent by their mothers, and sometimes prawns could be enticed from cracks in the stones. One boy swore he saw Lauretta with a mussel basket but Jacqueline, pale as death and great with child, insisted she was too young. Where was the truth? The only truth was this: that Lauretta was gone, and no one saw her go, and her body was never found, and the Coroners' Rolls recorded a natural death by drowning.

'A natural death!' Jacqueline cried on her knees in the chapel, her face wet, her hands like claws on the rail. 'How *can* death be natural?'

Brother Darenth muttered the words of comfort then was called away, and the chapel fell silent but for her cries. Cool hands touched Jacqueline's head from behind, gripped her skull gently, stroked her hair.

'Cry, child, cry,' Arthur said, kneeling beside her. 'I know it hurts. I've lost children of my own.'

He stroked Jacqueline until she was quiet. She slipped to one side on her knees, her belly looking big enough to burst. 'Life dies,' he murmured. 'Life is born again.'

'I don't want it,' she murmured. 'I don't want my baby, I can't bear it to be born. I can't bear it to die.'

He put his ragged arms round her. 'Poor Jacqueline. I know.'

That evening she returned to her house and found George sitting alone at the table. They had no family, no one except George's mother upstairs. The house was deathly silent. Then George jumped up, his bowl and pewter spoon clattering. 'Where have you been? We've been worried sick about you!' *We*, Jacqueline noted, not *I*. Arthur had warned her that George listened to his mother more than he did to his wife.

She sat with a groan. Nothing was comfortable for her now, standing, lying down, sitting, her back ached and the hours she'd knelt had grazed her knees. But she did feel better, calmer inside herself. 'You know,' she said, 'you can't keep on being so silly about your brother. People are beginning to think it's your fault. You'll have to make up with him.'

A voice spoke from the stairs. Margaret had come down without either of them hearing, her white hair knotted in a bun, her scrawny hands clasped in front of her. 'Arthur is no longer my son. I disowned him years ago, before we even knew you. Don't talk of what you don't understand, girl. It's a family matter.'

'You're on her side,' Jacqueline told George.

'It's not a matter of sides,' George said reasonably. He touched Jacqueline's tummy fondly. 'We still have a family. You'll have a son.'

Jacqueline looked at Margaret. Yes, if she had a son the family name would go on.

'Arthur has a son,' she said.

'Arthur's not married,' Margaret scoffed. 'It's not his. I've heard it's just an ale seller's brat, the girl's a shrew. He's never even seen it.' She put her hand on George's shoulder. 'I'm sure she'll give you a boy.'

Jacqueline went into labour that night – from grief, chatted the women who came round to help and drink and talk through the night – and George was banished to the attic room. At dawn when he got up, there was no word, Child's wife lay snoring with her head against Peyton's wife, so he went down to the shop room and worked, and it was afternoon before his mother came down.

'You'd better come up,' Margaret told him, and fear gripped George by his guts.

'What's wrong?'

She said nothing. George ran upstairs trying to pull his leather work apron off, it would not come off, the knot had jammed, and he stumbled into his wife's room cursing the apron. She lay against the pillow with the babe in her arms.

'Sssh,' she said.

George tiptoed to the bed. 'He's got my eyes,' he said.

'George,' she sighed. Neither of them noticed the mouse in the corner hungrily nibbling a stale crust.

George boomed, 'What a lot of hair he's got. He's got your hair, it's chestnut!' He never could be stopped once he'd started something, my George. He looked delighted.

'George,' Jacqueline said firmly. 'Listen.'

'He's a fat baby, isn't he? How much does he weigh?'

'He isn't a *he*, that's what I've been trying to tell you. Look.'

George stared. He grinned. His new girl wrapped her fingers round his thumb, her blue gaze gleamed at him through her fine brown curls.

'We've got a family again,' Jacqueline murmured. 'I'm going to give her my mother's name. I've called her Alice.'

Getting clumsily on her knees in the Bridge Chapel, Jacqueline gave thanks for the birth of her healthy baby daughter. It was evening and the figure of Christ on the Cross was draped with its white linen shroud ready for the night.

Arthur watched her from the entrance to the bell turret. His teeth showed as he grinned. It was raining and the rain made a pleasant cold sound down the darkening stained windows. At last Jacqueline got to her feet and put up her hood against the rain as she went out. Because he did not move, she did not see him.

Arthur lived in a small stone cell set in the wall between the turret and the chapel doors. It was barely longer than he was as he lay down on the matted straw, his pillow a piece of wood and his blanket woven from nettle. As darkness fell he closed his eyes and slept.

He slept, and dreamt.

He dreamt that he awoke.

He dreamt that he sat up.

The blanket slipped from Arthur's shoulders and he shivered. There was something he had forgotten. He got to his feet and went to the main door, the chapel silent but for the rain. He opened the door and the sound of the rain redoubled. He turned back to his cell for something he could not quite remember. His blanket, he didn't want to catch his death of cold. He wrapped the blanket round his shoulders and stood on the chapel steps in the rain. The rain had swollen the river and added its weight to the ebb tide, his bare feet tingled with the vibration of the bridge and the chapel. He heard a voice.

'Yes?' he replied. 'What do you want?'

Arthur walked through the rain sheeting along the roadway towards one of the few lights still showing, the Hoop alehouse. The door was shut. He pressed against the wood with the flats of his hands. He said nothing. He put his head against the door, the rain beat on his back. A woman's voice called, 'Who's there?'

'It's me.'

'You all say that. Get off, I'm closed.'

'Moll,' he said. 'Moll. Moll.'

The door opened. Straw clung to Moll's hair, one of her eyes was closed, the place stank of spilt ale and unwashed skin. 'I thought we weren't good enough for you,' she said.

Arthur came inside. 'Have you looked after him?'

She spat at him as she retreated. 'No thanks to you.' Her face changed. 'You've come back for him.'

'Where is he?'

She shook her head, but her eyes flickered to the corner where the steps were. Upstairs, in the attic probably. 'Don't, Arthur. He's all I got.'

Arthur looked around him. 'I told you I'd come for him one day.'

She got between him and the corner, threw her arms round him. 'Give me a squeeze, Arthur, like you used to. I miss you.'

He looked at her upturned throat, caressed it with his thumb.

'What's the matter with you?' she said. 'Don't hurt me.'

He looked her in the eyes. 'I've seen my death,' he said.

She shrank, made herself laugh, then said, 'That's my Arthur. I never did know what you was thinking.'

Arthur went to the steps. 'You're right about this place. It's not good enough.' He pulled a leather bag from his belt, tossed it. Moll gauged it to the penny by its weight in her hand. She looked horrified.

'God's wounds,' she said. 'Where'd you get this?'

'Stole it. The offertory grail.'

She called after him, 'I thought you were a saint now. Saint Arthur of London Bridge, you are. Suppose the priest finds out what you were up to?'

Arthur glanced down as though the answer was obvious. 'The priest helped me steal it.'

Moll laughed. Arthur jumped down, seized her hair, pushed his face close. 'Listen to me. Count it. I want you to look after him proper good. I want him in the bath house, hair cut, nails cut, I want him in good clothes. Nothing showy. Neat. Look after him, be proud.'

Tears trickled white lines down her face. 'I been a good mother to him, Arthur. I worked hard.'

'You're a good girl, Moll. Look after yourself. The bath house for you too, and one set of good clothes.'

'Neat, not showy. I will, Arthur.'

'But the best for my boy.'

'Yes, Arthur.'

'And clean this midden up. Get a girl to do it, not one of your whores, get rid of them. Hold one good girl back to keep you company. No more drinking.'

'Yes, Arthur.' She did love him, he had something about him. *I've seen my death.* She shuddered.

Arthur winked, touched her cheek with his knuckle as though he remembered she loved him, and climbed to the first floor. He opened several tiny rooms before finding the rickety wooden stairs at the back, built overhanging the river, and climbed silently on bare feet to the tiny crooked attic. The boy lay curled in the corner, half awake, half asleep. About nine years old. Old enough.

Arthur knelt beside him. 'Hello, Nicholas. You know who I am.'

The boy blinked sleepily. His voice was deep and slow with sleep. 'Mother said you'd come. Why did you leave me?' He seemed to wake a little more, his eyes filled with tears, anxious, impatient. 'Why don't you stay like the other boys' fathers?'

Arthur laid his hands on the boy's head. 'I can't stay. Come with me. There's so much more I have to show you.'

The boy spoke again in his strangely deep voice, blinking sleepily.

'Father, you can't show me anything that I don't know.'

Alice! My own name! I'm so pleased, I think it's the first time it's happened in my family for more than two hundred years, though it's such a popular name. Alice. I can't help taking an interest in her – I was there when she was born, as you saw. Being there when they come into the world always makes them special.

I saw Alice take her first breath. I heard her named. Look at her, those chestnut curls, those innocent round blue eyes. A beautifully made machine for living, a blank page, a child. Her experiences and the codes in her blood – I even sense my own! – will write her life. And the chances she takes. And the choices she makes.

Baby Alice is baptised by Brother Darenth at the black marble font in the chapel, and Alice is now a Christian.

Alice, my girl, can you hear me?

Nothing, only the dull background babble of voices, emotion, feeling that is always with us.

Does she have a soul? Doesn't everyone?

In a few weeks Alice's eyes focus and she notices the mouse. At first it moves too fast for her to see, but she learns. Soon her eyes follow the mouse and she learns to smile. She recognises her mother and smiles because Jacqueline loves her to, remembers her own childhood in her daughter's smile, wants Alice to be happy; as do we all.

Watching Alice makes me remember, too. Through her, I remember my own life vividly, and everything I've forgotten leaps into prominence. I remember my childish innocence, seeing things for the first time. The hugeness and greenness of trees, huger and greener than any I've seen since. Watching her, I see the marvel of a single fly buzzing round and round the room on a summer's day. I feel her pleasure and curiosity at crawling in front of winter's fire – a brick chimney has been put in – discovering everything for the first time, the fascination of a tassel on the rug, the dog's tail, a wooden toy that Alice turns clumsily at first in her hands, drops, learns to hold, learns to love.

I'm so afraid for her.

While Alice grows up from a baby to an infant, an infant to a child, a child to a young girl, growing her hair long, I die and live a hundred lives. I can't always be with her but I try, and I'm getting good at it. I have experience, I can choose what I am, I have become hardened. Almost no one has been on London Bridge as long as I have. Yet what happens still shocks me.

It's all right, Alice is safe. I couldn't bear anything to happen to her, could you? In fact she's one of those naturally lucky children and all the bad things that *could* have happened to her, didn't. You saw how George was very careless about that fire, once Alice crawled much too close to the flames, she was alone in the room, I was terrified her hair would catch fire, she'd be horribly burnt – but something caught her attention on the other side of the room, she crawled safely away, nothing happened. Once a spark landed on her gown, the wool scorched, a hole was burnt – and then went out. As soon as she saw it, Jacqueline screamed with her heart in her mouth, stuck her fist through the hole, and George would be more careful about the fire in the future. But another time *she* forgot the pot in the kitchen, bubbling and steaming fascinatingly with boiling water, and I saw Alice reach up – but her fingertips, by a hair, did not reach quite high enough to spill the scalding liquid down on her head. Then there's the traffic, always dangerous on London Bridge, carts shoving first this way then the other, but I swear Alice crawled after her ball between the horses' hooves without a scratch. And she even got her ball back. She catches colds but they never turn bad as so often happens with children. Her cuts and grazes heal, her gums are firm and pink, her teeth white.

Alice is blessed with a charmed life, it's obvious. And even as she grows up towards the difficult age, I know she will continue to be lucky because I can see she will be so very, very beautiful.

I alone saw Arthur Mason die.

It's night, the twenty-fifth of August, the very peak of the plague month, the year of Our Lord 1405, that the most shocking thing happened.

Starlit night, the moon soon to rise. The river like a snake of stars. It slides, ripples beneath the arches towards the eastern horizon, grows pale with the glow of the rising moon.

There it is, the first sliver of harvest moon, dark red, rippling like the river. Rising like a drop of blood. The rising moon elongates along its lower edge like a kiss, frees itself from the caress of the earth, takes its place among the stars and makes them dim with its stony radiance.

Everyone sleeps. The moon pulls the tide up after it, the river begins its rush upstream.

I can see Alice's window from the top of the bell turret, as always I watch over her.

Her mother makes her keep her window closed, even on the most sultry nights, for fear of the plague. Good. The moon gleams on the window glass, sends its radiance across the chapel steps.

I hear the creak of the heavy oak door.

The chapel door opens, thuds closed. A man comes down the steps, tall, thin, ragged. His long hair hides his face but I'd know him anywhere. Arthur. He walks at night sometimes. Sometimes he walks from one end of the bridge to the other. Sometimes he simply stands in the Square, arms crossed, and stares at George's house.

Tonight Arthur turns back. He returns to the chapel, I hear him climb the five-sided bell turret. I see the hatch lift up, his shadow climbs on to the top platform, its military-looking battlements also five-sided like the turret. The moon glows in his eyes as he looks over the battlements across the angular shape of the chapel roof, almost circular. I have the oddest feeling something in him senses me here on the highest point, the central pinnacle of the roof – in Islam the faithful are called to prayer from such places. An owl hoots elsewhere but he does not look away.

Arthur jumps on to the roof, does not risk the leads which may give way. He walks carefully along the battlements which ornament the five eastern facets of the chapel, holding lightly to the stone spear which rises from each second crenellation, disturbs a sleeping gull which flaps against the moon. Arthur pauses, swaying. He steps forward carefully until he comes to the end.

He stands on the final battlement. He stares at the moon. His shadow along the moonlit leads of the roof almost reaches me, his head almost touches the moon. Arthur takes a knife from his belt – the eating knife is all he has, obviously – and pushes the point into his neck where his earlobe touches his jawbone. The blood comes at once, I'm afraid he's cutting off his earlobe, but he saws the knife round his neck to his other ear, and I hear the breath and blood bubble from his throat. He has cut his throat. His lifeblood drops thirty feet or so without touching the chapel wall, splashes on the stone cutwater of the bridge pier and the starling.

I have seen this before. The blood sacrifice. The gift of life, atonement. *Pain, suffering, humility, sacrifice, strength*. Nick's oath. And I remember Nick saying, *Life is strength, strength is Gevurah*.

I remember the men chanting as they spill the girl's blood. *Deus. Ingeniator. Rex Mundi. Amen*.

The moon shines its reflection in the pond on the starling, shining above Arthur and below.

Nick saying, *Life, Alice*. Stroking my pregnant, swollen tummy gently. *Life, Alice, the mistake. Knowledge. Imperfection. The world.*

The knife drops from Arthur's hand. He raises his arms, and suddenly I am terrified. I am utterly terrified because I realise that everything I thought I knew is unimportant. I have been fooling myself. I'm tiny, and I have been blind. The moon stops, the river moves.

I feel the chill night wind. I feel the beating of my heart. I feel the wind on my eyes. I bear witness. I see the rows of watermen's boats moored away from the shore so that they will not be stolen. I see a single feather flutter on a bird's wing. I see the river rise up and burst into foam, I see the brow of a wave rise up under the moon.

I see an eye.

I see the eyes, the body, scales, *something*, blood, claws, nostrils, tenderness, *passion*, rise up.

I see into the eyes, huge, fierce, cruel, loving.

See more there than I knew there was to know. See them gaze down dazzled, sincere, yearning. Something more in them than innocence, something deeper than truth.

I see Arthur launch himself out, falling. See Arthur's body lie dead on the starling. See the river sliding quietly past the starling begin to lap over its stones, fill the pool to the brim, swirl round Arthur's body. Lift his arms and legs. Roll him down into the deep water. Gone.

The moon continues to rise.

The river swirls through the arches.

I did see it.

I don't believe what I saw. I can't. It's like Nick claiming Jesus Christ is alive, it's only a metaphor. King Arthur is supposed to be alive, too, awaiting his country's call. And Charlemagne, and Alexander the Great, and everyone else no doubt. Everyone wants immortality, everyone wants to live for ever. I don't believe what my own eyes saw that night any more than I believe my dreams. Except that I do believe my dreams. Well, I know my dreams aren't real. They just feel real.

I know what I see with my eyes is real.

I admit it. I saw. I don't *want* to believe it.

And yet I want to believe Jesus Christ is alive. That the Bible is true and there is a God. Truth to believe in. Certainty to cling to.

Then I do believe. I believe the Devil exists, but that God will win in the end.

But if Jesus Christ is alive, *really* alive as Nick said he is – the Lord dwells among His people, actually alive with us, in existence, hidden among us – how should I behave differently? How should I alter my behaviour?

Should I look after Alice differently? More? Less? Let her make her own choices, live her own life, leave her to her fate? What am I to do?

This I know. The road to Hell is paved with good intentions.

Arthur's dead. His body's gone. He can't do anything to harm her.

I love Alice so much it terrifies me. Terrifies me because I might lose her as the others were lost, and me powerless to do anything about it, to hold back the darkness in the world. By trying to do good, I enter into a relationship with evil, I might easily make the harm that I try to prevent. We create what we most fear: every nightmare knows that.

Truly this is Purgatory.

Nick! I call out with every ounce of my being. Nick, it's me you want. Take me! Hurt me! But leave Alice alone. Please. Please. Don't torment me like this, I can't bear it.

But this is what he wants.

Nick, I can't bear it.

No answer.

Nick?

Silence.

I die, live in the dark with my bones. Here I am still Alice, exactly as I was long ago. Poor murdered Alice buried beneath the marble undercroft floor with her broken leg and cracked skull, unable to hear her childrens' voices.

Thinking.

I strain to be born.

No answer.

Sometimes I think I hear the chanting of the Brethren and imagine the masons at the strange, intricate ceremonies of their order. The mystic rites and symbols of their ancient conspiracy. Perhaps they've even forgotten the meaning of them, forgotten what they're about. Achieved not innocence, but ignorance.

But some of them do know. One or two.

Time does not run down here in the earth. No night or day, no summer or winter. Sometimes I think my bones feel the distant tremble of the tide, I've counted a thousand tides or more, perhaps forgotten as many again. What's happened meanwhile? A year may have passed, or ten. God help me, Alice has no one to look after her. She may be dead, as dead as I. Or is she married? Is she still busy running her mother's errands? I imagine danger everywhere, all the dangers she does not see, all she does not know. She needs me and she does not know it. Oh, Alice, are you awake, are you asleep?

Sleeping.

The feeling of sleep.

I'm in her. *Sleeping.* I'm in Alice. For a moment I wonder if this is the moment of conception, she's married, I'm in her womb, I am to be Alice's daughter. A warm red glow, a sense of peace.

No, Alice is asleep, alone. I feel her chest move, her lungs fill. Her nightdress has ridden up over her knees, her feet are cold. Her nose is stuffy, perhaps she sleeps with the window closed; yes, I remember that she did. Still does.

This warm red glow is not her womb. I'm seeing the inside of her closed eyelids.

Alice is dreaming. I walk with her in the labyrinth of her heart.

The wheel turns, creaking, creaking, look at me, see me, feel me . . . I turn away, the walls of glass fall away, fall away behind me, I come from Southwark to London Bridge into the air, and young and innocent I sit beside him on the cart, the cart that rocks and sways and creaks, everyone is watching me, he drives the cart, I sit beside him on the cart between the shops, I cannot turn aside, his hand touches my knee, his hip my hip, he cracks the whip, the horse pulls hard, he turns my head, the people shout, his lips are hot, I whisper *no* but I cannot, he bears me down, tears me apart, my love, my love, the people watch, I whisper *no not here*, but I want, I want him to, want all of me, we fall down here beneath the arch, he fills me, I see his face, I murmur his sweet name as he fills me with his sweet seed, Nicholas, I am his wife.

NO!

Alice wakes gasping, sweating, ashamed.

It's disgusting, her secret dreams revealed. Her lust.

Was I any different? No. If I was a body with blood and youth coursing in its veins, I would feel the same way again.

But what made me recoil was the coincidence I saw, that no one else could know. The coincidence of the name in her dream.

Nicholas.

In her mind's eye I hardly saw him, impossibly handsome. But still, that name. Nicholas, Arthur's son.

(Did I shout? Did you hear my *NO*? Did *she* hear me?)

The room moves in the moonlight as Alice gets out of bed, then the bed rises as she kneels beside it. I am *of* her, but I am not her. I am of her even while she is awake, though it takes all my strength. She clasps her hands in front of her lips, praying. I feel the cold floor against her knees, the draught of cold air through the boards playing on her perspiring thighs. She clamps her nightdress between them, remembering her love dream, ashamed again. 'Dear Lord, forgive me, I did not mean to sin.' Her whisper is very pleasant, slightly lilting, light yet firm. 'It was a sin of my heart, my head could not stop me.' Young unmarried men who suffer the sexual seizure in the night must confess it to a priest, and so must she, but I catch a trace of her brain's thoughts even now that she is awake . . . Deceit. Alice means to hide what happened, naughty girl. How wonderful it is to be a human!

This time the bed does not seem to move as she stands, I am getting used to it. A human is in so many ways just like another animal, its body is an animal's body, its brain is an animal's brain, purely physical. And yet . . . I feel the depth of it, the power. And something more.

Something much more. An animal has no sense of wonder. Does Alice sense her soul?

Yes, she prayed. But does she *truly* believe? Alice believes in religion, has been taught to believe it. That's not the same thing. That lovely little *frisson* of deceit, she thinks she can lie to God. So she does not really believe God listens – except when *she* wants Him to, no doubt. I did.

She sits on the side of the bed, I glimpse her in the mirror, her pale, moonlit face, generous (too generous) mouth, deep blue eyes like Jack's. She wears her chestnut curls longer than I did, down past her shoulders – actually I remember I did wear it longer when I was young. I put her age at about fifteen, she should be married, no wonder she has these dreams. She looks at the window as a cockerel crows, she won't sleep again tonight. She scowls petulantly. Ah! She has my scowl, my temper! My Alice, you are so perfect. The cockerel crows again, dawn. As she wakes more fully, I begin to slip away from her, I cannot hold on, the scope of her mind overwhelms me.

I hang on.

She blows her nose into a rag, wipes it. I sense she feels irritation, something about a fire. She must light the kitchen hearth, a daily chore for her mother. Jacqueline? Is Jacqueline still alive? I get a misty impression of Jacqueline still very much alive and strict on the subject of fires being properly laid.

Hanging on to her. I don't want to go back into the dark. I love being her.

Alice leans forward to the mirror, licks her finger, smooths her dark eyebrows. The intimate business of the day begins, soon I will know her as well as she knows herself – better, for her body fascinates me. She lifts her nightdress, she has a mole to the left of her tummy button, and her nipples are very hard and pink. Before relieving her bowels, she pisses in the bucket so her turds don't stick, empties it out of the window but she's seen, one of the boatmen calls to her to show her virgin paps, she blushes. I glimpse a picture of the boatman in her mind, and an angry feeling. I feel her wipe her arse on the rag she blew her nose on, see her throw it out of the window. In her anger I sense her thoughts – as once I caught Crispin Whyte's thoughts. (*I hope you catch it, you*—) she thinks, a word I do not know. If she's near fifteen this must be about the year 1409, and fashions in insults change quickly. Her dress, too, is longer and fuller than I remember the style seven years ago, when Arthur Mason killed himself. That's a shock, remembering him. Alice flinches, then gives a little shiver and finishes dressing, slips her rather dainty white feet into house shoes, goes quietly downstairs.

She can hear her father stirring; George starts work at dawn.

Again I sense that feeling of deceit in her mind. George does not know about (*my lover*), he does not know about (*he kissed me*), he would not approve (*I love him*). Again I sense Nicholas in her thoughts, impossibly handsome, strong, the feel of his lips on hers. Concentrate on the fire, girl!

Alice bends over by the fire, rakes out the cold ashes, puts them in a pail to be taken up to the roof, the ash makes fertile soil (*Mother's garden*). She opens the window to let out the dust, the sound of traffic rushes in from the street below, heads and shoulders hurrying, a definite fashion for large hats, rather lovely. More traffic and even more people than I remember rushing across London Bridge, the whole structure and the houses shake, iron-shod horses and carts clatter and rumble. Suddenly there's a piercing shriek. Alice runs back to the window. (*What*—)

It's him.

It's no accident. Nicholas grins up at her from the Square. I can hardly see him, she cannot remotely think about him straight. All the old words, handsome, black curly hair, daring eyes. He gazes up at her, dazzled, she sees it, sees the effect she has on him, her heart races. He is here for her, no other. On his wrist paces the brightly-coloured bird that made the shriek. I've seen them before – I've seen a polar bear swimming in the Thames, for that matter – this is only a parrot from Africa, they can be made to prattle like magpies. To Alice, of course, the effect is magical and complimentary (*he did it for me*). She hopes her hair looks all right. She tries not to look too excited.

'Nick!' she calls down excitedly.

He whispers to the bird.

The bird caws, 'Alice . . . pretty Alice.'

He's taught it. *I* see through this in a trice, of course. I know what he's after, Alice's body. I have enough experience of men's minds, God knows. She doesn't. Grow up, girl. She claps her hands to her cheeks and simply trills with gullible laughter, then glances behind her (*Mother will hear*). Holds her finger to her lips, giggling. Nicholas, of course, has got her exactly where he wants her, and he knows when to stop. He bows deep – and lets the crowd sweep him away. Alice stands on tiptoe at the window to see him as long she can, and so he can see her. My, how we encourage them to manipulate us until we get what we want.

291

Alice sighs, turns from the window, dreams of marriage, makes up the fire, still smiling inside herself. Was I once like this? It's embarrassing – and lovely too. Precious innocence. So romantic! But marriage is not a bed of roses, my girl. Yet I was once exactly like her, wasn't I? I mustn't sound like an old woman.

But that name, Nick. He even looks like Nick. She shouldn't trust him. But we always do. He's as handsome as Jack, damn him. Even *I* can't help feeling—

Her father comes down, spears a crust with his knife. 'Good day, Father,' Alice murmurs without a thought, she must say it every morning, hardly sees him. But *I* look at him closely out of the corners of her eyes. George has put on weight, dark under the eyes, a man in his middle forties. And not so prosperous. He no longer dresses above himself, and why is his daughter not some serving girl or household slut raking out the fire? Because he cannot afford one. Alice knows rents are up, trade is hard, other cobblers have moved on to the bridge. I watch her hands pour a bowl of beer for him. George dips his bread in it. 'Alice.'

'Yes, Father?'

'Who were you talking to?'

Her heart bumps. 'Talking, Father?'

'Yes, you.'

'You know perfectly well!' Jacqueline interrupts, bustling in, chivvying her husband from the table. 'It was Nicholas, of course.'

'Nick,' Alice says without thinking, reddens.

Jacqueline shoots her a warning glance, I see the situation now. 'Nicholas, Nick, what does it matter,' she says, brisk. 'Can't she even see him from the window?' She moves about busily. 'Trade's a-passing, husband.'

'I know, I know,' George says fretfully. 'I don't want you to see him again, Alice. He isn't good enough for you.'

Mother knows how to handle Father. 'She doesn't encourage him. Nicholas is amusing and harmless.' I think Jacqueline rather likes that young man! 'Besides,' she reminds Geroge tartly, 'my father, as I recall, didn't think you were good enough for me.'

George blusters. 'Me?'

'He thought you were after my money.' Jacqueline shoos George out, closes the door after him and makes a face. 'You didn't have to shout Nicholas's name out loud.'

'Nick was in the street with a parrot!' Alice says excitedly. 'He must have got up early specially for me, don't you think? He can't help showing what he feels. He must have been thinking about me.' She pauses eagerly, wanting her mother's advice and approval, then bursts out, 'I can't bear not being with him!'

Jacqueline sniffs yesterday's butter. 'We'll make black sauce with this.'

Alice's elation falls like a stone, her self-importance pricked, she blinks back tears. She hates black sauce. 'I thought you were on my side,' she says. 'Now I hate you. I hate Father too.'

Jacqueline laughs, then looks exasperated, then looks sad. She puts her arms round her daughter, trying to remember herself thirty years ago. 'I know it's difficult,' she soothes. Alice is fiercely certain that Mother has no idea at all what she's feeling. This rage. Hunger. Despair. Love.

'Why is Father so determined to make me unhappy?'

'No, dear!' Jacqueline hugs her. 'We want you to be happy.'

Alice is going to cry, I can feel it coming. Doesn't she realise how lucky she is to have a father who cares about her? Alice stutters, 'When Nick – Nicholas' (*Mother likes me to call him Nicholas*) 'when Nicholas asked Father if he could call on me, Father said no.' Alice has got the hiccups. 'Father wants me to marry Edward Elcock. I *hate* Edward Elcock, he's stringy and his teeth stick out. Nick – Nicholas has perfect teeth, and he doesn't spit and he's always quiet, and he's respectful to Father but Father won't give him a chance . . .' She trails off in sobs. She's a clever one, Alice. Getting her way. She knows Mother hates her only daughter to cry, wants to give in to her.

'You know what your father's like,' Jacqueline temporises. 'Nicholas's mother wasn't always as respectable as she is now. Most people don't remember her as she was, but your father can't forget.'

'Mistress Moll's always been kind to me. Even when I was a child. She gave me a skipping-rope once. And a ball. She's kind.'

'Yes, she is. And she's been very good to Nicholas. Put him through school in Southwark, not cheap. Found the money to buy him good clothes, he was always properly turned out.'

'But Father says he doesn't have a trade and he's ten years older than me.'

'Not quite nine years.' Jacqueline gives away her feelings. 'And he's not short of money.'

'He's perfect.'

George says from the doorway, 'There's something your mother's not telling you.' He closes the door behind him, as though to stop his words escaping. 'Nick is my brother's son.'

'You don't know that!' Jacqueline explodes. 'That's tittle-tattle.'

Alice can't believe her ears. 'But you haven't got a brother.'

I understand it now. George hasn't told Alice about Arthur, who cut his throat when she was seven.

George sits at the table. 'You're missing trade,' Jacqueline says tartly. But George pulls Alice down on the stool beside him.

'I had a brother, Alice. He was no good. He was bad all through. He went with Moll—'

'Mistress Moll?'

'Just plain Moll, in those days. A woman very far from God. She kept a brothel.'

'It was an alehouse,' Jacqueline interrupts. 'The Hoop.'

George turns his back on her, speaks close to Alice. 'That boy Nick is Arthur's son.'

'You don't know that,' Jacqueline says.

George loses his temper. 'Be quiet, woman.'

She won't. 'Everyone knows who Nick's father is.'

George clears his throat warningly.

Jacqueline mutters obliquely, 'He had a father in the Church.'

Alice hates them both. Nick has told her they'll say this, Nick has primed her with the truth so that she knows her parents, especially her father, are lying to her. 'I even know who it was,' she tells them. 'It was Brother Darenth.'

Brother Darenth! I'm so surprised that Alice blinks. Her hand moves uncertainly to her forehead. 'That's what I heard,' she murmurs, 'may God have mercy on his soul.'

George says angrily, 'He was a fine priest, how dare you slur the name of a good man.'

Jacqueline is more fully involved in the life of the chapel than her husband is. 'Brother Darenth gave money each year for Nick's clothes and schooling. He confessed on his deathbed, I hear.'

'Arthur is the boy's father!' George shouts.

It's true. But how easily lies and deceit are sown in an unhappy family. Neither woman believes him because neither wants to.

The bell rings on the counter downstairs, rings again, impatiently.

293

'I don't want to hear any more talk about Nick,' George says in a low, ugly voice as he gets up. 'You won't see him again, Alice. And that's that.'

But of course Alice will. Almost any fruit is delicious as soon as it is forbidden, and George, vulnerable, over-protective and in pain – and no longer a great success at his trade – had put the women's backs up thoroughly. Of course, Jacqueline defers at once to her husband's wishes, Alice to her father's. They stand on the shoulders of generations of women used to getting their way, one way or another. They bide their time. Together they cook the black sauce that is George's favourite, and an Eastcheap capon. Jacqueline is tender in bed, Alice helps him at the counter. Nothing will ever change George's feelings about Arthur or Nicholas, but at least his vigilance relaxes. His women worship with George at his favourite church, St Mary Overie – Alice hopes to see Nicholas on the way, wears her blue gown with straight shoulders, walks head down, devoutly, every sense alert as we come past the dwelling that I remember as the Hoop but which looks so smartly kept now, white paint on the windowsills setting off the brown wooden beams, hanging baskets of flowers swaying above the heads of the crowd; but she does not see him, and here we come to Southwark, and I cease.

Darkness. Loneliness.

It is the first time in weeks I have been away from Alice. The darkness is blacker, the loneliness heavier. I've become so used to witnessing her bright life, to being part of the sensations her body imparts to her feelings and the thoughts in her mind, that sometimes it feels I *am* her. The soul she was born with – or, some would say, baptised into – is stronger off the bridge and I wonder if she changes at all. Do I affect her personality? Was she conceived off the bridge, is that how I am able to become part of her over the river? It is such a blessing I dare not question it, for fear it will stop.

In the dark I think about Nicholas. The one true thing I know about good and evil is that neither exists without knowledge. Now, Nicholas's father is Arthur – of course his father is Arthur, what's this cock-and-bull story about Brother Darenth that's been spread about in the meantime? Darenth was undoubtedly an accomplice, he knew, or sensed, something about Arthur. Something so strong that he lied in his deathbed confession. I remember the first night Arthur stood in the Square like a sleepwalker, hands reaching out as if to catch a prize that eluded his grasp. He looked like . . . not a sleepwalker. A man possessed.

Arthur returns to the Hoop and nine months later Nicholas is born.

Arthur loves his son, but gives him up. Never sleeps with Moll again, lives as a recluse in the chapel, but makes sure Moll cares for the boy. Nicholas must have learnt a lot about men and women in his first nine years.

And then Alice is born, and at once Arthur changes again. So Alice is important. Why more important than George and Jacqueline's three children who were killed? Because she is Alice. Because her name is Alice.

My name. Alice Mason.

Baptised by Brother Darenth. And suddenly everything that's chance, accident, random, begins to look like a plan.

Alice is born and Arthur, before the child is even baptised – he *knows* – gives Moll a bag of silver and puts the fear of God, or the Devil, into her to make her respectable. A proper education for Nicholas on top of what he already knows, which is surely enough about human nature, given the goings-on at the Hoop, to last a lifetime. But then there's even more. Arthur orders the boy, *Come with me. There's so much more I have to show you.*

And Nicholas replies calmly, *Father, you can't show me anything that I don't know.*

Why not?

Nicholas is Nick.

Gradually Arthur's relationship with Moll is forgotten. By the time Nick is eighteen, who except family would remember that the greying recluse of the Bridge Chapel had long ago fathered a strapping lad? Arthur has no more to give except his life, and the Beast takes him. Brother Darenth steps into the picture with his strange confession of paternity.

By now, the relationship between Arthur and Nicholas is all but erased. *Why?*

And there's another *why*. Why have I been brought back into a human form? I know the answer to this one. To have my life given, and taken away. To grow up, and be cut down. To watch my beauty eaten away, like a garment fretted by moth. To suffer. To feel suffering deeply as only a human feels it, to care, to grasp, to lose, to know I will die.

Alice gasps as brilliant sunlight flares in her eyes, the life of the bridge jostles her forward, blue wood smoke, the smell of roasting kippers, houses leaning together overhead. 'What's the matter with you?' Jacqueline is demanding. 'You've were so quiet in church, not yourself at all.'

'Sickening for something,' George says, admiring a man juggling knives.

But Jacqueline follows Alice's eyes. 'So that's who you're sickening for,' she whispers. She takes George's elbow, turns him away, they admire the juggler together. Alice steps back. Here's Nicholas. Nicholas in the doorway. He looks at her in that way he has, and Alice's heart hammers.

'Oh,' she says indifferently, 'it's you.' It's beautifully done. I have to admire her. I just wish it wasn't Nicholas.

He doesn't move.

She lets the crowd push her, takes a step towards him. Nicholas is twice her size, well in his twenties, broad-shouldered, gentle, shy, eager. His clothes brushed, his belt gleaming. Those deep, dazzled eyes. If he doesn't say something quickly Alice will simply melt for him.

'Hello, Alice.'

Alice swallows. I feel her tremble. 'Hello, Nicholas.'

This young man really is so handsome I almost want him myself. I know exactly what Alice is feeling. He has that vitality about him, Jack's vitality. I feel he might simply reach out and kiss Alice here, now, in the street!

She wants him to.

Her tongue touches her lips. 'We've been to church.'

He knows. 'You're wearing your blue dress.'

He's noticed. She smooths it, flustered, delighted. 'Did you look at me?'

'Yes. I saw you walk by.'

Alice realises the implications with the lightning speed of a young girl in love. He saw her go, he knew he would see her come back. He waited for her.

Time to put him down a touch. 'Oh, I suppose you stand there all day spying on everyone.'

Nicholas grins. He has a small scar on his chin that makes him look only very slightly dangerous. 'Yes. I stand here all day. I like to know everything about everyone.'

'I'm sure you don't know everything about me.'

His grin. 'I'm sure I do.' He raises his voice. 'Good afternoon to you, sir.'

'Sssh!' Alice hisses. But George has heard, begins to turn. Alice is much too close to Nicholas, steps back. But Nicholas steps forward at the same rate, takes her hand, bows. He lets George look at them. 'Pleasure to see you, Miss Alice.'

George grabs Alice's other hand, and for a moment I think a tug-of-war will ensue. But Nicholas's grip is suddenly light as the caress of a feather. Even so, George has to pull hard. It's obvious which one Alice wants to stay with.

Nicholas touches the back of her hand with his fingertip, she staggers against her father. George puts his arm round her, hustles her away. Alice looks back over her shoulder, she's going to cry.

'Don't you dare make a scene in the street,' George snaps.

Jacqueline hurries to catch up. 'Husband, it's you who are making a scene.' George's face is red and pinched, he won't be argued with. Alice's last glimpse of Nicholas is him still standing calmly in the doorway, arms crossed, watching her.

George pulls Alice past the counter. 'I don't want to see you again today. Not a word. No supper. Go to your room.' He turns to Jacqueline, outraged. 'Did you see the colour in her cheeks!'

Alice goes to her room. She puts her fists to her head, then throws herself down on the bed. Through her angry sobs, she feels humiliated by her father and angry enough to scratch him. I can hear the sound of the riverscape through the open window, the evening trade, fishermen's calls, the mellow creak of sculls and sails.

By now George is the only one who believes that Nicholas is Arthur's son. But of course *I* know it's true. Alice is suffering from forbidden love, always the tastiest. She loves her cousin, her father's brother's son. The Church would never permit such a marriage, it is profane. The children of such unions are idiots possessed by demons.

Through Alice's sobs I listen to the rattle of George's soling hammers downstairs.

George is the only one who knows. I imagine the dreadful things that can happen to anyone, a bee flying into his throat, his leather-punch slipping, a fall, a cancer, a lump in his blood, a death in his sleep.

Without George, who would stand up during the wedding ceremony – in the Bridge Chapel – and declare lawful impediment? Jacqueline? Never. Who else?

No one. Nicholas marries Alice.

Perhaps it doesn't matter. If anyone knows how intermarried we all are by now, I do. We're one family, one bridge, one nation. Alice marries Nicholas. If it *isn't* just chance, if there *is* a plan, it's only visible to those who made it.

But perhaps I do see one tiny corner of it.

Alice, and Nick. Their child?

The child I never had by Nick.

When George's only son, poor little Clement, died – was killed – Alice was born, a girl, the last of the line.

Nick wins. *His* child.

For goodness sake, Alice, stop crying, you make such a noise I can't think!

She stops. (*For goodness sake, Alice, stop crying, you make such a noise I can't think!*)

She heard me, just as Jack did.

Alice stands up, looks round the room. Looking for me. She wants to look under the bed but she's afraid to. Finally she laughs. 'I'm talking to myself!' she says. But no one, I imagine, likes the feeling of thoughts popping into their head without control. Too close to madness.

'Am I mad?' she says. She's not learnt to think properly.

This is my chance. I try to reassure her. Alice, I'm here to help you.

This time I catch her frightened thought (*Are you a demon?*) an instant before her words come. 'Are you a demon?'

No, Alice, I'm not a demon.

But of course a demon would say that. A demon would lie. The Devil is the prince of lies. Alice puts her hands to her head, covers her eyes. Red darkness. (*Go away!*) 'Go away!' she says.

There are some things every girl knows about demons, and I sense them bubbling up through Alice's mind, all these dark things we try not to think about, for humans sense they are true – and the Church insists they are true, for to deny night-flying and metamorphosis has been officially declared heretical. Thousands of women are known to have made pacts with the Devil whose empire is the world, despite all the efforts of the Church to wrest it from him in God's name. Women and girls are known to anoint themselves with Devil's grease, distilled from the fat of murdered infants, and their souls slip and slide through keyholes, cracked windows and chimneys, rise into the night air to bring mischief, harm and bad luck. The Devil is a huge man and they kiss him on his hairy arsehole, dance with him to the beat of horses' skulls and human bones, eat sliced turnips in parody of the Host, and impale themselves on his huge, freezing phallus in the sexual embrace. He impregnates them with his semen which he squeezes from the balls of dead men. To these women, who give birth to the worm-like creatures known as Drakes, the Devil is a man (I remember Nick recounting the Master's story of Hiram, King of Sidon and Tyre), but to men the Devil is a woman, a succubus. Each sex blames the other for these manifestations. We deserve each other.

Alice, I would never hurt you.

Then her thoughts come (*Who are you?*) and her voice asks, 'Who are you?'

I try to make her understand. I am Alice. I am you.

'You're lying!' she shouts without thinking. The room seems very bright as Alice takes her hands from her eyes. She looks round wildly. What should be so easy, convincing her of the obvious truth, seems almost impossible. Alice is too sensible, too normal. 'Where are you?' she calls. 'Where are you hiding? How are you doing this?'

Keep your voice down, your mother will hear you.

I try not to alarm her, but by now Alice is thoroughly alarmed. She walks quickly to the window, throws it open, looks out, sure it's a trick. Boatmen, children, who knows? I even catch a glorious romanticised mental image – my goodness – that I suppose represents Nicholas. But in reality there is only the placid blue river, high tide, fingers of golden sunset reaching through the arches below us towards the eastern horizon, the first dim stars growing.

'Nicholas?' She leans out, giggling. A few pigeons flap away, startled. Nothing else. The sunlight dies away. More stars. She looks down at the row of dark arches beneath her, pulls her head back into the room. Stands between the window and her bed – her room is not large – and turns round and round. Her thoughts are jumbled, chaotic, I can't catch anything except the feeling of Nicholas. She's searching for an explanation. Finds it, and it's just the one you'd expect. 'I'm in love,' she whispers. She says aloud, 'It's because I'm in love!'

I'm so proud of her, but I don't know whether to feel pleased or sad. She doesn't believe in me.

The door opens and Jacqueline looks in. I warned Alice her mother would hear her, I can't hide my irritation, Alice is endangering everything. Jacqueline looks round the room, frowning. 'I thought I heard voices.'

Alice says irritably, 'What voices? I can talk to myself if I like.'

Jacqueline looks at Alice's high colour, thinks she understands. 'Ah,' she smiles. 'I thought you had Nicholas in here.' Her joke, if it is a joke, falls flat.

'I can do anything I want,' Alice says furiously. 'I'm going to run away. Father was so rude to Nicholas but Nicholas was so good, he just smiled. I'm so *embarrassed*. I hate you both.' She throws herself into her mother's arms, almost knocking the basket from Jacqueline's hand.

Jacqueline soothes her. 'I was just going up to the roof to pick herbs for your father's supper. Why don't you come with me?'

Alice sulks.

Alice, stay down here, lie on your bed, think, sleep. I hope I may influence Alice more easily in her dreams than awake, she's so wilful.

'I'm not going to do anything anybody says,' Alice sulks to her mother.

'Suit yourself. Stay in your room like your father told you to.' But Jacqueline leaves the door open, and Alice hesitates, sighs, follows her. They climb the stairs overhanging the river, Jacqueline's big behind swaying and plump legs pumping. She stops to catch her breath, smiles down at her daughter. Alice hopes she'll never be like her mother.

It's much brighter on the flat roof, the western sky as blue as the sea, clouds drift in it like fiery islands. All over London, as night comes out of the ground, bells call the faithful to prayer. Jacqueline kneels on a mat, murmurs the responses to herself as Alice's fingers pull busily at lovage, borage, garlic, Alice doesn't care what. From the corner of her eye I notice how the apple tree I remember being planted has outgrown its mouldy barrel, been replanted, grown old, gnarled. Below us worshippers cross the Square to the Bridge Chapel. This new style of chanting is very pretty. The last sunlight lifts from the golden tip of St Paul's Cathedral spire, the dense pall of supper smoke begins to rise on each side of the river. But it's the time of year when London Bridge is still brilliant yellow, flowering rocket everywhere, a golden ribbon joining shore to shore. 'Your father likes cumin in his beer,' Jacqueline calls.

Alice leans on the railing, bored. Yellow loses its colour as the light fades. A boat drifts lazily through Chapel Lock, the tide begins its fall, slow at first. She knows perfectly well that the cumin is in the tub at her knee. Jacqueline stands beside her, close enough for Alice to feel her warmth, the size of her presence.

'It will get better, Alice, you know. It won't always hurt so much.'

'It won't get better. I love him.' Alice isn't tearful, she's determined. She won't let her mother stand between her and Nicholas. But I don't think Jacqueline wants to. 'I love him and he loves me and I want to be with him and that's all there is.'

'Yes, I know.' Jacqueline ignores the unpicked cumin, hangs the basket over her arm, leans beside her daughter on the railing. People are coming out of the chapel now, their heads and shoulders hurry below the houses that crisscross the street. 'Love does hurt. But it doesn't hurt for ever.'

She's so wrong! Love *does* hurt for ever! Oh, Jack, I still miss you, every moment!

Alice says, 'I'll find a way of being with Nicholas whatever you do.'

'Yes, I know,' Jacqueline agrees. 'All I'm saying is, that when you are with Nicholas, married to him, bear his child, you'll find that love does not hurt. It becomes unimportant. Dull. You'll become bored with it. There is so much more in the world than love.'

Alice shakes her head. 'What more?'

'I know it seems like that now. You'll see.'

But this is rubbish. Love is everything.

Alice tries to explain. 'All I know is that I love him.' But again her emotion overwhelms her, her blood courses rich and hot as brandy in her veins. 'If Father won't let me see him I'll kill myself!'

Jacqueline turns her head, her face in shadow. 'That's the last thing we want.' She grins, and only her teeth show. It's familiar. I've seen this before, somewhere.

I remember Arthur watching Jacqueline pray in the chapel. Arthur's teeth grinning in the shadows as he watched her.

Alice, get back to your room.

Alice's hands grip the railing tight. She won't move. I'm not ready for this. I can't hear George working. No hammering. Of course not, the whole bridge is

298

falling quiet, it's past sunset and the working day has ended. But I can't hear his footsteps on the stairs, I can't hear him moving in the rooms. I can't feel his presence. Nothing.

Alice, get back to your room!

She won't, she's so headstrong she won't listen to her inner voice.

Jacqueline says, 'I'm sure your father just wants you to be happy. He's just wrong about Nick, that's all.'

'Yes,' Alice says fiercely (I know this feeling so well!), 'he *is* wrong about Nick.'

Jacqueline says casually, 'You know best.'

Of course Alice thinks she knows best! Everyone does. Otherwise we'd just do everything we're told, believe what we're told to believe, live as we're told to live. But we *do* have a choice.

Alice, get to your room and lock the door. Push your bed against the door. Scream for help.

I try to peel back the grip of her fingers on the railing, I feel them loosen. She's beginning to give way, give way to doubt. The smell of herbs is very strong on the evening air, the scent of garlic and wood smoke.

Jacqueline says, 'Look, Alice. Look who I see.' Her teeth are smiling, her dark shadow moves against the last of the sunset, puts down the basket, takes hold of Alice's elbow. 'Look!' She points down.

It's Nicholas. Alice would recognise him anywhere, those broad shoulders, that curly dark hair – though *I* hardly see him at first, he looks like a shadow moving among shadows as he comes out below us into the street, so close to this house that it looks as though he may have come from inside. And did I not hear the soft clap of the counter flap closing?

'Nicholas!' Alice says. He fills her every thought. Just to be with him. Her hands grab the railing tight, I can do nothing, she waves to him, though for certain he will not see her against the night sky above him, even if he looks up.

Nicholas does look up.

He stands beneath the brazier that flames on its pole in the centre of the Square, lighting travellers on their way. The flames illuminate his face as he stands looking up at Alice, straight past the flames at her.

'Go down to him,' Jacqueline whispers. 'Stay with him awhile. Your father will never know.'

Don't go, Alice. Don't.

Alice hesitates. 'I don't know. Perhaps I shouldn't. Father told me to stay in my room.'

'Your father would want you to be happy,' Jacqueline smiles. 'Don't you see how much Nick loves you? You don't want to risk losing him.'

No, she's terrified of losing him. Nick waves. She waves down to him. He calls something Alice can't hear. She leans over the railing.

'Careful,' Jacqueline smiles. 'Don't fall. If you use the back stairs, you won't disturb your father.' Jacqueline kisses her daughter's cheek. 'Quick! Hurry! And hurry back!'

Alice kisses her, and runs.

And so much of me wants to do what Alice is doing. If I was Alice, I would do this, her dress lifted to her knees so she does not trip, running down the stairs that zigzag down the back of the house, the river below her turning this way and that. I used to run away with Jack, didn't I? I ran away with my dear Jack and talked to him and whispered with him and giggled with him beneath the arch of the bridge his father built, and let his hands caress me, and let him love me, and I gave him all of my love.

Dear Alice, I know exactly what you feel!

She runs across the Square and Nick holds out his hands and she throws herself in his arms. He swings her round, his mouth against hers, his strength holding her effortlessly. The feeling is so exciting that she laughs as she kisses him, grips his shoulders, feels his heat.

The flames make a roaring sound above their heads in the night breeze. This fierce, total feeling of giving is irresistible.

Nicholas slows her with his hands round her slim waist, slows her down. She doesn't want to stop. He sets her lightly on her feet.

He whispers her name, *my* name. 'Alice.'

And wouldn't it be worth it just to have him, whatever the consequences, here, now, just as she dreams it, to make that intensity of love, lust, come true? God, yes!

But I don't have her hot blood, and as he sets her down I try to see from the corners of her eyes. There's her parents' house behind us. The counter flap is closed but the little half-door beneath it is open. Something pale there. 'Alice, Alice,' Nick says. 'Walk with me.'

'Where?' Quite proper, but she's on fire inside. She wants him to kiss her lips again, to feel his hands lift her, his strength.

'Anywhere, Alice. To be with you.' He takes her arm in his, walks her to the chapel steps. She glances back.

'I don't know, my father—'

'Don't worry about your father. I don't want to hear another word about him.' His arm pulls her close as they walk. 'Only you.'

But that glance was enough for me. That pale shape was a foot, the shoe torn off with such force the toenails were ripped away, the ankle broken.

All that's behind us. Nicholas runs lightly up the chapel steps, lifts her with him. Alice hangs on to him. 'Where are we going? I should stay where Mother can see me.'

'Your mother?' Nicholas glances up at the roof garden, no sign of anyone at the rail. 'She trusts me. Don't you think you'll be safe in a holy place? I should think she'd thoroughly approve.'

He has that lovely deep, confident voice, and he sounds so reasonable. And he hasn't let go of her arm. We go through the ornately carved entrance of the newly decorated chapel, Alice bobs habitually to the altar, the crucified Christ decently concealed behind its linen shroud. I see the draught from the door make the shroud move. One corner flaps. *Go back, Alice.*

Jack's voice. Why doesn't Alice react?

Nicholas closes the door. Alice looks round. 'I thought you were chilly,' he explains. 'The night air's damp.' His solicitude touches her. She squeezes his hand. He kisses her. The air in the chapel is very still.

The white linen cloth flutters. *Alice, go back.*

All there is in her mind is Nick. His lips. His embrace. I can't get through to her. I don't think she hears Jack's voice.

Alice. Sweet Alice. Kissing Alice. Alice Lacknail.

He's not talking to this Alice, this body. He's talking to *me*.

I cry out, Jack!

'Jack,' Alice blurts.

Nick pulls back. 'There's no one called Jack here.'

She says demurely, 'You shouldn't kiss me in here, it's not right. I should go home.' Oh my God; her father dead on the floor and her mother very definitely possessed by a demon.

'Home?' Nick says. 'Not yet.' He smiles, slips his hands round both of hers, backs away, leading her forward. 'You've only just arrived. It's warmer downstairs. Come on. It's fun.' He takes a step down, another. 'I've settled it all with your mother. She doesn't mind.'

The shroud ripples as though a wind blows.

Alice follows Nick round the winding stair to the undercroft. The vigil candle glows on the altar, shadows move in the vaulted roof. The undercroft smells of stone and fish, she hears the tide rushing beyond the walls.

The floor is as I remember it, black and white flags of marble.

The candle flares up.

Jack's voice, *But you're lovely.*

It *is* Jack!

A glow suffuses the undercroft. *Alice, do you love me?*

I love you, Jack!

If I could reach out to grasp the flame, I would. To touch Jack. He's here. He's all around me.

Nicholas grins at Alice, puts his foot against the white samite corner of the altar, kicks forward. The altar swings round like an arm round a shoulder. He grins, handsome enough to die for, and he always knows exactly what to say. 'Do you dare? It's a secret.'

Jack's voice: *Alice. Go back. Our house. Nick's bones. Hurry!*

Nicholas, his foot on the stair, stops. He looks at Alice. He looks deep into her eyes, so deep that she gasps. I see into him, his eyes moving in the sockets of his skull, the intricate machinery of joints, tendons and muscles, see into his brain. See Nick, a burning man. The lips move over his blackened teeth, smiling.

Welcome, Alice. It's my time now. It's my turn.

Nicholas grins, kisses Alice's lips. 'Do you trust me? You want to come, don't you?'

She giggles, flattered. 'Of course I trust you.'

He winks, and she returns his smile. Nick takes the candle, leads her down. The steps are steep and she catches the hem of her dress between her heel and the stone. He stops solicitously, frees the piece of torn wool, inhales the scent of her legs. Then he swings her down and she sees the deep, narrow room, the tapestries, strange designs. She walks around, but he does not let her go. 'What is this?'

'Old stuff for old men.'

'But it's clean. They must come down here. Suppose we're found out?'

Nicholas stops. 'Are you frightened?'

'No. Of course not. I'm curious.'

'You should be.' Nicholas touched a golden eye on a golden tripod. 'How much do you love me?'

She laughs, looking at the woven stars. 'Oh, to the ends of the earth!'

From the corners of her eyes I glimpse the steps glow as though illumination pours up through the cracks that join the stones. Am I seeing the Light?

Alice! Nick's bones! Hurry!

How can I? I cannot possibly control Alice. I could not even unclench her hands from the rail.

'To the ends of the earth,' Nicholas murmurs. 'That's not nearly far enough. When we swear an oath, you kneel on one knee, like this.' He kneels like a knight swearing allegiance to his queen. 'You say, how much do you love me?'

Alice giggles again, I wish she wouldn't. Then she makes her face serious. 'How much do you love me?'

'From the surface of the World to its Centre.' Nick stands. 'How much do you love me?'

She kneels. I hear her murmur, 'From the surface of the World to its Centre . . .'

Nick lifts her easily by her hands. 'Now see.'

He sweeps aside the tapestry, and the winding staircase is revealed. *I have never seen this before. This must be what Durand saw. Down and down and down, round and round. It makes Alice dizzy to look at it. Nicholas picks her up easily in his arms, takes the candle in one hand, steps down.

Over Nicholas's shoulder, among the tapestries flying in the draught from below, I see Jack as he is now, made of the Light. The light of him illuminates the Sacred Lodge, Jack in the flesh as I knew him on the night of his death long ago, his blond hair cut in the style of those days, wearing his old-fashioned cloak that he took with him to the grave, before his bones were washed away, but clean and fresh again as though it was still, somewhere, now. Always now.

ALICE, FOR GOD'S SAKE HURRY! NICK'S BONES!

The light flickers, pales, fades. Jack reaches out his hands to me, is gone.

I understand what I must do. I concentrate. Alice's hands open and close helplessly. This isn't working. 'Don't worry,' Nicholas reassures her, misunderstanding, 'I've got you.'

The walls are pale, turn to chalk.

I try to shut Alice out of my consciousness. Dimly I sense her loss, her diminishment, as though her heart has skipped a beat. I have no more energy to spare for her. I reach up through the ground, up, up the winding stair, through the chapel, rise into the night air over London Bridge, look down on the watchman calling the weather and the tide, the brazier guttering the last of its embers, the houses round the Square.

Our house.

I feel that the rushing wind, the rushing tide, the night sky may sweep me away. I pull down with all my strength. Here's the counter flap, the little half-door swinging in the wind, banging against George's bare dead foot.

I rush forward, veins, arteries, brain – and George's body sits up.

Its head lolls back, the throat cut by one of his chisels. I whisper, I'm sorry, George. But there's no one here. His brain is vacant, without mind, without consciousness. I squeeze the heart, thick slow blood stirs, is forced to his cold muscles. I push the lungs, the mouth opens, draws a breath. His right eye is open, I fumble with his fingers to push his left eye open, to wipe the encrusted blood from it. I try to treat his body with respect, though I know it's just meat. George's soul, if he had one, is gone forward, or is overwhelmed.

The numb fingers fumble clumsily with the eye. This is never going to work. One eye must do. The hands drag at the counter, the body stands up.

I'm sorry, George. I'm sorry.

The shoulder slides along the wall, the arm pushes the body upright, it stumbles to the door at the back of the shop. Whatever killed George used great violence, one leg has broken bones, the bare foot drags behind it. The numb hands fumble at the latch, the body staggers into the back room. A lamp still burns on the table here. This clumsy body will set itself on fire if I am not careful. Reach out. Was George left-or right-handed? I reach out the left hand.

The fingers, clenched in the misery and agony of the moment of death, will not open.

I push the hand on to the table, drag the arm towards me. The rough wood of the table pulls the fingers open. I reach out for the handle of the lamp.

The hand knocks full into the lamp, oil splashes from the burning spout, fire runs up the arm.

The hand and arm are burning. If I'm not careful I shall set fire to the house. I swing the other arm round, try to pull the burning shirt off the skin.

A soundless shriek through the night. (*ALICE!*)

I know that cry. George's body flops forward against the table.

I am gone.

The rushing wind sweeps me down, down, down into the earth.

302

'Stop,' Alice is saying. 'Put me down.'

He's carrying her again, lighting the flambeaux that line the walls from the candle as he goes. They've left the winding stair that goes winding down to the centre of the earth, he carries her along a tunnel dug through solid chalk, her feet almost touch one wall, her head the other side. The chalk seems to slide very fast, very close past her eyes; Nicholas walks with long strides. 'Not much further now.'

Her foot catches an outcrop on the wall, her shoe falls off. She squeaks reprovingly, 'Nicholas!' He doesn't stop. They'll pick it up on the way back.

I sense she's a little angry with him for treating her so briskly. Apparently he put her down, but she tripped on the stair, almost fell. That frightened her. But she's excited too. And curious.

Alice, I'm with you. I'm trying to help you.

I hope the silly girl won't try and speak. She opens her mouth – but then closes her eyes, as if to see me better, and imagines me. (*I don't want help. I thought I was going to fall, that's all. You're my guardian angel, aren't you?*)

Would it help if she thought that? And suddenly I realise that, anyway, it's true. I *am* her guardian angel. But I don't have the nerve to pass myself off as an angel.

Yes, Alice, I am your . . . your guardian.

A happy feeling washes through her.

Alice, you must think about what is happening to you.

(*Isn't it fun? I never knew these tunnels were here. Nicholas knows everything. Isn't he strong? Go away now, guardian angel. I want to be alone with him.*)

I'm not doing any good here. Delay him, Alice.

(*But it's fun. I'm not afraid of him.*)

That's what I'm afraid of.

Alice tightens her arms, and does what she wanted to do anyway: puts her mouth against Nicholas's neck and kisses him.

The rushing wind. The rough wood of the table top against the eye.

I squeeze the heart, push the lungs, the body gasps a breath. The nose smells smoke, the ears hear the crackle of flame and spitting oil. The arm is burning, and the left side of the chest. How long have I been away? A few seconds. There's a pail of water by the drawing hatch in the floor – this end of the house is over an arch.

I push with the legs, the body stumbles forward, I push the arm into the bucket. Water spills across the floor, the bucket rattles as it falls over, but the fire is out.

The body drags itself upright against the back door, the steaming left hand grabs the lamp, the right hand knocks the latch open.

The back stairs leading up, the river below.

One short flight leads down to the hanging cellar, the windowless wooden construction behind most London Bridge houses used as a latrine or as a storeroom. George kept much of his stock out of the way there, skins, the wooden lasts for important people, tools.

The body staggers forward, almost overbalances into the river. The tide foams downstream below, so by a trick of the eye the bridge appears to forge upstream like a great ship.

The back door slams closed in the wind. Jacqueline's voice calls from upstairs, 'Who's there?'

I push the legs, the body half falls down the steps to the hanging cellar that protrudes from the bridge pier. The little door opens easily.

Jacqueline's voice calls down from the third floor, 'Is that you, Nicholas?'

The cellar is much larger than it looks from outside, dug back into the bridge pier. Among the rubbish of lasts, there's a broken chair, planks that will never be used, and a dusty shovel hangs from a nail. The right hand grabs at it, knocks it down. Pick it up, pick it up.

The left hand holds up the lamp, the eyes follow it into the darkness at the back of the cellar. The wooden floor turns to earth, rubble. One strong beam supports the weight of the house above, the roof of the cellar is made of joists and floorboards.

I am beneath the foundations of our house.

The legs bend, kneeling. Put down the lamp. Both hands grasp the shovel. Dig, dig—

Nicholas kisses her as he strides forward, his strength is intoxicating, desirable, his invulnerability excites her. Alice's heart hammers at his touch, she feels the caress of his fingers on her legs and shoulders as he carries her, she knows he needs her and this makes him more exciting than ever, the sense of power she has over him. He carries her as effortlessly as a child, her chestnut hair blows behind her from the wind ahead.

The tunnel widens, Nicholas halts at steps hewn in the chalk, puts her down, she kisses him eagerly. 'Wait,' he says, looking up. He seems to hear and see more than she does.

She leans against him. 'Where are we, Nicholas?'

He glances down at her. 'You will know when you see.'

He takes her hand, climbs the steps, Alice beside him feeling awkward because of her lost shoe. It's on the tip of her tongue to tell him off, send him back for it. Then the roof rises up from the steps, the walls turn away, and an ornate screen like the wooden rood screen in churches comes into view above the top step. But not wood. Pure gold.

The beauty of it takes Alice's breath away. It's the most precious thing she has ever seen, shimmering, gleaming, she sees herself inside it. She approaches herself breathlessly, her image fragments, splits, flows over the shining gold, statues, symbols, strange devices. And suddenly I remember something from long, long ago, *the quest of God. Not for God. Of.*

'Yes,' Nicholas says. 'It's real.'

Alice can see it's real. Her fingertips touch the warm, living gold. A golden angel – she looks exactly as an angel should, with long, gold, feathered wings whose tips almost meet above her head, her face tender yet strong, her straight eyebrows showing firmness, devotion, determination – holds a golden chain. The end of the chain is a massive fetter that encircles the neck of a demon, holds him imprisoned. The face of the demon is savage, mournful, full of hate.

She recoils. 'Who is he?'

'The demon Asmodeus, who built the Temple against his will.'

She turns back to the angel. I hear her thoughts with difficulty in this strange, terrifying, beautiful place. (*Is she you, Alice, my guardian angel? Is she what you look like?*)

But before I can reply – if I can reply – Nicholas takes Alice's arms, pulls her forward. The screen opens . . . and *you* know what you see. But I do not. I have never been here before.

'It is the Temple of God,' Nicholas whispers.

Alice shields her eyes against the glory of reflected light from the Shekinah, the golden sun of hammered gold above the white marble altar where the body lies.

'No,' Alice says abruptly. 'This is wrong. I don't want to go in.'

Nicholas teases her with his lips against her hair. 'There's much more I can show you.' There is a book on a lectern, the wind turns its pages. The Book. Again, everything that Nick had told me was true.

'I want to go home, Nicholas.' She backs a pace, stops with a jerk. He holds her elbows effortlessly.

'This is your destiny,' he says in his deep, low, masculine voice. 'You carry your destiny carved within you.' She shakes her head but he drags her towards the altar with one hand. 'Look. Look, and you will see—' Nicholas stops, staring. 'What?' he says, and draws deep breaths. *'What?'*

The floor is dirty, covered with mouse droppings. Nicholas snatches down with his free hand, scoops up a squealing mouse, crushes it. Alice cries out. He drags her against the altar, past broken chains, nibbled ropes, stares at the shape of the robed man, freed, unchained, unbound, lying in front of him. Peaceful. Asleep. Waiting. His hands clasped in prayer, His beard and hair carefully combed by the ministrations of a thousand, ten thousand, I cannot guess, little mice, their tiny teeth. Endless devout numbers and generations of them.

Nicholas picks up a tangle of heavy chain in his fist, stares at it. How long does it take a mouse to gnaw through iron? How many mice?

'Poor Nicholas,' the young girl whispers. 'I'm so sorry for you. What happened to you? What have you done?'

She's sorry for him! I try to warn her, but

The body of George falls forward, exhausted, its eyes against the earth and rubble of the foundations. I squeeze the heart, squeeze, squeeze, the body rises up and recommences its dogged work, the lungs gasp the dusty air. I pull the arms, the shovel drags stones and pebbles into the pile in front of the knees. Pull. Pull. Push the pile aside. Continue. The flesh is coming off the hands but they do not bleed, and there is no sweat.

Here's a change. The shovel pulls back black soil. Compacted ash. A layer of charred wood. This is the level the house collapsed to when it fell. Dig, dig!

Clean rubble again. The shovel's dug below the level of the fire. I widen my search, digging at the sides, hauling back the black earth.

The ears hear footsteps pass across the boards over the head.

I hear Jacqueline's voice. 'Nicholas? Aren't you in the chapel? Have you given her life? Have you brought her back?'

I wish I could scream. The body grunts as it digs. The heart stretches, quivers, almost bursting. Now a foul-smelling sweat does begin to drip, generated by the heat of the muscles.

Footsteps coming down.

The door of the hanging cellar opens. The body stops digging.

Jacqueline holds up a candle. 'George?' Her mouth opens. 'But you can't be.'

The arms clench, swing the shovel, the edge cuts through her head. For an instant I sense something of almost infinite evil reaching out towards me, towards *me*, leaving her. But then her body staggers back in its death agony, arms windmilling, knocks the door back, drops through the night air to the river below, is swept away. I feel nothing. It's gone.

The legs buckle, kneel. Here at last, a charred bone, blackened, part of a foot, a hand. Throw it in the river! Where's the skull? The skull matters most of all the bones, I remember Nick digging up the bones of his mother, Heylewise, from Garwynton woods, and how he was particularly careful with her skull, the abode of her soul.

Dig, dig—

She repeats her questions in a rising voice. 'What have you done? Who are you?'

Nicholas can't hear her. He stares at the form of his sleeping prisoner,

305

obsessed. Is His soul aware? He must be. *He is alive.* Sees all, watches all, knows all. Every sparrow, every fin, every eye, the life of every piece of blood and bone. He is all that we are. He is everything. He is us.

Nick picks up another length of chain, then another, lays them across the body, loops the links together to bind them.

She pulls her hand lightly from his.

I cry out: *Run! Run for your life!*

She runs.

Run, girl! Save yourself!

Nicholas turns. I think he is hardly Nicholas any more. His skin darkens, blisters, burns, yet I can feel the coldness of him behind the running girl. His legs bend against themselves, crouching, she falls down the steps, she feels the freezing touch of that gigantic hairy phallus as he jumps down. And she actually looks at it, hesitates, horrified, disgusted . . . fascinated.

Nick speaks with a voice and tongue not made for speaking, his words echo deep inside his chest. 'This is what was meant to happen years ago. Love me. Say you love me.'

She said it only a few minutes ago; she cannot possibly say it now. And this is the point: he doesn't understand her.

That terrifying image comes back to me from the day I was married, seeing the picture in Abbot's Littlebourne Church when I was myself little more than a child: the demon mating with the woman in the shadows, the ancient demon that denied us the right to live in Paradise.

But I married Jack instead.

Alice lies back. She's helpless. She knows the truth, she cannot resist. These impregnated women give birth to the creatures like worms, the Drakes.

I scream in her head: *Run, girl, run. Don't look back!*

Nick hears me, stops. He hears *me.* The demonic head turns upward as if seeing through the roof, and three hundred feet of chalk and clay.

Is that you, Alice?

There is a terrible roar and he flows upwards like the wind, the rushing wind.

Alice runs, her hair blowing in front of her. The burning flambeaux set at intervals make a dull roaring sound in the wind to match their pools of illumination as she runs past. Tunnels come down, join from side to side, but she follows the wind. 'I'm not lost,' she prays, 'I can find my way home.'

She must be on the right path, she sees her shoe. Picks it up. Her mother will be furious if she comes home without her shoe. Her foot hurts, scratched by the chalk floor.

She can see a hundred feet back along the tunnel. She hops on one leg, pulls the shoe half over her foot. It won't fit, too tight. She takes it off again, leans back against the wall, wipes her foot clean, pulls the shoe half on again. The cuts have swollen her foot.

Nicholas runs into view. He sees her and at once slows to a walk, puts out the palms of his hands. Peace. Walks slowly forward. 'What happened?' he says.

She screams, 'Stay where you are!'

He walks forward through the pools of illumination. 'That wasn't me, Alice. You know I love you.'

She backs away. 'I don't know anything.' Her voice rises. 'I never saw anything.'

'I never wanted this to happen,' Nicholas tells her desolately. This is the young man she remembers. 'I was born to be who I am. I can't help it.'

She snatches one of the flambeaux from the walls, waves it in front of her. 'Don't come any closer.'

'You know it's me, my love,' Nicholas says. 'You know you can trust me.'
He holds out his hand. 'Quick, come with me, we'll go together.'
She almost believes him, then backs away. He steps after her, snatching at
the flame with his bare hands. He grins. 'Don't look behind you.'
She looks.
There's nothing. It's the winding stair.
He pounces.
She throws the flames into his face. She tries to climb. The step's too steep,
she's close to the central pillar, the climb is almost vertical, each step is nothing
but a thin wedge of stone to cling to as it rotates round the pillar. She slips, bangs
her knees, hangs on.
Nicholas, dazzled by the flames, grabs her, misses, his fingernails tear
down the back of her dress. He shrieks, slides down her body, catches at
her ankle, falls.
He clings by his fingertips to the central pillar, his legs kicking in the wind
blowing past him to the centre of the world.
Nicholas stares at her fiercely, in terror. His eyes meet hers.
'Help me.'

Dig, dig.
Here it is. The shovel scrapes away the charred earth, reveals the smooth
blackened curve of a skull.
Nick's skull.
Most of the other bones, hands, feet, shins, thighs, hips, ribs, George's body
has thrown in the river.
The skull is heavy, full of soil. The body's hands grasp it, the arms pull up
with all their strength, black soil showers out as the skull and spine rise out of
the earth.
George's dead eyes stare into Nick's sockets of black bone. And I almost
think I see something still burning there, still feel the heat, the rushing heat
of the fire.
The cellar shakes, the lamp flutters, burns dim.
No time. I push the legs, turn clumsily. This body is almost finished,
shambles forward almost out of control. I feel the wind blow like ice on the
sweat that trickles from its skin. The skin breaks out in goosebumps.
Nick stands in the doorway. He is made of darkness, a terrible darkness.
I think I knew it even when we were children. I think I sensed the darkness
contained within him even then, the sorrow, the sense of loss. However much
he struggled against it, he could never overcome it.
I squeeze the lungs, tighten the chords, and George's voice speaks as
my own.
'Oh Nick, I'm so sorry.'
He looks into the eyes, knows me. 'Alice. I love you.'
'I know. But it isn't love, Nick.'
'I could have made you love me.' His human shape changes slightly, ripples
in the wind; this is not what he really is. 'I have read the Book. I know the truth.
I know who *my* Father is.' His hand sweeps out his cloak, which is darkness. 'I
asked you a question once, Alice. How can God, *En Soph*, who is perfect, create
imperfection? How can Light create Darkness? You never answered.'
I squeeze the lungs, they draw breath. George's voice grunts my words. 'I
see the answer now, Nick. Knowledge makes imperfection. A perfect God *must*
allow sin, without sin there is no choice. No good, no evil, nothing. We're still
scampering baby-naked in the Garden of Ignorance – I mean Eden. Without
sin, there's no freedom. No world. No me. No you.'
He growls. 'I do not require God's permission to flourish. This is *my* place.'

307

He reaches out one gleaming, hairy hand for the skull, his skull. 'Give it to me and I shall let you go forward. I shall let you go, Alice.'

Tears start in my dead eyes. I want it so much.

'I will dig up your bones from where I buried them, Alice, and let you go forward into the Light.' He reaches forward with his claws, his cloven hooves. 'I promise you.'

I hold up the blackened skull.

'Look at your tears,' he marvels. 'Give it to me. Go forward in peace, Alice.'

I pull the leg muscles, this body totters to him. He reaches out both hands, bending down to my height. I squeeze the heart, the lungs gasp. The legs run unsteadily but fast, the body runs forward below Nick's grasp, the hands throw the skull out over the river.

Nick gives a great shriek, lunges into the night, but the skull tumbles out and down.

The broken body of poor George falls to the river, the tide takes him to the Light.

I cannot go. These are not my bones.

'Damn you to Hell, Alice Lacknail,' Nick roars – and goes. I am, in my own way, a demon.

The rushing wind takes me—

'Help me.'

Nicholas clings by his fingertips to the central pillar, and the wind blows past him to the centre of the world. Alice tries not to meet his eyes, his fierce demanding gaze. Like me, she weeps. She has lost everything that meant anything to her. Love. Hope. Safety. Certainty. And, like me, she feels she will never recover. My Alice. My dear sweet Alice.

Nicholas says, 'Help me, Alice.'

She tries to look away, but she cannot. What will she do? I want to interfere but I must not. It must be her choice.

She reaches down for his hand.

I hear a sound high above. A regular tocking sound, drawing closer. Coming down the stair, round and round.

Alice stares over her shoulder.

From high up Nick's blackened skull comes bouncing down the winding stair, from step to step, with nothing to stop it.

Nicholas screams. The skull tumbles past Alice, will fall for ever – and Nicholas, with a shriek of utter despair, reaches out his hand and grabs it.

He looks up at Alice. 'Help me, damn you, or you'll never forgive yourself.'

Would she have reached down? I will never know.

A tiny mouse we had not noticed rushed forward, and sank its teeth into Nick's forefinger to the bone.

Nick's fingertips gave way, sliding, and he fell slowly at first, then with increasing speed, and he grew smaller until we could no longer see him, and the darkness took him.

Alice's tale

London Bridge, 7 February 1832

> London Bridge is broken down,
> Dance o'er, my lady lee;
> London Bridge is broken down,
> With a grey lady.

The voices of the workmen sounded mournfully through the early morning fog as Frank Laguerre walked on to old London Bridge.

Frank! The black cat leapt into his arms. You're late, as usual. Hold me. Stroke me.

> Build it up with silver and gold,
> Dance o'er, my lady lee;
> But silver and gold will be stole away,
> By a grey lady.

Frank looked down at the cat, and the cat looked at him steadily.

'You're smiling, Alice.'

This is my day. Today I am free. Can't you hear the pickaxes on the Chapel Pier?

'No one has called it the Chapel Pier for two hundred and eighty-four years, Alice. I checked. The chapel was converted into a private house belonging to a Mr William Bridger.'

A Mr William Bridger? A suggestive name, wouldn't you say? Significant. The undercroft was never touched, except to take out the chapel organ. No one went down there, the place was used for storing cheeses. Mr Bridger was a grocer, Master of the Worshipful Order of Masons and Poor Fellow-Soldiers of Christ and the Temple of Solomon, Bridge Ward.

> Build it up with wood and clay,
> Dance o'er, my lady lee;
> But wood and clay will wash away,
> With a grey lady.

'Are you the grey lady, Alice?'

I have a few grey hairs on my tummy. Walk forward. I like to hear the men sing.

'And the mouse was Noelle?'

The one we all forgot. The unimportant one. She matters most.

'Do you believe Nick was really the son of Deus? That Heylewise was deceived?'

I whisper, against thy will thou art an embryo, against thy will thou art born.

Frank heard no reply. The cat was just a cat. He walked forward slowly, stroking her between her ears to make her purr.

'And the golden angel? Alice? She was you?'

Perhaps I did hold a demon chained. But I think the face of the angel was Noelle's. Devout. Dedicated. Determined. Dutiful.

'Is Noelle with Him still?'

She will not be free until the Resurrection.

Here London Bridge stopped, only a narrow catwalk of planks led forward above the rushing tide to the island of the Chapel Pier. The pier stood proud of the river like a crumbling tooth, the dark figures of workmen clambering over it in the fog. Their pickaxes swung, the thud of sledgehammers demolishing the ancient stones echoed in the fog. More workmen sat round a brazier on the roadway, cooking their breakfast herrings on sticks, drinking beer. The foreman recognised Frank, beckoned him across.

'Strong old girl. Going to draw it for us? Won't be nothing here by summer.' He jerked his thumb over his shoulder to where the five pale, elegant spans of the new bridge upstream were braced across the river, already heavy with the sound of traffic.

'I had a dream last night,' Frank said.

The cat leapt from Frank's arms on to the stones, ignored the workmen, jumped down into the ruins. Down there the outline of massive walls was still visible, patches of black and white floor showing between the piles of rubble. 'Marble, that is,' the foreman said. 'Valuable. Didn't know they had marble back then, did you? That'll pay our wages this month. We're selling the rest of the stone to build houses. Careful there!' he bellowed as a navvy slipped. Forty men had been killed on the river building the new bridge, he didn't want to lose any more demolishing the old one. He stormed after the unfortunate man, swearing.

Frank picked his way carefully down the slope of rubble on to the old floor of the undercroft. He swept a clear space with his boot, sat beside the cat.

'What happened to young Alice?'

I looked after her, of course. I was her guardian angel.

'Did she believe what she had seen in the Temple of God?' Frank glanced through part of an ancient arched window still standing, past the new bridge to the Temple, its outlines now built over by an impenetrable tangle of lawyers' chambers, dark corners and narrow streets. Through the mist he could just make out the massive circular form of the Templar church.

Yes, Frank, Alice knew what she had seen. And I knew. I saw the earthly body of Our Lord Jesus Christ lying unchained, unshrouded, in the Sanctum Sanctorum beneath the Temple. His spirit is in Heaven, but His soul is alive among us in the world. I know Jesus Christ is alive, *really* alive. The Bible is true and the Devil exists and there is a God. Here, now, the Lord dwells among His people, actually alive with us, hidden among us. I am. Many are. And Him.

'Will the Resurrection come in our lifetimes?'

Oh, Frank! Yes. Yes. Yes.

'I want to see Him.'

Free me, Frank. I'm not like Noelle, my duty is done. My family is gone, I've no one to care for. Soon the bridge will not be here. Let me be with Jack. Tell the men to dig here. Free me.

Frank called the foreman. 'There's something under here.'

He stepped back, picked up the cat as the foreman called a navvy, watched the two men try the point of a pickaxe between two marble slabs. Frank rubbed his lips against the cat's ear, whispering. 'Will I see the staircase? Will I see the Temple of God?'

The cat purred softly, no more than a cat.

'Careful, Mick, careful,' the foreman muttered, working the point of the pickaxe forward. 'Lift a touch. Easy . . .'

Something moved in the corner of Frank's eye. He looked at the woman standing beside him.

'My God. You're Alice.'

Her hair was cut in a style unfashionable for many years and beneath chestnut curls and her straight, dark eyebrows not quite hiding her scar, her eyes were bright blue. She wore a shift still bearing the blood of childbirth, a Flanders cloak was draped from her shoulders, and on one foot she wore a red velvet slipper. Alice's other foot was bare except for a grass ring round her fourth toe.

She whispered, 'Let me go, Frank. Let me go forward to the Light.'

He gaped at her. Grasped her. 'Not until you show me the Temple of God. Swear that it's true!'

She smiled. 'I swear it's true.'

But he didn't let her go.

She touched his face tenderly. 'You asked me about young Alice, what happened to her. She climbed to safety, Frank. She married a pleasant man whom she loved neither too little nor too much, she brought up three daughters, she was a grandmother many times over, she grew old and she died in her sleep. One granddaughter married into the Dupont family, another into the Bridger family.'

Frank whispered, 'And they knew?'

She teased his lips with her fingertip. 'Dig down, Frank. All you'll find is water, and then mud, and then concrete. They knew what they were doing.'

'But I want to understand.'

'It's in you, Frank. I remember your great-grandfather. He was a painter too. And his great-great-great-grandfather was a mason. We're all part of it, Frank. It's in *you*.'

The marble slab lifted, showering earth. The foreman balanced it on edge, the navvy held it, then the foreman lowered himself into the shallow grave. 'What's this, painter boy?' His greedy tone turned at once to disappointment. 'Bones, that's all it is. Old bones.' He pulled them out of the hole, a woman's leg bones, her hips, skull.

Frank looked at Alice's face uplifted towards him, perfect, ecstatic. She was smiling.

'Chuck 'em in the drink!' the foreman swore. 'Old bones!'

'*Free me*,' Alice whispered into Frank's eyes.

Frank gripped her with all his strength. 'No. Not until you show me God. When will he come again?'

The navvy chucked the bones, the river swept them away, and an illumination grew in the mist as the sun rose.

Frank looked at his hands. He held nothing. He shielded his eyes.

Her voice whispered in his ear, then she was gone. The light blazed.

'*He's already here, Frank. Everywhere. Infinite. Mysterious. As are we.*'